T0344242

Swords
of the
Steppes

The Complete Cossack Adventures
Volume Four

Harold Lamb

Edited by Howard Andrew Jones
Introduction by Barrie Tait Collins

UNIVERSITY OF NEBRASKA PRESS
LINCOLN AND LONDON

Library of Congress Cataloging-in-Publication Data
Lamb, Harold, 1892–1962.
Swords of the steppes / Harold Lamb ;
edited by Howard Andrew Jones ;
introduction by Barrie Tait Collins.
p. cm.—(The complete Cossack adventures ; v. 4)
ISBN-13: 978-0-8032-8051-9 (pbk. : alk. paper)
ISBN-10: 0-8032-8051-3 (pbk. : alk. paper)
1. Cossacks—Fiction. 2. Steppes—Asia, Central—Fiction.
3. Asia, Central—History—16th century—Fiction.
I. Jones, Howard A. II. Jones, Howard Andrew. III. Title.
PS3523.A4235S96 2007
813'.52—dc22
2006035910

Set in Trump Mediaeval by Kim Essman.
Designed by R. W. Boeche.

Contents

Foreword

In the preceding three Khlit the Cossack adventures, printed in the third volume in this series, readers saw Kirdy being groomed by his grandfather to become a leader of men and a sterling Cossack. In the story that opens this volume, "The Wolf Master" (reprinted as *Kirdy* in 1933 by Doubleday) Kirdy is his own man at last. Khlit appears only briefly to send Kirdy on a deadly mission, and then the young man rides off alone, leaving even Ayub behind. It is the last time readers see Khlit, although he is mentioned in two more tales.

Throughout this series of reprint the editors at Bison Books and I have chosen to leave the stories themselves as originally presented, with the exception of minor adjustments for editorial consistency. Certain attitudes expressed by the characters or used by the author remain just as they were printed in the early twentieth century. It should go without saying that what is privately and even publicly acceptable in one century may make for uncomfortable reading in the next. Some of Lamb's character portrayals would today be considered anti-Semitic, sexist, or prejudiced against certain ethnic groups. Though Lamb may have been trying to capture the biased attitudes of his characters, or reflect those of his society, he seems to have been uncomfortable with some of these portrayals later in his life, for he left stories with the most offensive of these elements out of the only collection prepared for re-publication before his death. "The Wolf Master" features the worst of these scenes; Lamb was never to write another remotely similar.

Up until this novel it seemed as though Harold Lamb was readying Kirdy for a cycle of adventures of his own; in steps we saw him gain Khlit's curved saber and a title and learn to see through schemers, both men and women. Instead of providing further adventures, Lamb chose to conclude

"The Wolf Master" with a finale he could never have given Khlit, and as a result it is the last readers see of the young man.

It was not quite the end for the family of Lamb's recurring Cossack characters, however, for in 1929 Lamb returned to feature Ayub in a short novel of the Cossack's later years, "The Outrider," which is the second tale in this collection.

All the contents of this volume are rarities. "The Wolf Master" is rare enough, but the rest of the stories, gleaned from *Adventure, Collier's,* and other magazines, have never seen reprint. Herein you'll find a short series featuring the Cossack Koum, set a hundred years after Khlit and Kirdy. One tale introduces the bagpipe-playing Cossack, another introduces his friend Gurka, and a third, one of Lamb's best, is a novella of their adventure together. More tales of these two could have followed, but by this point in his career Lamb was busily co-writing screenplays for Cecil B. DeMille. He had become a respected and successful writer of histories and biographies, and besides, the pulp market itself was changing with the coming of the Great Depression. It's no wonder that Lamb wrote less short fiction, though we can regret it, for by the early 1930s, fifteen years or so after Lamb had begun writing for *Adventure,* his fiction had reached a poetic peak only hinted at in prior years. While he sometimes wrote for *Collier's* and other magazines in the '30s and '40s, he was constrained by space and editorial preferences and seldom got to spin more lengthy tales—or even to vary too much from a formula.

In addition to the stories mentioned above you'll find two tales of Stenka Razin, whom Lamb described as a kind of Robin Hood of the Steppe, and other stand-alone tales of Cossacks in perilous times. There's Borasun, with his delightful joie de vivre; Charnomar and Mark, American adventurers; and even another Demid, who journeys to another fortress of Khor— names recycled from *Adventure* for a short tale in *Collier's,* although the character is not the same Demid who adventured with Ayub. Perhaps the greatest surprise are the five tales of a World War II Cossack who is something like Khlit, gleaned from *Argosy* and *Collier's*—stories different in tone from Lamb's earlier work but enjoyable nonetheless.

The final story in this volume, long sought for in an early issue of a little-known pulp magazine, didn't turn up until mere days before this text was due to be turned over to Bison. "Wolf-Hounds of the Steppe" is, so far as I know, Lamb's earliest Cossack tale. Although likely penned only a half year before the first Khlit stories, it is heavy with melodrama, and there is an excess of offstage machinations in which the hero plays little part.

Still, there are hints within as to what Lamb would later be capable of, and it is included here in the interest of completeness.

Although there was no peril on this road to reprint, assembling these stories, like life upon the steppe, had its challenges. A big part of preparing manuscripts for these four volumes was the finding of them, for they were scattered through dozens of rare magazines, the longer stories sometimes divided in parts over multiple issues. Once in hand (a process which involved many years of searching), they had to be scanned, then formatted and proofread—for the scanning process, while immensely swifter than retyping almost close to a million words, isn't perfect. The letter *B* sometimes turns up as an *h* and vice versa; a capital *O* gets confused with a zero, and other little peculiarities pop up as well. The endeavor would not have been possible without the assistance of dedicated volunteers— all our efforts bolstered by other Harold Lamb fans who had located www. haroldlamb.net and written in to proclaim their appreciation for Lamb's work. So many of us thought we were the only ones who treasured these stories, but it turned out that there was a small, scattered army of us, and we tracked down the tales and exchanged them and hoped that we could one day see all of them collected between covers, as they deserved.

First among all of the volunteers was Bruce Nordstrom, who located every single *Collier's* and *Saturday Evening Post* issue in which Harold Lamb had written a story, not to mention a number of *Blue Books* and other magazines less well known. Bruce found these tales, scanned every one, and sent them my way, along with the text of *The Wolf Master*. Bruce was a private man, so I never prodded him for his real-world address. One day several years ago my e-mail letters to him began to bounce and his web site disappeared. I've never heard from him since. I wish him well but I fear the worst. All Harold Lamb fans owe him a debt of gratitude.

I have thanked Victor Dreger for his diligent research behind the map that appears in each of these volumes, but "diligence" is a poor word for what Victor did. He spent countless hours and many dollars tracking down old maps and searching them for the hard-to-find place names Lamb used in his Cossack tales. He found more information than could even easily fit on the map, alas, although Darrel Stevens' beautiful map somehow works in most of it. In addition to the maps, Victor has supplied me with texts and information and has proved an excellent sounding board about various features and problems that have cropped up over the course of the project.

Speaking of that lovely map, not only did Darrell Stevens go all out to produce it, he drafted four vibrant, exciting covers that captured the spirit of Lamb's stories with real class. Darrell went so far as to design the font used on each volume. It's hard now to imagine these stories without the accompaniment of Stevens' perfectly suited illustrations.

Jan Van Heiningen has been a true friend and scholar since he first found out about the project. It is he who discovered "Wolf-Hounds of the Steppe," and it would not be published within these pages without him.

Bill Prather, business manager for Thacher School (the copyright holder for Lamb's work) and a friend and true gentleman, has supported and endorsed my efforts even when the idea of getting this collection into print probably seemed absurd. Without his backing this collection could never have happened, and he deserves all of our thanks.

Alfred Lybeck, pulp scholar, wrote a wonderful retrospective of Lamb's work in the pulps (published in *Pulpdom* in July 1996) that serves as an excellent reference about Lamb and his publication history. It was of great aid up through the final days of manuscript preparation.

Lastly, I must thank my father, Victor H. Jones, who helped me track down more than a dozen Lamb *Adventure* texts in the years before his death, and a man I never met, Dr. John Drury Clark. Dr. Clark had hunted down a large number of Lamb stories from *Adventure*, placed a few between homemade covers, as some pulp magazine collectors do, and separated dozens more from magazines in preparation for binding. I purchased all of these from his widow. Dr. Clark's texts saved me years of searching and made preparation of the stories for these volumes far, far simpler than it would otherwise have been. I think Dr. Clark would have been happy that the time he spent preserving Harold Lamb stories has benefited all of us.

We may have reached the end of Harold Lamb's Cossack trail, but in an ideal world these books will be followed with a collection of Lamb's moody Crusader tales, most of which were written at the height of his powers, like the two outstanding Nial O'Gordon novellas and "The Making of the Morning Star," one of Lamb's very best novels. Its companion volume would be a book collecting Lamb's Arabian and Asian adventures, including three novellas narrated by swordsman-turned-physician Daril ibn Athir, and a prequel to Lamb's *Durandal* told by none other than Khalil el Kadr, Sir Hugh's loyal friend. It would be a simple matter to fill another volume with Lamb's tales of Vikings and sea explorers, including novel-length stories of both the search for the Northeast passage and the American expedition against the Barbary pirates, not to mention stories of John Paul Jones among the Russian fleet.

For now, though, you have four volumes of stories rescued from obscurity. It was sad indeed that such fine adventures were so close to oblivion, to disintegrating forever into a dry rain of brown flaking paper, and it is with great pride that we present them to you, in hopes that this vibrant, exciting fiction finds the audience denied it for so many years.

Enjoy!

Acknowledgments

I would like to thank Bill Prather of Thacher School for his continued support, encouragement, enthusiasm, and friendship. I also would like to express my appreciation for the tireless efforts of Victor Dreger, who pored over acres of old maps to compile a map of the locations that appear in the final version printed within this book. Thank yous also are due to the tireless Bruce Nordstrom, Dr. Victor H. Jones, and Jan Van Heiningen for aid in manuscript acquisition, as well as S. C. Bryce, who kindly provided a timely and time-consuming last-minute check of some key issues of *Adventure*, and Dr. James Pfundstein and Doug Ellis for similar aid. A great deal of time was saved because of the manuscript preservation efforts of the late Dr. John Drury Clark. I'm grateful to the staff at the University of Nebraska Press, for their support of the project and for efficiently shepherding the manuscript through the publication process. I'm likewise appreciative and delighted by the hard work of cover artist and map artist Darrel Stevens. My old friend Sean Connelly and his wife Kay provided a home base during an important final research trip to Indiana University. Thank you all for your hard work and dedication—you have helped bring Khlit the Cossack and his world to life.

Introduction

Barrie Tait Collins

Harold Albert Lamb grew up in an extended family of prominent artists in New York City and New Jersey.

His father, Frederick S. Lamb, was the head stained glass designer for the J. & R. Lamb Studios, the ecclesiastical art firm founded in 1857 in New York City by Harold's grandfather, Joseph Lamb, and his great-uncle, Richard. His uncle, Charles Rollinson Lamb, an architect-designer, was president of the family firm. (Although no longer under family ownership, the Studios is the oldest stained glass studio in the United States.) Both men were leaders in the art organizations of the times and in pressing for the recognition of art in public buildings and in America's cultural life.

In addition to demanding careers, Frederick and Charles also played important roles in the City Beautiful movement and reform politics in New York City as well as in successful conservation efforts to preserve the Palisades, the cliffs looming above the Hudson River for twelve miles north of the George Washington Bridge in New Jersey. Frederick was one of the commissioners appointed by New York State Governor Theodore Roosevelt to form the interstate park on New York's doorstep.

I knew of Harold Lamb from an early age because he was my mother's first cousin and grew up with her and her three brothers. My mother (an artist and stained glass designer successor to Frederick) remembered Harold as shy and quiet in contrast to his outgoing younger brother, Adrian (who became a noted portrait painter later in life in New York City). The brothers were close to their cousins and, as they grew older, tennis was a favorite sport on a homemade court at their adjoining summer homes on Lambs Lane, Cresskill, New Jersey. The two families lived in New York City the rest of the year.

Harold turned to the world of writing after graduation from Columbia University and gradually found increasing success. He moved to California, probably in the early 1920s, and married Ruth Barbour. An article later in his career in "Better Homes & Gardens" (October 1948) shows the new study with fireplace he added onto his Beverly Hills home to provide a quieter place for his writing.

With my early interest in history, geography, and "adventure" (a la Richard Halliburton!), it was natural for me to explore my parents' library and to come across *The Crusades*. It fired my imagination in ninth grade in a way I still remember. This, of course, led to reading many of Lamb's other books over the years. *Alexander of Macedon* is a particular favorite.

Although Harold Lamb grew up in New York City he only passed through it briefly on the way to and from short or extended trips to Europe, the Middle East, and Asia after he moved to California. In one of two letters I treasure from him he said he did not like the hectic pace that life had become in the city: "Being a recluse, the New York of today appalls me, and I spend as few hours there as possible, which is not right. In memory, my native city has become a blurred vista of preoccupied people hurrying to cocktail parties or away from the parties to trains and theatres."

I remember meeting him when I was beginning my nonfiction writing career in the 1950s in New York and he was already a very successful writer. "Uncle Harold," as my brothers and I called him, was a slim, scholarly, distinguished-looking man, still somewhat shy but gracious to a young aspiring writer-cum-"niece." He was always an inspiration to me because almost everyone else in the creative Lamb family was an artist! We exchanged several letters in his later years, and my "Aunt" Ruth also kept me posted occasionally on his trips.

Harold Lamb's life and writings always seemed magical to me, but the knowledge that most of his stories were well grounded in fact and personal knowledge of the faraway peoples and landscapes and described so vividly fascinates me to this day. I am happy that others also continue to read him with great pleasure.

WOLF'S WORLD

Th

Ural Mountains

Dnieper River
Kiev
Moskva
Donetz River
Don River
Kazan
Sietch
Sirog
Volga River
Rusk
Jaick River
Sea of
Azov
Kamyshin
S
t
e
p
p
e
s
Roum
Astrakhan
Charnomar
Blue
Sea
Sea of Khozar
Urgench
Kizil Kum
Desert
Aleppo
Bokhara
Roof of
the Wo
Tabriz
Samarkand
Damascus
Balkh
Jerusalem
Alamut
Herat
Hindu Ku
Persian Desert
Karadak
Isphahan
A
r
a
b
i
a
Indus River
Bandar Abbasi
Red Sea
Gulf
of Arabia

Lena River

Dead World

Khantai Khan Mountains

Lake
Baikal

Lake
Kukulon

Onon River

Altur Haiten

Kerlulan River

Sinkiang

Changa
Nor

Black Irtish River

Karakorum

Lake
Balkash

Altai Mountains

Gobi Desert

The Great Wall

Talas

Kashgar

Tarim River

Yarkand

Taklamakan
Desert

China

Badakshan

Khoten

Baramula

Srinaggar

Tibetan Plateau

Leh

malayas

Dehra Dun

Lhasa

Lahore

Kukushetra

Agra

India

Indian Ocean

The Wolf Master

Chapter I
My Saddle's My Home

I've been to Roum, and I've been to Rome,
Through the Black Mountains,
On the White Sea!
My hat is my house-top, my saddle's my home—
Hai-a—come away with me!

Song of the Cossack Wanderers

The streets of the village were deserted. On every hand deep snow covered the steppe; even the thatched roofs of the cottages were blanketed in white.

It was old snow, that, on the roofs and the plain. And stretching in every direction from the cluster of dwellings and stables tracks were to be seen. Tricks of men and horses, of carts, and wide, clumsy tracks that bit deep into the gray coverlet of the steppe.

A throng of men, a multitude of horses, had left their traces around the village. But the painted doors of the taverns were shut and barred; the horn windows of the cottages showed no gleam of light, though it was the dull twilight of a midwinter's day.

It was a time of trouble, early in the seventeenth century. And to the good people of this village in the steppe, trouble had come indeed. Their faces pressed against the windows, they listened to the muttering growl of cannon and musketry in the distance.

The dogs in the stable yards barked half-heartedly at the sound of approaching horses. Three Cossacks, plying their whips on spent ponies, galloped up to the post tavern. The youngest, who rode in advance of the others, reined in at the door and pounded on it with a pistol butt.

"Hi, father of a thousand slaves! Horses—give us fresh horses!"

A blur of faces was visible at the window overhead, but no answer was returned to the impatient rider. The dogs that had clustered around to yap at him gave back suddenly. Like a shadow drifting over the snow, a gray borzoi, or wolfhound, that had been following the young Cossack in the white coat, turned into the tavern yard. Its ears were pricked toward the man and the horse, and only by a soundless snarl did it acknowledge the growling of the village dogs. Its massive chest and arched ribs were mud-stained, and it moved with the effortless ease of the wolf that had sired it.

A second Cossack now entered the yard and dismounted from a foundered pony that stood nose to earth, legs planted wide.

"Aside, Kirdy," he grunted. "I will deal with the dog-souls."

The slender warrior in the white coat give place to the newcomer who strode to the door and thrust his shoulder against the painted panel. He was little less than a giant, hatless, with a long broadsword strapped to his wide shoulders. Under the impact of weight the door creaked ominously, and the watchers within saw fit to open the window.

"The forehead to you, master," a heavy voice cried down at the Cossacks. "We have done no harm. We are people who believe in God. What do you seek?"

"I am Ayub the Zaporogian!" roared the giant, steam rising from his black sweat-soaked coat. "I must have a horse—three horses, for ours."

"*Ekh ma*, Master Ayub. By Saint Andrew and the good Saint Thomas, we have not a horse."

"How, not a horse?"

A shaggy bearded head was thrust out of the window.

"We are innocent people, by all that's holy. It is true we had some beasts, for the post service. But first the noble boyars and the splendid Polish knights came and took their pick; then the illustrious Cossack lords came and hitched what was left to their guns. In all the village you will find no more than these dogs."

"How long have the cannon been speaking?"

"Since the sun was at the zenith, noble sir. At dawn the army of Zaporogian Cossacks passed through our streets to give battle to the Poles and the boyars."

"Hark ye, innkeeper!" The warrior called Ayub wrenched his wallet from his girdle and tossed it against the door, so that the jangle of silver coins against it was audible. "That's for the man who finds us three nags, now—at once!"

The head disappeared, and the impatient Cossacks heard the low growl of voices in argument. When the tavern-keeper looked out again, despair was written on his broad features.

"Good sir, no horse is to be had."

The two Cossacks who had ridden four hundred versts in four days to be present at that battle looked at each other without a word and turned by swiftly mutual consent to the third. He was an old man with shrewd gray eyes. His long white mustache fell below his stooped shoulders, and the brown skin seemed stretched and drawn over the bones of his head. Through the tears in his sheepskins a red silk shirt was visible, and his baggy trousers were spotted with tar and mud, quite disregarded by their owner, who was drawing tighter the girth on his sweating pony.

He was Khlit, called the Curved Saber, and he had been Koshevoi Ataman of all the Zaporogian Cossacks. When he had finished his task he straightened and held up his hand.

Straining their ears, Kirdy and Ayub made out a change in the reverberation of distant conflict. The cannon had ceased firing, and only the sharper impact of muskets was to be heard.

Ayub swore under his breath.

"It is nearly over, out there. Our brothers have whipped the Poles."

But in the clear eyes of the old warrior there were uncertainty and the shadow of misery.

It was true that the three had come up from the Cossack steppes in the south, heedless of the fate of the horses they bestrode, as messenger pigeons seek out a spot behind the horizon, untiringly. Khlit had brought his grandson out of the mountains of Tartary, through the empire of the Moghul, past the settlements of the frontier for one purpose.

He had meant to place Kirdy among his old comrades of the Zaporogian Siech—the war encampment of the Cossack warriors—before he died. They had heard on the Don that the army of the *siech* had taken the field against foes, and they had turned aside again, seeking it. As they rode, the clouds of war settled lower upon the wilderness of the steppe, and now the clouds had broken. The time of trouble was at hand; the Cossack warriors were in the saddle, the battle was drawing to its end, and

they were no nearer than this village of the Muscovites, five miles from
the armies, with their horses utterly useless.

Khlit swallowed his disappointment in silence. Before long he would
see his old comrades and learn from them all that had passed. He did not
understand why the Cossacks should be fighting the Poles, or why the
Muscovite boyars should be in arms. And, beyond weariness and disappointment, a foreboding was in his spirit.

"Look at Karai!" said Kirdy.

The gray wolfhound had been sitting in middle of the courtyard, the
long tail curved around its feet, eyeing them expectantly. Now it rose,
ears pricked, and stalked to the gate.

"Horses are coming," the young Cossack announced after a moment,
and they went to stand beside Karai and peer up the empty street.

Behind them a level bar of orange light divided earth from sky in the
curious twilight of the northern Winter, when the sky seems darker than
the earth and the sun is a thing forgotten.

A black mass passed between the first huts of village and resolved itself
into a detachment of horsemen. Weary men on weary beasts they were,
some bearing lances, some sabers, some no weapons at all.

"They are ours," cried Ayub, staring between cupped hands. Then
he lifted his deep voice in a shout, "*Hai Kosaki*! Have you whipped the
Poles?"

The leading riders came abreast the tavern, and an officer reined to one
side to look more closely at the three Cossacks. He was hatless, a blood-
stained shirt wrapped around his forehead.

"Are horses to be had in the village?" he asked of Ayub.

"Nay—not a nag."

The leader of the detachment sighed and urged his pony on. Some of
the chargers, smelling the hay in the tavern yard, neighed, and a man
cursed blackly.

"Look here," demanded Ayub, "aren't you ordered to camp in the village? It's twenty versts to the next houses."

A bearded lancer, erect as a statue on a fine black Tartar stallion, paused
long enough to spit toward the rear and thrust his sheepskin hat on the back
of his head. In silence the advance of the Zaporogians moved on through
the village and out into the plain toward the south. Other detachments
followed, and—when men fell out to light blazing fires along the street—
Kirdy saw that these were men as wild as the riders of Asia.

Many of them were tall as Ayub, giants in sheepskins, their saddles and headbands gleaming with silver. Scarce one but bore some cut or powder stain, and here and there a Cossack walked, holding a badly wounded comrade in the saddle.

"By the Horned One," Ayub groaned, "they have not whipped the Poles. Nay, they have been pounded and broken. Yonder are some of the Perieslav company, with red *kalpaks*, and men of the White Kosh* itself. Ho, brothers—where is the *ataman*?"

A young warrior who had lingered to warm himself at the nearest fire looked up with a wry smile.

"Our father Netchai died a week agone. Colonel Loboda of the White Kosh had command, until he swallowed bullets the wrong way. God knows who is our *ataman*."

"Are the Poles driving you?"

The young Cossack tightened his belt, slapped his sword hilt, and put a booted foot in the stirrup of his gray Arab.

"Nay, not the Poles nor the boyars. Satan himself is back there."

With a sweeping gesture at the black sky and the gray wilderness, he sprang into the saddle trotted off to rejoin his companions.

By now the streets of the locked-in village were full of light and the roar of voices. Orders were shouted above the snapping of the flaming wood; foragers rode in, to pile hay, grain, and whatnot into the slow-moving carts of the *tabor*—the wagon train that made up the heart of a Zaporogian army. Black carts, glistening wet, slid and creaked past the watchers. Long sleds, drawn by lowing oxen, appeared with cannon roped fast.

Other sleds bore loads of wounded, who sat on bearskins, smoking short clay pipes, or lay prone, twisted faces staring up blankly at the cold stars. If the Zaporogians were defeated, they were far from routed. Some ate, as they rode, from saddlebags, and an *essaul* who had no more than three men at his back lifted his fine voice in one of the mournful songs of the South.

The tavern yard, trampled into mud, was improvised into a dressing station of the roughest sort. Tar was heated in buckets at the fires, and when a mangled leg or arm was carried in, a saber slashed off the useless mem-

---

Kosh—a Cossack camp or clan. In the seventeenth century each clan had its own villages and grazing lands, and the men of the clan joined their *kuren*, or barrack, in the army. Each camp chose its own leader—or *ataman*, colonel. The Koshevoi Ataman, or commander-in-chief, was elected at the council of the clans.

ber, and the stump was plunged into the bubbling tar. Others stripped off
coats or trousers and suffered cuts to be plastered with mud. The slightly
wounded were given cups of vodka mixed with gunpowder to quaff.

No surgeon was to be seen, and the only bandages were shirts or long
sashes. When the wounded had been treated they were bundled up in
svitzas—long riding coats—taken from the slain, and placed again on
the sledges of the wagon train, crossing themselves and breathing a jest
if they were able to speak.

"No, brothers, Satan's claws ripped my hide, but the grass won't grow
over me this time."

"It isn't my sword arm you painted with tar. And the Poles will know
it before another harvest."

More often it was:

"*Dai vodky*—Give me vodka!"

A warrior, stripped to the waist and bleeding freely from the lower ribs,
reined his horse into the station and sat staring about, frowning, resisting those who came to lift him to the fires.

"Here, you devil—take that!" he shouted through set teeth. "Where is
the *ataman*? Brothers, I want to see the *ataman* and hear his voice again
before I die. Nay, you dog-souls, I can still ride! Take me to the commander."

Although it was clear that his mind was wandering and he was bleeding to death, no one could move him from the saddle until Ayub came
and peered into his stained face.

"It's Pavlenko!" the big Zaporogian shouted. "Many's the time we've
dried out a barrel together. Come down, Pavlenko, and let the lads wrap
you up. You were always a quarrelsome dolt. Here!"

Reaching out swiftly, Ayub caught the saber of the delirious warrior
close to the hilt and pulled strongly. Pavlenko swayed and tumbled into
the arms of his former comrade. Heedless of the blood that spattered his
garments, Ayub bore him to one of the groups round the fires, while Pavlenko's charger snorted and pawed at the slush.

Kirdy, a stranger to these men, tended their fire in silence, followed
wherever he went by the wolfhound, Karai.

At the gate Khlit stood, peering at the passing *tabor*. For ten years he
had been away from the *siech*, and all these faces were unknown to him.
Even the *essauls* passed the old Cossack by without a glance of recogni-

tion. He had outlived his generation and his comrades lay now out on the steppe, bones stripped by vulture and wolf and dried sun.

He watched silently until a sled halted at the gate and three lancers lifted from it a slender officer in a red *svitza* heavily sewn with gold. The boots of this man were fine shagreen, though caked with mud, and he gripped firmly an ivory baton with a small gold cross.

"Way for the father, lads," they cried, and Khlit came to the fire to look keenly into the wasted brown face of the wounded chief.

"Colonel Loboda," he growled.

"Don't take my coat off, by ——!" The Cossack grunted through set lips. "It's of no account, my children. Where are the *kuren atamans*? Where's Ivashko the One-Eyed? Well, then, summon whoever is leading the Black Kosh."

Khlit, glancing through the gate, saw that the rearguard had dismounted in the street—some five hundred riders on black horses, wearing mail under their *svitzas*. Their chargers seemed fresh, and a kept more than a semblance of formation. But the officer who came at Loboda's call was only a youth, flushed and silent.

And at sight of him the veteran colonel, who had been placed on a bear-skin near the blaze, frowned thoughtfully. Loboda had been shot twice through the body and only by an effort of iron will could he keep his thoughts on the Cossack regiments clearly as the need was. He could not outlive the night, he knew, and the fate of six thousand survivors of the army rested on his choice of a new commander. From the young warrior who had taken charge Black Kosh, his eyes went to Khlit, and he passed a quivering hand across his forehead.

"Hey, are you Ostap? Nay, he went out of his saddle at the second charge. They had too many cannon—"

He broke off to listen. No longer were reports of muskets heard. The *ta-bor* had passed on, and snow was beginning to fall, drifting into the glow of the fires and sinking into the mud of the courtyard. Out of the curtain of drifting flakes a stout priest strode, booted and belted, his long black robe tucked up into his belt, his cape drawn over his head.

"Nay, Loboda, Ostap gave up his soul in these arms. His squadrons are scattered among the others. Stohari sent me from the *tabor*. He asks—" the priest hesitated—"that you come with the baton because the broth-ers are saying up ahead that you were cut down."

He looked curiously at Khlit, who had stepped forward.

"Colonel Loboda," the wanderer said again.

This time the *ataman* peered at him closely, and his thin lips parted.

"Nay—ten thousand devils! Are the angels sending couriers from above so swiftly? You are Khlit, you old dog! The Curved Saber—I played with that sword when I was a fledgling."

He lay back, still frowning.

"Well, if you have come with a summons—I'll ride with you. You died in Cathay, when I was an *essaul*."

The priest crossed himself and laid his hand on Khlit's shoulder. Then he bent over the wounded colonel.

"Nay, my son—this is a living man, whoever he be."

"It is true, Loboda, nodded Khlit. "Many winters have gone by since these eyes saw the Mother Siech. Alone among the Cossacks you know my face."

"Then bring vodka. We'll drink, eh, Khlit? Come lads, a stirrup cup to Loboda."

The strong spirits cleared his brain for a moment and he motioned for his cup to be filled again. This time Kirdy brought it, and kneeled to hold it to the colonel's lips. Loboda's eye, caught by the glitter of the jewels in the hilt of the young warrior's saber, blinked reflectively.

"That should be Khlit's blade—I know it well. Who are you, *oùchar*?"

"It is the White Falcon, Loboda," Khlit responded moodily. "The Don Cossacks gave him that name, and I brought the lad hither from the Don to show him to the sir brothers in the *siech*. The sword that was the blade of Kaidu is his because he can use it well—"

"If it had cut down Satan it would have served us," Loboda whispered. "But that time is past. Not a blade, but the wisdom of a wolf is needed now by the brothers who still live."

And he turned with an effort, considering Khlit and the red-cheeked priest who held in both hands the icon that hung from the silver chain at his throat.

"Will the Poles and the boyars follow the victory?" Khlit muttered, pulling at his mustache. "Have they many squadrons? What kind of leader?"

The sight of Loboda, who had reveled with him in the Cossack camp, had brought back to the veteran the memory of the times when he had led the army against Turk and Tartar. He spoke to the priest, but it was the colonel who answered.

"Back yonder they have the Tchortiaka, the Archfiend, for commander."

"*Aya tak*," nodded the priest—"Aye, so."

"He is a Cossack!" Loboda muttered, and spat weakly.

Khlit started and bent to look into the eyes of the stout priest.

"A Cossack wars against his brothers? That has never been!"

"Until now," put in the priest sadly. "But he is also a monk. And he calls himself an emperor."

If the quiet priest had not added his word to that of Loboda, Khlit would have thought the dying Colonel was out of his mind—it did not occur to the wanderer that Loboda might be finding excuses for the defeat of that day. A Cossack commander is the servant of the *siech* and his brothers. If he fails—as some must do—he gives up the baton of his own accord, and no voice is raised to blame him.

Sudden coughing choked Loboda, and when he could breathe freely again, his lips had grown pallid.

"Thirty thousand free-born Cossacks followed him to the north. Now only six thousand have breath in them—Khlit. He was a traitor. Batko Andriev will tell—Khlit, lead the brothers to the *siech*!"

"Nay, Colonel Loboda—I can no longer strike with a sword."

"Take this! Who is to take it, if you do not?"

The *ataman* held out the ivory baton, and for a moment Khlit bent his head in thought. He had no conception of the forces in the field against the Cossacks, of the route to be taken or Loboda's plans. Yet he knew that this night the council of the clans could not be summoned to choose a new *ataman*. The need was instant, and hesitation was not a part him.

"I will take it," he said gravely, his eyes on the face of his comrade.

Loboda put the baton in his gaunt fingers, and Khlit thrust it straightway into his belt, turning to the young officer of the Black Kosh.

"You hold the rear. Have you pickets out?"

"Aye, father—" the warrior addressed Khlit as the new commander without a shadow of doubt—"one on either side the road, half a verst in the fields. A detachment of thirty back along the road—"

"Go to the detachment. I will send a man, when we move on."

"At command!"

The youth of the Black Kosh grasped his saber and ran to the gate, calling for his horse. Ayub, hearing the stir, came in from the street, where he had been searching for a sled. When he saw the prostrate Loboda and the baton in Khlit's belt, he halted as if struck by a bullet. For months he had ridden beside the old wanderer, had shared blankets and porridge pot with him; but now he saw that Khlit had been made leader of the Cossacks and he spoke to him as the Koshevoi Ataman of the *siech*.

"Father," he said anxiously, "I have a *kunak*, a comrade who has been left at the fire because he is stubborn. As God lives, he must not be left to be tortured by the Poles—"

"A three-horse sled has been kept for Loboda. The horses are being fed, down the street. Bring it—put the Cossack in it, with the colonel. Take ten from the Black Kosh. Follow the wagon train, a verst to the rear."

The giant Zaporogian plunged back into the drift and Loboda raised himself on one elbow, a gleam in his sunken eyes.

"Aye," he whispered, "shepherd the lads—south, Khlit. Forget not the Cossack dead—swear to me that the traitor who betrayed us—"

A fit of coughing swept him and when it was gone he could not even whisper. Khlit understood what he wished.

"I swear that he will die by a Cossack sword."

And when the sled whirled up out of the snow curtain and Loboda was placed in it beside the unconscious Pavlenko, he was smiling upon set teeth. The dying men were covered with bearskins, a Cossack mounted the off-horse of the three and Ayub sprang into the saddle of Pavlenko's charger.

But Khlit sought out Loboda's black stallion that had been led in after the colonel. He reined through the gate in advance of the sled, and checked the stallion back sharply.

"*Hai-a!*" He lifted his deep voice in a cry that carried the length of the street. "*Kosh po sotnyam-ra-ab*! Kosh into squadrons—form!"

Dimly-seen figures started up, and the nearest running to their mounts, peered at the lean rider on the colonel's charger who gave a command like a chief of Cossacks. The appearance of the gray-haired warrior, out of the storm itself, had an aspect of the miraculous, and the tired men closed up the formation, dressed the ranks, and stared at their leader with expectancy.

When the clinking of bit chains, the creaking of leather and muttered words of the sergeants ceased Khlit rode out in front of the Black Kosh.

Although he could see no more the first lines of the leading *sotnia*, he knew that some five hundred riders were drawn up in place waiting for his next command.

"Pvar Kosh sably pet!" he roared. "Swords up! The salute of the regiment!"

A sudden scraping of steel, a rustle of heavy coats, and the firelight from the gate of the tavern yard gleamed on upflung sabers.

But Khlit did not take the salute himself. The Cossack who had reined in the sled at the gate snapped his whip, and the three horses plunged forward, passing the motionless ranks, and vanished into the white curtain where Ayub waited with his ten.

Loboda had taken for the last time the salute of his Cossacks.

"Sheath sabers! Dismount."

With a word to the sergeant on the flank of the first squadron Khlit trotted back to the inn yard where the hooded priest and Kirdy were standing by the hissing embers of the fire.

"Hai, batko—Hi, little Grandfather," the new *ataman* said, "tell me of this Archfiend who has broken faith with the brotherhood, and of the battle this day. Be swift, because we ride forth at any moment."

Chapter II
The Tale of Batko Andriev

When Ivan the Terrible, Tsar of Muscovy, Lord of Novgorod and of Sibir, died some twenty years before, he left in the world two sons—an elder, Feodor, and a lusty youngster Dmitri.

He left, too, a councilor, Boris Godunov, wise beyond his generation and ambitious.

Feodor was saint-like and weak. Boris reigned as regent in Moscow until the ailing Feodor passed to his grave. And a courtier of Boris's was believed to have slain the boy Dmitri. At all events, Dmitri vanished, and in the next years it was seen that a curse was on the land. Famine stalked from the tundras of the north to the deserts of the south. Men said this was retribution for the deed that opened Boris's path to the throne. Dmitri, the last prince of the line of Rurik, had been slain.

And when the usurper Boris died—as he soon did—men said that the murder of Dmitri had been a curse upon him.

There was now no one to sit in the eagle throne of the Kremyl at Moscow. The boyars would not tolerate the son of Godunov. The time of trouble began.

Then Dmitri reappeared, a living man, at the gates of Moscow.

Out of the Monastery of the White Lake he came—where he had been sequestered since he was a child. He had broken his vows as a monk and had wandered off to join the brotherhood of the Zaporogian Cossacks. A bold rider, a wild spirit at revelry, and a youth of wit and daring, he had won his place in the hearts of the Cossacks.

From their camp he had gone to Poland, to the powerful King Sigismund, who had ambitions of his own. Dmitri's name had remained a secret until then—until, gravely stricken by sickness, he had confessed his origin to a Jesuit priest, saying that a slave child had been slain by mistake for himself. He had shown a jeweled cross given him by his parents, explaining that servants had hidden him in the monastery during the life of Boris Godunov.

Whether or not the king of the Poles believed his story, Sigismund saw at once that Dmitri would be a weapon in his hand. Dmitri was honored, and at the news of the death of Boris was sent into Muscovy with an army of Polish nobles. He summoned his old companions, the Zaporogian Cossacks, and they rallied to him. Battles were fought, but the boyars of Moscow were as ready to receive the young Dmitri as to fight against him. The gates were opened to him.

Over a land famine-ridden, among a stricken people, Dmitri rode laughing to his throne. The widow of Ivan was sent for, and embraced him, acknowledging him for her son. It seemed as if the time of trouble were past and done with.

Dmitri plunged into the task of ruling as if it had been a new pastime. He was tsar—autocrat of many million souls. Instead of riding in the imperial cortege, he galloped through the streets on his Kabarda horses; he drank deep of nights sitting with the foreign officers. Sham battles between the stolid Muscovite regiments and the German mercenaries were his pleasure. Where the holy images should have stood in his bedchamber, he hung a grinning mask. Always he laughed.

His wife, a Polish princess, arrived in Moscow attended by other regiments of King Sigismund. With these and the Germans Dmitri surrounded himself. He placed taxes on the monasteries to pay his soldiery.

And when it became clear to the Cossacks that Dmitri was ready to give their land to the Poles and King Sigismund, they left Moscow. At once the tsar sent his armies after them.

"Four battles in the snow—three charges of armored hussars repulsed—a retreat of four hundred miles, and still the Cossack array is not broken.

Powder gone, to the last grains—horses bleeding at the veins from lack of forage—the brothers have not yielded."

So said the priest Andriev, while his black eyes sparkled and the white flakes gleamed like jewels in his long beard. Khlit lifted his head suddenly. Scattered musket shots sounded in the north, and the dog Karai got up to move to the gate.

"For a *batko*," said Khlit grimly, "you know much—of kings and thrones."

The beard of the stout little priest twitched as he grinned, and his red cheeks broadened.

"I? Nay I am no more than the little father of the Cossacks. Yet, *ataman*, when sin rises before the eyes like a gray fiend—I see! All these matters were told me by one who did not lie. *Ohai!*" Andriev shook his head savagely. "He did not lie."

"Who was he?"

"A Jesuit—the same black robe who took the confession of Dmitri in Poland—an enemy of all Orthodox believers. A servant of the red hats in Rome who would make slaves of the free brothers. Harken, Khlit—before the first battle near Muscow we made prisoners of some Poles who were on their way to Warsaw. Among them was this black robe. The brothers would have burned him, because his accursed people burned Netchai our father in a brazen bull. But he ran to me and prayed for his life, saying that he could reveal to us a secret that would aid the Cossacks. First he told me all this that I have said. And then—"

Andriev glanced to right and left and drew closer to the old Cossack.

"This Dmitri," he said "is not the son of Ivan the Terrible."

"Not the tsar!" Khlit peered into the round red face of the little *batko*.

"*Ohai*—he has been crowned as tsar. In the church of Michael the Archangel, he was blessed and given the three crowns, and the princes of Muscovy kissed his hand. I saw it. But he is an impostor—a youth of wit and daring, who broke his vows of the monastery and said that he was Dmitri, the son of Ivan Grodznoi."

The little priest crossed himself and sighed.

"His real name is Gregory Otrèpiev."

"Otrèpiev." Khlit repeated thoughtfully. For ten years his wanderings had led him from the *siech*, and all these events were strange to him. But in Cathay and Ind he had seen men staking lives and treasure for a throne.

"The empress-mother acknowledged him—"

"She is old—she was persuaded," Andriev responded sadly. "The Jesuit admitted it—when his throat was pricked with steel."

"Is he dead?"

"Nay, I had pledged him life. Yet when our father Netchai heard the truth he went to the tsar's majesty and cried out, 'False Dmitri!' Then swords were drawn, and Netchai was taken and given to the Poles to play with. They kindled fire and roasted him. And Otrèpiev began to hunt the Cossacks down—"

"Who else knows the truth?"

"King Sigismund, almost of a surety. Some of the Muscovite princes suspect, but while they eat from gold dishes at Otrèpiev's table they are well enough content—"

"Enough!" Khlit closed his eyes for a moment, striding up and down before the stout, hooded priest. In his mind's eye the old Cossack beheld stark treachery. He saw traitors in the palaces of the Kremyl; a Polish woman empress—the splendid armies of Poland encroaching on the fertile Cossack steppes, eager for land and slaves.

In truth Otrèpiev, the false tsar, was troubled by neither hesitation nor remorse. He had turned, as a snake strikes, upon the Cossacks, who had joined him as allies at his plea. Now, as a bone is thrown to a dog to quiet it, he would throw the Cossack lands to the Poles—as the reward of their aid.

Deep in his throat the *ataman* growled, and Andriev looked up.

"Aye, Father," the priest said, "it is a black hour. Did not the impostor Otrèpiev cast down the icons from the stand and put in their stead a grinning mask? God's anger is like a storm upon the Muscovites."

"Yet the Archfiend lives," put in Kirdy, speaking for the first time—and Khlit turned upon him to stare grimly at his grandson.

"What was Loboda's plan?" he asked of the priest.

"To draw back, like a wolf, into the steppes, to muster new forces—"

"Against the Poles, the Lithuanians and the Muscovites!" Khlit threw back his head and laughed impatiently. "Nay, we are bait, to be cast from one to the other! We are so many heads of men and cattle to be roped and sold! To draw back is to invite a thrust. We must strike," he added slowly, "at least one blow."

"With what?" Andriev stretched out his strong hands helplessly.

Khlit stalked to the gate and summoned a Cossack to ride back to the detachment, and order all patrols to draw in on the *kosh*.

When the veteran *ataman* returned to the fire he stopped beside Kirdy.

"It is time," he said. "We must take the road. You have no horse. You will not need one, lad."

To this Kirdy made no response, but the priest uttered an exclamation of surprise.

"An hour ago," Khlit went on quietly, "I made a pledge to Colonel Loboda—that the traitor should die by a Cossack sword. Then, I did not know his name. An oath is an oath. Otrèpiev joined the brotherhood of the free Cossacks. Then he betrayed his brothers and gave to the fire Netchai, the *ataman*. Death to him!"

Kirdy bent his head in understanding. Andriev cried out in protest.

"Nay, Father—do not send a Cossack, your grandson, to die. No man could win through the guards of the tsar, to stab him."

"Otrèpiev is not a tsar but a traitor. Nay, Kirdy is a match for any man with a sword, and a sword will deal with the false Dmitri." Khlit touched the hilt of the curved saber at the young warrior's side, the same that he had worn in other days. "My sword and my honor go with you, lad. This is the blow we must strike."

"But how—"

"How looks he—this Otrèpiev, *batko*?"

Andriev swallowed his misgiving and searched his memory.

"Shorter by half a head than this White Falcon, but stalwart. No older, surely. His face is shaven smooth, and his skin is brown. Like a restive horse, he always moves his hands or limbs."

"Aye, so. But he bears some mark upon him?"

"A mark? Well, there is a wart or mole under the right eye, near the nose."

Even while speaking Khlit had been feeling under his girdle, and now he handed a small leather sack to Kirdy.

"Jewels—take them to the Jews. Change your garments, hide your sword. You who have come hither from the Gobi can appear as a Mongol lord among the Muscovites. You only, among the brothers, can do this. Do not come to me until Otrèpiev is dead."

He had taken the rein of the waiting charger, and now he swung into the saddle as the Cossack who had gone for the patrols trotted through the tavern gate.

"Is the detachment back in ranks?"

"Aye, Father."

"Then take this *batko* up behind."

Although grief tugged at the heart of the old *ataman*, he walked his horse in silence to the street, Kirdy striding beside him. Then, pretending to adjust a stirrup strap, he leaned down.

"Kirdy, I cannot leave any of the brothers with you. They would be smelled out—Ayub beyond all. Your road is dark, Cossack, be wary."

Searchingly, questioningly, he glanced at the silent figure beside him.

"Aye, *ataman*," Kirdy's clear untroubled voice made response.

Satisfied, Khlit reined on, although for a moment he saw nothing of what was before him. For years he had led Kirdy through hardships—had seen him suffer—had tested his courage in a hundred ways. Out of the youth he had forged a weapon. And this weapon, so evenly tempered, had touched his own spirit at parting.

"I have made a Cossack of him," he thought. "But has he a heart?"

A moment later he flung an order over his shoulder.

"Forward, the *kosh*! Trot! Singers to the front—the song of the *siech*!"

With bowed head Kirdy leaned against the gatepost, Karai curled up in the snow at his feet. Eagerly he listened to the song of the marching Cossacks. He had crossed a continent to join these brothers, and within two hours he was left alone. A twinge of sadness touched him. But to the eye of an onlooker—if any had seen him in the murk of the falling snow—he seemed lost in contemplation. He had a task to perform, and with Kirdy that left no room for consideration of other matters. He must go to the false tsar and measure swords with him.

When the first patrols of the Dobrudja Tartars in advance of the Polish regiments entered the streets of the village, riding slowly with keen eyes peering into the snow curtain, they saw neither man nor dog, but only the deserted courtyard of a silent tavern.

Chapter III
The Eagle's My Brother

I've hunted the wolf—I've coursed the stag,
Over the prairies
Of Tartary.
The eagle's my brother, the wild horse my nag—
Hai-a—come and hunt with me!

Leashing his whip-end about Karai's stalwart neck, Kirdy glanced up and down the street and crossed it, seeking a huddle of cattle sheds that he had noticed when he entered the village. Stooping, he made his way among restless steers and vociferating calves until he was conscious of an odor more penetrating than that of fouled straw or penned cattle. With a booted foot he felt in a manure heap until he touched something solid and heavy.

"Up, *chlop*—up, animal, and tell me where the Jew's hole is." A man arose from hiding and bowed up and down like a marionette, breathing gustily between teeth that chattered.

"*Tlck! Tlck*! Be merciful, your Illustriousness. It is true that the Jews will give the noble-born warrior better plunder than we poor Orthodox believers. Only come—*tlick*—this way!"

The frightened peasant led Kirdy through the sheds and pointed out a nest of high wooden buildings that seemed to be falling in upon themselves. Kirdy climbed a fence that Karai leaped without effort, and made his way into a back door. Here the darkness was, if possible, more impenetrable than under the sheds, and the reek was of cookery and washed wool. With the tip of his scabbard Kirdy probed piles of trash and garments until Karai growled suddenly, and the Cossack reached down to seize a human leg clad in a long woolen stocking.

He changed his grip to the collar of his captive's *shuba* and warned the Jew in a whisper to be quiet and conduct him to the headman of the colony. The request was emphasized by a touch of the sheathed saber— Kirdy would not have touched the steel blade to such a being for any need whatsoever.

The invisible man went at a half trot through halls cluttered with quilts and pots, up stairs where rats scampered away, up a ladder where Kirdy was obliged to carry the wolfhound under his free arm, over a covered gallery into a dark loft and stale, warm air. A woman squealed at the glowing eyes of the wolfhound, and Kirdy voiced a warning:

"Strike a light, one of you. No harm, if you obey. Otherwise you will feel the fangs of the borzoi, the wolf chaser."

A patter of whispers was followed by a scramble, and flint flashed against tinder. A candle flamed up, and the young Cossack saw that he was in an attic filled with old men, women, and children scattered among piles of goods. From the rafters hung legs of mutton, strings of onions, and mysterious articles of Jewish attire. Half a hundred dark eyes fastened instantly on the tall youth and—in spite of deadly fear—gauged to a nicety the worth of his ermine coat, his wide velvet trousers, gold embroidered boots and splendid girdle.

An elder in a ragged *shuba* came forward, holding his head on one side, his long cap in his gaunt hands—an ancient being scarred with pock-marks, with one eye half closed and the other shrewd and brilliant as the eye of a fox.

"Yusyski is my name, your honor. Only tell in what way my people can serve the noble knight."

"If one of your brood leaves the loft, you will die, Yusyski. Come with me. Take the candle."

Placing Karai at the end of the gallery, where the gray dog sniffed and growled alternately—relishing the human nest as little as his master—Kirdy made Yusyski overhaul piles of garments upon the shelves. Here were articles of miserable and costly attire taken from lords and Gypsies alike because the Jews dealt with all the world and no one escaped their clutches. So far, Kirdy saw, they were not aware that the Cossacks had abandoned the village.

He made a selection of clothing with care, then overhauled a dozen outer coats, and Yusyski groaned when he chose a dark sable with voluminous sleeves and a lining of yellow satin. Sending the old Jew before him, he entered the gallery and went to the loft of the other building which was deserted. Here he stripped off his splendid ermine *svitza*, the gift of Boris Godunov, his boots, and in a moment stood utterly naked, his sword near his right hand.

And as swiftly he began to dress while Yusyski watched in subdued amazement. First Kirdy slipped a white silk shirt over his long, muscular body, then wrapped himself from ankles to neck in lengths of the same stuff; after putting on a sleeveless black tunic that reached to his knees—over wide damask trousers—he donned a short quilted vest, heavily embroidered. Finally he drew on the sable outer coat and a round velvet hat with a long peacock feather rising from its crown.

"I swear," cried Yusyski, "the noble Cossack has taken for himself some of the garments of the Cathayan prince who was frozen to death down on the Volga. It will cost the noble lord seventy gold ducats!"

In fact Kirdy now stood arrayed as a Cathayan or Mongol youth of high rank. He had not been able to find the proper velvet footgear, but contented himself with a pair of Muscovite half-boots which were inconspicuous and much more serviceable.

"A razor and warm water, Yusyski," he ordered.

For the last moments the Jew had been using his ears to advantage. He heard horsemen in the streets—heard Muscovites shouting back and forth—the creaking of carts and the stamp and ring of armored squadrons. Lights were springing up, visible through the cracks in the loft. It was clear to Yusyski that the Cossacks were no longer in the village and the tsar's forces had entered.

"Seventy ducats!" he repeated more boldly. He had heard Kirdy's wallet ring heavily when it was thrown on the floor, and he had guessed very closely at the contents. "Then we will talk of a razor."

The Cossack was occupied in tearing up his costly girdle and rolling a strip into a short sling—an act that filled Yusyski with despair—and from the sling, thrown over his left shoulder, he hung his scabbard and sword, within the ample folds of the sable where it could not be seen.

"Nay, Yusyski," he grinned, "the ermine *svitza* is worth more than all this. You are paid."

But good-nature made the Jew more insistent.

"*Ei-ei*, does not the Cossack know that his enemies are all around the house? If I send for them—"

"I know, Yusyski. Send, if you will! Shout!"

This compliance made the elder instantly suspicious. He gnawed his fingernails, glancing from the dog to Kirdy and at the row of heads that thrust out from the passage. Tongues clacked in the heads and Yusyski began to cluck back at his audience, his hands writhing to right and left and grasping at his earlocks. His people were giving him advice, to fetch the Muscovite soldiery and have the Cossack slain, and Yusyski was cursing them for putting him at the mercy of the Cossack's sword.

"You have robbed me. I shall send for the Muscovites," he cried, glaring with his one eye at Kirdy.

"Good! They will burn me, perhaps, but they will root out your hole."

The wily elder had already come to that conclusion, and he saw now that Kirdy was not to be intimidated. Beyond everything Yusyski feared that the soldiers would find the way up to his lofts. Covertly he moved the ermine *svitza* out of sight of his brethren and piled saddlecloths on it, threatening his followers with untold misery if they disobeyed him.

"Give me your purse, Cossack," he demanded, "and you can go unharmed. Slieb will show you a way."

"First, the razor."

Yusyski prepared to argue the point, but a glance at Kirdy made him scream an order at the individual who had brought the Cossack to the loft. Slieb fetched a knife with a sharp edge and a basin of water. Watched intently by eyes that were covetous and at the same time fearful, Kirdy shaved off his scalp lock and the middle of his mustache. He trimmed the ends carefully, and Yusyski, who had heard soldiers preparing to quarter themselves in the lower floors, was inspired to fetch wax. With this Kirdy coaxed his mustache into the thin drooping lines of a Mongol.

His swarthy skin, black hair and eyes all fitted into the part. He passed his hand over the muscles of his face, let his eyelids droop, and, folding his arms in his sleeves, said with the quick inflection of a Mongol:

"*Mai machambi yarou*! Take heed, merchant!"

The Jews crowded nearer to stare and chatter, and even the redoubtable Yusyski blinked. A man of stratagems himself, he could appreciate a trick. Even the sword, as Kirdy happened to know, bore a Mongol inscription, and except for the pile of wet Cossack clothing on the floor and the word of the Jews—which was of doubtful value—a Mongol prince now stood in the attic of the elders. There was Karai, to be sure, who smelled over his master's new attire with interest. But more than one wolfhound was in the steppe, and Kirdy was quite willing to risk keeping him.

"*Ei-ei*!" grunted Yusyski. "It is like magic. But now the noble prince will give the gold and we will swear to keep his secret."

"Not now. Come to me tomorrow at high noon by the tavern gate, and I will give you ten pieces."

"Ten!" Yusyski raised both arms over his head, and snatched back his dirty sleeves to argue.

"Enough!" Kirdy's patience was at an end. Taking out, one after the other, ten gold ducats from the wallet Khlit had given him, he showed them to Yusyski in his palm, and a portentous silence fell upon the crowd. "They are yours if you keep silence. Follow me," he added on an after-thought, "or give me away to the soldiers, and how many gold pieces will you have? Not one. The Muscovites will pocket them."

Yusyski's one eye blinked rapidly, and he clutched Kirdy's arm, leaping back in fright when Karai rose suddenly from the shadows and snarled silent menace.

"O my God, illustrious sir; not a whisper will pass our lips. But how do we know the glorious knight will keep faith?"

Kirdy kicked up Slieb.

"You know well that a Cossack keeps faith, Jew. Here, animal, lead out of your warren."

Recognizing checkmate, Yusyski abandoned Kirdy and rounded upon his tribe, spitting and loosing a flood of jargon as he made ready to justify himself and at the same time keep the ermine *svitza* hidden and claim a majority of the ten ducats—a task to which, judging by appearance, he was quite equal, in spite of heavy odds against him.

The next morning a handsome young Mongol, obviously of rank, breakfasted quietly at the tavern, looking with well-bred curiosity at the pack of officers that filled every available seat.

Here were Polish *litzars* in polished and gold-plated armor and feathered helmets—stalwart Muscovite boyars in mail covered with cloth-of-gold trimmed with fur—pale Lithuanians who kept well together and were more than ready to quarrel with anyone who got in their way.

In fact, more than one quarrel flared up, and swords were grasped angrily. Servants, seeking their masters, elbowed and snarled for precedence. *Heydukes* in *kaftans* and Persian *khalats* galloped up to the tavern and drained the last liquor from the barrels that had been tapped by their superiors and rolled outside to make room. In the court, within great kettles roasted the quarters of the cows and steers Kirdy had seen in the cattle sheds. Carts blocked the streets; peasants, driven from their cottages, stood in frightened groups, while the smoke of campfires rose from the plain on every side.

It was a large army, made up of many factions. Tartar patrols rode in from time to time but brought no word of the Cossacks. The snow of last night had covered the tracks of Khlit's squadrons and mystified the boyars. Complaints, arguments, and advice were plentiful, but no one seemed to be in command of this army.

Certainly no one gave Kirdy more than a passing glance. A colonel of one of the regiments, noticing that the young Mongol's hands were strangely muscular and his face lean for an Eastern prince, took the trouble to question him.

Smilingly Kirdy responded in fluent Manchu-Tartar that he had been journeying from the hordes of Central Asia to see the great emperor of the Muscovites in his imperial city. His followers and interpreter, he explained, had been lost.

"Probably slain by dog-Cossacks," the colonel muttered and was passing on when Kirdy detained him courteously.

"Is not the emperor of the Muscovites in this camp?"

"Nay. Two days ago he rode north."

"To his imperial city?"

"Aye, to Moscow."

"And are you, O *orda khan*, in command of these men?"

Visibly flattered, the Polish colonel shook his head.

"Not I. The prince Basmanof was left in command. I have heard that he is taking horse for the north. God only knows what is happening and who is in command."

Kirdy could well believe this. On the highroad he found the baggage sleds of the nobles in a hopeless confusion and the drivers at a wordy war; in the fields only the veteran Polish hussars and the light cavalry of Tartars preserved good order. When he learned beyond doubt that Basmanof had left the army, taking his suite with him, Kirdy was satisfied that the Cossacks were in no danger of pursuit. Their quick march through the village, where the tsar's army had expected them to bivouac, had saved them.

The Mongol was seen that morning, by certain Jews who had an interest in him, moving here and there among the regiments. A little before noon he bought a horse from a *boyarin* who had lost heavily at dice the night before—a shaggy mustang with a high Muscovite birch saddle. In this he appeared in due course at noon, as he had promised, by the tavern gate, and Yusyski, who had been weighing the relative chance of profit in betraying the Cossack, or waiting for the reward, greeted him with profound delight.

"*Okh*, never for an instant did I doubt the noble lord would keep his promise."

Kirdy, through narrow eyes, stared at him coldly.

"*Mantourami tsia*," he responded. "I speak naught but Manchu."

Little understanding, but guessing at his meaning, Yusyski wagged his head admiringly and counted the ten gold pieces from one hand to the other, hiding them swiftly in his wallet. Then Kirdy, as he had seen Khlit do the evening before, bent down to shorten still more the stirrup strap—because a Mongol rides almost squatting in the saddle.

"Tell me, Jew," he whispered, "is this in truth the army of Dmitri—the tsar?"

"Aye," said Yusyski, his eye on the wallet at Kirdy's girdle.

"And this Basmanof, who is he—the commander?"

"Aye," the elder said again, cautiously. "The prince Basmanof was the friend of Boris Godunov. When the boyars rebelled against him and the son Boris Godunov, the prince was swift to join the new tsar. Many hated him, but the tsar loves him because he is daring and can squeeze the last kopek out of us Jews. Now, my lord, give me another ten ducats!"

Kirdy laughed.

"I swore that you should have ten. No more."

When he rode on, the one eye of Yusyski glared after him as if in some manner the elder of the tribe had been cheated, although in reality he had profited greatly.

Kirdy, however, was thinking of anything but the Jew. He had seen Khlit accept the baton of a broken and driven army as the honor that it was; and now he had heard of the tsar and Basmanof leaving this great array, victorious, well fed and equipped—as if a plague had broken out in the village. If the false tsar was in Moscow he must go thither, but he decided that he would overtake the prince's suite and travel with it.

It was the third day before he came up to the camp of the prince's party, and he was a little surprised to find it out in the open, although settlements were fairly thick hereabouts.

He presented himself before Basmanof—a ruddy man with gray hair, who looked more than a little worried—and told the same story that he had improvised for the Polish colonel. Saying that his servants had been lost, he requested permission to buy a spare horse, rice and tea for himself, and fish for the dog. This was granted indifferently and he added to his stock a bearskin, spreading it beside one of the fires of the encampment.

During that night, awakened by Karai's sudden growl, he heard a rider come in from the north and go to the prince.

After breakfast the next morning he heard the Muscovites saying that Basmanof had ordered a horse saddled before dawn and had ridden off with only one servant to make haste to Moscow.

And Kirdy thought there was dire need if the prince had left his suite with no more than one equerry to attend him. He was certain of it when he failed to overtake Basmanof on the road, although he kept the saddle for long hours—the prince changing horses at each post station, and sleeping, apparently, not at all.

Yet the placid-appearing Mongol made such excellent time that he trotted through the river gate of Moscow at dusk of the afternoon that the erstwhile commander of the army had made his entry.

Chapter IV
The Whirlwind Casts No Shadow

The whirlwind casts no shadow, and the lightning makes no sound;
the viper strikes unseen and the flood sends no herald before it.

Afghan proverb

Not by chance did Kirdy arrive at the walls of the imperial city at the hour of evening prayer. He knew that men are prone to be more watchful in broad daylight or deepest darkness than at twilight. And it was vitally important that he should pass the sentries of the outer wall without attracting attention.

A Cossack, attempting to ride into Moscow, would have been cut down or sent to the cells of Uglitch. A Cossack spy, if detected, would have been pulled apart by horses.

Seemingly he did not notice the halberdiers of the watch but he was both surprised and thankful to observe that they were foreigners who paid no attention to him. For a while he rode through the Kitaigorod, or Chinese city, where he would be expected to go. He talked a bit with some Manchu silk merchants, then sought out a small inn where his lack of a retinue would not excite comment. He watched his ponies rubbed down and fed, and wandered forth with Karai at his heels.

He cast only one glance at the crenellated wall of the Kremyl with its bulbed towers and gilded spires. To seek an audience of the false Dmitri was out of all consideration. It was impossible. He had come to slay with his sword the man who had deceived people into accepting him as tsar.

Kirdy's only chance was to meet his enemy in the streets. He had heard that the pretended Dmitri rode recklessly from place to place, like a Cossack. So, with infinite patience he set about learning all he could of the new tsar's habits.

Outwardly, he was a prince of Cathay, amused at the wonders of the imperial city. He stopped to watch the guard change at the palace, and he noticed that the half-company of archers and halberdiers that marched from the barrack gate of the Kremyl was made up of Swedes and Poles— the bodyguard commanded by a French captain.

This officer, brave in ribbons and gigantic boots, was called Jacques Margeret—as Kirdy in learned time by following the guardsmen and listening to the comments of passers-by. He thought, too, Margeret looked both irritable and feverish. At the barrack the archers and halberdiers were dismissed, and the French captain went hastily to a nearby tavern.

Kirdy resumed his ramble, the richer by one more particular. The foreign soldiery was heartily disliked by the native Muscovites. Perhaps this was because the tsar allowed only foreigners in his bodyguard. It had been very different in the days of Boris Godunov, when the boyars thronged the palace.

"He eats veal," grumbled a bearded giant, glaring after the handsome Margeret.

"That is not the worst—the tsar dines, it is said, without sprinkling the table with holy water."

Others of the group took up the tale:

"He sets bears to chase the priests who would attend him."

The first speaker shook his head sagely.

"*Ekh*, that is sin. Beyond doubt there is a fiend in the tsar, because of evenings he walks the streets almost alone, going into the shops of Frankish jewelers and such places."

The Mongol prince moved nearer the speakers, as if undecided whether or not to enter the tavern.

"There is no knowing where he goes, Ivan Ilyushka," grumbled another. "He is everywhere, but who sees him? It was not so with his father."

"A-ah! Ivan Grodznoi did not make a jest of holy things."

The talk veered to the taxing of the monasteries, and the tall Mongol moved away, followed by the great wolfhound. In fact, the doors of the monasteries were closed; the very bells rang out somberly.

If half of Moscow was penned up and moody another half was in festival. The night was clear and cold—a full moon soaring above the cloud wrack on the horizon. A company of buffoons and dwarfs passed noisily, bound for the Kremyl, shouting at the solemn, long-robed townspeople. They halted themselves at a fire. Here a Venetian mountebank had set up a marionette theater, and the familiar images of an old husband and a young wife and Mephistopheles were dancing about on strings, to the edification of the onlookers—until the Italian ducked out from his stall to hold forth his hat and cry the merits of his performance.

The Mongol—this being an excellent place to overhear talk—dropped
a coin in the hat and watched gravely when the miniature actors began
to dance again on their strings, while a hunchback tortured melody from
an ancient fiddle.

Horses entered the narrow street, and when the crowd turned to stare
the sable-clad Mongol glanced sidewise. A party of boyars were escorting a sleigh toward the Kremyl, and in the sleigh was nothing but a long
casket-like object wrapped in silk. So solemn the riders, so fantastic the
tasseled sleigh with its inanimate burden—the procession seemed to be
a ritual of some kind.

By token of the bossed trappings of the horses, and the cloth-of-gold that
covered the wooden saddles, the riders were men of rank. The crowd gave
back, bowing, to clear the way, and the leaders were preparing to move
on, when a merry chiming of bells sounded, and a three-horse sleigh entered the far end of the street, rounding the corner at a gallop, in a swirl
of snow.

At a cry from the driver the three coal-black Tartar steeds checked and
slid to a halt, obedient to the voice rather than to any tug of the reins. The
bells jangled and tinkled musically as the horses stood, pawing at the trodden snow, their nostrils steaming. Kirdy eyed them admiringly before he
spared a glance for the owner of the flying sleigh.

Then he lifted his head, forgetting for an instant the part he played, the
boyars, and the horses. A girl was in the sleigh, a white bearskin wrapped
around her.

Instead of the silver headgear of a noblewoman, she wore a fur cap, as
dark as the eyes that gleamed with suppressed amusement at the cortege
her horses had blocked. She sat erect, her silk *sarafan* shining upon slim
shoulders, and all at once she smiled. So unexpectedly friendly was this
smile, the men around Kirdy laughed good-naturedly.

"*Ekh!*" one muttered "what a splendid beauty—and no one to sit at
her side, the *divchina!*"

The leader of the boyars motioned at her impatiently.

"Out of the way, wanton!"

The girl's smile vanished, and her cheeks became colorless on the instant. She searched the faces of the riders as if they were past all understanding. Kirdy knew that Muscovite women of rank were kept as closely
secluded as Mohammedan wives and he suspected that it was unwonted
for a young girl to ride through the streets after torchlight.

But the occupant of the sleigh allowed scant time for thought. Springing to her feet, she snatched the whip from the driver's hand and lashed
across the face the *boyarin* who had spoken to her. It was a long Cossack
nagaika, and the flick of it drew blood on the noble's cheek.

"A thousand devils take you!" he roared drawing back instinctively.

"Go past!" She pointed with the whip, eyes and lips defiant. "Go, sei-
gneur, and take your grave thieves with you."

The bearded riders came forward to cluster about the leader and whisper
to him. Whether they did not know how to deal with the young woman,
or whether they disliked the attention they were attracting, they reined
their horses past the sleigh, forcing the crowd still farther back so that
their own vehicle could edge by the three blacks.

But the leader, shaking off his companions, trotted back to the sleigh
and bent down to peer at the girl with the whip.

"I shall look for you," he said calmly, "tomorrow."

Paying him no further heed, she handed back the whip to the driver,
and then glanced with quick interest at Karai. The gaunt wolfhound had
come into the street to sniff at the horses' tracks, and approached the sleigh
at her call, placing his forepaws on the side of the vehicle. Kirdy strode
after him with an exclamation, because the driver had started back and
Karai was not tolerant of whips.

"He is more than half wolf!" the girl said.

She rubbed her fingers through the shaggy hair of the borzoi's throat,
and though Karai's ears went back instinctively, his tongue lolled out pa-
cifically.

"O Cathayan, have you come to the carnival?" she added with thoughtful, searching eyes on Kirdy.

He bowed, to imply ignorance of the Muscovite words, and began to
slip the leash of his whip around Karai's throat. Then, to his utter astonishment, the girl in the sleigh spoke in fluent Manchu-Tartar that is the
dialect of High Asia.

"O son of white-boned fathers, you are far from the land of many rivers and the heavenly mountains. Surely you are an envoy to the court of
the White Emperor."

Still stooping over the wolfhound, he pondered his reply.

"Daughter of distinction I have no honor here. In the city of the Ta-jen
I am no more than a wanderer without servants or friends."

If his ready answer surprised her, she gave scant sign of it.

"You wear no sword, O wanderer!"

Sweeping his long arm toward the throng, as if to indicate the uselessness of a solitary weapon among so many strangers, he would have withdrawn but the girl was not yet satisfied.

"Friends! Surely in this place a man has need of friends. Come with
me. We shall talk together, you and I—for I am of the Altyn-juz, the
Golden Horde."

Kirdy regarded her calmly. This girl did not appear to be a Muscovite.
And he knew that no European woman would speak the language of the
Altyn-juz, which was the great horde that ruled the pastures of High Asia
between Cathay and the farthest posts of Muscovy. Her eyes were dark
enough, but her skin much too clear for a native woman—and certainly
no woman of the tribes would dare ride alone and whip a *boyarin*.

He assured himself that this must be a girl of the half-world, a spoiled
mistress of some lord of the frontier who owned the three horses and the
sleigh. It would be better not to accompany her.

"I am Nada," she said gravely, as if she had followed his thoughts. "My
house is near the Kremyl wall."

Hitherto, Kirdy had not pondered the matter of a name. It would not do
to hesitate in naming himself to this girl, and he did some quick thinking.
The garments he wore were those of a prince of the Altyn-juz, the Golden
Horde. But the girl had just claimed this people for her own. She might possibly know the names of the reigning families—among the nomad chiv-
alry of High Asia the family ties are strict and descent a matter of pride
and knowledge of twenty generations. And Kirdy was not apt at lies.

"I am Ak-Sokol of the Sha-mo," he said calmly.

He had told the exact truth. He was the White Falcon of the Sandy Desert that was called the Gobi. He did not add that Cossacks and not Mongols had given him this name—the same in both languages. And he had
been born in the Gobi.

"From where, in the Sha-mo?" she asked instantly.

Now the Gobi is a vast deal of land, including such things as rolling prairies and burning basins of land—rivers and barren mountain ranges.

"From the place of shifting sands where the sun rises beyond the Mountains of the Eagles," he responded, again taking refuge in the truth. He
knew the Gobi.

Nada's dark eyes gleamed with inward excitement or amusement. Clapping her hands suddenly, she laughed.

"O White Falcon, you please me. You have said well."

The laugh itself was mockery and the words hinted at unbelief. Because a Mongol prince is not supposed to endure ridicule, Kirdy saw that a chance was open to him to withdraw. He glanced up and down the street and stepped back, drawing Karai with him and silently cursing the dog's unwillingness to leave the sleigh.

"The way to your house is open, daughter of unwisdom," he assured Nada.

"And you will come—if you are not afraid of me. *Kai*, my lord of the Black Tents, prince of swords—now I know of a surety that you are the envoy sent to this court by my people. On the steppe I heard a tale that you were frozen to death, at the border river. My heart is glad that you live. Why do you take another name? Come and tell me!"

Kirdy wished that he could read Nada's thoughts as she seemed able to read his. Swift reflection gave him little comfort, because he understood that she must have known the envoy who was killed by the bitter cold down the Volga—as Yusyski the Jew had assured him. Now he wore the garments of the dead—who had borne another name.

So he did the simplest thing and seated himself beside her in the narrow sleigh. The hunchback by the fire took up his fiddle again, and the mountebank the strings of his marionettes. The crowd settled down to watch the play of the miniature actors, and the sleigh sped away while the bells chimed cheerily and Karai, his tongue hanging out on one side, trotted along behind looking every bit as wise and satisfied as Mephistopheles himself.

"I bid you to my bread and salt."

Nada, from between the two candles at the table's end, inclined her head to her guest. Kirdy took in his hand the cup offered to him by one of her servitors and bowed—a little stiffly by reason of the heavy sword slung within his fur mantle. Then before drinking he was careful to pour a driblet to the four quarters of the winds, as a Mongol should.

"*Paniha-boumbi*—my thanks to you!"

Well aware that he was being tested—though Nada gave no sign of it—he selected his food frugally. It was as natural that she should offer him refreshment in her house as that he should accept. The tea was seasoned with mutton fat, and he smacked his lips noisily over it; and he grunted loudly when he had eaten meat, to show a Mongol's appreciation of good things.

Meanwhile he took account of his surroundings—a dim hall with almost no furniture save the long table and benches, a roaring fire close at hand and straw underfoot. The wind whistled through cracks in the walls of hewn pine logs, and Kirdy had a curious impression that he was sitting within a forest rather than in a dwelling. The arched ceiling was barely visible, and the servitors of the place were certainly tribesmen. He did not think they were slaves.

There were no more than two—gnome-like old men, with hoods on their gray felt coats and horsehide boots on their warped legs. Even their swords were round and short, resembling hunting blades. He knew they came from the wastes of Asia beyond the frontier, and he believed they had served Nada for many years. No other woman was to be seen.

The very smell of the prairies had penetrated this room. Wooden saddles and sleeping-skins were flung against the wall. A hooded peregrine falcon screamed fitfully on its ring. The cups from which he drank were fashioned of birch.

"O my guest," Nada ventured when the last plate was pushed aside, "why did you lie to me?"

Kirdy looked up calmly.

"I have not lied to you."

"Are you really called the White Falcon?"

"Aye, so."

"No man of the Sha-mo ever came to the city of the White Walls before now."

"Then I am the first."

Kirdy turned toward the fire so that he would not look at Nada but could watch the two armed servitors who remained squatting in the shadows.

"O mistress of the house, you said that I was an ambassador. That is not the truth. Since when does a tablet-bearing prince of the Hordes come across the border without a swordsman at his back? I am no more than a wanderer, but in your thoughts—who am I?"

Above all things he wished to leave Nada without suspicion or doubt of him. And he knew by her silence that she was puzzled.

"You wear the garments of a prince of the Altyn-juz," she said, almost to herself. Kirdy smiled, and took refuge in a parable of the steppes.

"Because a goshawk wears the plumage of a brown eagle, is he an eagle?"

"Nay, but when a hawk soars like an eagle, the quail scatter on the ground. I think you are a spy, and I shall send word to the tsar's officers to take you."

Not long since, Kirdy had dared the Jews to give him up, but he suspected that Nada would dare do anything. She might well be a spy of the Poles and the Poles were in power for the moment. Leaning forward, he held his hands to the fire and made no answer, judging that if she threatened him she could not be sure of her own mind.

"Have you naught to say, O my guest?"

"This I would say: You spoke of the need of a friend; yet you will make of me an enemy."

From between the candles Nada glanced at him curiously. It was clear to Kirdy that the tribesmen might well have named her so—the Lily. Because her hair, streaming over her shoulders from the narrow pearl-sewn filet on her forehead, was light as ripe straw.

Upon this lightness of loose hair and the fair forehead of the girl the candle flames glowed, flickering when the wind swept the hall in tiny gusts. It was as if the splendid head of Nada were a moon, shedding light into the dim room. When Kirdy looked at her, he was troubled; the skin of his head and shoulders tingled, and words left his lips. In all his life he had not beheld a girl like this.

"Toghrul," she said clearly to one of her followers, "bind me this—foeman. Take him and bind him."

The two tribesmen drew their short hangers and came at Kirdy from either side, the one called Toghrul loosing a coil of woven horsehide at his girdle.

"O *Ak-Sokol*," he began persuasively, "thou hast heard the command. Hold forth thine arms and be bound."

Kirdy had risen from his bench, and after a swift glance at the youth's face Toghrul wasted no more words but cast a loop of the coil at his head. He saw that their distinguished guest did not intend to let himself be taken. Kirdy slipped aside from the rope and struck the tribesman in the chest, so that Toghrul stumbled and staggered back, barely saving himself from falling into the fire.

Meanwhile Kirdy had wheeled toward the door, only to find the other leaping at him. Again he dodged, but this time the flat of a heavy blade struck him over the ear, and he saw red. The dim room swayed, the firelight filled the air, and the whisper of the wind became a roar. Ripping open his mantle, he drew his long saber—that had been hidden until now—with a sharp slithering of steel.

He parried the second cut of the agile gnome and locked hilts. A second later the hooked scimitar flashed into the straw, and the man caught at his wrist with a groan. Upon the other servitor Kirdy leaped, and held his hand because Nada stood between them, her arms outstretched.

"*Hai-a,* my Cossack!" she cried softly: "The sword reveals the man. So does a Cossack leap and strike."

She came forward to look closely at the blue steel blade with its half-effaced inscription, and a word sent her two followers back into their shadow.

"I thought that you were a Cossack when you came to the sleigh, because you walked with a long stride. And your whip! Here, at the table, I doubted; but now there is no doubt. Can you use a sword?"

Without replying, Kirdy slipped the weapon back in its scabbard, which he held ready for use.

"You can!" Nada's lips trembled in a smile. "I prayed to the holy angels that they would send me a sword. I will not give you up to the Muscovites but you must serve me."

"O *divchina,* I am neither spy nor servitor. As you say, I am of the *siech,* free-born. I came to the city of the White Walls to slay a traitor. An oath has been sworn."

For a moment she pondered.

"And when you have slain this man? *Kai,* that is like a young warrior of the south—to follow a feud blindly, like a falcon that takes no notice of anything except its quarry."

"Then I go upon the snow road again, to the south."

Nada drew a bench to the fire and seated herself, leaning chin on hand, frowning a little.

"You said you came from the Sha-mo! I know it is true—you have no skill at lying."

"Aye, so. My grandmother on my mother's side was a princess of the Yakka Mongols, of the line from Genghis Khan. There was I born. But now I go to the Cossack *siech.*"

"Then you will need wings, O White Falcon. Because at midnight the city gates were closed, and now are guarded. None is suffered to pass out. So my men tell me."

Kirdy nodded without excitement. He never bothered his head about future difficulties, and he only wondered whether he could trust Nada to keep his secret.

"We have shared bread and salt," she said, as if answering his thought. "We are people of the steppe, and this is not our place. I do not know if we will pass again, alive, through the gates." Her eyes, wide and brooding, were bent on the fire. "O White Falcon, have you ever felt the storm wind rising far off, on the plains, when the black clouds mount up against the sun and the cattle become mad with fear? *Kai*, that has come upon me."

A breath of cold air stirred, and one of the candles went out, and Nada, glancing over her shoulder, gave a soft exclamation of dismay. Her hand went to her throat, and for the first time Kirdy saw that she wore a miniature icon, bearing a beautifully painted picture of an old man leaning on a wooden staff beside a wolf. He searched his memory and knew this for Saint Ulass of the wolves.

"A trap is set!" Nada began again, slowly, as if trying to see into the future. "For whom, for what? Toghrul, come here!"

The old tribesman came and squatted in the straw at her feet, like a dog.

"Didst thou see, Toghrul, the horses snort and rear when the boyars and their sleigh drew nigh us? Was that a sign?"

"Aye, Nada, they were afraid."

"But why?"

The lined face of the servitor puckered.

"Why not? There was a smell of the dead, of graves. It came from the sleigh."

"The casket in the red cloth was not a coffin—surely it was too small."

"I know not. The horses snorted and would have broken away had I not spoken to them."

"What else hast thou to say?"

"There is a *yang, yang seme*—a ringing of the bells. Even now it began, and the end is not yet."

"Nay, this is a festival night."

Toghrul considered and shook his head, speaking out with the boldness of one who knew his words were not idle.

"Not a festival, this! The Ta-jen with the little gods and the fiddle was merry in the street, yet the voice of the bells is otherwise. It is a voice raised to drive a devil away in the night, or to mourn because of bloodshed."

"I would have left the city, White Falcon, but the gates are shut and the order against leaving has gone forth. Is it not a trap? My fear is for you. If an oath has been sworn, you will not ride from Moscow until a man has died—but what if the trap is set for you?"

Her dark eyes were troubled, and Kirdy felt that she was indeed afraid. These three souls from the steppes were restless and alert, as he was. Intent on his purpose, he had no misgivings, and he did not think anyone but Nada knew that he was a Cossack.

"Go to the captain of the Franks, the man called Margeret," she cried. "I have talked with him, and he is a warrior who holds honor dear. Go to him and ask a written paper that will let me pass through the gates with three men."

Kirdy smiled.

"If the tsar has forbidden—"

"Who knows what the tsar has said? Margeret commands the first company of the bodyguards. His men are Franks, and they will obey an order from him. Go at once—oh, slay whom you will—break your sword and be cut down, if you will. Serve me only in this one thing, by the salt we shared—"

Seeing him thoughtful and unmoved, Nada stamped a slender, booted foot angrily.

"Fool! You will not forgive me because I played with you. But you will play the Cossack, and ride on and draw your sword and strike until life is cut out of you. Then you will be no more than a marionette that is tossed from the theatre. Abide by the oath, my wooden warrior, but bring me my paper before the dawn."

Chapter V
The Black Hour

Alone once more in the moonlit street, Kirdy reflected that he had been outwitted by the girl Nada. She had drawn his secret from him, had kept Karai with her—and might betray him to the very officer he was seeking. Nevertheless, he decided to go to Margeret. The captain of the imperial bodyguard would know better than anyone else the movements of the false Dmitri—might even be called upon to attend the impostor. And Nada's request would give him an excuse for arousing the officer at this hour of early morning.

He kept to the deep shadow in the narrow streets, with ears alert for the tread and clatter of the watch. He heard nothing except a flurry of hoofs when riders galloped through an adjoining alley, and a man laughed recklessly. Turning quickly, he beheld three black horses speeding through a lane of gleaming snow and the fluttering cloaks of men riding like fiends.

All the while the discordant tocsin of the bells rang out overhead, as if the great towers were calling to the graves to give up their dead.

Sleepy Muscovites stared at him in the taproom of the tavern and he was directed to an upper chamber, where the deep voice of the French captain was unmistakable enough. A Muscovite servant opened the door, candle in hand, and Kirdy sniffed at strangling fumes of charcoal. A brazier stood near the disordered bed upon which Margeret sat in shirt and trousers, his ruddy face blotched and gleaming with sweat.

At first Kirdy thought he was drunk. Margaret cursed steadily, shifting from one language to another as the impulse took him and paying no attention at all to his guest.

"He is sick," the servant observed tranquilly, "in the belly."

The Frenchman shivered, and his teeth clicked spasmodically. Racked by chills and the fever he straddled his bed and shouted for the sword that the servant would not give him.

"What is he saying?" Kirdy asked.

The serf yawned and listened.

"My master has been near to giving up his soul. The pains racked him when he came in. Then he grew worse all at once. That was how it was, your Excellency!"

"He'll die, right enough, in these fumes." The smoldering charcoal made Kirdy's head swim. "Carry the coals outside and build a fire."

The servant blinked bleared eyes and considered the matter at length.

"Why does your honor trouble about all that? If God sends my master death—no help for it. Besides, he appears to be stronger, now."

Kirdy's answer was to thrust his fist through the glazed paper window and kick the servant heartily. In his present state the foreign captain was incapable of signing any order at all; and the Cossack did not propose to watch him strangle in the foul air. So he forced Margeret to lie prone and covered him with all the quilts and skins in the chamber.

Grumbling, the servant brought wood and kindled a clean blaze on the hearth, eyeing askance the tall stranger who looked like a nobleman from

Cathay and paced the chamber angrily. Margeret ceased swearing and began to breathe more regularly. By the time the first gray light had crept
upon the white roofs he displayed an interest in his visitor.

"He asks," explained the servant, stumbling out of a doze, "what your
honor does in his room."

Kirdy explained carefully what he sought from the captain, and the
shaggy Muscovite interpreted the strange jargon that master and man had
hit on for mutual intercourse.

"He says your honor is mistaken. There was no order to close the gates.
You can ride forth with your young lady at any hour."

"Look!" Kirdy hauled him to the broken window and pointed through
it. The tavern was near the end of a street opening upon a drill ground and
one the gates of the Kremyl wall was visible, a knot of halberdiers clustered before it. The gate was shut, beyond a doubt.

The man blinked and scratched his head.

"Well, that is how it is. But it doesn't matter. My master says you can
go through, no one will stop you."

"Devil take the fellow!" Kirdy thought and added aloud: "The lady
must leave Moscow without delay; she has a quarrel with a *boyarin* and
is afraid. She must have an order from your master. It has nothing to do
with me, but I promised to bear her the order."

Margeret evidently knew her, because he smiled and nodded.

"Nada—a pretty lass. She watched me drill the pikemen by the Archangel. Nay, my lord, when I can stand I will do myself the honor of escorting her."

The closing of the gates seemed to puzzle him, but he dismissed it with
a shrug, the fever still burning in his veins. Then he glanced at Kirdy,
one eyebrow raised.

Near at hand had sounded the clang and slither of steel in conflict—
unmistakable to either Cossack or Frenchman. Voices were raised in sudden tumult. The street below was still in deep shadow, and Kirdy was trying to make out the nature of the fighting when he heard hurried steps
on the stairs.

An elderly man, with shrewd, pinched features, stepped into the room,
hugging a black velvet mantle around his thin body. When he saw Margeret he looked relieved—took a bit of snuff with a flourish and stared curiously at the young warrior garbed as a Mongol.

Margeret addressed him rapidly in French, and waved his hand from the newcomer to Kirdy.

"M'sieur Cathayan, this is the good M'sieur Bertrand from Kassa—a merchant by trade, a philosopher from choice. I have not the advantage of knowing your name—"

"The White Falcon." Kirdy smiled.

"Ah, Bertrand, this White Falcon—whatever he may be—has, I believe, ministered to me in good case. But what brings you here at this infernal cockcrow?"

"Listen!" The merchant held up his hand.

Kirdy, already at the window, saw a troop of horsemen spurring into the street in pursuit of human beings, half-clad and wailing, a man and woman. The leading riders came up with the man, who turned with drawn sword. A pass or two of weapons, and the fugitive went down silently with his skull split open. The woman screamed, and Kirdy swore under his breath.

She had been ridden down by the horses, and one of the soldiers, leaning from the saddle as he passed, drove his saber through her body.

"*Nom d'un nom!*" the merchant whispered, at his side.

"But what has happened, Bertrand?" demanded Margeret, trying to get out from under the covers.

The merchant took snuff again, glanced over the rose-tinted roofs and the gilded spires at the red glow in the east.

"Ah," he said, and considered, "the festival of mirth has ended, the carnival of death begun, *vieux!*" To Kirdy he added, shaking his thin head. "The tsar and Basmanof have been slain in one of the galleries of the Kremyl."

Chapter VI
The Trail

When the trail is clear the horse will follow it, even in darkness. If the trail be hidden, the dog will smell it out. But when the trail is at an end horse and dog look to their master, the man.

Monsieur Bertrand was a mild soul and a daring trader. He bought in Moscow damask stuffs, silks and red leather, paid for them in silver, and took his chances of robbery and shipwreck with all the equanimity of the philosopher that Margeret had named him. Having traveled for years along the rivers of Muscovy, he spoke the language well, and knew a deal of the half-oriental and wholly—to his thinking—barbaric court of the tsar. While Kirdy listened intently and the sick captain swore, he unfolded the tale of the Kremyl.

"It has been, messieurs, a night of more bloodshed than judgment. Only yesterday I met the unfortunate Dmitri in all health and hardihood upon the steps of the Kasna—that is how they call their treasury. He was at the head of some followers who were bearing forth certain jewels and moneys.

"A merchant at court must have his ear sharpened to catch intrigue. For weeks I have perceived a conspiracy against the tsar—" the worthy Bertrand pronounced it "Zar"—"and Dmitri must have been drunk as a trooper if he knew nothing of it. Some of the older princes and one Michael Tatikof lead the conspirators. Dmitri drank deep and laughed and feasted his eyes on jewels and fine horses. Good!

"Late in the evening this Tatikof, who had been from the city for several days, appeared at the head of a company of boyars. They concealed among their horses a sleigh. Upon this sleigh rested a casket. And, messieurs if you were to think for a thousand days you would never hit upon the meaning of that casket."

With a half smile on his thin lips, he paused to glance at the two listeners—he spoke in French, translating rapidly for Kirdy's benefit when he noticed the youth's eager interest.

"It was the coffin of the *real* Dmitri, the son of Ivan the Terrible. In the coffin reposed the body of the child dressed as when he had been murdered—even a toy in his skeleton hand. *C'est incroyable*—unbelievable—but this is—*la Russie*! Tatikof and others had suspected for some time that Dmitri was an impostor; but in what way could they prove their suspicions? Dmitri, the false Dmitri, had shown a jeweled cross; he had been acknowledged by the empress-mother; moreover, he had the army behind him—"

The Frenchman shrugged one shoulder toward Margeret, and, with a tentative glance at Kirdy, went on:

"Tatikof exhibited the body of the boy to the elder princes while the false Dmitri was reveling in the palace. The dead lay in judgment upon the living.

"Good! It was decided to slay the false tsar. You see, messieurs, it is an easier matter to prove a dead man an impostor than a living man a fraud.

And the army, except for the palace guards and the Moscow militia, was in the steppes chasing some Cossacks. A fool's mission.

"And Dmitri died like the reckless fool he was. Sound asleep. His gossip Basmanof was awake. Tatikof stabbed Basmanof in a gallery leading to the quarters of the tsar. Then the boyars entered the sleeping chamber of the false Dmitri, and now the impostor lies dead—"

"Name of a dog!" shouted the captain. "Dmitri, I do not believe he was a pretender!"

"My dear captain, he was a consummate and daring liar. In all the world, where will you find such another? Saint Denis—he had himself proclaimed emperor, and took a wife of the blood from Poland!"

"But, do you believe the conspirators, with their skeleton?"

Bertrand glanced at Kirdy covertly and took snuff.

"My dear Margeret," he said under his breath in French, "what do you or I know? I believe the Muscovite princes because they have the upper hand."

"We took oath to—"

"Be loyal to this Dmitri? Eh, well, he is now dead. I can admire his spirit, but I condemn his lack of wisdom. If he had not made a mock of churches and said his prayers to a ribald mask he would not have made enemies of the stiff old boyars. He gave his soul to the devil for a stake to gamble with."

Margeret, who had been tearing the coverlet between strong fingers, shook his head impatiently.

"But the palace guard!"

"Some of your sheep-headed archers were cut down. Be grateful, my friend, that you were not on duty. Saint Denis! I believe your dinner was tampered with!"

"The militia—"

"Slept and snored, but now has been won over by the boyars. It guards the gates and scratches its thick head. Meanwhile the boyars are hunting down the followers of the false Dmitri."

Going to the window, he gazed with some curiosity at bodies of halberdiers and mounted nobles passing through the square at the end of the street. Smoke was rising from different points in the city and veiling the clear light of early morning.

"I must go," he said thoughtfully, "to pay my respects to the victors, at the palace."

"And I," Margeret muttered, "to my men."

"Impossible! Your ailment is providential. Even if you could stand, you were better between the sheets. Margeret, you are an excellent soldier but an execrable diplomat."

"God's thunder! If my archers are to be put to the point of the sword—"

"Content you! I saw them penned in barracks. The boyars know the worth of your fire-eaters. Lie *perdu* until I can bring you fresh news."

Weakness rather than conviction forced Margeret to stretch himself on the bed again; but when Bertrand bowed and moved to the door, Kirdy stepped to his side.

"Merchant, take me with you!"

Bertrand tapped his snuffbox reflectively and pursed his lips.

"Ah, my prince, worthy people will avoid the streets this day. Why would you come?"

Kirdy swept his arm toward the rising sun.

"Thence rode I to set eyes on the great lord the Muscovites. If I may not behold him in life, I would see him in death."

After a second glance at the Mongol, the Frenchman bowed assent, rather grudgingly. He was a judge of character, and he discovered in Kirdy's eyes a certain smoldering eagerness that puzzled him.

The two took their way over the trampled snow, seeing much and saying little, each occupied with his own thoughts.

Kirdy reflected that a passport written and signed by the Captain Margeret would be worse than worthless, now, to Nada. He wasted no time in surprise over the end of the false Dmitri; it had happened and now he meant to see for himself the body of the impostor, so that he could say to the Cossacks without any shadow of doubt that the traitor who had cost the lives of thousands of the brothers was dead.

So thinking, he paid little heed to the bodies that lay in the narrow streets. At times they passed by a house that was beset by soldiers. Then Bertrand hung back and would have fetched a circle to avoid the armed men, but Kirdy pushed through the mob, saying that nothing was to be gained by slinking like dogs. In fact, the soldiery, seeing his erect head and imperious manner, often cleared a way for him and the Frankish merchant.

"Eh, it is terrible," Bertrand sighed, watched men run into a door under upflung shields, while arrows flickered down from narrow windows. "It is a massacre of the Poles."

There was real regret behind his sigh, because the shrewd trader fore-saw that this slaughter of the visitors would be ample excuse for the am-bitious and powerful King Sigismund to lead his armies into Muscovy, and that a great war would follow on the heels of civil conflict—with more plundering than profit for himself.

The more they penetrated the noisy streets, the less they were able to learn of events.

An officer of the town watch glared at them suspiciously and was ut-terly astonished when they told him the tsar was dead.

"*Okh*—who would give orders if not our great illustrious prince? How can he be dead?"

Pulling at Kirdy's arm, Bertrand hurried on, only to be stopped by a drunken halberdier who presented his pike and roared drowsily:

"Stand—enemies of the faith! Put down your weapons and bend the head!"

Him Kirdy quieted with a gold piece and passed on before the slow-thinking warrior reflected that more plunder might be had where the ducat came from. They saw a whole colony of Jews scurrying like hares into a dark alley where a barricade was being put up—a flimsy rampart of tables, benches and posts.

"It is a dark hour, my lords!" a blind beggar declaimed, shaking his shaggy head. "*Ai-a*, who knows what word is true and what is false? A priest said we had a new tsar—long life and glory to him. Give a copper for bread, my lords!"

"The belly endures no interregnum," murmured Bertrand. "Ah, here is a client who knows me."

He accosted a bearded noble who was forcing his way on horseback to-ward one of the Kremyl gates followed by a wild-looking array of fur-clad slaves and men-at-arms. This Muscovite knew nothing at all of events, save that he had been summoned to attendance by the councilors. But he allowed Kirdy and the merchant to pass through the palace gate with him and that was something gained.

Here there was less fighting but little more enlightenment. Kirdy saw a young woman with painted cheeks and mincing step—a being in volu-minous velvets and silk garments, who yet looked at him out of haggard eyes, led away between two files of guardsmen. With her were two elder men who walked proudly and held hat and gloves as precisely as if they were bound for a court audience instead of jail.

"The bride of the false Dmitri," Bertrand whispered. "The princess of Sandomir. A pawn, thrust in advance of king and bishops."

"She does not weep," Kirdy commented with approval.

The way into the tsar's quarters was barred to them, and they learned that the boyars were in council. It was a dwarf of the troupe of buffoons who told them where the false Dmitri lay—a jester of the company Kirdy had seen the night before.

"Nay, Uncle," the little man laughed, "which Dmitri doth your soberness seek? The skeleton or the corpse?"

"What difference?" retorted the merchant with a grimace.

"By the holy angels, a mighty difference! One that was no more than a fistful of bones yester-eve—that a starved jackal would turn from—now is an honorable relic, and worketh miracles by account of the priests. The other, that was our celestial Prince but a day agone, is now accursed cold meat that an honest butcher would spit upon."

"Where lies he—this false Dmitri?" asked Kirdy.

"*Ohai*—he lies for all to see. Come, Uncle Merchant, come my Lord of Tartary! I will show you! Permit me to conduct you to the royal seat. He lies in state."

Grimacing, the dwarf pushed and mumbled his way through the crowds, beckoning over his shoulder to the two, until he came to a dense throng, where elbows and fists were needed to clear a way. This was in front of a dark pile of stone, a silent monastery, where Bertrand informed Kirdy the empress-mother had taken refuge.

Here on a table lay two bodies stripped of all clothing.

The one on top, with its feet resting upon the chest of the other, was that of Basmanof. Kirdy recognized the harsh, lined features of the noble who had betrayed one master and had died in defense of the false Dmitri. He pushed closer to the table to look at the body of the impostor.

He saw a powerful figure, terribly gashed about the chest, and he caught his breath suddenly, while the dwarf chuckled.

"*Ohai*, my Lord of Tartary—we have fitted him for his long journey to the land of Satan."

Kirdy beheld upon the head of the dead man a mask. It was grotesque and evil, with the ears of an animal, the grin of a satyr, and the mouth of a monster. Through the holes of the mask the dead eyes stared up at the gray sky.

"Holy Mother," whispered Bertrand, "what mockery!"

The assassins had taken down the mask found in Dmitri's chamber and had placed it upon the man who had made a jest of the sacred pictures.

The men of the crowd, emotionless as so many statues, looked from the bodies on the table to the young Mongol, who pushed steadily closer to the head in the mask. A murmur went up as he stretched out his hand.

"Name of a name," the merchant cried, "do not touch it."

But Kirdy had lifted the heavy painted lacquer countenance and was studying the pallid features beneath—the strong features of a youth no older than himself, without a beard. A knife had slashed open the right cheek near the nose.

"Is this your tsar?" he asked Bertrand.

"Aye, that is Dmitri," the merchant nodded, and crossed himself. He started to say something more, but changed his mind and motioned to Kirdy to come away.

Kirdy replaced the mask, folded his arms in his sleeves, and withdrew through the crowd that opened to let him pass. The dwarf lingered with his fellows, and the two visitors walked slowly from the Kremyl grounds. Bertrand was chewing his lip and frowning, and when they were alone in a narrow alley, spoke to Kirdy abruptly.

"Why did you lift the mask?"

"To see the face," the young warrior made answer simply. "Men told me that the emperor of the Muscovites had a mole or wart on the cheek near the nose. I did not see it."

Several times Bertrand's lips moved before he found words that satisfied him.

"You have more boldness than discretion, friend! A mole! It must have been slashed away. The cheek was cut."

"*Aya tak*," Kirdy nodded, "aye so. It is an evil fate, that of the emperor of this people."

The Frenchman shrugged.

"Savages! Worse will follow, I fear."

Through Kirdy's mind the cry of the jester rang like an echo:

"*His long journey to the land of Satan.*" Aloud, he added to his companion: "Now I must sleep!"

For two days and a night he had not closed his eyes, and for many days he had not taken more a remnant of rest; he was a little bewildered by the fighting in the city, and the crowds from which he could not escape. He wanted to be alone, to think about what had happened. But he attended the older man to Bertrand's house near the tavern, and the Frenchman looked after him thoughtfully when he strode away.

Weary as he was, Kirdy was careful to lead his horses from their stable, where plunderers might find them, and take them with him when he sought Nada's dwelling to report his lack of success in getting the passport and to tell the girl all that had taken place during the night.

He found the house guarded by Toghrul and Karai and learned that Nada had gone out on foot to investigate matters with her other men. Kirdy gave the tribesman a message for his mistress and Toghrul prepared a bed for him in a corner of the dining hall—a bed of straw, with a saddle for pillow.

Almost at once Kirdy fell into a deep sleep, rousing a little when he heard voices. One of the voices sounded like Nada's, and he fancied that she was giving orders. A light footfall stirred the straw near his head, and he was aware of a scent that seemed to come from the open steppe—of flowers warmed by the sun.

Chapter VII
The Reflections of Monsieur Bertrand

Toghrul's almost soundless tread roused Kirdy, and he grasped at his sword hilt before he saw the old man squatting near him, waiting to be noticed.

"The lady says to thee, O Cossack," the servitor began at once "it is better to lie hidden than to walk in the eyes of men. It is much better to wait than to seek recklessly. So wilt thou abide her coming. The horses are fed."

"Has she gone forth again?" Kirdy was disappointed and a little vexed, though he did not show it.

"Aye."

"There is fighting. I must talk with her."

"When she wills."

"She is safer behind walls." Kirdy thought of the *boyarin* who had been lashed by her whip, a certain Tatikof who had promised to seek her out.

Toghrul pondered and made response gravely.

"When the end appointed by the unalterable decree has come, life is then lost, and for all there is an end ordained. What avail, to go thither or sit here? She will not be harmed now!"

"How long have I slept?"

"The sun was sinking, O Cossack—night came. And now the sun has risen."

With an exclamation the young warrior sprang to his feet. He had slept for eighteen hours, and there was much to be done. After plunging his head and hands in a basin of cold water brought by Toghrul he made a hasty meal of mutton and wine and learned that Nada intended to ride from Moscow that night. The guards, it seemed, had been removed from the gates, to deal with a conflagration that had broken out at the other end of the city.

"See to the horses, Toghrul. There will be looting."

"Aye. The *khanum* has said that thou wilt ride forth with us."

And all at once it seemed to Kirdy that nothing in the world could be finer than to ride with Nada and her men of the steppe. Whither? What matter? He was restless and uneasy here in the city, like an unbroken colt penned in with strange horses.

"I cannot do that," he said slowly.

Toghrul did not seem convinced.

"*Allah khanum yok—khanum Allah bir tzee,*" he muttered cryptically. "Allah said No to the woman—the woman said Yes to Allah."

"What words are these?"

"O Cossack, I said I shall water the horses and groom them, against thy need, this night."

Still afoot, still alone—he had left Karai perforce—and, still deep in moody reflection, fared forth into the mud and the snow and the anger of the streets. He went first to the imperial stables behind the Terem, looking for all the world like a Cathayan noble with an interest in fine horseflesh. So acute was his curiosity that he asked if all the emperor's beasts were in the stalls. As he did not stint gold pieces, he learned at length that the illustrious Tatikof had led out a half dozen Arabs, and that three Turkish racers had been missing since the night before last.

This matter he pondered, remembering the riders he had seen when the moon was setting that same night.

From the stables he made his way leisurely toward Bertrand's quarters and discovered that the worthy merchant was not at home. Upon this he sought Margeret's tavern, but contented himself with a table in the taproom instead of seeking out the sick captain. Here he sat, apparently lost in the contemplation of the intelligent Asiatic, sipping wine occasionally, until the afternoon wore on and Bertrand did not appear. He climbed the stairs and passed an hour listening to Margeret's roared-out comments on the madness that had seized the boyars.

At the end of the hour he had what he desired—a more or less detailed account of the false Dmitri's routine, habits, and especially his manner of exercising his horses.

He had taken his leave, ceremoniously, of the captain when he ran into Bertrand at the foot of the stairs. The merchant coughed, bowed, and would have passed on up, but Kirdy put a hand on his arm.

"Good sir, you think I am not—a Cathayan. Perhaps you are right. Will you honor me by sitting at table with me? They serve a Wallachian wine that is light and healthful."

Bertrand drew back into the shadow and tried to gaze into the lowered eyes of the young warrior.

"A plague on't! What are you?"

"A seeker, who will bring no harm to you."

"I think—"

But Bertrand kept his thought to himself and decided to accompany the Mongol noble. They faced each other over cups of spiced white wine, and the merchant waited for Kirdy to speak. He waited until his patience yielded to his fears.

"What master do you serve? Are you Tatikof's spy?"

Kirdy smiled.

"Let me tell you a story. Once there lived a sultan who was a very fox for wiles. He was called Motavakel Shah, and he summoned his enemy to his house thinking to teach him fear. A lion—one of his beasts—was let loose into the room by his servants. Though the lion ran past the table, the guest of Motavakel did not rise from his cushions nor utter a word. Then snakes were turned into the room, coiling past the feet of the host and the guest. Still the foe of Motavakel did not raise his feet or his voice. A dish was placed before him and under the cover of the dish were scorpions.

"'Nay,' said the guest of Motavakel, 'this is a night not of the lion, or the serpents, or the scorpion but of the sword!' And with the blade at his girdle he slew Motavakel and fled unhurt."

"Ah, a parable. Is your sword, then, hidden?"

"Good sir," Kirdy said quietly, "it is not you I seek. But the time for trickery is past; the moment of the sword is nigh. Answer, then, swiftly, remembering that what I seek from you is—truth! When you saw the body that lay under the mask, you were troubled by doubt."

"And you!"

"I also. The one mark that marked Dmitri beyond doubt—the wart—was gone. It might have been slashed away. But when a trail is hidden, a man has fled—who shuns pursuit."

Bertrand leaned forward breathing quickly, his eyes probing Kirdy's. "The false Dmitri has fled?"

"Leaving another body to hide his trail." Kirdy turned the porcelain cup slowly in his lean hand. "Perhaps. Every soul in the palace would have looked for the wart upon the face of the dead man. It was gone, and the slash was covered by the mask."

"*Tonnerre de dieu*! No Muscovite reasoned thus! What man are you?"

"One who has tracked beasts. Man is not otherwise. Tell me first why you doubted that the body was Dmitri's—the false Dmitri's?"

Bertrand glanced to one side, then the other.

"A little matter," he whispered. "Two, I should say. I saw his Illus—the impostor the day before. Eh, well. I noticed the cut of his hair, being exact in such conceits of dress. The hair on the body seemed to be longer than Dmitri's."

Kirdy nodded silently.

"Good!" The shrewd merchant warmed to his contention. "The late tsar shaved his chin. The body, also, was shaved, but the hair on the chin was soft and ill-cut—as if, *pardie*, this man had worn a beard until it was cut off hastily, to make him resemble someone else."

"Then, Uncle Merchant, was there a man in this court who looked like the false Dmitri?"

Bertrand chewed his lips reflectively.

"Aye, so. One Stanislav Bouthinski, a Pole. A secretary, I believe, to the ambassadors of that country."

"*Hai!*" Kirdy's dark eyes gleamed as if he had hit upon the slot of a stag. "You, my good sir, are no Muscovite. You have lived at other, and wiser courts."

The touch of flattery warmed the Frenchman, who said again that the Muscovites were savages.

"Bouthinski is missing. Today I searched for him and his people told me he must have fallen in the massacre. Many hundred Poles have been cut and trampled into the mud."

A new doubt struck him.

"But what of all this? Grant that the false Dmitri may have fled, leaving another body slain in his bed. Grant that this body is Bouthinski's—naked as a peeled turnip and slashed on the cheek. None the less, Dmitri is now proved false and pretender. How could he escape?"

"Three fine horses were missing from the stables that night. Three riders passed through the guards—and who could win out of the gates save this man who called himself the tsar?"

"It is possible."

"Aye, so. Men say that this false Dmitri was as shrewd as a fox. Surely he had scent of the conspiracy against him. He left the army and summoned Basmanhof after him. Then, leaving this body of his friend in his bed, he went from Moscow. Whether?"

Bertrand shrugged and felt for his snuffbox.

"Not to the Poles, I'll wager." He laughed grimly. *"Peste!* What a fellow! Destruction to all he touches."

"He would not flee to the Cossacks. He had betrayed them."

The merchant who knew the courts of Europe, the Cossack who had fought under the monarchs of Asia, measured each other with understanding eyes. Kirdy took time to think over all that had been said, because he wished to have it firmly in his mind in order to decide what to do next. Bertrand mused along a different line.

"St. Denis! I heard a rumor that the bride of the imposter did not seem to be dying of grief. It may be that she knows he is alive."

"I have heard that woman's tears are soon dried."

"Well, pardon me, but I have discovered otherwise, my friend. However, it is clear that he has not taken his bride with him, if indeed he lives."

"Could he win a following from the army in the south?"

The merchant shook his head and took snuff, wiping the brown grains from his coat carefully.

"After the massacre in Moscow the Polish regiments will turn on the Muscovites, and when the dogfight begins, the Tartars will plunder both. It is true that Sigismund's regiments—and they are many—were sent hither to support this Dmitri. But when the time came to draw the sword he abandoned the army and fled like a jade-robbing knave from the city. Even so—such is the charm of his presence—the Muscovite cavalry might have been won to his cause but he mocked the traditions of these stiff collars. He put an actor's mask on the icon stand. So now they say he has sold himself to Satan."

Bertrand smiled, contemplating the savagery of these pagans, as he chose to call them.

"But where are you going?"

Kirdy drew tighter his girdle and glanced out into the gathering dusk.

"Perhaps this dog-soul is dead; perhaps not. But if he lives, he must have taken refuge in the steppes. He has good horses, and I go to follow while the trail is fresh."

Leaving the worthy merchant utterly astonished, Kirdy hastened from the tavern and was turning into the open square where the great bell hung upon its stone dais when he beheld torches moving in the same direction.

Chapter VIII
The River Gate

Several riders, accompanied by a score of men-at-arms and link-bearers, were entering the street where Nada's house stood, driving some captives with arms bound before them. Hastening his pace, Kirdy drew closer and recognized the bearded Tatikof among the horsemen.

He passed behind the cavalcade, skirted the edge square to the mouth of an alley that led to Nada's stables. Then he ran as if a thousand fiends were at his heels. In the snow the footing was bad, and more than one log or wagon wheel made him plunge before he came out at the sheds and saw that they were empty. Nada's sleigh, too, was not to be seen.

A half-squad of Swedish halberdiers were standing talking by the gate-posts at the street end, evidently waiting for Tatikof and the company. Kirdy leaped to the rear steps of the house and pushed at the door. It was fastened—barred by the feel of it. He thrust his fist through the tallow paper of the nearest window and called softly.

Karai's delighted bark answered him.

He was half through the window when a figure appeared out of the darkness, and he recognized Toghrul's broad face.

"The *khanum* must leave the house by this way," he said quickly. "The Muscovites come for no good. Where are the horses?"

"Allah!" grunted the tribesman. "I saw warriors with long spears, and I sent Karabek with the five horses and the sleigh away at once."

"To the *khanum*? Where is she?"

"I do not know. Karabek says she is buying clothes at the Jew's bazaar. He will tell her of the coming of the Muscovites when he finds her—"

A warning hiss from the old man made Kirdy aware of footsteps approaching the side of the house, and he hauled himself through the window without waiting to see who might be approaching. It proved to be the halberdiers, with one of the boyars and a lantern. And they stationed themselves where they could watch both the house and the sheds.

"How many are with thee, Toghrul?"

"One, and the dog."

"Fool! The way was open to flee!"

"Nay, the house is in my charge. What do I know of these Urusses? Go thou and talk with them, for they beat at the door."

There was no escape by the rear now, and Kirdy saw that some men with firelocks and lighted torches were outside the only other window on the lower floor. The openings above were no more than slits to let in light and air. The log houses of Moscow had been built to keep out thieves and the cold.

Listening at the front door, he made out Tatikof's deep voice.

"Within there! I bear an order from the council. The lady Nada must go with me. Open!"

"The forehead to you, great lord! What seek you of Nada?"

"An order is to be obeyed. Open!"

"She is not here."

A moment of silence and then Tatikof laughed.

"She was seen to go in and only a Cossack has come out since. What man are you?"

Kirdy did not answer at once. Nada had no Cossacks among her servants; Tatikof's spies might have penetrated his disguise—but surely the servitors had been in and out since he left.

"*Nichevo*—no matter!" he responded cheerfully. "I have no quarrel with you, Tatikof, nor you with me, yet I swear to you one thing: If your men break into this house many will go to bed in their graves."

"And we will pull you out by the hair," the *boyarin* roared.

"Once you were whipped, but now you want a taste of the sword."

An ax thudded into the stout logs of the door, and Kirdy heard the Muscovite cursing steadily. He thought no more of explanations, because he believed Tatikof had come to seize Nada in the general looting. The *boyarin* did not look like a man who would forgive a lash of the whip.

It was true that Kirdy could have opened the door and allowed the house to be searched. But he knew that he could give no good account of

himself, and Tatikof would torture the tribesmen to find where the girl
had gone.

"The Urusses are angry," Toghrul observed at his elbow.

"Aye—blood is to be shed. Have ye bows? Arrows? Then go with thy
comrade to the openings. Send the first shaft at the bearded *mirza* with
the steel hat. In a little, come down and watch the window at the side."

The house was in utter darkness, and Kirdy himself in the dining hall
where he could listen to all that went on. Karai stalked from front to rear,
his eyes glowing yellow. In a moment a bow snapped, then another. A
man cried out. Muskets roared, but still the sharp snap of the bowstrings
was to be heard.

"Down with the torches!" Tatikof's deep voice ordered.

Kirdy knew that the lights were being quenched in the snow—knew
too that the moon was over the housetops and Toghrul had eyes like a cat.
The firelocks barked at the house, but the thick walls stopped the bullets,
and the Muscovites must have found the arrows too much for them, because the axes ceased work, and silence fell. Presently the two warriors
emerged out of blackness.

"O Cossack," Toghrul proclaimed moodily, "the bearded chieftain
wears too much iron. We hurt him but did not slay. Three are down, and
the other Urusses be very angry."

"They are at the back."

The axes began anew on the lighter door, and Kirdy posted the other
servitor at the side window, while he sought out logs from the hearth to
prop up the rear door. Toghrul experimented with his arrows at the nearby
window and discovered that he could do little damage, while the bullets
from the pistols of the Muscovites drew blood from him.

"The Urusses will not enter by the windows," Kirdy said to him. "The
door will not stand for long. It is better to run out than to be hunted from
room to room. Go thou and count how many are at the front."

He went himself and lifted down two of the three bars at the street
door, and ran back when he heard boards splintering on the stable side.
It seemed to him that the greater part of the assailants were at this point
where no arrows could reach them. From the window he could make out
a mass of forms in the haze of moonlight—Tatikof, his long sword drawn,
urging them on.

Then he felt Karai stiffen against his leg. A wolf howled faintly, not far
away. Again the sound drifted through the open window, nearer. Then
the door began to fly apart.

Footsteps pattered over the floor behind him, and he turned with bare saber outflung. Toghrul panted at him.

"Down the street the *khanum* comes. She cried out to me. Come now, Cossack!"

Together they leaped through the hall, calling to the other man to follow, and Karai, wild with excitement, jumped upon the door when Kirdy threw off the last bar. They heard the boots of the Muscovites thudding behind them.

"Follow!" Kirdy cried.

He kicked the door back and ran down the steps that Karai leaped without effort. Several halberdiers, leaning on their long weapons, started up, and two horsemen gathered up their reins. Kirdy knocked down the first spear thrust at him, jumped aside from a second, cutting the man deep in the shoulder as he did so.

Wrenching his blade clear, he parried a slash from one of the mounted boyars—a heavy man, too clumsy to wheel his horse for a second cut. He saw Karai leap silently at a third Muscovite—heard the fellow scream and a pistol roar.

Toghrul was before him now, speeding like a shadow through the gateposts. Down the street in a smother of snow the light sleigh of Nada was coming, a rider on one of the three black horses holding in the others. This, Kirdy thought, must be Karabek, and he had found Nada. It was brave of the girl to come back for Toghrul.

But he could not see Nada in the sleigh. Standing up, waving at him, was a young Cossack in a long black coat and a glittering girdle. Gloved, booted, and armed, the Cossack might have ridden thus out of the *siech*, the mother of warriors. Behind the sleigh, their reins caught in one of the youth's hands, Kirdy's two ponies reared and plunged, frightened by the clash of steel and roar of firelocks.

The sleigh came abreast the gate as Kirdy ran up, and the strange Cossack laughed at him. By that laugh he knew Nada, though her long gleaming hair was hidden under the *kalpak* and the upturned collar of her coat.

"Come," she cried, drawing back to make room for him. A second the sleigh halted, and Toghrul scrambled to the back of one of the ponies, jerking the rein free as he did so. A bullet whistled past Kirdy's head, and over his shoulder he saw Tatikof whipping through the gate, his feet feeling for the stirrups that he had failed to grip when he leaped into the saddle.

Kirdy acted almost without thought. He turned on his heel, ran at the Muscovite's big stallion, while Tatikof snatched at the sword on his far side. He did not draw the sword.

The flat of Kirdy's saber smote him across the eyes—his leg was gripped by a powerful arm, and he was off-balance, half-dazed by the blow. Tatikof fell on his back beside the stallion, and Kirdy, who had caught the saddle-horn, leaped up, finding stirrups before he gripped the rein.

Then he wheeled the powerful charger against the *boyarin* who had first fired at him, and who followed Tatikof through the gate. Two blades flashed and clanged in the moonlight—the shoulder of the black stallion took the flank of the other horse and the *boyarin* reeled, groaning. Calling off the raging Karai, the young warrior wheeled the stallion again, gripped firm with knees and rein, and raced beside the sleigh.

"Nay, come with me, Nada! I go to the river gate."

He saw some of the men-at-arms run out, and a bullet or two whistled past without harm. The other servant must have gone down at the door because he was not to be seen. Nada clapped her gloved hands and sank down on the seat.

"With the flat of the blade!" she cried gleefully. "In his beard Tatikof took it, and he went down like—like a speared boar. It was good to see!"

The rider of the off-horse whipped on his three steeds; the bells of the arched collars chimed faster and faster. They began to gallop, and then to race through the silent streets, as leaves whirl before the breath of the storm.

"It was so," the men of the guard at the river gate reported to their captain, Margeret, the Frenchman, next morning. "No vodka had been given us. But we saw them—three horses black as the pit, and the Cathayan standing up in his stirrups, with his hat gone and his eyes gleaming, and a Cossack in the sleigh singing like one of the angels from Heaven, and a wolf following them. It was so!"

No one had challenged them.

Throughout Mother Moscow the tale grew and passed from lip to lip. It was whispered at first then said openly that Dmitri who had been tsar had escaped the weapons of the nobles.

Warriors who had gone into the Kremyl remembered that a man had been seen to jump from the lower windows of the Terem into the courtyard. A groom of the imperial stables repeated that three Turkish horses had been saddled by order of the tsar and held in readiness. No one knew what had become of the horses—though the groom was put to the torture.

Then there came a rumor from Kolumna, the nearest town in the east, that Dmitri had been seen there the night of his downfall.

The elder princes of the council debated and gave out that this must be a lie. The body that had lain in the public square during these three days of bloodshed was solemnly burned, and the ashes fired from the mouth of a cannon. Tatikof was sent with a hundred riders to Kolumna, and there peasants pointed out the keeper of the road tavern as the one who had spoken with the false Dmitri.

"Bring him to me," the great *boyarin* said, and added sternly, "The traitor is dead, so you could not have seen him."

The tavern-keeper came, fear-ridden, and told his tale. In that evening four travelers had drawn up at his dram shop. They were escorting a sledge. They had loosed the girths of their horses but had not unsaddled. This was at milking time. During the night they played chess and did not get drunk or go to sleep.

Along in the cold hours—so said the innkeeper—other horses had galloped up. These were *dobra koniaka*—fine horses. From one, his great mightiness the tsar had dismounted, and called for veal and white wine. He had been served, while the first four riders were harnessing the ponies to the sledge; evidently they had been waiting for the coming of his serene mightiness. They all talked together, and then the tsar called for parchment and a goose quill and ink.

The others—fine young gentlemen—had remonstrated with him. They seemed to be impatient to get on. But the tsar laughed and wrote some words on the parchment, folded it and directed that it be kept until called for—

"By whom?" demanded Tatikof.

"By the serene, great elder princes or by Michael Tatikof, so it please ye."

The agent of the boyars started and frowned, and frowned still more when the master of the tavern produced the letter as evidence of his honesty.

"A hundred devils!" cried Tatikof, who was to read it. "Has anyone seen this?"

"Aye, your nobility! A *batko*, a priest it were. He read it to the travelers who came after the illustrious prince."

"May dogs tear you! Why was it read to others?"

"Because, when I told them the tale, they said I lied. I showed them the letter, and still they said I lied, because none could read. So they summoned the priest from the church, and he came and read it aloud, and then they knew I was telling the truth. There was no harm?"

"Harm!" Tatikof's red face grew darker. "Who were these people that had the letter read?"

The worthy taverner scratched his head and began to bow, because fear was growing upon him.

"Eh, they were fine folk. They were two young princes from over the border, only God knows where. One had long eyes like a girl, and a gold girdle—"

"And a dog?"

"Oh, aye, a borzoi it were, like a wolf."

"Dolt! It was a girl dressed as a Cossack, and a Cathayan."

The purple scar on the forehead of the *boyarin* flamed as he thought of Nada and Kirdy.

"What way did they go?"

"May it please your nobility, they bought meat and wine and forage for the horses and departed along the snow road, yesterday morning, eastward."

"Have any others seen this paper?"

"Not a soul! Only listen, I swear—"

The master of the tavern fell on his knees, and his mouth opened in dull horror. He had seen Tatikof draw and prime a pistol. The *boyarin* stepped forward and lowered the muzzle quickly, and the weapon roared in the man's ear.

"Devil take him!" Tatikof muttered, when his companions ran up at the shot, "I had not thought there were brains in his skull."

A second time he read the missive, though it was short:

> Veliki boyare domnui *[mighty nobles of the council]—greet-*
> *ing! We are grievously angered by the rebellion of our servants*
> *in the city of our governance, Moscow. The time is not distant*
> *when your insolence will be chastened by our just anger!*

It was signed simply *Dmitri Ivanovitch*—Dmitri, Son of Ivan.

And before he left Kolumna, Tatikof was careful to see that the priest who had been unfortunate enough to set eyes on this letter disappeared from human sight. This accomplished, he hastened on with his escort, eastward, to the frontier.

From time to time they heard of the sledge and the seven riders led by the daring impostor, and once they halted where the fugitives had camped. From this point on, there was only the one road leading to the Volga.

But they never saw the Volga. They approached near enough to see the smoke of a burning frontier post, and to pick up several fugitives who told them the Tartar tribes across the Volga had risen only a few days before. Muscovite officials along the frontier had been slain, and isolated garrisons massacred.

Clouds of fur-clad Nogai Tartars were visible on the skyline, restless and merciless as hungering eagles. By night, farms burned like torches along the river. Further pursuit of the false Dmitri was not to be thought of, when fire and sword gutted the border.

Bewildered, encumbered by the fleeing, driven by fear of the Tartar arrows, the boyars reined back to Kolumna, and it was weeks before Nogai prisoners were brought in by a patrol of Muscovite cavalry. The elder princes put the captives to the torture at once.

The Nogais swore that Dmitri himself had appeared among them and had shown them an apple and an imperial baton set with jewels. Surely he had been the great Khaghan, the Nogais said! He had summoned them to arms, they who lived by the sword and desired nothing more than raiding. For the rest, they knew nothing.

The captives were put on stakes and left to wriggle away their lives, and the council of the nobles met in solemn session. There was no longer the slightest doubt that the false Dmitri lived and had taken with him many of the crown jewels.

He had foreseen the conspiracy against him—and had fled before the boyars could seize him. He had slain the unfortunate Bouthinski in his own bed and had leaped from the window of the sleeping chamber. On fast horses, with his intimate followers, he had raced on to where the sledge with his plunder and stores awaited him.

Had he intended the Muscovites to believe him or had he tricked them daringly only to gain a few days' start? They did not know.

This strange being had valued a jest more than his own head because he had made a last gesture of defiance, at Kolumna—the letter to the boyars. And yet—these gray-haired princes cherished grave doubts—was not this letter a new scheme? The career of the false tsar had not ended. He had wealth, followers and allies of a sort among the tribes. What new evil would he bring forth to add blood to that already shed?

"As for Gregory Otrèpiev," Tatikof counseled them—the impostor's true name was known by now—"we cannot slay him. He, who has blasphemed against God, will fall by the hand of the Almighty. Yet the rumors that he lives must be answered. Already factions are forming against us, and soon brother may draw weapon against brother. Great seigneurs, let us say to the world that this Otrèpiev was a fiend. Though we slew his body he has appeared as a spirit."*

And Monsieur Bertrand, who was preparing to leave Moscow and its savages, coined one of his *bons mots* upon hearing this:

"If ever a fiend," he pronounced, "deserved to immortal, Otrèpiev, the False Dmitri, is he."

More than once Tatikof pondered the fate of Nada and the strange Cathayan, but they had disappeared as if the steppe had swallowed them with their horses and wolfhound.

Chapter IX
Black Smoke Ahead

When there is a black smoke ahead, the fool rides on the trail rejoicing; the coward turns back, but the wise man leaves the road and watches all things attentively.

Mongol proverb

The first day out of Kolumna, Kirdy and Nada covered seventy miles, for the horses were fresh and were shod against frost with cleats. The light sleigh slipped over the hard snow like a feather, and the big stallion kept up gamely. He was a Podolian breed, up to the Turkish racers in speed, and indifferent to cold.

Toghrul—who had plastered his cuts with mud and thought no more of them—observed the brown charger shrewdly when they halted that evening, off the trail, and remarked to Kirdy that they could not take the Pod-

---

*Rumors that the false Dmitri still lived were succeeded by a tale that he was a *vurdalak*, a vampire in human form. Captain Margeret has left in his memoirs a picture of the chaos wrought by the impostor—"The council, the people, the country divided one against another, beginning new treasons. The provinces, unable to know for a long time what had happened, revolted."

olian after the forage had given out. In the open steppe, only native-breds, trained to dig under the snow for grass and moss, could survive.

"Why do you say the open steppe?" Kirdy asked, looking up from grooming down the charger. "God grant that we overtake Otrèpiev before leaving the river!"

The trail for that day had followed the frozen bed of the little Okka, running through forests for the most part. They had passed two or three small villages where they had been told that Otrèpiev's party had passed on, to the east.

"A falcon is swifter in its stoop than the great golden eagle," responded the old man after a moment, "but the eagle is not easily tired. *Bak Allah!* We have six ponies; they have twenty. By changing saddles they can avoid pursuit."

"Canst thou follow the slot of their sledge?"

"Not here. There be too many tracks that come and go. Out on the steppe it is different."

Kirdy was silent while the two men cooked the supper and not until the fire had been replenished, and Nada had settled herself by it in a skin, did he speak.

"There must be talk between us. What road do you take?"

"'Whither goest thou?' the kite asks of the wind. Nay, *oùchar*, since you ran from my house with halberdiers tumbling all over you, like marionettes, you have given orders to my men. You lingered with the taverner at Kolumna—aye, and the priest, and it is no fault of yours that the boyars did not ride up then and take us." She laughed softly, pulling the paws of the bearskin over her slender shoulders. "And now after two days and two nights, you frown and ask the road of me!"

Kirdy kneeled beside her on his saddle cloth. Until now he had asked no questions of Nada—why she wore the garments of a Cossack—why she was fleeing to the east.

"I am no longer an *oùchar*—a fledgling," he responded in his slow drawl. "Once the Cossack brothers gave me a name. They gave me also work to do, and that is why I issued commands to your men."

"Did the sir brothers bid you go to my house when it was surrounded by foes?"

"Nay, my horses were there—I had thought so. Besides you might have been there, and Tatikof sought you with no gentle hand."

"Oh, it is clear to me now." Nada smiled, unseen. "You are a true Cossack, White Falcon. First you think of horses, then of the *divchina*, the maiden."

Kirdy pushed the ends of the branches into the fire. He found it difficult to choose words in talking to Nada. It was not easy to tell when she was making fun of him. Besides, he had never seen such a splendid girl before.

After two days on the snow road her cheeks, that had been pallid in the town, glowed softly. A light was in her eyes, and her small lips were dark with pulsing blood. In the glow of the fire and the wan radiance of the full moon that had risen over the tree crest, her head and hair were beautiful.

Even while she spoke to him she seemed to be listening to the sounds of the forest—to the snapping of wood under the growing cold, to the tinkle of ice falling on the snow crust, and the tiny scraping of an animal's claws somewhere in the darkness.

He wondered why she was more lovely in Cossack dress than in the *sarafan* of a noblewoman.

"When you drove into the street with the horses, Nada, you gave me my life. The boyars had penned me. Until death, I swear gratitude to you."

"Will you serve me?"

"In what way?"

Nada tossed her head scornfully.

"*Kai*, the Cossack hero is generous! He offers gratitude and then bargains like a Jew."

"It is not so," Kirdy said quietly. "To the sir brothers, I made a pledge. Until that is redeemed, how can I do otherwise than follow the path upon which I set my foot?"

"I have need, White Falcon, of a sword to guard me until I draw rein at my home. Such a sword as yours, for God has sent tumult and trouble upon this road."

Kirdy looked into the fire without answering once. He had meant to ask of Nada one of her ponies. By changing from the charger to this mustang he was sure of overtaking Otrèpiev within a week. He knew now that the false Dmitri had escaped from Moscow, and he was glad that the issue between them would be settled in open country where the Cossack was at home. How he would manage to get his enemy within reach of his sword he had not thought. Circumstances would decide that.

"Nada," he said, still pondering, "you wear the *svitza* and girdle of a warrior of the *siech*. You speak as one." They had ceased to avail themselves of the Manchu-Tartar, and it was clear that the Cossack speech was native to the girl.

"My father is a Zaporogian."

"Honor to him! What is his name?"

"Come and hear it!"

"I may not."

Kirdy bent forward to look deep into Nada's eyes. He stared so long that the blood darkened the girl's cheeks.

"I will wager my life there is faith in you," he said at last.

A shadow touched her brow, and she seemed to be vexed, for a reason he did not understand. But she listened attentively while he told her how he had to the Cossacks from the southern steppe, how the army of the *siech* had been betrayed by Otrèpiev, and how he had sworn to Khlit, the Koshevoi Ataman, that Otrèpiev should pay with his life for his treachery.

"The brothers are more foolish than wolves," she cried angrily. "For they fall into a trap; then they lick their wounds and begin to think of vengeance. It has always been like that, my father said. Why do you trust me?"

"I do not know."

Flinging herself back on the bearskin, Nada rested her head on her crossed arms and gazed up at the shining sky.

"*Kai*—give me horses, let me ride until a bullet brings me down! That is what you would say if you could find words. And the Cossack maiden must sit in her sleigh and pray for the young swordsman who has less sense than his charger that cannot get at the grass under the snow! You would never overtake Otrèpiev!"

"He may be a fiend, as it is said; but if he is a man I will find him."

"Did ever a hero of the *siech*," Nada asked of the stars, "swear so many vows or pledge so much in one short hour?"

This time Kirdy flushed, unaware that dark eyes were watching him under long lashes, and Nada hastened to make him more uncomfortable.

"In Holy Mother Moscow of the White Walls, I saw Gregory Otrèpiev many times. He rides like a hero and he is handsome, much more so than you are. The wife he took from the Poles is a painted puppet; he left her with little sorrow, nor did she remain at his side. Otrèpiev may be a fiend, but surely he is king of all the wanderers and monarch of the daring. I watched him at swordplay with the Frankish officers. He laughed and tossed their blades first to one side, then to the other, and to me he bowed the knee, saying that I was more beautiful than any Muscovite. I wonder who he is?"

"A soul," Kirdy responded in his slow fashion, "that feels neither remorse nor any fear. A man who could have been the greatest of emperors, if he had faith and honor in him. In all things he succeeds himself, yet brings death and torment to others."

A moment of silence followed, while Nada studied Kirdy from the shadow of her arm.

"And yet—alone among men he can play with crowns for stakes. A beggar, he sat on the Eagle Throne of the Kremyl! An exile, he wrote a letter bidding the boyars fear! If I—"

She paused and Kirdy remained grimly silent.

"If I were to meet Gregory Otrèpiev wandering in the steppe with his crown and his sword, I would share bread and salt with him."

"And pray for him?" Kirdy asked, smiling.

He had not meant to mock the girl, for he could understand her spirit. But Nada was not inclined to endure a smile.

"Aye, pray to St. Ulass the Good, for him—and for all outcasts."

"Where is your home?"

It occurred to Kirdy that if Nada's house was near at hand, she would not need the extra ponies. They were, in a way, his horses, but since Nada had saved them for him, and since she had two men to mount, he did not mean to claim them.

"In the Wolky Gorlo."

"The Wolf's Throat? Where is that?"

"Beyond the border, across the river where the sun rises."

"That is far."

"Aye, my White Falcon. I sought the aid of your sword upon the way, but since you have sworn an oath—" She glanced at him, with amusement vanished in one of her sudden changes of mood. "You do not know whither Otrèpiev draws his reins!"

"Nay, the trail is blind. Yet he must ride further."

"Soon the river turns sharp to the north. If he is for Kazan, which is the trading town of the northern frontier, he will follow it. If he strikes for Astrakhan, on the southern sea, he will turn off. But if he goes on, into the steppe—that way my road lies, to the eastward. Can you keep a bargain, Cossack?"

She pulled the bear's paws over her face, leaving only dark, grave eyes visible when Kirdy frowned blackly.

"*Kai*—I think you can, Cossack. You are a fool, but—" she chuckled aloud—"I will wager my life there is honesty in you! Well, we are agreed. If Otrèpiev turns north or south, I will give you one of your horses back, with gratitude, and you can ride off and be killed like a dog. If he keeps on, to the tribes, you must come with me. Nay—"

She forestalled a swift objection.

"Kazan and Astrakhan lie many weeks ride distant. But the river Volga he could reach before you can come up with him. I know the trail."

Kirdy nodded. She had spoken the truth. He wondered what course the fugitive would take on the Volga.

"If he crosses," Nada observed, "and he is bold enough to do that, you must go through the Wolky Gorlo to meet him. Now, my White Falcon, you must let me sleep. You have talked so much I am yawning. But is the bargain struck?"

"Agreed."

"Then you will see tomorrow that Nada can fly over the steppe as swiftly as any warrior of the *siech*."

She snuggled down into the voluminous folds of bearskin, wrapping the head and paws about her, and Kirdy strode away, too restless to sleep, wondering how he had come to talk so much. Usually he said little enough.

Presently Toghrul appeared out of the shadows with an armful of wood and stirred up the fire. And though he did not appear to look at them, his slant eyes took in the silent woman and the angry Cossack pacing from the horses to his blanket, and when old man returned to his sheepskins he kicked Karabek out of slumber.

"The *khanum* bids us to saddle when the stars are low, before the moon is out of the sky. By the beard of Azrael, it is as I said! Until now the Cossack has led, and when the *khanum* takes the rein there will be more than words. Two hands on the rein, and neither will yield to the other."

Nada, it seemed, had guessed Otrèpiev's course. They came the next evening to the great bend in the Okka and learned from a caravan of merchants who had just crossed on the ice that the sledge and seven cavaliers had taken the Volga road.

"They are merry—the young gentlemen. *Ekh*—what horses!"

And Toghrul proved to be right in the matter of horseflesh. For a while he pressed the three blacks with all the skill of the nomad he was. He would rub them down himself at night, water and feed them sparingly, sleep with them, and talk to them at the start before the rising of the sun.

Then he would let them walk for a while before trotting. At a word from him they would work into a light gallop, and the ground would flash past until Toghrul chose to bid his steeds halt. Then they would walk, stretching out their necks, until they breathed. Kirdy noticed that Toghrul managed by voice and gave little heed to the reins.

By now he was pretty certain of the tracks left by Otrèpiev's cavalcade, for the sledge had unusually narrow iron runners, and some of the ponies were unshod. He prayed that there would be no heavy fall of snow and that the ice in the Volga would be going out.

Winter was ending, and at midday the sun made the footing soft, so that mud began to appear on the trail—though everything froze hard at night. The villages were fewer—a scattering of *choutars* around a log church or fort, in a valley. The timber was thinning except for dense stands on the tablelands.

From passing traders, Finns or Armenians for the most part, who were coming in from the border with furs, he heard that Otrèpiev was still two full days in advance of him. It would be quite useless to take even three horses and try to come up with the fugitives before they reached the river.

Toghrul pointed out that they must wait over a day at the next farm until the charger was rested and the other horses had slept their fill.

"Why did you think that Otrèpiev would strike for the Volga?" he asked Nada.

"How? Does a stag not start up from the thicket when the wolfpack gives tongue? He would take the boldest course."

"That would be to cross the river. Why?"

"On the far side the Nogai tents are assembled here and there. The Tartars come in at Winter to trade their furs and plunder across the river when the ice is good. He can hide himself among them."

Kirdy knew this very well, but it surprised him a little that Nada should know what went on beyond the border. The Nogais had been driven out of Kazan and Muscovy by Ivan the Terrible generations ago, and they were far from peaceful. But the Tsar Ivan had massacred tens of thousands of their warriors in that day, and this had earned their hearty respect.

The trail brought them to the Volga at last, on a gray day when the sun had disappeared behind clouds. Kirdy searched the bank of the river that was like a dark valley between white hills. Toghrul agreed with him that Otrèpiev had crossed at once.

So the horses and the sleigh were led across, and the story that was written in the far bank drew Kirdy for an hour's searching of tracks. What had happened was clear as a minstrel's tale.

Here a Nogai yurta had been, where one of the tribes had Winter quarters. They had penned their cattle behind fences and had eaten the animals that died of starvation—for the Tartars never saved up for the Winter. Otrèpiev's party had gone into the yurta, and at least two days ago the whole had moved off—the Nogais loading their felt tents on wagons and driving their cattle.

A storm would hide the trail of the tribe, and once this was lost it would be a long and anxious matter to find trace of Otrèpiev again. On three sides of him stretched the steppe, with its treeless expanse of rolling ground, its vast spaces where the blast of the wind was more to be feared than Tartar arrows—its isolated burial mounds where spirits could be heard crying at night. Kirdy knew it well.

Nada, her coat collar turned up over her hair, her slim waist girdled tight, and her hands thrust into the wide sleeves, looked about her and turned to him curiously.

"Would you follow the Nogais, who have followed Otrèpiev?"

"Aye," he said.

She pointed to the leaden bank of the sky in the north that seemed to spread darkness over all the world.

"It is coming, the snow. Before morning, perhaps before night, it will end the trail. Look at Toghrul!"

The old man was stamping about by the horses, cursing the Nogai camp that had left not a bit of grazing on this part of the river; his impatience and uneasiness were unmistakable.

"Can I get hay at your Wolf's Throat?" Kirdy asked.

"Aye, and meat."

"Where lies this Wolky Gorlo?"

"Yonder."

Nada pointed inland, diagonally away from the track of the Nogais.

"Is it a Tartar yurta?"

The girl laughed gleefully.

"Ask the black-haired people!" she cried, dropping into the dialect of the tribes. "Ask—if they come near the Wolf's Throat!"

"In the name of Allah the Compassionate!" Toghrul's plaintive cry drifted up to them. "Are the horses to stand until their bones stiffen?"

Kirdy knew that he must go first to the Wolky Gorlo for food and forage for his horse, and then must take his chances at tracking down Otrèpiev in the open steppe.

"Come!" Nada called to him.

Toghrul drove as if possessed, swaying on his seat, singing to the three black heads and the manes that tossed like surf under the beat of the wind. The horses sped as if possessed by devils—or as if scenting their stables—over long ridges and the black beds of streams without sign of a road. Kirdy's charger gathered himself together and did his brute best to follow. The other man and the two mustangs were left far behind.

"Come!" Nada's clear voice came back to him "O Cossack, do you fear this road?"

The road, to be sure, was unprepossessing. Winding through barren uplands, it dipped among a nest of rock gullies where the charger stumbled and came up blindly. The gray sky pressed lower, and the sleigh was beyond sight; only the tinkling of the bells was to be heard. This ceased, and when the wind blew from her direction Kirdy caught the girl's voice lifted in song that mocked the oncoming storm.

A somber twilight fell, while Kirdy plied his whip and watched the landmarks on either hand. It seemed to him that they were descending sharply. Soon whirling flakes, heavy and damp, shut out everything except the horse and the trail.

He reined in the charger to listen, and to look for Karai. By the rock walls, rising in pinnacles and mounds on both flanks, he judged they were entering one of the long ravines that break the even surface the steppe.

Yellow eyes glared at him from a bend in the trail, and he snatched at the sword before he was certain from the behavior of the horse that it was Karai and not a wolf that waited his coming. The dog, contrary to his usual custom, pressed the charger's legs, his hair stiff on shoulders and neck, and his fangs a-gleam.

Wind devils whined above his head, the towers of black granite closed in on him, and the drifting flakes stung face and hands. The charger snorted and edged cautiously between two boulders.

The storm had set in, and all trace of the sleigh was lost. Nothing was to be seen, but Kirdy rode on stubbornly, sure that there could be no other way. He had the feeling of coming out into an open valley, when Karai bounded forward, and he beheld two eyes of light in the distance. A few paces more and he saw the glow of windows upon the falling snow, and the black mass of a log cabin.

Kirdy dismounted, and knocked with numb fingers on the door. Then he stepped aside, because he was now across the river, and it is not well to venture out of darkness into sudden light in the steppe, where Asia begins.

"*Ai Kazak!* Do you fear because you have come to the Wolf's Throat?"

Nada's voice from within challenged him, and he strode to the charger, leading him around the cottage to the lean-to that served as stable. When the saddle was off and the horse was blanketed he entered the cottage, stooping under the lintel.

By the white-tiled stove sat an old man, shielding a candle from the blast of air that swept through the open door. He rose, leaning on a staff, and peering at the young warrior.

"*Chlieb sol,*" he said, and bowed. "My bread and salt is yours."

Once he must have been as tall as Kirdy, because he bent over, resting heavily on his stick. He moved stiffly in his Turkish robes, but his boots and shirt were of Cossack make. Though his face was lined and his long hair gray around the forehead, he had the clear and alert eyes of middle age.

What held Kirdy's silent attention was the man's headgear—a white wolf skin, with a great broad head overhanging his brow. The white muzzle with the long fangs surely had belonged to a monarch of the wolf folk.

"Omelko am I," vouchsafed his host, "and it is a day of days that brings to my *choutar* a hero of the Cossacks."

"Health to you," responded Kirdy. "Rest I would have, and meat and forage for the horse. My road is far to the end."

Omelko hobbled to the stove and filled a long horn with hot brandy, offering it to his guest. Kirdy took it, and spilled a few drops to the four quarters of the winds, and lifted it.

"*Hai* to the Cossack brothers! To the heroes of other days."

"Glory to God, young warrior."

"For the ages of ages!"

Kirdy emptied the horn—not to do so would have been an insult to his host—and the blood warmed in his chilled limbs. Although he had never heard of a Cossack living beyond the river, he felt sure that this man was Cossack-born. If so, he was safe within the four walls of the *choutar* as in the barracks of the *siech*. He unslung his sword, threw off his sable coat, and stretched his boots toward the stove.

"A splendid borzoi," Omelko observed, "and full three-quarters wolf. How did you come by him?"

"Found him three-quarters starved beyond the Jaick and fed him. He has not left me. Down Karai!"

He knew that his host had taken note of his Cathayan garments, but Omelko, rubbing Karai's throat, was too courteous to question his guest before they shared food—or else Nada had already spoken with him. The girl brought them supper—mutton, with barley cakes, cheese and honey, and filled his horn with brandy in utter silence.

"Nada is a devilkin," Omelko remarked, shaking his head. "When she is off like that, there is always trouble. Last time she came in with her horse nearly dead—and a cavalcade of stag hunters at her heels. Eh, they drew rein at the Wolf's Throat!"

"Why?" asked Kirdy, who desired to know.

"No Tartars will enter the gorge, past the two rocks. When they trade, they leave their gear outside, and Nada takes it in, putting in place of it what we will give them. But for two days the storm will close all the paths."

The hut was built of pine logs, roughly smoothed, the chinks filled with moss and clay. The floor was sand, neatly raked, and there was a pleasant odor of herbs. Above the table Kirdy noticed a long yataghan with a fine ivory hilt, and an icon stand with a painting of the good Saint Ulass.

By the roar of wind in the trees above the gorge and the rattle of hard snow against the horn windows, Kirdy knew that the storm would last, as his host had said.

"That is Nada's sword," nodded Omelko, and his lips twisted under the beard. "*Ekh*, I would not let her take it, this time, because she is too swift to draw steel and she is no match for a swordsman. The blade of yours—I have seen it before."

"It was Khlit's—the Koshevoi Ataman's."

Omelko was silent for a while, ruminating.

"I am glad of the storm," he said, "because you will tell me of Cossack deeds and the wars of the heroes."

Far into the night the two Cossacks talked over the wine horns, until Nada, who had been sewing in silence on the other side of the stove, slipped away to her room. With the garments of a Cossack maiden, with the kerchief and *beshmet*, a shyness had come upon her, and Kirdy, glancing covertly from under his brows, wondered at her flushed cheeks and lowered eyes and wondered still more if this were the girl he had followed in that ride through the Wolf's Throat.

When he had stretched out on his coat to sleep, Omelko went to the shelf by the icon stand and took down a parchment-bound book, reading far into the night. At times he closed the book to gaze at the face of the sleeping warrior; and at times he raised his head as if to listen to the note of the wind.

Then Karai would spring up silently and trot back and forth behind the door.

Chapter X
Omelko's Dream

For two days it snowed. The paths indeed were closed to caravans or travelers, yet through the drifting curtain of the storm, riders passed from yurta to yurta. They were neither shadows nor ghosts; they were living men and Tartar messengers.

And as soon as the stars came out, during the second night, black masses of warriors moved out of the encampments.

It was noticed by the sentries of the Muscovite frontier posts that a star fell before the long hours of darkness were at an end. There was heard, too, the distant howling of wolves in every quarter. After the storm the great packs of the steppe were afoot.

In the Wolky Gorlo, long before dawn, Kirdy was roused by the stamping of the ponies in the lean-to. He went to the door and looked out. Clouds were drifting across the face of the old moon, almost overhead, but the white surface of the glen and the dark, timbered sides could be made out easily. Satisfied that the far-off howling came from wolves and not from the dreaded specters of men that ride at times upon the steppe about the places where they gave up their lives, he quieted Karai and stretched his arms. The frost had gone from the air, and the night was almost warm. Out of the darkness behind him Omelko, spoke.

"The gray friends are hunting. The pack has come down out of the heights."

Among the Cossacks, wolves were called grey brothers, yet these words stirred the interest of the young warrior.

"They hunt, aye," he said. "But one pack is like another."

"But that is the great one, from the heights. Often it passes through the Wolky Gorlo. It's leader is of large size with part of his tail torn off.

Kirdy knew now how the gorge had probably been named by Tartars who had reason to fear hunger-maddened packs of the steppe, especially in Winter. He wondered why Toghrul and Karabek slept on quietly in their felt tent by the lean-to. If the pack were approaching the gorge it would be best to light fires.

For a while he listened. The quavering note of the pack had changed, had dwindled and risen again savagely, and now seemed to come from a new quarter and to resemble the high-pitched shouts of men.

"The gray friends," Omelko's voice proclaimed, "have met riders—many men. They will not pass through the gorge."

But Kirdy, who had been putting on his boots and belt, had closed the door, thrusting Karai inside. Seeking out the bay stallion, he saddled him in the darkness and was ready to mount when he noticed a man peering in at the shed entrance. After a moment he recognized Toghrul.

"O Cossack," the old Tartar complained, "is the night so long that thou must even groom thy horse before the stars have set?"

He grunted when Kirdy mounted, and he saw the youth was fully clad and armed.

"Take heed!" he muttered. "The Nogais are on the move."

"Whether?"

"Am I an eagle to look down from heights, or a dog to smell the trails? One of their paths runs to the right of the gorge as far distant as two arrow flights. I will go with thee."

"Stay with the horses—thou!"

Leaving Toghrul muttering, the Cossack rode up the gorge, avoiding the drifts. The going was heavy, but the high wind had swept stretches almost clear, and the light was good. Half in hour later he came out on higher ground and reined in to search the neighboring knolls with his eyes.

Presently he saw what he expected to find—a tiny figure on a distant rise, no more than a dark speck that might have been a sitting wolf or a stone except for the glint of light when the moon's gleam struck a polished spear—tip slung on the Tartar's back.

Avoiding the watcher, Kirdy trotted down into a nest of gullies where the charger labored through drifts. He judged that he was well behind the sentry when he came on a broad trail stamped down by a score of ponies. The warrior with the spear still sat on his eminence, and Kirdy refrained from stalking him, knowing that more Tartars would come along the trail presently—if the sentry had not been withdrawn.

As soon as he heard hoofs, he wheeled the stallion and began to trot toward the river. Men approached from behind and a deep voice spoke at his elbow.

"Is the horse lame, that thou hast fallen behind the trail breakers?"

"*Yak*," Kirdy made answer. "No, I have word for thy leader. Where rides he?"

In the depths of the gully the darkness was impenetrable, except for the shimmer of starlight on the heights above them. Kirdy heard a pony trotting beside him.

"The lord," the same voice made answer, "rides with us. What word dost thou bring?"

"I have steel," Kirdy promised grimly, "to crop ears that be over-long."

The invisible rider snarled, a saddle creaked, and Kirdy reined a little to the side. But the tribesman swallowed his anger.

"*Bil ma'ida*! Surely thou art a servant of the Khaghan?"

Kirdy left it to the other's imagination whether or not he might be a servant of the tsar. And he drew aside to wait for the leader of the clan. It would not do to ride on, out of the protecting gully. The Tartars, having encountered him going in the same direction had no reason to suspect him.

It could hardly enter their minds that a stranger would appear at that hour between their advance and the main body—a stranger who spoke their language and asked for their leader. The sheer daring of Kirdy's action protected him, so far.

Ponies trotted past, and occasional riders came to peer at him, and to hear him ask again for the *soultan*. His nostrils filled with the odor of sheepskins, of mutton grease and sweat-soaked leather. These men had come far that night and, judging by the scattered words that reached him, were bound for the river.

"Here is the *soultan*," a Nogai called presently out of the darkness.

Kirdy wondered fleetingly why the leader was not one of the tribe, and why another answered for him. A white horse and a rider in loose, light garments took form in the obscurity, and a voice grumbled:

"What dog is this?"

Kirdy's pulse throbbed in his temples, and he ceased wondering. The man had spoken in fluent Persian, to himself, as if hopeless of gaining understanding from those around him.

"*Tourkat,*" grunted the Cossack, "one who speaks Turki."

"By the Ninety and Nine Holy Names, that is good hearing!" cried the rider of the white horse. "Oh, the smells unmentionable, the pains past bearing, the fear clinging like a shadow! Oh, the woe of these times—"

The breath left his lips in a gasp. Kirdy had reined the stallion around until the two horses touched shoulders, and during the outburst had drawn his sword silently. Now a quarter inch of a steel tip had pierced the man's back.

"Dogs there be, beyond doubt," the Cossack said grimly, "and fools likewise; but the greatest of fools is he who wags a loose tongue. Hold thine, therefore or feel the length of this blade."

The stranger said no more, nor did he move. Kirdy waited until the body of Nogais had passed, making astonishingly little noise, like men intent on what lay before them.

"Forward thou!" Kirdy commanded sharply.

And the pair who had lingered to accompany the stranger or to satisfy curiosity, went on again. Still Kirdy waited, moving the sword-tip a little, to keep his captive from thinking too much, until the rearguard had trotted past, with a long shout—to warn the watcher on the height that he should come down. It was a similar shout, much fainter, that Kirdy had heard an hour ago from the door of Omelko's cabin. He was grateful to the superstition that made the tribesmen cast a wide circle around the Wolky Gorlo. And he was just as well pleased that the riders of the rear had not seen him and the stranger. Reaching swiftly behind the other, he pulled a scimitar from its scabbard and thrust it through his belt. Then he felt for knives, finding three of different shapes in as many places. These he cast to the snow.

"Forward!" he said to his captive.

But he turned the head of the white horse, keeping the rein in his left hand and guiding the stallion by his knees. They walked back to the other gully through which the Cossack had entered, and down this they trot-ted—Kirdy removing the sword-tip generously.

In the east the stars were fading, and a kind of gray obscurity spread through the network of hollows and ridges around the Wolky Gorlo. When trees were visible against the snow, Kirdy peered at his captive and saw enough to convince him that the man was neither a Muscovite officer of the false Dmitri—as he had hoped—nor a Nogai chieftain.

At the narrow pass between the two boulders that formed the Wolf's Throat, he reined in and waited until full daylight. The Nogais, when they missed their leader, would have turned back before this.

"Eh," he thought, "it is true, then, they will not enter this place." Aloud, he added, "What man art thou?"

The prisoner salaamed, bending almost to Cossack's stirrup.

"Prince of swordsmen, Lion of the Steppe, I am thy slave—the inter-preter of dreams. Thus they call me Al-Tâbir."

He was a broad, round man, wrapped up in a half dozen *khalats* and vests, all gorgeous purples and blacks, with embroidered slippers and a sash that must have aroused the instant envy of all the Nogais. A small turban was knotted jauntily over one ear and the face under the turban was pale and round as the full moon. Kirdy had seen cows with just the same mild brown eyes of Al-Tâbir. He laughed, thinking that he had just risked torture to fetch this Persian—because the interpreter of dreams, smelling strongly of musk and civet, was as Persian as the gold-inlaid scimitar he had worn—from the tribesmen.

"May the dogs bite thee, Al-Tâbir!—what makest thou in this place?"

Taking heart from the laugh, the interpreter of dreams raised his head.

"Nay. I am truly Jahia ibn Muhammad al-Nisapur, cup-companion of the shah, whom way Allah exalt. Out of his courtesy the shah sent me to the great emperor of the Urusses. It was written that I should find this emperor dead and another seated upon the throne. This other, being pleased with my conversation, command me to attend him upon his ex-ile. I heard—I obeyed."

"Thou wert a man of Dmitri's?"

"Truly, his *sahab*, his companion. He revels well, but rides too much."

Kirdy tapped the sword blade that rested on his saddle peak.

"Al-Tâbir, in times past I have hearkened to Persians. I heard many lies and little truth. But thou, O my captive, shalt tell me truly what has happened. Or thy head will cease from thinking and tongue from lying. Where is thy master?"

"By the face of the Prophet, I know not. Yesterday he drank wine in the tent of the khan of the Nogais. He laid a command upon me to go with a warrior to another clan. I went."

"Wherefore?"

"It is my thought that he sent one of his companions to different tribes, as hostages, perhaps."

"The Nogais called you leader."

"Allah! Not a word of their talk is known to me. It is my thought that the tsar sent commands to them, and they looked upon us as emirs, greatly to be feared. They fear the tsar. So do I!"

Kirdy smiled.

"That I believe. Now think again, Al-Tâbir—what orders were sent?"

"Surely the command was to rise and arm against the Muscovites. The tsar makes war against his emirs. The Nogais will cross the river. I am content to be rid of them."

The lips of the Cossack hardened under the moustache, and his eyes narrowed. He had not expected that Otrèpiev would dare loose the tribes against the frontier posts. The man seemed able to breed chaos even in the steppe.

"Then the Nogais believe he is the tsar? Why?"

"*W'Allah*! Why not? He showed them jewels from the chests—even the gold apple, and the scepter that bears a ruby as large as my thumb. Their khan had never seen the jewels before. Besides, they were ready enough to make raids."

Kirdy nodded. All this was possible. The border would be fire- and fury-ridden, and the very ice of the Volga stained with blood. So, pursuit from Moscow would be checked.

"But," he said thoughtfully, "after a while the Tartars will know that he has no power, that only six men ride at his back—then they will plunder him."

Again Al-Tâbir salaamed.

"O youth, and scion of battles—in thee there is wisdom even sufficient unto thy courage! This thing the tsar has foreseen. Within a week he will ride from these pagans—may their graves be dug up!"

"Whither?"

"To the east."

"To what place?"

Al-Tâbir searched his memory, with an eye on the Cossack's sword, and decided not to lie. The young warrior knew a deal too much to make lying either safe or profitable.

"To the place where the sun rises. It lies behind the Mountains of the Eagles, and it is the country of the Golden Horde."

For the second time Otrèpiev had hidden his trail. Only, the first time he had slain a friend so that he might leave the body in his own bed; now he had slain hundreds, and the dead and dying along the river had concealed all trace of him.

No longer could the Muscovites follow him. Months must pass before the Nogais would be driven across the river again, and the caravan paths opened.

And now the way of pursuit was closed to Kirdy. Although the storm had ended, although the fresh snow on the steppe would reveal the tracks of the fleeing man—although Omelko had promised him horses, hay, and meat, he could not ride forth.

From the east, from unexpected places, the more distant clans of the Nogais would be coming in as vultures flock to a feast. No craft or skill would serve to avoid them. On the white waste of the steppe a rider would be seen by the keen eyes of the nomads even on the horizon; the Cossack's trail would be picked up inevitably. Moreover, it was extremely probable that the Nogais had left men to watch at the two openings of the Wolf's Throat into which Al-Tâbir had disappeared so unexpectedly.

Meanwhile Otrèpiev might do any one of a number of things. At any day, with his fast horses and his sledge with narrow runners, he could start on his journey into the unknown part of the steppe. Who could say what he would do?

Nature itself would hide him in another fortnight, because already the thaw had set in and presently the plain along the Volga would be a morass, the earth soft to its marrow, after the melting of seven months' snow; no rider then could cross the steppe near the flooded rivers.

All this Nada told Kirdy, quite aware that he already knew it, but moved by curiosity to learn what he meant to do.

"God gives," she said. "And here, surely, is the end of your road."

Kirdy, who had been sitting against the sunny side of the cabin, looked up at the clear sky, the fir-topped walls of the valley. Where the snow had melted from boulders the rock showed black and moist. From the low-hanging branches of the birches came a steady *drip-drip* of water. A pony neighed in the shed.

"By the grave of Otrèpiev I will know the end of the road, Nada."

"But he is far away! Only our brother the eagle, flying low, sees him. Only the wolf noses about his fire."

Kirdy smiled, and when he did so his dark eyes glowed.

"In such fashion the road ended at the City of the White Walls. And yet—we followed it hither."

"And is this not a better place than that town?"

"Aye, so."

Kirdy made response in his slow fashion, looking up at the girl frankly.

"Would you be alive outside, in the steppe—anywhere but here in the Wolf's Throat where the Nogais dare not come?"

"God gives, little Nada!"

"How did you capture the Persian? Tell me!"

"Eh, it was in darkness. I spoke to him, and was so glad to hear his own speech he came with me."

A slender booted foot stamped impatiently near Kirdy's knee.

"It was not like that at all. I can understand him a little. He is afraid of you, and he called me a *gul begam*—that's a Flower Princess, isn't it? Are you going to kill him? His sword is too light and curved, but the mare is splendid."

Kirdy looked up quickly.

"Don't let the Tartars harm him. I want him alive."

"Why? What good is he?"

"He can tell you the meaning of a dream. The science of the *tabir* is much esteemed by the Moslems. They glean prophecies out of dreams, and no doubt the prophets glean gold. Jania, or Al-Tâbir, is well born."

Upon this Nada went off to ply the captive with questions and Kirdy continued to sit by the hut, drawing lines in the trodden snow with the butt of his riding whip. He had gone among Nogais to try to get tidings of the man he sought; but he had satisfied himself that the entrances of the Wolf's Throat were watched, and he knew the uselessness of trying to escape when his trail would be clear to such keen eyes. Only by an effort did he restrain his impatience and settle down to watch for the chance that might open the way into the steppe.

That evening Nada held the entire attention of the three men. First she sang—the half-barbaric and wholly plaintive songs of the Cossacks that quickened Kirdy's blood and made her father call for more brandy. Then she teased Omelko to tell the young warrior stories of the past, and the lame man took fire at her persuasion.

"Eh, sir brother," he cried. "Once I followed the little Mother Volga. What is there to say? You know the way of a Cossack youth—to revel in the tavern, to mount when there is war. That was my blade."

He nodded at the yataghan with the ivory hilt, and the wolf's mask—that filled Al-Tâbir with fascinated dread—nodded likewise.

"A gray stallion I stole from the khan himself, from the stables of Bagche Serai. I rode to Kazan, which was then a Tartar city. In the bazaars were Greeks and God knows how many else. I drank for days, until I saw not one but several suns in the sky. I drank down the gray stallion—everything but my trousers and that blade. Why not? Other horses were to be had and I was young. But then began a great firing of cannon, and the Greeks said the city was besieged."

He stroked his beard and pushed aside the parchment book that was his companion of evenings.

"Eh, Falcon, what shall I tell you? I went on the wall, and many foemen felt the edge of my sword. After a time, when I could see the real sun, I heard that these foemen were Muscovites led by Ivan the Terrible. What matter?

"The walls of Kazan were stormed after much fighting, and the Tartar dead filled the alleys. Some of the tribesmen broke through, I with them. The armored boyars were all around—thick as flies in the slaughter yard. We tried to swim the Volga but there were boats, and I was taken up by warriors of the tsar who thought at first I was a Muscovite. In time men saw who knew me for the Cossack who had fought on the wall. They should have cut me down or blown me from a cannon.

"Instead they put my legs in the rack and broke all the bones. Then they carried me across the river and flung me out on the plain. Eh, that was an evil thing. Wolves came and sat by me but did not tear me. I could not crawl. Toghrul rode up—he was then a hunter of stags. He tied the ends of two saplings across his saddle-horn and wove branches to make a drag. So he brought me to this valley, where he had his tent."

"*Ekh ma'a!* Why should a man want to live when he can no longer ride? Yet I lived and in time could walk with a staff, as you see. He it was, my brother, who carried to the valley for refuge a Cossack maiden, a captive of the Tartars."

Omelko's grim head sank on his breast, and he sighed.

"Nay, I was no longer a hero, no longer a Cossack! Of what avail my life? She would not leave me, when the way was open. She was the daughter of an *ataman* and Nada was her child—she dying at the time."

From the sunken eyes of the old Cossack tears crept down his cheeks and he clasped his staff in gaunt fingers that still were powerful.

"How shall I tell this tale, sir brother? She was in all things like Nada, with a temper like a sword-edge and a heart that was like a very flame of love. She knew many legends of my people that brought me joy in the hearing, and before Nada was born she wrote them down in that book, and taught me the letters. Now I—who am no priest—can trace the legends, and many a time have I read them over to Nada."

For a while he was silent, his eyes traveling from the sword to the picture of the saint on the wall. To Kirdy there was nothing strange in the life of this girl, who had grown up tended by Tartars, who had hunted stag, and had dared to journey alone to Moscow to listen to the talk of Christians and bring back to Omelko tidings of the world across the river.

"God provided for Nada," Omelko said finally, "or she would have been lost to me. This was way of it. I dreamed one night that an old man came into my *choutar* and sat by the fire, saying, 'Omelko, my son, your suffering has been great.'

"Then, in the dream, my guest rose up, saying: 'I give you power over my children the gray friends, the wolves. They will hunt for you, and you shall be *koshevoi* of the wolves.'"

Omelko nodded at the gilded picture upon the wall.

"Surely that was Saint Ulass! Now, hearken, my brother—I woke up and went to the door. It stood open, and all about the *choutar* wolves were sitting like dogs.

"I saw, in the clear moonlight, the leader of the pack, a gray wolf with a part of his tail torn away. Often since then the great pack has come down from the heights, passing through the Wolky Gorlo. And then I say, 'A merry chase to you, brothers!'"

Kirdy pondered this in silence, and Nada met his eyes.

"It is true my Falcon," she said, "that the wolves have not harmed this *choutar*. At times, when I have hunted, I have seen the pack running about me. The Tartars believe that my father has power over the wolves, and they will not enter this place."

At this Omelko shook his head and reached for his glass.

"Nay, it is the good Saint Ulass who has protected you, my daughter. It is—" he added to Kirdy a smile—"to keep the tribesmen in awe that I wear that wolf's muzzle. Now, my Falcon, let us drink. Glory to God!"

"For the ages of ages!"

Chapter XI
Only a Ghost

Only a ghost, sitting on a tomb, enjoys the garlands of dead flowers.

Persian proverb

Days passed, and Kirdy fought down his impatience to be in the saddle. One sunny afternoon he heard the whisper of freshets, released from the barrier of ice, eating their way down into the valley from the heights, and he groaned, clasping his head in his hands. By now whatever trace Otrèpiev had left would be lost to sight, and soon the steppe would be closed to horses.

More faithful than the Cossack's shadow, Al-Tâbir had kept close to him in the Wolky Gorlo. The interpreter of dreams looked askance at the Tartars and Omelko, but for Nada he had heartfelt admiration. Now he believed he had discovered the reason of the warrior's brooding silence. He ventured closer and sighed.

"I have seen! Who would not despair? A mouth like the seal of Suleiman—hair blacker than the storm wind—eyes like a gazelle—teeth like matched pearls—form like a willow! I, too, would cast the ashes of longing upon the fire of life!"

Kirdy looked down at the stout little man, frowning.

"What dream is this?"

"A flower of the garden of blessedness!" The Persian raised plump hands and sighed profoundly. "Why should she wear a sword? Her eyes slay without mercy, and her voice binds with chains that may not be broken."

"Is it Nada?" Kirdy contemplated the sympathetic native without favor. "Then bridle thy tongue, because if she hears thee she will make trial of the edge of that yataghan without fail."

"Allah forfend, *sahab*—how can a man who looks upon her say otherwise?"

In Moscow the interpreter of dreams had noticed that the wives and daughters of the boyars were kept in seclusion and it did not occur to him that Cossack women were treated differently. But when he looked into Kirdy's eyes he saw that he had not made amends.

He had meant to condole, in a complimentary way, with one who—as he judged—had experienced the pangs of love for a beautiful woman. Instead, although the White Falcon had not threatened him, the skin of his back felt cold.

"Canst thou truly foretell events from dreams?" Kirdy asked gravely, but Al-Tâbir answered without hesitation:

"That gift have I. Six hundred times have I done so, and it is all written in a book by scribes."

"Then tell me the meaning of this!"

Kirdy repeated to the Persian the tale of Omelko's dream, and the coming of the wolves. Al-Tâbir remained in thought for some time, shaking his head the while.

"How can there be good in wolves?" he muttered. "They who are aided by the *djinn* will die. Take me from this place, young lord! Ai, a fear and a foreboding come upon me!"

In truth fear grew upon the interpreter of dreams, until he would not let Kirdy out of his sight. Al-Tâbir was far from being a fatalist where his life was concerned, and he was shrewd enough to understand that Kirdy could protect him from the people of the Wolky Gorlo, and that the Cossack had taken pity on him—as strong natures will protect weak.

That night Kirdy was kept awake by his restlessness and the Persian's wanderings. For Al-Tâbir ceased not to peer from the windows and mutter to himself. Karai, too, kept sniffing at the door, until the Cossack was brought to his feet by a moan from the native.

"*Ai-i!* Look!"

Kirdy flung the door open and peered out. As his eyes adjusted themselves to the gloom, he noticed shadows passing across the snow. Here and there, for a moment, twin balls of yellow fire glowed and vanished.

"Here, Karai!"

The Cossack called the wolfhound that had slipped out the instant the door was open. But the dog did not come back, and after a moment Kirdy started after him. Al-Tâbir, divided between dread of the wolves and unwillingness to be left alone, hung about the door until a sound within the cabin brought him around like a startled bustard.

Stooping over the stove, Nada was thrusting a length of knotted pitchpine into the bed of coals. Reeds had been wrapped about the stick, and when the end of the torch kindled, she waved it over her head, laughing at the Persian, who saw in this some new incantation.

Al-Tâbir retreated to his corner and left Nada to run alone after Kirdy, the long torch swinging over her.

"It is the great pack," she said over her shoulder as he strode to her side and took the firebrand. "Look, there is the leader."

They advanced slowly, because the wolves, though circling back restlessly, were too numerous to be driven easily—gaunt beasts high in the shoulder, and, by the look of them, more than half starved. Nada pointed to a wolf with only a remnant of a tail and caught Kirdy's arm.

"See the borzoi!"

Just beyond the circle of light Karai could be made out, moving silently toward the pack. To the Cossack's call the dog paid not the slightest attention, and when Kirdy started toward him Nada held back.

"It is too late. We must go no farther."

There was hardly a sound—a rending snarl, the spluttering of the pine. To Kirdy's surprise the wolves nearest Karai were sitting on their haunches in a rough half circle, and in front of them the scarred leader appeared of a sudden—a blotch of gray streaked with brown.

Karai no longer trotted; he moved into the torchlight stiff from nose to tail, his throat rumbling, his fangs clashing. The borzoi and the gray wolf did not face each other—for the wolf sprang too swiftly, and slashed open the dog's shoulder blade.

From that instant they were barely visible—Kirdy thought that the wolf rushed again and was thrown off. The clatter of fangs, the thunderous snarls, the impact of the shaggy bodies dwarfed all other sounds. The pack pressed closer, and the yellow eyes glowed more strongly.

Once the ring of beasts started up, as Karai almost lost his footing. But he was up and whirling on his hind legs in the same instant, blood spattering from muzzle and shoulders.

Again and again the gray wolf slashed at him, and Kirdy heard the unmistakable snap of a bone broken between steel jaws. Once more the wolfpack surged up, and now the leader was visible. The bleeding Karai had drawn away.

But instead of whirling on powerful legs, the gray wolf staggered. Blood streamed from its throat. Maddened and fearful to see, the wolf bristled, snapping its fangs—as if to drive back by menace the fate that inevitably awaited it. It was bleeding to death, the throat torn open.

Karai rushed in, and the wolf was thrown. Then the pack ran in, and a hideous snarling arose as the wolves tore the living flesh from the crippled leader.

Nada and Kirdy had drawn back to the door of the *choutar*, and the Cossack could make out Karai's great form, a little apart from the others. Then the borzoi was lost to sight, and the shadows once more flitted from side to side.

"Vain to call him now," Nada said quietly. "He will run with the pack. Look!"

The clearing was empty. From the wooded slope of the valley was heard a single howl, quavering and plaintive as the call of waterfowl. A full-throated chorus answered it, drifting farther away.

"At times he may come back," the girl went on, "but you are not now his master, White Falcon. Aye, he has slain and is hunting with the pack. A merry hunt to you, gray friend!"

Kirdy listened in silence. He had loved the wild Karai, and he knew that what Nada said was true. More wolf than dog, the borzoi had cast off the fellowship of men for that of his own kind.

"Go and sleep, little Nada." He raised his hand and a deeper note came into his voice. "May the holy angels watch over you!"

She looked up at him quickly, but for once could read nothing in his eyes or guess what was in his heart. On the threshold of her door she glanced back anxiously, and found his eyes still upon her. They glowed an instant, and then were veiled, as if ashes had been thrown upon a fire within them.

For once Kirdy sat quietly beside Omelko, who read aloud to him from the book of his dead wife, until Al-Tâbir snored lustily in his corner, and the young warrior put out his hand closing the sheets of the book of legends.

"Time—it is time, Omelko. Do not wake your daughter or the Persian drone. I must go upon the road."

Omelko sighed and looked at him inquiringly. During the last few days he had wished many times that the dark-browed hero were his son, that the White Falcon would remain at the Wolky Gorlo.

"The wolfpack hunts along the valley," Kirdy answered the unspoken question of his host. "The Nogais who have been watching will be afraid for their horses. They will build fires in the timber, or seek their yurtas. The way out of the Wolf's Throat will be open this night."

"And after?"

With his usual deliberateness—when there was no need of haste— Kirdy was filling his saddlebags, dried meat, barley, and other things of the Cossack's store. Omelko saw that the warrior would not answer the question. After all, who could know what the future held?

"Take what you need, my brother. Another horse."

Kirdy nodded.

"I will take two of the steppe-breds. Yours is the stallion."

"I shall give him to Nada." Again Omelko sighed. He was aware that Nada was fond of the White Falcon, because he knew the wayward moods of the young girl. "Do you draw your rein east?"

"Aye."

They went out to the stable and here Omelko bade Kirdy take two of the black Kabardas, saying that they were equal to a sultan's steeds and would fare for themselves. In darkness, Kirdy saddled one and strapped on the goatskin bags. On the led horse he placed the sack of barley, and a bow and arrows that he had bought of Toghrul.

"Well, you must go!" said Omelko. "But the road to the east has not been traveled before; they say only the ghosts of the dead camp beyond the Nogais. Go with God, my Falcon!"

Kirdy mounted, after drawing his girdle tighter and putting on the wolf skin cap that Nada had made for him. He wheeled the pony, but reined in and came back, to lean close to the lame man.

"Eh, it is not easy to part from friends. I would like to have a cross from Nada that she had kissed. Yet it is in my mind that if I bade her fare-well she would seek to ride a way, to show me the trail. And it is best otherwise, in this night of the wolves and the Tartars. Guard her, Omelko, for—for she is a dove and a brave heart. God knows I owe my life to her. Out in the steppe there is death as well as life. If I ride back, I will come to the Wolky Gorlo. *S'Bohun!*"

He did not urge the eager horses into a gallop, as usual, but reined them in, walking out of the *choutar*, so as not to disturb the sleeping girl.

And after he had disappeared into the darkness without a sound, no tidings of him reached the river, or the Wolky Gorlo. No tidings, except for the tale of a Nogai horde that had drifted in from the uplands of the Chelkar, scenting plunder. The tale was told at the great camp on the Volga to the khan of the Nogais, who was in great anger at that time because the emperor who had come out of Moscow and taken shelter in his tents had left him without warning or leave-taking.

"O shield of the faithful, Lord and companion of Ali—master of Tur— master of our herds, protector of our lives—Lion of the plain and the rivers, in this wise was the happening." So the Chelkar tribesmen declared, sitting in the tent of the khan. "And lo, it is a thing difficult of understanding and a mystery beyond thought!

"Allah had caused the morning to dawn, and the mists were not yet gone when we saw riding toward us a man with a wolf skin cap and a sable *khalat*, far distant as you could hear a loud shout. Now, on either hand of this rider ran wolves more numerous than a flock of our wild sheep.

"The wolves did not attack the two black horses of the rider, though their bellies were drawn. The leader of the wolves was a great gray beast. And it is not a lie, but the truth that our eyes beheld—the leader of the pack ran back to the horses, and for the time that milk takes to boil, trotted beside the man, doing him no hurt. Nor did the man strike the beast.

"We said, 'God is one!' And the rider passed from sight into the mists. Surely he was a *ghil* of the waste lands, a spirit of the dead that lacked a grave. Otherwise we would have slain him, for the horses were greatly to be desired.

"Now the sun was not on our faces that day, when we met a Nazarene girl, mounted on a bay stallion. Our young men rode about her and she whipped them, saying that she was the daughter of the khan of the wolves and we would eat woe if we hindered her. Among our hunters were some who said this thing was true.

"Lest the curse of the wolves be laid upon us, we did her no harm, only asking whither she held her way. It is likewise true that she said she sought the warrior with the two Kabardas. When we released her she went forward upon the trail of the man and the wolves.

"Now, in the next hour we beheld a fat Persian on a white horse, riding as if a fiend sat on the crupper. We had drawn our arrows to the strings when this son of many fathers cried out *thy* name!

"*W'allah!* He showed us a *khalat*, a gift from thee. And to one who understood his words he explained that he had been taken captive into the Wolf's Throat. Though he had escaped, his soul was sick from fear. We let him pass.

"We did no harm to the three remembering the Wolf's Throat where aforetime thousands of thy people went to their graves as to beds under the swords of the Muscovites. We hastened to thee. And this is truth— even as it is true that the spirits of our slain ancestors dwell today in the wolves of that pack.

"So we salaam before thee, asking leave to go, O Lord of our lives, to draw the sword across the river."

Chapter XII
The Trail Beyond the River

Snow still lay in the hollows and in the rock nests where the sun did not touch. But the earth was damp, and a soft blur of green was to be seen on the gray bushes that covered the hillocks. Spring had come to the steppe.

A warm wind rippled the forest of rushes that stretched down from the knolls into the flooded river. And this river, without a boat or sail visible in its dark surface, murmured in satisfaction, like a man full fed. Beyond its edge black pools of water also had their voices—the song of myriad frogs that felt the growing warmth. By the thin smoke of a fire two black horses snorted and tossed their heads as Kirdy parted the last fringe of rushes and strode toward his camp, a dead heron in one hand, a bow in the other.

With the bow he held an arrow, a light shaft with two tips that had struck down the bird rising in flight from the river mud. The man looked at the sun, sinking to the edge of the plain, and turned aside to a hillock where he knelt, gazing intently in all directions. In the bare plain that was like the bed of the ocean at sunset, nothing, apparently, was to be seen. But the Cossack noticed slender gray forms blending with the blur of the brush-wolves evidently full fed. For a moment he studied them with surprise. They had appeared around his camp at intervals during the weeks since he had left the Volga, and the leader of the pack was surely Karai, the giant borzoi.

The wolves had not attacked his horses, perhaps because Kirdy had lived for a while with the wolf master of the Wolky Gorlo, perhaps because Karai had once been the Cossack's dog.

Kirdy did not bother his head about why things happened on the steppe. He was grateful to the wolves because they had frightened off Nogai tribesmen who would otherwise have killed him for his horses.

If he had met one of the still more to be dreaded riders of the steppe—a spirit that had crept out of a murdered body that had not been buried—he would have reined to one side with a "Luck to you, sir brother!"

But, as he waited for the plucked heron to cook on the wooden spit over the fire where a handful of barley was already boiling in his one iron pot, he pondered men and their ways and especially the men he was following. He took out of a goatskin sack a worn leather horseshoe with the remnants of wooden cleats. Placing this before him, he added a silver coin with a hole in its center and a length of thin hemp rope.

These three things he had found by the ashes of a large fire to the north of his camp. Around these ashes at the edge of the river he had seen the tracks of a score of horses and the wheel track of a wagon. Now the men he had been following had with them a sledge with narrow iron runners, and a similar number of ponies. Back on the Volga their trail had revealed no wagon.

Moreover there was something curious about this trail. He had followed it back a little into the steppe and had spent a day in making wide circles without picking it up again. It ran to the ashes and it did not go away again. He had noticed many of the cleated horseshoes lying around.

He was certain that the man he sought, Gregory Otrèpiev, had camped at that fire for several days. The silver coin was a Muscovite coin, and the hole in it showed that it had been used as an ornament on a horse's rein or a saddle. The rope, too, was native workmanship.

Otrèpiev and his five companions had not turned back toward Muscovy. They had crossed the river and entered the unknown world that lay beyond it.

Kirdy knew this because the tracks had extended to the fire at the river's edge and had not left it. The six men had waited at their camp until they had hailed a boat, or a raft drifting down the river. The cleated horseshoes they had discarded because the horses no longer had to pass over snow. For the same reason they must have removed the runners from the sledge and fitted on the wheels that had been lashed to the sides.

So he was glad that he had found the campsite, after a week's careful search of the river's edge for that very thing. Only a tribesman or a steppe-bred Cossack would have discovered it and learned from it that on the other side of the river the trail would be that of a wagon and a score of unshod horses.

But he had discovered also this thing that troubled him, the worn leather shoe at his feet. A Cossack cares for his own horse, always, and Kirdy had cut out that same piece of leather at the Wolky Gorlo, and had nailed on those cleats. It was a piece of oxhide with the hair still on the inner side.

The shoe had been on the off forefoot of the bay stallion Kirdy had left at the Wolky Gorlo as a gift for Nada, the daughter of the wolf master. Nada was a wild girl, as apt to ride after him as to follow the trail of Otrèpiev of her own accord. Except the great dog Karai, Nada was the only living being that Kirdy cherished in his heart.

Nada tried to follow him? Had she fallen into the hands of the Otrèpiev party? Or—and Kirdy remembered how Otrèpiev's daring had stirred the girl—had she sought the false tsar of her own accord?

A horse like the bay stallion, he knew, was a magnet that might draw every thief along the Volga. The charger might have been stolen. Kirdy—although he had examined every inch of ground in the campsite—had seen no other traces of Nada.

His eyes gleamed under knotted brows.

"May the Father and Son grant that I come with them!"

But, however his spirit burned in him, he did nothing in haste. When he had eaten he threw the bones far enough from the fire to be sure that the wolves that came after them would not approach the horses. Then he led the ponies off to water and picketed them. He piled more brush on the fire and rolled himself up in his fur.

He slept lightly because he meant to start before dawn and several times the stamping of the horses roused him. He felt rather than heard movement in the black abyss around him, and—because it is not well to sleep when others are astir in the steppe—put on his boots and coat, feeding the fire to new life.

As he did so he caught the flash of animals' eyes. The gaunt gray form of Karai moved into the circle of light and flung itself down at the Cossack's side. Kirdy put out his hand and rubbed the wolfhound's throat and Karai growled softly, as was his wont.

"Well, brother," the young warrior smiled, "you have run with the pack, and I'll warrant you've had the pick of the girls. Will you come with me across the river?"

---

*This must have been the Ural River, then called the Jaick, the farthest landmark in Central Asia known to Cossacks or Muscovites.

Again the dog rumbled, the broad head stretched upon the bony paws, the amber eyes intent on the face of his former master. Karai was restless and uneasy, as if anticipating some evil beyond his ken. The other wolves remained without the firelight—gray shadows against the outer blackness.

When Kirdy saddled one pony and lashed the goatskins on the other a little after daybreak and went to the water's edge, Karai paced beside him. The Cossack had discovered a shallow stretch where the horses were able to keep their feet halfway across. The river* was in flood but the current sluggish, and the black Kabardas struck out for the far side without hesitation, the Cossack swimming Tartar fashion, holding to the tail of one pony.

They made the crossing and Kirdy looked back. Karai was still sitting on the western bank, and the wolfpack had come down to sniff at the tracks.

"Hi, Karai!" Kirdy called, and waited, hoping that the wolfhound would bark, or run up and down the bank. But the gray beast remained sitting until it threw back its head and howled like the wolf it was. The pack gave tongue, some of the wolves leaping off toward the brush. Karai took his place at the head of the pack. Once he stopped, on a rise, to look back across the river. The long, quavering hunt swelled and dwindled into distance.

"Eh, gray brother," Kirdy murmured, "you served me well. May you have good hunting!"

The loss of the wolfhound saddened him for a day. Karai had gone from his side to the steppe. Nada too had vanished as if the earth had swallowed her and the bay stallion. The Cossack quested far to the south, searching for the trail that must show where Otrèpiev and his men had landed. Then for a week he rode north without seeing so much the track of a horse. No human being appeared on the skyline.

For the third time Otrèpiev had hidden his trail—first by the body of a dead man, then by fire and sword, then by water. How was a man to be found in that wilderness of lush grass, of thickening brush and flooding watercourses? The Cossack was on the edge of the known world; beyond the river, he could still return to Ayub and wise old Khlit and say truly that he had followed Otrèpiev until all signs failed.

But Otrèpiev had once sworn that he would press on, to the Golden Horde. And this would be like the reckless spirit that had prayed to a grinning mask.

For the Golden Horde was no more than a name, spoken by wanderers. Some said the Horde was to be found beyond the Earth Girdle, others said the Horde was not made up of living men but of spirits, penned eternally behind a rampart far toward the rising sun.

All these matters Kirdy pondered for a day while he rested the Kabardas and repaired his arrows. Then, well content with his course, he set out. Lacking a trail, he turned his horse's head toward the rising sun.

The grass of the steppe grew long and tough, and the wind dried up the dark pools of water in the hollows. Instead of purple, the shadows lay gray on the plain, and haze was in the air, like a veil. The "whirling plant" rolled and tossed before the wind, often on the skyline black smoke appeared.

For the length of two moons Kirdy pushed steadily toward the rising sun. He passed through where the earth itself was gray, and a white froth spread around the pools of water—salt. Here the only game were antelope herds and wide-winged bustards, and man and horses suffered before he turned north to seek for a river.

If he was to go on, he must find good grazing for the Kabardas. He had fashioned his goatskins to hold water and made new saddlebags out of antelope hide—though he had little enough to carry. The barley was about gone, and only a few cups of brandy remained in the leather jug.

The land began to rise as he went on, and instead of finding grass he entered a barren and rocky region. During the two months he had met few human beings, because he avoided the larger clusters of tents, only riding up to the fires of two or three men—thin-faced nomads with long greasy hair, who tried first to bargain with him, then to beg. Their language he did not know, but he had no doubt whatever they were born thieves as well as idol worshipers and filth eaters. More than once he had to draw his sword.

When he asked where lay Altyn-juz—the Golden Horde—these creatures merely stared or shook their heads. But once or twice he saw them glance understandingly toward the east, and he thought they knew the name of the Golden Horde.

Although he did not come upon a large river, the nature of the land began to change again. The dry tamarisk growth yielded to thickets of birch and aspen. In the valleys now he met rivers flowing from the east, and since these were full in Midsummer he knew that far beyond sight they were born on the upper tiers of great mountains where the snow melted slowly under the touch of the sun.

"In the beginning," he said to himself, "the streams ran from the west."

It was the first sign that he was coming to a different land.

Kirdy knew cattle country—knew that this was a mellow, ripe land, well suited to cattle—and he began to be puzzled.

It was a rolling grassland, thinly wooded, with the lines of hills wandering here and there against the sky. Fish were in the streams and some of these he caught while the Kabardas rested and rolled and healed saddle sores. And at times the Cossack saw clouds of sheep near at hand—enormous masses. He heard dogs bark from behind the sheep. The sheep were heavy and fat-tailed—certainly they had not been driven far.

When he rode on again, he observed horses grazing on the uplands, and though they galloped off before the Kabardas, he made out that they were branded. They were shaggy beasts, swift-footed, evidently at home. Once he saw camels stalking on the skyline.

But no men were to be seen. Certainly the cattle and sheep were not wild—dogs did not shepherd mountain sheep. In the steppe the beasts of a tribe are always guarded, unless the owner is so feared that enemies dare not take what belongs to him.

And in the steppe, rich grassland such as this with abundant water in Midsummer is a prize to be fought for and held with bullet and steel until the coming of frost drives herds and men to the southern pastures.

At night the Cossack could make out no fires, or any smoke by day. The herds seemed masterless. Unless—and this puzzled him sorely—the flame he had noticed one evening had something to do with them.

It came out of a gully at deep dusk and flitted out of sight before he could do more than stare. It might have been a whirling plant afire and wind-driven, because the flame swung in circles. But there was no wind, and Kirdy thought that it was a man on a swift horse swinging a torch in his hand to keep it alight. He would have saddled and followed, but the Kabardas were spent after a day's run—and Kirdy had heard of the *ghils* of the steppe that led travelers astray in just this fashion.

That night he slept lightly and wished heartily that Karai were at his side to growl a warning of enemies.

Before sunrise he climbed a rise behind his camp and looked to the east. The air was cold, without haze. And the Cossack drew in his breath sharply.

Under the flood of crimson and the mantling clouds he made out a
dark line, jagged and yet symmetrical. A line of mountains at a great distance. And while he watched, the summits of the range began to glow as
if fires had been lighted within them. From rose and red, they changed
to orange and then to the glitter of sheer gold as the first rays of the sun
struck through them.

"A hundred devils!" Kirdy whispered, frowning.

There were many of these snow peaks at an unguessed height and distance. Often in the Caucasus and Mazanderan he had seen isolated snow
peaks, but never so many that looked like the crenellated towers of a battlement. Below them he could discern the veils of fog.

Then the golden glow faded, the mist seemed to rise and form a thin
haze that shut out the gigantic battlement of the mountains—if indeed it
really had been there. Kirdy had seen more than one mirage in the steppe,
and he had been told by the older Cossacks that such things were the work
of Moslem wizards, to betray wanderers.

"Herds without masters—a circle of fire—mountains that come and
go—Allah, here is either enchantment—or a very strange land!"

He looked again for the mountains at sunset, but there was no sunset.
The air was black, and the cold breath of coming rain swayed the white
stems of the birches. Kirdy led the horses into a ravine where he had noticed a shelving cliff on the sheltered slope. He had barely rubbed down
and tied the ponies when drops pattered on the outer rocks. Far off, thunder muttered and lightning flickered faintly. Kirdy looked for wood and
found under his stone shelf only damp loam. So he moved his almost
empty saddlebags and the furs out of the wet and prepared to sleep without food or fire. Pouring a cupful of the precious corn brandy, he lifted it
with a muttered:

"Glory to God!"

In the act of drinking he stopped to listen. The rain was coming down
in gusts, and the thunder was rolling ominously. Yet he thought he had
caught the slapping of hoofs up the gully. One of the Kabardas snorted.

A rending crackle and roar overhead was followed by a moment of comparative quiet, and Kirdy was sure that there was movement in the outer
darkness, more than the spatter of rain and soft rush of a freshet near his
ledge. Distinctly he heard the creaking of leather and ring of bit chains.

Then the white glare of lightning lighted up the ravine, the shining
drops of rain, the threshing trees.

On the slope across from Kirdy a horseman stood motionless as a stone figure—a squat man in a towering hat, astride a shaggy pony, peering ahead as if on the edge of a bottomless pit.

"For the ages of ages!" Kirdy concluded, and tossed down his *gorilka*.

This, he reflected, was the hour after sunset, the hour of ghosts. And surely the diminutive figure on the black horse resembled nothing human. The Cossack knew what he must do.

He touched the cross on the hilt of his saber and thrust his dagger into the ground near his boot. If the apparition of the mounted dwarf were a Christian soul riding the steppe in torment, the cross would give it comfort. If, however, it were a *ghil*, or evil spirit, it would climb upon the dagger and disappear into the earth—Kirdy jumped suddenly for the Kabardas. He had heard one beginning to whinny. In a second he had grasped both the velvety muzzles. And again came the lightning, revealing this time a score of strange riders. He could see the steam rising from their soaked sheepskins, and the flash of their eyeballs as they looked at him.

Then the pall of darkness, and sounds drawing nearer—guttural chuckling voices, sibilant whispers, the clatter of hoofs on rocks—and a harsh challenge.

"*Yarou-yarou!*"

Kirdy drew his sword with a sharp grating of steel that he intended them to hear, and then there was real silence for a moment.

"Kneel!" the harsh voice bade him. "Put down thy weapon."

The words were Tartar, and Kirdy heard with satisfaction. These riders, then, were not marauding Kara Kalpaks, or Turkomans—they were certainly not the Tartars of the Gobi. He answered promptly, because armed men on the steppe are tolerant of neither silence nor fear.

"Are ye men of the Altyn-juz—ye who ride in the night and the storm?"

"*Kai*—ask of the storm who we be! Kneel!"

The stamp of hoofs and the heavy-breathing near-winded ponies drew closer. Kirdy stepped forward and laughed.

"O ye men of the night! I am Ak Sokol. My mother is the steppe, my father the great river. Never will I take grass in my teeth and cast down my weapon."

"*Bil ma'ida!* Art thou in truth the White Falcon?" The speaker seemed surprised, even a little startled and Kirdy took instant advantage.

"Aye, so. I ride to the Golden Horde."

Afterward he wondered how these men could have heard his name.

"Verily all things are possible with Allah," the voice said musingly. "Even that a father of lies should have uttered the truth!"

"Aye, Sorgai," cried another, "here be the two good horses."

"And the sword," put in a third. "Slay the unbeliever and take what he has on him."

To this Kirdy made no response, because there is a time for silence as well as for insolent speech. And, as he had expected, the leader of the riders turned upon his followers angrily.

"With what words will ye answer the khan when he asks concerning the mission of this wayfarer? Nay, he shall not be harmed, but he must ride with us."

"Whither?" Kirdy demanded.

Out of utter darkness came the response:

"To Tevakel Khan, Lord of the plain and the mountains, Keeper of the Way, Master of life and death and khan of the Golden Horde."

Chapter XIII
The Cossack Rides in the Night

The Cossack rides in the night—there is no one to cry after him.

Proverb of the steppe

But not for long hours did Kirdy see the face of Tevakel Khan. The Tartar horsemen went swiftly south, keeping him in the center of their formation, and he made no effort to escape because he knew there were eyes close at hand that could see him when he could not make out the head of his horse—and because from their talk he gathered another captive had been taken a few days before.

When he thought of Nada he whipped on his horse, and the Tartars growled at him, asking whether he burned to kiss a stake or be torn by horses.

Once they were challenged by a wailing cry from unseen heights, and again, in a lull of the storm Kirdy saw a ring of fire moving toward them. This proved to be a pine knot, swung in the hand of a rider who spoke to his captors and galloped off.

Then, though the rain shut them in, he heard other bodies of horsemen moving in the same direction.

They circled around restless herds of cattle, and above the bellowing
of weary beasts Kirdy caught the long-drawn cry of distant horse-herders
and the barking of excited dogs.

Because even Tartars do not ride like fiends through a storm or leave
immense herds without shelter on the steppe, he knew that something
unwonted was taking place on the steppe.

They passed through the outer tents of a yurta and slowed to a more
reasonable pace. Coming to what appeared to be a massive wagon, they
bade Kirdy dismount and enter it, assuring him grimly that his horses
would be cared for—if he ever claimed them again. The wagon material-
ized into a wide cart with solid wooden wheels, the whole of it taken up
by a round leather dome that smoked at the summit.

Aware that he was being watched and that hesitation would avail him
nothing, Kirdy lifted the scabbard in his left hand and raised the flap of
the *kibitka*—the nomad wagon-tent.

A fire of camel dung glowed in the center of the floor on its clay bed.
The space around it was carpeted, the sides filled with bulky leather sacks
that looked like headless giants huddled together and smelled both sour
and pungent. From the far side of the fire a figure rolled out of a rug.

"By the Ninety and Nine Holy Names! By the beard of Ali, from whom
I am descended on the right side—my heart rejoices and my spirit up-lifted
at sight of the prince of swordsmen, the White Falcon!"

It was Al-Tâbir, the interpreter of dreams, and there was no doubt of
his joy at beholding the Cossack. He drew off the youth's soggy fur mantle and flung his arms around him.

"Now may Allah grant thee increase of joy. I wasted, in sorrow—the
blossom of hope was killed by the frost of calamity—"

"Enough. What seek ye here, Al-Tâbir?"

"Seek? I am sought. I am the leaf that drifts down the river of happenings. Happenings! I have fed upon disaster—"

"Is there aught to eat in this yurta?"

"Aye, and to drink."

Al-Tâbir made a wry grimace, and Kirdy saw that his broad, pale cheeks
were indeed wasted, and his cherished beard, that ran from under his chin
to his ears, ill-kept.

"Behold, O youthful Kai Kosru!"

He took up a lacquer bowl and slipped the thong from the vent of one
of the great sacks with a skill that hinted at considerable practice.

"Mare's milk, sour and fermented."

Kirdy gulped down the warm and heady liquid, which he knew was food as well as drink, and Al-Tâbir, after a mournful allusion to the vintages of Shiraz, followed his example.

"It brings oblivion," he said, with a sigh, "if you drink enough."

"Where is Nada?" demanded Kirdy, who had no sympathy with oblivion.

"Where? Nay, she is lost; she is no longer at my side. *Ai-a*, an ocean of the nectar of beauty, a rose heart—"

"Hast thou seen her—dead?"

Something in the quiet voice of the young warrior made the Persian roll his eyes around, and he noticed that Kirdy gripped the ivory hilt of the curved sword until his arm trembled. Taking this as a warning the interpreter of dreams hastened to explain.

"Nay. I rode with her to this place. Then she bade farewell and now the false shah is at her side."

Al-Tâbir glanced fleetingly at Kirdy's sword-hand and struggled inwardly.

"The lord who is called Otrè-pief."

Seated on the rug nearest the fire, moistening his throat ever and anon with the draught that was not a vintage of Shiraz but brought oblivion, the interpreter of dreams told Kirdy all that had passed since they left the Wolky Gorlo.

"Now when I drew my reins from the Nogais who are dogs-without-eyelashes I pressed on swiftly, desiring to come up with the woman who had gone before me. Solitude is evil, and solitude upon this northern plain is worse. By favor of the All-Compassionate and by the fleetness of my gray Arab, I did overtake the woman called Nada when she lost thy trail and was searching hither and yon—"

"She followed me?" asked the Cossack quickly.

"As a brown-winged falcon a hare. But thy trail was no more to be seen. Nada's brow grew dark as a storm cloud, and she sought until the light also had gone."

Kirdy groaned and beat clenched fists on his knees. He had suspected that the Nogais might decide to turn back after him and had been at some pains to hide his tracks in a network of pools that first day.

"Nada was clad as a Cossack youth," went on the interpreter of dreams with a sympathetic glance at the warrior, "and she was beautiful as a Circassian boy; she also had food, and that yataghan that hung upon the wall of her father's house. She was angry, but she took compassion on me and shared bread and salt. Then she said that since thy trail was lost she would turn to Otrè-pief, because it would come to pass that by companying with the Muscovite lord she would see thy face again—"

"Let no more than one lie escape thy lips, Al-Tâbir, and thou shalt taste steel in thy throat."

"By the beard of Ali, by the Ka'aba, and by my father's grave, I swear that these words be truth! Lo, for many days I followed the young woman. *Ai-ee*, my body ached from the rubbing of the saddle. We went from *aul* to *aul* of the plains-dwellers, Nada showing them the picture of the old man and the wolf that hung at her throat."

Kirdy remembered the icon painting of Saint Ulass and the wolf that the girl cherished—and the fear the Nogais had of the great wolfpack.

"The plains devils became afraid when they saw the picture—being image-worshipers no doubt. When we reached a broad river they led us to the tents of Otrè-pief on the near bank. The Muscovite lord looked twice at Nada and laughed. It is in my mind that he knew at once she was a woman, for he pulled off her hat and beheld her hair, like gold. The five companions of the lord who were drinking red wine raised their cups to her and asked of me if I had been to Paradise, that I rode thither with such a fair-faced houri at my side. They did not laugh when Nada spoke to them, naming them fools."

Al-Tâbir shook his head and sighed, his hand moving out toward the leather cup.

"Otrè-pief said, 'Nay, all begotten men are fools, and the wise are they that know it!' Nada looked at him and took back her cap, pointing across the river. She declared to the Muscovites that if they rode to the Golden Horde they would never find the way across the plain; and at the end of the plain would in any case be slain by the guardians of the Mountains of the Eagles.

"Then the Lord Otrè-pief questioned her as to how she knew of such matters. Whereupon Nada swore to him that once when she was a child she journeyed with her father as far as the Mountains of the Eagles, and there they had been obliged to turn back by the watchers who dwelt on the way to the city of the Golden Horde.

"The Muscovite lord asked what manner of city this might be, and she laughed at him, saying that a leader of men should not need to ask concerning the end of his road. She said the dwellers in this city had learned the secret of riches and happiness and all delights of existence. Then did Otrè-pief swear that she should lead them to the city, and he would turn back for no power of earth, though—so he said—no delight could be imagined greater than the joy her beauty yielded to his eyes.

"And when the cup-companions of this lord saw that he desired the woman above all things, they did not molest her but entreated her in courteous-wise and she did in truth beguile them with song and story and quip—with the tricks of her horse, and her merry ways.

"But when Otrè-pief would have caressed her, she showed him the sword girdled to her waist and said that if he would take her hand in his he must first overcome her at sword-play, and one or the other might die therefrom. Now the fate of men is in the hand of Allah, and Otrè-pief's pride was a great pride. It may be he was tempted to overcome her with his sword, because he fenced with his companions before her eyes. When he did so, she made light of him, saying that not long since she had held fellowship with a warrior who was his master at sword strokes. And it is in my mind, O White Falcon, that her thought did then dwell upon thee.

"So the pride of Otrè-pief was stirred, and he boasted, saying that he would make himself master of the city of the Golden Horde and would rule even as a king. Then he swore he would claim her as his. And to this she made response that if indeed he became king of the city of the Golden Horde, she would be his.

"With that the lord was content, because he ever had a mind to mighty accomplishments, and Nada led him verily across the dry lands toward the place where the sun rises. And to me she said it was a hunt—fools pursuing folly, and at the end of the road only God knew what. Yet I believe that she knew."

The fermented milk and the solace of companionship cheered Al-Tâbir, and he only wished he could make out the thoughts of the brown-faced warrior who sat across the glowing bed of dung.

"How came Otrèpiev to hear of the Golden Horde?" Kirdy asked, rousing from his silence.

The interpreter of dreams ceased to feel warm and comfortable. He rubbed his hands together and spread out lean fingers gracefully.

"I beguiled him with the tale at the city of the Muscovites."

"Thou?" Kirdy looked up in swift surprise that was not reassuring, and Al-Tâbir made haste to justify himself.

"Only hear me, prince of swordsmen. Forbear to cast the flame of wrath on the carpet of companionship. When the Muscovites commanded me to tell tales, I obeyed. Why not? It may be that a small matter of a lie or two escaped my tongue. But I told Otrè-pief of the Altyn-juz, and it pleased him."

"What tale was this?"

"The tale of Abou Ishak, of Samarkand, who was a great traveler, almost as great a one as I. Long ago a sultan sent him forth to seek for the Earth Girdle. Surely our wise men have said that the earth is girdled about by mountains—by a great rampart that holds in the water of the seas and the soil of the land. Now, behind this rampart in the west the sun sinks at the end of the day, and from the eastern rampart the sun rises at dawn. How could it be otherwise? Nay, do not frown, my lord. The earth is like a rope stretched taut about the circuit of the shield. The rampart is called Caf, in my speech, but among the northern folk it is called the Mountain of the Eagles."

Kirdy thought of the snow range he had seen the previous dawn and held his peace. Al-Tâbir refreshed himself and went on.

"Now this Abou Ishak—a man of some note in his day, and a writer of a book or so, though there was little faith in him—this Abou Ishak cried out with a loud voice that he did find the mountain Caf where the sun rises—a mountain rampart that may not be climbed by men, for near the summits only birds of prey live. And beyond the rampart he heard tell that certain spirits were penned.

"All this did I repeat to Otrè-pief. Then he asked of me if it was the Golden Horde that dwelt beyond the rampart—for into Muscovy had come tales of the Golden Horde that wanders near the place where the sun rises.

"Is not wine the better for spice—a tale for a little touch of fancy? I embroidered the garment of truth with the gold thread of imagination. I said it was so—the Golden Horde dwelt in a city beyond the rampart.

"Then surely madness smote this lord of the Muscovites, for he said to his companions that someday he would journey to the Mountain of the Eagles."

The young Cossack stared into the crimson eye of the fire and thought that Otrèpiev was not mad. The false tsar had foreseen the necessity of flight and had come to a place where the Muscovites could not reach him with vengeance.

"And yet," he muttered "the girl Nada is not a lying Persian. She told Otrèpiev of a city to be found beyond the mountains."

"Aye," the Persian smiled, no whit cast down by the Cossack's opinion of his people. "Yet she is a flower, a lily from the garden of paradise. Who would weigh her words for the dross of truth?"

Kirdy wondered if Nada had actually journeyed with her father to this place before now. A search of his memory revealed that Nada had said in Moscow that she had come from the country of the Golden Horde—certainly she spoke the language of these riders of the steppe.

"Hearken Al-Tâbir," he remarked. "One thing is certain beyond doubt. We are prisoners in the camp of Tevakel khan of the Golden Horde."

The soft mouth of the Persian fell open, and he peered over his shoulders into the shadows of the *kibitka*.

"All things are possible with Allah," he murmured, and then his brown eyes sparkling, "By the breath of Ali, by the everlasting Imamet—what a tale I shall tell in the courtyards of Fars and Isphahan!"

But the Cossack cared not at all for wonders. He wanted to find out where he was, where Otrèpiev and Nada were, and what their plans might be.

What Al-Tâbir had related simmered down to this: the Golden Horde was the race of tribes that wandered on this side the distant range. The mountains themselves might be called anything, and anything might lie beyond them. Nada had led Otrèpiev with the tale of a city. Where was she now?

"For what reason," he asked Al-Tâbir abruptly, "didst thou forsake the company of Otrèpiev?"

"I?" The interpreter of dreams roused reluctantly from imagination that painted him a greater man than Abou Ishak. "I was frightened. A week ago I had gone apart to look for forage. When I turned back to the camp I saw that a strong band of Turkomans had come up and dismounted."

"Turkomans? Here?"

"It is true—may Allah requite me if it is not true! I saw even the brands on their horses, their sheepskin hats. They rode off with my companions, and I whipped my horse to the north, away from them."

Only a few years ago Kirdy had been in some bitter fighting against the Turkoman marauders, and he knew that these tribes were justly feared. But their homeland should lie well to the south along the great Syr-Darya.

"Why?" he wondered.

"May they die without offspring! May their bones wither and their eyes cease to see! The Turkoman dogs be Sunnites—may they bellow in their graves."

A light dawned on the Cossack, who knew Sunnite and Shiite—although both zealous Mohammedans—love each other as a wildcat loves a wolf. In the eyes of an orthodox Sunnite, a Persian Shitte is more to be scorned than a *giour*, an unbeliever.

"Within two days, when I wandered without food, these un-eyelashed Tartars rode up and seized me, putting me to many indignities—"

"Enough! Sleep—hold thy tongue!"

Kirdy sprang up and seized his fur mantle. When he strode for the door, Al-Tâbir wailed and scrambled forward to clutch his girdle.

"Nay, what dost thou seek? I tell thee, these Tartars are all sons of devils! They look in and poke at me with spears. Their eyes are like cats'—"

Kirdy thrust him aside and threw back the flap to listen.

"Hearken, Al-Tâbir," he said grimly. "Dost thou yearn for Turkomans—a whole horde of Turkomans? Then abide with thy milk and prayers. I must go to Tevakel Khan. Dost thou hear the drums? They are horse drums and the song they sing is of war."

Chapter XIV
The Drink of the Fanga Nialma

Because on the far side of the border dignity rides in a saddle and disgrace walks afoot Kirdy lingered at the wagon tent until one of his horses was brought. This in itself was little less if a miracle, since the whole plain seemed to be alive with beasts.

The rain had ceased; mist lay in the hollows, and under a murky sky an orange glow spread in the east. Against this light the Cossack made out the dome-like tops of *kibitkas*, the tossing horns of multitudes of cattle, the black shapes of riders. He heard the harsh grunting of camels, the squealing of lions, the bellowing of bulls, the incessant, plaintive crying of thousands of sheep and unnumbered goats.

His nostrils tingled with the acrid smoke of dung and damp wood fires, the warm breath of trampled grass, and the reek of wet leather. Axles creaked, dogs howled, and unseen men shouted. It was a dawn of calamity, as if these inhabitants of the steppe had been driven together by flood or fire. But there was order in the chaos. Near at hand an old woman milked a complaining camel, and out of the nearest herd his black Karbarda was led up, saddled. Two warriors waited to see what he would do next—two broad and silent men clad in wolf skins, with lacquer helmets topped by a horsetail plume, with a leather drop that came down over their shoulders. Bows and arrows rested in carved wooden cases at hips, and each held a weapon Kirdy had never seen before.

This weapon was a battle-ax—a four-and-a-half foot staff, of ivory or bamboo, with a leather thong that passed around the wrist. The head was long, the edge slightly curved, the butt a steel point.

"*Oucheha keri kari,*" the Cossack said to the Tartars. "It is the dawn, and the drums summon to saddle."

The swift roll of the horse drums had ceased near him but had been taken up in distant *kibitkas*, and he knew it must be a summons to muster. Knew, too, it was infinitely better to make this assertion than to ask the question—because uncertainty is cousin to fear and for a captive to show fear is to invite taunts.

The Tartars regarded him impassively.

"*Ay-a*, the weapon-bearing men ride from the camp."

"Then I must speak with Tevakel Khan."

To a black dome rising out of a cleared space in the encampment they led him, and he loosed the girdle of his sword at the threshold. Older than the blade itself is the tabu against carrying so much as a stick into a tent of the Hordes of High Asia—and not for the khan's herd of ponies would any Tartar have stolen a weapon so left at the entrance.

The dome was of felt, rising on interlashed wattles, and a squadron could have formed beneath it. Within it was divided by partitions of painted leather into many compartments. By the fire in the central chamber knelt Tevakel Khan on a carpet.

"What gift, O Cossack," he asked, "dost thou bring to the Altyn-juz?"

He spoke placidly in the half voice of one accustomed to silence in his listeners. An old man, Tevakel Khan, with a thin, good-humored face and brilliant eyes—a straight figure in a horsehide jacket, the dark mane running down the middle of his back. His embroidered boots had very high red heels, and his black satin skullcap was neatly sewn with silver thread.

Considering him, Kirdy judged that he was not to be trifled with—a generous man, indulgent with increasing years, but with authority in his very blood. And the Cossack tried to think of some fitting gift. He had said that he came to the Golden Horde on a mission, and a present would be expected. But he had no gift

"I bring—"

He was about to say a black Karbarda stallion, but a glance about the compartment checked him. Behind Tevakel Khan were ranged sandalwood and ebony chests, rolls of splendid carpets, and saddles ornamented with silver inlaid on iron. The bowls on the little table from which the chieftain helped himself to dried raisins and tea and millet cake were of amber and jade. Tevakel Khan was wealthy—a horse meant little more to the nomad than one of the raisins he selected with such care.

"I bring a sword," he said.

Tevakel Khan looked at him expectantly. The Cossack requested one of the attendants to carry in the curved saber that he had left at the entrance, and noticed that the Tartar repressed an exclamation of pleasure when he beheld the jeweled hilt and the rich scabbard that the warrior held forth in both hands. Before Tevakel Khan could take it, Kirdy stepped forward and spoke.

"I am Ak Sokol, the White Falcon, and I have come to the Altyn-juz from the land of infidels near the setting of the sun."

The Tartar, sipping a bowl of tea, waited in courteous silence.

"The dog of a Persian," observed one of his household, "said thou wert near at hand on the plain, with two horses. He was fleeing from the Turkomans. Art thou his brother?"

The question was put with thinly veiled contempt, and Kirdy paid it no heed.

"Hearken, O Khan of the Altyn-juz," he went on. "Thy drums beat the summons to saddle. Thine enemies the Turkomans have come up from the southern plain to raid thy herds."

This was a reasonable surmise, and Tevakel Khan made an exclamation of assent. Pinpoints of fire glowed in his dark eyes.

"Allah hath caused desire to be born in the heart of Ilbars Sultan of Kwaresmia, the son of Arap Muhammad, lord of Khiva. He thought to find us with our eyes turned the other way, but he has come with a mighty following."

Not long since, Kirdy had waged a lengthy battle against Ilbars Sultan—the Leopard Prince. He seen the Turkomans wipe out five hundred Don Cossacks, and the memory rankled.

---

*Cossack.

"Ilbars Sultan has a high nose and keen eyes; he would rather slay men than carry off beasts and women. He is shrewd, but the blood lust blinds him."

A faint surprise was apparent in the emotionless Tartar.

"What words are these words, O Kazak?* Art thou a *fanga*—a wizard, to know what passes beyond thy sight?"

"Nay, I have seen the sultan when swords were drawn. I say to thee, O Khan, that he is terrible in battle."

"And is this thy mission—to praise Ilbars Sultan, the thieving dog, to my face?"

"As to that, I speak the truth. Yet I sought the Golden Horde to find therein an enemy. Within the year an oath was sworn that this enemy should die."

Whatever the old khan thought of this he kept to himself. Blood feuds were more to be cherished than religious faith, in the steppe. His eye wandered to the curved sword.

"What is the name of thine enemy, O youth?"

"He was khan of the Muscovites."

"Then he is not to be found within our grazing land. Harken, Kazak. Some have said to me that thou art a spy, sent in advance by the Turkomans. What are words? I bear thee neither ill will nor good. Give me then the sword and go in peace. I have said."

Kirdy inclined his head.

"And this is my answer, O Khan! Among my people it is a law of laws that a sword may not pass to another while the master of it lives. Lacking other gifts, I offer to bear the sword on thy behalf in this battle. When I have taken spoil, then I will have a gift that is fitting."

A murmur of impatience and anger arose from the listeners around the sides of the room—from the sons and grandsons of the khan, and his officers. They resented the appearance of the stranger at such a time, and more than resented his boldness. Even the quiet old man seemed surprised, but he meditated, his arms folded on his knees.

"Hearken, young warrior, to my second word. The lifetime of a horse before now, the Altyn-juz sought pasture in the west. We came to a river, and there found a lame man, a Kazak such as thou, whose only solace in life was a girl-child. Now this Kazak was assuredly a wizard, because the wolfpacks came to his tent of nights, and he talked with them. We shared bread and salt, he and I, and our talk was as brothers and friends.

That was long ago, yet I have seen no Kazak since. Abide, then, with me, but think no more of mounting for battle, lest my men slay thee, unknowing. With Ilbars Sultan is a *fanga*, and it will go hard with us. Tidings have come—"

With a gesture he dismissed the Cossack and turned to his household, crumpling the millet cakes in his slender fingers. Kirdy smiled as if greatly honored—though his very soul burned with impatience to be free of the tent and in the saddle—and took a seat among the sons of Tevakel Khan.

But when he heard the first of the messengers who had been waiting at the entrance, he forgot weariness and disappointment in sudden interest. The Turkomans were within a day's ride of the Tartar camp.

The messengers, who were soaked and weary with riding through the night and the storm, told tales of tent-villages seized by the foe—of old people cut down, warriors burned or crucified or dragged by horses, and young women that died within an hour of capture.

This was no ordinary raid on the part of Ilbars Sultan. The Turkomans, with their allies the Usbeks, numbered close to twenty thousand. They had followed the grass up to the north with their horse herds, and they meant to wipe out the armed men of the Golden Horde, to seize the cattle and pasture land for their own, and to keep the Tartar children for slaves.

In the face of calamity, the patriarch of the Golden Horde remained utterly calm. From the north and the west the Tartar clans were hastening on tired horses to the gathering of the Horde. To Kirdy, it seemed as if Tevakel Khan must give battle within the next two or three days.

If he retreated into the northern steppe he would lose the bulk of his cattle, many horses, and all his sheep—and these herds were the very life of the Altyn-juz. On the other hand, if he stood his ground against the dreaded Turkomans now, he would be outnumbered.

And if there was a battle, what would become of Otrèpiev and Nada? They were not far away—a Turkoman does not yield up such captives. And, unless the Cossack could free himself from the watch of Tevakel Khan this battle on the steppe would separate them again, as the black storm drives travelers asunder in the desert.

"In the night before this last the Turkoman did the two-sword dance in the chieftain's place."

A lad who had crept through the outer patrols of the invaders had just come in to report what he had seen.

"They have many ponies, and a great camp. While the sword dance was going on some of them made a great noise and a flash of fire with weapons they held in their hands, yet no harm came to them."

Tevakel Khan made a gesture of assent. Although the Altyn-juz had no firelocks, he had heard of them before.

"What does the *fanga nialma* of the sultan?"

"He drinks fire."

"A-ah!"

A sibilant moan from the listeners greeted this, and the boy glanced proudly around him, to take full credit for the ominous tidings he brought.

"The wizard drinks fire from a cup, sitting before Ilbars Sultan the Leopard," he went on. "My eyes beheld this. He sits on a white bearskin."

"A-ah!"

"He has five lesser *fanga*, to wait upon him and increase his magic."

"That is so," put in another, a burly warrior who had carried off the first prisoner from a Turkoman outpost. "The six magicians were found marching toward Ilbars Sultan, out in the steppe. They were clad in red velvet and sables and silver cloth, and their garments were sewn with jewels from skirt to cap."

Kirdy pushed aside the Tartar in front of him, to hear the better.

"*Allahim barabat yik saftir*," murmured Tevakel Khan. "God is just and merciful!" By this he meant that all matters were ordained, and what was happening could not be altered.

"The *fanga nialma*," went on the warrior, "held in his hand at that time an apple, and the apple was pure gold. He had changed it to gold."

"What else?"

"Six geese took flight from the grass at the moment when the six *fanga* appeared."

It was apparent to the old Tartar that mighty forces were opposed to him. The marauding Turkomans were evil, but this fellowship of magicians: drinking fire and changing fruit into gold, were more to be dreaded. But all at once it seemed to him that his captive, the Cossack, had become possessed of a devil.

Kirdy's dark eyes were blazing and the veins in his forehead stood out. The mention of a cup of fire had aroused his curiosity; the five companions of the wizard had aroused his suspicion, and the gold apple had made him certain of a strange fact. He remembered seeing, in other days, a gold apple among the crown pieces of the tsars.

"O Khan," he cried, "this *fanga nialma* is no more than a man, and I have found mine enemy!"

The Tartars shook their heads and whispered gutturally.

"Nay—he is beside himself!"

But Kirdy, on his feet upon the carpet before the khan, seized a bowl of wine and emptied it down his throat. Facing the warrior who had taken a prisoner, he asked:

"Was there not a Cossack woman among the five companions?"

"*Balmez*! Who knows? Yet, there was a woman dressed as a warrior."

"Aye, so. And this stranger—no hair is on his face?"

"*W'allah*! When did a wizard have hair on his face?"

"Still, I say that I know this man. He is cunning as a steppe fox, and he flees from Frankistan because he has stolen the jewels and garments of a king. I followed him hither."

Tevakel Khan considered and shook his head.

"*Kai*—can a common man drink fire?"

"Aye, so. I can drink fire from a cup. Bring hither my saddlebags— thou!"

A stir of interest went through the throng in the tent, and the khan signed for the captive's bags to be brought. The White Falcon, he thought, was possessed of a devil, but of what kind of a devil remained to be seen.

Kirdy asked for a small china bowl and breathed a sigh of relief when he found his leather flask of *gorilka* safe in the bag. There was enough of the white spirits left almost to fill the bowl. Deliberately he placed it on the carpet before the khan and went to the fire.

With his knife he cut a sliver from a pine stick and lighted it in the fire. He touched the light to the spirits in the cup, and a thin bluish flame danced on the surface of the *gorilka*.

Tevakel Khan rose on his knees to watch the better, and Kirdy lifted the china bowl in both hands. When the Tartars saw the smokeless blue flame they shivered.

"Glory to God!" said the Cossack, presenting the fire to the four quarters of the winds.

"E-eh!" breathed the watchers.

Tipping the cup toward him, Kirdy drank; but the instant before the spirits touched his lip, he let out his breath soundlessly. Unseen by the khan, the blue flame flickered out. The young warrior drank down the *gorilka*, and sighed. It was good, and it was his last.

For some moments the old chief remained buried in thought. He thought of the other Cossack who had power over the wolves, and he reached a decision.

"*Kai*—it must be thou art also a *fanga*. A wizard who bears a sword, with hair on his face."

Though Kirdy had not been prepared for this conclusion, he took instant advantage of it.

"Then grant me to ride in the battle. I will seek out this other *fanga* who drinks fire and destroy him."

The advantages of such an arrangement were apparent to Tevakel Khan, and he agreed at once, only demanding that Kirdy remain near him until the fighting began.

Chapter XV
Strike Like a Thunderbolt

Let your swiftness be that of the wind, your steadiness that of the forest. In raiding and plundering, be like fire, in immovability like a mountain.

   Above all, let your plans be dark and impenetrable as night, and when you move, strike like a thunderbolt.

Maxims of Sun Tzu

With the determination of a weasel, Al-Tâbir sought through the Tartar lines the next night for Kirdy. During the day Tevakel Khan had moved up with his clans to a ridge overlooking a long, shallow valley. On the opposite rise Ilbars Sultan was encamped, and Al-Tâbir felt uneasy.

To interpret dreams, to make verses at the courts of kings—that was his work. He was convinced that a prophet had no honor outside his own country. Because, at every fire he approached, the broad, dark faces of the wild Tartars peered at him suspiciously, and swords and javelins were flourished at his stocky legs. He blundered into a herd of restless cattle and fled to escape the prodding of the long horns. Dogs barked at sight of his *kaftan* and turban.

So Al-Tâbir was profoundly grateful when he saw one of the Cossack's Kabardas saddled by a fire where an ugly warrior in rusty chain mail squatted, working with whetstone and cloth upon the shining steel head of a battle-ax. This, Al-Tâbir knew, was the man who had taken prisoner the first Turkoman. But Al-Tâbir saw no prisoner, and the skin of his back prickled uncomfortably when he looked at the ax head. This was a fellow of violence, a dealer of blows—an unlearned soul, no fit companion for Jahia ibn Muhammad al Nisapur, who had written down six hundred true dreams in a book.

When the Tartar—Girai by name—merely lifted the corner of a thin lip at sight of the Persian, Al-Tâbir decided it would be safe for him to stay by the fire.

When Kirdy strode up, Girai raised a knotted hand to his forehead and lips, but Al-Tâbir gave tongue joyously.

"*Ai-ee*, young hero—prince of swordsmen—my deliverer! Let us sit upon the carpet of counsel and take thought for the morrow."

"How, take thought?" demanded Kirdy, whose mind was on other matters.

"Where shall I place myself in order—in order to see all that passes without molestation? I will make a song of thy deeds. But, to see everything clearly, I should be as a disembodied spirit, remote from these savages. When I seek the outer lines these unclean dogs drive me back. When the battle begins, shall I go to the standard?"

"Aye—a good place. The sword strokes will fall heavily there!"

Al-Tâbir squirmed and caressed his ample girdle.

"That is not what I want. To see the battle as a whole, perhaps the horse lines would be the best."

"Nay," Kirdy pointed out indifferently. "The herds are behind the ridge. Besides, the Turkomans usually sweep around an enemy—you would be trampled."

"Ah, the Turkomans. They be worse than these snouted pagans, because they cut innocent people open just to see them quiver. O the sons of nameless fathers! O that I were again in the hill gardens of Rudbar, where men have ears to listen and hearts to feel!"

But Kirdy was listening to guttural monosyllables from Girai, and now he sprang to his feet and seized the rein of the Karbarda.

"Eh—what has come to pass? Whither goest thou? We have made no plans—" Al-Tâbir was alarmed by this activity.

"The Turkomans have thrown a head into our lines. It was the head of Sorgai, a grandson of the khan, who rode out recklessly beyond his men, before our coming. Now Tevakel Khan is raging like a devil."

"Let him rage. Why should we go near him?"

But Kirdy was in the saddle, and Al-Tâbir, intent on keeping his only friend within call, clung to the stirrup, heedless of the Karbarda's snorting as he trotted through the groups of warriors up to the mound where the patriarch sat surrounded by his officers.

The mound was in darkness because Tevakel Khan did not wish his foes to see his anger. A musket-shot away, the camp of the raiders was in plain sight, for the Turkomans were enjoying themselves after their fashion. They had set up lofty stakes to the top of which they hung captives—women as well as men—by the feet. Warriors with torches were lighting the heads of the unfortunates. Archers were shooting shafts into the struggling and smoking bodies, and the hoarse shouting of the wild tribesmen could be clearly heard. It was answered by a groan from Al-Tâbir.

Stacked by the Turkoman tents were piles of plunder—rugs, weapons, and shining silver. Lean warriors, wrapped in grotesque finery, nankeens and furs and silk taken from the Tartars, stalked about in full view, while others roasted whole sides of mutton and beef over fires fed by broken tent furniture and wagons.

At times other men were visible, dripping red from head to boots, with stained knives in their hands—and Al-Tâbir wondered whether these had come from the butchery of beasts or captives. Wild cries and the roaring of flames, drifting smoke and the flash of bright blades in the sword dance—all this filled him with a dread of the morrow.

He looked at Tevakel Khan and shivered. The old man was grinding his teeth and clutching at his head, muttering.

"*Tzaktyr—kiari.* Burn—slay!"

Tevakel Khan had seen the blood of his grandson and the torture of his people, and for him there was neither rest nor sleep until he could take his sword in his hand and go against the invaders. But Kirdy, squatting at his side and paying no heed to the nudging of Al-Tâbir, scanned the extent of the Turkoman camp with experienced eyes and weighed chances. Before long the fires would die out, and then nothing could be seen.

The Cossack frowned. By dawn the Turkomans would be in the saddle, their best mounted men on the wings; they would circle the smaller array of the Tartars, making play with their long firelocks—Kirdy knew well how they fought, leaping in and slashing like wolves.

"Attack now!" he said under his breath.

The old man turned to peer into his eyes.

"What was thy word?"

"Attack now."

"*Kai*—it is dark. Yonder jackals snarl over their meat. That was the word of a traitor!"

"I have been asleep. Now my eyes are open. I see a way into the camp of the Turkomans." Kirdy spoke with utter assurance, knowing that, for a moment, life and death weighed in the balance. "After I drank the fire I slept, and the spirits of high and distant places came before me."

The Cossack was certain of three things: In darkness the crude fire-locks of the Turkomans would be of less service than the Tartars' bows; also, for a reason he had never fathomed, the Moslems of the south were reluctant to give battle at night. Also, if Tevakel Khan waited for dawn and the onset of the sultan, he would fare badly.

Tevakel Khan breathed deeply and ceased to snarl. He was aged and far from timid, and he was thinking that in the hours of night the power of the *fanga* increased greatly.

"Then, say!" he urged.

Kirdy was already shaping a plan in his mind.

"By fire, by the cattle herd, and by fear the Turkoman can be broken like a dry reed."

"I will make a whip from his hide—I will make a drinking cup from his skull."

"Aye, so. Now hearken, Tevakel Khan, to the plan."

Mindful of possible listeners, the Cossack leaned close to the chieftain and whispered. When he had done, the Tartar sat like a graven image, blinking at the distant camp fires. The shadowy figures of his men crept closer, to hear what he would say.

"God is just and merciful!" he ejaculated at last. "*Yalou baumbi*—mount your horses. Bring my shield and my horse. We shall go against the long-haired dogs."

"What has happened?" Al-Tâbir caught the flash of exultation in the Cossack's dark face. "Will we fly? That is good!"

"Nay, we draw the saber and cast away the scabbard. And that is best of all."

Now the interpreter of dreams did not lack cleverness. The set lips and blazing eyes of the young Cossack told him that it would be useless to protest; and he had found out that it was worse than useless to try to sneak out of the camp. So he pretended to be pleased and asked for a weapon, saying that he would ride between Kirdy and Girai. It seemed to him that in the company of such redoubtable warriors a man of peace and learning would be safer than elsewhere.

"Good!" cried Kirdy. "Then wilt thou point out to me the traitor Otrèpiev; but I myself shall find Nada."

It seemed to the agitated Al-Tâbir that everyone went mad that night, including himself. Dour Girai gave him a javelin and a short bow with a wooden quiver of arrows and watched the Persian's efforts to string the powerful bow with quiet amusement. Then they mounted, and the night was full of sound.

A fitful wind had sprung up in the last hours, whipping through the tall grass and muffling the thudding hoofs of unseen horses, the creaking of leather, the rattle of arrows in quivers. Masses of riders moved past Al-Tâbir, and the Persian tried to keep his teeth from chattering as he rode after the Cossack. He followed Kirdy back at last to the cattle herd—that had been picked up on the last day's march, and hurried in by Tartars who sought refuge from the sultan's pillagers. There were more than a thousand of the beasts.

And Al-Tâbir rubbed his eyes. Behind the restless herd he could make out dozens of new camp fires, and beyond them a solid mass of warriors drawn up around the oxtail standard of Tevakel Khan. He had left such a mass, out on the left of the herd, and from riders that came and went past the fires he judged that there was another third on the right.

Only the front of the herd was cleared of horsemen. Here was the black mass of the slope that hid the Turkoman camp from view.

"What is that?" Al-Tâbir startled and gripped his javelin, bow and reins all at once. His gray pony pricked up its ears.

"The Turkomans are loosening off their matchlocks," Kirdy grunted. "It is the end of the sword dance."

But Al-Tâbir was staring, fascinated, at the herd. Scores of gnome-like Tartars were at work there, and he heard a strange clattering and stamping that grew louder. Warriors ran up with bundles of reeds and brush, and others fashioned torches at the fires behind the masses of cattle. Then the torches began to flicker in and out of the herd.

"*Ai-ee!*" he cried. "The horns of the beasts are burning!"

It did not occur to him that the Tartars had been binding brush to the horns of a great part of the steers. He saw several of the Tartars trampled underfoot, and the blaze caught from one beast to another in the close packed, milling mass.

Then, to Al-Tâbir's thinking, all the devils of the night swooped down. The herds started to run away from the camp fires, and the Tartars around Kirdy howled and roared at it on their wing, so that the leaders plunged down the wind, over the knoll, and toward the Turkoman camp.

The bellowing of the beasts, the snorting of the frantic horses, the whining of the wind—all this swept Al-Tâbir along, close to Kirdy's stirrup. In the depression between the camps, the steers spread out but ceased not their maddened rush as hot embers fell on them.

Rushing to the summit of their slope, the Turkomens beheld the herd with its blazing horns. Their patrols tried to turn it, but that herd could not be turned. Then the Turkomans ran for their horses.

Thundering across the depression and up the slight slope, the cattle burst past the watch fires and scattered among the tents, the carts, the piles of plunder of the raiders. Firelocks barked at them, and arrows began to flicker among them, but the mass of them that surged over the tents— crashed head-on into wagons, rubbed blazing horns against flimsy felt. In another moment flames fanned by the rushing wind began to spring up all over the encampment.

To the best of Al-Tâbir's belief madness had given way to chaos, and he wondered into which of the seven hells of Moslem purgatory he had been plunged.

The *"Ghar—ghar—ghar!"* of the eager Tartars mingled with the *"Allah-hai!"* of the rallying Turkomens. Al-Tâbir was still between Kirdy and Girai, galloping through lines of tents and dodging frantic steers. He saw two warriors on shaggy ponies—two men with gleaming swords and bare, shaven heads. Prudently he pulled in his horse and watched the Cossack spur forward, parrying a slash of a Turkoman scimitar and slipping his blade into the throat of the shouting warrior as he passed.

Girai arose in his short stirrups, swinging the long battle-ax. The Turkoman who opposed him threw up his sword to guard his head. But the heavy ax smote through the guard and split open the man's forehead.

"Forward!" Kirdy cried.

They turned aside, bending low in the saddle to keep under the whistling shafts that flew from the shadows where men gathered. Their ponies leaped a tangle of bodies and flew up a clear slope toward the green standard of the sultan. Here the wind howled at them and eddies of smoke twined around them, as if to draw them onward.

A firelock roared and flashed, and Girai's pony sank, head down, at the crest of the knoll. But Kirdy, who had caught sight of Nada, rode on at a free gallop, his sword arm swinging at his knee.

The girl still wore her Cossack dress and hat for—despite Otrèpiev's authority—no woman of such beauty would have been safe in that camp. She was in the saddle of the bay stallion, without her yataghan, and the stallion's rein was held by two men, also mounted—companions of Otrèpiev.

One let fall the rein and rode at Kirdy. He was a young warrior, with thin, cold features, and his apparel was that of a Polish noble, a black velvet *kontash* thrown over silvered breastplate, a gilded eagle on his light shield. His horse was a splendid gray mare.

Kirdy tightened his reign and swerved to meet the Pole on his right side; but the other—a skilled horseman—darted in and slashed at his head.

The sabers clashed and parted, and before the young noble could turn his mare the Cossack had whirled his black Karbarda and crashed into him. The Pole kept his seat in the saddle by a miracle, but his sword wrist was gripped by steel fingers.

"Yield!" Kirdy demanded.

At the same instant both heard the flurry of hoofs behind them. The man who had remained at Nada's side was a Circassian, a follower of Otrèpiev, and not inclined to let slip an opportunity to use his weapon. Swinging his yataghan over his head, he darted at the Cossack's back.

"Guard yourself—White Falcon!" Nada shouted, her clear voice cutting through the uproar as a bell pierces the mutter of a throng.

Kirdy had no time to do that. He caught a glimpse of the lean Moslem, and the gleam of steel—and he swung himself out of the saddle.

"Hai!" The Circassian shouted once in triumph and again in anger, because his sweeping slash had met only air. The impetus of his rush carried him past, and before he could wheel, Kirdy, who had kept his left foot in the stirrup, had thrust the Pole away and was in the saddle again.

But—though his grip had numbed the young noble's right wrist—the Pole had plucked a dagger from his belt with his free hand, and the short blade slashed the Cossack's ribs. Feeling the bite of the steel, Kirdy smashed the hilt of his saber into the Pole's face. Both men reeled, but it was the Pole who fell, the Cossack who tightened his knees and groped for his rein with a numbed arm. And upon him all the fury of the Circassian descended.

The Moslem came on warily this time, and once his twisted blade cut Kirdy's forearm. Squatting in short stirrups, his long teeth bared, his dark eyes gleaming, he edged his horse closer, seeking to thrust under his foeman's guard with the shorter weapon.

And now Kirdy swayed in the saddle, his saber sliding off the yataghan.

"*Hai!*" cried the Circassian, and thrust.

But the Cossack, who had been watching for this, was not as weak as he seemed. The curved saber slashed down, and before the Moslem could recover, Kirdy had cut him through the temple so that the steel grated on bone and he had to strain to draw it free. So convulsively had the man gripped with rein and knees when he was struck, he remained for a moment crouching in the saddle—until his frantic horse, rearing, flung him to earth, a lifeless body.

Then Kirdy turned to look for the other. Instead, he saw Girai climbing into the saddle of the mare and a glance at the splendid figure in breastplate and *kontash* showed him that Girai had slain the owner before catching the horse.

"Dismount!" he heard Nada's voice. "Let me see your hurt." Kirdy shook his head.

"It was a trick. I can ride."

The girl, in her dark *svitza* and hat, looked slender and pale as if she had been wasted by sickness, and in the glare of the flames Kirdy wondered if this were indeed the Nada he had left at the Wolf's Throat, or some apparition that had taken form out of the steppe. He leaned forward to peer into her eyes, and the sight of her beauty warmed his blood like the rarest of wines.

"My yataghan," she begged at once. "The dog of a Circassian took it."

Kirdy bade Girai retrieve the weapon and its sheath, but when Nada took it in her hand, she shivered.

"There is blood—your blood upon it."

"Wipe the blade," Kirdy ordered the Tartar harshly, and Girai did so, on the end of the slain Moslem's turban.

"Nay," cried the girl. "It is an omen of death." And she looked at the young warrior steadfastly, as if she feared some power might, even at that moment, carry him from her side.

"Then take me to Otrèpiev!" he responded gruffly, because of the pain of the wound in his side.

And at that she flung up her head, her eyes blazing.

"Am I a spy? Nay, seek him among the hordes!" But Kirdy, leaning on his saddle horn, looked down into the tumult of battle. In that eddying of horsemen and maddened cattle and fire, no one could be found. He thought that if Otrèpiev lived he would return to the knoll where the standard had been, to seek Nada.

Only Girai—diligently stripping the slain of weapons—was near him. The Turkomans who had held the knoll had ridden off when the main body of Tartars came up—in fact, the standard of Ilbars Sultan was nowhere to be seen. Kirdy noticed a long cart near one of the tents and rode over to it, Nada trotting beside him.

It was not a Tartar wagon, and narrow iron runners were strapped to the sides. Perched on the fur packs that burdened it was a Muscovite saddle.

"Aye," laughed Nada, reading his face. "That is the *kibitka* of Otrèpiev. In it he keeps his treasure. Look and see!"

But Kirdy summoned Girai and bade him take stand by the wagon and allow no one to carry off what was in it.

"I give thee this as a duty."

And the Tartar came, swinging his ax, looking like a bear girdled with steel. He had everything from knives to breastplates hung to his belt.

"If this be truly the wagon of the *fanga nialmal*," he grunted, "he himself will have a word to say in the matter, because he is riding like a devil to this place—now."

Before he had finished speaking Kirdy was off and Nada with him. At the crest of the knoll the girl drew in her breath sharply.

"You are wounded. Do not go against him!"

Four horsemen were approaching the mound at full gallop. Two were Muscovite boyars in armor, wearing rich cloaks, fur edged. The man who rode in advance of the pair drew Kirdy's eyes instantly.

Beneath a silvered casque with a crest of eagle feathers, a broad, dark face was visible. High cheekbones, thin, restless eyes, and a sure seat in the saddle—all these bespoke power. And there was power in the body of Otrèpiev, and tranquility in his spirit, because he rode through chaos as if he were a king reviewing a host. Even his horse, a big-boned black, swept on with an easy gait. And, seeing Nada, Otrèpiev turned to fling a jest at his followers. Rising in his stirrups, he saluted her with a bloodstained sword.

Then he peered at Kirdy, who was urging his Karbarda down the slope.

At this instant, as quail dart from a thicket, a bevy of dwarf Tartars came out of the shadows and bore down on Otrèpiev, who turned his horse to meet them.

"Yarou manda!" Kirdy shouted at them, fearing that they might reach his foe before he did. But the Muscovites fired two pistols, and when one of the Tartars fell from the saddle, the others cried out in anger and closed in upon the four riders.

Horses reared, and blades flashed up. The shrill cry of the nomads mingled with the screamed oaths of the Muscovites. Steel clattered. One of Otrèpiev's followers went down, and Kirdy, plunging into the melee, saw the false Dmitri split the skull of a warrior. With all the impetus of the rush down the slope the Cossack's horse struck one of the Tartar ponies, and was jarred back to his haunches, Kirdy keeping his seat with an effort.

When he looked up, Otrèpiev had wheeled away, followed by only one man. The Tartars were springing from their saddles to snatch plunder from the two others, who were struggling weakly on the ground. Kirdy set his teeth and made after Otrèpiev, who had a bow-shot's start. Through a deserted part of the camp they galloped, beyond the glow of fire into the darkness of the plain.

"Stay!" Kirdy called angrily. "Will you fly from one?" Out of the murk the voice of Otrèpiev answered him:

"'Tis my hour for the road—for the long road to Satan. Follow if you will!"

Glancing over his shoulder Kirdy made out another rider at his heels, and, outlined against the distant glow of fire, the gnomelike figures of Tartars, casting about for the fleeing. Follow he did, with the Karbarda going lame.

For the first time he lashed the black racer madly, and the horse gathered himself together to plunge ahead into the rush of wind. The wind had a chill bite to it; the stars were hidden and rain pelted down as Kirdy, following the distant hoofbeats, swerved into a gully.

His horse stumbled and recovered with a long stagger and clatter of hoofs. Again Kirdy lashed him, but again he stumbled heavily. They dipped down into a nest of boulders, and when Kirdy reined in the done-up horse he could hear nothing of the men in front of him—only the rider coming up behind, who proved to be Nada.

Mustering what strength was left him after sleepless days and loss of blood, the Cossack caught her rein and spoke hoarsely.

"Unharmed he goes again upon the steppe. And what road will you follow?"

"I will stay with you."

Kirdy could see nothing at all, and the beat of the rain was like sword strokes on his bare head. With the rein of the Karbarda over his arm, he staggered toward the rocky side of the gully, to seek for shelter. Once he felt Nada catch his arm.

Stumbling forward, he tried to feel out the way.

Though his legs still carried him, he was half unconscious. Then he became aware that he was in a dry place—a shallow cavern, he thought. He heard the heavy breathing of the horses, the light step of Nada. Flinging himself down, he fell asleep at once.

The girl had taken the warrior's head in her lap, and with the long tresses of hair that had been kept dry under the sheepskin hat she rubbed the water and blood from his face. Because she also was weary and—for the first time in months—happy, she wept.

Chapter XVI
Tevakel Khan

Girai the ax-man sat on the saddle atop the treasure wagon of the vanished wizard and related over and over again the tale of what he had seen. This he did to establish his own worth and importance, but also to keep intact the contents of the wagon.

It had been placed upon him as a duty to preserve this spoil for the Cossack, and, being no more than one man, Girai knew that guile must come to the aid of his ax if he was to ward greedy hands from the bundles and chests that he sat on.

With the gold-embroidered *kontash* of the dead Pole wrapped around him, and the body of the Pole to point to in evidence of his tale, he held forth:

"*Hai*—in this fashion it was. We had slain many of the Turkoman wolves—the Cossack *fanga* and I. We twain rode up this height to where the standard was to be seen. In this place, as you may see, I slew the Frank, splitting his skull. Then out of the darkness appeared the woman dressed as a man and the Cossack bade me wipe clean a light sword and bestow it upon her. It was a good sword, though light. Then the twain rode to look at this wagon which contains the magic of the *fanga nialma*.

"No sooner had they touched the wagon than the *fanga nialma* came toward us, with a white pelt swinging from his shoulders and his horse snorting fire. The Cossack *fanga* shouted and reined at him, swinging the enchanted sword that cuts through iron or leather. If there were not magic in the sword, how else would it cut as it does?

"Then, behold, the *fanga nialma* fled for his life.

"But he cried out to the spirits of the upper air, and rain came, to be a veil in covering his flight. He vanished like a rat in a wheat field, and the Cossack also vanished; but by the gods of the high places, my brothers, it is not well to touch this wagon. I, who have permission, may sit in this saddle thus. Now, my brothers, bring me mare's milk and the fat tail of a sheep from a full pot."

After a time came Tevakel Khan with two sons, to look at the wizard's wagon. Though they yearned to investigate, after hearing Girai's tale they decided not to do so until all the rest of the spoil of the Turkoman camp was safely garnered.

The Turkoman wolves had been slashed and driven. The fighting eddied over the plain, as scattered wind gusts follow a hurricane. And the Tartars pursued like ferrets—for this was the kind of fighting they relished. The Horde had been thinned under the dreaded swords of the invaders, but a great number of the Turkomans lay headless in the high, wet grass. Their heads were piled into pyramids, about which vultures and crows flapped and stalked. The men of the Golden Horde cared not for slaves, and they had seen their women hung by the feet and burned the night before.

The younger warriors were still in the saddle, harrying the groups of the flying, when, at midafternoon, Kirdy and Nada rode in on lame horses, and Girai gave up his charge.

No sooner had the Cossack dismounted than word of his arrival was carried to Tevakel Khan. A carpet was placed near the wagon, and upon this the old chieftain knelt, while his surviving sons gathered behind him. Gravely he acknowledged Kirdy's salute, and without expression he stared at Nada, evidently believing her a captive.

"The fate of man is in God's hands," he intoned, and added: "Hast thou slain the wizard of Ilbars Sultan?"

"Nay—he has escaped to the east."

"Doubtless taking the form of a serpent or a rat," nodded the khan, who was familiar with the evasiveness of wizards. "Yet this, his *kibitka*, is in

thy hands. Thou hast, too, his woman. But let us see what is in the sacks."
Many and varied were the tales that had sprung up among the Horde of the
splendor and the daring of the departed wizard, and—though he gave no
sign of it—Tevakel Khan was afflicted with all the curiosity of a child.

First the saddle was brought to the chieftain for inspection, then kegs
of powder, which he recognized and distrusted. He believed that firelocks were uncanny, and since the firelocks of the Turkomans had done
them little good, he decided to sprinkle the powder on the earth, where
it could do no harm.

A pair of flutes pleased him immensely, and rich garments and jars of
rum and brandy likewise. But when Kirdy broke open a small chest and
showed him strings of pearls, the notorious gold apple, the gold staff with
jeweled tip, and rubies and diamonds of great size and luster, he fell into
meditation.

"Aforetime," Kirdy reminded him, "I made pledge that from the spoil
of this camp a gift should be found for thee—a fitting gift. Take then these
precious stones, for they are part of a royal treasure." Again the old man
scrutinized each flaming ruby—torn from more massive settings—and
the blue and yellow diamonds that must have come from Persia.

"Allah!" he grunted. "Of what worth are these? The garments I shall
wear, and the wines shall be drunk from the skull cup of Ilbars Sultan.
But these will not keep out the cold or warm the blood."

"They are thine. Do with them as thou wilt."

"They brought no good to the *fanga nialma*. Such things work evil. I
have seen it. I have goods enough. From the earth they came, and I shall
have them buried, and a horse slain upon the spot as an offering to the
spirits of the high places."

Kirdy glanced at Nada, who was fingering the stones curiously.

"The khan will bury them," he said. "Will you not keep some?" The
girl smiled, and then shook her head.

"Nay, White Falcon—they were stolen, and what would they avail us
here?" Now the jewels were the last of the things of the false tsar—and
Kirdy thought that he must have carried them from the palace the day before his flight from Moscow, sending them ahead in the sledge. Such articles as these might have been carried out under one of the immense coats
of the Muscovites, and Otrèpiev had counted on changing them into money
when his journey had ended. And Kirdy wondered, while he waited for the
khan to acknowledge his gift, whether Otrèpiev had turned back through
the shambles of the camp to seek Nada or these precious stones.

"Eh," said Tevakel Khan, "now come ye to my yurta and make choice of whatever thing thou desirest." A Tartar is avaricious where presents are concerned, but it is a matter of personal honor with him that the giver be rewarded. So he was surprised and not too well pleased when the Cossack said he would take only fresh horses and a man to show him the way.

"Whither?"

"Only the eagles know. I go upon the trail of my enemy, the *fanga nialma*."

Considering this, the khan shook his head moodily.

"Thou art bold, O Cossack. Thou art terrible in battle, as a man should be. Thou hast a golden-haired slave, and here in the Horde there is a place for thee, at the right of the fire. What more will a journey bring thee?"

"Vengeance."

"For death?"

"For the deaths of ten thousand, and the broken promise of a traitor."

The old chieftain made a gesture as of casting a stick upon a fire.

"With the slayer of his kin a man may not sleep under the same sky. Bind thy wounds, that they do not open—choose from my herd what pleases thee, and go. Yet if thy rein is drawn again to the Altyn-juz, the place on the white horse skin of my yurta is open. I have said it, and my word is not smoke."

Aware that this was a favorable moment to leave, and that the good-nature of the old man might not last, Kirdy placed his hand to his forehead and lips.

"And the woman!" Tevakel Khan observed suddenly. "What is to be done with her?"

"She desires to go with me."

"Then thy peace will be troubled, because she came from the camp of thine enemy. It would be better to slay her with thy sword—thus!"

He moved the scimitar that lay across his knees significantly.

"Nay, she is a Cossack, and her father is the master of the wolves, thy friend."

"Allah!" Tevakel Khan considered Nada and thought that here was a matter of wonder. It seemed to him that this feud was no ordinary pursuit of blood, but a struggle of wizardry. He chose rather to hear the ending of it than to have a share in it himself, and he gave Kirdy leave to go.

When the wounded Cossack and the young girl walked away through the charred camp, the sun was near setting, and the red light brought to the mind of Tevakel Khan another matter, most vital. His faded eyes gleamed, the wrinkles in his broad face deepened, and he bade his sons bring to him the scholar who did his writing.

When the native was seated at his feet, thin brush and paper roll in hand, the master of the Golden Horde began speaking.

"Write thus! To Arap Muhammad Khan of Khiva, lord of dead wolves and king of grave-jackals, greeting from his foe Tevakel Khan of the Altyn-juz!

"Understand that upon this day, the fifth of the month of the Ox, I mounted and rode against thy camp and thy son Ilbars Sultan and thy warriors, sword in hand.

"Thou couldst not see the flames devour thy tents, thy heroes overthrown and trampled, their heads piled into heaps.

"Thou couldst not see thy wise men and wizards fleeing like sheep, brother parting from brother—thy horses taken by my grandchildren, thy weapons cast before my tent pole, thy standard the plaything of girl-children—nor the skull of thy son Ilbars Sultan that was, a drinking cup ready to my hand.

"Since all these things thou couldst not see, and since not a man of thine hath escaped to bear thee the tale, I, Tevakel Khan—I tell it thee!"

This was the Tartar's valedictory to the hated Turkoman, and when he had satisfied himself that Al-Tâbir did not understand the writing, Tevakel Khan gave the letter to the interpreter of dreams to bear to Khiva, instructing several of his warriors to accompany the Persian as far as the first outposts of the Turkomans.

Chapter XVII
The Gate in the Mountain

It was several days later that Kirdy and Nada camped near a Tartar cemetery—a place of gray, moss-coated rocks and dense rushes—and listened to a harangue by Girai the ax-man, who had offered to accompany them. A half dozen rough-coated ponies grazed outside the firelight, with the bay stallion that the girl had kept. Their packs now held little except meat and salt, and Girai's cooking implements, and furs.

Squatting at a little distance from them, the Tartar spoke gravely, his hideous face outlined by the glow of the fire against the loom of a rock.

"*Kai*, it is so. Here the grazing land ends and the thick forest begins. After the rains it was a small matter to follow the trace of thine enemy; but in the forest a trail is lost if it be three or four days old."

Kirdy merely nodded, and Nada, lying outstretched on a bed of moss, hands clasped behind her head, looked only at the canopy of stars that seemed nearer now they had left the mists of the plain behind. Girai peered at his master uneasily.

"Thou hast seen. Once, in the first day, thine enemy sought to turn west. He fell in with riders going to the camp of the khan. They knew him not. They sold him a sheep and perhaps other things. As far beyond this spot as a man can see, thine enemy the *fanga* dismounted. His companion cooked part of the sheep. The horses rolled and grazed.

"For a while they watched from a high place, doubtless seeing others of my people. So they knew no path was open to them toward the setting sun. They turned then to the rising sun.

"Now they ride toward the Mountains of the Eagles, and through these mountains they mean to go."

Kirdy looked up.

"How knowest thou?"

"If a buffalo makes for a ford does it not mean to cross the stream? It is so! These twain have drawn their reins toward a gut in the range. They will go through."

"Is there a way?"

The ax-man rubbed his knees and looked everywhere but into the Cossack's eyes.

"There is a way."

"Can this *fanga* find it without a guide?"

Girai grinned.

"Nay, Cossack, hath he not a guide? One who knows all the ways of the earth?"

"Who then?"

"Shaitan, who sits atop yonder rampart. He beckons the rider and surely the gate is open when the Yakka Shaitan, the Lord of the Night, beckons."

The Cossack grunted and tried another tack. Girai had spoken of the snow range not as mountains but as a rampart, which implied a citadel or fortified place somewhere above them.

"Is the gate barred?"

"Is the pass to the wolf's gully barred to the lamb? Nay, the pass is open."

"What pass?"

Girai waved a scarred hand impatiently.

"Yonder pass, high—high. There the eagles and the vultures sit and wait. Fools may go through the pass to the other side. Yet the eagles are wiser. They sit and wait for food."

"Beyond the pass, is there a fortified place?"

"Ask the kites! They know, and we—we do not know. Only at one time there was a city beyond the rampart. It was the city of the Golden Horde."

"And now?"

"It is a *kuran tengri*—a place accursed. In three lifetimes no man of the Horde has crossed to the side of the rampart where the sun rises." And that was all Girai would say. Considering his words, Kirdy saw a little light. To the Tartars all lofty peaks are traditionally sacred—they went to a mountain summit to pray, and ran away if a storm came up. The snow range that was now clearly visible, even in the starlight, was a natural barrier.

That Girai and his fellows should be superstitious about the Mountains of the Eagles was to be expected.

Now Girai had used the words *kuran tengri* to describe what lay beyond the pass above them. This meant a forbidden or haunted spot, but a place of spirits as well. Such a name usually, the Cossack remembered, had a cause.

If there were indeed a city beyond the pass, it might be a city where the Horde had met with calamity in almost forgotten days. If so, the Tartars would naturally avoid the site. Asia has its lost cities where once devastating sand or plague has entered in—or an invading horde. Time would have erased the memory of calamity, though not the dread of the place.

So much Kirdy knew. And this would account for the tale of the Persian, that the mountain rampart was unscalable, and that beyond it the sun came up. Yet Al-Tâbir had also said that Nada knew of a city on the far side of the range and had told Otrèpiev of it. He looked at the silent girl.

"Nada, why did you send Otrèpiev to chase shadows? Who knows the country beyond these mountains?"

"*Ai-a*, White Falcon!" She stretched slender arms toward the stars and turned on her side to smile at him. "Am I a vampire to lead men from the trail? I spoke the truth."

She watched Girai replenish the fire and go off to the ponies.

"The ax-man is troubled. I think he is afraid. And you—you are like all men. When your enemy escapes you turn to me with a black brow and say, 'Why didst thou in this fashion?' Long ago my father wandered in the steppe and crossed the path of this Horde. And the mother of Tevakel Khan liked me and told me many tales—of a city that had once belonged to the Horde. I told her of Moscow, and she swore that this *khan tengri* was more splendid than that, with higher walls. They who entered this city found peace. And that, surely, is greater than Moscow. I think the hag wanted to steal me, but Tevakel Khan forbade."

"Girai says that Otrèpiev is heading for the pass that leads to this place."

Drowsily, Nada nodded, resting her head on her arm.

"Aye, my Falcon, and if he finds a city and a strange people, he will make himself master of them, as he did of the Muscovites. When the Turkoman riders were seen coming toward us on the plain, he robed his followers in rich coats and sables and took the scepter in his hand, greeting the dog-thieves as servants come to his aid."

She laughed delightedly.

"*Kai*, so it happened they were astonished and a little afraid—when six wild geese flew up from the grass at their coming. I saw it. Luck played into the hand of Gregory Otrèpiev, but his boldness saved my life."

Now she glanced fleetingly at the silent Cossack.

"O White Falcon, I made him a promise that if he should make himself king of the people beyond the mountain I would then bend the head to him and sit at his feet as queen."

"That was ill said."

From beneath long lashes dark eyes took stock of the young warrior and his growing anger. Nada fairly purred.

"'Why didst thou in this fashion?' So the Cossack says in his heart, being blind as a wounded ox. Have you tamed me, Cossack? Have you bound my tongue?"

"It was ill done, to send Otrèpiev astray!"

This seemed to please her the more.

"Ill done! It was his fate that he should go! A new kingdom to be conquered! What if he had but one man to ride at his heel, his treasure lost, his courtiers slain? The rampart is high—the more reason to climb it; the city beyond is unknown—so he went to find it. That is his way. Besides," she added tranquilly, "where else could he go? You have seen, and Girai has growled it out, that only the mountain pass was open to him."

"Nay, yours was the spur that sent him forward."

"True! How much better for him if he had lingered at that first camp, eating mutton until you came, with your sword, on a Tartar's pony—"

Kirdy winced, because the diminutive beasts of the Golden Horde were ill suited to his height, and Nada, secure on the great-limbed charger, had pointed this out more than once.

"—and cut him to pieces," the girl concluded pleasantly. "As it is, he goes free into the unknown."

"You led him across the dry lands."

"Should I leave him for the kites? Nay, he could never have found the way. And you blame me for that?"

Now in his heart Kirdy had no blame for any act of the girl; a blind rage was seizing him. Al-Tâbir had said that Nada had joined the company of Otrèpiev because she knew that, sooner or later, Kirdy would come up with them. Rage whispered that Al-Tâbir lied, to curry favor—that Nada loved the false tsar and the glitter of his deeds. Jealousy whispered that Nada was now riding at his side, not because she wished to be with him, but because she sought to lead him astray from his pursuit.

And in this moment Nada's mood changed, as a leaf blown by the wind whirls and rushes back upon the gust. Her long eyes, intent on the fire, grew troubled, and she put her hand lightly on the Cossack's arm. Under her fingers the man's muscles were like iron, and he did not dare look at her, for the anger in him.

"Kirdy," she said after a moment, "look!"

She pointed up, beyond the dark network of the forest, to the wall of darkness that was the bare, rocky heights above the timber line. Out of this black wall rose at intervals the snow peaks, gleaming in the clear starlight. To the girl—as well as to Girai—they resembled watchtowers built upon a wall of sheer immensity.

"Tevakel Khan is old and wise," she whispered. "Do as he counseled. Go back to the Horde. Your wounds have not closed; there is fever in you."

Now he looked at her with burning eyes, his lips set upon clenched teeth. And she frowned and tried to shake his arm.

"Go back, Kirdy. You did not hear the tale of the wife of Tevakel Khan. Only now—"she hesitated, then—"I fear that Gregory Otrèpiev will indeed be master of the country beyond, and blood will fall between us—yours or mine."

Once Kirdy laughed, and at the sound of it she drew back, lips parted.

"Remember the omen of the yataghan. Your blood was on it when it was given me." But the Cossack rose suddenly to his feet and cupped his hands about his eyes to peer at the heights.

"Kirdy," Nada went on impulsively, "let Otrèpiev meet his fate, wherever he has gone. He will not return. I fear, for us."

"Nada," he said slowly, "there is no fear in you. Your beauty is such that you command and men obey, like slaves. It burns, this fever."

His hands clenched, and his arms flung out so that bones and sinews cracked.

"That is the way of it! Your thoughts are bent on this traitor because he has played the part of a king. What thought have you for the Falcon, the Cossack? He serves to protect you—to groom your horse—to bring wood for your fire. When the wolves howl, the borzoi is caressed by his mistress; when the sun shines, the Cossack is good enough for your jests. The Cossack is bloody—the Cossack is revengeful—and in your dreams you cling to the man who has slain multitudes for a whim—"

Springing to her feet, Nada faced him with blazing eyes.

"Stop! I have given my love to no man."

"Nay, only you can know if Otrèpiev be man or fiend."

"I—"

Nada caught her breath, and the sound of it was surely a sob. The next instant she had grasped the hilt of the yataghan and drawn the weapon with a thin slither of steel. With all the strength of shoulders and arm she struck at Kirdy, and the twisted blade stopped over her head as if bound by chains.

The Cossack, laughing wildly, had caught her wrist with one hand, and when she sought to snatch the sword in her left hand he drew her forward and turned her about so that her head pressed back against his shoulder and his left hand grasped her girdle, holding her helpless. Her sheepskin hat fell off, and the loosened tangle of silk-like hair swept against his throat.

"Look!" he said between his teeth. And Nada ceased futile struggling to stare up at the heights.

In the maw of blackness between two of the peaks a red eye of light was visible.

"It is in the pass," Kirdy went on grimly, "far above the tree growth, where no Tartars venture. That is the fire of Otrèpiev, and when you beheld it you said to me, 'Turn back!' You would have led me from the trail."

"As God lives, that is a lie. I did not see the light."

But Kirdy merely laughed between his teeth and released the girl, turning his back upon her as if the yataghan and her anger, and his, did not exist.

"Hi, Girai! Make ready the packs. We will go upon the road."

Nada stood utterly still, one arm pressed against her heart, and presently she sheathed the sword, and came to Kirdy but did not touch him.

"You are wild with the fever," she said quietly. "Pour water on your head, walk about, and then sleep. Then in the morning go whither you will. I—I have no place to go, except to the Tartars, and would you have me do that?"

"Nay, you shall not leave my side until the end of the road."

She waited while Kirdy and the Tartar made up the packs and saddled the ponies with experienced hands in the darkness. Girai, after a glance into the Cossack's face and another at the gleam of light above them, made no objection to entering the forest on horses that had not slept.

The three mounted and moved off in silence, leaving the glen with its starlight at once. And when they entered the gloom of the forest, they were no longer three. Girai turned aside and made off toward the valley.

"Eh," he said, a week later, at the encampment of his clan, "I saw the light. It was the eye of Shaitan, looking out from the gate in the rampart."

Chapter XVIII
The Law

In elder days the wise men foregathered and said: Thus and so shall be the Law. And a woman, fair to see, came and spurned the Law, dancing upon it with light feet.

And thereupon the youth of the land came and made an oath, saying: Thus and so shall be the Faith between us.

When they had parted, a girl-child with flowers in her hair laughed at the Faith.

Yet when the old men and the youths girded on their armor and went with their chariots to a distant battle, the women kept the Law and abode by the Faith. And who shall say why this was done?

Nada could be surprisingly patient. Her father had taught her that there is an end to everything. She talked, low-voiced, to the big bay charger, who pricked up his ears and surged forward gallantly when she noticed him; she crooned at the eagles that flickered past the forest mesh, and she hunted wild turkeys with a bow while she waited for the black rage to leave Kirdy and the ascent of the Earth Girdle to end.

At evening—for the Cossack pressed on, and cooked only one meal in the day—she plucked a turkey or roasted a deer's quarter and made barley and cheese cakes for them both, while Kirdy attended to the horses. Only once did he speak.

"This companion of Otrèpiev—who is he?"

Nada, bending over the fire, made answer quietly.

"One of the tsar's dogs."

Then Kirdy knew that the man with the false tsar was an executioner—one of the torturers kept by the Muscovite lords. Otrèpiev had chosen a motley court to go upon his exile, and now, except for the interpreter of dreams, only this man garbed in black and armed with a two-handed sword—Kirdy had caught a glimpse of him during the fighting in the Turkoman camp—remained at the fugitive's side.

Nada's quick eyes missed nothing of the ascent. She knew when the birches and alders gave place to blue firs that they were near the end of the forest and near the spot where the fire had been seen. Ahead of them the mountain slopes closed in, and down this gorge a bitter wind howled as if it were a watchdog chained in the cut of the mountain.

She knew when Kirdy found the scattered ashes of the fire two days old. For an hour he examined the earth in a wide circle about the spot, and though Nada could see nothing at all in the ground, a sudden tensing of his dark brow and flicker of the thin lips told her that he had made certain that Otrèpiev had gone up the gorge. She had learned to read his face, if not his thoughts.

"Sleep, Nada," he ordered her. "We will rest, and the horses will roll and graze."

By this she was aware that the fever had left him and she did sleep, drawing her sheepskins about her against the chill breath of that wind—the sleep of the young and weary. But at times she heard the Cossack moving about, and the crackle of a growing fire, and the neighing of horses led to water. Near at hand a stream tore down the mountain side between black boulders—a stream that foamed, milky white. And Nada, who knew nothing of glacier-fed streams, was astonished because this one had roared past when she lay down in the late afternoon, and did no more than murmur when she roused at sunrise.

Kirdy, who never seemed to sleep—after that first night in the storm when she had held his head on her knee—led the way into the teeth of the wind.

That day they left the last stunted trees behind, and the short grass changed to a mossy growth that clung to the rocks, and the sides of the gorge became sheer cliffs that rose higher until the face of the sun was hidden. They saw the bones of a horse from which foul-smelling vultures flapped up lazily.

Once they circled the pool under a thousand-foot waterfall—the source of the stream that had given them water for the last day. The sun's rays reached the summit of the narrow fall and tinted the spray in an arc of color that made the girl gasp.

Then, when the roar of the fall had dwindled to a distant reverberation, Kirdy heard her singing against the voice of the wind:

> Tell me, brother Eagle, is it far to my home—
> Far to blessed Mother Volga's shore?
> I am hungry, brother Eagle, hungry and cold.
> I will ride no more—no more!

And, though he pushed ahead without a word, he was troubled. This was the song of Cossack captives, who went in chains to distant lands. He wondered why Nada had chosen it, and whether sickness had touched her.

That night she slept like the dead, and Kirdy tended the fire at her feet—the glimmer of a fire, fed by the wood one pony had packed up from the forest.

And while he watched, he listened to the twin voices of the Earth Girdle—the strident cry of the wind gusts and the moan of the waterfall.

In spite of the wind's breath, the fire burned badly, unaccountably so, and when he filled the pot with water and tried to boil the Tartar tea brick in it, he could not do so. Kirdy set this down to the working of the evil spirits that must frequent such a place.

Although he got up, to walk stiffly up and down between the boulders, drowsiness clutched at him and was not to be shaken off. So, when at last he seated himself by the unconscious girl, his head slipped forward on his chest. He had to struggle for breath. Almost at once the two voices of the pass swelled in volume, and strange words came to the Cossack's ears:

> Ai-a—come and see! The night birds await thee!
> Many have come! Come thou!

That was the cry of the night wind.

> Oho-ho-o! What lies beyond the Gate?
> A grave. She will ride to the end of the road,
> but if ill befalls thee, what of her?

Such was the warning roar that came up from the fall.

> She will lead thee astray—wait and see.
> We have seen her before and we know.
> Fool—she trusts thee. Turn back!
> What hope is there for the blind?

Then the wind's note changed swiftly to the clang of war cymbals and the monotone of the fall to the mutter of drums. The Cossack heard the clashing of shod hoofs on stones, the snapping of standards, the creaking of great wagons drawn by yoked oxen, and the roaring battle shout of riders.

The pass was filled with moving shadows and sound. Under the space of starlight above him gleamed the weapons of a host. He heard the snarling of laden camels, the snorting of horses, and the clang and clash of shields.

This, he thought, must be the Golden Horde coming up from its city. And surely he heard a deafening shout:

> Make way—make way!
> He comes, the Khan of all the Hordes!

Kirdy sprang up, his limbs chilled and stiff. He peered around him and saw that the line of sky between the rock walls was gray. The roar of the fall had dwindled to a whisper and the fitful wind was no more than a mocking whimper. At his side the horses were stamping and snorting, and Nada, roused by his sudden movement, lifted her head and smiled at the dawn drowsily.

"If such be the watchers," the Cossack thought, "at the gate, what will be the folk of the city?"

Before now he had slept on the upper slopes of a mountain range, and at such times dreams had troubled him; breathing had been difficult, and the fire had acted strangely. Whether all this were caused by evil spirits—

dreaded by the Tartars—or by the wind and the cold of the heights, he neither knew nor cared. The night was past, the day at hand.

"Did you hear the cymbals and the drums, White Falcon?" the girl asked.

"Aye."

"The Tartars say that is the Horde, marching through the gate. When they hear it, down below, they are afraid."

"Nay, little Nada—it was the wind, and the thunder of the fall."

"Listen!" She smiled at him in the gloom of the gorge. "Now the voice of the fall is only a little voice, and the wind barely stirs."

"Then it may be that the city is near, and the guards upon the wall sound cymbal and drum at the dawn hour."

"Do they drive camels through the pass at that hour? Nay, this is the gate!"

She pointed at the sheer rock walls, now growing gray, and Kirdy saw that the pass fell away, to the east. They had camped almost at its highest point. The thought struck him that Otrèpiev and the Muscovite might have turned back and passed them during the night and the two horses, clattering among the stones, might have made the uproar.

But this he did not believe. A man like Otrèpiev would not have passed a fire without investigating, or a half dozen ponies without trying to seize them. Also, the Cossack was certain that a horse coming up the pass—a living horse with a rider—would have roused him from his stupor.

If it had been a dream, Nada would not have heard the same sounds, and his ponies would not have been aroused and restless before the first light.

No, he had listened to the passage of an armed host, an array not of mortal men but of ghosts. And it was this Horde of the dead that the Tartars feared. Whence came it, and whither did it ride? What matter? The dead were the dead.

"They paid us no heed!" Nada mused. "*Ai*, Kirdy, it was surely a warning."

By now the light was strong enough for him to look closely into her eyes, shadowed by weariness and yet bright with a kind of fever. And he groaned, clutching both hands upon his belt. They were at the gate of the Earth Girdle; beyond might be a barren land where food could not be hunted down.

In his anger, a few nights ago, he had ordered Nada to ride on, with him. Better for her if she had struck him down with the yataghan! Better, perhaps, if she had kept at Otrèpiev's side.

"Go back, then, little Nada," he said gruffly. "Aye, the Cossack is mad—he has hurt you. How can you go on, in such a land as this where the spirits ride as a regiment? Take the horses, and—God keep you!"

He took her head in his powerful hands, pressing against the tangle of soft tresses; but his head hung upon his chest, and he did not see her eyes open very wide, or the sudden flush that darkened her skin.

"Whither?" she asked quietly. "Could I, a woman, ride alone with horses through the tribes?" Again he groaned, thinking that Girai the ax-man, who might have been relied upon to protect Nada, had run from them.

"Aye," he said, touching the icon at her bare throat.

"The good Saint Ulass will guard you, as among wolves."

"Foolish Cossack!" she smiled. "Now we are past the gate, and is there less of peril before than behind? Fool, to have crossed the Earth Girdle! Nay, I think we are near the end of the road. Come and see."

As Nada had prophesied, the sides of the gorge fell away, and the trail dipped sharply. Rounding a turn a little after sunrise they came out on a point of rocks and reined in, Kirdy silently, the girl with a quick cry of wonder.

Over the rim of distant mountain ranges the sun glared at them, and all the way to this far-off horizon were ridges and the purple shadows of ranges. Here and there in the nearer valleys the golden beds of lakes flared.

So great was the elevation of the point on which they stood, they could discern no trees or animal life below them. Instead of the gray-green steppes, they stared down at red cliffs and gorges, still mist-shrouded. Red and gray and barren, this land beyond the Earth Girdle might have been shaped by blind and tortured giants.

Nada shaded her eyes and looked down.

"See, my White Falcon, here is the city."

Kirdy nodded; he had seen it at once, and now he leaned on his saddle horn, studying it.

For more than a thousand yards the mountain fell away steeply beneath him—sheer cliffs, at places. At the foot of this descent a plateau extended. The top of the plateau, or table formation, was fairly level, and he thought that it towered far above the lower valley.

At the plateau's level, the mountain was limestone. And the city of the Golden Horde was the same red and white stone, with bits of gray granite and other rock that glittered—quartz or porphyry.

It was a ruin.

From where the Cossack stood, the twisted streets looked like gullies—the dwellings, piles of crumbled stone. He traced out terraces and bastions without being able to decide whether they had been wrought by men's hands or by nature. There were patches of green growth and glints of water.

But running down in long zigzags from the point of rock was a road, or rather the remnant of a road, covered at spots with rubble and fallen away completely at places. This road was the only way down from the pass.

Tevakel Khan's nomads would no more have built that ramp down the mountain side than nature itself could have done so. At one time men had hewn it out and built it up.

And so, at one time, men must have lived on the plateau. By now he could see the lower valley through the mist—the dense mesh of forest growth that seemed no greater than moss—the lighter green of the valley bed where the mist was clearing, and the brilliance of a lake that looked like a jewel.

The men who had lived upon the rock plateau could have grazed their herds thousands of feet below—or perhaps the plateau was a citadel, a refuge in time of war. Beyond doubt there were water, wood, and game in the valley.

But he could see no solitary sign of man.

Chapter XIX
The End of the Road

"Gregory Otrèpiev," Nada mused, "would have gone down to that city. He would like to see what the ruins are and what people live there."

"Eagles live there," Kirdy made answer, "and vipers—not men."

"We will soon know. At least someone has gone down the trail."

That much the Cossack had already ascertained. He had seen tracks in a cascade of soft earth, where one horse had rubbed against the slope and another had trampled the fresh dirt. They were halfway down the traverse road, and the worst of it was before them. That slide of earth told a story of frightened horses rearing back, and riders hovering over eternity.

But Otrèpiev had gone on, and Kirdy meant to follow. He bade Nada dismount, and took the rein of the bay stallion. The hardy Tartar ponies kept their footing wisely, but the charger was all nerves. The Cossack talked to him, and Nada coaxed, and it was one of the ponies that missed a short jump and hurtled, screaming, down the face of the cliff, with a thunder of rock and loosened dirt.

The charger took the jump with a yard to spare, and it needed all Nada's weight on the rein to keep him from plunging ahead with the sudden spurt of a high-strung horse that thinks danger lurks behind him.

"Well done!" Kirdy cried, as the girl quieted the bay stallion. "Here Otrèpiev lost one of his mounts." A speck on the valley bed had caught his eye—a cluster of vultures that had dined on something.

Obviously something a day or more old, because a score of the flapping creatures rose into the air to investigate the Tartar pony that had finally stopped, an inert huddle, not so far away. The distance was too great to make out whether they had been feeding on a horse or a man, but Kirdy prayed that it was a horse and that Otrèpiev, who had led him across the Earth Girdle, still lived on the plateau, now near at hand.

And Nada read his mind with a single glance.

"What will you do, White Falcon, when you meet with Otrèpiev?"

"Bid him to sabers."

Both had jumped to the same conclusion at once. If Otrèpiev and his companion were living and on the plateau, they might well have noticed the fall of the pony and the miniature avalanche that set a hundred echoes flying. If they happened to be on the cliff side of the city, they might have seen the two pursuers.

"So the Cossack says." Nada tossed her head. "And what, O my hero, if both fools die—and I am left alive with the tsar's dog, who has been trained since birth to torture, and who carries a sword as long as himself? Take heed! If you must fight Otrèpiev, agree with him as to that. But first do you and he and the other band together to journey safely back across the Earth Girdle."

Kirdy frowned and shook his head. The sun was well up by now and the glare of it against the white limestone had made him throw off the tattered sable coat, so that he walked in a worn red shirt, slashed and stained where he had been wounded. His lean head was dark as the long hair that fell over one shoulder—Nada, considering him, thought that he did look like a falcon, swift and merciless.

"If Otrèpiev were a true Cossack, or even a *boyarin* of honor, I would do that," he made response curtly. "But he has betrayed men too often."

"And if he comes to you sick, asking aid?"

Kirdy laughed grimly.

"Let him first do it."

"He has another with him, and he himself is a match for you. What if the other draws and strikes when your blade is turned against Otrèpiev?"

Again the Cossack laughed shortly, touching the splendid hilt of his curved sword.

"God gives. I desire only that."

Under veiling lashes, the girl looked at him steadily, and a sudden purpose made her tingle.

"Nada," Kirdy said gravely, "whatever happens, you must not draw that plaything, the yataghan."

"Could I draw against the man in black with the sword that is longer than I?" she demanded reasonably. "And would you suffer me to stand against Otrèpiev?"

She sighed and fell silent—unwontedly silent. Kirdy became grimly intent on their surroundings. They had reached the foot of the ramp, and here a shelving ledge allowed them to walk opposite the plateau.

They discovered what had been concealed from sight until now. Somewhere in the mountains a river had its source, a river that foamed down in flood when Winter loosened its hold on the heights, but that now was no more than a bed of round stones far below them.

This river ran, in season, between the mountainside and the mass of the plateau where the city stood. During countless ages it had eaten through the soft stone and clay until it formed a chasm. The chasm was thirty yards or so across—its depth unguessable.

And now there was no doubt at all that the city on the plateau had been built by men. The ruin of a wall ran along the rim across the defile. The wall had been built of hewn stone blocks, and the Cossack knew that this city of the Golden Horde had been invulnerable to attack. No enemy, advancing down the ramp and forming, shelterless, along the ledge, could have stormed the city wall.

The other three sides of the plateau looked unclimbable. Probably there was—or had been—a way down from the city to the lower valley. But this other road, being hung on the face of a cliff, could not be stormed. The city, then, could not have been taken by an enemy from without. Why had it been abandoned? Kirdy was too busy finding a way across the chasm to wonder.

His search for a while was fruitless. The river that had cut the plateau from the mountain a thousand centuries ago, had done its work well—except at one spot. Here he had noticed twin gate towers rising on the other side. Since these towers must have defended the entrance, he led the way along the ledge toward them, praying that the bridge, or whatever it might be, was still standing.

So at midday they reached the gate and found not a bridge man-made, but an arch of limestone that spanned the chasm.

Once the river must have plunged underground here—or dipped below a broad shelf of rock to thunder over a fall. The rock bridge had been worn by the elements until at the middle a tall man's arms might have spanned it. Also, it had been eaten down to the center.

In the white dust atop the limestone were the tracks of a horse and two men, leading fairly through the opening between the towers—where a barrier of wood and iron must have stood in other years.

"Go last, Nada!" Kirdy swept the ruined wall, the expanse between the towers, with a swift glance and started down the natural bridge, leading the charger. If his enemies were hidden in the ruins with so much as a pistol or a bow between them, he would fare badly; but he felt no fear, and the proof of it was that the charger followed him willingly, with only a pricking of ears and shortening of strides. The ponies ambled across indifferently, and Nada brought up the rear, laughing.

A blazing sun, beating on the white dust of streets and the gray and red ruins, half blinded them, and a vagrant wind clutched at them. They stood within sight of what had been the *registan*, the open square of the city.

Here a gray scum of tamarisk impeded progress, and the crumbling stone was covered with thorn and creepers. A sluggish gray snake with mottled red back crept past their feet. Remembering that little water remained in the goatskins, Kirdy investigated a pool of water that lay between two houses. It was bordered with sparkling salt incrustations, and small plants covered with brilliant orange and red berries. A glance convinced the Cossack that the water was undrinkable, the berries inedible.

Then his head jerked up, and the horses moved restlessly.

"O—ho—o! O—HO—O! O—ho!"

Someone had laughed and started up the echoes again. It was a mad, exulting laugh that seemed anything but human. It might mean that they were both watched and mocked, or their presence entirely unsuspected. Nada shivered and drew closer to Kirdy.

"Let us go to the palace. I think it is yonder on the height. From there we can see."

Taking the horses, which were as precious as life itself, the Cossack wound through vine-cumbered alleys and over fallen walls to an edifice that was marked by several stone columns, still standing. He avoided the *registan* and the wider streets, and only paused when in a bed of clay or sand he saw scattered bones that had fallen away from the skeleton of a man.

Not long before, he had come upon rows of tombs—square chambers of granite sunk into the earth and surmounted by stone pyramids. Several of these tombs stood open, and he had gone into one.

"An evil fate came upon this place," he muttered to Nada. "Here be many bodies lying in the houses, and few in the tombs. How did it happen that the men of the Horde died in dwellings and were not buried?"

Nada only shook her head. But when they had climbed out of the alleys to a brick roadway that led up to a granite-flagged courtyard, she gasped. The place was large enough for the tents of a whole tribe.

Slender aspens and twisted oaks, thrusting through the stones, had grown to full stature in the years since the city had been deserted. And from the courtyard a stairway of veined marble ascended to the pillars.

At the summit of the stair Kirdy pushed aside a mesh of undergrowth and stepped through to what had been an anteroom of the palace. From here other stairs led up to the central hall, marked by the columns still standing and by others like prone giants, fallen across the ruins.

He was hidden from the sight of anyone in the city below by the fringe of tamarisks and trees around the knoll. But by climbing to the dais at the far end he had a view of the more distant portion of the city, and the first thing he saw was a line of smoke rising from an open spot. A horse was picketed near the smoke, and the horse was not saddled.

"*Hai*," he cried, "there is the camp of Otrèpiev." Although he watched attentively for some moments, he could see no men moving among the ruins. Nada sat down, chin on hand, to gaze up at the Earth Girdle they had left that morning—the bulwarks of mighty mountains, rising into wisps of clouds, through which appeared at times the snow of the summits. The sun shone out of a blazing sky, and eagles, floating against the gray veil of mist, were sharply etched as black jewels sewn upon silk.

So Nada mused. But Kirdy, striding up and down the dais, was burning with impatience.

"It is the end of the road," he laughed. "I shall seek the false Dmitri, and you—"

"I shall stay here with the horses."

He turned in his stride to frown and think. He did not want to part from the girl, but to take her and the horses—no, the danger was below.

"Abide here, then," he advised her, "and if God sends misfortune to me and I come not by the next dawn, take the stallion and go up the pass without halting."

"God and His holy angels keep you, White Falcon."

So she responded, without looking at him, her lips close pressed and her eyes shut. She heard the grating of steel as he tried his sword in its scabbard, and his steps moving away, down the hall of the columns.

He left the palace at a spot where he could not be seen, and struck through the hollows until he reached the edge of the *registan* again. Here he sighted the thin line of smoke and ran, crouching, from ruin to ruin, stopping at times to listen with his head close to the ground.

But Nada remained without moving, chin on hand, gazing up at the Earth Girdle, listening to the horses that were grazing upon the bushes and scattered grass. So she sat, wondering why she had determined to stay where she was, in spite of the grief that chilled her veins and heart, until a voice near at hand aroused her.

"So, little Nada, you have kept your promise. Behold, I have kept mine!"

Blinking—for the sun was full in her eyes—she turned and saw Gregory Otrèpiev sitting on a block of marble upon the dais and smiling at her.

His powerful arms rested on his knees, and the woman in her took note of the rents and tears in the long coat that covered his rusted armor. A scruff of beard had grown over his chin, and his long blue eyes gleamed from his dark skin.

"My court," he said, "is small, yet when you sit at my feet I am more honored than any emperor."

Her lips parted to cry out, when she remembered that the Cossack was far beyond hearing. Then, too, she saw Otrèpiev's courtier. A man taller than Kirdy leaned on a five-foot sword, holding in the crook of his arm the silvered casque with the eagle crest of the false Dmitri. His black satin garments were gray with dust, and his drawn, sun-blackened face was expressionless as a mask. His lips smiled.

"My armorer, my counselor, my equerry and executioner!" Otrèpiev waved a scarred hand at the torturer. "Faith, lass, he stands upon the edge of madness. 'Twas his laugh enriched this silence a while ago and spurred your Cossack on to stalk my camp. I love him like a brother." His restless eyes roamed the ruins. "By the Horned One, here are five good horses!"

"Have you ever kept a promise, False Dmitri?"

"Rarely—only when it suited me. The weak promise when they have no other surety. Nay, I said to you—'I will make myself master of that city beyond the Earth Girdle.' Have you forgotten? I think not. So I sit on what is left of the throne."

"Yet you are not master here."

Otrèpiev considered her.

"I could find fault in you for telling me of this place—Satan's play-ground! What a city! Majestic it may be, but empty—too empty."

"Have you not seen, or heard, its people?"

"If you mean the wild Cossack—I saw him climbing up the pass with you. It was a goodly sight, but it puzzled me. In the battle of the tribes I saw him riding at me, and how was I to know whether the pair of you came to render allegiance or put me in my grave? Which was it?"

Nada's dark eyes surveyed him steadily, and she did not speak.

"Well," Otrèpiev mused aloud, "if the fellow is your lover, you must have lost your wit. When I found your city to be an empty shell, I occupied myself with preparing a reception for my pursuers, watching you descend that accursed path. I sent my faithful servitor to set up a camp within plain sight—a smoking fire and a foundered horse. By now your Cossack is squatting on his haunches near it—we saw him circle it. But I was here, behind this dais, before you came. When he returns to you we will be waiting."

"The people of this city are the dead. We heard them ride upon the Earth Girdle."

"Doubtless. They did not trouble my dreams. But we shall strike east from here. The valley below has a pleasant look."

"You are not master of this place, Otrèpiev, because it is peopled with the dead!"

The man on the marble throne slab smiled.

"I remember now, little Nada, you said that peace was to be found here. A beautiful girl may be pardoned a bad jest—"

"But you are not dead, Otrèpiev—how can you be lord of this Horde?"

"Ah, you are grinding wheat to look for chaff. What matter, if you have come to sit at my feet?"

The close-set blue eyes blazed upon her restlessly.

Whenever Otrèpiev spoke, neither eyes nor hands were still, and yet his voice was full and deep. A man of great physical strength, acting impulsively, he made no secret of his delight in Nada's beauty and youth. He addressed her as a child to be humored—a woman to be desired.

He glanced down at the ruined hall of columns.

"Eh, little Nada, the weeds and lizards keep the court of ancient kings. Was this place built by an emperor of Cathay, or by the Macedonian, Alexander, who made himself master of the world? I might have aroused the Muscovites as he did the Macedonians, except for one thing—superstition. The beast would not come out of its stall! I showed them the path of glory, and they hearkened to the chants of bald priests. I brought to Moscow a Polish bride, and they cringed. Fools!"

He shrugged and smiled wryly.

"How fared the lady of Sandomir? She was a painted stick beside you, Nada, lass. Eh—eh!"

The girl stood up, tossing back the mass of gleaming hair from her shoulders. The heat of the day had been so great she had thrown off her *svitza* and was clad only in white linen shirt and slender embroidered vest, over the loose Turkish trousers.

"A handsome Cossack—hi, Feodor!" Otrèpiev looked up at the silent headsman.

"I am here," Nada said, "at your feet. But if you would so much as touch me with your hand, you must first overpower me with the sword."

Otrèpiev frowned, and then his brow cleared.

"Why, so you said in the steppes. I will do it at once, my lass."

"And will you wear mail, my lord, in facing a woman's sword?"

For an instant Otrèpiev hesitated, and Nada laughed at him.

"Do you fear the Cossack, then, O my emperor?"

"Not I—nor shall you mock me."

Otrèpiev cast loose his cloak, and the tall Feodor assisted him out of the rusty mail shirt.

Otrèpiev turned to the brief bit of weapon play with the relish that he felt in anything that diverted his thoughts. His restlessness covered black brooding, and he dreaded to be left to himself; when another was with him he talked constantly, and until his flight from the Tartars he drank heavily of the spirits among his stores. He had been morose since the defeat of the Turkomans, whom he had expected to sweep over Tevakel Khan, but Nada's coming had restored his good humor. It was a good omen— the girl and fresh horses.

"To one, death," Nada breathed, "to the other, life!"

Otrèpiev lowered his blade and glanced at her keenly. Her face was ashen, and her lips trembled as she spoke the Cossack salutation before a duel.

"Answer me one question!" he demanded. "Do you love this Cossack?"

Nada flushed and met his eyes fairly.

"Aye—the White Falcon has my love. When we met in Moscow he was master of my heart, and it was to follow him that I joined you in the steppe. You—the traitor that played at kingship. In the steppes he took leadership among the Tartars, and it was he who overthrew you and the Turkomans. But he has thought that I serve you, and he has no faith in me."

"The devil!" said Otrèpiev thoughtfully.

The next instant, with eye and foot and hand, he was fighting for his life.

Nada had sprung at him as a Cossack rushes, recklessly, raining cut upon cut. Surprised, Otrèpiev gave ground a little, and settled himself to parry the flashing blade that darted at his throat and slashed at his side.

Again he stepped back, and Nada pressed in, her eyes narrowed, her lip gripped between her teeth.

Once he parried and tried a quick twist of the saber that should have disarmed her, but the yataghan slid clear.

The brain of Otrèpiev fought coolly, telling him that his saber was heavier than the girl's weapon, his strength greater. He only needed to ward off her first rush, and then—

Again Nada pressed him back, making no effort to parry, but striving to thrust inside his close-drawn guard.

"The girl is mad!" he thought, and then the evil impulse of desire that always lurked behind his brain seized upon him. The struggle had stirred him—he wanted to drive his blade past Nada's weapon, to strike it deep into her breast. To slay always delighted him, and, after all, if this wild Cossack lass loved the warrior, she might work him harm. Aye, better deal with her as he desired!

A moment later Otrèpiev stepped back, smiling, and lowered his saber, glancing at the darkened tip.

Nada's yataghan clattered on the stones, and she bent her head, fumbling with a long lock of hair that had fallen over her shoulder. Gathering the golden tresses in her hand, she pressed them against her side, where Otrèpiev's saber had pierced under the heart.

Then she sank to her knees and lay down, as if utterly weary, on the stones. Tall Feodor came and bent over her with professional interest.

"Not enough," he spoke for the first time, "my prince, your blade did not go deep. To make sure, another thrust is best." Otrèpiev stared eagerly at the girl's drawn face, the pallid lips, and the circles under her eyes.

"Keep back, you dog," he muttered at his follower.

And after a moment Feodor touched his shoulder.

"Great Prince, guard yourself!" Startled, Otrèpiev heard the impact of boots on the stones, and looked up as Kirdy leaped a fallen column.

The Cossack must have seen Nada as he leaped, because he came at them without pause or spoken word. He was panting from the long run, and his sword arm quivered.

He swerved toward Otrèpiev, and his heavy blade rang on the Muscovite's saber as the other stepped back to put space between them and Feodor.

"Slash him down, dog!" he panted at the headsman, who was swinging up his broadsword silently.

Kirdy heard and swerved away as Feodor struck, the long blade hissing through the air.

"From two sides!" snarled Otrèpiev. "Come at him from the other side!" As he cried out, he parried swiftly, because Kirdy had put him between himself and the headsman.

For an instant Otrèpiev could do no more than ward the whirling blade that sought head and throat as a wolf strikes. Meanwhile Feodor circled warily, swinging up his broadsword. Kirdy did not seem to notice him—certainly did not glide away as before.

Feodor tensed his arms, and the Cossack leaped high in the air, turning as he did so. His saber hissed down and in, and for an instant Feodor stood poised on massive limbs.

The man's head fell down on his chest, held only by one of the throat muscles—and the throat had been all but cut through.

"Ha!" Otrèpiev gasped.

He heard Feodor's sword and then the giant body fall to the stone flags; but his saber was locked fast by the Cossack's blade. For a moment the eyes of the two, beaded with sweat and bloodshot, glared, and then Kirdy wrenched free.

A wave of hot anger swept over Otrèpiev, and fear beat at his heart like a hammering pulse. With a cry he sprang forward, and his right hand, grasping the saber, flew off and slid along the stone slabs. Kirdy struck twice at the bent head of his foe, and, cut through the temples on either side, the body of Otrèpiev stumbled and dropped beside his henchman.

Kirdy wasted no second's thought upon him. Running to Nada, he cut the fastenings of her vest and drew it off, then gently pulled away the hand and the clotted tresses. With quivering fingers he felt the narrow wound.

Then he turned her on her left side, to check the inward bleeding, and as he did so, her hand touched his arm and felt up it until she could stroke his head.

"The end—" her lips moved— "of the road."

The Cossack glanced around wildly. To heal such a wound in a comrade he would have given a draft of powder mixed in vodka. But he had neither powder nor vodka, and he did not know what more to do, except to bring water.

"O Father and Son, hear me," he cried. "The spirit of little Nada flutters like a pigeon in the storm wind. It goes, her spirit, from my hands. Hearken, O White Christ, and thou, souls of the Cossack heroes who dwell in the regions above—there is faith in this maiden, and knightly honor. Did she not draw her sword bravely? Is it fitting she should die by the sword of a traitor and a dog?"

When he returned with water, Nada drank a little, and signed for him to bend closer.

"I love you, White Falcon—even your shadow and the horse you ride. I stayed behind because I feared he was hiding nearby. Truly, then, I thought I might slay him, so they could not fall upon you. But—promise me you will not leave me, White Falcon. Hold me in your arms and take me from this place, down to the valley, my Falcon."

The rush of words ceased and her lips quivered.

Kirdy looked up. Already vultures were dropping down on the columns and the throne slab. The wind threshed through the dry growth, and up the Earth Girdle clouds of driven dust hid the pass and the heights.

"Aye, little Nada," he said, gently, "I promise."

Here was something he could do. Yet no living man could carry the suffering girl up that wind-whipped ramp to the desolate pass—or make the horses follow. They had made the descent, but they could not go back that way. When he had circled Otrèpiev's bait of a camp, and had noticed that the fire was left to die and the horse likewise, he had suspected the trap set for him and had gone back instantly, running like one possessed when he heard the clash of weapons. But before then he had seen what Otrèpiev had discovered, a road winding down the east face of the plateau.

So, only stopping to bind Feodor's great sword and Otrèpiev's helmet on the charger's saddle, he tied up Nada's wound with strips of his shirt and lifted her in his arms, keeping the stallion's rein in his fingers. The ponies trailed after, and no sooner had they moved away than the vultures closed in upon the bodies of the false Dmitri and his solitary companion, the torturer.

"It was a dog's burial," Kirdy thought, "but it is well suited to Gregory Otrèpiev, because he has left his bones in the hall of a king. Bold he was, but not a good Cossack. He kept faith with no one, and he handled a sword badly." Weary beyond knowing, Kirdy strode on into darkness and wind. The night had brought the first of the Autumn's storms, and gusts of rain whipped the mesh of the forest over his head. The burden of the unconscious girl had numbed his arms long since, but as long as he could feel Nada's heart pulsing slowly under his fingers he kept on.

When neither wind, nor the bitter air of the heights that hinted at snow penetrated to him, he halted and laid Nada down in the darkness, upon ferns and pine needles. When he was able to raise his arms again, he took down the broadsword from the stallion's saddle, and groped for branches and fallen wood.

A fire kindled and fed to roaring flames, he shook the stupor of sleep from his brain and hacked down young firs, working incessantly until he put together the framework of a low hut and covered three sides with branches. Then he took the saddle from the stallion and the packs from the two ponies that had followed patiently, to be unloaded. He watched them go down at once toward the muttering rush of a stream.

Then he hurried back to listen to the girl's even breathing. And the glare of exhaustion and anger left his dark eyes.

"She sleeps, the little Nada," he smiled. "Eh, there is faith in her, in all things. When the Muscovites would have taken her captive, she met them

with the sword. With the dawn she will open her eyes." He glanced up
at the whirling sparks. The hut was in a grove of gigantic deodars, whose
branches rose beyond the firelight, whose tips threshed under the wind
gusts that could not move the massive trunks.

A light flurry of snow came down on the Cossack—snow that powdered
the hut without melting. He looked out at it thoughtfully.

"Aye, the pass through the Earth Girdle is closed. And here there is no
road of any kind."

He was in a new world, where the sun rises. And Nada had given him
her love. What matter the way, if they could ride forth together with no
shadow of doubt between them and all the unknown ahead?

It was the next Summer that Girai the ax-man came to the yurta of old
Tevakel Khan and squatted down at the edge of the white horse skin, an-
nouncing that he came as a bearer of tidings.

"Upon thee, O Khan of the Altyn-juz, Lord of the Lesser Horde, master of the plain, mirror of the faith, tree of the fruit of understanding—
the salute!

"The words of caravan men from Cathay have reached my ears, and
this is the tale:

"Where the forest meets the desert, far—far—these men beheld a pair
of the *tengri* that come down at seasons from the heights and are visible to
mortal eyes, as is well known. The tale was that one of these spirits was a
man, wearing a silver helmet and bearing a sword as long as a spear. The
other was a woman with hair like gold, glittering in the sun. Their faces
were dark, yet in their voices was no sorrow. They asked, 'What land is
this?' And the men of the caravan, being fearful, kneeled at a distance.

"Because, O Khan, this twain spoke in pride and had the bearing of
kings. So the caravan men went away swiftly, leaving gifts, thinking that
they had seen the *tengri* that come down from the high places.

"And my thought is this—that the two are they I led up to the Earth Girdle in the month of the Ox. They followed thine enemy the *fanga nialma*,
and surely they have overcome him, since they carry his sword and helmet. They have set at naught his magic. And now, being spirits, they wander without fear. That is my word, O Khan, my master."

With the tranquility of the very old, Tevakel Khan considered this,
looking into the fire.

"It is evident," he said at length, "that this youth and maiden have crossed the Earth Girdle and passed through the city of the dead. It is known to me that in former days this city was built by our ancestors. And treachery arose in it as a viper lifts its head. The Khan of all the Hordes was slain, and his warriors, and brother fought with brother, until no more than a few families lived to flee. So, it is accursed and the unburied dead ride about it at night."

"And the youth and the maiden?" Girai demanded, for his curiosity was very great.

Tevakel Khan smiled.

"Surely they are living mortals, or the caravan men would have seen them at night, not during the hours of the day." He meditated upon this for a moment and came to a conclusion.

"In this twain there was great faith and little fear. *Kai*, the wolves harmed them not, and the dead passed them by. To such as they, God hath given the keys of the unseen!"

The Outrider

Chapter I
A Cossack of the Don

Ayub was in Winter quarters. That is, he had built himself a hut in one of the *balkas* of the river Dnieper. The *balkas*, being gullies under the flood level, were filled with brush and willow growth and were likewise sheltered from the Winter winds that swept the surface of the steppe.

A Cossack—and Ayub was a Cossack of the Don—was able to get shelter and rations for himself even on the shore of an ice-bound river. Ayub had built his hut of wattle and clay, but it kept out the wind; his fireplace was part oven and he slept on top of it. He had made himself a sturgeon spear and had haggled out of the village Tartars a hunting bow with double-headed arrows. When he needed silver he worked at the town of Kudak, a league down the frontier road, at the smithy when the smith was drunk.

But Ayub preferred his hut under the black willows, and the silence of the *balka*, to the bustle and argument of the town. He was lonely, not for the peasants and tradespeople of Kudak, but for his brother Cossacks.

He was two score and ten years old, and most of his life had been passed in the war encampments of the Cossacks. He had had many brothers-in-arms. Khlit, called the Wolf, and Kirdy, who had wandered in out of the East. But Khlit had vanished again, going off somewhere alone after Kirdy was lost in the steppe. And Demid, the sword slayer, had laid his bones in the deserts by the inland seas. Ayub was left solitary.

True, he could have gone to the camp of the Zaporogians—where the picked men of the Cossacks reveled and gathered together to ride to the wars. But the pain of rheumatism was in his bones; at times his sight grew misty. He was an old Cossack, a man who had served his time, a gray-beard who liked a seat at the fires where others would listen to his tales and see that his cup did not lack vodka.

Moreover, the Cossacks who spread their blankets in the barracks now did not know him. Men who had gone with him on that ride with the witch of Aleppo—who had raided Arap Muhammad Khan—they were gone elsewhere, if they still lived. Among the Zaporogians, Ayub would appear as a stranger. And he did not relish that.

Most important of all, at the moment he lacked both a horse and a sword. He had drunk up his last horse at Kudak, and his saber had been stolen that night when he was stretched out in the straw of the tavern stables. Perhaps Gypsies had taken it to sell to the Jews. Gone also was everything worthwhile in his garments—his silk neckcloth and the Persian shawl that had served him for a girdle.

"To the devil with them all," he had thought. "I'll find others."

But finding others was not so easy as in former years, not so easy in a trading post like Kudak on the frontier. Once Ayub would have gone on the bend and turned out the whole garrison of such a town and come out of it with an officer's sword in each hand, singing the march of the Don Cossacks. He did not lie when he told how he had stolen a racing horse from the sultan's string near Stamboul.

No, he could not wander off to the Zaporogians in a shabby gray coat, unadorned, and a black sheepskin *kalpak*, without a horse between his knees or a saber on his hip. So he had gone, alone, into Winter quarters to see what God might give, there on the ice-bound Dnieper, that year in the mid-seventeenth century.

It was a dull twilight, that one. The snow seemed to give off more light than the sky. The dry rushes crackled under his heavy boots when he plodded into the gully, towing behind him a long bundle of brush looped in his lariat. It was not cheerful work, gathering firewood for himself, alone, but he knew how cold it would be before morning. The cold was the breath of the steppe itself—that almost treeless plain stretching from river to river, hundreds of leagues to the east. Ayub knew it well—a glory of lush grass and wildflowers in the early Spring; a parched plain, wind-tortured in the Summer heat. And now under heavy snow, almost untracked. The *saiga* antelope had vanished elsewhere, the cattle of the frontier posts were penned, and only the wolfpacks ranged the white expanse with the herds of wild horses.

No king was master of the steppe. It stretched, partially desolate and forbidding, to the warmer shores of Charnomar, the southern salt sea. The river was its western border, and to this bank of the Dnieper the great landlords of Poland laid claim; but beyond the river was only what men called the wilderness.

And no Cossack could remember when the steppe had been different in any way. Over its surface moved at times fighting men, but not disciplined armies. They were bands of Tartars on the raid, Cossack patrols looking for spoil or vengeance, moving villages of slant-eyed Kalmuks. Along the rivers outlaws hid and banded together to fall like vultures upon the boats that passed up to the rapids when the ice left the waters. Into the steppe men fled from pursuit, and out of it at times were driven captives to be sold in Warsaw or Stamboul, as the case might be.

"*Hai*," Ayub grunted, all thought of the wilderness and other years leaving his mind. He dropped the rope and squinted through the shadows of the gully.

A pony stood before the entrance of his hut, and the pony was saddled. Unless it had strayed from the road, he had a visitor.

"Who are you?" he shouted.

And a soft voice answered from the hut—

"*Ai kunak*—O brother—it is no one, only a message."

Ayub went nearer without haste and looked at the horse, a shaggy little beast with only a sheepskin for a saddle.

"Eh, show yourself. Don't hide like a dog."

A spark flickered in the darkness of the hut entrance, and in a moment a boy's smooth face appeared, outlined in a red glow. The stranger was blowing upon tinder held in the hollow of his hand. When he came out a lighted horn lantern swung in his hand, and Ayub saw that he was a Gypsy lad, wrapped in fox and marmot skins. Without saying anything, the Cossack took the lantern and inspected the one room of the hut.

"The saddle is there, *kunak*," the Gypsy whispered.

This saddle was the one valuable thing Ayub owned—a fine bit of Persian leather work, of gilt shagreen with silver inlaid horn. The night the Cossack's sword had been stolen, he had been sleeping with his head on the green saddle.

"What was the message?" he asked.

The Gypsy's eyes lingered on the saddle and lifted sidewise to Ayub's lined face.

"A good horse is to be shod," he said, and repeated emphatically the words, 'a good horse.' "I have seen him, a piebald Kabardian racer, of the breed of wolf chasers. Swift-paced and enduring and wise I know him to be."

Ayub shook his head.

"What lie is this, O thief of the pastures? No such horse is in Kudak."

"Only listen, Cossack. I have seen him in the tavern stables. Zut! Strangers are in Kudak, barons, nobles, and they are outlanders. Omelnik the smith lies drunk in the alley of the tavern." The Gypsy felt in his girdle and showed the Cossack a silver coin. "This was given me, to find a smith. We must go, now, or the Pole will be angry."

"What Pole?"

"He who gave me the half-thaler—the owner of the Kabardian."

"But what are Poles doing out here in the steppe?"

"Do I know?"

The Gypsy moved his shoulders idly and smiled. No love had ever been lost between the Cossacks of the steppe and the soldiers and landlords of great Poland.

"Listen, O my brother. The horse is, as I have said, a good horse. Tomorrow—soon—the Poles will mount and go on. They are many, with splendid sleds and enough baggage for a king. Go with them for awhile and surely it will happen that thou wilt find the Kabardian unguarded and then—where would they find thee?"

"Am I a horse stealing Tzigani? To the devil with thy tricks!" Ayub frowned. "Still, I would like to see the horse, Poles or no Poles."

He would be given silver and could drink brandy at the tavern. As for the horse, he would not put his hand to that kind of stealing. It was one thing to lift ponies from the Tartar herds or the Turkish lines; it was quite another matter to sneak off with a merchant's beast in camp.

Ayub swung his leg over the Gypsy's pony and they moved off at a foot pace down the gully. As they climbed to the road the chill wind whirled through their garments, and both the Cossack and the Gypsy glanced over their shoulders. It was an old habit—to look up and down the gray stretch of the river, to see whether the shore was clear.

But no dark figures showed against the white line of the far bank, and the old warrior and the boy went on without speaking.

A bundle of pine knots chained to a stake flamed beside Ayub as he worked by the horse. With a chisel he cut a piece of stiff leather to fit one of the stallion's hoofs, and then shaped three narrow strips of the iron-like leather.

"What are those?" demanded the Cossack who watched him.

"Cleats," Ayub explained, between the nails in his teeth. "Eh, the snow is hard."

The other Cossack wore a wolf skin cap and a black wool coat and varnished boots; Ayub suspected that he was an under-officer of a cavalry regiment that had not seen much service out on the frontier. His name was Chort. Also he was the aide of the man who owned the horse.

And the piebald stallion was, as the Gypsy had said, a splendid beast. Higher than most Kabardians, his slender forelegs and arched loins promised speed, and the powerful shoulders and hard flesh told of endurance. His lean muzzle swerved and brushed Ayub's shoulder.

"*Akai,*" grinned the big Cossack. "He watches me! Who is in command of your detachment?"

Chort's plump and ruddy face twisted reflectively.

"I don't know."

Ayub warded off a swish of the wolf chaser's long tail.

"You're wet behind the ears! An *essual* of light cavalry doesn't know who to take orders from! Isn't your officer in command?"

"The sir colonel? The little father?" Chort pondered. "If God grant it, he's in command."

Under his wide mustache Ayub grinned. He had known officers who liked to lick the cup and at such times were not in shape to give an order. But this was a large detachment—he had seen carts upended down the length of the street, and horses were picketed all around the church. Moreover, he had seen the fires of a Tartar bivouac. Now the frontier was snowbound; even the Gypsies had not heard of any raiders coming in from the steppe. He wondered what the detachment intended doing and why it was in the town of Kudak.

"Who else gives orders?" he asked.

"Well, there's his Excellency the Prince, and his high Mightiness."

"What kind of men are they—soldiers?"

"*Tá nitchevo,*" responded Chort. "What's the difference? They're ambassadors."

"Not kings—emperors?" Ayub pushed the stallion aside and rubbed his knees.

"Nay, they are ambassadors of his serene Majesty, the King of Po-land."

"Devil take your serene mighty ambassadors!"

Ayub was sure the Cossack officer was making game of him. Ambassadors went to the courts of other kings and lords, not to the edge of the steppe.

"Hai, they must be going to Satan, or off the end of the earth."

He stopped abruptly because Chort, who had been staring at him, open mouthed, was now gazing fixedly over his shoulder—and had jumped to his feet, taking the pipe from his lips.

Ayub turned around and found himself looking squarely into the eyes of a stranger. The big Cossack stood four inches over six feet, and the stranger lacked no more than two inches of his height. An officer, Ayub knew at once, by the silver crown in his lynx skin hat, and by the sheen of the long gray cloak that swung from his wide shoulders. An officer, moreover, who had chosen his garments with care. Ayub noticed his knee boots of soft red morocco and the linked silver plates of his sword belt.

But the officer turned his attention to the horse. He ran his hand down the piebald's muzzle and picked up the rear foot that the Cossack had shod, looked attentively at the cleats. Then he lifted, one after the other, the remaining three hoofs and made certain that similar cleats had been nailed on them all.

"Well done," he said briefly, and pulled a wallet from his belt.

Out of it he took a silver Dutch dollar and gave this to the Cossack.

Before Ayub could think of anything to say, the officer turned on his heel and walked out into the darkness. Chort released pent-up breath.

"That's the sir colonel," he whispered, "the little father."

"He comes like an owl, without a light. May the fiends take me, if he's a Russian, to come out to look at a horse. Or a Pole," Ayub added, "to leave his glass and fire and walk out in this cold."

The silver coin burned in Ayub's fingers. Within the tavern there was a fire, and no doubt spirits were being poured like water, with such a company in the taproom. He dropped his tools and hastened into the dark-ness after the colonel.

Threading his way through the wagons he approached the door, through which came the murmur of voices and the strumming of a *bandura*.

"Eh, things are warming up," he thought, eager for his first taste of brandy.

A shadow loomed up beside him, and a harsh voice challenged:
"Not tonight. Go!"

Ayub made out the figure of a guard, armed with what seemed to be a long pike.

"How not tonight?" he asked bluntly. "My gullet's dry as the hide of a dead cow."

"Because there are nobles within. It is not permitted."

The Cossack swallowed a hot retort. These Poles came from afar. They claimed, no doubt, to be masters of this town of Kudak and all the Cossack settlements along the frontier. But the Cossacks had grazed their cattle over the steppe and had hunted these lands and fought off the Tartars for generations without bothering their heads about the Polish nobility. And Ayub was thirsty.

The sentry, being kept out in the cold, was in no mood for beguilement. A dozen years ago Ayub would have pushed in through the door and let happen what might happen. Now he held his peace and went around to the rear where a door opened into the clatter of a busy kitchen.

"Hi, thou vagabond!" a woman's voice hailed him. "This is no night for the likes of you steppe dogs. Away with ye!"

Had the tavern-keeper said that, Ayub would have dropped him into the well. But the wife of the tavern-keeper was a shrew with a high voice and the kitchen was filled with other women.

"Eh, old woman," Ayub muttered persuasively. "Look, here is silver."

"To the devil with thy silver. We are serving his high Mightiness. We'll have no Cossack drunk on the floor."

"May the foul fiends sit upon ye," Ayub muttered. "When a song is wanted, or a wagon to be mended—'Where's that fine lad, the Cossack?' Now when his Mightiness is sprawled out in the room, it's, 'Get out, dog!'"

Nursing his growing rage and trying to forget both thirst and emptiness, he swung away from the door and made his way again through the wagons to the front. Here, as he was seeking for the street, he stopped suddenly and sniffed strongly. The black bulk of a sledge was beside him, and from the sledge came a familiar smell. Ayub went closer and sniffed again.

"*Gorilka*," he muttered. "Corn brandy." He went on to the next loaded sledge. "Honey mead and wine. His Mightiness takes his cellar with him."

While he pondered, strongly tempted—if the kegs were not chained he could get one on his shoulder easily enough—he heard the brisk step of the sentry behind him.

"Off to thy kennel, thou thieving dog!"

And in the gleam of starlight, Ayub perceived the steel end of a lance thrust toward him. He said nothing, nor did he move. The anger that heated his veins rushed into his head. In all his fifty years Ayub had never turned his back to a weapon. The sentry, who did not know this, advanced with a swinging step and prodded at him—and that was more than he would endure.

Ayub's arm shot out, his hand closed on the lance shaft behind the head, and he jerked it toward him. The guard, unprepared for this, swung forward with the weapon. And Ayub's other fist crashed against his cheek bone. The man went over backward with a grunt and the lance fell on the snow.

But the sentry was no weakling. Rolling over and drawing his sword, he rushed at the Cossack. And the butt end of the lance smote him above the belt.

Before the other could draw breath or gain his footing again, Ayub had wrenched the sword away and caught the soldier and hoisted him to a massive shoulder. Then, in spite of his captive's shouting and squirming, the big Cossack strode toward the well.

Ayub found it covered with boards, and he was trying to work these loose, when other men ran at him in the darkness. He dropped the battered guard and turned on his new assailants, his fists beating at them until they caught him by the legs. Ayub was no stranger to a mauling fight, and he locked his arms around two of his foes, thrusting his head into their faces. For a moment the group swayed around the well.

Light flared before the Cossack's eyes, and the other men wrenched themselves away. Steel gleamed under his chin, and he saw that two powerful men in a dark uniform held him against the stones of the well with drawn swords. Behind them half a dozen others peered at him, and under a sputtering torch a young noble eyed him with some curiosity.

"What kind of a bear baiting is this?"

The youth drew a sable riding cloak closer about his shoulders and a gold chain gleamed for an instant at this throat. He seemed provoked because the brawl had ended so abruptly.

"Your Highness, he was putting Platovsky down the well."

The guard emerged into the light, bending over, one arm clasped to his middle, his eye bleeding. When he stood before the youth in the sable cloak he straightened, not without a grimace of pain.

"True, your Highness. He was lurking about, trying to get in the tavern, stealing from the carts. I did not like to use steel on such an animal."

"Devil take you!" shouted the Cossack. "I pulled one blade away from you. Give me a saber and I'll put you down again." He turned to the noble. "My Lord, I'm no peasant, but a man who has served—aye, before these pole-bearers of yours were whelped. God is my witness, I've led a regiment into smoke."

The man in the sable cloak lifted his brows, staring at Ayub's shaggy head and shabby gray coat, the worse for the fight. A sudden gust of wind swept the group and he shivered.

"Strip him. Give him fifty lashes and let him go."

Ayub took a step forward and a soldier caught his arms. But he was passive now, and his anger had changed to a gnawing fear. To be stripped and lashed by strangers! If the Turks had taken him captive, that was to be expected. But to be laid out like a slave while Poles looked on over their cups—Some of them had run out with great beakers in their hands and were even now quenching their thirst. The odor of the hot brandy came to Ayub's nostrils.

"My Lord," he begged, "if you are a soldier, grant that I may have a sword and face this man of yours with steel."

The young noble seemed surprised, but before he could speak a voice sounded curt in the shadows beyond the torches.

"Your Highness!"

Ayub saw, walking toward them, the officer who had come to look at the mare, the little father, in whose gray eyes and ruddy, weather-lined face, there was no hint of amusement. In one hand he held the sentry's lance, in the other the sword.

"Are these your weapons, Platovsky?" he asked.

"Aye, Sir Colonel."

"Did this Cossack take them from you?"

The soldier who had been on guard started to speak, then drew himself straighter and nodded. Silence fell upon the group by the well.

"What the devil has this to do with whipping the animal, Stuart?" the youth of the sable cloak demanded.

"A peasant would not have faced weapons, Prince Paul. Besides, this man is here at my summons—shod my horse an hour ago. He may not be a thief."

"But he's a rogue, Stuart—a masterless rogue. If your horse is shod you'll not need him more. *Par dex*, we must have some entertainment."

"Then give him a sword," responded the man called Stuart.

"A duel? A hussar of the guard to face a horse-shoeing vagabond? Oh, 'tis impossible."

"Nay, not impossible," said the colonel quietly, "when the hussar has lost his sword and his lance. Platovsky was on duty."

Men who had been drinking withdrew the cups from their lips and Prince Paul flushed.

"Lord Prince," cried Ayub, "I've faced not only hussars, but a Tartar khan, and more than one sultan, stirrup to stirrup. Only not in a tavern yard."

The thin lips of the youth were touched by a quick smile.

"Rogue thou mayest be," he exclaimed, "but a royal liar thou art. It would be sport—if Platovsky is willing—"

"Only give him a weapon," the hussar responded, "and he will boast no more."

By now the taproom had emptied and a score of men gathered at the well. Some were under-officers of Stuart's regiment, and Ayub saw Chort's red face beside the slender figure of a Tartar *mirza* in *kaftan* and helmet. A strange gathering, he thought. But he was glad that he would not be laid out and lashed.

Servants brought fresh torches and hung them on stakes while Ayub was taking off his heavy coat and rolling up his sleeves. Chort did not come forward to offer his sword, but one of the hussars gave Ayub his blade—a long, straight weapon, similar to Platovsky's.

The Cossack would have liked a curved blade better, and a horse between his knees. He knew that his eyes were not as clear as they had been once, and that his strength would fail in a few moments. Platovsky was in no mood to deal with him lightly, but it did not occur to Ayub to draw back and take his whipping. Only one thing he wanted.

"*Dai vudka!*" he cried.

"As I live, the old clown wants a drink!"

Several beakers were thrust out to him—for a man who stood between life and death was privileged to ask that favor. Ayub selected the largest and seized it in both hands. His head went back and his beard went up, and when he surrendered the beaker he sighed gratefully. The men nearest him nudged one another and whispered, pointed out the corded muscles of his heavy forearms, and the way he selected his ground and took stock of the lights. When he tried the spring of his blade, prince Paul exclaimed:

"Perish me, Stuart—your vagabond acts his part. Ten silver crowns that Platovsky ends him!"

The man called Stuart made no response. Evidently the prince was accustomed to calling his own wagers.

The hussar stood motionless, ten paces away, his sword tip buried in the snow. He had watched every move of the old Cossack but had not troubled to remove either his coat or his fur cap. Ayub, feeling the hot brandy warming his veins, gripped the hilt of his sword and called out:

"To one life! To the other death!"

"The devil!" Murmured Prince Paul. "Begin, gentlemen—or vagabonds."

Platovsky engaged at once, his point sliding forward with effortless ease. A swift slither of steel, a twirl of the hussar's point, and Ayub sprang back, avoiding barely in time the thrust that would have passed below his heart. His lips were drawn back from his teeth and he breathed heavily, while Platovsky, expressionless, seemed not to exert himself at all.

"Look, Stuart," the young noble cried, "your animal gives ground. Faith, again! The ten crowns are mine."

The throng pressed closer, because Ayub had been forced back to the well. The mist of their breathing rose against the smoking flare of the torches.

"Eh, the rogue is pricked," muttered one of the soldiers.

But Ayub had not yet been hurt. Unskilled in the niceties of fencing and realizing Platovsky's power, he leapt suddenly to one side and slashed down at the hussar's guard.

"He uses his blade like a saber," Prince Paul remarked.

With his great strength the Cossack lashed at his adversary. But a hussar of the guard regiment was at home with the curved blade as well as the straight, and Platovsky hardly moved his elbow. Only his wrist turned, and his eyes flickered under drawn brows. The clatter of the blades sounded louder and swifter, for Ayub was slashing recklessly at his foe.

Well content to let the Cossack tire himself out, the husar stood his ground. Ayub's bearded lips drew back from his teeth and his broad cheeks glistened with sweat. He was laboring now, panting as his arm lashed back and forth. His arm burned with a weariness that was like fever. The watchers saw no slackening in the savage sweep of his long blade, but Platovsky parried a cut and lunged up at his throat.

"Double your ten crowns, Stuart?" Prince Paul asked idly.

"Aye!" cried the colonel suddenly.

Someone laughed, as the hussar thrust again, and Ayub crouched like a cat. Then without a sound the giant Cossack leaped up and forward. He rose nearly his own height in the air, gathering his knees under him— and his sword swept up, and down.

It was a trick of the Moslem swordsmen, this leap and slash, and men who had faced it once took care to jump aside. Platovsky did not move. Instinctively he flung up his arms to parry; a quick thrust might have saved him. The Cossack's sword beat down his blade and thudded into his head. The hussar fell heavily to one side and lay without moving.

"U-ha!" Ayub roared. "I said I would put him down again. If this sword had been a saber, he would never rise."

He bent over his adversary, and the watchers stirred out of their amazement to gather around him. The cut, partly deflected by Platovsky's frantic parry, had slashed through the fur cap and had laid bare the skull. Blood soaked the man's hair and streamed upon the snow. But after several moments the injured hussar was still breathing regularly.

"Don't put him to bed in the snow," Ayub remarked, wiping the sweat from his eyes with his long sleeve. "Carry him in and give him vodka and gunpowder to drink, and he'll be looking at the girls again in a week."

Prince Paul and the officers had gone into the tavern. The rest of the crowd followed Platovsky in. No one said anything to Ayub or offered him a glass. Left to his own devices, he put on his coat, shaking his head.

"A fight doesn't warm them up at all," he thought. "They won't talk or offer brandy."

"Hi," the Cossack Chort called out from the door. "The sir colonel wants to see you in his room."

Chapter II
The Colonel

Colonel Duncan Stuart, late of Scotland, and long service in the Thirty Years' War, sat in his shirtsleeves by the open door of his stove and nursed a short clay pipe into cool smoke. There were lines about his eyes and his

firm lips, and his skin was darkened by exposure to cold and wet, but he
was not more than twenty and eight years old. In that age of almost universal war, lads in their teens were given rank, and Stuart had earned his
colonelcy.

He spent many evenings alone, a stranger among men whom he did
not understand, serving a foreign king for money, as did many another
younger son of a Scottish family. He could not respond to the vivacious
talk of the Polish gentlemen over their glasses, and at present Prince Paul
was in a petulant mood, thanks to the misfortune of the hussar Platovsky. Stuart was in command of the military escort of the ambassadors,
but he had discovered that all the hussars of the guard were men of noble
birth who did not take kindly to discipline.

With frank curiosity he gazed at Ayub, who could not stand upright
because the beams of the ceiling were too low for his height. Except for
his head, which was shaved, all but the tuft of hair on the crown, Ayub
might have been an old Highlander. Just so the men of the northern clans
stood—firm footed, hands on hips, open-eyed.

"Sit," he said, motioning toward a bench near the stove.

A peasant would have been dismayed by such an unexpected request,
but the Cossack flung himself down, dropped his *kalpak* on the floor and
spread his booted feet toward the blaze.

"Why did you want to fight the soldier? He nearly put an end to you."

"Well, Sir Colonel, we're always fighting the Poles. They call us devils in stinking sheepskins."

"But his Highness, Prince Paul, is an ambassador, and our men do not
seek quarrels." Stuart motioned with his pipe toward the east. "You've
been in the steppe. Do you know the roads yonder?"

Ayub grinned under his mustache.

"To Hindustan—or the edge of the world."

"To the south—to the sea?"

"Aye, so."

"As far as the city of the Great Khan?"

The Cossack looked up quickly.

"The khan who is master of the Horde and lord of the Krim? Eh, Sir
Colonel, the only Christians who have seen the city of the khan are the
captives, and they've never come back. Once I heard a man say he had
been there, but he lied."

Colonel Stuart reflected for a moment.

"We are going thither."

"*Ekh ma!*" Ayub laughed. "How?"

"Prince Paul and his Excellency, the under chancellor, are ambassadors from the court of Poland to the khan."

Light dawned upon Ayub. After all, Chort had not been pulling his leg. Off the edge of the world to Satan's city. That was it.

Since the day when Genghis Khan and his Mongol host came out of the East and overran the steppe, and the riders of Tamerlane followed, the khan of the Horde had been master of a corner of the earth, down on the southern sea. In times past the khan's people had been called the Golden Horde, but now they were called the Krim, and they gave their name to the land.*

And the Krim was truly a corner of the earth, for it stretched into the sea so far that only in one place could it be entered upon land. One road led into it over this neck of land, a league in width. And across this roadway of earth, Ayub had heard, stretched a deep ditch, filled with the water of the sea. Only a small wooden bridge permitted men to cross it. A wall from one arm of the sea to the other defended the sea moat, and a stone gate stood at the end of the bridge—a gate well guarded by the Krim warriors. It was called the Golden Gate. He did not know why.

More than this, Ayub knew that the city of the khan was called Bagche Serai, the Palace of the Garden. No snow covered it in Winter. Horses could graze on the nearby plains in every month of the year. The gardens of Bagche Serai were always warm, and there, the Cossacks said, the khan had gathered the treasures of centuries of raiding and the fairest women of a dozen lands.

He had met the riders of the Horde at times when the khan lifted his standard and invaded the steppe. Like wolves the wild Tartars came up from the sea, and like wolves they struck at drowsy towns, slashed and stowed away their loot and were gone again into the steppe. But no army had followed the khan into his lair, and only the sultan of the Turks ventured to call upon him for aid.

"Why does the King of Poland send to the khan?" he asked suddenly.

---

*It is still called the Crimea, a great peninsula containing some ten thousand square miles of land, connected with the mainland of modern Russia only by a neck some five miles wide. As late as 1800 this strip was still known as the Golden Gate, and it was narrower then than now.

Colonel Stuart bent forward to take up a glowing coal with the fire tongs. There was an urgent reason why the Poles journeyed to the khan, but this he did not see fit to reveal to the Cossack.

"Our orders are to press on without delay," he responded. "Do you know the road? Is it clear?"

"No road at all, now," Ayub enlightened him. "Only snow trails. When grass comes, it is different; then you could go down the Dnieper to its mouth in boats, or cross the steppe anywhere. Now you will have to feel your way, like a horse crossing a stream."

"Still, the snow is open."

Stuart had been told at court that the khan was the neighbor of Poland, and that once the frontier was crossed he would be in Krim country. He had discovered that there were two or three hundred miles of Winter-bound steppe to be crossed first.

"Aye," said the Cossack dryly, "but it's no Summer garden to pick flowers in. What are your men like, Sir Colonel?"

"Thirty armored hussars of the guard, six Cossacks from the Wallachian light cavalry with their officer, an *essaul*, and fifty Tartars of the Dobrudja regiment with their *mirza*. Then the servants of the ambassadors, a dozen or so."

"Well, you have a little of everything. Only Chort's men aren't Cossacks—they're town Cossacks, used to sleeping in feather beds, who don't stray far from their wives."

The ghost of a smile touched Stuart's thin lips.

"Even so, we are able to beat off marauders."

"Aye, so, in the Polish streets, maybe. Out yonder it's different. The Nogais wander with their tent villages."

"What are they?"

"Tartar clans. At war they follow the khan, but otherwise they do what they like. They're wolves."

"Tribesmen fear the hussars. Besides, would the Nogais attack ambassadors?"

"Will a panther leap from a tree? Only God knows. You have too many sledges. They'll string out like lame cows. Hai, you ought to get rid of half your loads and fill up with barley and chopped hay. Your horses aren't the kind to dig under the snow for grass. But," Ayub added hastily, "don't throw away any of the brandy."

A knock sounded on Stuart's door, and in a moment a magnificent figure appeared, a man in a uniform of sorts. On his arm he carried a white lambskin *kalpak;* a fur tipped *kaftan* hung over his broad shoulders and his doublet was laced with bright scarlet; his boots were polished, but he wore no spurs, and from his belt hung a curved Turkish knife instead of a sword. Long black mustaches were brushed upward toward his ears. Ayub had seen his kind before—a *heyduke,* or servant, dressed like an Asiatic warrior.

"Jackal in a panther's hide," he muttered under his breath.

The *heyduke* glared, and his mustache moved irresolutely, until he caught Stuart's eye, when he produced a knotted purse and bowed respectfully.

"His Highness," he said loudly, "begs that the lord colonel will accept the twenty silver crowns wagered this evening."

Stuart nodded and tossed the purse on the table. With another bow the *heyduke* withdrew. As the door closed behind him, Ayub heard a single word vociferated in the passage.

"Animal!"

"Are you in service now?" the colonel demanded suddenly.

"Nay."

"Will you serve me, go with me to Bagche Serai?"

For a moment the seamed brown eyes of the big Cossack gazed steadily into the gray eyes of the Scot. Ayub had taken a fancy to the man called Stuart who had saved him from a hiding at the hands of the Poles. And here was a chance to see the inside of Bagche Serai. What a tale that would be! He could go to the Zaporogians and relate what he had seen. And the chances were that the Poles would get through with a whole skin. They were the ambassadors of a powerful king, and the khan would respect ambassadors.

"Nay, Sir Colonel," he said slowly. "I couldn't ride with the Poles. I'd go along with you, but I don't drink out of the same cup with them."

"No need. I have other duty for you—to ride ahead with a Tartar patrol, mark out the road, select halting places and observe any enemies."

"*Tien!*" cried Ayub. "That's a *tien.*"

When Stuart lifted his brows, he explained.

"The shadow—that's what you mean. We Cossacks send ahead a light chap on a *koulanok*—the fastest horse of the regiment. He watches the high grass for Tartars and rides back with word to the regiment. Because he's light and the *koulanok* goes like the winged fiend, he gets away safe. Hai—I'm no shadow."

Stuart eyed his massive visitor reflectively.

"I have a horse that will carry you, at a pace, too. A black stallion I bought in Poland. As for a sword—"

"Sir Colonel, grant me two more Dutch dollars and I'll attend to such things as that. I have a good saddle."

"Then you will serve me?" Stuart's eyes became penetrating. "You are not a servant, but you will obey my orders."

Ayub rose, bent his shaggy head toward the icon stand and crossed himself on breast and forehead.

"Aye, Sir Colonel. May the foul fiend himself take me, if I do not obey."

Stuart motioned with his pipe toward the purse lying on the table.

"Take that, then. Buy yourself weapons and a good coat. Come to me here, an hour after noon tomorrow. And come sober."

Ayub swept up the purse and his *kalpak*. "*Insh'allum bak Allah*," he muttered. "God forbid otherwise."

He left the colonel's room with a swagger.

"Eh," he muttered to himself, "he's a Frank, the little father, but why shouldn't I serve him? He put a sword in my hand—he promises a good horse and gives a purse without counting it."

Ayub himself did not look into the purse, but thrust it into his girdle. He had come to Kudak with the Gypsy's whisper in his ears, intending to lift the piebald horse if possible from the Poles. Now this was not possible, because he had sworn service to Stuart. But the journey to the court of the khan appealed to him more, and he was impatient to outfit himself. When he closed the door behind him he remembered the *heyduke* and the fine white lambskin *kalpak* and he decided to add this to his outfit the first thing.

Questing around the inn yard for the officer's servants, he heard voices in the kitchen and thrust open the door. A haze of tobacco smoke hung under the low roof and in this haze on the tables were sitting a half dozen *heydukes*, making up to the women. These, having finished their labor of the evening, were giggling and exclaiming at the talk of the brilliantly uniformed creatures from the great cities. But when they saw the big Cossack with his hands on his hips, they all fell silent.

Ayub looked from face to face until he recognized a pair of scimitar-like black mustaches, brushed up. This was the one who had called him an animal from behind the door.

"Down on thy face!" he roared. "Bend thy forehead to the shadow of his serene great high Mightiness."

The *heyduke* glanced right and left and fumbled with his dagger. But some of his companions had witnessed the duel of two hours ago, and the others had heard about it. The *heyduke* thought better of drawing his weapon.

"Only liste, sir—" he began.

Ayub strode over to him and caught the breast of his tunic in a hand that was like a bear's paw. With the other hand he cuffed the *heyduke*'s ear.

"It is for me to speak and for thee to listen, O thou ditch-running whelp of a she jackal! Only listen to this—" and he swung his fist on the servant's ear, then released his grasp of the tunic and put all his weight behind a blow of the other arm.

Ayub weighed very close to two hundred and fifty pounds, and the *heyduke* spun from his feet, crashed into a bench and lay groaning upon the sand of the floor.

"Hi, little grandmother," cried the Cossack, "the moon is up and I have had no more than a swallow. Fill me a stone jug of the white corn brandy."

Swiftly—for they feared a tumult in the kitchen otherwise—the tavern women hastened to do his bidding. Ayub picked up the *heyduke*'s white lambskin hat, sniffed at it and tried it on. He thrust it to one side of his skull and left it there, tossing away his own worn hat. He took up the jug, quaffed deeply from it and eyed the other *heydukes* expectantly. But they sat silent and motionless in their laced velvets and fur edged *kaftans*, while the brandy crept into Ayub's veins.

"And you also listen," he felt moved to say, "to my words. Here you sit making sheeps' eyes at the girls and emptying your masters' cups. But where will you be the next moon? You will be out on the steppe, d'ye understand, my fleece lambs?

"And what will you be in the next moon?" he went on without waiting for an answer. "Well, listen—out there, in the mists under the moon, Tartar magicians will creep up when you are snoring and they will go around you and around. Your blood will change to ice, and there will be chains around your limbs, although you cannot see any chains. And then, only listen—"

He tossed up the jug and drew several gulps from it.

"Then, while you lie like ghosts in the snow, the riders of the Horde will come, in the mists. You will hear their war shout—'Ghar-ghar-ghar!'—and you will see their lances with the hair tufts under the points so as to catch running blood. You will see their lances sticking into your comrades, and all the white snow will be red as your own pantaloons, my poor *heydukes*. Then the women of the Horde will come riding up and they will take off your little earrings and your *kaftans* and cut off your heads and pile them for the vultures to come and dine upon. And then the grass will grow, next thaw, between your ribs. And after that nothing at all will matter, my *heyduke* lambs, because—" his voice sank to a whisper—"you will be dead."

Even the man who had been cuffed ceased groaning to listen, but when the Cossack ended his prophecy a simultaneous groan burst from their lips. Well satisfied, Ayub corked his jug and went off swaggering across the moonlit snow, on his way to haggle with the Gypsies whom he suspected of stealing his sword. The evening had begun auspiciously, and he lifted his voice in song:

> *When your bread is warm in the oven, my girls,*
> *When your bread is warm in the oven,*
> *Be quick.*
> *Don't burn your fingers,*
> *With fire!*

His dark figure merged into the haze of mist, and the sentry who had taken Platovsky's post heard his voice grow fainter in the distance:

> *When a kiss is warm on your lips, my girls,*
> *When a kiss is warm on your lips,*
> *Take care!*
> *Don't burn your hearts,*
> *For a man!*

Chapter III
The Ambassadors

A week later Ayub dismounted and thrust his hands into his girdle. Slowly he took stock of his surroundings—on one side a straggling growth of dwarf pines; on the other several log cabins and sheds. The hamlet was deserted and the surface of the snow unbroken.

"The end of the road, eh, brothers?"

"Allah *birdui*," one of the Tartars murmured. "God gives!"

For a week they had followed a fairly good snow road, running through the fishing villages and the outlying settlements and past the herds of some friendly tribes. Ayub and his four Dobrudja Tartars had had little to do except ask what lay ahead of them, and to select whatever shelter might be had for the ambassadors.

The Tartars followed Ayub obediently, even with respect. He could talk in their own dialect, and when one of them had disappeared for a day— probably to ride back and loot some house—the Cossack had forced him to walk all the following day tied to the tail of his own pony. After that they kept together. And Ayub was now a figure to command their respect.

The Cossack's old coat had been replaced with a long *svitza* that swung down to his knees. His girdle was a Persian pearl-sewn shawl, and from this girdle hung a long yataghan in a gilded leather sheath, two Turkish pistols, a powder pouch, a knife and a wallet for his pipe and tobacco. How he had achieved all this with twenty silver marks, Ayub did not choose to explain.

"Two of you ride around the woods," he ordered. "Thou, Toghrul, take the horses, and thou, Ahmak, gather up the best wood before the nobles come." The three whose work lay with the horses looked silently at Ahmak, who had to find wood—a woman's task. Ahmak had been the deserter of a day.

Ayub stared thoughtfully out beyond the cabins at the rolling ridges of ruddy white that stretched to the sky. It was late afternoon, near sunset, and the breath of the open steppe grew colder. Beyond this hamlet the road ended. After this the Cossack would have to ransack his memory for the trails that led south—and cross long stretches of open plain, choosing a route that the sledges could follow. As a forest dweller finds his way through overgrown land by crossing clearings and questing along animal and cattle paths, the Cossack of the plains would have to pick his way by memory over land hidden under three feet of snow.

"These Polish Tartars don't know where to turn their reins," he thought. "The devil! A blind Nogai on a lame horse could take us through."

He trudged over to look at the best cabin. The door stood open, wedged so by a mound of drifted snow. The small horn windows were shut, as

always. Ayub entered the single gloomy room and inspected the cold stove.
A broken caldron lay on the floor, and the heavy frames of massive beds
had been drawn close to the stove. But the quilts and sheet were gone and
he could not find any cooking gear.

Nor any clothing. And the rafters overhead were bare. No hams or onions or dried sheaves of corn hung from them. The few furnishings seemed
to be untouched, and the holy pictures were on the wall, in their stand
above some candles. Ayub took off his hat, crossed himself and went to
look at the next log house.

It was in the same state as the first, except that odds and ends of rope
and sacking lay on the sand that composed the floor. Ayub looked carefully at the sand near the door. Here and there the print of an iron heel
was visible, and the marks of smaller feet shod in soft leather. Long tracks
and whorls showed where heavy sacks had been dragged to the door. One
thing he picked up, a child's wooden doll with a long beard and black hair
painted upon it and a miniature robe of coarse wool sewn over it. Ayub
tossed it away and scratched his head under his *kalpak*.

He did not feel cheerful. There should be people in this hamlet. They
had gone, somehow, with all their animals, food and utensils, but without
their most prized possessions, the picture stands. Even a doll remained,
but nothing worth picking up.

"They went off," Ayub muttered, "before the last snow—three and four
days ago. They didn't go toward the river."

Along the frontier sudden removals were common enough—to escape
raiding Tartars, or an epidemic, or just because the men wanted to go
elsewhere to other lands. Yet these cabins were large and comfortable.
Ayub wished that the fresh snow had not covered all the tracks outside.
He could not make anything out of the cabin floors.

"If it wasn't for the pictures—"

He shook his head gravely, and went out. The two Tartars had come in
from their patrol and were investigating the dwellings.

"Hi, you thieves!" he cried. "What did you see?"

"No horses, no men, no tracks."

Evidently the place had not been visited since the snow fell.

"The *tabor* is coming," volunteered the other rider. By the *tabor* he
meant the wagon train with the main body.

Ayub nodded and went over to the clump of pines on the lee of the woods,
where Ahmak had been preparing camp. Here the horses were tethered,
the saddle cloths unfolded and tied over their backs, and Ahmak squat-

ted by piled brush. At a word from the Cossack he fell to work with his flint and steel until he had struck a spark into a pinch of powder. A tiny flare, and wisps of smoke began to curl up. The dark faces of the Tartars turned expectantly toward Ayub.

He took his *kalpak* upon his arm and faced the south, lifting his free hand.

"Brothers, Cossacks," he cried in his deep voice, "the fire is burning. Come and warm yourselves."

Three times he repeated the words, facing the other quarters of the compass. It was the brief ritual of every evening, and every Zaporogian Cossack did likewise in the steppe, bidding to his fire the spirits of other Cossacks slain in this waste land. They would be cold, those spirits, and unseen and unheard; they might hasten toward him and gather around the flames.

Ayub seated himself on his saddle where the snow had been cleared away, and lighted his pipe. A jangling of distant bells, and the creaking of runners over hard-packed snow told him that the main body was entering the hamlet, but his work was over. The Poles would see his fire, and the cabins and their servants could do the rest. In fact, voices soon shouted back and forth, and the dark masses of the sledge train, from which steam rose from the horses, filled the open space between the wood and the hamlet. Men hastened up to light torches at his fire. The stamping and neighing of horses in the grove, the ringing of axes, and the crashing of broken branches indicated that the military escort was making itself at home under the shelter of the trees.

"The White Beard comes," observed one of the Tartars.

Bells chimed melodiously, and a closed sleigh drew up before the largest cabin. Servants hastened toward it and opened the door, upon which was painted a crimson coat of arms. From the traveling sleigh descended a bent form in a dark velvet cloak.

This was the under-chancellor of Poland, an aged dignitary of the court, who was addressed as his Mightiness. He was the elder envoy, and the Tartars called him White Beard. He glanced around the encampment, frowning, and moved stiffly toward the cabin that was being made ready for him. He did not set out until the *tabor* had gone far ahead, and his fast sleigh, escorted by a detail of hussars, had easy going over the beaten track. Ayub only caught fleeting glimpses of him, and wondered why such a grandee of the court tried to make the journey across the steppes.

The Cossack ate the supper his Tartars had cooked, and when they rose
to go as usual to the camp of their companions, apart from the Poles, he
checked them.

"Nay, Ahmak, thou wilt stay by the horses. I go to the fire of the little father."

The broad face of the Tartar warrior grew sulky. He gritted his white
teeth and shook his head.

"*Ai-a*, am I to have the duty of a boy as well as a woman?"

The others stopped and looked at Ayub, who strode over to Ahmak
and grasped the thin beard that dangled from his chin. The Tartar felt for
the dagger in his girdle, but before he could draw his weapon, the Cossack wrenched his head around and flung him to the ground. Ahmak
drew his knife and got to his knees. Then he hesitated, because the Cossack loomed over him, dangerously silent. When Ayub abused them, the
tribesmen smiled and retorted cheerfully, but when he said nothing they
did not know what to expect. It was Ahmak who spoke first.

"Thou art a wolf. Kai—I have sat in thy shadow, and I obey."

He shook himself like a dog and sheathed his dagger, then went and
squatted by the fire, with a muttered "God is one." His companions moved
off silently into the darkness.

"Thou hast heard the order," Ayub reminded him. "If I, coming back
to this place, find thee not, I shall seek for thee and make of thee something that is less than a boy or a woman."

"I have heard."

Ayub glanced at his follower appraisingly. The stocky little warrior
seemed saddened, and his lips moved as he squatted over the embers.

"What has come upon thee?" he asked finally.

"It is not good, this place."

"How not good?"

But Ahmak only closed his eyes, and the Cossack swung away impatiently. He sought through the damp smoke of the grove until he found
the round yurt that belonged to Colonel Stuart. Ayub had persuaded his
officer to buy this at Kudak—a small shelter shaped like a dome, with a
hole in the center. It was a light wicker frame that folded together in several bundles when not in use, covered with strips of heavy felt. When a
fire was going inside, the yurt was comfortable in any cold, and its shape

enabled it to stand up against the wind.

Stuart, just returned from dining with the nobles, was taking off his cloak and putting on a short sheepskin jacket.

"How is it?" he greeted the Cossack.

"Not good, Little Father." Ayub sat down on a log and stirred the ashes of his pipe moodily.

"Why?"

Ayub thought of the deserted cabins, now lighted by candles and resounding with the talk of the nobles, and of the ill humor of the Tartars.

"Who is in command, at need?" he asked.

The Scot smiled.

"I am in command of the military escort. As to the journey, Prince Paul gives orders, but his Excellency, the chancellor, has the final word."

"Two heads are worse than one. After this, the road is harder. We have too many sledges, too much baggage. Harken, Sir Colonel—we have only grain enough to feed the horses for eight days. It is four days' ride to the sea. But if a storm comes, we will have to stay under shelter two or three days and perhaps more. If a wind comes with the snow, out yonder, we will lose horses and men."

"Well, Ayub, we must take what the road sends."

"But why does a noble like his Mightiness come into the steppe when the roads are gone?"

"He was sent by the king."

"Then why were hussars given to escort him? *Ekh ma*, they cannot wear their steel armor; they must carry all their ironware in the sledges and dress themselves in furs. Their horses are heavy."

"That also was ordered."

"No good ever came of orders like that. What does the court of the great king know about a place like this? Devil take it! The horses are nervous, won't sleep. The Dobrudja men are ready to quarrel. There are fiends of some kind about, because the cabins have been abandoned with the candles still under the holy pictures. Only listen!"

Ayub held up his hand. Above the murmur of voices from the nearby fires could be heard the sough of wind in the pine tips, and the rustle of dry snow blown against the sides of the yurt. And a faint whining, far in the upper reaches of the air, over their heads.

"Don't you hear, Sir Colonel?" the Cossack whispered. "The vampires are crying, because they are hungry."

Stuart could hear the shrill whimper clearly. It was like the high note of a violin, trailing off into silence.

"Aye, the wind is rising," he assented.

Ayub shook his head and crossed himself.

"Nay, that is how the spirits call when they speed over the trees. Then, along in the night, they come down and stand on their feet—perhaps white-faced women, perhaps little children with lights shining in their heads. They cry and cry, until you go out to them, and when you are far away from your fellows—"

"Faith," laughed the Scot, "there is naught in the air but a storm gathering."

"Didn't you ever see a vampire, or a table goblin, or a wolf-woman begging at twilight?"

"Not I!" Stuart picked up a thin bottle and poured two glasses full.

When he had downed his brandy Ayub grew more cheerful.

"Well, it's an omen, anyway. Perhaps the spirits of darkness, perhaps a storm."

He left his officer feeling more at ease. When he reached his fire he found that it had died to ashes and beside it lay the squat figure of the Tartar Ahmak. He lay face down on his sheepskins and he was whimpering drowsily, like a dog in pain.

Duncan Stuart listened to the voice of the wind over his yurt, watching how the whorls of smoke were drawn up through the central opening as if pulled forth by an invisible hand. Although he had not let Ayub see it, the prospect of a storm did not reassure him.

He did not regret engaging the Cossack. Ayub doctored his horses, interpreted for him, filled empty hours with tales of the steppe. Moreover, Ayub was the only guide with the column, as Prince Paul had neglected to search for others when they left the Dnieper.

Prince Paul had all the gallantry and the heedlessness of a Polish gentleman. And the expedition had been chosen more to impress the khan than for any other reason. The hussars were the famous cavalry of Poland, picturesque in their helmets and dark armor, and the eagles' wings fastened to their shoulders, when they went forth in full regalia. The Dobrudja Tartars were sent to show the khan that other tribes served the King of Poland—so also Chort and his town Cossacks.

And Stuart suspected that he himself had been ordered to accompany the prince so that a Frankish officer would appear in the train of the ambassadors. At least his position as commander of the escort was an empty one. Prince Paul was officer of the hussars, and this left only the Cossacks under Stuart's orders, because the Tartars would listen to no one except their *mirza*.

But no one realized better than Stuart how much depended on the expedition. Mighty Poland had wasted her strength in continuous war. Now, attacked at the same time by the Swedes of Gustavus Adolphus, and the Russians, she had fared badly in the north. Her armies were thinned, her treasury overburdened, her frontiers dwindling.

Meanwhile the Turks had come up from the south and overrun the border states. Tidings had reached the court of Sigismund of Poland that the sultan was gathering greater forces to advance again in the Spring. And to make this blow decisive, the sultan had sent to the khan of the Krim, bidding him come with fifty thousand horsemen of the Horde.

The Turks themselves had no good cavalry, yet if the khan threw himself across the steppe into the heart of Poland, there would be no forces to withstand him. Poland was prostrate, and in her need, had sent envoys to the khan.

That was why the under-chancellor and Prince Paul must press on without stopping in Midwinter. The ambassadors of the sultan were already at Bagche Serai, and there was no knowing when the khan would decide to ally himself with the sultan.

Ten thousand pieces of gold had been entrusted to the ambassadors. Much of this had been raised by the sale of jewels of the nobility, and it was to be given the khan, to buy a peace. There was no other alternative. The khan made no treaties with Christian kings, but if he accepted the gift he would abide by his word, as long as he respected the Poles. If, however, he discovered the real weakness of the mighty commonwealth, he would not be too tender about pledges. So the king had sent as envoy the arrogant Prince Paul and the venerable under-chancellor, and the escort composed of varied arms of the service. And King Sigismund had ordered Colonel Stuart, one of the most notable cavalry leaders, to go to the court of the khan.

"Faith," Stuart thought, "'tis no light task to buy a peace."

The wind was still rising, and the dry snow swept against the edge of his yurt like the spray of surf. Above the rustle of the trees, he caught a snatch of song from Prince Paul's quarters, and even a deep shout.

"Vivat Imperator!"

"Long live the king!" Stuart reflected. "And may the envoys live also!"

Chapter IV
The Price of Peace

It seemed to the colonel that he had not been asleep long when he was called.

"Little Father—Little Father!"

Someone was slapping the entrance fold of the yurt, and Stuart pulled on his boots. Picking up his sword, he thrust himself through the opening. A glance through the trees showed him the red half circle of the old moon. It was near the last watch of the night. Ayub stood before him.

"The Tartars are gone."

"Yours—what the devil?"

"All of them. Only that undersized goblin Ahmak is left, and he is weeping and howling—drunk."

"The *mirza* too? Bring a lantern."

"No need of that," Ayub vouchsafed. "I heard the horses stirring and left my blankets. Those three dog-born dogs of mine were saddling their nags. Eh, they went off when they saw me. I thought that was not good, and I walked over to the Tartar camp. Not a rope left."

"Did they take any of the sledges?"

"Nay, Chort's lads were on guard at the *tabor*. The Tartars rode away on the other side of the wood, and no one saw them go."

Stuart went first to look at the site of the camp, then a short distance into the steppe with Ayub. The tracks led directly away from the wood. In silence the Scot returned to the hamlet and roused Prince Paul. The hussars were more than ready to pursue the tribesmen, but Stuart pointed out that the *mirza*'s men had the faster horses and, besides, had headed away from the trail. They had an hour's start—Ayub's detail had been the last to leave-and pursuit was useless. Useless also was any speculation as to why they had gone. Clearly, they had planned their move beforehand, but they had not tried to take anything from the *tabor*. The officers gathered around the breakfast table for consultation.

Stuart pointed out that a storm seemed to be coming nearer, and advised remaining at the hamlet. The strength of the escort had been cut in half, but they had grain enough now, and food to spare.

"*Par dex!*" cried the Prince. "Shall we hug the stove for a gray sky and a few deserters?"

The under-chancellor decided that they would go forward, as usual.

So Ayub mounted and rode out. He took with him Ahmak, after tying the Tartar's ankles together under his horse's belly, and binding up his follower's weapon's upon his own saddle.

"He would lie to the nobles," he explained to Stuart, "but he will tell me the truth about his fellows, the little darling, before sunset."

For the greater part of the day Ayub had no time to spare to question Ahmak. Their course took them through a network of gullies and buttes where deep drifts had formed. This was a place called the Dry Lands, and in Summer a meeting point for raiders who were going to cross the Dnieper. Ayub remembered the way through, but at times he had to cast to right and left to make certain that he was not leading the *tabor* astray.

It was noon before he came out into easier going, where the ravines yielded to shallow valleys and finally to the gentle sweep of the open plain. He pushed on swiftly, to look for a good halting place, where wood might be found. Ahmak, who was now able to sit erect in the saddle, followed him without complaining.

"Why didn't you go with *mirza*?" Ayub asked. "Why did you drink?"

"I was afraid." The little Tartar answered indifferently. "It was written."

"Well it's also written—"

The Cossack fell silent and reined in his horse. For a moment the two riders gazed at each other, their heads bent, listening.

Through the whine of the wind overhead came a new note, like the slow beating of distant drums. When the wind freshened it grew louder.

"Guns," Ayub said.

For awhile the reports were only heard at intervals, then came the thudding of an irregular volley. This could not be hunters after wild horses, or the young soldiers loosing off their pistols haphazard.

After the volley, silence.

"Come," Ayub called to the Tartar, and wheeled his horse, urging the black stallion to a trot and then a gallop. For nearly half a league he rode back over his own trail. Once the wind brought to his ears an uproar of voices. Then, silence again. But the Cossack had located the conflict—beyond a low ridge where he had stopped to look at the surrounding plain.

Approaching this ridge, he drew rein to listen. Then he dismounted, and assisted Ahmak to do likewise. On foot he hastened up the last of the slope, toward a fringe of gray tamarisk. At the brush he threw himself down and crawled forward with the Tartar. For a moment they stared in silence at the shallow valley beyond the ridge.

Outlined against the white surface of the snow they saw the *tabor*. The head of the wagon train was tangled in a rough half circle. Behind this group of sledges and animals, the rest of the train strung out like the tail of a kite—abandoned.

Within the half circle Ayub saw the Poles with their servants, and Chort's few Cossacks. Some of them had on breastplates and helmets, and had harquebuses and pistols. They were on top of the sledge loads, their horses within the barricade. A few of the Poles were in the saddle, and Ayub recognized among the riders Colonel Stuart's gray cloak and the piebald horse. He thought he made out Prince Paul's bay mare, but the under-chancellor's traveling sleigh was not visible.

Gathered beyond pistol shot of the *tabor* were groups of riders—small men on rough coated ponies, armed with scimitars and long lances. On their arms they carried round shields, most of them painted red. Their heads were covered with furs—bearskin and wolf. Ayub was so near one of the bands that he could have thrown a knife among them.

But many wore under their sheepskins fine link armor and carried Turkish pistols in their girdles. Their dark, square faces were beardless.

"Nogais," the Cossack muttered.

The story of what had happened was clearly written in the snow. The tribesmen had come down on the *tabor* from the neighboring heights, had taken it by surprise because only the leading sledges had drawn up together to resist the attack, and the circle was not completed. At least once—and Ayub remembered the volley he had heard—the Nogais had charged the *tabor* and had been driven off. Four or five bodies lay in the space near the sledges.

What had happened to the men in the rearmost sledges he could not tell. Perhaps they had reached the half circle, perhaps they had been cut down. The Tartars were looting the sledges beyond musket shot. They had gathered into three bands, on different sides, and were watching the dark mass of the Poles' barricade, like wolves sitting on their haunches beyond the horns of angered cattle. They had made their first attack and had been beaten off—Ayub wondered who had thought to close up the sledges in time—and were taking what loot they could while they pondered what to do next.

More of the Poles appeared in armor. The hussars were taking advantage of the lull to don the heavy steel that had given them the name of "iron men." But Ayub thought that some were missing. He could only make out about forty men in all within the *tabor*. The Nogais outnumbered them some three to one, but the better firearms and fine armor of the Poles made the issue an even one.

"If the Tartars are looting," the Cossack reflected, "they may ride off at sunset."

He lay in the snow without moving, and Ahmak was silent as a shadow at his side. The slightest stirring of the bushes would draw a dozen eyes upon them, and they knew the folly of trying to ride between the bands into the *tabor*. The shaggy ponies were as quick-footed as hunting dogs in the hard snow, where Ayub and his charger might break through to the horse's knees. Ayub was in no haste to move.

At intervals harquebuses were discharged from the sledges, and smoke rolled over the ground toward the riders, who scattered at the flash of powder and moved back a little. Some of them went off to join their comrades who were breaking open the loads on the captured vehicles and cutting the horses loose from the traces.

A Moslem on a white horse circled near the *tabor*, waving a black velvet cloak, taken from the Poles. A flash and a flurry of smoke greeted him, but he flung the cloak over his shoulders and rode off, shouting triumphantly.

And then a trumpet blared from the barricade. The mounted Poles began to stir, the horse's heads shifted, and long lances uprose.

Ayub muttered under his breath and rose on his elbows. The lances began to move, and presently the hussars appeared, out of the open space, and formed in two ranks, nearly thirty of them. The first line half wheeled and began to trot toward the nearest group of Tartars, while the second followed at ten yards.

"Devil take them!" groaned the Cossack.

This was no trick to draw in the tribesmen; the hussars meant to charge. Their heavy chargers moved more swiftly, floundering here and there; the long lances came down to the level. Above the shoulders of the iron men flapped the great eagle wings, the eagles of Poland and the emblem of the cavalry.

Ahead of them, his sword at his shoulder, trotted Prince Paul. He wore no helmet, and his dark head was lifted with all the pride of a caste that knows not fear. For several moments the gray cloud of Tartars had watched in utter silence, but now clamor resounded over the plain.

Bows snapped and arrows flew among the Poles. The Nogais nearest the oncoming hussars wheeled away and scattered, while the tribesmen in front of Ayub charged down the slope in a mass.

A deep shout of triumph resounded from the iron hussars, as they drove the fugitives of the first band. But most of the Tartars kept beyond the long lances, and their heavy bows made play at short range. For the most part the arrows broke against the armor of the Poles, who drew the pistols from the saddle holsters and fired at the second group of tribesmen.

Then for a moment the gray figures of the hussars were hidden behind wreathing black smoke. And into this smoke the Tartars rushed like wolves.

"*Ghar-ghar-ghar!*"

Their war cry rose, shrill and exultant, and horses screamed in agony.

When the smoke thinned, the hussars were hemmed in, nearly half their horses down. The heavy chargers, plunging through deep snow, could not keep pace with the darting ponies of the clansmen, and they were marks for the flying arrows. The hussars had no time to reload their pistols. They fought furiously with lance or sword.

Ayub watched with both horror and anger.

"May the saints guard them! They went into deep snow in armor."

He had expected the Poles to make good the barricade, standing in the sledges, until darkness, when the Tartars would have withdrawn. More horses went down, and the remaining hussars would not desert their dismounted comrades. Led by the swiftly flashing sword of Prince Paul, the knot of them began to move back slowly toward the *tabor*. And then they were hidden by fresh throngs of gray riders.

Ahmak tugged at his arm, muttering to him to mount and ride away. The Dobrudja Tartars were afraid of the Nogais and Ahmak thought that the iron men were doomed:

"*Nà kòn!*" the Cossack assented. "To horse."

They ran back down the slope and leaped into their saddles. Ayub delayed long enough to toss Ahmak his bow and short sword, then he urged his stallion up the rise.

"Nay," he cried, "I must find the little father."

The Tartar's face twisted ruefully and he clucked his tongue, but he followed Ayub, who galloped toward the *tabor*. They were a pistol shot away when they saw Stuart. For a few moments the Nogais had left the *tabor* to its own devices and the colonel had rallied a small party to aid the hussars. Three of Chort's Cossacks and a half dozen *heydukes* followed him. He saw Ayub and Ahmak, and waved at them to come on.

The struggling mass of horsemen around the hussars was no more than a stone's throw away. Ayub drew a pistol, looked at the priming in the pan.

"*U-ha!*" he roared. "Do we lack powder and steel, lads? Make way for a Cossack!"

But slant eyes had seen the advance of the little party, and fifty stocky riders turned in their saddles to ply their bows. Arrows hissed among the Christians. A horse reared with a shaking scream and one of Chort's men dropped like a stone into the snow. Ayub and several others fired their pistols. Then a group of Nogais bore down on them.

This was too much for the *heydukes*, who had been hanging back. But Ayub did not see them flee. Out of the haze of smoke a gray figure, crouching in the saddle of a white horse, made for him, a steel lance point gleaming above a red fringe of hair. The old Cossack felt for his other pistol, and changed his mind, grasping his sword hilt instead.

He jerked his horse to the right, and the Nogai swerved toward him. When the lance point was darting at his head, Ayub shifted his heavy body with surprising swiftness to the left, his weight on that stirrup. The lance passed over his shoulder, and he thrust the blade of his yataghan into the Nogai's side.

He looked for Stuart, and saw two tribesmen rushing at the Scot, who parried the scimitar stroke of the first man with his long straight blade. The Tartar slipped to one side, dodging the officer's slash, and Stuart turned in the saddle to meet the other rider. The first Tartar checked his pony in its tracks and lifted his scimitar to strike the Scot in the back.

As he did so Ayub heard Ahmak's bow resound at his side. An arrow thudded into the head of the tribesman, who slipped from the saddle with a snarling scream.

"Well done!" Ayub roared, and the little archer shouted triumphantly.

The man he had brought down was the owner of the black velvet cloak—the one flourished at the Poles—and the cloak had a gold buckle set with gleaming stones. Ayub remembered it vaguely, but Ahmak seemed to covet it, for he sprang down from his saddle and wrenched it from the fingers of the dying man. His greed made him forget all caution.

A pony whirled past Ahmak, a lance thrust down, and the Tartar was pulled over—dragged through the snow, with the steel point of the lance fast in his throat.

Ayub gained Stuart's side in time to see the Scot's adversary turn and flee.

"Eh, Little Father," he cried, "where are your men?"

Stuart's followers and the Tartars alike had left them. The flight of the *heydukes* had stirred the Nogais to pursue them, and a score of riders were scattering down the valley. The three who had come against Ayub and Stuart were accounted for, and for these few seconds the Scot and his follower were left unnoticed.

Ayub looked around swiftly. The *tabor* was deserted, and on the other side of him, the Nogais were closing in upon the last hussars. Not one of the Poles remained in the saddle, and during this moment of triumph the tribesmen were intent on striking down the living and stripping the dead. The old Cossack made up his mind at once.

A glance at Stuart's set face, and he leaned forward, wrenching the rein of the piebald horse from the Scot's left hand. Then he struck the horse with the flat of his blade, urged on his own beast, and turned back toward the knoll from which he had first seen the conflict.

He heard a swift oath and the Scot's deep cry—

"Loose the horse, or I'll cut you down!"

"Slash, Little Father," Ayub shouted, "and you'll soon follow me down. Only look in back of you!"

Stuart turned in the saddle. A dozen Nogais were detaching themselves from the throng that had made an end of Prince Paul and his hussars. Only a faint clash of steel could be heard, where the exultant tribesmen were tearing plunder from each other's hands. The *heydukes* were being overtaken and killed, one by one.

"The Poles have all—" Ayub panted—"turned up their toes. No good going back to be stretched out like a dog."

For a moment the Scot was silent. Then he shook his shoulders and reached out calmly for the rein, and Ayub, after a glance at him, gave it up. They had passed over the ridge and were galloping along the trail that the Cossack had made earlier in the afternoon—to the south. Behind them, a long musket shot away, the Nogai riders appeared.

They fell into single file, pushing rapidly along the narrow trail, but for the time being the longer limbed horses of the fugitives increased the distance between them. Stuart's piebald was fairly fresh, and carried less weight than the Cossack's stallion, yet the powerful black charger galloped steadily through the heavy going, the snow flying up like spray under its hoofs.

The light failed steadily, the gray sky darkened and the Nogais became a blur against the snow. But Ayub knew that night would not hide the trail from the keen eyes of the Tartars. Evidently their ponies were tired and the tribes were content to follow, certain that they would come up with the fugitives when the swifter horses lagged. The Cossack pulled his charger back to a fast trot, and pondered.

"No cover, no place to hide—can't hide our tracks," he muttered to Stuart.

"They will stick like burrs to a dog's tail, because they want our horses."

The Nogais did not seem to be any nearer; by now they were lost to sight in the murk. The two riders felt as if they were speeding through a lifeless plain. The horses' hoofs were muffled in the snow, and no stars were to be seen.

"Were the Poles mad," Ayub asked presently, "to ride out from the *tabor*? Where was his Mightiness?"

"The Tartars cut him off, with his escort," Stuart said grimly. "They brought his head to the *tabor* and threw it among our men."

He had been riding near the center of the sledge train when the tribesmen came over the crests. Chort, at the head of the train, had brought the first sledges into a half circle, and Stuart had taken command here, ordering the hussars to dismount and use their firearms. Most of the men had reached the barricade safely, bringing in the sledges with the gold. The first charge of the Nogais had been broken.

Some of the Cossacks had shouted to the Nogais that they were envoys, on their way to the great khan, and a rider on a white horse with a green saddle cloth had come up as if to talk to them. Instead he had drawn the head of the under-chancellor from beneath his arm, and had swung it by the beard into the nearest sledge, riding off unhurt in the confusion among the Poles. Prince Paul, maddened by the insult, had called to the hussars to arm themselves and go out to the Nogais.

"They followed him," the colonel said quietly, "against my order."

"Well," Ayub grunted, "they were brave and now they are dead, and we are like to share their bed this night. I said, Sir Colonel, that the omen was not good."

"More like," Stuart pointed out, "the Nogais had sacked those cabins and camped nearby—"

"*Aya tak!* 'Tis so, by God!" The old Cossack struck the saddle horn with his hand. "And those weasels, our Tartars, sniffed blood in the air and went off." He shook his head sadly. "Eh, the blame is not yours!"

"Two nobles and forty—two Christian souls slain, and the gold lost—the mission destroyed." Stuart laughed harshly. "It is on my head, the blame—and I live."

The attack on the column, the savage fighting and the swift flight had given him no moment for thought, but now the massacre burned in his memory. He had been in command of the escort, and it had been wiped out by tribesmen.

"Nay, Sir Colonel," Ayub said gravely, "you are young and this is not your country. The Poles gave orders, not you. If I had a good head to think with, I would have spied out the tracks of the Nogais in the cabins. Or maybe I would have searched Ahmak's toes this dawn to make him talk. But I have no more than an empty keg on my shoulders, and now I am running like a dog with a panther hissing at his tail. *Tfu!* You are wise, Little Father. Do you see any way to escape?"

He bent his huge body to stare into Stuart's face. The Scot looked around at the bleak expanse of white and at the curtain of darkness that hemmed them in, and behind which followed the riders of the steppe.

"Not I!" he laughed.

As if it had been an echo of his voice, the high-pitched shout of a Nogai came down the wind—a shout to announce the picking up of the trail, or a taunt—

"*Ahai, caphar*—ho, unbelievers!"

Ayub tightened his knees, and the black charger flung up its head and trotted faster. Hearing the men's voices, the horses had lagged, and the pursuers had come closer.

Chapter V
Enemy's Shelter

Stuart, on the fresher horse, had taken the lead. The Cossack's big charger had been trotting through snow for the greater part of a day and the half of a night, and its strength was failing. It stumbled frequently, pulling up with a snort and a quick heaving of flanks. If the two men had been mounted on ordinary cavalry beasts they would have been overtaken by the ponies of the Nogais before now.

From time to time Ayub glanced over his shoulder, trying to pierce the pitlike gloom. The tribesmen, he knew, would not loose their arrows until they were certain of striking down the men without injuring the horses. They were too wise to scatter in pursuit, and they would not give the fugitives a chance to use their swords. The Cossack and the officer had a pistol each, but in the darkness they were worse than useless—the flash would reveal them to their adversaries and the dense smoke would hide the ensuing rush of the tribesmen. Avub had seen the Nogais charge the Poles through such smoke.

The piebald wolf-chaser neighed suddenly, and then again, thrusting down its head.

"That is a good omen, Little Father," the Cossack called.

He stared around him, then down at the ground. Bending over, he looked again, and jumped off without slowing up the black horse. Rein in hand he ran beside it for awhile. Then, gripping the saddle horn, the rein over his arm, he swung himself up again, grunting with the effort.

"Turn to the right, Little Father," he urged, and Stuart obeyed in silence.

After a few minutes, his eyes still bent on the snow, the Cossack spoke again.

"Now to the left a little."

"What is it?" Stuart asked.

"Many horse tracks, all around. A whole herd—wild, maybe, or a Tartar's herd. By day I could know."

"Will yonder devils lose our tracks here?"

"Nay, they will not lose the trail. But they will have to dismount and stick their snouts down, and so they will fall behind."

Ayub uttered an exclamation and turned his head. For some time the air had been growing colder; now it seemed warmer, and the black sky lighter. Something stung his face and beat against his eyes.

"Faith," Stuart said, "nothing is wanted. We are already marked for dead men, and here is the snow to bury us."

The snow was dry and hard, and it whirled around them, shutting them in so that soon they could not see beyond their horses' heads. And presently it rose from the ground, swirling around them.

"Eh," the Cossack observed, "the Nogais won't look for us any more.

They'll ride for shelter, if they know any place near; if not, they'll let the horses pick the way." He pondered for a moment. "Drop the rein, Little Father; urge on the spotted horse, and let him lead. That's the best thing to do."

The two horses drew together until the stirrups rubbed, and the piebald seemed to turn down the wind, after Stuart tossed the rein on his neck. But he trotted slowly and then fell of his own accord into a walk.

So far the cold had not troubled the men, but now the icy breath of the storm chilled their backs. Stuart dismounted and walked for a while, to stir the blood in his numbed feet.

"Don't do that, Sir Colonel," the Cossack remarked. "If you walk, the horse will follow you. If he is left to himself he'll go to a wood, or perhaps a ravine, and then we may be able to gather a fire."

There was no sign of any break in the plain. At times they went down long slopes, or circled around a knoll, but the dense veil of drifting snow made it seem as if they were still walking over the level steppe. Both of them knew what the storm meant—the cold steadily increasing until morning. By then the horses would be exhausted. And the wind came in such gusts that they could not tell whether they were wandering in a circle or not.

Once or twice the piebald wolf-chaser lifted his head and pricked his ears. Finally he whinnied, and Ayub grunted with satisfaction. The horse had heard or scented something.

"*Ahai muslimin*—" a wailing voice pierced the silence. "Ho, ye believers!"

And from the other side of them a second voice made response—

"Is it thou, Ismail?"

Leather creaked faintly near at hand and was echoed by a jangling of iron. Ayub and Stuart reined in and waited. They could see nothing in the drifting veil of white.

"Do not wander!"

A shout came from farther off, and then the silence remained unbroken. Ayub crossed himself on breast and forehead.

"Lost souls—spirits seeking for shelter," he muttered, "or those dog-born dogs of Nogais."

He noticed that the piebald went forward again more swiftly, and he wondered whether the charger were following the horses of the tribesmen. Then the cold crept into his limbs; the ache of hunger settled in his body. The best thing, he thought, was to let the horse go on.

When his bones pained him, and the cold settled in his old hurts, his thoughts turned to the tavern of Kudak and the delight of hot brandy.

"*Tfu*," he told himself, "all that fine wine of the *tabor* is being guzzled by these sons of Satan, and I did not even fill a flask. They'll find gold enough to cover their wives with necklaces, and not a ducat in my pouch. Devil fly away with them!"

The sky seemed lighter, and the snow had moderated. But it was not morning, because a silvery half-light filled the air. The clouds had broken away and the glow of the old moon had penetrated to the plain. By this dim radiance, through the thin veil of the storm, he saw that Stuart rode crouched in his saddle, his shoulders bent. The snow had drifted against the crupper and the officer's back, and had coated one side of the spotted horse. Stuart's cloth greatcoat was less protection than the sheepskin-lined *svitza* and the massive flesh of the Cossack.

"Eh," Ayub thought, "the lad is suffering, but he does not curse or berate me."

He drew up to the Scot, when the piebald horse turned sharply to one side and quickened its pace. Ahead of it something high and dark took shape through the drift—something shaped like a dome, coated white on one side.

Beside it the piebald halted, and Stuart laughed hoarsely.

"A haystack!"

Ayub tumbled out of his saddle and ran to the horses' heads, gripping their muzzles as well as he could in his numbed hands.

"Please to dismount, Little Father," he whispered. "Take the horses and don't let them whinny. Perhaps there is a hut near this stack. The men out here don't leave their hay in pastures."

While Stuart climbed down stiffly, Ayub swung his arms and beat his fists together until he could move his fingers. Then he disappeared into the gloom.

The Scot had his hands full with the horses, which were snorting and pushing up to the stack, and when he quieted them he heard Ayub's high pitched call.

"A-a-ay, Little Father. This wa—ay!"

Leading the horses, Stuart walked toward the sound, and made out what

seemed to be a smaller haystack before him. It was a domed yurt, like the
one he had lost, but with a rough shed and corral of twisted branches built
against its protected side. He went around it until he reached the entrance
flap. Ayub's voice came from within.

Looking under the lifted felt, he saw the big Cossack, sword in hand,
shaking the snow off his *svitza*. The light came from the glowing embers
of a fire in the sunken stone hearth beneath the central opening of the
tent. The earth was covered with greasy carpets, and the place reeked of
smoke and sour milk and leather. On the divan at the side crouched an
old man who wore a stiff leather jacket with a horse's mane hanging from
the shoulders, his shaven head covered by a green skullcap, and from under it his black eyes stared at the intruders without expression. A broad-
faced, handsome girl was hanging a pot over the embers and putting on
fresh dried dung from a pile in one corner.

"Nogais," Ayub said. "Warm yourself, Little Father, and don't let them
run out, while I look around. That young lioness is heating up broth."

In the half hour that he was gone the two Tartars said not one word.
The girl built up the fire until the mutton broth steamed, and from time
to time when her back was to the old man, she stared intently at Stuart
out of her slanting eyes. Her head was bound in a neat white kerchief, and
her shoulders were weighted by strings of pierced silver coins of all kinds.
Ayub came in with a gust of snow.

"Satan still has us in charge," he grunted. "Other yurts are near. I saw
some tracks going toward them. Those dogs we heard yelping out yonder
must have come in ahead of us, and our nags followed them. But this storm's
a regular *buran*, and they won't stir out of their nests for awhile."

"Is this a Nogai village?"

"That's what it is." The Cossack went over to look at the woman's cup-
board, where cheese cakes were hung in a leather bag, beside heavier sacks.
"Mare's milk; kumiss, they call it," he explained, prodding a sack. He
sniffed at a heavy clay jug. "*Gorilka!* Eh, thou grandfather, offer a greeting to thy guests!" He tipped up the jug and took several long swallows.
"*Allah kirbadiz partalouk!* Allah protect your shadow!"

The old Nogai spat out one word.

"*Caphar!*"

Silently the girl brought out two porcelain bowls and filled them with
broth, setting the cheese cakes between her unbidden guests. Ayub handed
the jug to the officer.

The fiery spirits and the hot broth warmed them, and the Nogai woman filled the Cossack's bowl three times before setting the pot aside to cool. Stuart could eat but little, but the heat of the yurt brought on a drowsiness that he could not shake off.

"Stretch out and sleep," Ayub advised him. "I'll smoke my pipe and talk to the grandfather and his bride. I'll wake you after dawn."

Stuart loosened his belt, but kept his boots on, and he placed his sword and pistol by his right hand. Lying on the carpet of the divan, he watched Ayub light his clay pipe with an ember. The reek of the Cossack's tobacco mingled with the burning dung, and smoke eddied under the blackened dome of the yurt. But before the young officer's eyes passed the vista of the fight in the steppe—the winged hussars engulfed in the gray horse— the blood-streaked beard of the chancellor—Chort, kneeling with an arrow in his throat. And the wind buffeted the heavy folds of the felt near his head, as if the storm itself were striking at him.

All the next day the storm raged. The cold increased, until the small fire failed to warm the windswept yurt, and Ayub departed without explaining to Stuart why he went. The Scot heard him moving about in the corral, and at intervals a loud thump sounded. When at last he appeared he carried an armful of wood, and explained that he had found a supply near some distant yurts. He had seen no Tartars, and said they were all holed up like foxes.

Ayub had been tipping up the jug and helping out the *gorilka* with the fermented mare's milk. This combination made him restless and cheerful. When he had a roaring fire going, he went out again and returned with the frozen leg of a lamb on his shoulder.

"Nogais always hang them up, out of reach of the gray brothers."

The eyes of the old tribesman kindled for the first time when he saw so much meat, ready to be eaten without payment. It was a fat leg and tied to it was the massive tail of the sheep, with a half dozen pounds of fat in it. This was the prized portion of the sheep, and the Nogai gorged himself, when his visitors passed over the tail for the leaner meat, upon the greasy fat, until his leather jacket swelled visibly. Even when he belched he went on stuffing. Probably not for years had he tasted this delicacy, reserved for the distinguished or the richer men of the clan. He ate it all, and his girl wife dined after him on the broth.

When they had finished, Ayub filled two leather sacks with the mutton stew and took them outside to freeze. For the third time he vanished. The old Nogai was asleep after his debauch, and the girl was sitting quietly by the fire watching the officer. They had not been harmed, and they accepted the visitors with the fatalism of their race, taking pains to hide their curiosity.

The light was failing, and Stuart went to the entrance to watch for the Cossack, half minded to truss up his hosts and go and look for Ayub, even though nothing was visible ten yards away.

But the big warrior showed up again, this time with a low *kibitka* in tow—a small cart on runners, the wheels removed. He lugged this up to the corral and swaggered into the yurt.

"We are ready for the road now, Little Father." He grinned. "I found the sled over in the village, and brought it out myself. We'll load the wood into the *kibitka*, with the sacks of mutton and some hay. Then, when the storm is over, before the first light, we'll harness up two of old grandfather's nags and saddle our horses and go before these devils in sheepskins are stirring."

"What about the two Tartars?"

"We'll take them, too. They'll sell for ten ducats in Kudak. Now, if we had some fresh *gorilka*—"

He glanced longingly back into the drifting snow, but Stuart spoke to him sharply.

"Ayub, is your head clear?"

"Ay, Sir Colonel!"

"Then stay here with these two. I'm going to look at the horses." At the entrance he paused to ask another question.

"If the storm lasts tonight, and stops tomorrow, in daylight—what then?"

The Cossack pondered, swaying a little as he warmed his shoulders at the fire.

"We'll have to trust to the horses again, ride like the devil."

Before the twilight ended Stuart inspected the commandeered sled and satisfied himself that the harness hanging in the Nogai's shed was sound. Then he busied himself loading the wood Ayub had confiscated into the *kibitka*, with the sacks of mutton. With a handful of hay he rubbed down the horses. This done, he made sure that the saddles were hanging on their pegs and that the chargers were well covered with felt blankets.

He knew that they had a chance to escape if the snow stopped before daylight, but if not—if the Nogais saw them riding off their chance was gone. Even if they could throw the warriors off their track by some miracle they could not cross the open plain without supplies. Strangely Ayub, who had been moody before there was any danger, was now heedless of what might happen. The jug, no doubt, kept him from worrying; but the nearness of his old enemies, and the fight in the steppe, had stirred his blood. Stuart had taken stock of the situation and had weighed their chances with the care of a man who is not disturbed by danger. That night he told Ayub that he would watch, and the Cossack was soon snoring on the divan across the fire from the Tartars.

From time to time the girl, as if accustomed to do so, woke and put more wood on the fire. Once, after listening to the snores of her aged master, she came close to the officer and smiled at him shyly.

"*Caphar!*" she whispered, but the word was approval rather than reproach.

The fire flickered up and by its light Stuart saw that the Nogai bride had not been idle during the last day. To the silver coins in her necklaces she had added two new gold pieces. And he wondered if in any way they had come from the treasure carried by the *tabor*. They were bright pieces of irregular shape, badly minted, and she glanced down at them proudly. He lifted one from her breast and inspected it. The inscription was Turkish—a sultan's seal.

"Othman?" he asked, and she nodded vigorously.

They had not come from the treasure of the Poles, but Stuart reflected that this girl could not have had them long. She seemed to value them immensely, and he did not understand why she had chosen to add them to her ornaments just then. She pointed at the snoring old man and held up three fingers. Evidently the Nogai had three similar coins. After a moment's thought, Stuart went to the divan and shook Ayub's knee.

The Cossack sprang up, his hand groping for his sword, and the girl would have fled had not Stuart caught her wrist.

"Ask her where the Turkish pieces came from. Nay, do not take them."

Ayub listened, his head bent down to the girl's white kerchief while she whispered rapidly.

"A man called Abd-al-Rahman brought much money, like this," he explained, "in the last moon. He gave with an open hand, and he rode a white Arabian horse, with a green saddle cloth, and he wore Tartar garments. But he came from Stamboul, the city of the sultan, to give the Tartars money."

"The man who carried the chancellor's head to the *tabor* rode a white

Arabian with a green saddle cloth, and he was richly dressed."

"Ahmak noticed that," the Cossack assented. "The girl said he gave the money because the great sultan loves the Tartars, and so Abd-al-Rahman went with them to raid the Christians."

Stuart nodded. The Turks, then, were sending gold to the tribes even in Winter, and officers to lead them on raids. If they did that with the Nogais they would surely have envoys in the court of the Krim khan.

"Does the Nogai chieftain serve the khan of the Krim?" he asked, and Ayub pondered.

"Well, they fight over cattle, Little Father, and they have more feuds than a dog has fleas, but the Nogais go to war under the khan's standard."

He stared at Stuart and at the jug, wondering what had got into his officer. But the Scot, frowning, went to the entrance and looked out. Suddenly he swung around, shaking back the dark locks from his face, his gray eyes alight.

"Faith, Ayub, an omen. The stars are out!"

The Cossack ran to look for himself and then hastened to kick the old Nogai and pull on his gloves.

"*Nà kòn!*—to horse."

The wind had not died down, and the cold was like flame touching their faces. Except to the south the sky was clear, and they harnessed the Tartar's ponies to the sled without delay, loading it up with bundles of hay. Among these bundles Ayub stowed the old man and the girl, wrapped in sheepskin robes. They made no effort to escape—in fact helped with the loading, since they had not expected that their lives would be spared.

Ayub saddled the two chargers, swearing under his breath when his fingers touched any metal. When he took the rein of the leading pony Stuart rode up to him.

"Make the Tartars show the road, or we will not get through the drifts." And when the Cossack would have started off, he checked him. "Nay, this way."

"But that is the south, Little Father, the way toward the sea."

"Aye."

"Down there is the Krim khan and his city. The outposts cannot be more than three days' ride."

"Aye, we are going to the khan."

Slowly Ayub shook his head.

"How, going? The ambassadors have turned up their toes—the gold is gone. Why should we go?"

"It is the order of the king. The others are slain, but we are free to go."

The Cossack swung his short whip in silence for a moment.

"Impossible to go on! The Krim warriors would make saddles out of the hides of unbelievers, unless they are ambassadors. And ambassadors always have papers and servants, and they make lying speeches. We can't do all that."

Stuart fumbled with a gloved hand under his coat and drew out a sheet of parchment that had been rolled and creased. When Ayub bent to peer at it in the starlight he saw closely written lines, and at the bottom a seal.

"That is from the hand of the king," Stuart explained, "and the order he gave me was to reach the court of the khan, at all costs."

Again the Cossack shook his head.

"Easier to keep a wolf out of sheep, than the Krim Tartars out of a war. Nay, 'tis not to be done."

Stuart put away the paper.

"In Kudak you said that two riders might get through where the detachment of Poles could not go. But I do not order you to go. Give me a horse and some food, and I will go on."

"May the devil take the king and all the Poles!" the Cossack groaned. "Impossible to abandon a comrade. You could not talk to the Krim, and they would take your head to put on a gatepost." He shook his own head gravely. "Little Father, I have seen men rush to embrace Death as if into the arms of a fair young woman, but I have never seen a man turn his rein toward the court of Satan."

Still muttering, he turned the head of the lead horse, and the sled creaked over the snow, past the distant black yurts of the Nogai encampment.

Chapter VI
The Turks

Four days later they heard the roar of the sea. It was near sunset, although no sun could be seen. Mist rolled in from the water, among black outcroppings of rock; the snow lay only in pockets and in the steep gullies under waving brush. The ground reeked of mud and salt and damp, and the tired horses floundered over slush and stones. The clamor of waterfowl filled the mist. The air, after the icy breath of the steppes, seemed hot.

They followed the narrow road that led along the shore, by fishing villages and shallow bays, until the throbbing of the surf diminished and the path led them beside what seemed to be a canal. Sometimes this strip of water narrowed until a horse almost could have leaped it, and at times it widened into reed-bordered lakes where herons passed silently overhead. The mist thinned away by degrees, and the outline of the land loomed dark against the gray sky.

The canal became straighter, its banks high and sheer. And on the far side uprose the level line of a wall. No human dwellings were visible on the wall and, although Ayub listened for the tramp of horses, nothing could be heard moving.

The old Tartar—Stuart had sent back the pair to their village with the sled when the road to the sea had been reached—had said that after they came out on the shore a ride of three hours would bring them to the gate of the Krim men. The deserted canal seemed to be the sea moat, but no gate was visible until darkness set in and the Cossack pointed out a glimmer of light ahead of them.

As they drew nearer the glimmer became brighter. Moving lights took shape, and the glow of fires. They heard a murmur of voices and the stir of animals.

On their side of the canal a street of sorts stretched to the moat—twin lines of mud and thatch buildings that seemed to house the offspring of bedlam. Around the fires men of all races were visible. Ayub saw the thin faces and the ragged *kaftans* of Jews clustered among the muddy sheepskins of herders, and the striped cloaks of bearded Persians who snarled at all the rest.

Dogs and children wandered between the fires. A Circassian horseman trotted down the street, singing a high-pitched love song. The air smelled of horses and dung, and the love song was blended with the whistling and bubbling of camels. Here and there the broken stone wall of a caravansary took shape by the fires, with covered carts and lines of rough coated ponies beyond.

All of the men except the Jews were armed, but the Cossack noticed that no guards had been posted. At the end of the street the fires gleamed in the water of the moat and revealed the shadowy outline of the crenellated wall on the far side. A narrow bridge ran across the moat to the gate of a dark building on the other side. Little could be seen of this, ex-

cept two slender towers that might have been watchtowers or the minarets of a mosque.

Ayub stared up at it, fingering his beard.

"Eh, Little Father, the gate is closed. See, the caravans have taken to
shelter for the night. In the morning, perhaps, they will go in."

"We will go in tonight."

They had no more food, the horses were nearly done. To beg quarters
from the rabble of the *serais* would be to earn mockery and to lessen their
dignity in the eyes of the throng. To sleep in their cloaks in the muddy
field would be little better.

The Cossack nodded slowly.

"Aye, so. Shall we ride in among the dogs and send a message to the
gate?"

"Nay, we will ride to the bridge. Is the envoy of a king to dismount
among herders?"

He pulled up the head of the piebald charger and trotted forward, Ayub
following a little to one side. The Cossack tightened his girdle and drew
off his right glove, trying the blade of his yataghan to see if it were free in
the sheath. Once within the light of the fires they could not turn back,
and there was no guessing how the Moslems would greet them.

But they entered the head of the street unnoticed, and trotted between
the buildings, amid a snarling of dogs, until a boy's shrill cry drew attention to them.

"*Giaours!*"

Then silence fell about the nearest fires. Men rose hastily to stare and to
finger their beards in utter amazement. They seemed not to believe their
eyes. They would have expected to see the companions of the Prophet himself ride armed among them, more readily than two Christians emerging
from the steppe at night, unheralded and palpably without escort. Few of
them had ever seen a man like Stuart before, and dark eyes fastened hungrily upon his gray cloak and stained red boots.

He did not turn his head, and he was halfway down the street when
a clamor of excited comment uprose. Then, when it was evident that he
would keep on to the bridge, men jostled to hasten after him and the dogs
scurried ahead. Swordsmen swung into the saddles of waiting horses and
cantered through the herders and slaves who raced afoot. Some snatched
up torches and beat a way for themselves.

Stuart and the Cossack reined in and walked their chargers out on the bridge because it was built of timbers laid loose across the beams, and a gap might have been left for the unwary. But the torches of their escort gave them light, although the throng halted and spread itself expectantly about the end of the bridge.

From over their heads came a harsh challenge, and when Stuart kept on without heading it, an arrow thudded into the boards by the forefeet of his horse. Ayub looked up at the towers, lifting his arm.

"*Elchi!*" he shouted. "An ambassador! O ye men of Krim, send word to the gate."

A second arrow flashed down, and the Cossack's charger snorted. Voices gibed and mocked from the crowd that jostled beyond the bridge, but the towers were silent. The glow of the torches revealed the face of the fortress clearly—a seemingly solid wall of blackened brick and the lofty pointed doors, strengthened by knobs of iron. Although he strained his eyes upward, Ayub could see nothing moving on the tower summits.

It was not easy to sit quietly in the saddle beneath bows that could slay them unseen, and the watchers from the caravans did not make matters easier.

"Since when did *giaours* send ambassadors to the Krim?" a voice taunted.

Minutes passed, and the crowd grew more vociferous. Evidently it dared not come upon the bridge, but it made no secret of its hatred of unbelievers, and prophecies were bandied back and forth in shrill speculation as to the fate that awaited the Christians.

"O ye without wit," one proclaimed. "O blind dogs, wearers of hats, eaters of filth, know ye not the gate is closed between sun and sun?"

Ayub gritted his teeth in a rage because he could not retort, because their lot would be no enviable one if they had to turn back now. But Stuart became impatient and, ignoring the threat of the arrow, reined his horse forward, drew his sword and smote the timbers of the door with the pommel. Echoes answered from within, and the caravan men ceased their shouting to listen.

Whether the watchers above had sent tidings of the strangers, or the Scot's tattoo roused the guards within, the great doors creaked and swung outward. A man strode through the opening. By his green turban and the robe thrown over one shoulder, Ayub recognized a *mullah* who had visited Mecca. With a thin arm he lifted the lantern he carried and looked briefly at the Cossack and searchingly at the officer.

"What seek ye?" he cried.

Ayub answered—

"To be taken to the khan."

"Whence come ye?"

"From his Majesty, the King of Poland."

"There is no majesty save that of Allah and no power save of his be-stowing. What token was given thee?"

"The letter that will be placed at the feet of the khan."

"Hai!" The gaunt *mullah* threw back his head and laughed. "What words are these? No word hath reached this place of the coming ambas-sadors. Nay, they have never come in my time or my father's time from the Franks. Who led thee hither, and where are thy men?"

Sensing the mood of the *mullah*, the crowd howled and began to push forward upon the bridge. To show Stuart's missive now would be to yield to the *mullah*, and the least sign of weakness would be fatal. Ayub edged his horse close to the bearded servant of Islam.

"We will ask of the khan, 'Where are our companions?' Forty and two were beset and slain by the tribes on the road hither, and we alone may tell the tale of it. Give us safe escort to the khan, or thy head will lack ears and thy mouth a tongue!"

The dark eyes of the *mullah* moved restlessly, and he motioned back the listeners who had edged forward.

"Think well," he said, "if thy words be true. If not—" he laughed soundlessly and turned, throwing his robe back upon his arm—"come, if ye dare!"

Stuart reined his horse forward, and the two passed through the open doors into a stone passage where the flicker of the lantern fell upon nar-row embrasures and round holes high overhead. This part of the fortress seemed to be older than the rest, and had been built in the days when bows and liquid fire were the weapons of defense.

They crossed an open courtyard and here their guide bade them dis-mount. Throwing open the door of a bare chamber and pointing to a fine carpet, he said:

"Tomorrow ye shall mount for the ride to the khan. Meat and wine shall be brought, for ye are infidels. May Allah direct your steps aright."

They did not see the *mullah* again. When the sun was high the next day a Tartar *mirza* appeared and bade them make ready for the road, since he would conduct them to the khan. He was a dark, diminutive figure, clad in crimson and gold, and his horse was a blood Arab of price. He seemed astonished that the Christians had no goods or gear with them, and he exclaimed admiringly at sight of the piebald charger. He led them at a trot through the crowded courtyard and out to a highway where the earth was dry and free from snow.

Then the *mirza* let his Arab gallop. The four warriors who attended him fell in behind the Christians, and they thundered past the caravans that had set out before them, taking not the slightest trouble to turn aside for man or beast. The mule trains were hurried to the side of the road by anxious owners, and the slaves scuttled into the muddy ditch, to stare fearfully at the flashing robes and the tufted spears of the Tartars.

When he had scattered the foremost string of beasts, and had left an echo of mournful profanity in the air behind him, the little *mirza* looked around with satisfaction and reined in to a more sensible pace, motioning Ayub to ride abreast him.

For the rest of the morning they talked, and when they dismounted at noon to let the horses graze, the Cossack sought out Stuart and flung himself down in the brown grass.

"Not good, Little Father!" He shook his head and sighed, and the Scot waited in silence for him to relate his tidings in his own way. "May the devil take the sultan and all the Turks, and these wasps of Tartars, too! May the foul fiends sit upon them. May their hides be made into dog whips!"

The Turks, he said, were already at the Krim court. A *wazir* had arrived in the last moon with a galley load of gifts, and an army corps had followed him—eleven thousand janissaries and *sipahis* who were to march under the standard of the khan, up into the steppes and into Christian lands. They were preparing to take the field already, while the snow was still on the plains, before the Spring rains made a marsh of the grasslands.

This was bad news and Stuart considered it gravely. If the sultan had sent such a strong division out to the Krim peninsula for a flank movement, the Ottomans must be preparing to move with their full strength against Poland. There were fortresses along the southern frontier that could hold the main army of the Mohammedans in check—for a time. But Stuart, a cavalry officer himself, appreciated the havoc that would be wrought by this detached army, and especially by the fine Tartar cavalry of the Horde.

As usual, the Polish ministers had blundered. They had sent an ill assorted mission into the steppes, and it had been sent too late. The Turks were first in the field, and the tidings of the massacre of Prince Paul and the chancellor's party would only make the khan contemptuous of the fighting qualities of the Poles. And Stuart had seen enough of the steppe-dwellers to understand that a hint of weakness would draw the Tartars out of their fastness with fire and sword.

"Even the gold will work ill," he said to himself, thinking of the Nogai women who would soon be wearing His Majesty's gold thalers.

Better if it had never been sent. And noblewomen had brought their jewel caskets, and churches their candlesticks to make up the treasure.

"Is this true?" he asked Ayub.

"The red *mirza* is still rubbing his belly because he ate sugared mastic in the booths of the janissaries."

"Has the khan sworn to support the Turkish envoy?"

"Satan knows—at least they were hunting together. They have left Bagche Serai. Eh, no good ever came of trying to wear another man's boots. We are not ambassadors, and they will plant us on stakes for the sport of the women."

"*Aida—aida!* Hasten—hasten!" cried the *mirza* of the red *khalat*, swinging into his stirrups again.

He cried out impatiently, because Stuart took his time, and he seemed to look upon his charges more as captives than envoys. He set out again at the same breakneck pace, although he must have seen that the horses of the strangers were tired. He rode with the short stirrups of the Mongol and the easy, swaying seat of the Arab, and he did not draw rein until they had left the sun-warmed fields and plunged into a forest of dwarf oaks.

Here the trail narrowed and—because the oaks were still in leaf—they rode in shadow, sometimes stooping to pass under a gnarled branch. Presently the *mirza* dropped back until he could touch Ayub's arm.

"Look, *caphar*, yonder are some of the sultan's men."

Ayub had seen them already, a dozen horsemen who had been sitting by a stream, and who now were climbing into the saddle hastily. Their officer was an *agha*, by token of his white and gold mace. They were bigger men than the Tartars, clad in heavy garments and riding slippers. They had no shields or spears but carried long pistols in saddle holsters. Ayub knew they were Turks.

The *agha* made quite a fuss about drawing up his men as the Tartar detachment came up to him, and he called out to the red *mirza* the usual "*Salaam aleikoum!*"

The *mirza*, too, was inclined to be friendly.

"I greet thee, O companion of the road," he made response, his hand on his hip, and the head of his pacer pulled well up.

The Turk turned in his saddle, smiling, and suddenly snatched a pistol from its sheath. Ayub saw the hammer fall, and then smoke beat against his eyes, while his ears rang from the explosion.

The weapon had been thrust almost into the *mirza*'s side, and the little Tartar swayed, catching at his saddle horn. He reached for his sword hilt with a quivering hand and half drew the blade. Then he groaned and fell forward upon the neck of his horse. Other pistols roared, and Ayub drew his yataghan, shouting with surprise and anger. But he made no other movement.

One of the Turks ran up and gripped the rein of his charger, and another pointed a pistol at his head. The Cossack saw that Stuart, just behind him, was caught in the same fashion. Through the haze of white smoke he made out the Tartars of the escort fighting savagely. The *agha* and eight men had closed in around them, and one of them had fallen.

Although wounded by pistol balls, the others clung to their seats, wielding their short sabers, and snarling defiance. One of them, beset by three men, slid under his horse, stabbed a Turk's charger from beneath and emerged on foot on the other side—grappled with another adversary and pulled him to the ground, under the wounded horse that reared frantically. When Ayub looked that way again, they were both dead, the Tartar warrior's head crushed and his hands locked around the hilt of a curved knife that he had pulled from the Turk's girdle and driven under his ribs.

The other three fought without asking or giving mercy, and without any thought of flight. One of them was hacked with scimitars until the blood, draining over his horse, made the animal rear and throw him. The last survivor held off his foes and plunged from the road, to the rocks of the stream, where he made good his ground with saber and shield until he fell with a pistol ball in his head.

When the smoke drifted away between the trees, three of the Turks were dead and as many badly wounded in the body. The seven who were still unhurt gathered around the captives. They took Ayub's and Stuart's sword and pistol and brought them to the *agha*, who was nursing the sliced flesh on his jaw where a Tartar sword had grazed him.

He motioned for the saddlebags to be taken from the Christians and he seemed astonished when he found nothing but food and the Cossack's kit.

"Eh," he said in broken Nogai dialect, "where is the rest—the baggage?"

"Ask the wolves!" retorted the Cossack.

"Where are the others of thy band?"

Ayub pointed at the bodies on the ground, and the officer stroked his jaw in silence.

"Art thou indeed from the king of Poland?" he asked presently.

"*They* could have told thee!" Ayub motioned toward the dead.

"Thou wilt be like that, soon," the *agha* muttered, "thou and the young Frank."

And then, because his jaw pained him, he spat suddenly into the Cossack's face. Ayub lunged toward him, but the officer's baton smashed against his forehead and he reeled back in the saddle. Stuart pushed his horse forward, and the Turks ran up, but Ayub gripped his friend's arm.

"Do not strike, Little Father."

At a sign from the *agha* the soldiers tied the feet of the captives—ankle knotted to ankle beneath the horse's belly. Ayub watched from beneath shaggy brows, while his captors dragged the bodies of the Krim men into the trees. He heard shovels striking into earth; then the saddles were taken from the Tartar ponies, and the *agha* had his own saddle changed to the white pacer that had belonged to the *mirza*. He mounted clumsily, and the high-strung horse, excited by the conflict and the smell of blood, sidled and half reared. The wounded officer struck him over the head with the heavy baton.

Because the young horse was restless, or because his men delayed over the work of burial, the leader of the Turks called to two of his men to mount. He signed to Stuart and Ayub to follow, and set out, whipping the white Arab into a gallop before the swift-paced horse had time to find its gait. The two soldiers closed in behind the captives and when Ayub glanced back at them, one fingered his long pistol meaningly.

The *agha* seemed both anxious and in haste. When they came out of the wood into a rolling plain that stretched to the blue line of distant hills, he looked around on all sides—at the distant tents of herders and the road ahead of him. Then he turned off into a narrow trail and settled down into a steady trot.

Duncan Stuart, with his ankles aching from the ropes and his shoulders and thighs stiff from long hours in the saddle, was almost happy, although he looked utterly indifferent. He had slept through the night, although the Turks had given him no better food than barley soaked in water and had bedded him down in the dirty straw behind the horses. They had passed the night in a hut where the trail entered a ravine, and the Turks had taken some pains to hide the glow of their fire.

It was clear that the *agha* did not wish his captives to be seen. The treacherous attack upon the Tartars could have only one cause. The sultan's men had been sent to intercept the ambassadors and to do it secretly. How word of their presence had reached the Turks, he did not know. Perhaps there had been spies at the gate of the caravans. Perhaps the Tartars had sent one of their riders ahead.

But surely the envoy from Constantinople could not have bound the khan to an alliance, since the Turks had hunted down the Christian envoys. And, for some reason, the Turks must find his presence dangerous if they risked discovery in this manner.

Stuart did not know what was in store for him, and he expected no gentle treatment. Ayub had passed more than one hour on the road relating the tortures favored by the Ottomans, and flaying a man limb by limb was not the worst. No doubt the Turks meant to question him, and he had no delusions as to how this would be done.

It was clear that he was being taken to the Turkish camp, since his captors took such precautions to hide him from the eyes of the Krim men. Indeed, if the story of the attack on the *mirza*—the true story—were known to the Tartars, matters would not go well with the Turks. Stuart wondered what the khan of the Krim was like.

He noticed that day that they saw few horsemen in the hills. Women in bright *khalats* and children stared at them from a distance, and here and there old men were out with cattle herds. But they encountered no bands of horsemen and no one approached near them. Probably from afar they looked like three officers with two troopers following. Only once did they pass Tartar soldiers, when the trail, climbing the foothills, entered a ravine so narrow that Stuart could touch the sheer walls of granite by stretching out both his arms. The defile was no more than the bed of a stream, filled with worn stones. But when the weary horses scrambled up the last ascent they came out into a place that made Stuart catch his breath.

It was the summit of the pass—a level expanse of gravel as hard as a parade ground. In shape it was rough square, a long musket shot across, but instead of being the open summit of the hills, it was a valley surrounded by cliffs so lofty that Stuart had to raise his head to look at the summits. And these blue-gray cliffs rose in tiers to jagged rock masses against the cloud-flecked sky. On some of the ledges he saw the dark mouths of caverns and myriad clefts.

But these rock walls fell away in four places, as if the giants who shaped this plateau on the heights had hewn them asunder. Through the gaps he could see the horizon far below the hills. And through these ravines the wind surged gustily, sending the dust devils dancing over the ground.

"Ho, *caphars*," grinned Zain ad-Din the *agha*. "Look well, for this is the second gate—aye, the Gate of the Winds!"

And faint, clear echoes answered "Ho *caphars!*" flinging the words back and forth between the rock walls. The whole place was a subdued tumult of sound that trailed away like the ripple of water. In the center of the arena stood Tartar yurts, and here in the sun sat a few score warriors talking with a patrol of horsemen in round steel helmets and chain armor who carried long lances—a detachment of Turkish *sipahis*, the best of the sultan's cavalry.

"The two roads meet here." Zain ad-Din pointed to the other ravines. "Look well, for ye will not see the pass again."

Stuart had already noticed that paths zigzagged up the rocks, leading to the upper ledges. On the highest pinnacles tiny black figures moved against the passing clouds. For the most part the ledges and paths were deserted, but at need several thousand men could have stationed themselves on the heights of this citadel of rocks. If cannon had been placed at the summit of the ravines, the defenders of the Gate of the Winds could have maintained themselves against any siege. The plateau was large enough for several regiments of cavalry.

They had come out of the smallest of the ravines, and they must have been sighted from the heights above, because a Tartar officer mounted his horse near the yurts and cantered across the dusty arena toward them. Zain ad-Din spoke to his two troopers and hastened off to meet the officer. They met and talked a hundred paces away, and the Tartar, glancing idly toward the captives, saw only four men halted in the deep shadow of the cliff. The sun beat into the valley and the heat simmered over the dusty ground, although the breath of the wind was chill; it seemed natural enough that the *agha*'s men should keep to the shade—and no one saw that his two troopers had loaded pistols in their hands.

The Tartar officer of the guard seemed more interested in the *agha*'s white Arab than in the waiting men, and presently he turned back to his tents.

"Eh, Sir Brother—" Ayub broke a silence that had lasted for a night and a day—"let us ride toward the tents. We will fall with bullets in us, or steel. But that is better than the skinning knives that we will feel when we stand before the dog of a captain general of the Turks."

Stuart glanced at him quickly. In the Cossack's seamed and blistered face was a gleam of desperation. That morning the Turks had bound their wrists with ropes of twisted leather thongs and the heat had made the bruised flesh swell until it was agony to move an arm, or hold the reins.

Ayub had sunk into a black mood.

"Wait," said the Scot quietly.

But Ayub only shook his head, his bound hands caught in his beard. He saw no good in waiting. His bones ached and he had not eaten since Zain ad-Din had spat in his face.

"What is it you say?" Stuart asked him.

"'The Cossacks still have powder, and their strength?'"

"*Ekh ma!*" Ayub lifted his head. "It was said long ago by an *ataman* who was surrounded by enemies. 'There is powder still in the powder-horns—the Cossack strength is not broken!' That is what the brothers call out when matters go hard with them."

"And how is it with us?"

"We have no weapons. Nothing ahead but the knives."

The brief gleam of interest passed from the big man's face, and Stuart saw that he had failed to rouse Ayub from the moodiness that was like a sickness.

"One of us must reach the khan," he said. "For that we were sent. When did a Cossack turn aside from the road because he feared the end of the road?"

"By God, never!" Ayub smote his two hands upon his saddle horn and cursed the stab of pain that made his arms quiver. "I do not fear the Turks, and I will not leave you, but a bullet is better than the flaying knife that lifts your skin a little at a time."

"Will you go on with the *agha* like a tied dog?"

But even the taunt did not make Ayub angry.

"Zain ad-Din is a fox," he muttered. "He has the tongue of a woman. Just now he went up to the Tartar officer on that Arab—and came away unharmed."

"Why not?"

"He was riding a Tartar horse of price and the other knew it, yet he was not made to dismount."

Stuart looked up quickly.

"Nay, one white Arabian is like another—and Zain ad-Din has his own saddle."

"The *tamgha*—the brand on the flank. All Tartar clans have their brand marks. The mark on the white Arabian is a circle with a spear through it—and such horses are not often given as gifts," Ayub answered indifferently.

This gave the Scot food for thought, and he looked for the *tamgha* himself on the flank of Zain ad-Din's stolen mount. As the Cossack had said, the outline of a circle could be traced through the heavy Winter coat of the animal.

Zain Ad-Din led them through the southern ravine of the Gate of the Winds and, as soon as the gorge yielded to the open mountainside, he turned off into a cattle trail. Here they had to ride in file, and it was some time before Stuart could speak to Ayub again.

"Before we reach the Turkish camp," he said, "just before, we will do as you have said. It may be tomorrow or the next day, or the next, and until then we will watch for a chance to get free. If there is no chance, faith, we'll make one."

Ayub bent his head to listen, and looked around anxiously at the Turks, although not one of their captors understood a word they said. His bound hands quivered on his thigh.

"How make one?"

"We have no weapons and can't use our hands. But something will aid us."

"May God give it! Only, what?"

Stuart started to speak, and smiled. Leaning forward, he rested his hands on the sweat streaked mane of the piebald horse.

"He took us out of the storm and he will aid us now."

The Cossack looked keenly at the spotted horse, which favored a lame foreleg as he trotted stiffly after the *agha*'s smooth-paced Arab. The horses had been pushed hard the last two days, and ill fed. Their coats were rough and plastered with mud.

"Zain ad-Din's nag will run down the wolf-chaser now," he said, "and even the trooper's mounts will keep up with you."

"I trust the wolf-chaser." Stuart thought for a moment. "It is better to take the chance than go like sheep to the butcher. This is a trick that the *agha*'s men will not know. When we are in broken country, with woods or brush near, I will call to you, and push past Zain ad-Din at a gallop. The Turks will follow, and they may fire with their pistols. They will have their eyes on me and you must make no move—until Zain-ad-Din spurs after me. Then turn swiftly, and make for cover, to the side. Even if the troopers have fired their pistols, they may miss. 'Tis no easy thing to send a ball straight from a galloping horse."

Ayub nodded, his tousled mustache twitching in a grin.

"You to go one way—I another. Well, that works sometimes. But those sons of dogs may all follow you, and you have the king's letter."

Again a faint smile touched the Scot's lips. Zain ad-Din had searched their garments and boots, but Stuart's missive still lay where he had placed it, folded under his broad leather belt. He had not taken that belt off, and the Turks had not seemed to think that an envoy's papers could be stuck under a belt. The *agha* had no reason to search more carefully because the envoys were prisoners in his hands, their secrets soon to be drawn from them.

"I trust the wolf-chaser," he responded. "If you get clear and I fall, go to the nearest Tartars, ask to be taken to the khan, and tell how the Nogais slew the ambassadors, and how the Turks dealt with his officer in the wood. Bid them search in the wood for the bodies. As to the message from the king, the real ambassadors are dead and there is nothing you can say. But I know the Tartars a little, and if the khan discovers that his men have been set upon and slain, he will do nothing until he has avenged them."

"*Aya tak*, that is so. But if you escape, how will you talk to the Krim men?"

"I cannot talk to them, not to a soul in all this land of the Krim."

Ayub waited for his friend to say more; however, Stuart remained silent and it was Zain-ad-Din who broke the silence.

"Ho, ye hat wearers! Look! The road—this is the end."

They had been passing through a nest of boulders, and the *agha* had gone ahead to the brow of a ridge that overlooked the mountainside. When Stuart and Ayub joined him, they stopped instantly.

The ridge gave them a clear view for miles to the south, into a plain that stretched without break to the horizon. And this plain was green, from crops or grass. They saw scattered huts by groves of fruit trees, and far off the gleam of a winding river. The sun, on this side of the range, burned into their faces, and the mild breath of the wind was warm. A faint heat haze veiled the horizon.

This, Stuart thought, was the pasture land of the Krim, always free from snow. What drew his eyes at once and made Ayub mutter in his beard was the great encampment below them.

It was not one camp, but two, a half mile or so apart across the river. On the east of the river, the ground was covered with the domed tents of the Tartars, in the clear places masses of animals grazing. The sun glinted on the horns of cattle, and the bright robes of riders moved like flecks of color against the gray-brown horse herds. Smoke curled up from scattered fires.

To the west of the river appeared the huts and pavilions of a different sort. Some of the pavilions with their red and white sun curtains seemed as large as castles. The lines of regular streets ran through the camp, and a breastwork had been thrown up around it. In a cleared place the sun reflected upon brass. Stuart thought that cannon were parked here. Streamers and banners marked different sections, and there were few horses to be seen, but many men on foot in more somber colors.

"The camp of the Kapitan Pasha," said Zain ad-Din. "Aye, Murad, the Pasha of the Sea."

Chapter VII
Comrades

The nearest portion of the Turkish camp was less than two miles away. The path they were following ran close to the river on this side. Across the stream some Krim men were watering their horses, and others were more to the left, apparently flying falcons at the herons that started up from the rushes, but not a Tartar was on their side of the river. The path was clear to the gate of the breastwork, where some guards sat watching peasant carts go in and out. Zain ad-Din was well content. He had obeyed orders, had found and taken the envoys of the Christian king and had brought them safely within sight of his sultan's army. The evidence of his attack upon the Tartars was well hidden, and the two Christians, half-starved men on wearied horses, had nothing more to hope for. Zain ad-Din, as he trotted down the winding trail, wondered whether the Kapitan Pasha would reward him with jewels, or a new command.

"Thou seest," he cried, thrusting his baton into the Cossack's ribs. "There is peace and agreement between the host of Krim and the Ottomans. Soon the Moslem scimitar will strike, and thy brothers' heads will fall like cut grain, and as for thy sisters—"

"I know them well," growled the old Cossack, roused by the taunt. "And they will fall by the men, sword in hand. But as for thee, knowest thou thy sisters?"

The face of the lean *agha* darkened and he clutched at one of the daggers in his girdle. Then his teeth gleamed in a smile, and he spurred on the white pacer.

"Hasten—hasten! Thy fate is near."

Even the troopers urged on their jaded horses, for the breath of the plain was hot, and the breastwork less than a mile away. Already some of the guards had turned to gaze at the five riders.

Stuart watched the distant figures through narrowed eyes and laughed over his shoulder at the Cossack.

"Well said, O my brother. The Cossack strength is not spent."

"Well, we will look soon at our fate. Why did you not try the trick back in the thickets of the hill? There is no cover here and in a moment the dogs yonder will be leading our horses."

"Wait."

The Scot's lips tightened and he moved his hands between the ropes. A group of janissaries who had wandered out to the fruit trees waved at them and shouted. Beyond this grove the plain stretched as flat as a desert floor to the half mile distant river.

Stuart turned in his saddle and smiled at his friend.

"What was it you said before the duel in Kudak?"

"What, eh? To one of us life, to the other death!"

"That was it. Well, now is the time, Ayub. When the *agha* starts after me, go for the river, and don't look back or turn aside. Go with God."

Ayub answered mechanically, "With God," before he realized that the Scot had struck the piebald horse on the side away from Zain ad-Din with his heel. Surprised and hurt, the spotted horse lunged forward into a gallop. It passed the *agha*'s Arab and took the road, its head thrust out, its flanks heaving.

Zain ad-Din watched, at first with curiosity and then—when he urged on the pacer and the gap between them did not diminish—with anger. It was no part of his plan to have his prisoner a runaway into the Turkish camp.

"Stop!" he shouted, and lashed on his Arab.

The swifter horses drew away from the three following. For a moment they all held their places. Looking over his shoulder, Stuart saw that the *agha* was about ten yards behind him, and some fifty yards ahead of the other three.

Suddenly and without warning of any kind, the Scot flung himself back in the saddle, crying out to his horse as he did so. The wolf chaser plunged and came to a stop, all four legs gathered under him. At the same instant the horse wheeled and reared, lashing out with its forelegs.

And the lashing hoofs and all the weight of horse and rider came down on Zain ad Din.

The *agha* had tried in vain to check the rush of his own horse when he saw the wolf-chaser rear in front of him. But he was too near, the time too short. His Arab half wheeled, and the result was to throw the white horse.

The crash sent the piebald charger reeling back. If it had fallen, with Stuart's ankles bound beneath, the Scot could not have escaped from the saddle. With a stagger and lurch the spotted horse recovered its balance, quivering all over. Then Stuart reined over to Zain ad-Din.

The *agha* lay motionless, blood dripping from his open teeth. He had fallen on his right side, and the scimitar sheath in his girdle was caught under one leg. Stuart, hearing hoofs thudding close to him, slipped his feet from the stirrups and flung himself toward the unconscious man.

With his hands bound together, it was his only chance to grip the scimitar hilt, and grip it he did, although he hung by one knee from the saddle. The rope that bound his ankles kept him from falling clear, and the piebald horse stood quiet. He drew the sword with one hand. And then with an effort that sent a wrenching pain through his hip and shoulder, he swung himself up far enough to catch the saddle horn with his free hand. Another pull and he was back in the saddle, just as the Turkish trooper who had hastened toward him, slashed down at his head with a sword.

Quickly as Stuart flung up his own blade to parry, he could not quite check the blow. The steel blade, near the hand guard, struck his lynx skin cap and grazed his skull.

But the rush of the trooper's horse carried him past, and when he wheeled and came in to strike again, Stuart had found his stirrups and had raised his scimitar.

"Allah!" the Turk cried, and slashed with all his strength.

But a blade in the hands of a skilled swordsman—even though his hands were tied together—overmatched the Moslem soldier.

Once the horses reared, and the steel rang out. Twice the blades clashed, and then the Turk fell, cut across the eyes, and Stuart wrenched his scimitar clear.

He turned to look for Ayub. But the Cossack was not riding for the river, had not left the road.

Instead, two riders were locked together in a crushing embrace, while their horses danced and wheeled like two ships moored together in a swift current. Without trying to guess what had happened, Stuart raced the wolf-chaser back to them.

He saw that the Turk held a knife in one hand and a pistol in the other, and was twisting desperately to free an arm. Ayub had thrown his bound arms over the trooper's shoulders, pinning the other's forearms to his sides. The curved knife was moving spasmodically an inch from his ribs, but the giant Cossack, exerting all the strength of his shoulders, squeezed his enemy's bones in a vise-like grip. The Turk was panting, and foam puffed between his loose lips.

"*Hai*, Little Father!" Ayub grunted. "Don't cut—thrust him under the arm."

Stuart drew back his scimitar as the soldier with a convulsive effort discharged his pistol toward Ayub. But the ball went wide, although the spraying powder blackened the Cossack's cheek. Then, seeing death inevitable, the Turk turned his eyes up and dropped his knife.

Instead of thrusting him through, the Scot pulled the trooper's scimitar from its sheath in his girdle, and with it cut the ropes that bound Ayub's wrists.

"Take one sword—here!" he cried. "Now cut these cords."

When the Cossack had sliced the leather thongs from his throbbing wrists, Stuart wasted no second of precious time upon the Turk. Instead, he turned back and galloped to the white Arab that had regained its feet and was standing near Zain ad-Din. The pacer snorted and sprang away at his coming, but in another moment suffered itself to be caught. He drew the dangling rein over his arm, wiped the blood from his eye and shouted to Ayub to ride toward the river.

A glance over his shoulder showed him that the guards at the gate of the camp were running about and pointing toward him. Behind him, from the grove whence the janissaries had been drawn by the sound of fighting, a pistol roared, and the ball whipped past him, over his head.

He urged the spotted horse on to the river, drawing up to the Cossack, whose horse was stumbling badly. The Turkish trooper lay huddled as if sleeping in the high grass, and Ayub was wiping clean his blade with his foe's turban cloth. Riders—*sipahis* with lances—were galloping out of the gate, but the river was less than a quarter mile away and at the far bank the Tartars who had been spectators of the fighting were watching expectantly.

Stuart slowed the spotted horse to keep pace with the winded stallion.

"Why didn't you ride off as we agreed?" he demanded of the Cossack.

"Eh, why did you turn back into the *agha*? Impossible to ride off and leave a comrade to fight three Turks! They'd have cut you down. *Hai*— you went into Zain ad-Din like a Cossack!"

Ayub struck his horse with the flat of his blade and galloped headlong into the stream without pausing to look for fords. Rising in his stirrups, he shouted at the Tartars.

"*Hi*, ye men of the Krim! We are ambassadors to the khan!"

Chapter VIII
Diplomatic Truth

Arak Buka, Khan of all the Hordes, descendant of Mohammed, Lord of the Krim, and Master of Bagche Serai, sat on his heels and looked with pleasure at what lay before him. Two antelopes, a young panther and a black marten lay outstretched in front of the pavilion opening, and they had fallen to Arak Buka's bow that morning. The khan was seventy and six years of age, his black eyes gleamed out of a mass of wrinkles, and the hair hidden by the black velvet cap was white, but he could still sit in the saddle from sun to sun and bring down beasts with his hunting bow.

More than hunting, he relished leading the Horde afield, as he had done for half a century. True, the *ordus* were commanded by his four sons and some twoscore grandsons; but not one of his offspring would have dreamed of defying the authority of that thin and aged veteran. A dozen of them in gold-trimmed *khalats* sat behind him, and behind them were grouped as many *mirzas*—officers of high birth—and beyond them the slaves who hastened to bring snow-cooled wine to the carpet of the khan, who munched sunflower seeds and hemp as he contemplated the result of his morning's hunt.

"Take them—thou and thou—" he nodded to four officers who rose and hastened to press their heads to the carpet at his knees at this signal favor.

Then, because the aged khan watched them, the four *mirzas* hurried to pick up the game, and carry the carcasses off on their own shoulders.

The khan chewed on his string of hemp, his eyes closed.

Only one thing marred his content. His brother, the sultan of the Ottomans, Lord of Stamboul,* had sent a strong force of infantry, with a dozen cannon and some regiments of supporting cavalry, to aid him in the new war upon the unbelievers. And this division was commanded by a certain Kapitan Pasha who was a notable leader upon the sea. In fact, this right-hand officer of the sultan had spent most of his life on galleys and had matched his strength against the Barbary pashas.

But it was clear to the khan, although he kept his own counsel about it, that this captain general of the Turks knew little about handling cavalry. Murad Pasha had come with his galleys more than once to besiege the coast cities of the Krim, but Arak Buka did not hold this against him. That had been the war of brothers—and what would life be without war?

Murad Pasha now demanded that the khan advance at once with his cavalry division and the Turkish infantry division, across the steppe while the snow roads were still good. That was very well for infantry, but it would be hard for the horses.

The khan was willing enough to march into Poland, and for the time being he was at peace with his brother, the sultan, but Murad's insistence made him angry. His horses were not in condition for such a march. So he had assembled some fifteen thousand of the Krim riders and occupied himself with hunting, fully determined not to move north until he was ready, Murad Pasha and all the Turks to the contrary.

While he chewed drowsily upon the hemp, a shaven *mullah* stand-

---

*Constantinople.

ing beside him reading aloud verses from the Koran, the khan's eye was caught by a mailed figure that dismounted a stone's throw from the wide entrance of his sitting pavilion, and advanced toward him, kneeling outside the ropes. He held up his hand and the *mullah* ceased reading. He nodded, and the bearded Tartar who held a spear across his knees as he stood by the entrance—and by that token was officer of the day's guard—cried out to the messenger—

"Speak!"

The man lifted his hands to his helmet and bent his head to the ground. Then, still upon his knees, he cried out:

"Two Franks have come to the *ordu*. O Khan of the Horde, O *sayyid*, O Pole of the Faith, and Lord of Krim, these Franks are envoys from Poland."

A murmur of whispering filled the pavilion, and Arak Buka opened his eyes.

"What dogs are these? Is it not known that I have lifted my standard for war? Send them away."

The messenger bent his head.

"I have heard. And yet, O Lord my khan, they have with them a letter. Will the Soul of the Krim see the letter?"

Slowly the bony jaws of the aged man resumed their chewing, and his eyelids drooped.

"What is a letter brought by dogs? Have they gifts?"

"Naught have they but their horses, good horses. Their coming was in this manner: They were riding across the plain with three Turks, and then they were seen to fight with the Turks, of whom all three were left on the ground. Then they turned their heads toward the river which is the boundary of our camp. They have also," the methodical Tartar added, "another good horse, taken from the Turkish officer."

Arak Buka stopped chewing, and his thin fingers caressed a worn gold bracelet upon his wrist under the gray silk sleeve. He was still a splendid figure, and he had all the fire of impetuosity and recklessness with an insatiable desire for gifts and spoil.

"Do ambassadors fight like leopards?" he said. "Let the horses be led before me."

When the Tartars of the guard were running up with the leg-weary beasts, two black-robed attendants hastened up the slope to the pavilion entrance. They carried staffs, and they wore turbans with crowns like sugar loaves, and they cried out loudly—

"The Master of the Stirrup of the Pasha comes to the footstool of the Majesty of the Krim!"

Behind the wand-bearers advanced a Turkish officer with an ermine-bordered cloak, worn upon one shoulder, behind him other officers. They salaamed deeply, breathing heavily from the haste of their coming, and the khan's fine eyes looked at them with some surprise.

"O Lord of Bagche Serai," the Master of the Stirrup cried, "we beg that thy generosity will give into our hands the captives who escaped from an *agha* of the sultan."

Arak Buka had been looking over the horses, and his eye lingered on the big wolf-chaser and wandered to the white Arabian.

"There is blood on that one," he observed.

The Master of the Stirrup stepped forward.

"Aye, by Allah, the blood of a believer. That is the *agha*'s horse."

Again Arak Buka looked at the brand mark on the pacer's flank, and something seemed to puzzle him. Finally he spat out the hemp and handed it to the nearest *mullah* to eat, as a sign of favor.

"By Allah, there is too much talk," he grumbled. "If the Franks are indeed ambassadors, they were sent to me. Let them come before me."

The assemblage of Turks bowed, to hide their anger. They had not been invited within the shade of the pavilion where the Tartars sat at ease on the carpets, and the sun did not improve their mood.

When Duncan Stuart and Ayub were escorted to the pavilion entrance by spearmen of the guard, there was utter silence. Many of the Krim lords had never seen a man like the Scot. He had had neither time nor means to clean the dried blood from his head and cheek, and Ayub's shaggy countenance was black with powder. Their swords had been taken by the guards. But they stood erect, half a head taller than the largest of the Turks.

After Arak Buka had considered them awhile, he asked for the letter that had been sent him, and Ayub interpreted to Stuart. The Scot felt under his belt and drew out the square of parchment folded many times. Slowly he opened this, and when he stepped forward, two Tartars sprang to catch and hold him by the shoulders. They led him to the carpet of the khan and motioned him to place the missive at Arak Buka's knees.

This he did, and the aged Tartar gazed at it curiously.

"Read!" he commanded.

A long-robed *mullah* picked up the parchment, studied the seal and

shook his head. He handed it to another who fingered his beard in silence.
A third reader of the Koran announced that it was not written in Arabic,
or Syriac, or Turkish, or even Greek.

"Read it thyself!" the khan commanded Stuart, and Ayub prompted
his friend.

The Scot took the missive and looked into the dark eyes of the master of the Krim.

"This is the message, O Khan of the Horde," he explained slowly.

> To thee gives greeting Sigismund of Poland. Long has there
> been peace between the Commonwealth and the Krim; nor is
> there now any cause for conflict between them. Many enemies
> has Poland, and long has the Commonwealth been at war.
>
> The eagles of Poland are strong, their wings untiring. They
> will rise from the conflict as they have done before, victori-
> ous, and they will drive the spoilers again beyond their coun-
> try. The foes of the eagles will count their dead and grieve—
> as they have done before.
>
> Not of his own will does the khan of the Krim move to war,
> but at the will of the Ottoman sultan. Is the khan a peregrine
> falcon, to be hooded by a master and loosed at game when the
> master pleases? It was not so in the day of Tamerlane when
> the Golden Horde were lords of the steppe.
>
> Is the khan less than his ancestors? Is—he indeed a blind fal-
> con, not seeing that the hand that feeds him takes his prey
> from him. The Ottoman sultan looks upon him as a servant
> and sends commands to him by an officer. Let the khan con-
> sider and act wisely.

When Ayub had translated the last word there was a general silence.
Never before had the Tartars listened to such an exhortation by Christians—and Stuart's eloquence lost nothing in Ayub's vivid rendering.
The *mullahs* muttered together, for they had been preaching a holy war
against the Franks, and the apparition of two wounded envoys was not to
their liking. The few Turks who understood looked astonished.

The aged khan, kneeling on the green carpet of the dais, lifted a finger
to his lips and meditated, while he fixed the words in his memory.

"I have heard the message of the khan of the Christians," he said calmly.

"Now I will hear how the message was brought to me, to this place."

And when the Cossack turned to Stuart, he added curtly—

"Let the Kazak speak and the young officer be silent."

He closed his eyes expectantly, and the two boy slaves who moved the feather fans behind his head became very attentive, for the old Tartar was never so alert as when he pretended to doze; they knew this to their cost.

Ayub thrust his hands into his girdle and looked around at the rows of thin, dark faces that stared up at him without expression. It had been easy to interpret Stuart's message, but what was he to say? His throat was dry with dust, and there was nothing in his head but pain. Behind set teeth Ayub cursed all ambassadors and all the Poles. He was no fox to beguile a multitude with tricks.

"O ye men of Krim," he said hoarsely, "since when have ye suffered envoys to stand like foundered horses, without wine to cool their throats? Spirits are better than wine."

They stirred restlessly, because to offer food or drink was to acknowledge strangers as guests. A bearded *mirza* whispered to Arak Buka and then signed to a cup-bearer, who poured white liquid into a deep bowl and came forward to the Cossack. Ayub took it in his hands and sniffed. The bowl was filled with distilled spirits mixed with mare's milk. He stroked down his mustaches, and lifted it joyfully, booming forth—

"Health to ye!"

He handed the silver vessel back to the cup-bearer, who hastened to fill it again and offer it. It was a custom of the Krim to refrain from offering wine until a guest made a sign that he wished no more, but Ayub was not aware of this.

"Health to ye!"

Again he lifted the silver bowl, and again he emptied it with deep swallows without lowering it. A murmur rose from the watchers. The guests in the khan's presence were expected to drink down all that was offered them, and not to do so was to slight the hospitality of the Krim. But this giant emptied bowls as if they were cups.

Ayub felt Stuart's eyes upon him questioningly, and he gave voice to his trouble.

"Sir Brother, the khan has commanded you to be silent, and me to explain how that writing was brought."

"Tell the truth," the Scot responded quickly, and then Ayub saw before him the cup-bearer again, holding out the silver bowl.

"Well," he muttered, "our fate is near, and 'tis better to have this milk vodka under our belts."

His own girdle irked him, and he loosened it, then gripped the vessel and drank it down, more slowly this time, and the Tartar servant looked into it and held it upside down, to show the watchers that for the third time it was empty.

The Cossack's heart began to beat strongly, and heat crept into all his veins. Spreading his feet wide, he looked around at the assemblage, surprised because the lines of faces had merged into a dark mass. He shook his head, and the mass began to revolve slowly about the tent pole. And, staring at the great gilded pole, Ayub fancied that it also was turning upon its axis. He had eaten nothing for two days and had drunk down enough of the fermented milk and pure spirits to make a bullock reel.

"No more!"

He heard Stuart's voice, blurred, as if from a distance, and he shook his head to quiet the throbbing in his ears. He began to speak and found that all hoarseness had left his voice. In fact, it carried to the lines of the outer guards, and filled the tent with its roar.

"O Lord of the Krim, Eagle of the Steppe, Master of all the Hordes, this is how the letter was brought. We were many, and we had many wagons filled with gold to be brought to thee, and a prince and a White Beard to repeat to thee the words of the Christian king. Aye, ten thousand pieces of gold and other gifts that would have filled this yurt."

Ayub waved a stalwart arm in a sweeping circle.

"The jackals that hunt beyond thy gate, the gully-lurking jackals, the Nogais, came upon us without warning and slew and seized, and we twain are all that lived when the swords of the Nogais were sheathed."

And he related the details of their ride through the storm and hiding in the village of their foes.

"And why did these jackals tear us? It is true that the Turks sent gold and an officer to lead them against us. Nay, the kites are fattening upon the body of that officer! And what did the dogs of Turks do then? When we had entered thy gate, they shot down thy men, our escort."

He told how Zain ad-Din had come up to the *mirza*, and how the Tartars had died, and it seemed to him that the throbbing in his ears became a roar. In fact, scores of the listeners were upon their feet, some crying out in anger, and some—the *mullahs* and the Turks among them—mocking him. These were in the majority and their shouts drowned his voice.

"Proof, let there be proof!"

"What lies are these? The *giaour* was sent hither with lies!"

"To the stake with the Nazarenes!"

"Ho, ye Muslimin, is a snake to creep among us? Strike him with steel. This is no envoy."

In all the clamor one word penetrated to the Cossack's understanding.

"Proof!" he roared above the tumult.

He stretched his arms out and pulled back his long sleeves. "Look, ye Muslimin! Were these scars made by a girl's bracelet?"

His swollen wrists and the torn and matted sores on his hairy forearms were mute testimony to the ropes that had bound him.

"Will ye have proof?" he went on when the outcry had dwindled because the watchers had become curious. "Then ask the men of the Horde who were watering at the river and saw us beat down the Turks with their own weapons. Ask them what weapons were in our hands! And then send riders on swift horses, back to the road at the oak forest, and bid them dig up and bring before the khan the bodies of his men."

There was silence then, because Ayub had spoken in the presence of the khan, of Tartars who had been killed by the sultan's men, and every listener bent forward to hear what the old chieftain might be pleased to say.

Arak Bukas opened his eyes and, without paying any attention to Ayub, signed to the Turkish Master of the Stirrup to come forward, and a way was opened for the officer who flung back his dolman and salaamed low, remaining on his knees.

"Is it true," asked Arak Buka, "what thou didst say at first, that these Christians are the prisoners of the sultan?"

"May Allah be my witness, it is true."

Ayub stepped forward unsteadily.

"Send to the oak forest!"

But the khan took no heed of his words, and before he could speak again, the officer of the Tartar guard advanced to the dais.

"Speak!" murmured Arak Buka.

"Murad Pasha comes, O my khan, to sit with thee."

Like an eagle stooping to earth, Murad Pasha came, calm-eyed, amid a throng of horsemen and glittering, lofty turbans. His attendants brought gifts to the khan—a brown and white *kafalka*, a peregrine falcon with a silver chain, and a gold box of musk, and a lump of sweet-smelling ambergris as large as a man's head. The pasha himself wore only the uniform of the *sipahis*, although the crest of his turban was that of a minister of the Ottoman Empire. A sallow-faced man, broad and tranquil and merciless—and unafraid. He took as if by right a seat on the blue carpet beside the khan and leaned back on the pillows that the slaves hastened to bring.

It was sunset by then, because the Captain General of the Sea had not hurried, and the Tartar slaves moved among the throng, lighting the lanterns and raising them upon spears. The throng had grown to a multitude and thousands of eyes stared into the open front of the pavilion, watching every movement of the two leaders of Islam, while the khan feasted his distinguished guest from trays of almonds and mastic and melons. Neither spoke of the Christian prisoners, and only outside the tent did men dare whisper of what had passed.

The khan had taken the falcon upon his wrist for a moment and then handed it to one of his officers.

Stuart could learn nothing from the faces, for the old Tartar seemed only concerned about his hospitality, and the pasha about nothing at all. The khan's musicians were sent for and disturbed the twilight with the whining of flutes and the squealing of bagpipes, and blare of horns. The envoys, seated among the lesser officers below the dais, were left to themselves, and this was not a good sign.

It was Murad Pasha who spoke of them, looking in their direction, idly.

"*Allah kirbadiz partalouk!* May Allah protect thy shadow, O my Uncle! I have heard that men of mine have taken captive two *giaours* who say they were sent to thee. As to that I know not, but keep thou the Nazarenes, as a gift from my hand."

Arak Buka nodded slightly, and after a moment the pasha added:

"Soon, if God wills it, we shall mount for the journey against the Christian cities, and the gathering of spoils. Let this evening be rendered pleasant and our eyes refreshed by the slaying of the two Nazarenes. If indeed they be envoys from the insolent king, their death will be a fitting response. If they be liars, the stake is a good sitting place for them."

The old Tartar thought for a moment.

"Is it thy desire?"

And the Turk's fine teeth flashed in a smile.

"Verily, it would please me, for it is written that the faithful shall be made glad by the downfall of unbelievers."

A soft murmur came from the listening readers of the Koran.

"True, true!"

"My officer, who took them," Murad added indifferently, "saw the letter they bore, but who can read what is written upon it? Nay, only the two giaours can say what is written."

Arak Buka raised his hand to his lips and shook his head as if this thought had not struck him before.

"How did thy servant come upon these dogs, O my nephew?"

There was no relationship between the Tartar and the Turkish pasha, or the sultan whom he called his brother by custom, but the words implied trust, and Murad clapped his hands together, calling out to his more distant followers. From beyond the lights an officer hastened forward and cast himself down at the dais. And Ayub started, seeing that he was Zain ad-Din, pallid from loss of blood, but resplendent in a new tunic and *kaftan* and his *agha*'s helmet.

"O, my uncle," the Pasha explained, "here is the servant to answer thy question."

"Speak!" Arak Buka closed his eyes as if wearied by the many lights.

"By the threefold oath, by the grave of the Prophet I swear," cried Zain ad-Din, "that when I rode with two followers I came up with these twain crossing the ravine that leads to the Gate of the Winds. We rode up with our pistols in hand and took their weapons, and then bound them and led them to the Pasha's camp. In the plain across the river the young Nazarene tricked me and threw me from my horse, and the twain escaped to the river. The rest thou knowest."

"Said I not," Ayub whispered to his comrade, "that the *agha* had a woman's wit? He has been told all that was said here before him. And the khan has not sent to look for the bodies."

"What would it prove if he did?" the Scot asked quietly, and Ayub could only gnaw his mustache.

Arak Buka considered, his eyes still shut and his thin face tranquil.

"They brought thy horse also," he observed.

And Zain ad-Din remembered that the khan was acquisitive where horses were involved.

"May it find favor in thy sight, O Majesty of the Krim, he cried, "if thou wilt accept the horse as a gift."

"A good horse." The old Tartar nodded approvingly, and even commanded that the Arabian be led before the pavilion entrance for him to see again. The pacer had not yet been relieved of its saddle. "Is that the horse?"

"May it please the Sword of the Faith, the white charger was mine and is now thine."

"How was it bred? Has it been long in thy hand?"

"As to the blood strain I know not, but I had it of a dealer of Sivas, and for four years it has carried me."

"Nay," murmured Arak Buka, "the white horse bears the brand of the Ghirei clan of Tartars. Look upon its flank."

Zain ad-Din's dark eyes lowered and lifted again. In ten seconds he had meditated swiftly; he did not know of any brand, but he did not dare question the khan's word.

"That mark? It was on the horse when I had it of the dealer."

"*Kai*, this horse is no more than a two-year." Suddenly Arak Buka leaned forward, his gnarled hands on his knees, his slant eyes blazing, and words hissed from his lips. "Thou hast lied! The horse is Tartar bred, and one of that breed is only taken from us by the sword. Thou hast slain my *mirza*."

The white faced *agha* swayed on his knees, and Murad Pasha spoke swiftly.

"So, Zain ad-Din, thy tale was false, and—thou has struck down a servant of the khan to gain the horse. For no other reason than that, thou hast the blood of a believer upon thy hand."

His lips curved, and his dark eyes stared at his officer from drooping lids. Only his hand, caressing a dagger sheath, was tense as the talons of a hawk.

Zain ad-Din started to speak, and involuntarily his eyes sought Murad's. The blood seemed to drain from his cheeks, leaving his face a set mask, and his lips a line of pain. Twice he bent his head and murmured:

"God is one! It is true that I have slain a *mirza* of the great khan to gain this horse."

Immediately Murad rose, his brow dark.

"O dog of the dunghill! Thou knowest the law of the Horde? For the thief and the slayer, death."

The *agha* folded his arms.

"I have heard, O my pasha."

The pasha spoke to one of his officers, who came forward with a *sipahi* and took Zain ad-Din by the arms. And the *agha* rose to his feet at once. He salaamed to Arak Buka, who watched him silently, and then turned to leave the pavilion. His step was firm and he seemed less stirred than the two who walked at his side. At the entrance he waited for the throng to give way.

Then he knelt, beyond the ropes, and for several moments lifted his hands and bent his body in prayer, his eyes toward Mecca. So still was the assemblage that the murmur of his voice carried to the pasha—

"*Allah u kerim*—God *the* merciful and compassionate—"

When the murmur ended, and he knelt with his clenched hands against his forehead, the *sipahi* stepped quickly behind him. In the gleam of the lanterns the arc of blue steel showed for an instant as the soldier lifted his arm, the point of the blade turned down. A quick thrust downward, a check, a final lunge. Zain ad-Din's body jerked forward, and a sigh ran through the crowd.

The *sipahi* bent forward and held up in both hands the *agha*'s severed head, holding it by the ears.

"Thou hast seen!" Murad leaned toward his host. "A life taken for a life."

"Aye," said Arak Buka, and thought for a moment. "Now give me back the ten thousand pieces of gold that would have been mine."

Surprise made the Turk frown.

"O Lord of the Krim, believest thou the tale of the gold and the message that none but the Nazarenes themselves can read?"

The old Tartar indulged in one of his spells of silence, until his eyes opened and he smiled as if he saw a solution of the matter.

"I have heard, O my nephew, that thou art schooled in the writing of Stamboul and the writing of the Franks."

"Indeed, O my khan."

Stretching forth his hand for the missive that had been given to a *mullah*'s care, Arak Buka offered Stuart's parchment to the Turk.

"Then read, thyself, and satisfy thyself."

Murad took it in his hands and glanced at it eagerly.

"This is the common language of the Franks, by which one race writes to another and it is called Latin."

He scanned the lines, at first curiously, then with a swift and amazed stare. Motioning for a lantern to be brought, he bent over it, glancing hastily at the seal and then returning to the written lines. And Stuart, watching from the outer shadows, caught Ayub by the arm with a grip that pressed into the Cossack's muscles.

When he had finished, Murad Pasha looked up, his broad face flushed with triumph, and his dark eyes alight.

"O my khan, this paper is not a message to thee. It is no more than an appointment to the rank of colonel, signed by the king of Poland."

A single exclamation resounded from all who had heard, and the old Tartar rose suddenly, his hand clutching at the hilt of his scimitar. His slant eyes glowed and the lines on his bronzed head deepened into a mask of rage.

"*Hai*, I have listened too long to thee, Murad Pasha. I have heard thee say thy men seized these ambassadors, not knowing. And then like a snake thou hast come to bid me slay them. Thy men were taking them to thee, not to me. Am I an addled old woman? Am I blind?"

"Nay—" the Turk held out the parchment in both hands—"the words are written—"

"Am I a twice begotten fool? God forbid! Would two Nazarenes ride into the Krim without a letter to me? I am tired of lies. I am weary of hearing talk to lead my horses into the snow!"

Murad Pasha was a man who loved best the boldest course, and now he stifled his anger while he weighed two alternatives and made his decision. He did a very simple and reckless thing. Turning away from the furious Tartar, he spoke to the throng that were now on their feet in a tumult of shouts; he threw back his head and laughed.

"O ye men of the sword, too long has this dotard ruled ye. Verily he is aged as a gray horse. He is a child, grasping at trinkets, and easily beguiled; he is a falcon with dim eyes. Choose, ye Muslimin! I have set up my standard. Come thither, ye who will ride to the holy war. And let the others who are fools come to the standard of the blind khan."

Arak Buka became quiet instantly, and before any one could speak, he stretched out a lean arm, pointing to the pavilion entrance.

"Go!" he said slowly. "Here, thou art the guest of my yurt. Go to thy camp and arm thy men and then watch to see who will come to thy standard."

Throwing back his heavy *svitza*, Ayub bared his steaming chest to the cool night air and looked up at the sky aglow with starlight. He was in the saddle of his own horse again, and beside him Stuart rode the piebald wolf-chaser. Ahead of them trotted a Krim *mirza* on his pony, the guide appointed them, to show them the way to the guest pavilion.

"As God lives, Sir Brother," the big Cossack said, loosing long pent up breath with a sigh that was like a bellow, you will never touch death as near as that, until the grave takes you."

The throbbing in his head was echoed by the rising mutter of drums that grew louder as they penetrated the lines of yurts. Lanterns bobbed past them, and dust sifted over them. From far off came the other mutter that, once known, is never mistaken—the swift thudding of hundreds of horses at a gallop.

"And what now?" said the Scot.

"*Ekh ma*! The khan has received us as ambassadors, and no man of his dare lift hand against us. We are safe in our skins."

"As long as he is the khan."

They reined in, because their escort motioned them back. Past the end of the tent alley a dark mass rushed, visible in the starglow. Dust rose thicker, and they heard the creaking of leather, the jangle of bit chains. They saw steel lance points flash and vanish, as a regiment of horsemen went past at a gallop.

A little farther on they had to edge by the picket lines where warriors were saddling their shaggy ponies and riding off almost in silence, as if commands were things unheard of. Nor did any lights go with them. Stuart sniffed the damp air like a hunting dog nosing out a high scent, and Ayub peered about him curiously. The roar of the drums did not lessen, and now wild pipes wailed.

"Thousands are moving out," Stuart said, "and they are riding light."

"What is it?" the Cossack asked the *mirza*.

He did not answer, but turned aside to ascend a rise where the great drums thundered, and the pole and crosspiece of a battle standard rose, with its drooping buffalo tails against the stars. Here no lanterns gleamed, and they were challenged by unseen guards.

The *mirza* turned in the saddle then and pointed toward the west— as Stuart calculated quickly from the stars. Beyond the Tartar lines the plain was dark as far as the distant lights of the Turkish camp. But Stuart made out the banks of the river, and the water itself where it was churned

to white foam by some unseen power. And he knew that the mounted regiments were crossing the river.

Suddenly the drums above them were silent, and other sounds reached
them—a faint ululation of voices, and a single shrill cry—

"*Ghar-ghar-ghar!*"

The whole night seemed to be astir and moving toward the west, where
now sounded the faint thudding of musketry.

Stuart's hand clenched upon his belt as he studied the far-off flashes
that lighted up clouds of rolling smoke. The cavalry of the khan was attacking the pasha's camp. Arak Buka had not waited for any discussion,
but had launched his horsemen across the river at once. Ayub had come
to the same conclusion.

"Devil take him, he's gone to tear down the standard of the Turks!"

More lights appeared, and a ruddy glow outlined the rampart of the
distant camp. The Turks were starting fires, to drive away the darkness.
The deeper reverberations of cannon rolled over the plain.

"Will the Horde storm the rampart?" Ayub asked the *mirza.*

"*Kabadir, amamja.* Perhaps; God knows."

But the Tartar remained motionless as the Scot, his slant eyes fixed
on the plain. Although the wanderers were aching with hunger they did
not think of food. Stuart was the first to see tiny black figures moving
in front of the fires. They seemed to move very slowly and the musketry
fire increased.

Then the sounds dwindled, although the fires did not die out. No more
Tartars were crossing the river. The far off murmur swelled and sank. The
shooting lessened and finally ceased.

"They are in," Stuart said, "or they have been beaten off."

Lights appeared in the dark plain, moving back toward the river, like fire-
flies crawling through the grass. It was an hour before the nearest of them
reached the water, and Stuart noticed that they moved at a foot pace.

On the near bank slaves were lighting piled up brush at the fords to
mark the way and presently the first men came out of the plain, walking
into the water up to their waists. Their turbans and heavy breeches revealed them as Turkish infantry. But they carried no arms or packs and
they came on in huddled groups.

Beside them rode armed Tartars with bundles slung upon their cruppers. When the Turks hung back at the water's edge, the riders mocked
them, laughing and whirling long lances over their heads. More of the

dark columns moved into the firelight—captives, sullen and surprised. Few were wounded, but all seemed dazed, as if stirred out of their sleep. Among them marched dismounted *aghas* and officers of the pasha.

Through them galloped a warrior of the Horde, a gold mace in his hand, and an ermine *khalat* thrown over his knees. His shrill shout reached the height where Stuart watched.

"*Ohai*, ye men of the Krim! The door of looting is open! Arak Buka Khan has pulled down the standard of the Ottomans—aye, he will send them back to their galleys, barefoot and without arms!"

As if in answer to these tidings, the kettledrums roared over their heads. Duncan Stuart sat back in the saddle with a long sigh of contentment. He had carried out his orders, and his mission was accomplished. And the result was more than he had hoped for. Because now it was certain that the Tartars would not ride beside the Turks to the Christian frontiers. And, being young, he felt the thrill that comes to the man who has faced odds and gone ahead in spite of them.

"Well for us, Sir Brother," Ayub mused, "that the khan took that camp. It was a rich camp, and these wasps of Tartars will think we brought them good fortune." For a moment he pondered what had happened. "Only, Murad Pasha must have been struck by madness to make up such about your letter. It was a poor lie."

"Nay," Stuart smiled. "He told the truth."

"How the truth?"

"The paper was my commission as colonel, from the hand of the king, and Murad Pasha read it aright."

Gripping his beard in both hands, Ayub peered at his companion.

"But the message, the message you gave the khan?"

"I made it up as you interpreted. And God knows," the young Scot added quietly, "that every word of it was true."

Ayub snorted, and shook his head slowly from side to side. He put his hands on his lips and looked up at the stars. Then he gripped the arm of the man whose life he had saved and whom he loved as a son.

"Devil take you!" he muttered in his beard. "You're a true Cossack—won't turn aside for anything. Said I not that we twain could find a way through where the ambassadors could not?"

"We two—" Stuart gathered up his reins and leaned forward to stroke the shoulder of the piebald wolf-chaser—"and a good horse."

Koum

The *essaul* reined in his horse and looked around.

"We can halt here," he said.

The seven Cossacks of the detachment also glanced about them, at the rolling plain with its brown grass and occasional clump of poplars down in some gully. Here and there a knob of red rock uprose. Ahead of them, within a stone's toss, the cinnamon-colored river moved sluggishly between its borders of dark rushes. They were on a bare knoll, and they could see across the river.

All of them searched the far bank with their eyes. Nothing moved. Only banks of yellow clay and sand stretched above the rank steppe grass. From the banks light gleamed fitfully; but it was no more than the reflected glow of the sunset behind them upon some bits of quartz.

For a moment the Cossacks whispered among themselves, and one of them addressed the *essaul*, who was in command of the detachment.

"Look here, Father Kirdiak, we ought to have a fire."

"Can't be done," Kirdiak grunted, and then reflected. They had shot an antelope back in the hills, and they had had a long, hot ride to the river. "Don't you know this is an outpost of the cordon? Over the river yonder are Tartars and other devils."

"But the captain won't come out this far, and who will know?"

"Well—" Kirdiak pushed his *kalpak* back and scratched his shaven forehead—"all right. Only make it behind the mound."

Promptly the Cossacks dismounted. They lifted their packs from behind the saddles, stretched and yawned. While two of them led the horses down to water, the others scattered about the knoll and reappeared with armfuls of thorn bush, withered tamarisk and roots. One had even found some dried dung.

"Camels." He smiled as he passed the stout *essaul.*

"Was there a trail, Ostap?"

"A path?" The young Cossack shook his head impatiently. "God knows, Father. We'll have a look in the morning."

Kirdiak thought of going down to examine the ground where the dung had been. If there was a trail passing over the steppe here, he ought to know about it. But his legs were stiff, and he felt very comfortable stretched out on his sheepskins. It would be dark down in the gullies, he told himself—better to have a look round in the morning. So he struck a spark into a handful of dry grass and lighted his pipe.

As he did so he looked longingly at a clay jug beside him. The jug contained a gallon of corn brandy, and Kirdiak had brought it along in case God should send an emergency, when he and the detachment might have need of something to drink. Otherwise, it was forbidden to drink spirits when on duty. The detachment knew that he had the jug, and so he dared not let it out of his sight.

"Hi there, Borchik!" he called to one of the men who had been watering the horses. "Go and watch by the river."

The tall Cossack hastening toward the fire turned aside and picked up his musket. Without a word he disappeared through the brush into the gloom.

Kirdiak stretched himself out on his massive back and pulled at his pipe. He could hear the whispering of the river, the croaking of frogs and some of the Cossacks arguing about snares they were going to set for the waterfowl. They would have fish, too—much better than the dried meat and rusks of their rations.

They were all registered Cossacks. That is, they were enrolled in the frontier force which served along the vast borderland stretching from the Caspian Sea up to the white tundras of the polar sea. They were the trail breakers and the guardians of the Empire of All the Russias, which moved slowly and inexorably as a juggernaut car into the east.

Already in this Midsummer of the year 1806 the frontier had passed over Mother Volga and was stretching its posts toward the salt deserts of the southeast.

And ahead of the posts moved the *stanitzas* of the Cossacks who had once been a free people along the River Don. The older men among them remembered well how the Empress Catherine had abolished their liberty and had broken up the *siech*—the war encampment of the Zaporogian Cossacks. So the cordon of Cossack villages moved away from the forts and soldiers of the tsars, out into the ranges. Here they had no tithes to pay, and they could worship in the old fashion as they pleased. Only they had to defend themselves against the Kalmuk and Kirghiz Tartars who had grazed over these same ranges.

Behind them the Empire smiled indulgently at their trek because it helped enlarge the frontier and beat off the Tartar clans.

Kirdiak's detachment had been ordered out by the *stanitza ataman* who wanted to have an advanced post at the river, twenty miles from the villages of the *stanitza* with their cattle and maize and melon fields. A horde of Tartars could gallop that twenty miles in two hours, and the *ataman* instructed Kirdiak to watch for any tribesmen crossing the river, which was then shoaling in the Midsummer heat. The Cossacks of the detachment all had picked horses, and at least two of them were to start back with the news if Tartars were seen in force.

Kirdiak was pondering this idly, when he sat up suddenly—his pipe falling from his teeth and his hand grasping at the long pistol in his belt. A strange figure stood against the sunset glow beside him, although he had heard no tread on the ground.

He drew out the pistol but did not lift it. He saw that the man wore a long, black lambskin coat with torn sleeves, and boots of soft, unpolished leather, and a high black *kalpak* like his own but much the worse for wear. Over his shoulder was slung a musket, and from his wide belt hung some bloody pheasants, a curved Circassian dagger, a tobacco pouch and powder horn.

"Christ save us!" Kirdiak muttered. "Why didn't you speak?"

The stranger looked around the knoll.

"What's in the jug?" he asked in a deep, ringing voice.

"A little—" the *essaul* remembered his dignity. He picked up his pipe and got to his feet. His bullet head only came to the stranger's chin. "Eh, what's this? What's your name—why are you wandering out here?"

The tall Cossack glanced down at the sergeant.

"I am Koum," he said, and walked away toward the embers of the fire where the antelope steaks were sizzling in a pan by the kasha pot.

"God be with you, Uncle!" The other men greeted him.

"*Chelam vam,*" responded Koum. "The forehead to you, brothers."

When the sergeant came up, they all got out daggers and caught up the steaks, wrapping strings of fried garlic round them. While he ate, Kirdiak scanned the stranger, tossing some loose brush upon the embers so that the fire sprang up.

Koum had taken off his *kalpak*. His head had been shaved—all except a long lock of black hair on the top. So was his chin shaved and the middle of his mustache trimmed, leaving the ends hanging down in shaggy bunches. His brown eyes slanted a little at the corners, and the hard skin of his face had dried and wrinkled from years of exposure. The muscles of his full neck wrinkled under his long jaw. His shirt, open at the throat, had been soaked in tar.

"Black as a she-devil," Kirdiak thought. "No one could see him at night. He walks like a hunter, but he wears a long sword. He's had a bath, too, by God, and a Tartar barber trimmed his head like that—so Allah can pull him up by the scalp lock when he dies."

He drew the cork out of the jug and at once small bowls and silver cups appeared in the hands of the Cossacks. But Kirdiak filled his own cup first and offered it to the stranger.

"*Koshkildui!*" Koum said in his deep voice. "God be with you!"

That was a Tartar greeting, Kirdiak reflected. He noticed that the stranger had claw scratches over his right hand and wrist. So Koum owned a hawk—carried the falcon around without a glove.

"Look here, lads," he muttered, "we'll have a cup of the brandy because we have a guest."

Koum handed back the sergeant's cup, which Kirdiak filled and drained before he poured out measures for the men.

"Health to you, Koum!" Ostap laughed, drinking. "How do you live out here?"

"How not? There's meat enough—aye, buffalo and antelope and the water fowl."

"But how did you find us?"

"Only village girls would light a fire against a red sunset. The smoke can be seen. You're young—you still smell of milk. Besides, it's not good."

"How, not good?"

"This sunset, like blood. Aye, the Tartars say it means Allah has hung the banners of death in the sky, and someone will die before the sun is seen again."

"An old woman's tale," grunted Kirdiak. "If a man dies, it happens that way. A sunset can't do good or ill to any one."

"A red moon is worse," put in one of the older men.

Brandy gurgled from the jug, and tongues were loosened. Some said it was a bad sign when horses stumbled or snorted, although it was good when they neighed. Others maintained that the worst of all was to see a vampire, whining in the darkness.

"That may be, but a sunset means nothing—nothing," persisted the sergeant who was a stubborn man and, besides, had served years in the regular army where an order was an order and the officers took no account of omens. "Harken, Koum—how is it along the river here? Do the Tartars raid often?"

"Nay," said the stranger slowly. "The Black Hats are moving to the north, looking for better grass. Now, the White Sheep are on the range across the river."

"What white sheep?" demanded Kirdiak.

"Tek!" Koum shook his head. "You are new to the steppe, my brother. They are Turkomans of the White Sheep clan—real wolves. Now, the hordes used to raid twice in the year, at harvest time, just like this—and when the snow hardens. But you can't tell what the Turkomans will do. They slash and rush off like wolves, or perhaps they make war without warning. They are slayers—eh, they carry off even eight-year-old girls. But they kill all the younger ones, and the very old people."

For an instant the sergeant thought of the hundreds of people back in the new *stanitza*, putting roofs on their cottages, and working in the fields still full of stones. They had maize and melons and cattle, but little else.

"Is there a Turkoman village near?" He nodded toward the river.

"Nay—two hours ride is their *aul*, by a salt lake. At times they come over to hunt, one or two of them. They took my horse and shot my dog once when I was off with the hawk. Down there is a ford, where they come over."

Again Kirdiak meditated upon the camel dung and the path and the ford so close at hand. He wished he had not let the men make a fire—but then they would have had no steaks. He leaned over and thrust the cork into the jug. "What are you doing?" rumbled Koum.

"No more brandy. We've had enough."

"It's bad luck, *essaul*." Koum shook his head ominously. "Never cork up wine until it's all been drunk. The devil watches out for a thing like that. *He* will have it in for you if you don't pour out the rest."

One of the older Cossacks muttered assent. Kirdiak, however, was stubborn.

"Against orders to drink at a post," he said bluntly.

"That won't change the bad luck," responded Koum. "I'll drink the half that's left—then the bad luck won't come."

"Devil take you!" roared the sergeant. "The jug is half full, with corn brandy, not red wine. Hey, it won't go down the gullet of an antelope hunter."

Koum stood up and stretched his long arms.

"Tck! Kirdiak, you may be a sergeant of the new army, but it's clear that you never learned how to drink like a Cossack. When you were nuzzling your mother, I was in the *siech*, in the brotherhood of the Zaporogians. You have heard of them, when the *bandura* players sang. They didn't drill in the village street—one, two, halt! Nay, by the hide and hair of the horned one, they went to war. They crossed the great sea Charnomar in their *ka-yuks*. Even the sultan trembled when the Zaporogians took to the road. And the khan of all the hordes was glad to call them brothers."

The younger men of the detachment glanced up, grinning. For the *bal-alaika* players and the blind men sang of the glorious time when the Cos-sacks had been free, and of the deeds of the *atamans* of long ago—of Khlit who had been called the Wolf, and Demid who had raided Aleppo. Few Za-porogians survived. Koum must have been young when he had belonged to the last brotherhood of the war camp.

"We may drill," muttered Kirdiak who was ruffled by the veteran's boasting, "but we have long muskets and we can use them. We have horses, too, and we don't let the tribesmen lift them."

"I'll get mine back from the devils." Koum's white teeth flashed in a smile. "Only wait a bit. But take heed, *essaul*—the Turkomans are real wolves. If they take one of you, they'll send him back with a pair of high, red boots. They'll strip the skin off him, below the knees, and turn him out to walk in the salt desert." He pondered, frowning. "Nay, it will not be easy for you, out here. The signs are bad. Don't you know it's tempt-ing God not to drink up what has been opened? In the *siech* they used to drink from barrels, not jugs. A man who couldn't empty your jug and dance the *trepak* after it, or jump from one side to the other of a run-ning horse, would be sent back to the villages. In the old time they knew how to drink and how to love the girls. Ask the beauties of Stamboul or Aleppo if that wasn't so. Do you know why the cavalry of the sultan and the khan of the Krim—aye, and the Cherkess and the Persian shah is so fine today?"

"Nay," growled Kirdiak, "but—"

"Because there's Cossack blood in all of them. The Cossacks of the *siech* embraced their Moslem mothers—"

A shout of laughter interrupted Koum, and voices called out to the sergeant to open the jug again.

"Drink health to the Zaporogian. He's right, Father—it's a sin to hoard up the jug. Borchik hasn't had his cup yet."

Kirdiak, however, got to his feet angrily and spat.

"Fools! You can listen to the old beggar's lying. I'm going to sleep. By God, it's for me to give orders here. Ostap, go and relieve Borchik. And one of you tie up the horses near the fire and sleep outside of them."

Carrying the jug and without any other word to Koum, he went off to his sheepskins.

"The Little Father's got his hair up," laughed the oldest Cossack. "Well, Uncle—"

But Koum rose to his feet, throwing down the half dozen pheasants from his belt.

"Here's a gift for the pot. I see there's no welcome in this post—no fun at all. God send you fortune, to change the bad luck."

He picked up his musket and strode away into the gloom, when he heard a step behind him.

"Stop, Uncle!" Ostap begged. "Don't go away angry."

"I wasn't boasting," Koum muttered.

"Well, come and watch with me. Show me where the ford is."

After a moment the Zaporogian halted and leaned on his musket.

"I'll watch the river with you, if you'll tell the sergeant—tell him we'll divide the time between us. He need send no one out until daylight."

In a little while Koum joined the young Cossack in the darkness under some poplars, against a sandbank from which a long stretch of the river was visible. A full moon, rising above the dunes of the east bank, cast a vague radiance over the plain. Distant hillocks stood out clearly, while the river itself lay in the murk between black masses of rushes.

Ostap wondered how Koum had found him, and how the hunter had come within a stone's throw of the poplars without being seen.

"Borchik was wild." He laughed. "Because he did not taste a drop of the brandy."

But Koum would not talk. He lay back on his elbow in the sand, and before long Ostap, who felt the drowsiness of youth after a full meal of meat, began to yawn.

"You sleep," Koum advised him presently. "I'll call you in time to watch. If I walk around, don't pay attention—only if I fire the musket."

Ostap muttered a protest, but presently wrapped his sheepskin coat over him and stretched out in the sand, dropping off to sleep in a moment. After listening to his breathing a while, Koum got up and moved about among the poplars. Ostap did not even check his heavy breathing.

Two hours later the moon stood high over the river. Tiny gleams of light ran along the shallows and vanished. The edges of drifting clouds high over the steppe showed white, until they passed across the river, sinking everything in a half shadow.

A dry breeze ruffled the deep pools, swaying the dense rushes along the bank until they looked like silver. The rustling of the poplars merged into the croaking of the frogs and the hurrying whisper of the water. Soundlessly an owl passed over the moving rushes.

Koum sat again on the sandbank. But now the clay jug rested between his knees, and at intervals he lifted it up, and a slight gurgling could be heard. Each time he had to lift the jug higher. He did not rouse Ostap, who was sleeping peacefully.

Not for many moons had Koum tasted corn brandy like this. He sighed gratefully and checked a sudden snort. The skin pricked along his scalp and he threw off his heavy *kalpak*. He felt more than comfortably warm, and slid the lambskin coat from his shoulders. Such a fine night it was, he thought, for hunting along the river. But he had to watch for these village girls who called themselves Cossacks.

The round moon glowed down upon his bare head. A golden moon. And what a river it was! Over there the owl skimmed the rushes again, and something slid into the water. A shadow slipped past the poplars and Koum sniffed. A red fox. And he couldn't even fire off his musket without bringing curses on his head. Koum tipped up the jug again. Strange that the brandy didn't come out of it any more!

Across the river he heard a plunging and rushing among the high reeds. Only one thing made a sound like that—wild pigs rooting along the bank. Over there was tender roast pig, and here he was, sitting like an old mama by a cradle. To the devil with it all!

Koum got to his feet restlessly, and planted his legs wide, to keep from
swaying toward the rushing river. A strange thing he saw. There behind
him the devil had hung another moon in the sky. But this did not fool
Koum. He knew that the pig was across the river. So he loosened his long
sword and laid it on his coat. Then taking up and priming his gun, he hastened toward the shallow ford. His black figure was only visible when it
crossed the strip of moonlight in midstream, and he made no sound that
could be heard above the wash of the river. The cold water ran into his
leather bag trousers.

Climbing out on a sandbank, he stepped into the mesh of rushes where
the frogs were holding their chorus. Quietly as he advanced, the pig took
alarm. A sudden splashing ahead of him changed to a rustling that went
away swiftly.

"They've gone into the *balka*," he thought, "and I may have a shot at
them if they turn up the side."

He hurried after the pig into a long gully, full of high grass and brush.
The bottom of the gully was in deep shadow, only the steep clay bank
on his left being in the moonlight. Upon this Koum kept his eyes as he
went forward, twisting among the brushwood. He could still hear a faint
scampering.

The *balka* turned first one way and then the other. Once Koum thought
he saw the pig far ahead up the bank. He walked slowly now, his wet boots
making no noise in the sand. Among a nest of boulders he stopped to listen. Then he laid his musket down, and squatted over it. Squinting up
into the sky, he held his breath and began to count.

Along the moonlit bank, clear against the luminous sky, mounted men
were picking their way toward the river. And Koum did not trouble his
head about the pigs any more. A single glance at the shaggy sheepskin
cloaks and turban head wraps—the dark round shields and thin ponies—
showed the hunter that these were Turkomans.

Koum counted fifteen and thought that a couple more were riding off to
the side. Half of them carried long flintlocks, not slung over their backs.
Tartars would not move at night, and only the prospect of a raid would
bring out Turkomans before daylight. They were arguing in low voices
and as they passed over his head he caught a few words. "*Choupak bir Ko-
zaghi*—those dogs of Cossacks. . ."

What devil of ill omen could have brought a war party to this place on
the river, at this time? They must have seen the smoke of the sergeant's

fire, and watched the Cossack detachment at sunset. Now, when they thought the Cossacks would be deep in sleep, they were going to cross the ford and rush the camp.

Suddenly a chill chased up Koum's back. The Cossacks *were* all asleep, even Ostap. Why in God's name hadn't he roused the youngster when he went off after the pig? Now here he was, cut off without a horse.

He did not move until the riders had disappeared down the bank, and he had made certain no more were coming after. If they had been Tartars he might have whined like a vampire in the darkness, and scared them back to their tents. But these were gray wolves, following the scent of blood. Well, the omens had given warning that blood would flow before sunrise.

Koum could only see one moon in the sky now. Getting to his feet, he scrutinized the bank of the gully to his right, in shadow. Slinging his gun on his back he began to climb the highest point, pulling himself up by roots but keeping his feet clear of stones. At the edge of the clay bank he turned his head cautiously. Nothing was to be seen except the summits of the dunes and the dark patches of brush. The Turkomans had reached the river bank.

Scrambling out, he crawled up among the rocks of the height and peered toward the river. He could see it clearly, some three hundred paces distant, between the masses of rushes. But he kept his eyes upon the stretch of moonlight in the center of the ford. Quickly he thrust his gun forward, powdered the priming, sighted it, and waited.

No help for it. He had been on watch, and the detachment was asleep. He had forgotten to call Ostap when he went off, and now he must shoot off his musket, to give the alarm. If he fired, the wolves would see the smoke. They would come back, find his tracks easily in this accursed light. Some of them would watch the ford, while the others would ride him down like a hare.

A rider appeared in the ford. Then others after him. Koum's head buzzed as he sighted his gun again. Too far off in that half-light!

"To the Father and Son!" he muttered, and pulled the trigger.

At the crash of the musket behind them, the heads of the Turkomans turned toward him. They remained motionless, while he peered at them under the smoke cloud—they were astonished no doubt, and hesitated whether to go on or turn back. Then a red flash came from the dark-

ness under the poplars where Ostap had been sleeping, and Koum saw the
Turkomans turn their horses toward the gully.

Without waiting to reload, he ran back from the rocks, down one long
slope and up the next. He headed away from the river, keeping close to
the *balka*, until he dared run no longer for fear of being seen. He glanced
down into the gully, and saw that it had become shallow, opening into
a kind of bowl filled with poplars and brush. Well, he had no choice. He
must head in here.

Digging his heels into the dry clay, he ran down the slope, leaped through
the brush and plunged in, under the first trees. As he did so the hunter
swerved. Something light had flashed before his eyes, and when he threw
himself to the side, he felt steel rip through his loose sleeve.

"*Ghar!*" A hoarse voice screamed into his face.

Swiftly Koum swung forward the muzzle of his heavy musket. It struck
something yielding—knocked it back. A second time he dodged a knife
slash, stumbling over broken ground as he did so. Grasping his musket in
both hands, he leaped high in the air and smashed the butt of the gun forward as he came down. It struck fair upon something that crunched under
it. And that something fell heavily to the ground, moving jerkily.

Koum steadied himself on his feet, and swung the butt of the gun
down again with all the strength of his shoulders. Bones snapped under
the impact and he heard a deep groan. Stepping aside and paying no heed
to the spasmodic movements of the wounded man, he bent his head and
listened intently.

By the river shots boomed out, but the hunter was listening for the
tread or stamp of a horse. The Turkoman who attacked him would not
have gone far from his mount. Koum could perceive no sign of a horse.
He saw, however, something else.

In the center of the poplar grove the ground was clear, and in the shafts
of moonlight a small horsehide tent was visible. Koum reloaded his musket
and strode forward. He came upon trampled ground, strewn with bundles
of sheepskins and furs, and a few pots. And he swore under his breath.

"Eh, it was a hunting party," he thought. "They camped here, and saw
the Cossacks. Well, it's true they will come back."

He heard a scattering of shots and a faint shouting. He started to make
his way out of the depression, but stopped and shook his head. Useless to
go up on the steppe with the horsemen coming in. And when they came,

they would find their wounded comrade. Nothing for it but to hide in the grove until daylight, and then trust to luck. Yet his luck had been bad—

Hoofs thudded closer, and a shrill voice hailed—

"Ai-a, Ahmet!"

Koum stepped into deeper shadow, gripping his gun. Then horses galloped by, tearing through the brush. The grove seemed to be filled with them, going past. A shadowy rider leaned down, and caught up a bundle of furs and swerved away. A white horse plunged to a stop in the flecks of moonlight so near he might have touched it with the muzzle of his gun. Backed against the bole of a tree, Koum did not move.

"Ai-a, Ahmet, shaitan chavassar! Hey, Ahmet—may the black devil ride you!"

The lank Turkoman on the white horse shouted angrily, and flung himself to the ground. He darted into the tent, and Koum leaned his gun against the tree, pulling his knife from his belt.

He strode toward the horse, which snorted and drew away. Then the tribesman ran out of the shelter, carrying a bundle in his arms. Even in the gloom he saw the Cossack, and dropped his burden, leaping forward with a curved sword swinging in his hand.

Koum turned on his heels and flung himself at the Turkoman's knees, as the sword and long sleeve swished over him. And as he struck the man, he thrust up with his long knife. The blade stuck in flesh, but came out as the two men rolled on the ground. Koum buried his knife again in his antagonist, under the ribs. The man choked and curled himself up, while the Cossack felt on the ground and picked up the sword the other had dropped.

"You won't get up, *shaitan*," he muttered, running his hand over the bundle the Turkoman had dropped. Nothing but stinking robes. The sword, however, felt like a good one. Koum put it under his belt and picked up his gun, listening the while. Other men were riding past.

He went over quietly to the horse, and this time caught the bridle. Swinging himself into the saddle, he found the flat stirrups, as the horse sidled and reared. Tightening the rein, he felt the neck and shoulders of his new mount.

"A good one," he thought. "A real steed." Now, at least, he could risk a dash down the *balka* to the river.

Near at hand a gun roared. Hearty voices cried—

"Strike, strike, brothers!"

Koum turned his head, astonished.

"By God, the village girls have come over the river. The fools!"

Lifting his deep voice, he shouted:

"Cossacks! This way—down in the *balka*. Here is their nest!"

A moment more and horses pushed in under the poplars. Ostap trotted in front, peering from side to side.

"Hi, Cossack!" he called. "Where is that nest?"

"This way," Koum answered, and drew back quickly as the young Cossack struck out at him, suddenly. "Can't you see, you wildcat?"

"Ho, Uncle," laughed the youngster, "I didn't know you had a horse. Look, brothers, there's the camp!"

Some of them flung themselves from the saddle to ransack the tent and the ground. Finding the dead Turkoman, they began to pull off the best of his garments.

"There's another back of you, five lance lengths," Koum told them.

"What devil brought you here, Koum?" demanded Kirdiak, panting. "Did you see us chase them? We shot one up on the dunes, and Borchik has his horse. Omelko was shot in the ribs as we came over the ford—he's back on the other side with Andriev who lost his horse."

Koum made a quick reckoning. If two Cossacks were out of it, they had only six, with himself, against about twice their number of tribesmen.

"*Essaul*," he said earnestly, "don't be stubborn now. Give the order to go back to the camp, at once."

"By God, can't you see *they* are running from us."

"They were afraid of a trap, because they were shot at from behind, at the ford. They had not counted your heads, yet. Now they will turn back on both sides, and cut you off from the ford. Harken!"

Kirdiak lifted his head. On the dunes above him he heard a wolf's howl, then another, and a third. They came from different points, and the sergeant knew that they were not wolves. Scattered in groups of twos and threes the tribesmen were calling to the others. They had halted and soon they would turn back. Probably this man Koum had killed was their khan—such a fine horse he had. Aye, the Turkomans would be drawing a ring around the sunken grove. Kirdiak tried to remember how many they were—he had seen a score or so. Well, if seven Cossacks rode against them in the open, that would be bad. Worse to hide in the trees, until they were surrounded. He scratched his head and tried to think of a plan.

"Come on, Kirdiak," muttered Koum impatiently. He had been examining the saddle under him, and had found to his satisfaction that it was a good one. "I'll show the way."

"Where?" demanded the sergeant.

"Down the *balka*."

Kirdiak nodded, relieved. He rounded up the five Cossacks who were turning over everything in the camp, looking for more trophies. When they were all in the saddle, tying bundles on their cruppers, he bade Koum lead the way.

"Shut your mouths, lads, and don't fire off your guns."

In single file they trotted out of the wood, into the brush of the ravine. No saddles creaked and no scabbards clacked against the riders' legs. Their figures merged into the obscurity of the ravine. Behind them shaggy heads appeared at the edge of the *balka*, and the howling of the wolves changed to strident calls.

Koum felt his way down to the spot where he had first seen the Turkomans. Here he was sure of his ground, and cantered on through the tall rushes, splashing across the ford. As the Cossacks followed, a dozen muskets flashed from the dunes behind them, and the balls whistled harmlessly overhead. Kirdiak remained to watch the ford with the oldest of the Cossacks, but Koum, after turning into the poplars to pick up his coat and other things, rode on to the knoll where Borchik was stirring up the fire again.

The moon had vanished into haze, and the air had grown cold. A thin mist hung over the water, and in the east the sky was lightening, before sunrise. The men's faces could be seen under the dark *kalpaks*. Standing about the fire, they talked and laughed excitedly, gazing enviously at the white horse the hunter had brought back with him.

"Eh, Uncle," cried Ostap, "it's a Kabarda—a steppe racer. It must have been the khan's."

Koum looked over the horse with satisfaction. It was much better than the one he had lost, although he did not say so. He took off the saddle which was covered with red morocco and ornamented with silver coins. His left arm was dark with dried blood where the Turkoman had slashed the skin.

When he had put a halter on his Kabarda and tied the horse with the others, he poured some powder from his horn upon the slash, and bound his torn sleeve around it. Then he glanced up at the sky and yawned.

"Hi, Ostap," he called. "Here's a sword for you, a nice blade. I took it from the khan over yonder but I don't want it."

Stretching himself out in the grass beside the badly wounded Cossack, he put his head on the saddle and pulled his coat over him.

"Ostap," he muttered, "don't let the sergeant take my horse. You lads can watch now, without harm coming of it—"

He was asleep almost at once. The men of the detachment looked admiringly at the shaven head and powerful body of the Zaporogian who had gone alone, somehow, over the river and had killed the Turkoman khan with a knife by his own tent.

The red sun seemed to leap over the line of the dunes, and the gray surface of the river became tinged with fire. The veil of mist shredded away, and all the uncertain, fantastic shadows of the last hours vanished, revealing only ordinary sand and tamarisk clumps and rock buttes from which a warm red glow grew, and faded into plain daylight. After the night, the wide steppe became quiet and drowsy again.

Kirdiak walked up, with the white-haired Cossack, and went straight to his jug, which now lay in its place by his sheepskins.

"Well, lads," he said, "we drove the Turkomans and killed three of them, we took two horses and some other things. We got a knock or two but that's nothing. And as for these omens, you see that the sunset and the cork in the jug meant nothing at all." He glanced around triumphantly. "*Nitchogo*—nothing at all. And now, lads, we'll drink a health or two. No harm now."

He caught up the big jug, frowned, and shook it hastily. Then he jerked out the cork—shook it again close to his ear, and turned it cautiously down. A single drop fell from it.

"As God lives, Father," cried one of the men, "we have not looked at it. Not one of us has gone over to it."

Slowly Kirdiak's brow grew red, and he began to snort. But the other men swore they had not laid hand on it.

"Then it was you, you hedgehog!" he cried at Ostap. "You had the watch."

The young Cossack shook his head. "How could I, when I was asleep?"

Kirdiak turned on his heel and glared down at Koum snoring gently under his coat.

"May the devil take him! Eight men's rations of brandy he had, down his gullet! The son of a dog is full! Look here, Ostap, I didn't see him cross the river—how did he get over?"

Ostap wiped at the blade of his new saber with a greasy rag.

"Allah knows—I don't. I was asleep when his gun went off—*bang!* I sat up and there were the Turkomans sitting their horses in the ford. 'To the Father and Son,' said I, and fired my musket. Then I ran back, and you gave command to chase the Turkomans. But I didn't see Koum until—"

"He was drunk, the hog's belly. And if we had not chased the Turkomans he would have left his hide over there."

"But we found him on a horse, a good horse," objected Ostap. "He was all right. He waited and called to us—"

"Well," grumbled Kirdiak, "then he is a wizard."

"Nay." The oldest of the Cossacks came forward with his clay pipe in his hand. He leaned down to pick a burning stick from the fire. "Don't you see, Father, and you brothers? It's not like that at all. Koum changed our luck."

"How—changed our luck?"

The white-haired Cossack held the brand to his pipe and puffed.

"The signs—they never lie. Didn't the Turkomans look for us, and look into the blood sunset? And aren't three of them dead before sunrise? Didn't we cork up the jug when it was only half empty? Aye, we did. And we'd all be lying with our toes up, if Koum had not changed the luck by drinking the brandy down. Then didn't he find a wonder of a horse? Look at it!"

Kirdiak looked at the white Kabarda, and said nothing more. But the old Cossack shook his head pensively.

"You're a good officer, eh, Father. You say build a fire here, and go on sentry post there, and charge, lads! That's what an officer should do. But luck settles the thing for us, and that's the end of it."

The listening Cossacks nodded, and a murmur of assent ran around the fire.

Over the River

Koum sat on the oven. He wore only a shirt, and his powerful bare legs hung down the side of the oven, which felt pleasantly cool. The big Cossack was sewing up a tear in his breeches, pushing a bodkin methodically through the soft leather and stopping work at times to sing in a voice that reverberated in the walls of his small hut.

It was a hot afternoon, and both the Cossack and the hawk on its perch beside him were drowsy. There was nothing to do until the evening meal.

The hut was comfortable enough, with its thatch roof keeping out the heat. A gallon jug buried in the sand of one corner held plenty of cool river water. Dried fish hung from a roof beam, with strings of onions and some pungent herbs. A fine saddle covered with red morocco leather stood on its peg, and to the wall beside it were nailed skins of the white and black steppe fox, with sables and wolves. Boots, firewood and a sack of barley occupied the other corner.

Over the head of his cot Koum had placed a picture of the wonder-working Saint Nicholas, framed in gilt and imitation silver. On a long shelf beneath it, with some tallow and a tin of powder and bullet mold, lay the Cossack's most prized possession—a bagpipe.

This bagpipe had belonged to a fellow Cossack of the war encampment, whose bones had dried in the grass long since. Koum remembered vaguely that this brother had been an outlander from some island in the Western Ocean. All kinds of men had joined the brotherhood of the Cossacks in these first years of the nineteenth century—after the wars that had raged like grass fires over Europe. Tartars, Gypsies, even noblemen, had become Cossacks.

The bagpipe, with its sack of soft black leather and its polished pipes ornamented with carved beasts' heads, had whiled away long hours for

Koum. He had a musical ear, and he drew strange melodies out of the droning wail of the pipes.

Koum lived alone in this hut. He hunted over the steppe, with its herds of wild horses, its black-nosed buffalo and small antelope. He found lesser game, wild pig and waterfowl along the deserted river, and his nearest neighbors were the Turkoman clans across the river. Koum was careful to keep his distance from these neighbors.

"*Crei-I!*" shrilled the falcon, moving along its stick.

"Not time to eat, little warrior," muttered the Cossack. "Don't you see the sun?"

Ruffling its feathers, the bird gazed at the white sand, its eyes half open. Koum yawned and scratched his shaven head, from the center of which a long scalp lock hung. Then he reached out his arm for his sack of tobacco. Abruptly his hand stopped, outstretched in the air.

Down the gully he heard his horse neigh. Koum knew the habits of his animals as well as his own, and his Karbarda was no spoiled stable horse, to make a fuss in the shade in midafternoon.

Thrusting his legs into his breeches, Koum wound a shawl scarf round his hips and caught up his musket from the wall. Without delaying for boots or *kalpak*, he ran out of the door.

"*Crei-i-i!*" screamed the hawk, clawing at its cord.

Koum had built his hut in one of the *balkas*, or wooded ravines, that led to the river. In this gully below the level of the steppe he had wood and some grazing for his animals, and his hut could not be seen from the plain.

Leaping up steps cut in the clay bank, Koum came to a nest of boulders under the branches of a tall poplar—his lookout post. His eyes went swiftly over the miles of rolling crests covered with high brown grass, and he muttered in astonishment.

A hundred paces away a woman was riding on a spent horse. And Koum had never seen a woman like this in the steppes before. Her long skirt trailed down over her boots and she seemed to have one leg curled around the saddlehorn. A ruffled cape covered her shoulders, and the hood had been drawn up over her hair. Moodily she swung her whip against the flank of her sweat-stained mare.

Behind her followed a man without a hat. He wore a blue coat short in front and long behind and much bedraggled, and his head hung on his chest. Far behind the two a bearded postilion limped, leading a shaggy pony overburdened with bundles.

Once in Sarai on the Volga, Koum had seen noble people like these two, with white skin, riding around in carriages. They were Muscovites—Russians—and he could not think what they were doing here, beyond the frontier, in the waste lands. They could not be hunting, because the only weapons they had were two great pistols carried in holsters on the man's saddle. Still the Cossack could not let them stagger along like this without water.

He walked out from his shelter, and the woman screamed.

Koum stopped, embarrassed. He did not know how to address such people.

"Hi, noble born," he called out, "where are you going?"

The man, who at first had drawn out a pistol, seemed relieved. Urging his tired horse up to the Cossack, he began to talk all at once in the Muscovite speech. Koum could make out only that God had sent a calamity upon them, and they were lost. But Koum looked at the woman. She was shorter than the Cossack girls, and white as clean linen, with two spots of red on her cheeks. She had fine eyes, and even in her weariness she showed her beauty.

"Well, don't fear, noble born," he said cheerfully. "Here is shelter, and how can you be lost?"

He led the way down a path into his *balka*. It surprised him that the gentleman should dismount stiffly, holding to the saddle, and go over to untangle the lady's skirt from the saddle, and lift her to the ground. She went into the hut and sat down on the bed, without greeting Saint Nicholas.

Koum offered them cool water from his jar, but the gentleman shouted, and presently the servant came in with two silver cups gritty with dust. They drank a little water, when the servant who had been lugging the packs from the pony hastened up with a bottle of brandy.

"My house is your house," said Koum, bowing. This was the customary greeting of the Cossacks to a guest.

Filling the two cups with brandy, the Muscovite handed one to his lady, and she sipped at it, while he gulped his. To Koum's surprise they did not offer any to him—although they must have seen that he had no brandy. The man seemed to feel better, because he stared round the hut and began to talk loudly to Koum.

All the Cossack could understand was that the visitor was a count—Dolbruka—and an official accompanied by his wife on his way to Uralskaia, a frontier post.

"Uralskaia—how far? Tomorrow?" he shouted, angry because Koum could not make out what he wanted.

"Don't be a fool," remarked his wife. And she spoke quietly to Koum, choosing words that he knew.

They had been traveling with Russian soldiers down the Ural in flatboats, when she had asked the count to ride for a day along the shore, to exercise the horses. They had wandered from the river, and in trying to get back, their servant had led them more astray. For two days they had made their way over the steppe, with only these few packs they had brought along. Finally they had come to this little river and had found a place to ford it.

"May the dev—" exclaimed Koum. "Did you go over the river?"

"Yes," said the countess, flicking at her skirt. "The country was bad—worse than before. Then the Cossack rode after us."

"A Cossack?" muttered Koum, who had seen no familiar face for a month.

"Like you, but finer, quite an intelligent man. He spoke French, and told us we must turn back quickly, at once. He said it was dangerous, because the pagan Moslems were watching us and perhaps they would rob us. So we went back at a gallop. And when we reached the river again we saw the pagans following after us. They were dirty and they fired off their muskets. Then the Cossack laughed and said we must ride on, very quickly, until the sun set. He said to go straight toward the setting sun and not to turn back, and he would stay at the ford to play a game with the insolent pagans who wanted to rob us. So he stayed behind to shoot at them, at the ford. We heard the guns going off for some time. It was terrible, and we had no water, and only Christ's mercy saved us from being followed again by the pagans. Do you understand, Cossack?"

He understood very clearly what had happened. He could see the three ignorant Russians scrambling over the salt steppe, the Turkomans' country. Until the watchers of the herds noticed them, and a group of the wild tribesmen rode after them. He could see the strange Cossack holding the narrow ford with his musket, until they were safely off.

He wondered what had happened at the ford after that. But he knew that the Russians had been saved not only from being stripped to the skin but from torture for the man and slavery for the woman.

"Tell me, noble born," he muttered. "Where is it, this ford?"

The Russian shrugged her comely shoulders.

"How can I tell, Cossack? One place is like another. We were lost. But now—" she smiled comfortably—"surely you can show us the way to Uralskaia."

Koum looked about him helplessly. He felt ill at ease, talking to these strangers, who knew so little of the steppe and who paid no attention to good Saint Nicholas in his gilt frame. Even while he pondered them, the woman spoke rapidly to the man in a queer staccato and he answered with a word or two of the same language. Koum had never heard French before—the polite speech of the Russian court.

"Look here, gracious lady," he observed, when she had finished. "Why is it that the count and his man did not stay to drive off the Turkomans? They had two pistols."

"Eh, what?" The gracious lady frowned. "How could I ride unattended in this place?"

Koum did not know. He had never beheld so beautiful a woman. Above her stately head even the bright picture of the saint looked dull.

"This dog must be humored," she said to her husband. "He must guide us back to the villages. Lord, he is as uncouth as a Tartar, but the hut is clean. We can sleep here tonight."

But she spoke in the French that Koum did not understand. The Countess Ileana had never met Cossacks before today, yet her intuition judged Koum's character quickly. And she made the strongest possible appeal to him.

"We are your guests—" she smiled—"and we thank God that we found your house, because tomorrow you will guide us to Christian people where we shall be safe."

Slowly Koum shook his head.

"Impossible," he said.

The Russians stared at him.

"Eh," cried the count, "we will give you silver."

"Listen," said Koum, "silver has nothing to do with it. You don't understand, noble born. I must ride toward the river at once. Wait!"

Pulling on his boots of soft leather, he hastened from the hut down the *balka* to the water's edge. Running a few paces through the rushes, he caught up a line and tugged at it. A flurry at the other end of the line— and he pulled it in, to find a young sturgeon hooked and already weary of fighting. Killing the fish and drawing it carefully from the hook, Koum hurried back to his guests.

"Here is something for food," he explained hastily. "There is barley in that sack, and if you want game, you will find pheasants snared up in the brush beyond the trees—there. Do not stir out of the *balka*—this place. If I do not come back before the first light, mount and ride. Your horses will be rested. Go away from the rising sun, and go quickly. You will not find Uralskaia, but you will come at sunset to a Cossack *stanitza*, a frontier village—"

"But we could not find a village," cried the woman, flushing angrily.

"How can't you? There will be tilled fields, cattle—the herd girls will see you. Anyway, light a fire, and they will come to you—"

"Nay, you must come." The countess hid her annoyance, and her fine eyes became imploring. "I—I will not be safe without you."

Koum's great hands gripped his girdle. It seemed to the Count Dolbruka that a little money offered to the Cossack would make him reasonable. So he felt in his pocket and held out a piece of gold. "For you—more at Uralskaia," he said.

"May the devil fly away with you!" roared Koum. "Cross yourself and spit twice, and pray to Saint Nicholas to save your hide!"

Shaking his head, Koum strode out.

Running down the *balka* he disappeared, and came back presently astride his white horse. Dismounting, he caught up the saddle, flung it on the horse, thrust on the headstall, and picked up his black coat and lambskin *kalpak*. He had brought back with him a dead pheasant, taken from a snare. This he tied on the perch of the screaming falcon, and filled the bird's water cup.

Into his saddlebag he put a full water bottle and some black bread and garlic. He slipped the strap of his musket over his shoulder, picked up the powder horn and doffed his headgear a second before the holy picture, muttering a prayer.

"Ask *him* to show you the way," he grunted to the Russians.

As he was turning away, his eye fell on the bagpipe. He remembered that in spite of all the good Nicholas might do, his hut might be burned to the ground within a few hours, and he picked up the bagpipe, tying it with the bag behind his saddle. Then he leaped into the saddle, snapped his whip and was off up the *balka*.

"*Bras de Dieu!*" cried the count. "What an animal! Well, he has left us."

The woman listened to the thudding of hoofs that dwindled into the distance. Silence returned to the ravine and this silence held for her a dread of things unknown and unseen.

"You were a fool to offer him gold," she said.

The man poured himself another glass of brandy. He too was afraid of this endless plain and the dry mist that hung over it.

On its perch, with red eyes, the falcon gripped its meat with a claw and its beak ripped flesh from between the feathers.

But Koum, as he headed his horse along the back track of the travelers, had forgotten about the gold and the angry eyes of the countess. He was only anxious because he had been delayed so long in starting out. It was already late in the afternoon.

How could he explain to the Muscovites that the Turkomans would follow their trail unless held back by something? The count and his man could not fight, even for their lives. But it would be a sin to let such a fine lady fall into the claws of the tribesmen.

He must find the Turkomans, if they had crossed the river, and find out what had happened to the other Cossack.

So he rode on at a fast canter that ate up the ground, with his eyes searching the skyline hidden in gray mist. He soon was conscious that the trail quartered widely, wandering in and out of the gullies.

"A fox," he muttered to himself, "would go straighter than those Muscovites. Well, it's as God wills."

An hour later Koum was nosing about like a dog in a criss-cross of trails. The tracks of the Muscovites had brought him to the river again, some six miles from his camp. Here the clay bank shelved down steeply to a broad, shallow stretch, strewn with sandbanks and rocks.

On top of the bank stood a kind of bastion of worn limestone, and here Koum found signs of the other Cossack—scattered bullets and sprinklings of powder grains, and the scratches of iron heels on the soft stone. There were dark stains of blood, surrounded by innumerable drops, and some bits of sheepskins. In a sandy depression where a man had lain, stretched toward the river, he found a Cossack *kalpak* of clean white lambskin with a red felt crown.

"Eh," Koum said to himself, "that was *his*, and he did not take it away with him.

Behind the limestone ledge he found the hoof marks of a shod horse that had been tied to the branches of a stunted tamarisk, and had plunged and circled about without being able to break away.

"He tied his horse here," Koum thought, "and went up to the stone to shoot at the Turkomans. He stayed there a long time. After that he fought hand to hand, scattering blood."

Along the sandbanks by the water lay a network of tracks—made by the horses of the Christians and the unshod ponies of the tribesmen. Koum mounted his own horse and circled back over the plain behind the limestone bastion. Here the tracks told a clear story.

The three Muscovites had come up earlier in the day, at a walk. And a solitary horseman had followed them at a gallop—riding the same animal that had been tied to the tamarisk. Then the travelers had ridden off in the direction of Koum's hut; but the strange Cossack had never left the river.

And still there was not a single body upon the scene of the fight, not even a knife or strap on the ground. If the Turkomans had killed the Cossack, they would have stripped him, and perhaps amused themselves by disfiguring the body with their knives. They would not have carried it off with them.

Koum pulled at his mustache gloomily. The worst possible thing had happened. He understood now why the Turkomans had not pursued the Russians. The Cossack had held them so long at the ford—and perhaps had wounded so many of them—that they had not killed him here. They had carried him back, a prisoner. And now they would string him up somewhere and torture him slowly, before going to sleep.

Well, the count and his lady were safe. He thought that all he had to do would be to ride back to the hut, guide the noble born, and have a smile from the lady, a gold piece from the man and a good debouch at Uralskaia.

Instead, he rode down to the ford.

The first thing he saw on the other bank was a twisted dead branch with a fork projecting toward him, like a claw lifted out of the sand. A sign of ill omen. Koum grunted dismally, and spat twice as he passed the branch, being careful to ride well around it. The tracks of the Turkomans also avoided it.

"Eh, was it for them, the sign?" he wondered, "Nay, it must be for the other Cossack."

Still he was uneasy, and he watched attentively for further signs. A raven flew across overhead, and Koum held his breath. But it did not croak. So he could not make up his mind whether the signs were good or bad.

He put his Karbarda into a long gallop, for the plain was as level as the sea here, with only scattered white salt beds glimmering in the strong sunset glow like mirages, through the beds of dry rushes and dark *saksaul*. The Turkomans and their captive had disappeared. Koum put the whip to his horse and sped on. He must get near enough to the tribesmen before dark to see their fire.

For two hours he rode due west. Behind him the gorgeous colors of the sunset flung up to the lofty sky, as if great glowing banners had been cast aloft by the hands of the unseen gods. The whole steppe seemed to be no more than the floor of an immense empty chamber whose wall had been painted with fire. The figure of the solitary Cossack was a black speck crawling across space.

Rising in his stirrups to ease the cramp in his knees, Koum talked to his horse.

"Hi, brother, art thou weary? The eagle flies over thee—hasten! Hey, brother, the wind passes by thee, and says to thee, 'Come!'"

Urged on by the Cossack's voice, the Turkoman-bred racer changed from canter to gallop and back again, untiring. For a few moments the plain grew brighter, and the eastern heights shone with an orange fire, that changed swiftly to blood color. As if a veil had been drawn behind them, the plain darkened around the horse and the Cossack when the sun went down. And a blue haze spread from the foot of the heights, up toward the summits. Then the light vanished and a tracery of stars gleamed overhead.

But Koum reined in the horse and let him breathe. He had seen what he sought—a dark group of horsemen ascending the bare foothills among larger masses of cattle and sheep.

The Turkomans were riding into their *aul*.

Never before had Koum been within sight of the *aul*—the dwelling place of the clan. It stood upon a low plateau under the foothills, cut up by the dried beds of streams and rock strewn gullies. As the Cossack walked his horse forward he made out, in the starlight, some rude domes topped by long poles from which streamers of rags hung. These were tombs, and around them bunched innumerable sheep and cattle.

Beyond, he could see torches moving between low huts and walls whitened with lime. From time to time a strident voice shouted, or a horseman trotted by. The *aul* was awake and astir.

Koum knew what lay yonder under the mantle of starlight. A deep well, and a pool of filthy water. A tomb of some holy man, guarded by a handful of *mullahs* and dervishes. Perhaps three score families of Turkomans in their flat clay dwellings and horsehide tents—the men robbers and slayers by choice and heredity, the women of less account than the horses. Sharp eyes and sharper weapons on the watch, suspicious of each other but merciless to strangers. Koum remembered that his own horse had come from this *aul*, having been acquired by a hand-to-hand fight in which he had slain the Turkoman who owned the horse.

By the sounds and by the subdued glow of small fires, he thought that the tribesmen were eating. As yet he had seen no trace of the captive Cossack. But the torture would come after the eating. And from this torment Koum must release the prisoner, if it could be done.

How it might be done Koum did not know. He had one musket and a tired horse, and there were probably a hundred muskets and swords in the *aul*. If he were seen, they would drag him down like wolves. He could not think of any plan.

But he could rest the Karbarda. It might have to carry double, later. Dismounting, he tied the horse in a dark gully and looked around him cautiously. Near at hand camels were dozing, grunting and bubbling. And the black dome of a tent stood by them. Koum walked over to the tent quietly and listened. After a moment he sniffed and moved closer to the entrance gap.

A strong, sourish smell came from the tent which seemed deserted. The Cossack bent his massive body and went in. He traced the smell to a side where goatskins and leather sacks lay piled. He picked up one of the skins which gurgled cheerfully under his hands.

Pulling out the peg that served as a cork in one leg, he tilted up the skin and tasted the liquid in it. As he had thought, it was kumiss—the fermented mare's milk that served the nomads for wine and food. Koum drank deep.

Then he sat down on a sack. He had a little time, and it would be bad luck to leave the skin half empty after tasting it. He drank again and felt refreshed. There was quite a bit of kumiss in the skin, and when Koum had finished he sat still. His head hummed, but he could hear someone approaching the tent. His eyes had become accustomed to the darkness, and when the visitor stooped through the entrance, he made out the slender figure, the tight-fitting garment and white hair veil of a young girl.

Presently she stopped, with a hiss of indrawn breath, and Koum thought she had heard or smelled something strange. So he sprang up, groped for her, grasped her shoulders and yowled in her ear.

"*Shaitan, khanum—mumtaz khanum!*—Woman, I am a devil—I love you, woman!"

The girl wrenched herself away, darted from the tent and began to scream when she was a little distance off. Koum also left the tent, going the other way, back to his horse. No one would pay any attention to a girl's outcry, but the Cossack chuckled as he reflected that the next day the *mullah* would probably be called in to write a prayer against a black seven-foot Tartar devil that waylaid women. Then he tried to think of a plan, but could not.

He guided his horse up a little rise near the graves, so he could look into the *aul*.

And when he did so the shaven hairs bristled on his scalp. The torture had begun.

A great fire lighted the center of the *aul*, where there was a little clear space before the tomb. A lance length in front of the white wall of the tomb a heavy stake had been planted in the ground, with a crosspiece fastened to it and upon this cross the captive Cossack had been tied with his arms stretched out. He had been stripped to the girdle and his long white body glinted in the firelight.

Round the fire a dark mass of tribesmen sat on the ground, shaggy heads moving restlessly.

"*Yah huk—yah hak; yah huk—yah hak!*" the wailing of a dervish went on like a tireless drum, and already some of the heads began to sway in time to the chant.

As soon as the mood seized them, the Moslems would start upon the Cossack with their knives, or perhaps heated irons. Once Koum had seen a victim of such torture—a man with empty eye sockets who ran from side to side in the plain with hoarse cries coming out of his open mouth, while his hands tore at his bleeding stomach. The skin of his stomach had been slit open and sewed together again very skillfully and what had been put inside the slit Koum never knew. But the vultures were hopping around the dying man . . .

And Koum felt the chill of fear in his blood. In another moment they might start with the knives, and here he was out of reach. He caught the strap of his musket. A lucky shot would save the other Cossack from his agony.

But the bullet might miss—and Koum did not want to wipe out a Cossack like that. He thought of spurring his horse into the *aul*, trying to reach the man and cut him loose. No chance of that. They would both be roped, dragged down.

A strange thing had happened. An hour ago Koum had not been able to think of a plan. Now a dozen plans buzzed and sang in his head. He would pretend to be a ghost coming out of the graves. He would play a ghost march, to draw the attention of the Turkomans. Then he would steal away—creep round behind the captive Cossack and cut him free. Aye, he would even let the Cossack know that aid was coming. While he mused, Koum took up the bagpipe.

An unearthly cry rent the night, echoed by a wailing moan. It was as if all the devils of the winds had come together, out of the sky. The howling of wolves, the roaring of trumpets and squealing of pigs could not have made such sounds.

In the *aul*, men scrambled to their feet and peered into the darkness. The dervish ceased his howling.

After a minute Koum put down the bagpipe. It was time to change his place. But a new sound caught his ear—a bellowing and rushing of hoofs. The wailing of the pipe had stampeded the cattle sleeping in the nearby fields.

He trotted down from the hillock toward the dark shapes that rushed past. A horseman galloped out of the darkness, shouting, and—seeing the Cossack—swerved toward him. Koum heard the rasp of steel drawn from a sheath, and saw a bearded face snarl in triumph.

Beneath him, the Karbarda braced itself, and the two horses came together. The Turkoman slashed at his ribs with a curved knife, but the Cossack slipped to the far side of the saddle. The long arm of the tribesman in its wide sleeve swung past harmlessly, and Koum gripped the other around the waist with his right arm.

Swiftly the Cossack's left arm shot behind the Turkman's head, his fingers clamping upon the bearded chin. With his shoulder under the other's knife arm, Koum wrenched with all the strength of his back. He pulled the man's chin half around, cutting off a wild cry.

The Turkoman groaned and tried to strike down with his knife, then kicked at his horse to urge it on. But he was anchored in Koum's arms, which wrenched at him again and a third time. Bones crackled and suddenly the Turkoman's head became limp in Koum's fingers. His neck was broken, the spine snapped clear.

Panting, Koum looked to right and left, and lowered the big body in its greasy sheepskins to the saddle, catching the rein of the other pony as he did so. Leading the dead man's horse, he urged his own beast at a walk across the fields, until he came to some white boulders and a stunted tree.

Here he tethered the restless horses, and squatted down to stare over the ground on all sides. A few sheep galloped past, and on the knoll he had quitted ten minutes ago, dark figures moved slowly. Searchers were looking for the source of the demoniac music.

Koum chuckled silently, and lifted the dead Turkoman to his back by one arm. He loosed the strap of his musket and laid it against a rock. Guns were no use in the dark—only got in the way. But he kept the bagpipe in his free hand.

Slowly he made his way not toward the mound but to the *aul*. In the starlight he looked like some humped, eight-legged creature dangling horns before him. Circling refuse heaps, he crept along the wall of a hut, and waited until a group of men walked by. Then he went forward hastily in the shadow of an alley.

"Now they will find a sign," he muttered under his breath.

Carefully he lowered the Turkoman to the ground and pulled his legs straight. Then he stretched the dead man's arms to each side, and stopped to listen. A harsh voice called from a roof top.

"*Hai*, Yussouf, has aught been seen?"

Another voice mumbled a response, and Koum heard a step behind him. Without looking up, he fitted the wind tube to his mouth and filled the bag. A dim figure stooped over him, staring down at the dark mass crouching on the ground.

"*Y'allah!*" The newcomer muttered. "O God!"

Koum's bagpipe skirled and wailed, filling the alley with sound. The inquisitive Turkoman leaped high and ran. Koum's pipe shrieked in triumph, and into its madness, Koum wove snatches of a song—a staccato march known to all the Cossacks. Now the prisoner would know that a friend had seen him.

Almost at once Koum ceased playing the pipe and hastened into the protecting shadows of the alley. Behind him silence reigned. But he knew that men would come into the alley cautiously, to behold the devil who made the wailing music, and they would find the dead Turkoman. The path he had taken led into the deeper gloom of trees, and Koum made a half circle before coming out into the starlight. He could no longer see the firelight reflected on the high dome of the tomb, but he saw that he was standing in a small graveyard and judged that he was behind the tomb itself.

In the direction of the alley he heard an outcry and angry shouts. Taking off his *kalpak* and tucking it through his girdle, he moved forward cautiously to the corner of the tomb.

By shifting his head a little he could look out into the cleared space. The fire had been allowed to die down, and by the glow of the embers he could see that most of the Turkomans had left the place. Those who remained were talking uneasily, their attention upon the tumult in the alley. Boys ran by with newly lighted torches.

Twenty feet away from Koum stood the cross facing the other way. The prisoner had not changed his position—only his head moved slowly from side to side. Koum could not see his face. Between the cross and the fire, within arm's reach of the captive stood a tall tribesman with a sword and knife in his girdle.

Now was Koum's chance to cut the other Cossack free. Not much of a chance, but the only one he would have.

Slowly, he slid around the corner of the stone tomb. He kept erect because he knew that anything crawling along the ground would catch the eyes of the men out there more quickly than a man moving slowly on his legs. He was flat against the wall, edging toward the shadow cast by the cross.

For a moment he was in full view of the squatting Turkomans, and he would have been seen if any one of the dozen round the fire had looked carefully at the wall. He took another step. Another. He had six feet more to cover, when a boy galloped by the fire, waving a torch. Koum's head buzzed, and he held himself motionless. Still, not a man looked at him.

Stepping into the shadow of the cross, he moved forward a pace—touched the stake and stood against it. He could hear the other Cossack breathing quickly. Did the prisoner know he was there? Koum dared not whisper a word.

He felt along the back of the crosspiece. The wrists of the Cossack had been bound to it with hemp cords. Carefully Koum drew out his knife.

The tall tribesman in front of the cross spoke suddenly. "*Yok, chambla, yok.* It's bad, no good."

No one responded, and the Turkoman yawned, and turned his back, picking at his nose. Koum touched the other Cossack on the ribs with his knife blade. The prisoner stiffened, planting his feet. Then, swiftly, Koum cut the hemp cords, pressing his dagger's edge into the wood.

The cords dangled over the cross bar, but the other Cossack held his arms motionless as before. The big Turkoman had turned suddenly, staring behind the cross and sniffing loudly. He had one blind, white eye, but the other glared into the shadow, and he started to draw the curved knife.

In that instant the Cossack upon the cross moved. His right arm thrust down. He caught the Turkoman's sword hilt and ripped the blade clear. As the tribesman struck with the knife, the Cossack thrust the point of the curved sword beneath his beard, and the Turkoman staggered back screaming.

"Y'allah—al——"

The Cossack whipped round the post, glanced once at Koum, and stumbled against the wall of the tomb.

"Lead!" he cried.

Cries of amazement went up from the fire as the watchers beheld the cross empty and their comrade wounded. Koum ran behind the tomb and stopped, hearing the clash of steel at his back. The Cossack had turned at the corner to strike at the first tribesman to leap after him. Twice he struck, knocking the pursuer's sword down and slashing his head.

"This way!" Koum called to him.

Instead of heading back into the graveyard and the trees, Koum ran clear round the tomb coming out into the alley where the throng had gathered about the dead man.

"Put this over your hide," he told the Cossack, slipping off his lambskin coat. The black garment covered the man's white skin, and the Turkomans in the alley only saw two dark figures walk across and disappear among some tents. Meanwhile the pursuers at the tomb were shouting for torches to search the cemetery.

"I can't run," whispered the Cossack. "Leg hurt."

"No matter." Koum put his arm under the other's shoulder and walked beside him, heading down toward the rocks where he had tied the horses. "Luck's with us."

As he sighted the tree and the waiting beasts, he saw torches coming out of the tents through which they had run. He did not ask the prisoner if he could ride—he would have to stick to the saddle. He gave the Cossack his own horse, mounting the Turkoman pony himself.

They walked the horses at first, then struck into a gallop, down the slope, until the *aul* and its torches were far behind. Then Koum chuckled and reined in. The Cossack beside him heard a sound of blowing and presently a demoniac wail split the darkness.

When Koum had finished his parting salutation to the Turkomans they galloped on, heading toward the river. Koum knew that a whole regiment might chase them in vain in the darkness, and they could swim the river when they came to it. His head felt warm and comfortable, and once or twice he snored unexpectedly. Then he settled back in the high saddle, and sighed.

He woke suddenly when his pony stumbled. Straightening himself in the saddle, he felt to see if his musket and bagpipe were safe; then he stretched and yawned.

"How is it?" asked the Cossack beside him. "Are you still drunk?"

"How, drunk?" demanded Koum.

"Soused, playing hide and find in the *aul*. But you saved my hide for me."

"As God lives, you son of a dog," Koum rumbled, "I haven't taken a glass—" He thought of the kumiss sack, and remembered vaguely playing the bagpipe to distract the wolves back yonder.

The other Cossack nodded. He was a tall man, a good man with the sword, Koum reflected.

"Perhaps not a glass, but you've had a jugful somewhere, *bratik moi*. When you were behind the stake you were breathing fumes like a cellar. No wonder the Turkoman smelled you out. Fire would have caught on such a breath. Look here—didn't you know they were looking for you?"

Koum was silent, trying to remember just what had happened at the *aul*.

"The guard in the watchtower saw you riding up at sunset," went on the other Cossack. "They were searching for you down below. I heard them tell of it. When you played that music of yours, they all ran to the spot. They put me on the stake and lighted a fire, as bait to draw you in. I called to you, twice. Didn't you hear?"

"Nay," Koum shook his head. It seemed to him that the plan he had made to fool the Turkomans had not been so fine, after all. And he be-

gan to feel angry, because his head ached and crawled as if lice were biting his brains. He peered from side to side. By the cold feel of the air the
night was more than half gone. Ahead of him lay the river and the outline of the far bank looked familiar. "Look," he cried. "You've brought us
back to the ford again. The Turkomans will look for us here."

"Well, they're not here," the Cossack answered casually. "And I left
my *kalpak* over in those rocks."

"Your *kalpak*! By God, don't you know I was riding back to my *choutar*
to see the beautiful lady before she goes off. She's like the moon."

"She may be that, but I heard her say to her husband that we Cossacks
were animals."

"That's a lie, you foster son of a hog!" Koum began to snort, because it
seemed to him that this Cossack was mocking the lady.

"Don't get your hair up. The countess is fair enough, but if we go back
to your *choutar* she'll make more trouble for us. Better sleep here——"

"May the dogs bite you!" The hot blood rushed into Koum's head. "I'll
sleep where I like. I am Koum, the Zaporogian. Aye, the Tartars beat their
foreheads on earth when they see me, and the man doesn't live I can't put
down with my hands."

"Well, Koum," said the other Cossack, "I'm Gurka, the sword slayer,
and I could cut you open like a hare——"

"Death to you!" Koum howled with rage. He jerked his horse up to
Gurka and struck out with a heavy fist.

The blow caught the Cossack on the shoulder, turning him half round.
It cast his weight upon his injured leg, and he groaned and fell from the
saddle. Still holding to the sword he had brought from the *aul*, he got to
his knee, panting.

"You fool," he muttered. "Go down to the river and cool off your head.
Don't come back until you've soaked it well, and then I'll cut your hide
for you if you want."

Koum had dismounted and drawn his long knife. But his throat was
afire with thirst, and he ran down to the water's edge. He stretched himself out on the stones, sucking in the cold water. Then he thrust in his
head several times.

He walked back slowly, wiping the water from his eyes and wringing
it from scalp lock. All at once he remembered that Gurka had been hurt,
and he felt ashamed because he had struck at him.

Gurka was standing, leaning on the scimitar.

"Well," he said sternly, "what now?"

"I did not think—forgot your leg was bad. We won't fight. We'll bed down over there, back of the rocks. It's true what you say, Gurka—these Muscovites cause too much trouble. So we'll wait until they are gone. Only I was not drunk. Saint Nicholas looked out for me."

Gurka laughed and turned to his saddle.

"Then he did wonders."

This pleased Koum.

"Aye, he's like that." Swinging himself into the saddle, he sheathed his knife and fumbled for tobacco. "We'll have a pipe, eh, *kunak*?"

As he filled the clay pipe, he reflected admiringly that Gurka was a fine Cossack—had cut down two men with three strokes of a blade after being trussed up on a cross. And he thought of everything, made plans as easily as Koum could spit.

Although it was cold and Koum wore only a shirt, he felt warm and comfortable. His enemies might be within hail, but he wasted no thoughts upon them.

It was good to have a *kunak*, a real comrade to talk to. And after his sip or two of mare's milk and the fast ride over the steppe, Koum felt well content with the day.

The Post in the Steppe

Gurka paced the dusty street in front of the tavern. Most Cossacks would have waited inside the tavern, as long as they had any silver in their pockets for brandy or vodka. But Gurka was restless.

Hands thrust in his belt, his white *kalpak* pushed back on his head, he stared up the wide dirt street lined with log houses. He paid no attention to a pair of girls who passed near him, their long *beshmets* swirling in the wind puffs—although they glanced back at the tall Cossack with the face of an officer and the sword with gold inlay on the hilt.

"Devil take him," he muttered, "he's off again."

Gurka thought that he had waited long enough for his comrade. Koum had a way of disappearing for hours or days at a time, after entrusting his valuables to Gurka. But Koum was a hunter, a *stiepnik*—born in the steppe—and had only a child's notion of time. Moreover the hunter, accustomed to his hut beyond the frontier and the fellowship of a horse and falcon, felt uncomfortable in this great town where hundreds of human beings walked in and out of buildings, thronging the markets and the drinking places. Yesterday noon Koum had left his musket and bagpipe and the white Kabarda horse with Gurka, and had departed on foot without any explanation, or any indication whatever of the hour he might return. "He's like a child, the son of a dog," Gurka muttered, going around the inn to the stable yard. "Unless he's tied up he's always in trouble."

Leading out the white horse, Gurka saddled him. The saddle had a red morocco cover rather the worse for wear but much esteemed by Koum, who had carried it off with the horse during an affray with a Turkoman clan. Gurka mounted and trotted forth to find the hunter. He went first to the earth rampart of the town where old-fashioned cannon stood pointing out into the endless brown plain. Here, amid dust and swarms of flies,

Tartars and fishermen thronged the native market, and a line of drowsy camels knelt under their loads.

Gurka rode past stalls of fruit and wool and paused to look carefully around the horse market. Koum had no money on him, he knew, but the hunter was quite capable of bargaining a pony out of his friends, the Kahnuks, and then trading the pony in for vodka.

There was no sign of Koum in the markets, or any fighting. Gurka went on to the town jail, a log pen open to the sky within which a score of men slept or argued, watched by a Russian sentry. Several were Cossacks—strangers.

Gurka reasoned that if Koum had left the traders and had not yet arrived at the pen, he must be in one of the numerous taverns. The Cossack passed by the better places with painted wooden doors, and drew rein at a log house by the river, where he heard singing. Dismounting, he made his way into a smoke-dimmed room, below the level of the street, reeking of frying fish and onions.

Koum was not singing. He sat peaceably enough in a corner, an empty pipe in his teeth, working with his knife at a piece of pearl shell. His broad head was shaved in the old Zaporogian fashion, except for a long scalp lock, and it was almost as dark as his tarred shirt. His long lambskin coat, the Cossack *svitza*, was not to be seen.

"Well," remarked Gurka, "where did you spend the night?" He sat down on the bench, running his whip between his fingers.

"*Cosatka chata*," grunted Koum, without looking up from his carving. "In the Cossack's palace."

This meant the sand or mud outside the tavern doors. The name came from the Jews and shopkeepers who were accustomed to find the men of the border snoring on the earth by the doors.

"Where is your *svitza?*"

"What is it to you?" Koum held up the shell, from which he was shaping a belt buckle. "I drank it up, of course."

A grievance rankled in Koum's brain. He had not wanted to ride down the river to this town. They had been fine and comfortable in his *choutar*, with plenty to eat. But Gurka wanted to make plans—to sit with the officers of the garrison, drinking tea and wine.

True, Gurka had been a gentleman once, even a noble, a *barin*. Once he had owned wide lands and horses and servants, off in a place called Hungary. After he had lost all that in the wars he had come out to the frontier—joined the Cossacks. So it was natural enough that the Hungarian should want to talk to the officers and their ladies; but the hunter, without saying anything about it, felt aggrieved and went off to the dingy drinking places by the river.

"Look here," remarked Gurka, "you've got to come with me this afternoon. I've talked with a lieutenant, an aide to His Excellency. They have a mission for us."

"A what?"

"Something for us to do over the frontier. I don't know what, but they'll pay."

"They'll pay—when the devil rings for church with his tail."

But Koum ached with hunger, and the odor of fish and onions tormented him. After a little persuasion he borrowed back his *svitza* from the tavern-keeper for long enough to visit the general. On previous occasions he had discovered that a visit to Russian officers meant either work or punishment. Yet he and Gurka had not three silver rubles between them, and they must do something to get money. These people of the town would not give even a starving man food without payment.

The officers at Sarachikof led a dull life, being isolated upon the salt plain where the sluggish Ural River runs into the Caspian. Their fort was the farthest point of the Russian Empire, to the southeast. Astrakhan with its theaters lay eight days' fast riding behind them, and Moscow six weeks' journey. Their military district extended for some thirty thousand square miles—no one except the clerks in Moscow knew just where—and in this miniature empire of sand and grassland the officers were supposed to minister to the wandering Tartar tribes and to guard the caravan route through Khiva from the east.

This duty fell in particular upon the stout shoulders adorned with gleaming epaulets of His Excellency, General Andriev Lermontoff, whose inclination lay rather toward Gypsy singers, card clubs and the opera—and who in consequence deeply resented his exile where not one of these luxuries could be had. Of course the imperial minister of state at Moscow should have known that the military forces attached to Sarachikof were incapable of keeping order within such a desert; but after the manner of bureaus, Moscow demanded reports of the commander's activities. And these reports were the bane of Lermontoff's easy life.

He had discovered some amusements in Sarachikof, and had gathered in various sums of money. But he avoided moving on expeditions—it was no easy matter to enter the desert beyond the Ural—and sent reports of patrols and garrison posts which did not as yet exist. These reports to Moscow hung over his well-groomed head like ghostly swords. Because no one knew better than Lermontoff that decorations and disgrace alike came out of the ministry at Moscow. So far, he had avoided both.

On the day when he summoned the two wandering Cossacks to appear before him, he had a vexatious problem to solve.

After finishing his dinner he wiped his plump hands on the tablecloth and motioned for a soldier to hold a wax-light to his pipe. Loosening his collar, he blinked drowsily at the empty dishes and at the stout lieutenant of dragoons who sat at the end of the table, ready to write down anything the general might command.

"You came from up the river," said the general, "and so you do not know the country here. But still you ask for service. Well, I need two men who won't run off."

He did not look at the two Cossacks who stood opposite him, and they made no answer.

"This is how it is. My town is on the edge of the sea, and the caravan road from the east—from Samarkand through Khiva—circles the sea and approaches us from the desert yonder." He sighed, drank a little brandy from a glass and nodded toward the river. "The merchants who have come through from Khiva complain that the tribes have attacked them. They say some caravans were taken--looted and carried off. That's a pity."

Lermontoff glanced at Koum, who grunted uneasily.

"They're horned devils," the Russian went on, "these tribesmen--Black Hats and Tartars. *Akh*—they come right up to the river and raid ships that have put in to the shore for the night. No doubt some of them come into the horse market here, to steal and to spy on us. But the worst is the raiding of the caravan road."

The commander did not add that letters had been written to him from Moscow, ordering him to retaliate against the tribes and protect all caravans from Khiva. How could he lead a column of infantry out into the salt steppe, where no good water or firewood or food was to be had? The nomads would keep out of his way, or hang on his rear like wolves, to harass him. He was aware that Moscow set great store by the new caravan trade out of Asia—but Moscow was a long way off, and the emperor was occupied in fighting a man named Bonaparte, a usurper back in Europe. Lermontoff had no intention of moving beyond the range of the cannon of Sarachikof.

"Now, my lads," he went on. "There's only one post across the river— a Cossack troop eight versts along the road. After that, nothing. But the Cossacks say that sixty versts east of them the road passes an old fort on a mound. It is known as the Kurgan. The Tartars are afraid of it; they won't camp in it, although they camp near it and go up in the day for water."

Lermontoff considered, rubbing his beard.

"I'll send you two fine lads out to the Kurgan. You'll be given all the bread and dried fish and barley you need, with a packhorse and plenty of powder and bullets. You'll establish a post at the Kurgan, watch the move- ments of the Tartars and communicate with the caravans when they pass. Try to find out who the raiders are, and one of you ride in each week to re- port to the river post. Do you understand?"

"Yes," said Gurka crisply. "I can write a report. But your Excellency knows that this is work for a strong detachment with artillery."

"What is your name?" Lermontoff was amazed that a vagabond Cos- sack should be able to write and to criticize an order. "Are you registered— what rank have you?"

"My name is Gurka. I am not registered, but—" he smiled—"I have seen service, your Excellency."

He had held the rank of captain in Suvarof's campaign in the Alps, and he had fought through Austerlitz.

"Well, Gurka, no detachment can be sent. My cavalry was called for the western mobilization. I want a pair of galliards at the Kurgan, who will use their eyes and not run from shadows. Eh—you'll have ten sil- ver rubles paid this minute for a drink or two, and twenty each month, as long as you report."

"Not enough," said Gurka promptly. "This is hazardous work, and your Russians won't undertake it."

With a wave of his pipe, Lermontoff agreed.

"Double pay then—twenty to each of you."

"*Pas de l'argent ici, les sales bêtes,*" muttered the lieutenant, in French. "No more money here for drinks, because these stinking animals will go off with it."

Gurka, who understood this, made no response and Lermontoff an- swered in the same speech:

"What matter? If only they will get to the Kurgan and occupy it!" To Gurka, he added, good-humoredly, "No more vodka money. Report to the supply officer tomorrow for your rations. I'll wager you fine lads will get yourselves plenty of antelope steak and catch some wild horses. Don't fail to spy out where the Tartars have their *auls*."

"Would your Excellency," asked Gurka seriously, "also desire us to enlist Tartars to serve under us?"

Lermontoff blinked his moist eyes and seemed pleased.

"Certainly, my lad, if you can. Look here—I've heard that a caravan from Bokhara is coming in, under Ismail Bey. You'll have gold, if it gets in safe."

"Then," the Cossack pointed out, "we should have written authority to enlist men and to protect caravans for Sarachikof."

"Good!" The general dictated a brief order to his aide and signed the paper when it was written out. Handing it to Gurka with ten rubles, he waved his pipe again. *"S'Bogum*—Go with God!"

The two Cossacks bowed and strode out. When the door closed behind them the lieutenant laughed.

"Do you really expect them to go, *mon Général?*"

"Yes, Rostov. Did you notice the elder's head—shaved like the old Zaporogians? The young one's a fire-eater. They'll go just to boast of it."

"The Tartars will tear them out of their skins. You did not explain that the Kurgan is really a tomb of some kind. When those mad tribesmen find two unbelievers cooking meat over the grave of a saint—"

"We shall not have to pay the forty rubles."

Lermontoff signed for the soldier at his back to fill his glass.

"I wonder why Gurka asked for an order—imagine enlisting any one out there! Still, it will read well in our report. Write it out, Rostov, lad. After the usual, begin. 'The command of their high Excellencies, of ninth September, has been obeyed to the utmost. A picked detachment of mounted Cossacks has been sent to occupy the Tartar fort sixty versts east of Sarachikof, on the Khiva road. The commander of the detachment will use every effort to enlist the Tartar tribesmen, and their high Excellencies may rest assured that the Khivan caravans will suffer no further molestation.'"

Lermontoff signed the dispatch with a sigh of relief. The order to guard the caravans had been troubling him for weeks, and now at the price of a few rubles he had earned a year's peace. Before then the Cossacks would be killed off, and—after a reasonable time—he could report the tragic fate of the detachment.

"So," remarked Rostov, throwing down the pen, "Ismail is on the way with his—"

A sudden gesture of Lermontoff checked him, and he remembered the soldier attending them.

"He may not get through," he added.

But the general shrugged.

"He's a fox, Ismail is. And he'll be well guarded. I warned him to cross the river cautiously at night and stop in the old *serai*."

The moist eyes of the general gleamed pleasantly. He was contemplating the arrival of a true treasure—a treasure such as a homesick campaigner in this isolated crossroads of Asia might well look for.

Two days later Gurka and Koum were trotting easily over the dry plain, their long shadows going before them. Behind them the packhorse jogged methodically under its load of provisions, cooking pot and pan, and a small felt tent. Dust rose over them and hung motionless in the air. They were crossing a sandy depression where fragments of ancient shells sparkled in the dunes. Ages ago this depression had been the bed of a great inland sea, of which the Caspian and the Aral were the remnants.

From time to time Koum swung over and lashed the pony, because he wanted to reach the Kurgan that evening. He had redeemed his *svitza* from the tavern-keeper and had bought a new supply of tobacco with his share of the ten rubles. Although he grumbled he was really well content, because he was out in the steppe again and he had seen plenty of antelope that day.

"It always happens like that," he ruminated, shifting his musket sling to the other shoulder. "When you poke your snout into the city the Russians find work for you. They beat you, or perhaps they call you a fine lad, and send you off to some black work too dirty for them. . . . Eh, why did you ask the old fox for that order?"

Moodily, Gurka shrugged his wide shoulders. He had expected to be taken on as a courier at Sarachikof, and he did not care for the desert.

"Always get a written order if you can," he responded absently.

"Well," Koum argued, "who will read it? It's in Russian, isn't it? No one can read it but the Russians and they aren't here—not a bit. And who will you enlist? Call in the jackals and say 'Dear little devils. Here's the written order of his High-Well-Born-ness, for you to enlist and serve us instead of trying to snatch our meat?'"

He chuckled, shaking his head. Gurka frowned.

"I don't like it, Koum. That general was not drunk—he had an idea in his head. It's a mad notion to send two men to hold a fort."

"The Kurgan's a ruin, not a fort."

"Whatever the accursed thing is, we can't do anything for the caravans—two men and one musket!"

Koum was indifferent to the military aspect of their task.

"We can get some good skins, and then hide when anything shows up. Then we'll ride in to the Cossacks for the forty rubles at the end of each month."

"A fine mission!"

"Well, you planned it. And why is it so bad? We might be walking and carrying our saddles, instead of riding in them."

"I'd rather be walking back over the river."

With sudden anxiety Koum looked up. "Do you feel unlucky, Gurka? The signs have not been bad. Horses haven't stumbled, and we've seen no *myzga*—"

What the Cossacks called the *myzga* or steppe mist was the mirage, often seen in the salt desert. Gurka looked ahead curiously and pointed.

"The devil! Isn't that the steppe mist?"

Beyond the depression white lines gleamed in the air, through a gray curtain. High up, as if hung in the sky above rolling ramparts, a dome took shape. Koum spat hastily to both sides, and crossed himself, drawing out the miniature picture of Saint Nicholas, the Wonder Worker, that he always carried hung about his neck. For a moment he stared in silence.

"No," he said. "That is a height with salt showing through the brushwood. Must be the Kurgan."

After a while, when they had climbed out of the depression and the hot air ceased to rise in front of them like a quivering curtain, they saw that the apparition was really their post. Only the stone dome showed above the top of the mound. Before sunset they dismounted at the summit and went to inspect the Kurgan.

The great mound rose about two hundred feet from the plain—steeper and higher on the west, whence they had approached, than elsewhere. The summit, roughly circular, measured sixty paces across. All round it the ground rose and fell, as if a gigantic mole had burrowed there. Gurka counted nine distinct small mounds, so old that tamarisk trees grew on their slopes.

In the center lay the fallen stones of a small, square structure whose inner dome, built on more solid foundations, stood intact, although the entrance gaped open.

"What birds roosted here?" Gurka asked curiously.

About the dome gray, weather-cracked poles leaned crazily. Bits of ragged clothing hung from their tops. By the entrance strange objects had been placed—a dried-up goatskin, some tarnished silver armlets, bones of animals, and even a broken pistol coated with rust. Gurka entered the round chamber under the dome and found nothing at all. The stone flags of the floor were bare; the wall had no windows and the hollow of the dome revealed nothing except the traces of whitewash.

"It's not a watchtower," he remarked to Koum. "No man could stand on that dome."

Koum shook his head. He had been staring intently at the array of curios by the door without touching them.

"It was made for the dead," he said, striking a stone slab with his boot. "A grave, here—lots outside."

"But they call it a *kurgan*."

"A Tartar word—means a tomb or old castle. You ride by these mounds all over the steppe. No one knows who built them. This here is the grave of a holy man."

He motioned for Gurka to come out, and carefully rubbed over the print of their boots at the entrance.

"The men of the caravans left these gifts—" he pointed to the rags and the objects on the stones. "Some have been here a long time—the bowl of barley only a few days. Don't touch them—it's said to bring bad luck."

And, after sampling the water in the well by the tomb, he led the pack-horse out of the mounds. A stone's throw down the slope of the Kurgan, in a sandy depression screened by tamarisks, he dumped the loads.

"We'll have to carry the water down here, and we can't watch the road," Gurka objected. "Up there, the tomb is dry and warm—a better place."

"Worse," grunted Koum, opening the packs.

"How worse? What the devil ails it?" The Hungarian waited in vain for a reply. "The dead won't bite us, will they?"

"They might." Koum began to root up tamarisk brush for the fire. "Vampires do—aye, and the spirit wolves."

Gurka only swore fiercely, and Koum went on preparing supper quietly. He could not explain to the Hungarian why he would not sleep within the mounds of the Kurgan, because it was not clear in his own mind.

"Look here," Gurka remarked when they were eating the barley soup. "Don't you think your guardian, Saint Nicholas, could watch out for your tender skin if you slept up there?"

Koum turned this over in his mind.

"Well, he could. But I'd be a fool to go into trouble."

The big hunter did all the work that evening, roping and currying the horses and setting up the small tent before the fire went out. He felt at peace with his surroundings, secure and drowsy. The uneasiness that had troubled him in Sarachikof had vanished. When he had finished he arranged his blanket in the sand and got out his saddle pack.

Gurka did not want to sleep. He went up to the Kurgan's summit, pacing restlessly among the mounds. The sickle of the new moon stood behind the domed tower. Off in the west a yellow gleam marked the line of the plain. The throbbing drone of insects came up from the grass—hushed at times by the whisper of a breeze.

He stretched himself on a mound, picking out the form of the Great Bear among the stars. They glowed like living eyes. The tomb looked larger than in the day. It was a strange place, the Kurgan, he thought. He knew that Moslems often were buried close to the grave of a holy man. But these mounds did not look like a cemetery. Whatever men lay under him had been buried all at the same time, hundreds, perhaps thousands of them. Was this where Tamerlane had fought a battle? Or unknown pagans?

In the black entrance of the tower he thought that something moved. At once his ears strained to catch a sound.

And near him he heard a subdued snuffling and breathing. As if some animal were trying to free itself, and come out of the ground.

Suddenly a wailing and moaning burst upon his ears. Gurka sprang to his feet and ran down the slope of the mound, out of the Kurgan. The weird melody was coming from the tent, and at his sudden approach it ceased.

"What's the matter?" asked Koum's voice.

"Nothing," Gurka laughed.

He had forgotten Koum's cherished possession, carried about in the hunter's saddlebag. Koum had not played the bagpipe for weeks, but now he sat with one leg outstretched, the leather bag pressed in his arms.

In the full light of the next day the Kurgan looked both dusty and desolate, and Gurka wondered why he had fancied that it held life within it. Koum, who had wasted no thought at all on the mounds during the night, now wandered around on foot, to look at the sites where caravans had made camp. He pointed out that they formed a kind of ring about the Kurgan, because all were just beyond arrow shot from the grave mounds.

"They had to water many horses, many camels," he said. "Aye, they carried the water rather than sleep up there."

"Then they were fools. Look here. This Kurgan is older than Islam—the mounds were not made by Moslems at all. Why should they fear it and make offerings to it?"

Koum shook his head. Why did the men born in the steppe fear the old and unseen? Why did they make gifts to the spirits of this barren place?

"Well," he observed, "what made you run away after the last light?"

"You lie, you cow-herder," Gurka flushed. "I was half asleep when your accursed pipe sounded."

"Don't go to sleep up there, after sundown. You wouldn't wake up."

The next day the two Cossacks rode east along the caravan trail to look for signs of the tribes. They found nothing except the monotonous track outlined by round camel pads and dung. After twenty miles the road turned south, toward the blue line of distant hills. Here they crossed the dry bed of a river, and beyond it they came upon the scene of a fight.

Scattered among the gray bushes and sprawled between boulders lay the bodies of two dozen men—tatters of wool and fragments of leather hanging upon bleached bones. Except for the skeletons, only some bits of rope and sacks were to be seen. Everything else had been carried off. Tracks of wolves and the claw marks of scavenger birds on the ground showed why the flesh had vanished from the bodies.

Koum went over the ground with interest, explaining that this had been a raid on a party of horsemen or a caravan camped by the river before the late Summer heat had dried it up. The raiders had taken away everything, except the worthless garments of the slain. Even boots and belts were missing.

"Tartars did not do it," he said. "They would bury the dead toward Mecca."

"Who was it, then?"

"I don't know. Someone from afar."

Nothing more was to be seen at the river, and after breathing their horses they rode back to the Kurgan—Koum pointing out how other caravans had circled wide of the place of the massacre.

Several days passed without a sign of other men in the plain. At Sarachikof the Cossacks had been told that two caravans were on the way from Khiva, but they were not sighted from the Kurgan. Gurka began to grow restless, and Koum took him off antelope hunting.

They rode into the grasslands toward the north, where the antelope grazed—gray shadows drifting along the brown earth. The animals would not let them come within range, but Koum turned aside on his pony and disappeared into a gully.

Gurka, on the swift-paced white horse, circled back to get behind the herd. He rode in toward them at a gallop and the antelope, instead of running straight away, fled in a wide circle that brought them closer to where Koum had hidden himself with the musket. Usually the hunter, firing from a rest, would bring down an antelope, and when Gurka came up he would be cutting its throat with his long knife.

"Eh," he sighed, "if we only had a golden eagle and dogs, that would be sport."

"An eagle will not pull down a running deer."

"Nay, it flies over the antelope's head, beating with its wings. The antelope turns and twists to escape, and the dogs come up and pull it down. That is the way!"

To Gurka this chasing of foolish antelope seemed a child's sport, and he would not have done it if they had not needed the meat. When Koum showed him tracks of wild horses, he only shrugged indifferently, and in the camp at the Kurgan he did nothing. This did not trouble Koum, who was accustomed to making the fires and cooking. The experienced hunter knew that if trouble or hardship came, Gurka would take the lead at once, and would do the work of three men. But he knew that the younger man was growing weary of sitting in one place and staring at the sky. If only Gurka could have a frolic with the sword—a long ride and a brisk fight. Since there was nothing of the kind to be done the old hunter tried craftily to draw Gurka into talk about the wars in Europe.

"It can't be," he remarked, "as you say. Now at that battle--what is it called?"

"Austerlitz."

"Well, you say thousands and thousands of soldiers were crowded to-gether on your side, in companies and brigades and the like. And they marched ahead against the other fellows, the French, all in step in bri-gades like that. Then the French pounded them with cannon, all the day, until half of them turned their toes up. What kind of soldiers were these soldiers of yours?"

"Good men." Gurka thought of the dogged gray infantry, and especially of the horse guards, all noble-born, all mounted on black horses who had cast away their lives before the lines of French guns.

"Then why did they act like *duraks*, like chuckleheads? If the other fel-lows were too strong, they ought to have looked around and found some shelter and pounded with their muskets."

"How could they, when they were ordered to advance?" Gurka smiled.

"They could do it in Cossack fashion—ride to the side and dismount and clear the way with muskets. Then get to the saddle and chase the other fellows."

"Our cavalry had no muskets, only sabers and pistols. Besides, we could not turn off, because we were all crowded together. You've never seen a battle, Koum. The generals make plans, and maneuver the masses of sol-diers. If every man did what he wanted and never obeyed an order, the army would become a mob—running away."

"Well," Koum pondered this. "Your generals did make plans and you obeyed orders, but you ran away like a mob."

"Bonaparte was leader of the French—he's a magician. Our generals made mistakes."

"Weren't they Cossacks?"

"Cossacks! Don't you know that three emperors commanded at Auster-litz? Bonaparte, and the Emperor of Austria, and Alexander of Russia."

"Nay." Koum nodded understanding. "Well, that's why forty thousand were killed. A little officer, a *sotnik* out here can get forty men killed if he makes a mistake. An emperor can do a thousand times as much."

Gurka did not laugh. Sometimes at night visions of that foggy day of Austerlitz seized upon his mind and drove away sleep.

"Weren't the Cossacks there at all? They didn't march in step crowded together like cattle."

"No—" Gurka smiled—"they were on the wings, and they got off well enough."

"That's it. They are better than the soldiers because they're wolves—they strike and slash, and you can't corner them in front of cannon. If an army of Cossacks went against this Bonaparte of yours, they would tear at him, and pull him down, even if he is a magician." Koura fingered his bagpipe reflectively. "Aye, if you had given the command at Austerlitz to the Cossacks, you would not have lost all your lands. But why didn't you stay in the army, instead of coming out to the frontier?"

"I came—" he laughed—"to look for a pot of gold under a rainbow. Count Gurka of Zaratz, fortune seeker—now occupied in killing flies on a dusty grave. *Requiescat in pace!*"

"I've seen rainbows," Koum observed, "but the gold is all back in the cities."

As if to ridicule both of them, the steppe itself answered them that afternoon, when a veil of dust raised by distant winds hung over the plain. Upon the particles of sand in the air the strong sun beat, and above the haze forms began to take shape. White domes appeared against the glare of the sky, and light flashed upon the waves of a mighty river. Shadows of beasts and men seemed to walk upon the waves. They were like a procession of dead souls, making their endless way through the elements without a Charon to guide them. The Cossacks came out to stare at the pageant in the sky. They saw laden camels and masses of horsemen threading through the blue river.

"It is the *myzga*," said Koum. "Eh, there is your rainbow; but down under it you would find the carrion we saw by the dry river."

Gurka gazed in silence. It was his first encounter with a mirage, and this impalpable city with its river rushing through the air stirred him deeply. Koum, who believed that the *myzga* was a procession of dead souls moving from one resting place to another in the sky, tried to decide if the omen meant good or evil.

"Hard to tell," he mused. "We'll meet men and camels, and we'll go to a city by a river."

The next morning, however, revealed nothing more than the familiar gray plain. The Cossacks went off after antelope and bagged one far to the north. It had been a hard chase and they rode back slowly. When they rounded the last hillocks and glanced at their camp, they drew rein quickly. A caravan had come up and occupied the Kurgan.

The new arrivals were camped within the mounds, about the dome of the tomb. Below the slope groups of camels knelt, heavy bales rising on either side of them. Close to the tomb the round summit of a desert tent showed.

"From the east," muttered Koum. "By God, they've gone into the Kurgan."

Going forward at a foot pace, he studied the men working about the camels. Instead of turbans or *kalpaks*, they wore round caps, and their voices sounded in a meaningless sing-song.

"Kitaians," the big Cossack muttered. "Men from China."

The loads of the caravan seemed to be tea or rice, and since Koum could not speak with the Chinese camel men, he dismounted to go up the Kurgan to the tent. As he did so, he heard Gurka hiss softly, and looked up. Between two of the mounds lounged a half dozen men with long muskets. They wore long cotton and quilted *khalats*, and the toes of their short riding boots curled up. In their shawl girdles were thrust long curved knives, and Koum bristled like a dog at sight of wolves--for these tall warriors were Turkomans, the most treacherous breed in the steppes.

"Too late to ride off," Gurka whispered. Nothing was more certain than that the tribesmen might shoot down two Cossacks who turned their backs to flee. "Go on up. We'll talk with the chieftain."

"Take the horses," Koum assented. And he hailed the men above. "*Ohai*, my brothers. Where is the *bimbashi?*"

One of the Turkomans spat with deliberation and leaned forward.

"What do you seek, Kozaki?"

"We are guards," Gurka put in swiftly, "of this place. We were sent here by the Agha Khan of the Russians, and over there is our camp."

Someone shouted within the Kurgan, and the warriors motioned the Cossacks to come up. The small eyes of the tribesmen fastened greedily on the white horse with the red leather saddle. They made no effort to stand aside, and Gurka, who was leading, thrust one out of his path. The man's retort was an oath like the flicker of a knife, but as Gurka went on without turning his head, he followed with his hand on his knife hilt.

Koum saw that more Turkomans were gathered about the Cossacks' tent, ransacking it, but he said nothing. Gurka was approaching the caravan tent--a great pavilion of white felt with the entrance flap tied down. At least a dozen guards stood about this at regular intervals, and one of them motioned the Cossack away angrily.

"Over there is the *bimbashi*."

The leader of the caravan was sitting on a rug in the shadow of the tomb, with a score of Turkomans lying around him, sleeping or pretending to. He wore a striped silk *khalat* and his shaven head bore no covering of any kind. His broad face, pitted with smallpox scars, turned to one side, like a vulture's, because he had one blind white eye. A necklace hung down upon his greasy bare chest—a strange necklace made of dried human fingers and women's ears strung between boar's tusks and huge gleaming opals. His broad leather belt was studded with flashing emeralds and rubies of great size.

Gurka, walking up to him, noticed that he carried these tokens of his victims, and evidence of his wealth for all to see. His weapons were two long pistols, the stocks inlaid with silver and ivory, laid on the rug upon the side of his good eye. A man, evidently, who liked to make display of his power.

"*Keifunuz eyi-mi, bimbashi?*" Gurka greeted him. "How is thy health, O Chieftain?"

The man on the rug responded in the same fluent Turkish. "It is good. What are you doing here, Cossack?"

"By command of the Agha Khan at Sarachikof, we watch the caravans. We seek news of raiders, for the Agha Khan wishes to protect the Khiva merchants."

"With two men—with one gun?" The pock-marked face twisted in a sneer. "Look. I have sixty men and I fight, many times."

"Yes. What is thy name?"

"Who does not know Ismail Bey the Bokharian?"

"What goods hast thou, Ismail Bey? Tea?"

"Tea, and other things. Rich—more than gold." The Bey waved his hand at the white felt tent.

"What is in it?"

Ismail smiled.

"How foolish are thy words, Cossack! Shall I tell thee what is only for the ear of the Agha Khan? Nay, I think you are scoundrels!" He considered a moment. "But be at peace—go to your tent."

Gurka turned indifferently to stroke the soft muzzle of his horse and in doing so he glanced inquiringly at Koum.

The big Cossack looked thoughtful. Many things about the caravan struck him as curious—the Chinese camel men, the camels themselves half again as many as the loads, the strong force of lawless Turkomans, the camp within the usually inviolate Kurgan, and the violation of his own quarters. He was worried about his bagpipe, which he had seen the warriors passing from hand to hand with interest. Reaching back, he freed the carcass of the antelope from his saddle and laid it before the knees of Ismail Bey.

"A gift, *bimbashi*." He did not speak Turkish as well as Gurka who had learned it in childhood, and he was just able to follow the talk.

Ismail grunted and touched the antelope, showing that he accepted it, before signing to a man to take it away. But he did not invite the Cossacks to eat with him. Koum, in withdrawing, spoke casually to Gurka.

"It's bad. Tell him to order his men out of our place."

"Are thy men dogs, O my Bey," asked Gurka coolly, "to prowl in our tent? Send them away!"

Again the leader of the caravan smiled. He shouted in a dialect that the Cossacks did not know. But Koum, watching the men behind the rug, saw them lean forward expectantly.

"What now?" Gurka asked him.

"Tell him to take his horses away from the grazing ground below our tent. That belongs to us."

A third time Ismail Bey assented courteously. He said that the Cossack's horses were weary, and he would yield them the good grass. When he shouted his command, the Turkomans who had been at the Cossack tent moved off reluctantly to drive their beasts from the grass.

Turning their backs on the Bey and his followers, Gurka and Koum circled the white felt pavilion, scenting as they did so a faint odor of incense and perfume. Leisurely they descended the slope of the Kurgan, and Kourm retrieved his cherished bagpipe from the ground, inspecting it anxiously. Gurka saw that their saddle bags had been turned out and many articles were missing.

"To the devil with them," Koum observed. "They are jackals, hunting in a pack. After we've taken off the saddles and roped out the horses, they'll fill our hides with lead and take everything. The best thing is to ride off swiftly now. If they follow, it may be we can keep them off until dark."

"Agreed." Gurka nodded.

He did not know the hunter's reasons for flight, but he felt that Ismail's men would make bad bedfellows. Down here within stone's throw of the mounds they could be picked off at any moment by the Turkomans—after they had separated from the valuable horses.

A glance at the sky showed him that they had two hours or more of daylight left. In the field below them the Turkomans were moving sluggishly among the horses, like men who were only awaiting a signal to cease their efforts. He picked up his grazing rope and stretched himself, yawning. The Russians had been mad to post two men here—

"Now!" whispered Koum.

As one man, the two Cossacks jerked the reins back over the heads of the startled horses, leaped into the saddles, and plied their whips. The fast ponies sped down the slope, as a clamor of voices arose from the Kurgan.

Kourn swerved to the left, to avoid the men in the field and to shift the direction of their flight.

"Not together—pull away you fool!"

Gurka swerved aside, to separate from his comrade, just as a scattered volley roared from the Kurgan. Heavy lead bullets whined over their heads. But men riding downhill make a poor target, and the Cossacks, bent beside the straining necks of their horses, only feared that the beasts would be hit.

"May they burn, the fiends!" Koum screamed.

Moving toward him, Gurka cried out to him, to know where he was hit. He had heard the thud of a bullet striking something solid.

"The sons of dog-born dogs! Only look!"

Koum raised his arm, his face dark with rage. In his hand dangled the bag-pipe, a bullet hole through the leather sack. Gurka laughed.

But in a moment he began to reflect. A glance over his shoulder assured him that a half dozen Turkomans on rangy horses were starting from the Kurgan in pursuit—proof, if any were needed, that they had meant to kill the Cossacks. They were nearly half a mile behind, and Gurka knew that his fast horse would keep him ahead until darkness. But Koum's mount, carrying a greater weight, was dark with sweat and laboring already to hold the pace.

The open steppe offered no hiding; it would be useless to try turning into the shallow gullies or bare hillocks. Koum was heading straight to the south, still muttering over his damaged treasure.

"Hi, Koum—time to change," Gurka called out.

Drawing into a trot, the two Cossacks swung out of the saddles, and hurriedly changed ponies. Leaping to the horses' backs, they settled themselves in the saddles and found the stirrups, using their whips again. Gurka, the better rider as well as the lighter weight, devoted all his attention to nursing the brown pony along. Allowing Koum to pick the way, he kept his eyes on the ground, until the big Cossack called to him.

"Hi, Gurka—look at them."

Glancing over his shoulder, Gurka was surprised to see that the Turkomans had come up halfway in the last twenty minutes. Their lean, shaggy ponies covered the ground with a tireless gallop. The riders had taken their muskets in their hands, and Gurka could make out faces and beards distinctly.

"Go on," he said between his teeth. "This clod of a horse holds you back."

Koum shook his head.

"Nay, Gurka. Only look yonder. There's a height where we can hold them off."

The height was a line of rocky knolls with green brush showing above them. Gurka did not think that one musket would keep the tribesmen off for long, but his tired mount would have a chance to breathe and what else was there to do? Koum had been heading for the knolls, so that the Turkomans were strung out in a long tangent behind them.

Whipping their horses, the Cossacks galloped toward the highest point of the rise and started up the slope, only to find that the tired horses could not force their way to the top of the hard clay bank. Swearing roundly, Koum slid from the saddle and poured powder from his flask into the pan of the flintlock. The Turkomans, who had closed in rapidly, were within easy shot. They did not hang back to shoot, but raced forward to get within short range.

Koum fired quickly, bringing down a horse without harming the rider. Swiftly he reloaded, while Gurka drew his sword.

"Ghar—ghar—ghar!" the Turkomans shouted, swinging their guns over their heads.

And then the Cossacks heard a strange snapping and whistling in the air. Invisible birds seemed to dart down from the crest of the knoll. Feathers sprang into sight, quivering in the ground. One of the tribesmen yelled, clutching his leg—the ragged turban of another dropped off.

One after the other, the Turkomans fired, above the heads of the Cossacks. They turned their horses and darted off, plying their whips, the dismounted man jumping up behind one of his companions.

Gurka looked at the summit above him. Over the dry grass rose huge ungainly hats, high felt crowns with wide flapping brims. Under the hats dark faces appeared, and leather-bound arms clutching bows.

"*Hi kunak!*" Koum called out. "They are Tartars, brother," he added to Gurka.

The Tartars stood up, short stocky figures in long sheepskin coats, talking excitedly. When Koum put aside his musket, they helped the two Cossacks with their horses to the summit. In the grassy ravine behind the ridge stood round felt tents, with herds of fat sheep and ponies and a throng of the nomads, men, women and children, watching the event on the height.

The Tartars had been gathered around the dinner kettles before the skirmish with the caravan men, and now they went back to their food, kneeling on the ground and thrusting their hands into the thick broth, to seize bits of mutton or rice. They paid no attention to the Cossacks, and Gurka wondered if he had got away from wolves to fall into a lair of panthers. These nomads were hiding in the ravine—they had brought in all their herds, and a rider passing by the hillocks would have seen no sign of them. The smoke from the embers drifted into the haze of dust stirred up by the breeze. It was the sunset hour and the red murk of the day cast only a faint light into the depression.

But Koum had no misgivings.

"They won't bite. Eh, they are Kara Kalpaks—Black Hats—cattle raisers. I've stayed in their tents during a blizzard." He was trying to repair the damage to his bagpipe by cutting two short wooden pegs to fit in the bullet holes. When the pegs were in he inflated the bag and tried a few notes. The unmelodious wail that came forth caused the Black Hats to turn in startled concern, while the nearest cows lifted their heads. A man came over and argued angrily, until Koum put down the pipe.

"Well, you see it won't sound right," he sighed. "They say it will stampede the herd. They say if we want food we must come before it is all eaten."

The Tartar led them into the largest of the round tents, where a huge candle burned in dense smoke. Behind the fire on a rug covered bench sat a fat man in a *khalat* of horsehide painted red. This was Tavka Khan, master of the little horde, and he waited patiently until the Cossacks had eaten. Then Koum washed his hands in a basin brought by a young woman and asked for wine.

Tavka Khan shook his head. He had no wine, being, he explained, a true Moslem, but he had kumiss—fermented mare's milk. And he opened wide his watery eyes when the big Cossack downed bowl after bowl of the heady drink.

Since Gurka could not understand their talk, Koum enlightened him from time to time between bowls.

"The khan is angry because we led Ismail's jackals here. He turned aside from the road yesterday because he heard that Ismail's caravan was coming after him. He says Ismail is a black-boned robber."

"The Bey has his own caravan to guard," responded Gurka. "These men must be afraid."

"Not so. They are fighting men, but they do not raid and they have few muskets. They plunder the Russian merchants along the river, of course. But Ismail—"

Koum asked the old Tartar a question and listened with growing interest to his emphatic answer.

"Only think, Gurka! Ismail's a fox—a steppe fox. This is what he does. He brings a rich trade from Bokhara to sell to the Russians. Then at Sarai or along the Volga he lays in a few things to take back. But here, on the eastern road, he attacks the westbound caravans, killing every one. Aye, he takes their camels and goods. He wiped out a Tartar caravan at the river crossing last Spring, where we found the bones. That is why these Black Hats keep out of his path."

"He's going west now, not east."

"Aye, but they think he would drive off their cattle to sell at Sarachikof—only two marches away . . . Devil take him—he's the raider! He's the one who has been eating up the caravans."

Gurka thought of the sixty warriors at the Kurgan, with fast horses and many muskets. Few merchants could afford, or handle, such a guard. And the Chinese camelmen would tell no tales.

"Why doesn't Tavka Khan tell this to the Russian officers!" he asked.

The Tartar made hot response, his eyes flashing as he clawed at his thin red beard.

"He says," Koum interpreted, "he has no witnesses to the slaying, and the Bey trades with the Russian generals. Besides, the Russians don't set foot over the river. They claim this grazing land of Tavka's—make him pay a head tax and send Cossacks to collect it. But they don't protect him.

They protect Ismail, so Tavka loots their ships when he can to get money to pay the tax."

"What kind of man is the Bey?"

"He's a dog—not a good Moslem. Wears pigs' tusks and eats unlawful meat. He's not a Tartar, not a Turkoman—but the tribes fear him because he slays like a mad dog."

"He speaks Turki like a man from the east."

"God knows. But we're well out of his hands."

"Nay—" Gurka smiled—"we are going back to the Kurgan tonight."

In the act of handing his bowl to the woman to be filled again, Koum turned his head.

"What's that you say?"

Gurka had passed an unpleasant afternoon. He did not relish being chased like a wandering horse, and now he saw an opportunity to strike a blow himself.

"Don't you see, Koum? We can go back with these Tartars and rush the Turkomans. They will not look for an attack."

For a moment Koum considered and shook his head.

"Nay, brother. There will be a moon—a half-moon on the steppe. And those sons of dogs have too many guns."

"Too many for the day. At night a gun is no good. The light will be strong enough for the Tartars to use their bows. If they don't shirk, it can be done. And then we'll open up that treasure of the Bey's. I'd like to get my hand in it."

Slowly Koum sipped at the bowl. He also had a score to settle with the men who had damaged his beloved bagpipe. By now he had drunk enough kumiss to look at matters with the eye of an opportunist.

"Well," he muttered, "glory to God, why not try?"

Visibly excited, Tavka Khan listened to his urging, without being won to consent.

"*Ai Barba,*" he responded. "No, uncle, who has ever attacked Turkoman raiders? They are wolves with long teeth. If they came against us, aye— then we would fight."

"Some day they will come, O my khan." Koum's mellow voice was deep with feeling. "And then, by Allah, they will pick their time and leave all of you without graves, for the jackals to bury in their bellies. Even thy moon-faced women, and young sons, tender as saplings. How much better it would be to lead thy men against them now and take their camels, their horses and that rich treasure concealed in the white tent?"

After filling and lighting his clay pipe he handed it to the khan, who took it and drew upon it until his lungs must have been filled with smoke. Nor did he let out the smoke, except as it filtered after moments from his nose and ears. No true Tartar would waste the precious smoke.

"Aye, true it is," he muttered, "that the one-eyed wolf guards something of great price, concealed from other eyes. By day he carries it in camel hampers, and at every halting he places it within the white tent. He takes it to the Russians. No one else has seen it, except his men of Cathay."

"O my khan, he said himself it was more than gold. Think of six camels loaded with more-than-gold. Yah Allah—what a thing! And consider moreover that this captain of Cossacks, my *kunak*, will be at thy side to tell thee of stratagems. Once he held the baton of command in a great battle of the Franks in which forty thousand died."

The bleared eyes of the old Tartar studied the spare figure and lean face of the Cossack Gurka. The Black Hats had their affrays with the Cossack posts, and each stole horses from the other, and held the other in respect. In a storm, or upon purely friendly visits, each welcomed the other. Tavka Khan perceived in Gurka the quality of a man who knew how to command. But he himself was old and heavy; he could not see very well and he liked to sit in the smoke of the tent fire.

"*Ai, tzee!* He is a khan, as thou sayest; yet I—"

Koum saw that it was time to use his final argument.

"Listen, now. When a dog is mad doth not Allah shorten his days, so that death comes upon him suddenly."

"Aye, so."

"Well, now—this night—it hath happened that Allah sealed the seal of death upon the life of that dog Ismail Bey, the ill-born. It is certain. For he sleeps with his men in the place of the doomed. He eats and he scatters his filth upon the Kurgan itself, above the mounds and the grave of the holy one."

Tavka Khan clutched at his beard.

"Is this true?"

"By Allah, his carpet is spread against the tomb. Allah will aid thy hand in his punishment."

Fumbling in his girdle, the Tartar drew out a case of pearl shell shaped like a half-moon. Inserting his thumb and forefinger, he helped himself to snuff and passed the case to Koum who did likewise.

"I am young again," cried Tavka. "Tonight I will ride against Ismail Bey!"

He was as good as his word. In fact, influenced perhaps by the copious drafts of kumiss, Tavka became so convinced of the righteousness of his cause that he would take no more than fifty men and the Cossacks—explaining that these fifty were his best men and the others must remain to guard the horde, in case the fifty should be killed. Gurka approved this, saying that in a night attack it was better to have a compact body of experienced fighters than a throng.

They started about midnight, to reach the Kurgan when the moon was low. Although they pushed on at a fast trot, Gurka heard no clinking of stirrups or rattling of bow cases. The Tartars seemed to be black shadows floating through the haze of moonlight. The ponies' hoofs struck soundlessly into the sandy ground.

Tavka sang quietly to himself something about the blood of brave men in a vase of gold, and fair women carried off on the saddles of raiders. He sang the charms of the women in detail, until he reined in and beckoned to Koum.

"It is time," he said, "for the *Kosaki bimbashi* to tell us the plan he has made."

"Gurka," the big Cossack interpreted, "they want you to tell them how to attack the Turkomans."

Already Gurka had pondered this, going over in his mind the site of the Kurgan and the disposition of the warriors with it. Obviously he must count heavily upon surprise, because Ismail's men once aroused and armed could hold the mounds even in that treacherous light against an inferior force.

"Will these fellows fight foot to foot with Ismail's?" he asked.

"Nay," Koum laughed, "but they will ride their horses through the Turkomans. They will not leave the saddle. Wounds will not stop them, yet if they are beaten in the first attack it will be hard to bring them forward again."

Gurka nodded—he had suspected as much. The riders of the horde all carried the weapons of horsemen, short bows and small, curved sabers, and many had lances with tufts of horsehair.

"Tell Tavka Khan," he responded, "that most of the Bey's horses are below the Kurgan on this side. There will be some guards out with them, and probably a watcher on the Kurgan. The camels with the Chinese are on the other side, near the road. The Turkomans will be sleeping within the mounds. We will not rush on together. You, Koum, will go forward on this side, drive in the horse guards and stampede the horses—then circle the mounds, making an outcry and shooting. You will have six men."

"And what—"

"The rest will follow the khan, and I will take them in a circle beyond sight of the Kurgan—you must hold back until we do this—to the road. When you make your onset, the Turkomans in the Kurgan will wake and run to that side. They will not see us come in at first, and we ought to be on their backs before they can hold us off with musketry. Meanwhile, your circle will bring you in among the camels—start them up, make a tumult, then join us."

When this was explained to him, Tavka Khan approved of it.

"We will draw the dogs this way by the bleating of a goat," he assented, "then we will rush upon their backs with a panther's spring."

"But watch for Ismail," Koum urged Gurka. "He's a magician—full of tricks. Besides, we'd better get hold of his belt and trappings before these fellows see him."

Gurka, however, was thinking of what the white tent concealed. It must hide something of great value, because Ismail would not mount such a guard over it without reason. Probably he sold or traded this treasure to the Russians. It might be camphor, ginseng, or rare drugs from the East. Evidently Ismail had to conceal it from the Moslems; perhaps he brought it all the way from China. Opium—but that would not fill such a pavilion. Jade—but why would heavy pieces of jade need to be housed in a tent at night?

What kind of treasure smelled like perfumes, and rode during the day in camel hampers, and was kept at night in a guarded tent? Nothing— and yet there it was. Koum and Tavka did not bother their heads about it. They would see it before long. And the other tribesmen jogged along by him as impassive as armored dwarfs, their wide-brimmed hats hiding their faces.

Behind them the moon sank lower, while vague shadows moved ahead of them, over the dry grass. Gurka recognized a nest of boulders by a stunted tree and pulled up.

"Time to take your men," he whispered to the big Cossack.

With his half dozen, Koum turned off to the left at a foot pace. He would have to give the others time to make the circuit of the Kurgan and he must judge the time nicely because they could not signal to him when they were in place. He had left his long musket with the horde, and had armed himself with a lariat, a heavy, three-foot cudgel and his knife. Also he had his saddle pack.

With the Tartar khan beside him, Gurka swung off to the right, pointing as he did so to the dim shape of the mound. Tavka Khan grunted assent—probably he knew the place. His men were stringing their bows, whispering among themselves. Swiftly as they covered the ground, little could be heard above the rustle of the grass under the rising wind.

When he thought he had made a half circle, and the mound of the Kurgan showed dark against the moon, Gurka touched Tavka on the knee and wheeled his horse. To breathe the animals, he reined in to a walk. It was hard to tell how far he might be from the caravan. Nothing seemed to be alive in the steppe ahead of them, and for a moment the Cossack wondered if Ismail had left the place.

"*Hai!*" muttered a man beside him.

Thin and faint in the distance, Gurka heard an unearthly wail. Such a cry as a forlorn vampire wandering in quest of blood might make. The back of his neck grew cold, until he remembered Koum's bagpipe which was audible even if damaged.

Then a far-off cry caught his ears, followed by a shot. He tightened his knees and sent the white horse forward at a gallop. In silence the Tartars pressed after him, until they entered the dim shadow of the Kurgan.

And then shouts resounded on the summit of the Kurgan, while men appeared running along the mounds clearly outlined against the glow in the sky. A spit of flame darted toward them and a musket roared. Gurka swore savagely, realizing that he was too far from the Kurgan and that Ismail and his men were aroused and armed. If Koum had only waited five minutes more before sounding his pipe!

Camels surged around him, and men fled away. He felt his horse rise to the slope of the mounds, and he drew his sword. A half dozen muskets roared above him.

A rider pushed close to him, and a hand caught his rein.

"*Kosaki bimbashi!*" a voice cried plaintively.

More guns flashed and bellowed as the Cossack turned angrily on the man who had stopped him. The hand clutched his arm and pressed warningly. Gurka bent forward, looking from side to side.

Ismail's men were thronging upon the line of the mounds. The steppe fox had not been caught asleep. The Tartars had stopped abruptly, but no

one seemed to have fallen. Instead they were using their bows swiftly—
Gurka heard the incessant snap and hiss of them—and their shafts were
striking into the clearly visible Turkomans, not forty paces away.

Men dropped back from the skyline, screaming as the arrows from the
powerful bows tore into their bodies. The musket fire dwindled, as the
clumsy pieces were discharged into the shadow. Gurka heard the slugs
whine over his head.

"Ahai!" shouted Tavka Khan.

The Tartars dashed forward again, slashing with their short sabers
at the men on the mounds, thrusting down with their lances. Cries and
snarls and the thudding of horses' hoofs sounded around the Cossack who
was striking silently with his saber.

He turned toward the flash of a musket and saw the Turkoman lift the
weapon to parry his slash. Checking his arm, Gurka leaned forward and
thrust, the point of his blade piercing the man's beard and throat. The
Cossack freed his sword and turned warily in time to ward off the slash
of a long knife.

His horse swerved, and he saw two men rolling on the ground, locked
together in a death struggle. Horses swept by him and a shrill voice chanted
"Yah Allah—yah All—"

Out of the murk a long robed figure staggered, reeled against his horse
and vanished. Seeing a Turkoman climbing upon a pony, Gurka wheeled
toward him and struck him from the saddle before his feet were in the
stirrups. Over the tumult shrilled the lament of the bagpipe, and, hearing it, Gurka remembered to look for Ismail.

The tomb was deserted, the rug bare. But Gurka thought that he recognized the thin figure mounted on a horse, moving away toward the moon.
A Tartar appeared riding at it, and the figure lifted an arm that flashed and
roared. The Tartar dropped from his pony, landing on his feet. As Ismail
trotted past, peering into the murk, the Tartar swung his arm around his
head. The next second Ismail was jerked from the saddle as if an invisible hand had pulled him to earth.

Gurka rode over to him and saw that, although wounded, the Tartar
had managed to cast his lariat and pull down the chieftain. Now he was
winding his rope about his struggling prisoner.

"Hi, Gurka! The dogs are running. Come to the tent."

Before the white felt pavilion Koum was beckoning him. A glance
showed Gurka that all the horsemen had swept from the mounds, leaving

only the huddled bodies of the dead and the injured dragging themselves to shelter. Tavka Khan appeared on foot, panting and exclaiming, and laid his hand on the entrance flap of the tent, now deserted by its guards.

In a second Koum was out of the saddle, jostling stout Tavka, to be first to enter. Both became aware of a light within, and of quiet sounds made by living beings. They hesitated, gripping their weapons, until Tavka raised a corner of the flap and peered in. Grunting, he flung the flap wide open and strode in.

"Women," Koum cried. "Ismail had wives!"

The floor of the pavilion was covered with soft rugs and cushions. Candles fastened to the heavy pole shed a flickering light upon a group of slender women crouched at the far end. Tavka and the two Cossacks went over to them and stared, amazed. What need had Ismail of nine wives, all young, all clad in damask and silk, all wearing ornaments of heavy silver and giltwork? Their fingers were henna stained, their eyes touched with kohl, and they smelled of attar and musk and aloes.

"Not wives," Tavka muttered. "Girls."

Bending down, he pulled off a few veils, revealing fair, painted faces— thin Persian cheeks and slanting Chinese eyes. Swiftly he turned over the bundles of clothing and trinkets with his foot. Then he looked at Koum moodily.

"There is no treasure here, he said. "Only these slaves."

Slaves! Koum bethought him of how Ismail guarded his living treasure in screened camel hampers and pavilions and how he carried his stock-in-trade to the Russian market and did not bring it back again. True, the Moslems frowned upon the slave traffic, but it was carried on more or less openly, and Ismail would not need to take such precautions to hide his human goods unless—

"Look, Gurka," he exclaimed. "Ismail sold these dancing girls to the high, well-born Russians. That is why he hid them like jewels. Aye, they are more than gold. What a fox he is!"

Koum scratched his head, and remembered that if Ismail had no wealth in the white tent, the trader must have it all on his own person.

"Where is the dog?" he shouted. "Hi, Tav—"

But the fat Tartar had come to the same conclusion a moment before Koum and had vanished from the tent.

Strangely enough, Ismail also had disappeared. Koum searched the Kurgan and asked questions in vain. Not until broad daylight did Tavka Khan admit that he had the Bey among the prisoners with the horse herd, and by then the scowling Ismail had been stripped of belt and wallet, rings and embroidered vest—although Tavka denied any knowledge of jewels or gold found on his captive.

By then the fighting had ceased. The Turkomans had left a dozen men killed and badly hurt about the Kurgan, with most of the muskets. The survivors, who had managed to get a number of horses and stray camels, had scattered like wild dogs among the dunes and hollows of the steppe. The Tartars, having pursued them out of sight, gave up the dangerous task of trailing them and rode back to count the spoils. They had lost only two men killed, with as many badly wounded, and they had rounded up all the camels.

They were delighted with events. Not only had they thrashed the hated raiders and avenged their slain clansmen, but they had gained rare weapons, powder and ponies, besides the camel freight and the Chinese camelmen, who remained by their beasts, little moved at this abrupt change of masters. Moreover Tavka Khan had extracted a small treasure from the Bey's garments, and meant to ransom Ismail for a stiff price in Bokhara.

Koum guessed at this, and demanded what Tavka had left to the Cossacks.

"Now," responded the fat chieftain, "thou hast again by our aid thy *kibitka.*"

He meant the Cossacks' tent, and when Koum cursed him roundly for a thief without honor, he ruminated. Tavka was honest enough in his way, but he could not bring himself to hand over horses or jewels.

"You are brave, my brothers," he observed. "Aye, Gurka is like forked lightning, striking down all who come against him. I love you more than fat sheep, more than fat, swift-paced ponies. Thus, I will give to you *all* the girls."

Although some of his men, who had been inspecting the slaves, wanted them, Tavka did not think they would be of service in the horde. Plainly, they were not strong women who could endure in the steppe. And to sell them in the distant cities would be a difficult and somewhat hazardous matter for the Tartars.

"Those dancing girls?" Koum stared. "What would we do with them?"

"They are young, moon faced—good for many things. Now, I have given them to thee."

And, argue as the Cossack would, Tavka refused to change his mind. He had satisfied his conscience and rid himself of a source of possible trouble, and he was content. Being weary with his exertions he went to sleep presently, and Koum strode off to find Gurka.

"The khan," he said, "has given us for our share all the girls in the tent."

"May the devil take him! Refuse the slaves—ask for horses. We can sell them in the town."

"No use. He won't give up even a pony, only the girls."

"Then we have nothing."

"Nay, Gurka, we have the girls."

"How? You did not accept them?"

Koum shoved his *kalpak* to one side and scratched his shaven head.

"You don't understand. Tavka has given them to us—they are his gift. He will not take back his gift, so now the nine *bayadere* are in our hands. We must do something with them."

"What? Rope them out, to graze? Give them swords and drill them for recruits?" Gurka laughed.

But Koum was thinking. These singing and dancing girls—choice ones, from remote lands—had been meant for the Russians. Had not Tavka assured him that Ismail sold one or more on each trip through Sarachikof? Unlike the Cossacks, the Russians had secluded their women until a very few generations ago—Koum himself had seen the ladies of the nobility traveling like the *khanims* of Asia in closed carriages. The officers looked twice at young Asiatic girls, and in remote posts like Sarachikof, personable women brought good prices. The traffic was secret, of course; but the Cossacks knew about it, as they knew everything that went on in the steppe. Girls like these in the tent would bring six hundred silver rubles each.

"Look here," he observed, "they are worth more than fast horses. The high, well born generals in Sarachikof have been buying them from that dog Ismail."

Gurka's gray eyes flashed angrily, at the thought that officers would buy Moslem slaves.

"I might take one or two," Koum ventured, "into the town at night and sell them to Lermontoff and the other stall-fed cows."

To his surprise the Hungarian became even more angry, his lips tightening in a half smile that had no mirth in it.

"I'm a Cossack, and a vagabond now," he said quietly, "but not yet a woman seller."

"What's the harm? You trade horses, Gurka, and why not—"

"Shut your teeth!"

For a while Koum mused upon his comrade's nature, and gave it up.

"Eh," he suggested at last, "then tell me what's to be done with them."

"Take them back to the river—turn them over to the Russians to look after."

It was Koum's turn to be angry. Snatching off his *kalpak*, he snorted, pounding the grass with his clenched fist.

"So that's all the plan you can think of, with all your education? May your hide be salted down! So we're to take in these *bayadere*, the nine of them, and bow down to Lermontoff and his crowd and say, 'Please, your Illustriousness, here's a few girls for your Excellencies to take care of, and all for nothing at all, not a kopeck do we ask. We fought the Turkomans, just to bring them to your Excellencies!'" Picking up his hat, he stamped away, muttering, "They'll be taken care of just the same. What difference if they're sold or given away?"

To relieve his feelings he went down and watched the young men of the Black Hats burying the headless bodies of the Turkomans in a distant gully. The heads were to be dried and set up on stakes on the scene of the massacre to the east. Their own dead the Tartars were burying on the slope of the Kurgan facing toward Mecca, in order to benefit by the sanctity of the tomb.

Koum wandered off to inspect the captive Ismail, and it cheered him a bit to find the raider in the sun with his ankles bound and roped to a stake. Deprived of his padded garments, he seemed to have shrunk, and his eyes stared up malevolently. All the wealth had been torn from him, literally; even his breeches had been ripped, and the grisly necklace of teeth and human ears had vanished.

"How is thy health, Ismail Bey?" Koum asked. "Is it good? Then bethink thee that we, who rode over thy camp last night, will take thy fair slaves to Sarachikof to sell for gold."

But the pleasure of mocking Ismail was dimmed by a calculation of how much Tavka must have taken out of the garments of the trader, and Koum became moody. He went off to his own tent and found little to comfort him in the disorder evident at the hands of the Turkomans. Even his kit had been rifled and he had no hope of recovering any of the missing articles. He took up his bagpipe and remembered that it had been spoiled by the bullet. Putting it away in his saddlebag, he drew out his clay pipe and rooted in his pouch for tobacco.

When he lighted it, the pipe tasted bad, and he swore fervently as he threw it down in the sand. If he only had a single mug of brandy or vodka!

"He shies like a horse whenever I speak of girls," he meditated. "He made a fine plan to capture the Kurgan, and he went through the Turkomans as a scythe-man goes through wheat, but now he won't make a plan to get gold out of the girls."

The big Cossack yawned and rapped his fist against his head.

"God gave me bone here—nothing to think with. Why is it Ismail had to hide his slaves? Well, there are priests in Sarachikof, who would make an outcry if they saw them. And Lermontoff has a wife, an old wife. That's it—the officers are afraid of their little mothers."

Beyond that point Koum's thoughts did not carry him, and he fell to musing upon the old and better days when Cossacks were able to do things in proper fashion—when hogsheads of brandy would be broken in after a victory, and the earth itself would resound to the high silver heels of the warriors beating out the *trepak*, and no one would dream of turning over nine girls to Russian officers.

Gurka, who had gone to sleep in the heat of the afternoon, woke up at sunset. The air had grown cool, and the ruddy glow in the western sky reflected upon the dome of the tomb, as if it held the embers of a fire. But the sound that had roused the Cossack came from beyond the mounds--a subdued wailing and chanting, accompanied by a rhythmic tinkling and chiming of tiny bells. Turning his head, Gurka saw no living thing near him, and he sat up, frowning.

All the summit of the Kurgan had been cleared, even the debris of the fighting bad been picked up and the white tent had vanished. For an instant Gurka wondered if the spirits of the place had put in appearance at last and driven off the men. Then he heard a hoarse, familiar voice raised in song—

> *Oh, Brother Eagle,*
> *I am far from my home—*

Rising, Gurka saw that the Tartars had moved everything beyond the line of the grave mounds, and he remembered that they feared the Kurgan after sunset. They had pitched the white tent again on a level place and were kneeling round it, listening with satisfaction to the strange sounds that came from within. Tavka Khan, installed on Ismail's carpet, snuff box in hand, looked up, smiling, as Gurka approached. Not one of them would approach the tent.

Lifting the entrance flap, Gurka stepped inside. The candles had been lighted and one of the slaves was circling slowly on the carpet in front of Koum, who rested comfortably among the pillows, a smoking pipe in his hand. Other girls were accompanying the dancer, with flutes and silver staffs set with tinkling bells.

"One—two—" Koum waved his pipe, "Round and round—Hi, Gurka!"

"Are you drunk!"

"How should I be drunk? There's not a cupful in the camp. Nay, this is a *tamasha*—a festival. The Black Hats won't come in because these girls belong to us. Look at this one—" He pointed to the veiled dancer, whose dark eyes regarded the tall Hungarian anxiously. "Not every Cossack, even in the old days, had a troupe of singers like this. *Hai, yartak bish yabir, tzee Kosaki khoudsarma*—Ho, young women, here is your Cossack master." And he waved the pipe at Gurka.

"*Chapir—chapir, choulbim bir Agha!*" One of the slaves cried, going down on her knees and pressing her head to the carpet. "Be seated, be seated, we are your Excellency's slaves!"

The experienced dancers recognized the bearing of an officer, and the fairest of them tried to catch his attention by revealing graceful arms.

"See how they take to you, the lambs!" Koum grinned. "Ask them to make a feast of sugared fruit and rice—they have their own food in those packs."

"Enough of this," cried Gurka, his handsome face reddening. "We'll eat with the khan. And tomorrow you and I will leave the Kurgan and start back to your hut."

"Well, as you like. It's your mission."

The Cossacks, however, did not forsake their post the next day. Before noon animal herds appeared in the south with riders, and reports of muskets were heard. The newcomers proved to be Tavka's horde, retreating from the ravine, harried by a score of mounted Turkomans. They came in to the Kurgan with all their animals and laden camels, and they explained that they had been afraid to remain longer at the other camp because the tribesmen were appearing in greater numbers.

Tavka Khan summoned the two Cossacks. He told them that he had stayed at the Kurgan to rest his men and horses, but especially to keep the surviving raiders from water. Holding the well at the Kurgan, and the spring in the southern ravine, he had counted on forcing the Turkomans to ride off to the nearest water, and leave him free to withdraw in safety with his herds.

Now, instead of going away, Ismail's surviving men had lingered, and had somehow got more horses and powder. They held the spring, which would supply them with water, and they could follow his trail, driving off animals and shooting down men with their muskets.

"*Hai, Barba,*" he complained, "I do not know where to turn my head."

"Thou art heavy with sleep and fat." Koum laughed. "Thy hands are burdened with spoil."

"Nay," responded Tavka moodily, "Misfortune will overtake us, because we defiled the Kurgan with blood. Who can avert his fate?"

He was as moody and uncertain as he had been joyful the night before last. To reassure him the Cossacks led a band of the younger Tartars out toward the raiders. When they drew near the brush-covered hillocks scattered shots greeted them, and when they circled the position they were fired on again from some rocks. The Black Hats could not use their arrows and would not rush the muskets.

Drawing off, Koum pointed out to Gurka a fresh band of riders—black specks coming up fast under rolling dust. Ismail's men were being reinforced. When the Cossacks drew off, several tribesmen rode after them boldly for a final shot. Evidently the Turkomans meant to stay within reach of the rich prize at the Kurgan, and without doubt they expected allies to come on the scene before long from some distant *aul* or some caravan that had left their camels in camp to hurry to the scene of the fighting. How the tidings had spread over that barren plain was a mystery; but whispers traveled from river to river, and from well to well.

"Like that," Koum pointed over his head. On motionless wings, scrawny vultures were wheeling around the Kurgan.

With a fight in prospect, the Cossacks would not leave their ally. And as Tavka would not think of abandoning either his spoils or his own herds, they must make off at once. They might hold the Kurgan for days, but more raiders would come up continually and in the end not one of the horde might escape.

That afternoon Tavka talked it over with the Cossacks and agreed that their best way out was to head west, toward the river. It would be a two days' march, with the cattle, and this meant a dry camp the first night— but they would be moving away from the raiders, and the Turkomans would not carry the fight beyond the Russian posts.

"Today we ride," Koum repeated, "and tomorrow we carry the saddle. That's how it always is."

A little after midnight the sheep and cattle were sent off along the trail with a group of boys and young men to guide them. Three hours later the camels were loaded and started with the Chinese and the Moslem girls, who had been placed in their accustomed hampers. Water skins were filled and loaded on the same camels. With them went the Tartar women and children on their camel train, guarded by a troop of horsemen.

An hour before the first light the main body of fighting men, some hundred strong, mounted and abandoned the Kurgan, taking Ismail with them. When the Bey found that he was heading toward the west, he laughed harshly and cursed his captors.

"The vultures will tear the flesh from thy bones, O Tavka Khan," he cried, "but first, before thy death, I will take off thy skin to make a mat." And he said again that he would wipe his feet each day on the mat.

By midmorning they had caught up with the cattle and the camels. After that they could go forward only at a foot pace, and at noon they had to halt to let the sheep graze and lie down. They went on in drifting dust, harried along by a chill wind. And they saw that the Turkomans were following.

Bands of riders appeared on either flank, without attempting to close in, so that the Cossacks could only guess at their numbers. Beyond doubt they were waiting for others to arrive before opening fire on the horde.

Overhead the vultures circled tirelessly, until a lame sheep or a sick cow fell behind the herds, when they swept down to hover over the doomed animals and come to the ground, to wait until they dropped.

"Their death will be easier than thine," Ismail taunted the khan, who said not a word. Encumbered by his women and all his possessions, Tavka could not muster any spirit, and his men, although they displayed no emotion, shared his gloom.

Already the animals were lagging, and it was thirty hours' march to water.

"Well," Koum retorted, "thou wilt not see it, Ismail."

The pock-marked face of the captive chieftain wrinkled savagely, and he spat into the sand.

"My eyes see what is hidden to thee," he said, strangely.

Before long the Cossacks learned what Ismail had in his mind. Early in the afternoon a single rider appeared on the trail ahead of them. He came up at a rapid trot, without hesitation, and they made out by his coat and military saddle that he was a Cossack. Passing through the herds, and gazing curiously at the camel train, he sought Koum and Gurka.

"I've come out to warn you high flying eagles," he said, dropping his rein and swinging his leg over the saddle horn. He explained that he was Ostap, a registered Cossack, at the river post. "Tell me, what kind of brandy have you been licking up?"

"As God lives," Koum declared, "we've had well water."

"Then what are you doing? Night before last a Turkoman came in carrying the Bey's bone necklace. He swore by the Koran that you had fetched Tartars and ambushed the caravan. Aye, he said you tortured Ismail and seized all his young wives." Ostap glanced around. "Where are they?"

"Why didn't you throw the Turkoman into the river?" demanded Koum.

"How could we? He brought military tidings and asked for the general—besides, he had a token from the Bey. We escorted him in to the Russian officers." Ostap rubbed his chin, smiling. "It was like kicking a hive. Such a scurrying about and scolding. Ismail's His Excellency's pet— at least they've been asking for him every day. Why did you do it? Did you get many weapons—good scimitars? Any gold?"

Koum started to make a hot retort, and instead began to reflect. Meanwhile the soldier Ostap scrutinized the motley array about him curiously.

"You've got Ismail's camels," he remarked. "But the devil himself couldn't squeeze out of your fix. You'll be given a hundred lashes each to begin with, and then you'll sit on your buttocks in the pen.

"But Ismail's the raider," grumbled Koum, "we were sent—"

"One dog barks at another. Where's your proof?"

"Look behind you," said Gurka briefly.

Turning in his saddle, the Cossack from the cordon looked at first casually, then with interest, at the bands of sheepskin-clad riders scattered along the horizon.

"That's bad," he grunted. "They'll overtake you."

"They're hanging back—waiting for more men."

Spitting out the seeds he had been chewing, Ostap reflected.

"Aye, for the men from the northern *aul*." He explained that this Turkoman village, about a day's ride from the Kurgan, mustered more than a hundred riders, who often visited the Kurgan. "That's why we could not hold a station out there."

"Did General Lermontoff know that?" demanded Gurka.

"We told him, often."

"Then why did he send two men to the Kurgan?"

Ostap shook his head.

"Don't know. He wanted to, that's all. But if you complain, he'll hang you."

The Cossacks were interrupted by scattered shots from the pursuers; and to keep the Turkomans at a distance, they took some of the best muskets and rode from the point in the rear. At this matching of long-range shots Koum could more than hold his own.

But after sunset the raiders drew in closer and wounded several horses. At moonrise they disappeared, except for a single fire lighted upon a distant knoll. The Cossacks knew better than to make a sally out to this fire, which had been placed there either to tempt them or to guide the tribesmen coming in from the *aul*.

They took turns at watching with the Tartars until early morning, when Koum and Ostap heard shouts and haphazard shooting near the fire. When nothing further happened they returned to the horde and roused Gurka, who was sleeping near his horse.

Ostap believed that the expected reinforcement had reached Ismail's men and had been greeted by shouts and gunfire and that the attack would come before long. The horde had covered half the distance to the river, but the animals were tired and would move slowly the next day; they could never reach the Russian lines.

"After the first light," he went on, "we can't get away; but now there is still time. We can ride off and they will not see us."

Gurka shook his head.

"No," he said. "Tavka's men saved our hides—we'll stay with them. But you go."

For a moment Ostap considered, frowning.

"If I had not seen those devils skin a captured wolf and turn him loose, I would stay. Don't tempt God, brothers—come away!"

When the two refused, he put up his pipe and led his horse out into the haze of moonlight. They watched him circle the camp and head toward the river. After he had gone Koum got out the bagpipe and tried to make harmony come from the damaged sack, until Tavka Khan appeared beside them, saying that he had taken the chance of starting off the herds and camels but that all the men must go with them this time. A grunting and lowing and a trampling of horses testified that the beasts had to be clubbed and driven to take to the road again.

The Cossacks could see the dark figures of children running after truant sheep. A little girl passed, leading a pony upon which an old woman sat, rocking and moaning to herself. Tavka Khan pretended to take no heed of this, but the sorrow of his people, revealed in the dim light, tore at his heart, and he spoke with the calm of a stoic.

"Is there no plan, O *Kosaki bimbashi*, by which thou canst save my horde?"

Reluctantly Gurka shook his head.

They could not take cover in this treeless plain, without water and adequate arms. If they scattered under the cloak of darkness, they would be tracked down the next day.

"Only one," Koum answered gravely. "Take the horses and ride swiftly ahead to the river."

"*Hai*, there are not ponies enough for the young children and the old people. Besides, without our herds and tents, we could not live through this coming Winter."

Koum closed and strapped his saddle bag and stood up, stretching his long arms.

"Eh, Tavka Khan, it is written that each man's grave is dug in its appointed place. We will go and find out."

When they moved off to guard the herds, howls resounded from the distance, echoed by mocking laughs. Then the flare of a torch came out of the haze behind them. The light swung in circles, and presently Gurka saw that a horseman carried it. He had no weapon except the knives in his girdle and no others followed him.

"*Aman!*" he cried. "*Aman.*"

He was an old Turkoman, a greasy cloth wrapped round his long hair, and he did not draw rein until he was within spear's length of Tavka Khan. "Peace—I will not harm ye, who will soon be dead," he shouted, swinging the torch to keep it alight. "Nay, I bring a message. Release Ismail

Bey—set him on a horse and loose him, and ye will not feel the knives of torture. If Ismail Bey is slain, the jackals will howl and turn away when they see your bodies. We have sworn it on the Koran."

Tavka Khan shook his head, snarling.

"I trust the jackals more than any word of thine. As for Ismail, his hour is at hand."

"Is that thy word?"

"Aye, so."

The messenger wheeled his horse, flung his dying torch at them, and darted away into the murk. Tavka Khan fell into heavy silence, knowing that while the tribesmen might try to save Ismail, nothing would keep them from massacring the Tartars.

After sunrise no one thought of escape. They moved at a walk beside the stumbling herds. Young girls and boys, mounted on cows, gazed fearfully about them. Only the camels, striding along under their burdens, seemed indifferent to thirst or weariness or the peril on their flanks.

The Turkomans, twice as numerous as the day before, and certain now of their prey, trotted forward in several bands, keeping just beyond range of Koum's musket. The morning passed, and they delayed their attack to mock the men of the horde who were heading toward a line of hillocks where trees showed green on the skyline. This height would offer some protection—perhaps water.

But the Turkomans had seen it, and just before the advance riders of the horde came within galloping distance of the broken ground, the bands of raiders moved forward and closed in ahead of the laboring horde. Cut off from the hillocks, Tavka could do nothing but form his beasts and men in a circle and make ready for the final struggle. As he did so the tribesmen began to shoot; a herder fell from his saddle, and a camel began to moan and jump about. The cattle surged ominously, their horns clashing together. Tavka Khan shouted, knowing that they would stampede in another moment.

"We must ride at the dogs!"

"Wait!" exclaimed Gurka, catching his rein and pointing.

The reports of the muskets ceased, and all the men, Tartars and Turkomans, looked toward the line of hillocks. From that line horsemen were emerging.

They came at a shaking trot and they tossed about in the saddles strangely; they wore gray uniforms faced with red, and they carried muskets slung on their backs. One of them held a flag, and another a sword pressed against his shoulder.

"*Urusse!*" grunted Tavka.

"Russian mounted infantry," added Gurka.

The first troop was followed by a cavalcade of officers—the sharp eyes of the Cossacks noticed the thoroughbred horses and the glittering points of braid--with their equerries and servants. Some of the servants were *heydukes* dressed as Turks and Circassians. Then, rumbling through the dust, came a field gun with its caisson and cart. Last appeared wagons piled with tents, escorted by a dozen Cossacks.

"It's a general," shouted Koum. "No one else travels like that in the steppe. Look, brothers, he has a cannon." Suddenly he grinned. "Devil take me but he's come after his girls."

The arrival of the small Russian column nearly balanced the numbers on either side. The precious quarter of an hour in which they could have launched an attack upon the Tartar caravan was wasted by the Turkomans who feared that greater forces might be hidden behind the hillocks. They scented a trap and drew off swiftly to the sides, and paused, uncertain whether to charge or retreat.

Then a solitary Cossack galloped from the Russian column toward the horde, and Gurka, recognizing Ostap, went swiftly to meet him.

"I found His Excellency," explained Ostap, "camped back there five versts away. He did not know the tribes were fighting. I told him a few Turkomans were attacking a caravan—we heard the shots—"

"What is he doing?"

"*Ekh*, he's looking at the Turkomans. He's just had his breakfast—"

"Tell him to fire the cannon. They will run from a cannon."

"Now, brother, how can I tell him to do anything?"

Gurka glanced impatiently over his shoulder at the restless masses of tribesmen, and put spurs to his horse. He shot toward the Russians, who had halted in some disorder, and sprang from the saddle before His Excellency. Lermontoff, seated in an open carriage lined with yellow silk, lifted a plump finger to acknowledge the Cossack's salute.

"May I be the first to congratulate your Excellency," cried Gurka, "now that you have arrived in time to save the caravan. Tavka Khan places himself under your protection. Will your Excellency begin the battle by cannon fire, or by a charge?"

Lermontoff chewed his mustache and looked about him, frowning. He had not expected to see such masses of the nomads, and he was uncertain as to what to do. Seeing his frown, the officers of his staff preserved a discreet silence.

"Send them a ball or two," the general remarked to an elderly colonel, who was brushing up his drooping mustache and fingering his sword.

"Does your Excellency," inquired that officer bending down respectfully, "give the order to fire the cannon?"

"Certainly," snapped Lermontoff.

The colonel drew himself up and shouted to a captain of the staff, who turned and galloped off with his pelisse flapping behind him. A moment later the clumsy gun was wheeled forward, swung into position, and the horses led away. The charge and ball were rammed down, and a cannoneer, squatting on the tail, sighted carefully—then rose to ask a question. The staff captain hesitated and came back to the carriage, saluting.

"At what does the General wish us to fire?"

"At those devils!" Lermontoff pointed with the stem of the pipe he was filling, muttering, "*Durak*—fool."

The captain hastened back, and the gun which had been pointed at Tavka's caravan, was swung around to the Turkomans. Gurka wondered if these officers had ever set foot in the steppe before. The soldier with the linstock stood up, the others ran back, and the gun roared, smoke shooting over the dry grass. Every one peered at the black speck speeding the air, until it dropped among the horsemen, raising clouds of dust.

"Again!" cried Lermontoff.

A second time the cannon spoke, and the Cossacks amused themselves by dismounting to do some long distance shooting. The Turkomans turned and galloped off on both flanks.

"Major Vasilivitch," commanded the general, "take your troop—teach them a lesson."

The officer at the head of the mounted infantry saluted, lifted his sword and shouted the order to charge. Hastily the Cossacks got to their horses and caught up with the Russians, and the line trotted past the interested Tartars. When the Turkomans showed signs of hanging back, Vasilivitch prudently ordered a volley fired. Meanwhile the cannon had been moved forward, and the tribesmen galloped off, unwilling to face it.

"Again," observed Gurka, who had remained by the carriage, "I congratulate your Excellency upon his success. Now will your Excellency give command to escort the Tartar caravan back to the river? The herds are without water."

Not until they were in motion, with the hillocks behind them, and the Cossacks posted there as a rearguard, did he draw a long breath of relief.

It was dark when they reached the river at last and saw the lights of Sarachikof on the distant shore. And Lermontoff decided to halt for the night where he was—in the midst of the bellowing cattle, forcing their way down to the water, and the Tartars unloading the protesting camels. His men were tired, and it would look more military to encamp by the tribes and make an orderly crossing the next day. Besides, he had certain matters to settle with the khan and the two vagabond Cossacks.

Lermontoff had not been able to set eyes on them after the return march had begun, because they were with the rear detachment. For miles the Cossacks had fought off prowling Turkoman bands. At the river Lermontoff sent a sergeant to find Koum and Gurka. The sergeant returned empty-handed, reporting that Koum had been setting up a large white felt tent near a string of kneeling camels, and that armed tribesmen had prevented the sergeant from entering the tent, although a light showed within. But the *essaul* Ostap insisted that Koum had gone out on the river in a barge with some others. By way of excuse the sergeant added that the whole place was in a tumult as if Satan's stables had been turned loose.

Whereupon the general swore and ordered the sergeant to take a squad with bayonets, and to bring in after dinner the khan Tavka, and the Turkoman chief Ismail with the two missing Cossacks.

Being hungry after his two days' campaigning, Lermontoff dined well. By the time he finished his roast mutton and onions, he unfastened his collar and tasted wine and began to feel pleased with events. After all, he had gone on an expedition, he had been in action against the tribes. All this would go into his next report. Moreover—and this would not be in the report—he now had in his hands all the property of the wild Tavka Khan, who could be made to pay a round sum for its release . . .

By the time he had finished his fruit and cordial, Lermontoff saw himself awarded the order of Saint Anne, with a sword of honor, for distinguished military service. Then he wondered where Ismail's slaves were quartered.

"They were brought in on the camels," Rostov, the aide, answered his question, "and were taken into the large white tent."

Lermontoff nodded pleasantly. Out on the steppe he had felt worried, but now matters were cleared up nicely. He did not think he would invite the colonel to his tent for the inquiry.

"Have you got them all—the prisoners?"

Rostov explained that Gurka had been found in the quarters of the khan, while Ismail had been bound, gagged and wrapped in a rug, and Koum had just now been brought over from a tavern in Sarachikof.

"I will see them all."

The four were ushered in, Ismail free of bonds, his green eyes vindictive, Tavka Khan unarmed and palpably worried—falling on his knees before the table. Only Gurka seemed indifferent. After glancing at each in turn and identifying Ismail, Lermontoff drew from his pocket the chieftain's missing necklace and singled out Gurka.

"Now, my lad," he said grimly, "you have something to answer for. Ismail Khan is a well known merchant who makes yearly trips to Sarai, and he was entitled to protection. Three days ago one of his men brought me this necklace of his, with a message that the Bey had been attacked without provocation at the Kurgan by two Cossacks and a Tartar horde. It's plain enough that you've plundered him—you've still got his goods, which it is my duty to confiscate until a full inquiry can be made. Do you understand?"

"I understand," Gurka responded at once, "everything."

"And you?" The general glanced at Koum.

The big Cossack had more experience with Russian military administration than Gurka, and he turned his *kalpak* uneasily in his great hands.

"But, Excellency," he muttered, "you don't know how it is." And he explained how Ismail Bey had tricked the Russians by raiding the caravans on his return to Khiva, and how the evidence of one of his massacres was to be seen beyond the Kurgan—how Tavka Khan and natives in the town could bear witness to this, while the necklace itself was a trophy of his crimes. "Your Excellency saw with his own eyes this morning how the wolves were hunting."

Lermontoff listened, frowning but attentive, and asked Rostov to make note of what the Cossack said. He had heard something of this from Ostap and he saw his way clear now. He would hang Ismail, and report to Moscow the seizure and death of the raider. But he did not wish to exonerate the Tartar khan or the two Cossacks.

"Do you think, my lad," he demanded, "that you know more than the government? You were sent to the Kurgan to guard the caravans, not to loot them. *Ekh!* Your looting made it necessary for me to lead a column over the river, and if I had not done so, you would have left your hides out there. You ought to be lashed—" he paused to glare at the hunter—"but I'll let you off, if you leave Sarachikof at once."

"Do you admit your guilt, Cossack?" put in Rostov, making notes.

"No," said Gurka abruptly.

The word rang out like a gunshot, and fat Tavka, fearing anger and punishment, climbed from his knees in dread. Lermontoff's hands clenched on the table.

"And why not?" he cried.

Gurka came forward and placed his open hands on the table.

"Because," he said, "we two Cossacks were sent by you to do the work of a cavalry troop, without aid. At our post Ismail's men fired upon us without warning. We have your written order to enlist followers, and we did so, calling upon these Tartars. You understood all this because you directed your men to fire upon the Turkomans."

Silence settled upon the room, while Lermontoff's heavy face became darker by the second. Striking his fist on the table, he found his tongue.

"I'll have you lashed!"

"No," said Gurka again, "because we are volunteers, not under your orders. If you should, I would challenge you to a settlement with pistols."

The aide got to his feet, seeing the glitter in the gray eyes of this mad Cossack, who somehow bore himself like a man of rank. But Lermontoff was thinking of many things—of ridicule, and of the report he had sent in about the occupation of the Kurgan. The last thing he wanted was talk, a public scandal.

"I did not realize," he said uncertainly. "The Cossacks say you are a count, Gurka—a former officer—"

"It doesn't matter."

"Ah, but you should have made yourself known. Now, of course, there is no blame to you. You are free to leave Sarachikof."

Koum pulled at his sleeve, but Gurka faced the general without moving.

"Tavka Khan," he said, "is afraid. He tells me he has paid you a yearly tax for protection, while until now you have done nothing but send Cossacks to collect the payment from him. Now he surrenders Ismail to you, and gives up Ismail's ransom. But he is afraid you will take his cattle and camels. I have assured him you will not. Is that true?"

Lermontoff waved an indulgent hand.

"Of course, my dear fellow!"

"Then will you write out an order, that Tavka's herds and goods are not to be molested?"

For a moment the general hesitated. The sergeant who had come in with the prisoners was watching him, and he knew that keen ears outside the tent might be listening to all his words. After all, his report to Moscow was the main thing—that and Ismail's slaves. He dictated the order to Rostov and signed it: handing it to Gurka, who gave it in turn to the khan. Tavka took it in both hands and touched it to his forehead.

"That is all. Good evening, General Lermontoff." Gurka turned on his heel and walked from the tent.

Lermontoff signed to the sergeant to lead Ismail out, and asked Rostov to see that the Turkoman was locked up under guard. Alone in the tent with Koum, he beckoned to the Cossack and whispered—

"Ismail's slaves, where are they?"

"Safe, your Excellency. Tavka Khan gave them to us—"

"I know. Ostap told me the tale. What—what have you done with them?"

Rubbing his head, Koum eyed the general doubtfully.

"Eh, Gurka's full of ideas. He said I must bring them in to you, at the governor's palace, but—"

"Hss! I don't want that." Lermontoff visioned the Moslem girls being escorted through the streets to his gate. "I don't want them at all. Ismail lied, you understand, when he said he sold one to the officers here. Do you understand?"

Koum nodded, and watched with growing interest while the general went to his cot and opened a leather valise. From it Lermontoff drew a silk bag and from the bag he poured a half dozen gold coins into his hand.

"Will you swear to say nothing of Ismail's slaves—you and your comrade?"

"As God lives, I'll say nothing more."

"They are safe, and no one has seen them?"

"True, by Saint Nicholas."

Lermontoff filled his fist with coins and gave them to the big Cossack, who took them incredulously.

"What is this for?"

Thinking of the white tent, Lermontoff smiled.

"Have you forgotten I promised you gold if you brought in Ismail's caravan safely? Now you must hold your tongue—better go away at once."

"At once," Koum assented, tucking the money beneath his coat, within his shirt.

Hastening from the tent, he ran into Tavka Khan, who was examining the written order with Ostap's assistance.

"Hold on, eagle!" The *essaul* caught Koum's arm. "What is this? The khan wants to know if it is his death order. Gurka's gone off and I can't read."

"It's for Tavka to keep all his animals and goods, everything. But he had better move off before sunrise, just the same."

The stout Tartar smiled and patted his sides.

"*Ai*, the brave Cossacks have brought me good fortune. Come to my *kibitka* at any hour and I will make place for you among my sons."

Ostap winked and nudged the hunter.

"Now tell me—what about *them*?"

He pointed toward the lighted tent of the slave girls. To his surprise Koum closed his lips, glanced over his shoulder at the general's quarters and clutched his belt. Then he strode off into the darkness.

Hastening through the camp, he found Gurka spreading his blankets near the horses.

"Saddle up, Gurka," he whispered. "Now."

After peering into the hunter's face, Gurka led in his horse and lifted the saddle without a word. By the time he had rolled his pack and fastened it in place, Koum was already mounted.

"What—" Gurka began.

"Hss! Don't speak, brother. We must go."

Riding out of the camp, the two Cossacks headed north along the river, away from Sarachikof. Not for an hour did Koum open his lips or draw rein. Then, after a glance around, he turned down toward the river to a sandy stretch concealed in tall rushes.

After rubbing down and tethering the horses, the Cossacks got out their blankets. Koum removed his boots and filled and lighted his pipe. He looked up at the stars, and listened contentedly to the whisper of the water in the rushes and the drone of insects.

"Eh," he observed, "this is best. Around the cities and the armies it's not safe. Still, your mission brought us good fortune. Aye, we are rich."

He fumbled inside his shirt and began to pull out gold coins, showing them to Gurka before tucking them away in his tobacco sack. "Fourteen," he counted up.

"Look here!" Gurka raised himself on his elbow. "You didn't ask for pay did you?"

"No, he gave them. He asked us to hold our tongues and ride away from Sarachikof, and we've done it. Now they are ours."

Gurka shook his head.

"Didn't you sell him one of the girls?"

"You would not have it, Gurka. It's foolish to give up all those girls to the officers, I thought. So after I had them in the big *kibitka* I led them out, quiet-like from the back, and rowed them over in a barge. I took them straight to the church, to the little fathers. 'Here, priests, I said, 'are Moslem slaves without a master. Take care of the stray lambs.' Then I stopped for just one glass of brandy, and the soldiers arrested me. Nay, the little fathers can't give up women to the general. That's why I wanted to ride away at once, before Lermontoff found out."

Gurka laughed, and Koum fumbled under his coat again.

"Here," he said with satisfaction, "feel this."

Stretching out his hand, Gurka touched a wide leather belt in which hard pointed objects had been set. Holding it close to his eyes, he recognized in the faint moonlight the belt of Ismail Bey with its precious stones.

"What! Did you take this from Tavka Khan?"

"Nay, he gave it to me, in the afternoon. He was afraid the Russians would seize his horses and camels. He wanted me to give it to Lermontoff, to buy him off. But after you lashed him with your tongue, he wrote the order, and after that I thought it would be a sin to hand over such a treasure."

"Well!"

Gurka settled back in his blankets. After a moment he chuckled.

"You can't say now that the omens at the Kurgan harmed us."

The pipe in the hunter's mouth glowed fiercely.

"Why should they harm us? You said we ought to find a pot of gold at the end of a rainbow. I didn't know that, but here is the gold." Koum nodded sagely. "As for the Kurgan, I kept you from sleeping there, and you're living; but Ismail slept there and he'll be kicking his heels in the air, eh, Gurka?"

Gurka, however, was asleep. For a while the hunter pondered, harkening to the croaking of toads and the faint rustling of small animals moving near him. Then, yawning, he glanced at the horses, and knocked out his pipe. Getting to his knees, he muttered a short prayer to his guardian saint, Nicholas.

After that, for additional safety, he rose and traced a circle in the sand about their blankets. In the center of the circle he stuck his dagger with the cross shaped hilt upright, and three times he spat beyond the circle, to ward off the evil spirits. Seeking his blanket, he listened to Gurka's steady breathing.

"He's like a child," he thought. "Needs someone to look out for him."

The Devil's Song

They were drifting down the river. Thirty and seven of them, sailing the ships of the Volga pirates, drifting through the red glow of sunset.

Southward they were going, on the Spring flood—the ice was breaking out far behind them south through the grass steppes—to raid Gorod town.

Zamourza the Tartar sniffed the night coming on, and he lifted his head where he lay curled like a bear asleep. Zamourza could cut the skin off a man with his knife. Ay, he was deft enough with a knife, but he had in him the skill of a wizard. He could hear the whispering of the dead where they lay.

Now he lifted his head, for it was his way to look around once at the ending of a day, to fix in his mind all that was there before Allah drew the curtain of night over the earth. He looked at the setting sun, and that deep red sky.

"*Yah ahmaut*," he murmured. "Allah hath hung the banner of death in the sky."

When the sun touched the dark line of reeds on the bank, a crane winged past it. Zamourza nodded, puckering his lined face. He listened and heard a wolf howl on the other hand. The omens were clear. "One of us," the old Tartar thought, "will die. A great one. The wings of the wild birds pass over him, and the wolves drink his blood."

Satisfied of this, Zamourza got to his feet, to see if a sign would be evident as to who the doomed man might be. And, standing behind him, framed against the loosening sail, he saw Stenka Razin.

Stenka Razin, lord of the river, master of the *bourlaki*—the river-men. Taller he was than Zamourza by two heads, heavy and powerful as a gray buffalo. Like Zamourza's, his skull was shaved except for a scalp lock;

his short beard was black and lustrous. He held in hand the oak staff with the iron spike that served him better than a sword. His crimson shirt was embroidered with gold.

Under that shirt, Zamourza knew, on Stenka Razin's left shoulder the word CAIN had been branded. Stenka took pride in that branding. Sometimes when the whim seized him, he would pull back his shirt and show these letters to a man, saying, "See, dog, that is what I am." And he would kill the man. Because the letters reminded him of the ten years he had spent in Kazan Prison in the hands of the Muscovites.

Now he hunted down the Muscovites, the tsar's men of Moscow, to pay for those years and that branding. They hunted him along the Volga, putting a price on his head and laying traps for him—without success. Some said that Stenka Razin had sold his soul to Satan for immunity from steel, fire, or bullets. But they lied. Stenka Razin kept alive because he was as wary as a wolf and as merciless.

"*A-ha-a-y,*" a voice hailed from the river.

Like a cat Zamourza slipped to the rail and looked over. A canoe was putting out from shore toward the pirate fleet, instead of scurrying away like the other shore craft. And it headed for Stenka Razin's boat. An old peasant pulled at the oars. In the stern sat a woman, cloaked, holding a bundle.

When she turned her head the hood fell back, and her hair gleamed gold.

"O seafarers," she called, "will you take me down to Gorod town?"

Some of the Cossacks came to the rail to stare, and one laughed. Here was a lass with a shining face, who asked Stenka Razin to sail her down to Gorod!

The *ataman* himself glanced at the girl. "Help her in," he said.

The Cossacks lifted her over the rail, and stared anew. With the bundle the girl was hugging a goat—a white goat with gilt horns, and a red cross painted on its back.

Zamourza inspected it curiously. He had never seen a goat marked like that. And the girl, its mistress, showed no fear of the wild Volga men.

"Girl," demanded Stenka Razin, "what are you?"

"Are you the master?" Her gray eyes turned to him, and she smiled. "Why, I am Nada, and if you'll take me down to Gorod I'll ask God's blessing on you and this ship."

Once a Gypsy wench had tried to trick the *ataman*, and he had crushed her throat in his hands before escaping. He asked suddenly, "Who sent you?"

"Ekh—no one." She laughed.

Nada or Gretchen or Zuleika, Zamourza thought it would all be the same to the *ataman*. For under her white cotton dress was a soft, slim body and surely her eyes did not shun Stenka Razin.

The *ataman* was in a mood to play with a woman that evening, and this girl pleased him. "Then, come," he said.

He led the way aft, to the roofed in cabin, and the goat followed arrogantly as goats do.

"*Precor pro nobis*," a drunken voice droned.

It was Pop Theodore—Chvedor, the lads called him—lying on the deck muttering a Latin prayer. When this renegade priest had been licking the cup, he had a way of chanting that Stenka Razin liked. He was a learned man.

"Souse the Pop," the *ataman* roared from the cabin. "Be quick with him."

Zamourza and another Cossack hurried to the priest, for Stenka Razin did not relish being kept waiting. The Tartar did not know why Stenka Razin went through this form of a wedding with all his girls—even the steppe Gypsies and that Persian slave he brought up from the Caspian. Always the *ataman* had Pop Theodore marry him. Sometimes when the mood was on him, he demanded lighted candles and a hymn chanted . . . he got rid of them quickly enough after he tired of them.

Zamourza and the Cossack grappled with the priest, who knew what was coming. They swung him over the side, holding to his hands and ducking him while he choked out curses, until he was sobered and stood shivering on his feet. "May the black she-goat litter on your graves," he mumbled. "There's no woman on this boat."

"There's one now, little father," said the Cossack. "Come."

Inside the curtain they stopped abruptly, and even Theodore was silent. Stenka Razin had lighted the candles, and the incense in the jeweled bowl. Soft brocades and cloth-of-silver glimmered upon the walls. But this was familiar enough to the Volga men. They were looking at the girl Nada.

She sat on the couch, fingering its silk coverlet with delight.

"'Tis the couch of a prince," she laughed. "I fear me to sleep upon it."

Her light hand passed over the tray beside her, the tray filled with sugared ginger, cherries and mastic.

"Nay, master," she chattered, "I think you are no merchant."

Frowning, Stenka Razin watched her.

"I think you are a warrior—"

Stenka Razin passed his hand suddenly before her face.

"—and so you will safeguard me upon the river."

And Stenka Razin drew one of the long pistols from his girdle, pointing the muzzle at her. Still she smiled and her eyes did not change.

Slowly the giant *ataman* lowered the pistol. "You are blind, girl," he said. For the first time he noticed the three men at the entrance, and growled, "Get out!"

"Yes," she said quietly, "didn't you know? I thought, master, that all the river knew Nada and her goat, Omelko."

Omelko, she explained gaily, guided her footsteps by day and night. He had been marked, so that people with eyes could pick him out from other goats if he strayed from her. "Master," she asked, "what is your name?"

He hesitated. "Cain," he answered.

"A strange name." She frowned. "What are you like?"

She leaned toward him, and her hand passed lightly over his shaven head, his shaggy brows, and the scar along one cheekbone. She felt the iron muscles of his throat, the spread of his shoulders. For a second she faltered. "Will you take me safe to Gorod, Master Cain?"

Stenka Razin moved his head from side to side, like the great horned buffalo scenting the wind.

"Eh, girl," he said gruffly, "no harm will come to you."

He brought her water to bathe her face, and he watched while she ate— although he heard Filka giving commands to beach the boats for the night. He listened to the thump of the poles working the boat in, and the scraping of the bow among the rushes. When Nada slept, the incense drifting over the tangle of her golden hair, he put a sable wrap over her body.

He heard Filka's voice, mellow over the water, singing the familiar Devil's Song:

> *From the white island*
> *On the Mother Volga,*
> *Stenka Razin's brothers*
> *Sail with a merry song.*

Nada stirred drowsily, and the giant Cossack left the cabin, treading lightly.

"Stow that song, Filka," he growled, and the growl carried to the boat of Filka Chortyaka, his lieutenant, near by.

Filka only laughed, thinking that the *ataman* had been licking the jug.

> *Stenka Razin's the captain*
> *And the Devil is the admiral—*
> *Sing a song, Princess,*
> *For we are merry today!*

Stenka Razin went to the rail. "Still your tongue, you son of a Turkish bathboy," he roared. And this time Filka was silent. He came splashing through the rushes, and hauled himself over the rail.

"What's biting you, *ataman*?" he laughed. "Can't a man sing?"

"Not that song," said Stenka Razin. "Not here." And he strode aft. Filka peered after him curiously.

"Eh, say, what's come over him?"

"He has a new woman," grunted a Cossack, stretched out on the deck.

The priest Theodore had been thinking. "Either a woman," he whispered, "or a witch."

"How, a witch?" demanded Filka.

"Well, she came out of the river at sunset. She follows after a goat with gilt horns."

"Perhaps, little father," suggested a Cossack, "she's a vampire on the hunt—a *vurdalak*. A hungry vampire, the kind that bites behind the ear and flies away before sunup. I saw—"

"It's clear," decided Pop Theodore, "she's cast a spell on the *ataman*."

Filka had a bold spirit in him—he feared neither man nor devil. But he obeyed Stenka Razin. Now he looked at the red spark of the *ataman*'s pipe, and chewed his lip. "So," he whispered, "he's not as he was."

Zamourza said nothing. He was thinking of the omens he had seen at sunset.

"Eh, little Nada," Stenka Razin ventured the next day, "why don't you stay here, on the boat?"

He was at the tiller of his ship, and the bellying sails of his fleet filled the river. They were making speed down the Volga, to reach Gorod that night.

"It's better," he added, "than the shore. You don't need eyes on the boat, Nada."

He didn't know himself why he wanted this girl at his side. It was something in the way her gray eyes looked at him.

Nada shook her head slowly. "Nay, Master Cain," she said, "I must go to Gorod town."

"Why?"

To follow Petr Noga, she explained, Petr Noga, the young tsar's officer of the Moscow guards. He had been sent with his men down to Gorod, to garrison that frontier town against Tartar raids. And he would marry her in Gorod.

"Hmm," said the *ataman*. He had heard that Petr Noga was now *starosta*, governor. A keen soldier, and ambitious.

And the blood came into Nada's white throat. Even, she whispered, if Petr Noga couldn't marry her, she would be near him in Gorod. She could listen to his voice, and hear men praise him. For everyone loved Petr Noga.

"Ay, he told me," she confided, "not to go upon the river until he sent for me. He told me how the river pirates slay and burn. Have you seen them, Cain?"

"Yes," assented Stenka Razin.

"But he didn't send. I had no silver to buy passage on a merchant's bark. I was weary with waiting and I took Omelko and came."

Stenka Razin said nothing more.

When the shadows lengthened over the river, and Nada went below deck, Pop Theodore staggered aft.

"Eh, *ataman*," he whispered, "the brothers are talking. They say this girl is a witch. They say she has cast a spell on you, *ataman*. Ay, she will bring evil fortune upon us." He wagged his head ominously. "Tonight you're going against the Muscovites. Then throw her over the side before night comes on and her power increases."

When Stenka Razin did not answer he went back to the men gathered about the mast. It was Filka who gave commands at the sunset hour. They all knew what must be done before a raid.

They headed for the shore, where any soul on the river could see them. They moored the boats in among the rushes.

Then, after lanterns were lighted, they hung the lights on wooden poles stuck into the mud; silently they lowered the tall masts, and with their swords cut bundles of rushes, which they fastened to the rails of the boats.

"Push off," Filka called, "for a warm night, lads. We'll kindle up Gorod."

The Cossacks poled out into the current, leaving the lights behind them. Keeping close to the bank, they drifted downstream, drawing the boats together and roping them. So that even a Tartar watching from the bank would see no more than an island of rushes moving down.

When the town came in sight around the bend, Stenka Razin's voice was heard. "Tie up to the poles, here."

The long poles were driven into the muddy bottom, and ropes passed around them. And the boat leaders climbed from rail to rail, to Stenka Razin's deck.

Silently, they massed around the giant *ataman*.

"Why do we wait?" jeered Filka. "Yonder's Gorod with its gate wide and the Muscovites snoring."

"We'll bide here."

"Kiss a bear's snout, *ataman*," grinned Filka, "but don't hang back in a raid."

A Cossack laughed softly. "We'll fire it, and fry the boyars in it."

"Nay," growled Stenka Razin.

They pressed closer.

"And why?" murmured Filka. The Cossacks thought it was strange that their *ataman* hung back.

"I'm going over," Stenka Razin told them. "Wait here for me."

He went to the cabin, and led out Nada by the hand. He lifted her into the canoe at the stern, and dropped the goat in after her. Then he followed.

"I'll cut the skin off any fool," he called back, "who follows me."

Filka peered after the canoe until it vanished into the haze. He licked his lips and moved his fingers softly together. Bewitched or not, Stenka Razin was losing his grip on his men. And Filka was no man to hang back when his chance came. He looked about him until he found Zamourza.

"Hey, animal," whispered the lieutenant, "I'll fill your hands with gold this night."

The Tartar merely grunted.

"The *ataman*'s lost," Filka breathed. "The witch holds him in her hand.
By Allah, you saw. Now go after him, and if he ventures into Gorod—
there's five thousand silver ducats will be paid for his head—for one word
to the Muscovites. And I'll fill your hands with gold. You can go back to
your people; you can have a white tent and many wives, many horses.
You hear?"

"Ay, lord." Zamourza rose, and stepped into the next boat. Filka watched
until he saw the shadow of a canoe drift away with a man in it. Then he
went back to the Cossacks.

"Eh, brothers," he said, "listen to Filka Chortyaka. That was not Stenka
Razin, our *ataman*. The young witch has sucked his blood. That is another man, a shadow whining in the night—"

By the far bank, Stenka Razin was drawing close to the log wall of Gorod.
He could make out the square watchtowers against the stars . . .

With the goat leading, they plodded into the muddy street of Gorod,
where only a tavern door or a passing torch showed light, Stenka Razin
turned once, sharply, feeling that a shadow passed behind him; but neither he nor the guards saw Zamourza slip by.

"Where will you go now, girl?" Stenka Razin asked.

"To Petr Noga," she cried.

Stenka Razin had sensed a shadow behind him, and instinct urged him
to turn back. But the street was dark, and the Muscovites dumb as cattle.
He asked the way to the *starosta*'s house of a passing priest.

"Is it a small house or a great one?" Nada asked. He could feel her quivering against his arm. For now the fear of the blind had come upon her,
the dread of unfamiliar things.

They did not reach the house. Petr Noga came out of it, with a torch-
bearer going before him, and a sedan chair borne by Tartar slaves at his
side. Behind him followed a half dozen guards.

When Nada heard his voice she ran forward.

"Petr!" she cried. "Blessed be Saint Nikolka—I've found you."

She was reaching out her arms to him. And Petr Noga's face flushed. He
had a small, clipped beard, and he wore the blue coat of the Moscow *strelsui*, and he stared at Nada as if seeing a spirit come out of the night.

"Why, girl—how did you come?"

Nada's face was straining up, her eyes closed. She felt the coldness of his
words, and the helplessness of her blindness.

Stenka Razin, watching from the shadows, saw the door of the sedan open. A woman's head emerged, with the plaited hair and painted cheeks of the Muscovites.

"Petr," Nada whispered, "have I made you angry?"

He patted her hand, glancing at the sedan. "Who brought you hither, girl? 'Tis no place, this, for one who is blind."

"Cain," explained Nada, turning, her hand feeling beside her. "He was here."

Impatiently Petr Noga glanced at the man beyond the torchlight.

"Cain?" he laughed.

The woman spoke from the sedan: "Hurry, Excellency—it is so cold."

"He is the master of many ships," Nada explained quickly, "and he brought me here himself. Please, Petr, tell me—"

But the officer had looked again at Stenka Razin, and his eyes narrowed. He took the torch from his servant's hand and walked over to the Volga pirate. Suddenly he drew his sword and shouted to his men, "Take him!"

Stenka Razin lifted his steel-tipped pike and backed to place himself against a wall. The guards were lumbering forward with sword and halberd. Nada had picked Omelko up in her arms.

"*Ataman*," a voice whispered behind Stenka Razin, "come this way—run."

He knew Zamourza's voice, and he turned. The Tartar was running down an alley, and Stenka Razin followed, while the Muscovites charged after him.

Zamourza saw a glow of light in an open door—the door of a log tower—he turned in there, calling over his shoulder, "Here, *ataman*—"

Stenka Razin brushed past him, ducking into the low portal. And they swung shut the heavy log door. Stenka Razin set his back against it, and jammed his heels into the dirt floor, as the first Muscovites flung themselves against it, outside. He grunted as he braced himself. Zamourza quested about, snatching up a heavy hand-ax.

"There's a table," said Stenka Razin. "Shore up this door."

"Yield yourself," they heard Petr Noga's voice "Stenka Razin, the tsar's justice."

"Come and take me," roared the Cossack. Then he laughed. He had looked around for another door, but had seen only kegs and sacks stacked against the log walls—evidently the tower served as storehouse. By the fragrance in the air he knew there was good drink here.

"Come and drink a cup with me, you dogs," he called to them.

They were beating with their halberd butts against the logs of the door without effect. Stenka Razin listened a moment, then went over to smell the kegs. He selected one, found a pewter bowl, and drew white liquor from the wooden cock. "*Gorilka*," he muttered.

He drained the bowl of corn brandy, and started to fill it again, when Zamourza tugged at his arm.

"*Ataman*," he begged, "don't drink."

Stenka Razin paused, frowning. "What brought you here, Zamourza?"

The Tartar was silent.

"You followed me."

Zamourza murmured assent. "Ai, *ataman*," he said plaintively, "why did you come among the Muscovites?"

Stenka Razin looked into the bowl, and drank. "Because of the eyes of a wench," he snarled, "An elf of a girl—a child I could break in my hands. Because she was blind."

He listened for the Muscovites at the door, and heard nothing. Either they had gone for axes or more soldiers, or they meant to wait until morning before breaking into his stronghold.

"Here, you wolf," he grunted, "drink this, before they cut the life out of your body."

Sipping at the bowl, Zamourza shook his head. "*Ataman*," he observed, "it is written that a great one will die tonight. I am only a slave. But who is the great one?"

And he told about the omens he had seen on the Volga. Did they point to Stenka Razin, or the young khan of the Russians, or to Filka? Surely it would be one of the three.

"We'll find out," Razin laughed.

"Listen," said Zamourza suddenly.

Not far away a bell was sounding, tolling fast.

"By Allah," Stenka Razin grinned, "they're ringing the alarm in the church for me."

He could hear men running. He heard a muffled roar, then another.

"Cannon," he laughed.

Then came a burst of sharper reports, and the shouting increased. Zamourza listened intently, his ear to a crack. Then he ran up the ladder that led to the floor above.

"Come up, *ataman*," he called after a moment. Stenka Razin glanced at the barricaded door. It stood unharmed and quiet as before.

He swung himself up the ladder, which creaked under his weight.

Their tower overlooked the wall and the dark plain beyond. But the wall was not dark. Torches flared and smoked, where matchlock-men trained their clumsy weapons over the parapet, out at the darkness. Other figures were ramming powder and ball into a brass cannon.

"*Ghar-ghar-ghar!*"

A distant, steady cry pulsed through the uproar below them. Stenka Razin shaded his eyes against the flare of the lights. Beyond, he could discern dark masses that moved over the plain.

"Tartars," he said.

Zamourza nodded. "*Ai*, the horde of Mirak Khan, the Kalmuk."

Stenka Razin was silent, thinking. When grass came along the Volga, the settlers turned their cattle out to the plain to graze. At such a time, when the ground was dry enough to bear horses at a fast pace, the Tartar hordes beyond the Volga were apt to raid. They came fast, at night, avoiding the frontier posts, until they reached some settlement on the river.

Zamourza grunted with satisfaction. "Now they have no eyes for us, *ataman*. Now we can go unseen back to the river gate."

But Stenka Razin was watching the Muscovites with a calculating eye. These halberdiers and matchlock-men were town militia, trained to march and stand in line and fire off their weapons at command. The sudden raid had frightened them—they were clucking about like a barnyard at the coming of a fox. Their officers did not seem to know what to do.

Stenka Razin had licked up his fill of corn brandy. He was in no mood to turn his back on a battle.

"Nay," he said, "we'll do more than that."

Zamourza followed his chief with misgivings, down the ladders, and out to the street.

At the main gate the young *starosta* and a bewildered Swedish captain of artillery were listening to the uproar, trying to decide what next to do, in the face of an invisible foe that loosed deadly arrows out of the dark.

Through the group around him Stenka Razin strode, staff in hand, towering over the smaller Muscovites.

"Eh, fledgling," he hailed, "what are you doing? Douse the flares on the walls—don't waste powder until they attack." He grinned at the young officer. "So the wolves have come out of the steppes?"

Petr Noga's hand tightened on his sword. "You're under arrest—"

"Tfu!" The Cossack spat. "No time for that. I'll help you, *starosta*."

"I ask for no aid from you."

"You'll need it. But put out the flares—don't make marks of your men."

Stenka Razin's deep voice had the ring of command in it, and he knew how to jest. The men were listening to him, and the Swede shouted an order to extinguish all fire along the parapet. And to load the cannon and stand by.

"It's Mirak Khan with his Kalmuks," Stenka Razin explained. "He's fond of gold, as a hog loves corn. Buy him off before it's too late. If you shed blood enough, he'll tear down your wall, and kindle up all the town. He'll pile your heads over there by the church, and take the women off to his tents."

"We'll escape by the boat," said Petr Noga unsteadily. He was in command of the garrison, and the responsibility weighed on him.

Stenka Razin looked amused. "Ay, so—in the fishing boats, Excellency? My men are waiting out on Mother Volga with thirty and seven of their little ships. They'll be glad to see you, with all these merchants and gold and gear. They'll feed the fish with you."

The two officers stared at him. Somehow they did not doubt him—they knew that the Volga pirates were bound down the river, and they had heard that Stenka Razin never ventured far from his band.

"If you are a Christian," the Swede said stiffly, pulling at his yellow mustache, "you'll summon your followers to aid us against these devils."

Stenka Razin laughed. "I'll save your hides, if that's what you mean. Mirak Khan knows my face—he'll listen to me. Only give me some of your coins, for a gift."

"You mean—to ransom Gorod?" Petr Noga asked.

"Ay, so."

"How much?"

Stenka Razin rubbed his shaven head. "Five thousand silver ducats—that's the price of my head, or yours."

"You'll take the ransom out to the Tartars?"

The Cossack nodded.

"Why?" demanded Petr Noga.

"Because I brought a blind girl to Gorod. And I've no mind to let the Tartars ride over her. Look!"

His eye had caught a flame in the sky, that rose over the dark wall and dropped, sizzling, into the mud. Another burning arrow followed, in a red arc, lodging in the roof of a hut. Petr Noga stared at it, and made up his mind. Better to pay the ransom than to see Gorod sacked.

He ordered his lieutenants to collect the ransom from the town merchants. "Put it in two saddlebags," ordered Stenka Razin. "Put the bags on a white horse. Get me a white camel hair *svitza*, to cover my shirt, and be quick about it." Then he turned to the *starosta*: "Where is Nada?"

The girl had been sent to the church, where the priests were praying, with the other people, Petr Noga explained. Stenka Razin said they'd go to the church, he and the *starosta*, for a word with her.

They set out together swiftly, because the Cossack gripped fast the young *starosta*'s arm, and he walked with long strides.

"Listen, you cub," he breathed, "there's one thing more you'll do, or Gorod will burn like a hayrick. You'll wed that blind girl, Nada—"

"Drunken hound!" Petr Noga tried to get at his sword, but Stenka Razin held his arm in a vise.

"You made love to her up north. Now a painted tenpenny slut makes sheep's eyes at you, Petr Noga, and you won't look at Nada. Eh—isn't it so?"

"Nay—"

"Ay, it's so. Now, you unlicked cub, this girl is a flower, a saint—" the big Cossack choked, and spat. "Now you make love to her again, and say before the priests you'll wed her, and Gorod will be safe. I swear it."

Petr Noga's brain whirled dizzily. He had cared for the girl Nada, and now, when he heard her voice again—if only he could stave off the attack of the wild Tartars—if he—

They came on Nada standing by a post of the church.

"Nada."

"Oh, Master Cain!" She groped toward him. She had lost Omelko, and fear tugged at her heart.

"Nada," he said with an effort, "I'm going away. I'm a pirate, a blood-licking dog, and the name of Cain is burned on my hide—"

Trembling, she shrank back.

"But Petr Noga's here, girl," Stenka Razin went on. "When he saw you first he had troubles on his mind. Ay, fighting and raids and such. But now he's looking for you—" Stenka Razin eyed the officer like a wolf—

"to tell you how his heart's full of love for you, and he'll be asking you to marry him."

"Ay, Nada," said Petr Noga, quietly, "we'll be wed tomorrow."

And he took the girl's groping hands in his. A smile touched his lips, but her face was like that of a saint in a holy picture. Stenka Razin looked at them once and swung away.

Some, who were standing at the gate that night, said afterward that he was roaring drunk. But Zamourza, who waited, holding the rein of the white horse, did not think so. Stenka Razin came up, his heels stamping in time to the tolling of the bell. He looked at the saddlebags that the merchants were filling with coins and golden jewelry. He slung the bags over the saddle, and pulled the white cloak across his shoulders.

Then he swung himself into the saddle, and yelled for the gates to be opened.

To the tattoo of the drums, and the tolling of the bell, Stenka Razin trotted through the half-open gate, with Zarmourza running beside him. Hastily the log gates swung shut behind him.

Stenka Razin rode on, and he nudged Zamourza with his foot.

"Eh, tell them my name," he said. Just beyond the circle of torchlight he could make out figures on shaggy ponies, and the flicker of steel lance tips.

"*Ahai*, men of the tents," Zamourza wailed, "the Lord of the River goes to his ships. Make way!"

No arrow sped toward them, and Zamourza drew breath anew.

"Hark to the yang-yang of the bell," he chanted. "Hark to the drums. This is the mighty khan of the sea, friend of Mirak Khan of the steppes."

"Ai!" a voice exclaimed. The fame of Stenka Razin was known in the steppes.

"Behold how the Muscovites bow down to him," Zamourza chanted. "They are his slaves. They pay tribute to him. And he says to Mirak Khan that this town of the wooden wall is under his hand. Let Mirak Khan go back to the steppes, with his cattle."

Stanka Razin hurled the torch away from him, and reined in, to listen. He heard hoofs moving away, and the trampling of driven cattle. When he was sure the Tartars were retreating with their plunder, he stretched his arms and laughed. "Eh, Zamourza," he chuckled, "those militiamen didn't know that Tartars won't storm a wall."

With that he turned his horse's head toward the river. They came out on the bank opposite his boats just as the first light streaked the sky.

Zamourza quested about until he found a fishing boat, which he ran into the water. As Stenka Razin came up, carrying the saddlebags, he touched his arm.

"*Ataman*," he whispered, "look twice before you step into your own boat. There is one waiting who would put a sword into your back."

"*Hai*," said Stenka Razin, "so Filka has been throwing his brawn about."

He said nothing more, but hot rage darkened his face.

The Cossacks in the boats had not slept that night. They had heard the tolling of the distant bell, and the echoes of the fighting, and they had wondered into what kettle their *ataman* had fallen. Some of them had wanted to row in, to find out; but Filka, assuming command, had reminded them that Stenka Razin would flay alive any who followed.

They saw the fishing boat coming out, and recognized Zamourza— then Stenka Razin in a new *svitza*. Filka rubbed his fingers together softly, perceiving these two alive.

Stenka Razin stepped through the screen of rushes to the deck of his boat and threw down the saddlebags. Coins and flashing gold scattered around the boots of the watching Volga men.

"There, dogs," said Stenka Razin, "is the ransom of Gorod."

Filka saw this, and saw the blood lust in the eyes of the *ataman*. Without warning, Filka thrust aside the man in front of him, and leaped at Stenka Razin, drawing his sword as he did so. The sword swung up, glittering.

Stenka Razin needed no warning. He caught the flash of steel, and lowered his head. Like a gray buffalo, his body plunged toward Filka, as his arms thrust out the steel-tipped staff.

The point caught Filka in midair, under the ribs. He screamed as the point came out of his back. The sword in his hand struck Stenka Razin across the shoulders, without force behind it—and clattered to the deck.

Stenka Razin put forth the strength of his shoulders, and swung up the pike with the dying man on it. He tossed Filka into the water, jerking his staff clear of the body as it vanished. Then he strode into his cabin.

But Zamourza crept to the rail, and looked into the water, reddening with blood. The splash had startled a wild crane, and the bird winged overhead. A wolf that had come to the bank to drink at sunrise lifted its head and turned back into the rushes. So Zamourza saw the omens fulfilled.

And in his cabin, Stenka Razin sat on the couch that bore the impress of Nada's body—even the scent of her hair. He stared at the guttered candles. His hand, passing heavily over his face, touched the brand on his shoulder.

His head swayed from side to side, like a buffalo in pain. For he was lonely—lonely.

Mark of Astrakhan

I am Barbakosta, the stag hunter. My dogs are worth looking at. Now, I have no horses. But when I was younger I had a fine string—Circassian breeds.

It is true, your honor, that I would rather sit here in the sun against the wall of the tavern than *jigit* around yonder where the young fellows are showing off their horses to the girls. They did not steal those ponies from the Circassians up in the foothills. They bought them from the Gypsies. They pretend they stole the horses, but that is a lie.

In my day I got many a fine nag from the Circassian *auls*. When it was dark, with knives in my belt, I would crawl up, like a shadow into the stone-walled pastures of the villages. That was the way of it, your honor!

Pistols—like those long horse-pistols in your honor's belt—are not good for anything in the dark. They flash and roar, and you can see nothing for a moment afterward, and God only knows where the bullet has gone. That is bad.

I have sat for an hour waiting for sunrise near a thicket where a stag has slept the night. It was no easy matter to stalk anything in those days of matchlocks. Now, your honor has a fine flintlock with a long barrel. Eh, I would like to try it out. I can still see an eagle under the clouds against the snow cap of Mount Kasbek, yonder. Once I had a *kunak*, a friend who called these mountains the Caucasus. He said, too, that my name was Uncle Konstantine.

Yet he was not a liar. He was a man of his word, a hard man—altogether after my heart. Your honor knows that when we Cossacks have a friend we would pull out an eye for him. This one came to me out of a snow-storm after he had traveled from the edge of the world.

Nay, that is truth! It is also true that he drank, cup for cup, with Stenka Razin, lord of the steppe, *ataman* of the Volga brigands. That was a night of fear. Never were men so feared on the steppe as these two. And in the end God rewarded them in a strange fashion, one with death, the other with banishment. And they were ready. They desired nothing more than that. Such men they were. A little your honor may have heard of them at the battle of the Volga mouths. Always battles and hangings are written down in books by the chroniclers. But what is said of the men?

What does your honor know of the terror that came to Astrakhan, or of Chvedor, the black priest, or the young lass that became a Cossack?

Here, then, is the tale:*

It was a bad night, that one. Snow covered the trails on the steppe, and it was so deep you could not feel the way with your feet any longer. The wind picked it up and whirled it in the air—the east wind that comes off the sea.

And it moaned, the wind, as if the *Tchertiaka*, the arch-fiend, were riding across the stars. Only you couldn't see the stars at all. It cut through sheepskins as if through cotton.

Nay, you could not feel the way and when you opened your eyes you could not see anything at all. Perhaps a pony could have taken you from one place to another, but I had no pony. Mine had strayed, I thought, when the storm began, and I was seeking them. It was many days, as you shall see, before I learned that Bassangor Khan and his Nogai Tatars had made off with them.

I searched, keeping direction by the wind and the beating of the surf on the edge of the sea. And I went forward toward a dark shape that turned out to be not a horse or a clump of sedge, but a man.

He was not a Tatar. He had a cloak wrapped over his head and great boots that came above his knees, the tops turned down and flopping when he made a step. A horse would not endure a rider who wore boots like that.

When I peered at his face I saw it was dark and broad, with a thin black mustache that ran from ear to ear. His teeth were chattering like the fangs of a wolf at bay. But this was not at all on account of fear.

---

*The events related by Barbakosta took place in the years 1670–1671 and are preserved in the journal of an unknown officer who visited the Caucasus. The author has attempted to give the narrative as Barbakosta first told it.

Nay, I put my hand on his coat and it was wet. Not from the snow's touch, but soaked with water. And God is my witness, it was no night to be upon the steppe in wet garments.

I asked him what he was doing, and he shook his head, not understanding. I thought of the missing horses and of my cabin, and decided to lead the stranger to my place. I was born on the steppe, and my days have been passed beyond the border among the tribes of Islam—Circassians, Tatars and others. Because of that, I learned to look at matters through their eyes.

They have a word that explains everything that happens—*kismet*. And perhaps it was written that I should come upon this stranger, nearly dead with cold on the edge of the steppe by the sea.

"Well," I said to myself, "a life may be saved if the stranger is given shelter."

And in the end I was rewarded for this thought, as you shall see.

"Come!" I said, and gave him the end of my shawl girdle to hold so he would be able to follow me and I would know if he tumbled into a drift.

He fell more than once, but he did not drag on the girdle and he did not complain when I lost the way and circled back to find it. Yet, I think if I had not found him, he would have made his way to the Tatar tents or to an *aul* of the hill people. That was the kind of man he was.

Before very long we sighted the lantern I had left in the door of my cabin. When the door was shut and the stranger stood by the smoking stove, he swayed like a hamstrung pony.

I heated some *gorilka* steaming hot, but his fingers were numbed so that he could not hold the cup, and I held it until he got it down. Then I made him sit on the stove while I pulled off his heavy morocco boots, being filled with curiosity because his garments were such as I had never seen before on a man. The cloak was velvet and had belonged to some Moslem officer, but the coat was that of a Frank, a Christian from Europe. His *sharivari*, bag trousers, were voluminous black damask, such as a Circassian or a Cossack might wear.

He had on nothing else except a shirt of clean white linen embroidered with small crosses of St. George, and an Armenian must have made that. When everything was off he lay down on the stove to dry himself.

His limbs were not long, but massive as a bear's. His ruddy face with its black mustache and deep-set gray eyes seemed to be stone. Not a smile or frown crossed it, and by looking at him I could not tell whether he was suffering or pleased in the least.

"*Zdorovènky bou-ly!*" I said, dipping a cup for myself. "Health to you!"

The gray eyes of the stranger considered me, and I think I puzzled him as much as he did me, though he did not show it.

"*Touloumbash!*" he said presently, and was more surprised than ever because that was his way of saving "*tch l'oum 'a basha,*" which means pasha or master of the drinking in Osmanli Turkish.

Now I had picked up a good deal of Turkish from the fur merchants in Tiflis and Astrakhan and others, and I asked him in that tongue if he had come from Constantinople.

He nodded, and I asked if he were not a Christian, a Nasrani.

Again he assented, and I became more surprised, because the stranger wore the garments of half Asia and knew Turkish, and looked altogether like a Cossack except for his eyes, which were tawny gray.

I asked him where he came from, and he considered, searching for words. It became clear to me that Turkish was not his own language.

"*Mour dan,*" he responded. "From the sea."

Somewhere before then I had heard other men say, 'from the seas,' and they were pirates.

"From what sea, effendi?"

In this fashion I addressed him because it seemed to me that he was a man of rank, possibly a chief in some tribe of Frankistan. And in this I was right.

"That one." He pointed over his shoulder toward the east where we had been wandering, and he thought of a question himself. "What in the name of all the —— is it called and where is it?"

I became more curious than ever. Here was the stranger making his way out of the sea into the snow, and asking me in the oaths of a Turkish slave galley where he had come from. Eh, I have been in many tight places. I have been in the salt desert and the Mountains of the Eagles, but it has never happened that I did not know the place and the way in and the way out as well.

"*Mour Mazanderan,*" I responded. "The Sea of Mazanderan. The Franks call it the Caspian."

It is, of course, an inland sea. Men say it is like no other in the earth because it lies down in the earth itself as if a great pit had been dug in other days and filled with salt and water. You cannot go from it to any other sea; only up the great river Volga into our steppe. No tall ships journey on it—only our barks and sailing skiffs and the oar galleys of the Moslems. And in other days it had been a sea of the Moslems, until a man came who took it from them.

"The ——" he said. A very little I explained to him. The Caspian was like a bear sitting up on its haunches. And it sat on Persia with its tiny hills and garden valleys. To the east, where the forelegs of the bear might be, were the waste lands—the gray sand deserts and the nomad tribes. To the north was the steppe, around the head of the bear and the river Volga, with the great town of Astrakhan which was held by the Muscovites, where the river runs into the sea. And my cabin was on the west where the steppe runs into the peaks of the Caucasus, about two weeks' ride from Astrakhan.

And all about the Volga on the breast of the steppe is the country of the Cossacks, of the Jaick and the Don, who once were free men, but are now under the rule of the Muscovite.

While I explained this to the stranger I filled and lighted my water-pipe, giving him the stem.

"Tell me your name," I bade him, "and your tribe."

I could see that the sea and the country I described to him, all of the world I knew, had been unknown to him, and my curiosity grew the more.

He thought for a moment, and then said—

"Mark."

"Is that all the name?"

"It is enough."

"And where are your people?"

He tried to tell me in his slave galley Turkish, but I could not understand. Ships he mentioned and a long, long journey over the sea and then islands.

I asked then how many days it had taken him to come from his country, and he told me as many days as were in one Winter and one Summer, and this seemed to be a lie. Who could journey for a year without going over the edge of the world?

Nevertheless, he told the truth. He had come from beyond the edge of the world, and the name of the place sounded like Marak. He was telling the truth, but I could not understand.

Very patiently he sat on the stove, the stem of the hubble-bubble pipe in his hand, like a bear—a big bear in the prime of life, stripped of its fell. And before long I noticed what I should have seen long ago—that his eyes were sunk and his belly drawn in with hunger. He had not eaten for a day and a night and the part of another day.

I was ashamed because I had not given him food, and I set about making barley gruel and roasting the quarter of a wild boar that had been hanging outside under the rafters. It was a hard Winter on the steppe, that one; but my cabin had a good stock of meat.

"*Chlieb sol*," I bowed to him when the boar's meat and the gruel was ready. "I bid you to my bread and salt, Mark."

As for him, he got up and put on his shirt; then he bowed, not as we Cossacks do, bending the head to the girdle, but with a downward thrust of the shoulders and a slight outward sweep of the right hand. Then he began to eat very slowly for all his hunger, and when he had done, the shank bone of the boar was picked bare, the bowl emptied of gruel. For a while we drank brandy until the last devilkin of frost had left our fingers and our hearts were thumping soundly. Mark went to sleep where he sat, on the stove, and I put sheepskins, over him, kindling up the fire good and plenty.

When a man has come over the edge of the world, and has been cast into the waters of an angry sea, and has been upon the steppe when the wind is like the archfiend, he has need of sleep and a fire under him. A good fire.

The storm lasted for three days and, when it ended, the snow had covered everything except the tips of the sage bushes. Even the deer were snowed in the *barkas*, the little gullies of the foothills. A man could not walk in that snow until its crust had hardened.

Mark went to the door and looked at the white hills and the cloudless blue sky and the pinnacles of the great mountains to the south, and I could not tell whether he was pleased or grieved. But it was clear that he had not seen such a land until now. He liked to sleep on the stove, but he always left my place clear for me. The rents in his coat he sewed up very neatly, and he greased his boots with bear's fat. Nor would he help himself to brandy unless I was drinking.

Our next bout with the spirits was a long one. Mark kept pace with me, cup for cup. In time I became both sad and gay, and sang a song of the Cossack people:

Glorious fame will arise,
Among the brothers, among the Cossacks,
Till the end of time.

Mark liked the song. He kept time, beating with his hand. And when I had done, he sang. His voice was deep and throaty, but it rang out finely in the cabin. And the song had a beat to it that I liked. When he had repeated the first words of the chorus I joined in—though the words were unknown to me—thus:

Blow high; blow low—what care we,
On the coast of the high Barbaree.

That night it was Mark who put me to bed. Eh, he had a hard head on him.

In time I went into the valleys again to hunt and to discover where my ponies were, and brought back many Ufa marten skins and some skins of the little black mountain bear, so we did not lack for meat—or barley or honey, for that matter.

One day I came back to the cabin about sunset, and on the trail I saw the tracks of four ponies that looked like mine. The door was shut and I could not see through the horn windows, so I circled the *choutar* and found that the four horses had gone away again. Then I discovered a great deal of blood sunk in the snow before the door and many footprints. Some were the horsehide riding boots of Tatars and some were Mark's broad prints. I thought that there had been trouble, and it was a bad thing.

If Tatars had come, they would have slain Mark and taken away everything I had in the hut. Usually the Nogais did not trouble me because I did them no harm; but the Winter was a hard one and many of their ponies had died. So they had come for the food and the weapons and the garments in my place, doubtless having watched me go out that morning, unaware that Mark was in the cabin.

Most of all I was sorry for Mark. He had worn no weapon, and had never shown any inclination to use one of mine. I had taken the matchlock with me and the four Nogais must have had arrows. From the amount of blood, it appeared that he had killed or hurt one of them, and that would have been his end.

So I thought. But Mark was sitting on the stove, the stem of the hubble-bubble in his hand just the same as ever, except that his eyes were like bits of light in his dark face. I looked around at the weapons in the cabin.

There were the nine Circassian daggers hanging in place, and the rusted yataghan that a dying Turkoman had let me have. But the heavy scimitar was on the stove beside Mark. I took the blade from the sheath; it was not bloodied, but had been cleaned painstakingly with sand and oil, so that the blood was all gone from the channels.

This had been the weapon Mark used, and I wondered what had happened in my cabin.

"Eh, Mark, how was it?"

The four Nogais had all entered the hut on foot. They were surprised to find Mark sitting on the stove. At first they moved around without touching anything. Then one of them caught up the cask of brandy and another threatened Mark with a knife. He took down the scimitar from the wall before they realized what he was doing, and when they ran at him he put two on their backs. One was cut between the shoulder and throat and one in the groin.

When this had been done the two others carried their wounded brothers to the horses without being molested by Mark, who stayed in the cabin when he saw their bows. It was well for him he did that. They did not try to enter the door again because they were afraid of his sword. Afterwards he went out and watched them ride to the south.

"*Shabash!*" I cried. "Well done!"

If the food and the weapons and the pelts had been taken from the cabin, we would have been no better off than hamstrung rabbits. On the other hand, Mark had wounded two of the Nogais, and their brothers would certainly come from the camp to make an end of us twain. The Nogais are great thieves, but they do not take up the sword unless they have a blood feud. They had one now.

That evening when I had thought it all over, I told Mark we must go from the cabin.

"Nay," he said at once. "I will go, if it's my hide they want. Why should you leave your cabin?"

"Where, *kunak moi*, would you go?"

Aye, I called him my brother-friend. It is not every man who will stand up to four armed Tatars in a hut for the sake of the belongings of another man. The Tatars would not have hurt him if he had sat still.

After he thought about it, he said he would go to Astrakhan where I had told him there was a Muscovite governor and many officers from Frankistan. Then I said I would go to Astrakhan with him. Why not? For three years I had not talked with my brother Cossacks, or heard tidings of what was going on in the world.

Already the ice was breaking up in the rivers and the sun was eating through the crust of snow. We would be able to make our way along the trails, and when we reached the northern plain the snow would be gone. It was not pleasant to walk on our feet but it was better to do that than to be buried in the snow.

The next morning I made a bundle of the pelts. It was very heavy, but Mark carried it easily on his shoulders. Before setting out, I gave him the scimitar, saying that a man who went unarmed in this country would not live very long. He thrust it through his belt and smiled, the first time I had seen him smile since he came out of the storm.

The nine daggers I put in my shawl girdle and took the harquebus on my arm, with a pack made up of the barley, salt, a cook pan, tallow and flint and steel, also powder and bullets in a separate leather sack.

"Now for the road!" I said.

So we closed the door of the *choutar* and set forth for Astrakhan, neither of us minded to turn out for any one. We had finished the brandy the night before, and it was indeed the will of God that kept us on the trail, because a dozen suns were floating in the sky over me. Hornets were buzzing in my ears and flies crawling up and down my back.

And that morning I knew who Mark was. We had come to understand each other well enough in Turkish and as we went forward he talked.

This place called Marak had nothing to do with his name. It was America.

A strange place, by all the ——! It lay beyond the great sea, beyond Frankistan where the Christian tribes of Europe have their camps. Mark had been born in a frontier *stanitza*, called Virginia, where *tabak** was grown as at Astrakhan, and the white men fought against nomad tribes that were very much like our Tatars.

When he was old enough to own a gun, Mark went to an island off this coast of America on the other side of the world with his father, who was a governor of the island.

There they were raided by other Franks, who were Spaniards and came in ships. The Spaniards must have been like the Turks of Constantino-

---

*Tobacco.

ple, because their sultan was an emperor who claimed dominion over all this new world and had multitudes of slaves. His ships were full of gold and silver, like the galleons of the sultan.

Mark was not made a slave because he escaped from the Spaniards and found his way to another island where was a city named Tortuga.

Here were gathered a brotherhood of men who had come to band themselves together in this way. They had voyaged to the islands to hunt wild cattle, which were plentiful. The meat of the steers they smoked and dried and sent away in ships. Before long they found that they could take plunder easily by going out in their sailing skiffs and lying in wait for the treasure ships of the Spaniards. Then they began to build and to capture tall ships of their own and to go against the fleets of the Spaniards.

The men of this brotherhood were called the *buccaneers* of America, although the Spaniards called them pirates and the hornets of Tortuga.

They grew in number and power until the other kings of Frankistan began to encourage them with gifts of powder and weapons and money to make war on the Spaniards, because these kings were not strong enough to stand against the Spaniards in the new world.

"Eh," I explained to Mark, "your brotherhood is like the fellowship of the Cossacks. When the Muscovite nobles and the Poles wish us to fight the Turks, they make gifts to us. When we do any plundering on our own account, they call us pirates and cry death to us."

"That is so," he assented.

I had spoken in jest, but it was indeed as he said. Did not the buccaneers choose their own *ataman*, or chief, to lead them? Did they not take new names when they joined the brotherhood of that coast, as we do? They had no wives in the camp at Tortuga, and when they had made a successful raid they scattered their plunder in a fine debauch, as the Cossacks do. Why not? What does it avail a man to store honey and mead in cellars and gold in chests?

When we have such things we go into the streets, and all who pass by may drink or eat at our will.

"Eh," I thought, "my *kunak* does not always sit on the stove. There is cold blood in him, but fire as well. He will kindle things up in Astrakhan."

And, in truth, he did so. Though not as I had thought. I had seen much of his spirit, but not all. It would have been better for us if we had stayed in the *choutar* in the Caucasus in spite of a feud and Tatars.

"How did you come, *kunak*," I asked, "from this nest of pirates in the sea beyond the edge of the world?"

"I did not come. I was brought, Uncle Kosta. Among the Spaniards was an emir of the sea who had slain my father and my mother. I sought his ship for a long time among the islands of the Americas. In the end I found it—in company with three others."

He looked out over the glittering snow with narrowed eyes, as in that day he might have gazed over the shining sea at the four ships of his enemies.

"I cut him down in his own cabin, but before night I and the men who survived were prisoners of the Dons. They brought us to Algiers to be sold as slaves to the people of the Barbary pashas. I was taken by a Persian *mirza* who was far from his own country. He went in a galleon to Constantinople and from there into another sea. Then we crossed beneath high mountains into a land of many cities—Mazanderan, I think. Persia was not far away when the *mirza* was taken sick and died. I have known worse men than he."

Mark thought for a while, and shifted the burden on his back.

"I never saw Persia, Uncle Kosta. They put me into an oar galley that was being fitted out in that lake you call the Caspian. There was talk of a war on the lake. Some pirates had come down from the north, and the Mohammedans were sending galleys against them. When we did go out of the harbor, a storm came up, and the galley, besides being ill-built, was not the craft for a storm. It broke up on a sandbar and I swam ashore."

"You have a horned soul in you, Mark. You are not easily killed."

In fact, luck was with us for a while. At the Kuma River we traded our pelts with a wandering band of Kalmuks, for horses.

It is true that the nags were not roundbellied Kiptchak stallions. They were all bones and sores and evil temper, and our saddles were strips of felt. But all cattle were lean at that time, and hunger was like a curse on the steppe.

The tribesmen were in a black mood. Before long they would be able to glean milk out of the mares and make themselves drunk—aye, even the babes at the women's breasts—from the fermented milk. Then they could take honey from the wild hives and fish from the streams. But not yet. I was glad to get across the Kuma with a whole skin.

We gave the ponies some barley, and before long the steppe showed green in patches, and they were able to graze after a fashion. Because here on the Caspian the steppe is not like our Cossack land. The *al-kali* grass is poisonous to horses, good only to be burned so that soap can be made from the ashes. And when we looked to find wells in rocky pits, we found only layers of shining salt.

Almost in a day the snow ended and the steppe became brown. Waves of sand appeared at the sea's edge, where we followed one of the *Kozaki khoda*, the Cossack paths to the north. Aye, sand and crumbled shells and, in the air—gnats. And the ceaseless croaking of frogs.

But one evening we saw a thing that astonished me. The sea was a Moslem sea, and it had been so for the ages of ages. We were watching the round moon come up over the dry lakes of shining salt when Mark pointed out to the gray line of the sea where his quick eye had picked out a sail.

It was not a skiff, but a bark, and it was going north. We could hear the men in it singing with a light heart.

"That sounds like your song, Barbakosta," Mark said after he had listened.

It was so. A puff of wind brought it clearly to my ears.

> *Glorious fame will arise,*
> *Among the Cossacks, among the brothers,*
> *'Till the end of time.*

I shouted at the bark and, though they must have seen our fire, they paid no attention. The wind was blowing away from them and they did not hear. If they had heard, we might have been spared many things and less blood would have been on the path that lay before us.

But who can escape what lies before him? It was our *kismet* that we should go to Astrakhan, on the white island in the river Volga.

When we saw the gray breast of the Volga and the masts of the ships and, behind them, the wall of the town with its domes and clock towers, Mark was glad.

We could see the house of the governor within its wooden wall and the stone fortress that is the Muscovite citadel with its churches. But all the rest was Asia. The domed gray tents of Tatars, the huts of Armenians, the mud caravansary of the Hindu traders—all these clustered like hornets' nests outside the Muscovite wall, filling the north end of the island on which the city stood. Mark was glad, and yet one thing grieved him. While we waited for the ferry barge to cross the river we saw a fleet of more than twenty sailing craft depart up the river. And every vessel was crowded with Muscovite soldiery in their black and white greatcoats. They were armed with harquebuses and the ships were armed with brass cannon. Flags snapped on staffs at the prows, and when they drew abreast the governor's house there was a great hullabaloo of trumpets, and a gun went off—*bang.*

Mark watched them for as long as he could, and I think he was sorry that we had not come in time for him to go on one of those boats on the expedition.

"Where are they bound for, Uncle Kosta?" he asked me.

"They go where they go, *kunak moi.*"

And I could tell him no more than that, because all around Astrakhan the steppe is like a desert—a red and gray desert.

And when we reached the *serai* of the Armenians, I thought no more of the fleet of boats going up the river. Mark wanted a new pair of trousers and a hat and such things before presenting himself at the governor's house and, after looking at him very shrewdly, the Armenians gave him all he wanted. They were very excited about something or other, but would say nothing at all to me. And as for understanding their talk among themselves, the devil himself cannot understand Armenians when they wag their beards and toss their hands and shriek at each other.

There were some Circassians around the big fire in the courtyard of the *serai* where the horses were quartered, playing their interminable fiddles and singing under their breath. They went off without a word when I began to question them, and they were not the sort to give up the fire to anyone else.

So we went to sleep in the gallery above the horses, no wiser than when we came. All night the hubbub of voices went on, quarreling all over the place, even the camels squealing and grunting, and Jewesses screeching at their men who were trying to keep out of the way of the Circassians and their knives.

I was glad when morning came and the town gates opened. Mark started off through one of the gates toward the citadel and I went to the Tatar tent village to look for old friends. It had been agreed between us that he was to seek some post of employment in the garrison because we could not live in the town for long without money, and we had not a kopek between us—only the two nags.

In the steppe we got along splendidly without silver or copper, but here in Astrakhan, among our kind, we had to give money. Eh, that is how things are!

I had not expected to find so many Nogai Tatars still at Astrakhan, because the ice had gone out of the river and the steppe was in flower to the north, the cattle fattening up splendidly. You see the Nogais come to Astrakhan with the first snow for shelter and to escape the Kalmuks,[*] who hunt them down like ferrets. During the Winter the governor of the town gives the Nogais arms, firelocks and such, to protect themselves against the raids of the Kalmuks, who come across when the river is frozen.

With the last of the snow the governor takes the weapons away from the Nogais so that they will not be tempted to use them against Muscovites on the steppe. But these Nogais still had firelocks, and they had sent their women and children from their yurtas.

Their chief, Koum Agha, was known to me and I sat down in his tent on the carpet with several other old men who were all drinking mare's milk, flavored with bitter herbs. When Koum Agha offered me a bowl of the milk, I knew that he remembered me. He was a thin warrior who shaved his head and carried it a little on one side because of a sword cut that had injured the neck muscles.

When I had listened to the talk for a while, I understood that the Nogais were making ready for war.

"Eh, Koum," I asked, "what is upon the river?"

"*Kazaki!*"

"How, Cossacks?"

"They are upon the river, Barbakosta, and upon the steppe like the fire that springs up with the night."

It was nothing particularly new for the Nogais to have a quarrel with my people, and I asked what leader they were going against, thinking that horses had been stolen on one side or the other.

"Khaghan Kazaki, Stenka Razin."

The chief of the Cossacks, Stenka Razin! Three years ago I had been in the bazaar of Astrakhan and I had seen Razin, the little father, the nourisher. *Ekh*, a tall man with dark eyes, his face pitted with smallpox scars,

---

[*]Kalmuks and Nogais; Tatar tribes conquered a hundred years previous by Ivan the Terrible, now furnished irregular cavalry to the Muscovites.

his *svitza* pure white ermine, strings of pearls wound around his *kalpak*, his sword hilt gleaming with diamonds. Wherever he went a crowd gathered, and at times he tossed handfuls of gold coins to the children.

He had despoiled a Persian city, and he cast away his riches so that every one could be jolly. He was a pirate, and he had the gift of holding the love of men. They brought him their woes and he laughed, saying—

"Come with me!"

But I did not see what quarrel the Tatars could have with Stenka Razin who lived on the Volga and the sea.

"He comes," Koum explained, "the great leader. He comes against Astrakhan with a horde. Tomorrow or the next day or the next he will be beating at the walls. Already he has taken Kamushink and the other *kibitkas* of the Muscovites. The steppe is afire, as I said."

"Your words are smoke, Koum Agha," I told him. "Stenka Razin has made a truce with the Muscovites."

"Unless, by God's will, a goat does not breed." He meant that all things happened only by God's will. "A truce is easily broken, Barbakosta. *Ai-iy!* This thing is true."

By then I had remembered the bark that we had seen manned by armed Cossacks and sailing toward Astrakhan, and the boats going up the river with the Muscovite soldiers. I remembered the tumult in the *serai* of the Armenians. Indeed, as the old *agha* said, this thing was true.

Long ago a Muscovite general had put to death Stenka Razin's brother, who was serving under his command, for slight cause. And Razin had sworn that until the day of his death he would be an enemy of the Muscovites. Men came to him then as now, and he ranged the Volga, escaping pursuit, boarding the barks of the merchants, laughing when flames soared up.

They sent armed regiments and barks with cannon from Moscow to take him and he slipped away to the Caspian to a refuge in the islands where they besieged him in vain. Eh, he was a wolf, the leader of a pack!

He descended on the Moslem shores, and the women of Kinderly and Kietu had cause to weep. With his six thousand he took the city of a sultan. But there was splendid wine in that city and, when his men were drunk, the Moslems came back and slew all but six hundred. The Muscovites did not know this and they had had their fill of his sword. They offered him peace and swore that he would not be molested and his men would be pardoned.

He accepted the truce and came to Astrakhan, laughing, as I have said, with his handful of followers, clad like princes. *Ekh moi*. They gave a pearl for a glass of brandy and the Jews waxed wealthy overnight. Even the Frankish merchants crowded around the Cossacks to buy a silk carpet for a few kopeks or a gold chain for a cask of mead.

When they found out that his band was no more than these few, they began to think. When they thought that he was stripped of his power at last, they became imperious, saying that he must command all his followers to enter Astrakhan and not leave it. And this thing he did, though not as they had desired.

"If you so love fire and the sword," he said to their envoys, "I will make you glad."

With that he went away into the steppe, and men rode from far places to join him until he had an army again. Astrakhan was cut off from the northern world and, as Koum Agha said, the steppe was his. In this way he fetched all his followers to Astrakhan as the governor had commanded!

"And you, Koum Agha," I asked. "What will you do?"

"*Tchoulbim padishah*," he responded. "We are servants of the emperor."

"You did not go in the boats."

"Fire is for the hearth, water for the bowl."

By this he meant that the Nogais were not accustomed to fighting in boats as the Cossacks were, and I asked if he had heard how the flotilla had fared against Stenka Razin. The Tatars have a way of finding out what is happening on the steppe before anyone else knows, and that was why I had come to his tent.

"God is one!" he said with conviction, and I waited until afternoon when riders came to the tents and there was swift talk among the Tatars. It was then the hour of sunset.

Finally Koum took me aside and clicked his teeth, shaking his head to show that he was troubled.

"Go away from the tents, Barbakosta. The town is not a good place for you. The boats of the Muscovites have all been eaten by your Kazak Khaghan."

So Stenka Razin had got the better of the fleet!

"Was it a great fight?" I asked.

"*Yok!* Nay, a very little fight. Only the Muscovite officers were slain, and by their own men who went over to your chieftain." Again he shook his head moodily. *"Ai-iy!* I see wolves, full fed. I see vultures gathering in the sky, and the earth red with blood. Go now, Barbakosta."

But I did not want to go without Mark, and he was somewhere within the Muscovite city. I hurried, because the ten gates of Astrakhan are always closed when it is dark.

A strong body of horsemen were coming out of the Motsagolski gate near the Tatar tents, and these were Circassians, riding fine Kipchak and Kabarda ponies, clashing cymbals and kettledrums as they came to make their rounds of the island. They ride well, the Circassians, and these were pleased with themselves. But I knew they were not the fellows to stand a charge or to drive one home——.

It was not pleasant in the narrow streets, with women hanging out of the upper windows and the smells of many kinds of greasy cooking arising from the doors and the dogs snarling among the piles of refuse. Only overhead where the glow was leaving the sky, the stars began to shine down, bright and warm. So it was in the quarter of the Circassian women—courtesans if ever women were—only the smells were of musk and mastic and fruit. Here and there one of the beauties opened a screen casement to look at me, but they mocked my sheepskins when they saw I was not an officer.

They had big, dark eyes and white skins and small mouths. They needed no paint to make them shine—those tall, supple women with hair like ripe straw. I saw more than one Muscovite underofficer going in their doors to eat dinner, but I did not see Mark. Nor was he in the wide central place called the bazaar street, where a mob of people moved around in groups and lanterns bobbed in and out like glow flies on the steppe. Aye, here were Hindu turbans and the small velvet caps of Kitayans* among the merchants closing up their stalls.

When the dark angel, Gabriel, blows his horn, some men will be found bartering goods, and when the dead of all the ages come out of their graves, a Jew or an Armenian will still be sitting on a carpet, testing a *dinar* with his teeth to see if it is a sound coin.

Then I remembered that Mark had gone to the governor's house, and thither I went, too, through rows of barracks where many soldiers were gathered around fires, through a palisade gate, into a grove of tall poplars

---

*Chinese.

and so to a square wooden building with a double-headed eagle painted over the door and two halberdiers standing guard. I went where the shadows were deepest because those who saw me shouted evilly, and I knew that a Cossack with a gun was not a welcome sight within government grounds.

At the edge of the trees I hid behind bushes and watched for a long time all that went on within the house. It shone with candles, and many people were eating dinner at a long table, waited on by serfs with iron collars about their necks. By and by some ladies came out of the door wearing enormous puffed-out skirts and Turkish shawls, and the officers bowed them to the sedan chairs that were in waiting under the poplars.

I looked chiefly at the officers, and they seemed to have come from different parts of Frankistan, and were all very gay. Muscovite lords, too, appeared at the windows, and I heard later that many of these had fled from their estates up the river to the protection of the governor at Astrakhan.

More candles were brought, and they began to play at cards and chess, and I grew more and more impatient because the night was wearing on and Mark was not to be seen.

Then he came out with a gray-haired colonel who wore a breastplate and a wide sash and long boots. This, Mark explained to me afterward, was a Roundhead. By this he meant an English *kwajahbahadur* or praying soldier who had rebelled against his king and had to fly from the country. Ironsides was another name for him.

They headed through the grove and I joined them, bowing so that the colonel should think I was a servant and whispering to Mark what I had heard from Koum Agha.

"Eh, Uncle Kosta—" he shook his head—"his Excellency, the governor has had no news from the flotilla."

By this I knew that Mark had been told about the war with the Cossacks and the coming of Stenka Razin.

"The Armenian are flying down the river in boats," I pointed out. "The Nogais are of two minds what to do. It is true."

Not by words can you tell when a thing is true. *Ekh moi,* if birds fly up in fright from a thicket, is not an animal stirring in the brush?

Mark looked at me.

"How could such a well-equipped fleet be wiped out by pirates, Uncle Kosta? Why did you not bring the word to the governor at once?"

"Because by dawn we must mount and ride from this place. If I had gone braying to the Muscovite princes, they would have asked questions and shut me up in a room."

Then Mark spoke to the colonel, and the praying Englishman swore under his breath unhappily.

"We are not leaving Astrakhan, Uncle Kosta," my *kunak* then said to me. "I have volunteered to serve in the defense of the town."

That was like a saber cut on the head! I could think of nothing to say until we reached Mark's new quarters—the colonel going back at once to bear the report to the governor—in a clay house near the barracks. Again I urged him to come with me to the steppe, and he said that I was free to go, but he had given his word to stay with the Muscovites.

It is true that I was not a follower of Stenka Razin, but I was not at ease in Astrakhan. Koum Agha had given me good advice. But how could I leave Mark, my *kunak?* He had talked with his countrymen and had eaten bread and wine with them, and his heart was uplifted. He smiled and said he would appoint me a sergeant of artillery, since he had now a hundred men and many guns under his orders.

"Good!" I said at last. "We will remain in this place. It was written. But I would rather pare the devil's hoofs than be one of the Muscovite soldiery. Let me be your servant. Otherwise they will hang me later because I am a Cossack."

So I stayed in the hut the next morning, sweeping it out and tending the fire in the stove like a serf. Again I prayed Mark to go away with me, but he would not, going off instead to drill his men at the guns. He gave me some silver to take to the Armenians to make payment for his new clothes, and I went with a heavy heart.

Not an Armenian remained in the *serai* except some that had been knifed during the night by Moslems.

Eh, it was truly as if a steppe fire had been sweeping down on us, fanned by a whirlwind! Such a fire as drives all the steppe dwellers into flight before it—the little red foxes, the marmots out of their holes, the wolfpack and antelope taking no heed of each other, and even the *bougày*, the great, gray, long-horned steer, master of the wild herd, lord of the plains.

The foreign merchants, many of them, and all Circassians who were not penned within the garrison, were crowding into boats. They were lugging along bales and women, and the women were lugging brats and pitchers and bundles on their heads. Every other minute a bark would hoist sail and begin to move down the river toward the sea. And some of the skiffs were so crowded that the sailors were dipping water out in pails when the waves splashed over the sides.

If they had known what was awaiting them on the sea down below, they would have stayed with us.

But they had heard that morning of the rebellion of the soldiers that had been sent against Stenka Razin in the fleet, and they were mad with fear. I saw a Jew, watering at the mouth, running down to the shore, clad only in his long cap and half a sheepskin and carrying his own weight in rolls of silk, snatched up from —— knows where. A Muscovite guard shouted at him and pricked him with a spear, and he dropped the silk and began to weep because he could not carry it away with him. Then he feared that he would be left on the shore, and waded into the water. He could not swim, and an oar hit him on the head, so that he was not to be seen any more.

Then the same Muscovite pikeman came up to me with some soldiers and said I was a spy because I had been standing on the shore watching what went on.

"Bind the dog of a Cossack," he ordered.

I gave him the silver that had been meant for the Armenians, and they let me off because they wanted to go to a tavern and drink brandy. Eh, they had not been paid for a year, and had nothing but beer and watery vodka to drink.

"Don't hang around here, Uncle," they said. "You will be flayed. Go across the river to your mates."

Instead of that, I doubled back through the gate of St. Nicholas, intending to find my hut and stay in it like a bear in his snow shelter when Winter is on the steppe.

Nay, the narrow streets were full of eyes, and men who, the day before, had passed me with a friendly word, now took occasion to cry after me to show their zeal for the Muscovite cause. A patrol of riders, black-faced Kalmuks with spears slung across their shoulders, heard the cries and closed around me, taking me to the poplar grove where others of their tribe had brought one of Razin's boys, a prisoner.

He was a young Zaporogian, as I knew by the long scalp lock and the wide Turkish trousers. He had been tortured a little in the hands and arms, and was hot with fever.

"Brother, Cossack," he cried, "give me brandy! By ——, the Kalmuks, the sons of dogs, are going to cut the skin off me."

The tribesmen had nailed a small beam athwart the tree and had bound his bleeding arms to this cross-piece and his ankles to the trunk of the poplar. They tied me to a tree just opposite him, not on a cross, but sitting on the earth, my back against the trunk, saying:

"*Agha ckapir!* Be seated, your Excellency!"

When they told me that the *khaghan karaüli*, the governor, had ordered all Cossacks found within the walls to be tortured, I knew that there was little hope for the Zaporogian or for me. The young warrior cried out again for spirits to help him endure the torments. A throng of Muscovite soldiers off duty and townspeople had come into the grove to watch, but no one brought a pitcher of brandy. Aye, there were ladies at the back of the crowd, leaning on the arms of gentlemen merchants.

When the Kalmuks took off the Zaporogian's boots and began to strip the skin from his instep with their long knives these ladies screamed and put their fans before their faces. One of them fainted, but the others did not go away. It was hard to understand.

The Zaporogian warrior had a horned soul in him. The pain did not make him whine.

"When Stenka Razin comes, you will remember me," he shouted at the watchers. "The little father will make a torch out of your town. Death to you, dog-brothers!"

Some of the Muscovite soldiers went away, murmuring when the tribesmen reached the Zaporogian's ankles. The Kalmuks relished their work, and the sight was not a pretty one. If only I had had some silver or a weapon! But I had left all in the hut because I was playing the part of a servant.

And when the Kalmuks had finished with the Zaporogian, they would begin with me. I called to the Muscovites, saying that I was the servant of an officer of the governor's, and they gave me only kicks for an answer. Mark had come to Astrakhan only the day before and his face was not known in the city.

So no one went to seek him, and after a while I grew ashamed of shouting when the Zaporogian was dying without a groan. If it was written that I should be flayed alive by Kalmuks in this place, how could it be otherwise? And after all, Mark was no more than a wanderer from the sea who had taken service with the Muscovites. How was he to countermand an order of the governor?

But it was not written that I should die then. There was a stir in the crowd and Mark pushed his stocky form through the inner ring. Eh, it was a joyful thing to see his broad, lined face and his big boots that flopped when he walked. Another officer was with him—a young ensign who wore a fine new uniform of white damask, the breastplate silvered and the iron headpiece crested with plumes. Mark had seen me tied to the tree when he was inspecting the palisade gate, and had come to investigate.

When he saw the Zaporogian, he started, and the ensign grew white all at once in the face. Then Mark pointed to me and spoke to the young Muscovite, who shrugged his shoulders and gave an order to the Kalmuks, and they cast off my cords and set me free.

"Eh, Mark," I told him, "that poor devil on the tree wants brandy to help him out of his skin. Have you any more money?"

Mark turned to the ensign and they talked in a language I did not know. I learned afterward that Mark conversed with the Muscovite officers in French, a dialect of Frankistan that is well known in the northern cities. And I learned, too, what passed between him and the ensign.

First, Mark asked why the prisoner was being tortured, and the ensign said it was the order of the governor who wished to teach the rebels a lesson.

"His own men may profit more by the lesson than the Cossacks," Mark pointed out. And it happened that the tormenting of the young warrior did stir up uncertainty among the soldiers of the garrison. Because they knew that Stenka Razin would hear of it and, when he did, every Muscovite in Astrakhan might have reason to regret his mother had given him birth.

"An order," said the ensign, "is an order."

Mark asked if the order was that the Zaporogian should be killed, and the ensign said this was so. Then Mark took a long pistol from his belt and powdered the pan without pointing the muzzle at any one. Turning suddenly on his heel, he raised the pistol and fired and the Zaporogian's head dropped at once on his chest. He had been shot through the brain, but so great had been his suffering that the sweat still ran from his mustaches and chin, although he was dead in a few seconds.

"Now," Mark assured the ensign, "the savages can skin the prisoner."

The crowd went away, and the ensign and the Kalmuks looked bewildered, but it could not be said that Mark had countermanded the order.

Word of what he had done was taken to the governor's house and, before long a Polish colonel came to us on the ramparts—from that time a flea did not stick to a dog as close as I did to my *kunak*, Mark—and began to blow out his cheeks and talk angrily.

He had a red face, that colonel, and a fine *kaftan*, embroidered with gold thread and a splendid ivory baton. He was so fat that he panted when he climbed the steps to the rampart, yet he was the officer commanding the garrison. A group of underofficers walked behind him and, whenever the colonel would speak, one of them would come forward and bow and smile. When the Polish colonel frowned at Mark, they all scowled and fingered their mustaches.

"Eh, Lieutenant—" this is what I heard of the colonel's talk from a cannoneer—"it has been reported to me that you have changed the loading of the guns. As you are a civilian without experience in the arts of war, you have not known better than to put wadding in upon the powder without balls. It is reported to me that you have done so, or perhaps have put the wadding behind the powder charge and the ball, which amounts to the same thing."

Ekh moi! What had happened was that some soldiers had related how Mark had put the prisoner out of pain and others had repeated that he sympathized with the Cossacks, and the people in the governor's house had passed on the story that Mark was a traitor who, no doubt, was charging the guns so they would not go off. And the colonel had heard that Mark had changed the charges in the cannon. That is how a rumor grows in such times!

As for Mark, he did not look at all uneasy or angry. He asked the colonel's permission to discharge one of the guns and the colonel agreed. So a slow match was brought and Mark himself trained the gun-carriage to bear on a sandbar in the middle of the river. Then the match was touched to the breech and there was a great roar and billows of smoke, and the sand out on the shallows sprang up like mad.

They all saw that nothing was wrong with the charge; but Mark went on to the next cannon, and the fat colonel had to go with him to each gun until all were fired off.

The Polish colonel grunted, and looked at Mark a long time. Then he swore at the underofficers and stamped off, pausing at the steps to speak under his breath to a German lieutenant who wore a black coat with red ornaments and had a habit of brushing his mustaches to make them stand up like bristles instead of hanging down as God ordained.

This lieutenant waited until the Pole and his staff had disappeared, then he walked up to where Mark was showing his men how to load the guns quickly. Mark was not sitting on the stove any longer. He showed the Muscovites himself just how everything was done, and then the lunkheads would get matters mixed. They were surly and slow, and I saw that Mark was studying them as he explained things through a sergeant who acted as interpreter. He was very patient and, before that morning had ended, the Muscovites had learned that they must do what he said, swiftly, without muddling. For four hours he made them load and draw the charges from the guns, and they were very weary. I think they expected to be flogged, but Mark had his own way of doing things.

This had not pleased the German, who only watched a few minutes before he took his stand where he was in the way of the cannoneers.

"Please to stand aside, *barin*," the sergeant urged.

"I am on duty," replied the German who was called a Walloon, rumbling in his throat and brushing up his bristles. "The *hochwohlgeborener*, the high well-born, has said that this is not the time for adventurers to seek promotion in the garrison."

He meant the fat colonel, and he intended to cast a slur at Mark. Now Mark had told his name to the governor and favor had been shown him, so the foreign officers of the garrison were jealous of him. And the Muscovite officers were sulking because the governor had given the important posts of command to the foreigners. He trusted them more than he did the Muscovites.

"It is a time," repeated the lieutenant, "when we should think only of the defense of the city, not of personal advancement by intrigue."

And he looked hard at Mark, who had taken off his coat and was working in his shirtsleeves among the men.

"Stand back, Rudolph," he said. "You are in the way."

The men began to look up from their tasks and the drill came to a stop. The eyes of the lieutenant, Rudolph, began to glitter and he put a gloved hand on the hilt of his long rapier.

"My dear sir, do not shout at me. I am on duty."

Mark had not raised his voice to the officer, and now he made a fine bow.

"My dear lieutenant," he whispered, "kindly go to the ——."

"*Achtingkrist!*" roared Rudolph. "You threaten me? We will have a word or two about that. We will have a meeting, Master Nameless, before night. Will you choose rapiers or barkers, sir?"

It was all plainly to be seen. The Polish colonel and the Dutch and German officers disliked Mark, who had only the English colonel for his friend. They had selected the man Rudolph to quarrel with him so that a duel would be fought. It seems that Rudolph was a good man with weapons, a veteran of a great war that they called the War of Thirty Years in Frankistan. Nor did he lack courage. Like a boar, he bristled and roared.

Mark looked at him intently for a moment, and his gray eyes twinkled.

"Sir," he said gravely, "is not this a time when we should think only of the defense of the city, not of personal quarrels, especially of intrigue? Astrakhan, I fear me, would be lost without Lieutenant Rudolph."

The Walloon brushed up his mustaches fiercely and opened his mouth twice to reply, without finding words. Then he remembered his mission.

"*Akh,* I understand." He scowled and rumbled again in his throat. "You lack courage. In short, sir, you are a coward."

And he turned his back to await Mark's reply.

But Mark was engaged in teaching the men again. He had seen through the lieutenant with the eyes of his mind, and wasted no more words on him except to send the sergeant who acted as interpreter after Rudolph to remind him that when the siege was over, he would be at his service, and that he preferred pistols to swords.

I had seen Mark turn on his heel and fire a bullet into the brain of the Cossack prisoner, twenty paces away, and I knew that he was a match for the man called Rudolph. That evening at dinner, the governor, who was a just man, explained to the officers that Mark had refused a commission in the emperor's service.

The governor was very polite to Mark, and when the other officers learned that he had seen service in America, they became civil, and the Polish colonel urged him again to accept a lieutenant's commission. But Mark would not and in the end this was a good thing.

Many bottles were opened at the table, and all were in good spirits. That afternoon they had seen Stenka Razin's fleet.

It came, the Cossack fleet, sailing down the Volga, with the men singing and the minstrels playing. Aye, it was a strange attack. I counted fifty-two vessels and about seven thousand warriors.

When we expected them to land below the island, they turned and rowed back around a bend in the river. They came *so* near we could hear their laughter and the words of their song. They were big men, some in rags, some in Persian finery.

The governor and his officers did not know what to make of this. Some said Stenka Razin had lost heart when the moment came to attack the shore; others believed that he wanted to scout around the city. But all agreed that he had gone off without trying to get a foothold anywhere.

Then the governor asked for advice, and they held a council when the ladies had left the table, as on the previous evening. Some of the Muscovite women were dark-browed and beautiful, but all were painted red and white, and this is not the way of our Cossack maids.

The Polish colonel was all for crossing to the mainland and moving to attack Razin with the Circassians and the Tatars, saying that we had nine thousand Muscovite infantry, as many hundred Poles and Swedes and four thousand native cavalry. But the governor said his duty was to defend the city, and we did not know where to find Razin and his men.

To this the Muscovite officers assented, but insisted that the Nogais should be sent to harass Razin.

When Mark was asked his opinion, he said that he had just come to Astrakhan and knew little of the situation, but it seemed to him that the governor should offer amnesty to all who had joined the Cossacks and for-giveness for past offences to make sure of those who were wavering be-tween him and Razin.

All except the Roundhead English colonel shook their heads, and the young ensign, who shone like a bride in his new uniform, swore that he would rather die than lower himself to treat with pirates.

So the governor did nothing, except a little of many things. He did not advance on the Cossacks, but he sent the Nogais, and Koum Agha vanished like a bat into the night and was not seen again. Nay, he fled into the steppe, as I would have done in his place. And the governor issued casks of *tabak* and mead to the garrison and promised them a month's pay—who had not seen a kopek for a year. Surely the kopeks had gone into the governor's wallet, because the feast that night was a great feast. The table was covered with gold and silver plate, and the serving knaves carried stuffed quail and sturgeon and mutton in great platters.

And at the end of the feast came two envoys from Stenka Razin—a gray-haired *ataman* and a priest.

They offered the governor the lives of all within Astrakhan if he would surrender to Stenka Razin.

Now the governor was no coward; he was bold enough, and foolish. Pride made him foolish. He hung the Cossack colonel to a tree and cut off the head of the little father, the priest.

But I did not see this. Mark and the English colonel were walking on the wall, inspecting all things and moving their regiment to the south side of the town, which was the weakest because it faced the length of the island. See—the island is long and covered in places with woods. Without this south side of the city wall are the quarters of the Armenians and the others. On the other three sides the wall presses close to the river, within pistol shot of the shore.

And here at the end is the governor's house where it overlooks the river to the north.

Mark and the Roundhead agreed that the city with its high stone wall and great towers could stand off an attack by a hundred thousand men. The cannon of the Muscovites were splendid, shooting balls as big as a man's head, and there was powder enough to last for years. If Stenka Razin's boats approached the shore they would be blown out of the water. If he landed below Astrakhan and tried to storm the south wall he would be advancing up a narrow strip of land under heavy fire. His cannon were small brass falconets, firing a ball no bigger than a man's fist. Such cannon could not make a breach in our wall.

And Stenka Razin's followers were not as many as the soldiers of the garrison.

"What do you think, Uncle Kosta," Mark asked, "of the Muscovite soldiery? Will they stand?"

"Eh *kunak*," I said, "the Muscovite is like no other man. It is hard to make him angry, but when he is angry it is just as hard to make him laugh again. They will grumble for ten days, then they will rebel if God wills. If Stenka Razin had attacked this afternoon they would have fired off the guns and stirred up their blood. Then they would have fought well enough behind a wall. As it is, I do not know. The governor has been a hard master."

This Mark repeated to the Roundhead colonel, who shrugged his shoulders.

"If the men do turn against us, God help the women!"

They both glanced back at the governor's great house where the Muscovite noblewomen were all quartered. The officers in the banquet hall had fetched in some Gypsies, and a likely looking lass was dancing the *chapak* for them on the long table, while Rudolph and the Polish colonel were beating time with their swords.

"Listen, effendi," I said to Mark.

Somewhere in the town men were singing.

> *In years gone by,*
> *Trai-rai-ta-ra-tai!*
> *The peasant was a huntsman.*
> *Trai-rai-ra-ta-tai!*

And then, as if some devil in the air had drawn a shroud over everything, the damp river mist drifted up and settled around the wall, hiding the lights in the great house, the watch fires and even changing the moon into a round silvery lantern.

"Listen, effendi!"

It was late, late when I warned Mark thus for the second time.

The round lantern of the moon was a lantern no longer; only a spot of silver in the mist. The camp fires were embers. Only the government house blazed with candles.

Bending over the wall, I heard jackals yelping down by the shore and the hooting of an owl in the shadows of the Armenian *serai*. By and by wolves began howling down the island.

Mark and the Roundhead colonel looked at me, and after a moment they remembered what I knew very well, that there were no wolves or jackals on the island.

"What is it, Barbakosta?"

When I heard the keels of boats grating on the small stones of the shore— my ears are sharp, like a dog's, to hear sounds at night—and the trampling of heavy feet in the Tatar town, I went close to them and whispered.

"Effendi, it is death."

Mark, too, had heard the sounds of men moving in the mist, and he became aware that the Muscovite sentries were not giving the alarm. Sentries? The Circassians should have been watching the shore and we had outposts in the Tatar town. The yelping of jackals had been the Cossacks of Stenka Razin calling to scouts who had gone ahead to talk to the Muscovite soldiers in the outposts, and the hooting of the owl was the reply.

The Cossacks were coming up from their boats to the wall of Astrakhan. Eh, had I not gone with them in their skiffs when I was a boy to steal horses from the *auls* along the Persian shore? That was how they did things. I wanted to go down with Mark to a small postern door beside the great Motsagolski gate, so that we could hear them talking and find out where they would attack, but the officers had no thought except to muster their men. It seemed as if the Cossacks were moving toward the Vosnasinski gate where the Roundhead colonel had his headquarters, and he went off that direction.

Mark went up to the nearest sentry who was leaning over the parapet, listening with all his ears. He ordered the man to fire off his gun, and the sentry jumped as if someone had stuck a knife in him—jumped and ran off, dropping his firelock. This Mark picked up, pulling the trigger. It only sparked and clicked, as the powder had fallen out of the pan.

Then Mark said something softly and called the sergeant who acted as interpreter, and the man ran up at once, although he had been off duty.

"Bring a slow match!" Mark ordered, and the Muscovite bawled out loud for a light.

None came, and it appeared that the cannoneers had let the matches go out. Then my *kunak* drew his sword and spoke very quietly to the sergeant, and the man began to bow as if had been frightened to the soul, which was indeed the case. He went off to fetch embers from the nearest fire, and Mark went among the groups of cannoneers, lashing them with his tongue in slave galley Turkish that many of them understood. Eh, he said things! Those who did not understand, saw his sword, and by degrees they began to take their stations.

The thought came to me of my firelock in the hut within the governor's palisade. It was time that I had a weapon.

"Eh, Mark," I whispered when I could get his attention, "these sons of jackals are not to be trusted. Leave them and come with me."

But he would not. And still no trumpet had blared the alarm. As I ran down the steps on the wall I heard steel clashing faintly over toward the Vosnasinski gate. Mark had told me to warn the governor's people that Cossacks were afoot on the island. Of this, however, there was no need because I had not gone halfway to the hut when one of his cannon went off with a roar, and I knew that the sergeant had brought the fire.

Other cannon began to talk, and I thought that now the Muscovites would show fight if their officers knew how to handle them.

"*Matier Boga molis zanas!*" I cried. "Holy Lady, pray for us!"

Why did I pray that the Cossacks be driven away? Well, I was alive and Mark was alive; yet if the men of Stenka Razin found us fighting among the Muscovites, we would be cut open like rabbits in a wolfpack. I knew this as well as I knew that I was standing in my own boots. Because then I had seen the head!

An old man's head, the forehead bald, the long white hair clotted under the chin and dripping red. Instead of a body under it, the head had a staff and the staff was a spear, stuck into the ground, and the head had belonged to a Cossack priest—the one Razin had sent as envoy to the governor of the Muscovites. It peered at me, the eyes wide open under the poplar trees.

Ekh moi! When I had my gun I ran back very fast toward the Motsagolski gate toward Mark. As I passed the barracks the white ensign was trying to muster his company in line, first pleading with them, then threatening. The soldiers in their dark coats were shuffling their feet and looking all around at the officer and at the cannon on the wall. They were like cattle in a herd when a solitary wolf is scented near at hand. The beasts toss their heads and move together, not knowing whether to stand their ground with the monarch steer or to flee.

All at once one of the men levelled his gun and shot the ensign, who fell to his knees. As soon as this happened, a dozen ran up and let off their guns into his body. When I could no longer see the fine white uniform, I ran on until a man in a breastplate stumbled against me within an alley, black as the pit itself.

He called out, and it was the voice of the Roundhead colonel.

"Are you hurt?" I asked, because his knees were wavering strangely.

"Barbakosta!" he groaned.

A candle flared up in a window above us and his face became visible. He had been badly hacked in the hand and across the forehead. I thought of the ringing of steel I had heard near his post on the wall. He cried out something several times, but how was I to understand?

Wrenching a long piece of white linen from his shirt at the throat with his good hand, he plucked one of my daggers from my girdle. Dipping the point in his own blood at the wrist he traced two words on the linen and handed it to me. Then he gave me a push toward the wall. What was I to do?

He was too heavy to carry, and his wounds made him weak very quickly. With a sigh he looked around and went to sit down on the threshold of the house where the candle burned.

Eh, he did not lack courage, that gray colonel. Again he waved me off and I went, thrusting the strip of cloth into my girdle.

At the wall Mark's men were serving the cannon, but it was apparent that no other cannon were being fired. And we were not long in learning the reason. Two officers, the Walloon Rudolph and a Muscovite lieutenant, ran up to Mark's place on the wall and urged him to come with them to the governor's house.

Their men had mutinied, and when Mark would not go, they asked what they should do.

He said—I asked the sergeant what his words were—that he must stay at his post of command as long as the guns could be served, and, as for them, they had better bring their men to order.

"The Cossacks have entered the Vosnasinski gate," they said.

When Mark shrugged his shoulders they started off, but not along the wall. They began to run toward the governor's house when they were clear of the wall, and in the end it did them no good. Just then I heard singing from the streets behind us, and I knew well that song.

> From the White Island
> On the Mother Volga,
> Stenka Razin's brothers
> Sail with a merry song.

Between the reports of Mark's guns laughter came from the darkness in front of us—roaring, drunken laughter. And the song was taken up somewhere to our left in the Tatar town.

> Stenka Razin's the captain,
> The black devil's the admiral—
> Sing a song princess,
> For we are merry today.

The sergeant began to tear at his head, crying out that cannon balls and steel could not harm our foes. Aye, it fairly made my skin creep to hear those roaring voices out of the mist almost under the muzzles of our guns. And when the sergeant cried out, the men all stood still and looked at Mark. The guns ceased speaking, and Mark took his sword tip in his left hand, the muscles on his chin standing out, his gray eyes glittering.

> *Red wine and jewels,*
> *Dark blood and fire—*
> *Hi, Stenka, Razin, our father:*
> *Sarin na kitchkou!*

This was the rallying cry of the Volga brothers, the children of Stenka Razin, and when they heard it, the Muscovites looked unhappy, scowling at Mark. I moved to stand between him and the outer parapet, slinging my gun over one shoulder to free my hands. Then I pushed him off the inner wall.

Beneath him were a flight of steps, leading into a tower. He fell, but his feet were under him and he leaped down the steps with me on his shoulders. Before he could gain his balance I had thrust him through the tower door and slammed it shut behind us, setting the bars in place.

"*Kunak moi,*" I said into the darkness where he was breathing heavily. "No doubt you would like to stick old Uncle Kosta with your sword. Very well, go ahead. My hands are open, but I will not return up yonder to be pulled into pieces by the Muscovite pack."

He was silent for the time it takes to empty a flagon of brandy. Then he laughed.

"*Shabash!*" Which means well done or the work is over. "What now?"

I explained that at the foot of the tower there was the postern door. This would let us out into the Tatar town, and in the mist we could easily escape notice by the Cossacks until we had gained the shore where we could steal a skiff and go over to the mainland. If we were challenged, I could answer that we were wounded Cossacks going back to the ships. Our horses were lost to us, of course, but at that moment our skins were the things to think about.

Two soldiers had been posted in the lower tower; I did not hear them, and they had probably run away. Our friends, the cannoneers were pounding on the door beside us before Mark agreed to my plan.

Cautiously we descended the winding stair until we saw the glow of a lantern below, and then we stopped short like dead men. The two sentries were not there. A young woman was standing holding the lantern, looking up at us wide-eyed, and the long pistol in her other hand was pointed at me.

"——!" shouted Mark.

She was in truth a strange girl. She was thinner than the Cossack maids, too young to have reached the years of wisdom. Her whole body was wrapped in a gray cloak, a white collar covering throat and shoulders. The hood of the cloak did not hide bright tresses of hair like sun-bleached grain.

Aye, she looked like a nun from a holy convent in that strange garment of gray and white. Yet, when Mark cried out, she lowered the pistol and answered him. Now her voice trembled, but her hand had been steady enough. I could not understand their words which came bursting out swiftly. By these very words I knew she must be a woman of Mark's tribe in Frankistan.* She was a beautiful child, altogether fair and clean.

Mark went down the remaining steps three at a time and put up the bars on the door that opened into the city street. Then he looked at me, his broad face twisted by a kind of excited grief.

"Barbakosta," he said. "This is the niece of the Roundhead colonel. She came to seek him and took shelter in this place when she heard the singing in the streets. I am going to find Colonel Bailly."

"If that is the name of the Roundhead," I answered, remembering the bit of linen that had escaped my mind until then, "you would not find him in this world. Here is what he gave me. Is it meant for you?"

He took the white strip with its red lettering and turned his back so the girl would not see. I think the writing was about her because Mark only said when he had crumpled it up in his hand—

"Aye, Uncle Kosta, it was meant for me."

He spoke quietly to the girl who stood looking at him without a word. The noises around the tower seemed to bewilder her and she took his arm in such a way that I saw she did not mean to let it go in a hurry.

Then he blew out the lantern and ordered me to open the postern, saying that they would follow me down to the shore. *Ekh moi*, I had got Mark away from the traitors, his men. But I knew I could not make him leave the blue-eyed lass. Here we had been on the point of escaping without a scratched skin, and now we had a woman to take through Stenka Razin's pirates!

---

*Europe; the Western world in general.

No time was to be lost, and I merely said to myself—

"Old Konstantine, you may lose your skin if that is your *kismet.*"

And I opened the door. It would have availed more if I had said a prayer. A torrent of Cossacks poured in on us, slashing with their swords, crying—

"*Von sabliouky—smiert!* Use your blades—death!"

Aye death was upon us then. I was knocked back upon the steps, and from that place I could see Mark's form against a distant glow of torches. He had pushed the girl behind him and was using his blade in truth. Two of the leaders he put down, and was thrust back against the far wall by others, who howled when they saw their comrades cut open.

I could hear the cannoneers shouting at them from the wall above the postern, and the thought came to me that the Muscovite sons of dogs had warned the Cossacks that an officer was trying to escape through the postern. If it had not been for the Frankish girl, we might have gone free.

Drawing two daggers, I ran into the stumbling warriors and slashed them at the girdles. Eh, in the darkness two daggers are worth twice two swords. A big man struck me with his fist, and the darkness became red light before my eyes so that I could no longer see him and expected to be cut down at once.

A pistol roared behind my ear, and I heard him fall. Aye, the girl in the gray cloak had fired that pistol, but it did us little good. Mark's sword was broken, and three of the Cossacks, heavy men in damp sheepskins, grappled me. We went down in a mass, all of us.

Then someone cried for a torch and, when the light came, we were jerked to our feet and sabers were swung up to make an end of us.

"By the ascension of Mahomet!" roared one of them. "Here is a lass, such a lass!"

They began to stare at us, and when they discovered that I was a Cossack and Mark a foreign officer and the girl something altogether strange, they scratched their heads and decided to take us to Stenka Razin.

Ai-a, have you ever seen the *bougày,* the great wild steer of the steppes? Have you seen him, the master of the herd, standing on a knoll around which the other cattle are feeding?

He does not move his massive weight, his red eyes scan you as you approach, and you wonder what is in his mind or if he has a mind and, while you wonder, you feel afraid.

Just so did Stenka Razin sit among his colonels the next day when we were brought before him in the poplar grove. He was the master, the little father, and the Cossacks were his children and the prisoners were his slaves. I said to myself—

"Old Konstantine, yesterday the Muscovites were going to skin you alive in this very grove, but God alone knows what will happen to you today!"

For a Don Cossack, Stenka Razin was sizable, rather heavy. As tall as I—six feet and eight inches—he must have weighed two hundred and twenty pounds. Sprawled in an armchair, he sat in a fine red satin shirt, spotted down the front with spilled wine; his wide green nankeen trousers were stained with tar; the hilt of his sword was Venetian work, set with many shining diamonds. The black lambskin hat on the table beside him gleamed with a solitary Siberian emerald as large as my thumbnail.

"What sign is that on his arm?" Mark asked me in a whisper.

"An evil sign," I replied, "for us."

It was a thing like a diamond, burned into the skin, with one word printed within the diamond—*Cain*. In this way the Muscovites had branded him when he was a youth and they had taken him prisoner when one of them said he had stolen a horse. I do not know whether he stole the horse, but I know that he was branded and spent the ten years that were the prime of his life in the prison at Kazan. Since then he had sworn an oath that the Muscovites would not take him alive again.

Now he had rolled up the sleeve on that arm so that all the Muscovites of Astrakhan who were brought before him could see the mark and the word. Truly Cain once slew his brother, who was a mild man, but Stenka Razin had not slain his brother. The Muscovites had done that.

And when each of the governor's officers were set before the table, Razin looked at them and said whether they were to be thrown into the river or beheaded. None of the officers did he spare, so it was not long before Mark was led forward. Behind Mark was the young girl, Mistress Bailly, and I was last of the three.

"*Batko*," cried the Cossack warriors at Mark's side, "Father, this is the dog of a Frank who fired on us with cannon last night."

Razin had a great, broad head. Even the skin was dark—the eyes black under drooping lids, the long beard black, and likewise the hair on his chest that showed where the shirt was loosened. Aye, it was no easy matter to face him. To see him was enough to yield, to beat to him with the forehead on the ground.

But Mark did not lower his eyes before Razin's stare and, after a moment, the Cossack chief stirred his shoulders and the chair creaked.

"What more?" he asked.

Then did Chvëdor, the priest, speak in his ringing voice—a stout man who had given up the cassock for *svitza* and saber, and who sat, tankard on knee, at the side of Razin.

"Eh, father, this Frank put an end to the torture of Melko, the Zaporogian yonder."

Chvëdor was a bold spirit and more than once Razin had been on the point of hanging him, but the priest was merry and the pirate liked to drink with him. Now Razin glanced at the dead Cossack who rested as he had been left by the Kalmuks on the cross.

"Sit," he said to Mark, and no man could tell how he was minded to deal with my comrade.

One of the Cossacks ran up with a chair, and Mark seated himself gravely, a little apart from the chieftain.

The girl was led forward. Her hood had been pulled back on her shoulders, and the sunlight, coming through the poplar branches, gleamed in the tangle of her hair. A slim lass, flushing under the eyes of the drunken warriors. Like a lily she was, shining in rank steppe grass. So she swayed, standing before the *bougày*, the master of the steppe.

Aye, in that moment I felt grief and pity for her, the young maiden who had come from afar to the Volga and the children of Razin. I saw that she had taken the chieftain's fancy at once.

"To my *choutar*," he said, meaning the governor's house that he called his farm.

The eyes of the girl flew to Mark and she tried to run to him, but the Cossacks checked her. Then she closed her eyes and moved away without a word. Mark leaned forward, looking at the ground between his feet, and the muscles in his hands became rigid. It was clear to me that he would not let Razin take the girl without an effort to protect her; but at the time he said nothing, and I wondered. Before very long I thought of the reason. Mark had wished Mistress Bailly to be out of sight of the Cossack when he spoke. Eh, she was very fair, and no man seeing her could fail to desire her.

Meanwhile I was led forward, hanging my head. The Cossacks who had seized us in the tower had taken my gun and coat and a fine pair of boots, and I was barefoot.

"Father," said someone, "this is Uncle Kosta, an old dog who fought on the side of the Muscovites."

Though I looked searchingly at the throng, I could not see the man who had spoken, but presently the Muscovite mutineers began to give tongue. They had turned their coats inside out and had come to Razin on their knees, and he had given them the year's pay that was owing to them out of the coffers in the governor's house. They said that I had been the first to bring word of the loss of the flotilla; that I had been a spy of the governor's and had given the alarm the night before.

Eh, it was the Muscovite halberdier who said that, the one who had accosted me on the beach and had taken my silver for brandy money. He desired to gain the favor of Razin.

As for me, I spat on the ground toward that father of lies, and Stenka Razin moved impatiently in his chair.

"Fill Kosta's belly with sand," he said, "and throw him into Mother Volga."

The Cossacks, who had grasped my arms, were dragging me off when a voice made them stop and look around in surprise.

"Khaghan," Mark had said in his slow Turkish, "are you drunk?"

Most of the Cossacks, among them Razin, understood him and some got up from their chairs to stare at him. The chieftain lifted his pitcher of white spirits and drained it to the bottom; then he turned around to face Mark.

"A devil is in you, Frank. Nay, Stenka Razin is not drunk. Are you weary of carrying your head?"

"I have eyes, and I can tell you the truth. This man, Uncle Kosta, is not a spy. He came with me, out of the steppe to the river. His home is in the mountains down below among the tribes, and he can tell you much of the Moslems and their doings. Another thing I say to you: The shah of the Persians is gathering his war vessels together and fitting them out to sail up the Volga and make war against you."

"That is a lie," Razin laughed. "The shah is afraid of my shadow. Did I not put the torch to Baku under his eyes? Did I not take the horses he sent to the white-livered emperor of the Muscovites?"

"It is the truth," said Mark quietly. "I was a prisoner on a Persian galley."

Now when my comrade said a thing, as he did then, his scarred hands folded on his knee, his gray eyes unfaltering, it was not possible to doubt him. Stenka Razin did not doubt him, but the words bred anger in the big Cossack. He grew more angry when one of his lieutenants laughed.

This was a slender man who carried his head on one side and drank only red wine. They called him Filka Tchortyaka, Filka the Devil. It was his habit to goad Razin to do mad things, and for some reason Filka had taken a dislike to Mark.

"Drunk!" echoed Razin, shaking his great head. "Well, we will see. By ——, you will drink with me, Frank, cup for cup, in equal measure. If at the end you are less steady than I, you will be put in a hogshead of vodka and touched off with a torch, pouff!"

Even at that time his victories had stirred Razin to a reckless belief in his own powers. He was master of the steppe, but he fancied himself emperor of all that part of the earth. When he was quite sober, he was all that a Cossack should be—open-handed, full of frolic, eager for new doings. When he was drinking, a black devil seized him, and he had been drinking spirits all that morning. Even so, it was clearly to be seen that his Cossacks believed that Mark would be put in the hogshead.

"*Ei sokoly vina Atamanou*—hi, falcons, wine for the colonel!" they shouted, and those who had me in hand sat down to smoke their pipes and watch.

It was a strange duel. At first Chvëdor drank with them—drank the spiced *varenukha* and the white, sweet-smelling corn brandy. Every time two cups would be filled evenly and one taken to Mark, one to Stenka Razin's table.

By and by Chvëdor dropped out to go off into the town and plunder a bit. The prisoners were brought in a steady stream before the *ataman*, and it is true he showed no mercy to those who had white hands. The fancy struck Stenka Razin to have the prince, the governor, thrown from the clock tower, the highest in the town, and this was done. Then he sent for wines from the governor's house, and the afternoon was not half gone before he had emptied two bottles.

"*Ataman*—" Mark had picked up this word from us—"you have said what will happen if I do not keep pace with you in this drinking. But how if I do?"

"Ask for what you want, Frank," the chieftain made answer carelessly. "It will be yours."

"Good!" said Mark, and Stenka Razin looked at him for a moment from under drooping lids.

When the shadows began to stretch along the ground under the poplars, Stenka Razin's broad face grew darker and darker until it was purple. By some blow many of his front teeth had been broken out, and from his loose mouth trinkles of wine ran down on his shirt. Mark looked whiter and no longer said anything.

The *ataman* called for a pitcher of *gorilka* and tossed it down his throat, while Mark quaffed his slowly. Stenka Razin looked at him and grinned. Mark's head was swaying just a little from side to side, while the big Cossack was motionless as always.

"*Ekh*, my falcon," he muttered, "that last was bitter, was it not? We will have something sweet."

Throwing back his head he roared out a verse from one of the songs of Chvëdor, and Mark, thinking that this was part of the game, responded at once with his only song:

> *Blow high, blow low—what care we,*
> *On the coast of the high Barbaree.*

"Good!" laughed Razin, pleased because my friend's head seemed to be not altogether clear. "Bring mead, sweetened with honey."

That seemed to be more than men could endure—the goblets of sweet drink. The skin on my head felt chill, and I did not dare to look at Mark. The veins were standing out on his forehead, and steam was rising from him into the damp air.

Stenka Razin rose without holding to chair or table just as the sun was setting. He pulled a pistol from his belt and spoke to my comrade.

"Now we will see who is the steadier."

The long pistol looked small in his great fist as he levelled it at the tree from which the Zaporogian had been cut down. His shot showed clearly—a white flake where it had ripped the bark from the side of the poplar. The tree was fifty paces away. It was a wonder that he had been able to stand on his own feet, a miracle that he had hit the tree.

It is one thing to keep a quiet tongue and not to fall down when you are roaring drunk; it is quite another matter to shoot at anything with a pistol and hit what you aim at.

Mark, too, was drunk, but something within his mind was cold and clear. I think he had forgotten all about himself and me. The thing in his mind was the girl who had held out her arms to him and the bit of the old colonel's shirt inscribed with blood. He moved like a man who has been cut on the head—very slowly, doing one thing at a time.

He raised the pistol Stenka Razin handed him and fired. And the bullet struck fairly, near the center of the poplar trunk. The Cossacks raised a shout, and for a moment Razin's eyes glowed red. Then he went over and stood in front of Mark, hands on his thighs.

"*Shabash!*" he roared. "Well done!"

"Then give me the Frankish girl," Mark muttered. "She is mine."

Razin looked at him in astonishment.

"How, yours?"

"My betrothed. She is to be my wife."

Mark lied, yet he said the only thing that would have weight with Razin in such a moment.

"What is that to me?"

"Your word!"

"Well, my word is not smoke. Take the lass. She's fair, but I have a lovelier bit in my bark. By ——, you are bold. There is a horned soul in you, Mark." Razin turned to the watching Cossacks. "Look here, children. This Frank is Stenka Razin's *kunak*, his chosen friend! Do you understand?"

"Aye, father," the Cossacks cried.

"The whole world knows and the —— in purgatory knows, too, that Stenka Razin is no niggard. *Allah!* Where is that besotted priest, Chvëdor? Fetch him here, and do you, Filka, run and get the maid. We'll marry you, Mark, to the blue-eyed lass, and —— take you if you don't know how to look out for her after you are her husband."

Meanwhile my guards, who knew that I was a follower of the Frank, decided to release me.

We soon saw that Razin was a man of his word. Chvëdor came staggering and put a priest's embroidered chasuble over his *svitza* and took his stand behind the very table where the chieftain had been drinking. Torches were fetched, and the round lantern of the moon peered down at us between the poplars.

Filka escorted Mistress Bailly from the governor's house and all the Cossacks bowed to the girdle when she entered among them, carrying a candle. Mark went to her and they talked for some moments aside, and I do not know what they said. But the girl put her hand on his arm, and a little color came into her white cheeks.

Ekh, they had spirit in them—those two. A fine pair, Mark standing straight as a lance staff, looking every one full in the eyes, although the liquor must have been boiling in his veins; Mistress Bailly, trembling a little beneath the cloak, but outwardly indifferent to all except Chvëdor who began the ritual at once in his fine voice. Her hand was steady when she placed the candle on the table, and the flame burned bright. If it had gone out, it would have meant an evil fate for her and my comrade.

We Cossacks all watched the candle, and it did not go out.

"Christ be with you, my children," said the pirate priest at the end.

He knew the ritual well because he had married Stenka Razin a hundred times or more.

"The Father and Son be with you!" all the Cossacks shouted, and Filka the Devil, grinning like the fiend he was, fetched the whip with which the bridegroom should beat the bride to show her who is master. But Mark did not do this.

Razin began to enjoy the spectacle and to be pleased with himself. At such times he showed the princely blood that was in him, for he selected a scimitar and gave it to Mark himself, and the day came when that scimitar served us well in a fashion Razin little suspected.

In addition to the sword, he made Mark the gift of a boat—one of the Cossack barks that had come down the river. It was as long as five horses and as wide as one, and it had a single mast. There were benches and sweeps for ten rowers. The sides of the boat were splendidly painted with banners and figures of the saints, and the rump of the boat was roofed in like a hut.

The floor of the cabin was covered with Turkish carpets, and hung with fine colored lanterns and silk tapestries that had come from Ispahan. It had a divan with many pillows and ivory tabourets and incense burned in jeweled holders.

To this bark the Cossacks escorted us in their skiffs in the moonlight. When Mark and his bride stood on the roof of the cabin, the warriors raised a shout and let off all their firearms. Then Stenka Razin rose up in his skiff and greeted his new *kunak*.

"One thing I ask of you, Mark," he roared. "When I summon you to sit with me and drink a glass, you will come."

"I will come," said my comrade gravely, and even at the end of all things on the Volga he kept his promise.

This done, the Cossacks rowed off, singing to hold revelry in Astrakhan, while I sat down in the nose of the boat to smoke a pipe I had borrowed from one of the plunderers, and to think. In the cabin were sugared fruits and cheese cakes and red wine and white wine, and I could see the girl eating and drinking a little.

Mother Volga was very quiet that night, and no mist hid the stars. On all sides were anchored the boats of the pirates, each with its light, and canoes and skiffs came and went while the feasting in the town went on apace. The lights on the boats moved very gently when little waves came and went and the lantern of the moon cast a white light on the rushes of the shore and the towers of the city.

Meanwhile Mark had drawn the curtain that shut off the cabin from the belly of the boat and came and sat down by me. He had his short clay pipe, because the warriors had not plundered him, and this he lighted from mine, sitting on the wooden wall that runs around the nose of such a boat, his head propped in his hands.

"Eh, Mark," I said after a long while, "luck has come your way. If Stenka Razin did not have a whim to marry you, we twain would have been food for the fishes by now. It is altogether a miracle."

"I am not married, Uncle Kosta," he said shortly.

"How, not married?"

He explained that the lass had been weaned in a tribe and a land where the priests were not as ours and the churches different. He called her a Puritan, which is a praying person who has a knack of fighting. Chvëdor and our ceremony, the candle and the wedding feast and all the rest of it, he insisted, was not in the least like the weddings in that tribe of Frankistan.

"Nay, Mark," I answered when I had thought about this, "a priest is a priest even if he be full of wine. A promise is a promise in Frankistan or on the Volga. Did she not light a candle to set before the Holy Mother?"

"She was made to do it by Filka."

"You were not made to take her hand before the priest. It is true that you did not kiss her then, or beat her with the whip and I do not know if you have kissed her now. But you are certainly her husband."

"*Yavash!* Uncle Kosta, I have lived all my life among the brethren of the coast—a plunderer, a vagabond, a buccaneer! I have slept many a time in a bloodied shirt and have served no king." He laughed under his breath. "A buccaneer once, always a buccaneer. My wedding, a ribald priest on the heels of a drinking bout."

"You would have been a *galliard* among the Cossacks, Mark. Eh; the minstrels must know your name in that far-off sea at the edge of the world."

But Mark shook his head like a man who sees no use in trying to make a hard situation better with words. He said that Mistress Bailly was a flower, a saint, and how was he to care for her?

"Mark," said I, "you drove the Tatars out of my hut. You faced down the Muscovite mutineers with nothing at your back but your shadow. You drank, cup for cup, with Razin and the little father himself swore that you had a horned soul in you. But you do not at all understand how to go about consoling a young girl."

"Perhaps, Uncle Kosta, you might go and talk to her."

"I? A bear putting his paw into a hive! That would not make her glad! Look here, I have not heard her weeping."

"She is not. First she made me tell her about the fate of her uncle, then she thanked me and said she would sleep."

I looked at Mark who was puffing at a cold pipe.

"*Inshallum bak allah!* If I were in your boots, I would not sit out here and hold my head. I would sit by her and hold her hand and stroke her yellow hair. Then I would tell her she is beautiful—and as the saints hear me, that is the truth. Then I would not fail to kiss her."

"The —— take you! Uncle Kosta, you know nothing about such a girl."

"They're alike, all of them. If you don't order them around and show them some endearments they think you don't love them. Then they'll plague you like a demon until you take the horsewhip to them."

Again he shook his head helplessly. Yet that is the truth. When a Cossack maiden is married she fetches a whip to her husband to show that she is ready to serve him. Only if he does not use the whip, she'll get the upper hand, because those young girls are like pasture-bred fillies. They need the bit and spur, otherwise they toss their heads and get out of hand.

Mark explained again that they had gone through the ceremony because Razin made them, and because they wished Stenka to be free to leave the Volga.

"*Taib.* True, Mark. Yet I do not think that this maiden would have done that if she had not loved you."

He started as if I had flicked him with a whip.

"Not to be believed, Uncle Kostal"

"I have eyes, *kunak*," I said, beginning to be angry with him. "I know. What is the use of talking to you? I am going to sleep."

Mark had forgotten to bring me any supper. He had forgotten every-thing except his own uncertainty, and when I curled up on the planks he began to pace up and down in his heavy boots—going on tip-toe at times to listen at the curtain to discover if Mistress Bailly slept in peace, and making more noise in so doing than a buffalo going through underbrush to drink. Eh, he kept us both awake with his rambling and muttering.

When I dozed off at last, he shook me up to ask why I thought she loved him.

"Because she watches you when you are not looking and is altogether a different person when you are with her, you fool."

Again I dozed and then heard him splashing around in the river. He had gone over the side of the boat to swim like a dog, which is a custom of the Franks, hard to believe. It was nearly sunrise and I was very weary.

"Listen, Mark," I said angrily, "if you will sit in one place and smoke your pipe or think and not move around in the boat and the water all the time as if the flies were biting you, I will be able to snooze a bit even though I have had nothing to eat."

After that he was quiet, and I found him propped up against the side wall of the boat when it was light. Mistress Bailly was awake, and with-out making any fuss at all she brought us a fine breakfast on a tray.

When Mark had gone off to talk with Stenka Razin, she watched his skiff out of sight, and then, finding out that I knew a little of the Mus-covite tongue, she made me tell her everything that he had done—how he had found favor with the dead governor and had saved me from being skinned alive. I told her some handsome tales because there is nothing to be gained by sticking about facts when a beautiful maiden lends her ear, and we got along splendidly.

She told me that when she and her uncle had been forced to fly from their home, they had dwelt a little among various peoples of Frankistan and had journeyed to Moscow when they heard that the emperor was paying foreign officers to drill his soldiery and sail his boats. They had been ordered to Astrakhan when Stenka Razin took up the torch and the sword. She said that a new army was being sent down the Volga to crush the Cossacks.

"Will the Cossack chieftain let us go back to Moscow, Uncle Kosta?" she asked.

"I do not think so. His whim is to keep Mark at his side."

So it happened. While the Cossacks were feasting in the town and the merchants and citizens of the place doffed their caps and bent the knee to us, Mark was summoned at all hours to drink with Razin. He was made to tell about the buccaneers, and the hunters of Tortuga and the great treasure ships that crossed the seas to Frankistan. Such things Razin had never heard before, and his favorite story was the one in which Mark related how he had taken the galleon of the Spaniard, boring holes in the skiffs of his men when they rowed up to the enemy in the darkness so that his followers would not lose heart and try to draw back, once the swords began to talk.

Because such deeds were good hearing, Stenka Razin held Mark in favor, and the next days were pleasant ones. We went about clad in cloth of silver and in silks from Kitai,* with belts full of weapons, with wine casks open in all the streets and more meat than we could eat at night. For a bottle of spirits we gave a gold chain to a merchant, and the minstrels made a song about Stenka Razin. Even the shepherds and boatmen of the place had full bellies and wallets and no one mourned the dead Muscovite lords.

The sun smiled on us and we lived like princes in the fine boats of the Cossacks until the day a Terek Cossack rode a foundered horse into the gate of the Tatar city and flung himself, white with dust, from the saddle before Razin.

"Father," he cried, "the shah of the Persians has sent his fleet to sea to make war on you."

Then Stenka Razin laughed. The townspeople of Astrakhan feared that he would hoist the sails on his *chayaks*, his river skiffs, and go away up the Volga into the steppe where the archfiend himself could not find him, and they would be left without a defender.

On their knees they begged him to stay and hold the city wall against the Moslems who would carry off all the inhabitants and sell them into

---

*China.

slavery in Shamaki and Tiflis and Bokhara. Sitting in his chair under the poplars, with a tankard of mead on his knee, Razin heard them through, and laughed.

"We are dogs," he growled, "to bite the Muscovite boyars. We are not a garrison."

For his captains he had other words.

"Come with me, my children. We will frolic!"

It was in the minds of all who heard that he meant to leave Astrakhan to its fate and move up the river. But he had another plan. And at this moment it happened that his eye fell upon Mark, who was sitting with him, and he remembered the warning of my comrade.

"Eh, Mark," Razin said, "are you a prophet as well as a *kunak?* You said the Moslem jackals were getting together a fleet to come against me."

"That is true, *ataman*, as you see."

"Well, I will not await them here in Astrakhan. I will move down among the islands, and their women will wait in vain for the warriors of the shah."

Hearing this, the captains exchanged glances and Chvëdor made bold to speak. The Persian fleet had been seen coasting to the north within a few days of the Volga mouth. In the fleet were a hundred vessels, large and small, manned by perhaps twenty thousand warriors and slaves. The Cossacks, he pointed out, numbered seven thousand, not counting what was left of the Muscovite garrison, and the soldiers might do well enough behind walls supported by heavy cannon, but were little used to river warfare.

"By the black mass!" cried Razin. "I do not want the Muscovites. They would overcrowd our boats."

To other arguments he would not listen, and the townspeople thought him mad. They were pleased that the Cossacks were going against the Persians, because there were not ships enough left to them to bear away the inhabitants up the river, and they were thinking of their houses and goods and children.

As for the Cossacks, they were ready to follow Razin anywhere. Was he not their father? Had he not a charm that protected him against bullets, steel or poison? Did he not find plunder and sport for them wherever he turned? They would have gone with him against all Asia!

And so, in fact, the pirate boats were manned on the second day, sixty of them. Filka the Devil and two thousand men were left with the Muscovites who had joined Razin in the city, and the fleet moved off down the Volga after sending picket boats ahead to find the Persians. And with the others went the little bark that had been given to Mark.

Razin wished the buccaneer to come, and Mark was not the man to refuse. Nor would the Frankish girl leave him. Although two brass cannon had been put in the pretty cabin in place of the divan and a crew of a dozen outlaws were in the waist of the vessel, she sat on the rail of the cabin beside Mark, and in vain he urged her that she would be better in Astrakhan.

Eh, the same thought was in my mind. In a battle on the steppe if things go wrong you can turn your horse and go away, but you cannot run away on a ship. And if God wills that the ship should cease floating and should sink down in the water, that's the end of everything. I thought of what Koum Agha had said:

"Fire for the hearth, water for the cup."

A ship and a battle on the sea was not to my liking.

Mistress Bailly only smiled at Mark and waved her hand to the children, gathered on the shore near the city wall under conduct of some priest or other. They were delighted at the sight of so many little boats moving down the river and began to sing in their high, sweet voices:

> *From the White Island*
> *On the Mother Volga*
> *Stenka Razin's brothers*
> *Sail with a merry song.*

Our Cossacks all looked at the children and waved their hats, and took it as a good omen. At first they had grumbled because there was a woman on the boat. They were surprised that evening when a skiff came from the big bark of the chieftain with a command that Mark should attend the council of the captains. They had not known that Stenka Razin trusted Mark greatly, and now they treated me in friendly wise and asked me to share their kasha and hubble-bubble pipes. They were lean men from the uplands of the Don and Terek, river-men and hunters like myself—men of good faith, although given to quarrelling. They had been kissing the cup a-plenty in the town, but now that we were setting forth to pound the Moslems, they would not touch even mild red wine.

So we sailed down the Volga, five thousand going against twenty thousand, and we knew not what else.

Nor did we know where the Persians were or what channel they would enter. And this, the Cossacks told me, was no light trouble. Because Mother Volga has not one mouth but eighty, all reaching into the sea. How were we to find the Moslems?

What worried our leaders were the eighty mouths of the great river. These mouths spread over the steppe, running around innumerable islands, and some were not channels, but shallow streams down which barks could not sail. Others, nearly all, had sandbars and rocks that barred the way.

So, for as far as a man could ride on a good horse in a day, there was a wilderness in front of us—a wilderness of sluggish streams and marshes, of islands hidden by immense rushes and inhabited only by hawks and gnats and the evil spirits of the waste. Roving Tatars sometimes pitched their tents on one of the islands by a main channel and waited until a bark ran ashore, which often happened, and gave them a chance to plunder the goods of merchants and carry off the merchants to sell as slaves. In all this waste of rushes and rocks and yellow sand a man might lose himself and starve to death.

The Muscovites came there, it is true, to set their nets for sturgeon and strelet; but they had no love for the Volga mouths.

And here it was that Stenka Razin had decided to give battle to the Moslem fleet; beside an island that he knew well. This was an eminence of rocks on the summit of which he had built a wooden castle when the Muscovites besieged him in former years. It was called Shatiri Bogar, the Mountain of the Prince, and it lay beside one of the navigable channels.

Stenka Razin was shrewd enough to know that in the open sea his small Cossack craft would fare badly against the big sailing barks and sandals and oar galleys of the Moslems.

He had brought a score of heavy iron cannon from Astrakhan and barrels of powder and round shot and grape. And he planned to set a trap for the Persians.

"Eh," he said, "we will catch them in nets, like fish."

And that night, when the full moon came up over the Volga mouths, we saw what he meant. We came to the nets.

They stretched from the shore of one long island to another save for a space of the length of three spears that had been left for the boats of the merchants to pass. Piles made from the trunks of trees, sharpened at one end, had been driven down into the bottom of the channel in a ragged line, and between the piles nets of strong hemp were stretched.

There were three lines of these nets, a stone's cast apart—the two up-stream having openings in them so that the fish might swim through and be held against the lowest trap. Then the Muscovites would row up in their boats and sink hooks behind the heads of the sturgeon and slay them. Since there had been no Muscovites at the nets for many days, the traps were nearly filled with the long, twisting bodies.

And since the sturgeon were great and powerful, the nets were heavy, too heavy for any boat to break through.

Behind this triple line of nets Razin planned to place the bulk of his boats, manned with Cossacks who had muskets. So, in a way, they would be behind an entrenchment—a palisade in the river itself. And since there was no time to lose, he set a hundred men to work pulling up the piles and the hemp meshes from the upstream line, enough of them to close the gap that had been left for boats to go through.

But before this was done, twenty skiffs and barks and barges floated down through the gap, down the river for the distance of two musket shots, along the side of a great island in the center of which rose a rocky height. This was Shatiri Bogar, and its shore was hidden by a mass of rushes—the highest I had ever seen—like a forest growing out of the water.

In seventeen of these craft were the heavy cannon he had fetched from Astrakhan. And these boats were sent through the tall rushes in single file so that they made but one track which was afterward closed by a screen of rushes. They were beached and the cannon, the shot and the powder, landed. A command was given, and the Cossacks from the seventeen boats began to dig an entrenchment in the sand of the shore.

They worked swiftly, for this was labor they liked well, and the trick they thought to play on the Moslems made them merry. They arranged places for the cannon behind the earthwork so that a little after sunup, they had twenty guns on the shore of Shatiri Bogar, hidden behind the towering rushes.

And these twenty guns pointed at the channel. A Polish officer of artillery—Heaven knows whence he came or why he fled to the outlaws—commanded the guns and the thousand men who were in the redoubt. And the stout priest Chvëdor, sitting atop a powder keg, commanded the Pole, in order that everything should be as Razin wished. I wondered why the Cossacks did not man the wooden fort on the summit of the rock; but not so much as a lookout was posted there. The buildings looked empty because they were in truth deserted except by crows.

Aye, all these things I saw because our bark was one of the three that had drifted below the nets and had not been run ashore on Shatiri Bogar. I saw, too, how the trap was being made. First the cannon, then the nets would hinder the Moslem boats from going up the channel. But why should the Persians choose this of the half dozen main channels? And why could they not turn around and go away to another one when they discovered the lair of the Cossacks?

Razin, however, had thought of all things. At the council he said:

"*Hai*, my brothers, the trap must be baited. Who ever heard of a wolf putting his head into a snare unless there was bait? We will anchor three boats out the mouth of the Shatiri Bogar channel and when the Persians come up along the coast they will sight our boats and come this way."

To this the captains agreed—all except Mark, who had set such traps himself in that sea of the Spaniards at the edge of the world.

"Nay, *ataman*," he said thoughtfully. "I have seen the Persians and their leaders. They are fathers of treachery, and they are ever distrustful. If they behold three Cossack boats waiting for them they may take it into their heads to go elsewhere, thinking that these are scouts."

"Well, they may. They will ask their astrologers and, if the omens are favorable, they will press ahead. In that way they are fools. "

"True," assented Mark. "But who knows what the soothsayers will advise?"

The Cossacks exchanged glances and Razin gnawed his nails. He was bold. He had gone with five thousand against a great fleet. He was shrewd—he had blocked the channel, as I have said. But beyond that he cared not, trusting in his luck.

"Eh, what?" he asked.

"Send the three barks out into the sea athwart the course of the Moslems. When they sight the Persians, let them veer and sail confusedly as if the pilots were terrified or as if they had no pilots. Drawing back into this channel they will surely bring some of the Moslem craft in pursuit. And where some of them go, all will go."

"You have spoken well, Mark. You have planned wisely. Do you wish to be part of the bait?"

"Aye," said Mark when the eyes of the Cossack leaders turned on him.

Stenka Razin had asked the question idly, pondering whom he would send as captain of the three ships, which would be the same as a death warrant. When Mark accepted at once, he stroked his mustache and said no more. He would have gone himself, but the Cossacks would not have permitted it.

"Eh, be it so." Suddenly he remembered the woman on the bark. "What will you do with your wife? We will guard her on Shatiri Bogar."

Mark pondered and shook his head.

"Unless we bound her, she would not leave the bark. She will go with me."

And so in truth she did. All that morning I had been asleep in the nose of the boat where Mark would not see me and take it into his head to summon me to row with the Cossacks who were laboring at the oars—since the wind was the warm, south wind, and the boat would not go against it without the oars. When the sun was overhead and the thumping of the oars stopped, I woke up and found that a new Cossack was on the boat.

A slender youth with a white lambskin hat and white wool *cherkeska*, bound with a broad red sash. The boots of the newcomer were red morocco, embroidered with gold, and a pistol and a light yataghan were thrust through the red sash. Eh, that was Mistress Bailly and a handsome boy she made, standing on the rump of the boat beside Mark, looking intently to the south.

"*A-yar!*" said a Terek warrior who was sitting smoking beside me. "She is better so, the princess! Look!"

With his pipe he pointed to the south. Here the gray water was covered by a black mass moving along the shore toward us. Never have I seen such a number of vessels—high *sandals*, swift shallops, darting like spiders over the waves, squat merchants' barks and galleys—all with sails of every color, both square and triangular and all moving toward us while we sat on the water, rolling from side to side and making no effort to escape.

Even before I saw the green crescents on the white sails of the *sandals*, I knew this was the fleet of the Persians. Among the ships were many that had fled from Astrakhan and had been captured.

We were not far from the coast, but when I looked to the north whence we had come I saw only a gray line, shrouded in mist. We had followed the west coast but we had come many leagues from the river's mouth. On the rump of the ship I found Mark leaning against the pole by which he steered.

"Surely, Mark," I said, "it is time to hoist the sail and tighten the reins of the ship so that we will not fall into the hands of yonder dogs."

"Your place, Barbakosta," he responded, "is there in the bow."

Mistress Bailly smiled at me, and her eyes were bright. Mark, too, appeared taller, and his words had a bite to them. He was studying the clouds and the birds that wheeled over the masts of the Moslems—rooks and hawks that had come from God knows where.

Ekh-ma! The men from the Terek and the Don mocked me when I went back and sat down, not at all proudly, because the sons of jackals had heard the words of the Frank. One said—

"Messenger to the chieftain!"

Another put in—

"Ambassador Barbakosta!"

"Hi, brothers, to the oars! Barbakosta does not want to fall into the hands of the Moslems."

"Nay, he went to woo the *ataman*'s wife, the old dog! His fleas woke him up."

I had not thought before then that a Cossack on a boat was not expected to speak to the officer or to go up on the roof where the tiller was. Just then Mark gave an order and the men ran to the mast and began to hoist the long beam to which the sail hangs. The wind turned the boat and we ploughed through the waves instead of rolling around in one place.

But it was not part of Mark's plan to run away quickly. He turned the tiller and our bark bumped against the side of another so that some of the ropes were broken and the sail began to flap like a limed pigeon.

Soon I heard the "Hourra-ha-a!" of the Moslems who were closest to us in several long shallops. Our Cossacks mended the ropes that were broken and we sped away again, leaning over on one side because the wind was pushing very strongly.

The islands of the Volga mouths began to draw nearer, and I picked out the high rock of Shatiri Bogar before midafternoon. By then we could see the peaked turbans and the mailed corselets of the Persians in the shallops, and it was clear that the whole fleet was coming after us.

Slowly opened out the mouth of the river toward which we were headed. White surf fringed the rocks and the tall rushes wavered and bent like a forest under a tempest. Our boat leaned over more and more until the men beside me lay down on the floor with their feet braced against the lower railing, paying no heed to the spray that came over us. They watched the sail and said that Mark at last was trying to make the boat show its best speed.

The cannon in the Persian boats began to go off, and every time the man from the Terek would lift his head to see where the balls had struck.

"The birds are flying high," he said, and I asked why we did not return their fire.

He pointed down to the floor of the bark and shook his head, meaning that it was impossible to fire unless the deck were level; but our pursuers began to loose more cannon at us. Their great *sandals* had come up closer, and they seemed to have no reluctance to burn powder. This was because they did not wish us to escape and bear the tidings, as they fancied, of their arrival to Astrakhan. So said the man from the Terek, pointing to the shore that seemed to fly toward us. Thin, veil-like mist was gathering between us and the rock of Shatiri Bogar. Yet I could see the wooden house of Stenka Razin on the summit with the rooks settled about it.

Surely the Persians would fear nothing from that, because birds would not act like that if men were about.

"Look!" said the Terek Cossack, ramming his elbow into my ribs.

The largest of our boats had been hit more than once by the Moslem cannon. And I saw white splinters fly up from its side as it swung slowly, first this way, then that, its mast broken down. The leading shallops circled around it as dogs rush in on a wolf. Now the cannon of our comrades in the disabled boat began to speak, puffs of smoke darting out and drifting down the wind.

But it availed them little. A black ship with two masts, towering over the rolling *chayak*, headed toward it and struck it with a dull crashing of wood. The Persian *sandal* kept on after us, and our boat sank lower and lower until it could not be seen at all.

Mark had seen, but his face had not changed. The girl had grown pale and her eyes were smoldering. She sat on the deck at his feet where the railing protected her from arrows.

The roaring of the swell on the shore grew louder, the soughing of the rushes and shrieking of the gulls, and the breath and power of the sea seemed to sweep us into the gut between the islands. We fled. Crowding together, the first boats of the fleet were close upon our heels.

We passed the flank of Shatiri Bogar where the thickening mist and the rushes hid a thousand men with their cannon. We swept around the bend in the river beyond, Mark steering the boat past rocks and the gray shapes of sandbars. In the farther reach of the river we moved more slowly because the wind did not push as much. What became of the other boat I do not know. Perhaps it stumbled on a sandbar and sat.

For a space we drifted alone in a shroud of gray mist with our heads close to the water, listening. The Terek Cossack got up and looked over the nose of the boat, listening also. Mark jumped up to the railing, keeping one foot on the pole that steers the boat, attentive to things that were going on behind the gray veil. We heard firelocks booming far behind us, and I thought of the second boat.

Eh, we had led the dogs of *Tourki* into the nets, but we ourselves were in the trap. We could not go ahead. There was no longer a path through the nets. We could not go back. The oncoming fleet was at our heels. And now that the wind had ceased the river began to push at us, first this way, then that.

"To the oars!" cried Mark.

Four oars were thrust into the water, and Mark turned the guiding pole so that we moved toward the island on the far side of the river from Shatiri Bogar. We felt our way among rocks and shallows until we entered a hole in the side of the island—a cove, the Terek Cossack said. Big black boulders rose on either side and passed behind us. Then the oars were lifted and our boat sat on the ground, although the water still stretched a spear cast to the shore.

"Barbakosta," Mark ordered, "take one man and go to a high place on the shore. Watch the river! Bring us tidings!"

I took the tall man from the Terek and waded ashore. We carried our firelocks through the brush and shivered when the wind whipped through our trousers. We heard the shouting of the Moslems, the creaking of wood on the ships and the threshing of oars. We could see perhaps half the river, with black shapes moving up the stream.

And then the gray curtain was cut by red flashes and rolling white smoke upstream where the Cossack *chayaks* were in ambush behind the nets. All of the boats had small brass cannon and the balls tore through the close packed Moslems. But I heard no firing from Shatiri Bogar below the bend.

"Chvëdor is not a fool," my companion grunted. "He will not loose his iron dogs until the *Tourki* begin to flee down the river."

Then I saw the whole of the trap Stenka Razin had set. It was like the trap the Muscovites made in the water for the sturgeon—easy to get into, but no way out. The cannon on Shatiri Bogar were not to keep the Moslems from ascending the Volga; nay, to sink them when they fled.

For a time we sat and watched, and it seemed as if the Persians were trying to force their way through the nets, because we heard the clashing of steel and the war shouts—

"*Haura—haa-a!*"

More boats were coming up and these began to drift over toward us, oar galleys and *sandals* packed with men who were all watching the fighting up the river. They did not look happy. By and by we heard the Cossack cry:

"*Saryn na kitchkou!* Up, lads to the bows!"

The Terek Cossack let his pipe go out and rammed his arm into my ribs.

"Eh, Barbakosta, the brothers are warming up. They are getting their blood up!"

I had drawn careful aim at a tall *mirza* who stood on the rump of the nearest galley, a stone's throw away. He was a fine man in a black *khalat* with a brass knob on the top of his white turban that was shaped like a lily. Over his head was a canopy of striped stuff, and two black slaves stood behind him with peacock plumes on their noddles. And upon the mast near him dangled two Muscovites, taken from the boats that had fled from Astrakhan—now hanging head down, roped by the ankles.

From below the bend thundered Chvëdor's big cannon—*bong, bang, bong!* My *mirza* looked surprised, but he could see nothing, of course. One by one, the ships began to try to go back.

Bong, bang, bong! Thus spoke Chvëdor's guns, and all at once, as a flight of swallows start up from a thicket, the Persians became afraid. A galley broke off its oars against the side of a big ship; a sailing boat ran down a skiff. There was not room enough in the river for them all to turn and go out as they wanted.

Many of them started toward our shore, the *mirza*'s boat among them. At first a few, then throngs of Moslems began to run up the shore, shouting and holding their heads. That is always the way with the Tourki. When they are attacking or cornered they are brave fighters. But when they flee they rush blindly.

"It is time to go back to Mark," I said, and the Cossack from the Terek nodded assent. Indeed it was time, because they had seen us on our rock.

We ran down through the brush until my companion stopped suddenly, putting his hand to his side. Nay, he was not hit by an arrow, he was feeling in his pocket.

"*Stoy bratikou, lioulkou zagoubil!*" he cried. "Stop, brother, I have lost my pipe!"

"May the dogs bite you! If you go back, you'll never smoke *labak* again."

But the mad fellow turned and started up into the rocks to look for his pipe. I waited several moments, and then I saw turbans and cloaks on the height where he had vanished. Nay, I never saw him again.

To Mark I said that the Tourka boats were in a stampede like cattle, leaving the nets. And what was going on by Shatiri Bogar I knew not. Indeed it was not long before our eyes beheld what our ears had long been aware of. First a skiff rowed into our hole in the shore as if the fiends were behind it. Then a gilded *sandal* with its mast shot away.

These boats paid no heed to us. They ran on the ground and sat and the men swarmed to shore. Some began to shoot arrows at us, and we more than paid them back. But finally there came the oared galley of the tall *mirza*, with half its men lying bleeding on the deck. When he saw us, he shouted angrily, and the galley ran in beside us, and forty Moslems poured over the rail of our bark, ululating with blood lust, with steel in their hands and teeth. We shouted once—

"*Hai—Kosaki!*"

And we fired our muskets into them. I picked up a heavy boat hook with a long point and prong, regretting greatly my nine daggers. By breaking the shaft of the boat hook in twain, I had a good weapon. One man I pierced with the point and another I hooked through the ribs.

I was knocked into the nose of the boat, my boat hook lost. A gun lay here, and I loaded it, being protected for the moment by the mast. Mark was standing on the rump of the vessel alone with the girl, his scimitar flashing up and down—up and down, as he sprang from side to side. An arrow flickered into his thigh and he staggered.

At the same instant the girl fired a pistol down into the Moslems who were climbing over the dying Cossacks toward the stern. She drew her light sword bravely. But what is a blade in the hand of one unskilled? A giant black slave sprang up beside her and struck the scimitar out of her hand with his heavy sword. Then he hacked deep below her shoulder just as Mark reached him, stumbling, and cut off his head cleanly.

Hai, that was a good stroke! *"Shabash!"* I cried, and shot down a warrior who had run at Mark's back.

It seemed to me then that our lives would go out in another moment—Mark with his arm around the bleeding girl, raging back and forth on one leg; I with an empty gun and no other weapon. Then I heard a roaring voice:

"Steel to them! Strike on all sides!"

And a man jumped from the galley into our deck. A man with a ring-mail shirt half slashed from his shoulders and the tatters of red sleeves flying when he struck with a long curved blade that sang in the air.

Eh, the blade dripped red, and the man scattered blood as he crashed into the huddle of the Moslems.

His blade snapped off, and he thrust out with his fists, sending men flying. His big, bow legs bent and leaped, and he began to lash about with a battle ax he had caught up. No one could stand against him. Shields split and bones snapped under his blows. The Moslems who had been about Mark—among them the shining *mirza*—flung themselves on him until they all became a knot of arms and heads, twisting among the dead bodies in the belly of the boat.

For the last moment I had heard other shouts.

"Aid for the *ataman*! Slash them brothers, slash!"

Other Cossacks dropped over the rail and pounced on the knot of men. Pistols barked, and before my gun was loaded the deck was cleared of all Moslems save the dead and the dying.

That was how Stenka Razin came to seek Mark in the fight on the Volga. He wiped the sweat from his black brows and spat from bleeding lips. When he was certain that Mark was alive and not dangerously hurt he turned on the Cossacks who had followed him across the empty galley from two *chayaks* that had come up to the far side of the galley.

"Eh, dogs—fathers of a thousand slaves! You were late, late! The Frank was nearly done for when you came."

They were ashamed and hung their heads, until one of them looked around at that sepulcher of a boat.

"Aga tachomek chapar Frankistan," he said. "The Frankish lord is brave."

Then Stenka Razin saw the Moslems gathering on the heights above him, drawing their bows. Instantly he sprang into the water and waded

ashore, leaving a red trail behind him, heaving himself up on the shore
as the wild *bougày*, lord of the steppes, comes up out of a river, shaking
his horns and roaring to let other animals know that he is on the shore.
So Stenka Razin roared out of an open throat, running toward the uneasy bowmen. And, though they were many and his followers few, they
turned and fled.

That is how Stenka Razin fought—without mercy for himself, his men
or his foes. And yet he took thought in that red twilight for Mark, his
kunak.

We carried the girl ashore, Mark and I, as gently as we could, and laid her
on the sand, drawing off her *cherkeska*. I had thought to find her cut half
through, the life all gone. But Mark had thought to make her put on a
shirt of finely wrought ring mail.

The blow of the slave's sword had severed this under the armpit and
had driven many of the links into her white flesh, yet the steel rings had
checked the bite of the blade and the wound was no deeper than my thumb
joint. It had not quite reached the wall around the heart.

"Eh, Mark," I said to hearten him, seeing that his eyes were haggard,
"spit on some clay, put it on the cut and give her vodka and she will live
to give you more than one son."

Instead of that, he bade me go to all the fiends, and bathed out the girl's
bleeding side with salt water. She whimpered but did not cry out. Then he
bound her tightly under the arms with the white cotton turban cloth of
the Persian *mirza* which was the cleanest thing within reach.

When this was done she made him put her head on his knee and held
up her hands. He stroked her hair, but she pulled down his head so that he
kissed her many times on the eyes and lips. That was the way of it.

"See, Mark," I pointed out from where I was sitting at a little distance
so that the smoke of my pipe would not make the girl cough, "it is as I
said. Although you are a fool where such women are concerned, she wants
you for her man, if God gives her life."

"The saints bless you, Uncle Kosta," he whispered, and tears were
shining in his eyes.

And in the end her life was spared. Mark went as swiftly as a *chayak*
could be rowed to Astrakhan and from there, all the weary way up to Moscow, on the Volga, I accompanying him because I had no wish to leave my
kunak. He wanted a Muscovite surgeon to attend her, but she wanted no

more than his nursing, though he could not understand that. He had eyes for nothing except this young girl lying on the rug under the canopy, nor would he permit any one else to give orders on the skiff.

He was no longer a wanderer or a prisoner. In Moscow he held his head high and spoke proudly to the Muscovites who, having heard of his deeds at Astrakhan and in the Volga mouths, offered him a commission as colonel of a fleet. This time he accepted.

The battle of Shatiri Bogar was much talked about, because the Persians had been badly cut up. Men said that ten thousand of them had departed this life, trapped between Chvëdor's guns and the nets, and the Cossack took more spoil than they knew what to do with. Never since then have the Moslems launched a fleet on the Caspian.

As for Mistress Bailly, she was married again to Mark by a priest of her own faith, a little man in dull garments who read through his nose out of a book. Although she and Mark took pleasure in it, the ceremony was lacking to my mind. No candles were set before the Holy Mother and the drinking was not a cupful to the revelry in Astrakhan when the moon looked down through the poplars and the lover and lass stood between life and death while Stenka Razin frolicked.

Nay, should a promise be said over again? I thought of the promise Mark had made to Razin—that he would come and sit with the Cossack when he was summoned. For a time it seemed as if Mark and his new fleet would be sent against the Cossacks and the two fighters would exchange sword strokes instead of stories.

Then we heard that the Cossacks had been cut to pieces by the Muscovite army that had been sent from the north. It was in the north, too, that Prince Boriatinski broke the power of Razin. Eh, the Cossacks had suffered as well as the Moslems in that red evening on the Volga. The survivors scattered, and Razin was hunted from place to place.

Before long tidings came that he had been taken, in a hut on the Volga. He had killed fourteen of the soldiers that surrounded him. Then he came out of the door, leaving his sword within, saying:

"Take me, curs! I am ready to be killed."

It was a day in late Summer when the leaves were dry on the oaks that grew in the promenade before the great church of Saint Vasili the Blessed. Mark was walking with his lady on his arm, accompanied by Frankish and Muscovite officers of the tsar's bodyguards. I, as his servant, followed behind with a stick instead of a gun, to drive away beggars. Mark had on a splendid white *kaftan* and broad red boots and a wide Frankish hat with plumes, and many officers were the first to bow when they met him. But that evening a crowd came toward the Kremyl gate, escorting a file of halberdiers who surrounded a cart drawn by black oxen.

In the cart, leaning against the rail, his arms folded, was Razin. Eh, his finery was no more. His shirt was in rags, and his feet were bare; his hair had grown long on his head. The wild *bougày* of the steppe had been torn by wolves and the flesh of his purple face was sodden, his eyes dull. No longer did his followers crowd around him. Look where he would, he beheld only the eyes of hatred.

Yet he saw Mark and leaned over to stare at him and his lady.

"*Hai*, Mark," he said beseechingly, "my friend, come and sit with me in the prison. Come and talk over the wine cup these few days."

He had spoken in Turkish and none of the Muscovites understood. Mark looked long at Razin.

"I will come," he said.

Afterward, I went to him and said that this thing was not to be thought of. In the tsar's service a colonel could not go and drink with a Cossack pirate. It was known that Mark had had dealings with Razin in Astrakhan, but this had been forgiven him in view of his skill in handling the new ships. If he went to Razin like a brother now he would be suspected and treated in evil wise. That is how it is at a tsar's court.

But the lass, when she understood the matter, said suddenly that he was to go and visit Razin as he had promised.

And Mark laughed, looking down at her with pride.

"It is as you see, Uncle Kosta," he cried.

As for me, knowing that Mark was not to be persuaded from anything, I burned a gold candle before the good Saint Nicholas and went to the river gate where some Nogai Tatars of my acquaintance had a skiff that they were willing to sell. I bought it, and the Tatars too, for we lacked not gold in those days. I made everything ready to flee.

For three days Mark went to the prison, I carrying a keg of brandy behind him. Because of his rank, Razin's warders could not refuse him. And far into the night the two of them sat drinking, cup for cup, saying little.

At times Razin would tell of how he frolicked on the Volga and at times Mark would relate how the buccaneers made a kingdom in the islands that lie at the edge of the world. When the candles burned low, Razin would ask if Mark were coming again to sit with him.

"Well, *kunak*," he said on the third day, "soon the stirrup cup."

On the fourth day Mark came, indeed, and so did the priest and the executioners. The crowd around the prison and the open space where he was to die in the Kremyl was very great. The cart and the black oxen were in readiness, and even musicians had been summoned. Razin was given a goblet of mead and, as a last favor, allowed to smoke the pipe for which he asked.

With it between his teeth he climbed into the cart and leaned down to grasp Mark's hand. He noticed the musicians with pleasure and smiled.

"*Shabash!*" he said to Mark. "Well done!"

He did not think that such words were like to be a noose around Mark's neck. Stenka Razin waved farewell to his *kunak* with his pipe and called out to the fiddlers—

"Strike up, lads!"

The oxen grunted and the cart creaked and he started forward through the crowd, roaring his favorite song—the same the children of Astrakhan had sung when we floated down the river toward the Volga mouths:

> *From the White Island*
> *On the Mother Volga,*
> *Stenka Razin's brothers*
> *Sail with a merry song—*

So died Razin, lord of the steppe, our little father.

As for Mark, he went to the Kremyl and handed to the Muscovites his insignia of rank. Perhaps because he acted swiftly, perhaps because they knew he was planning to leave Muscovy, but surely because they did not know quite how to deal with Mark, the Muscovite lords did not try to make him a prisoner.

He went to his own quarters and took off the white uniform, putting on his old leather and armor and the scimitar Razin had given him. The young Frankish girl, his wife, was in readiness, and they rode out of the river gate on two good horses.

By the huts of the Tatars I stopped them, saying that a boat was in readiness for flight and my shack in the mountains by the Caspian was waiting for them.

"Eh, Uncle Kosta," Mark laughed, "it is as you see. A buccaneer is always a buccaneer and never a lord at court."

He reached down then to grip my hand and say that here our roads parted, since I was for the Volga and the steppe. He and the girl were

going into Frankistan, to the great sea in the west, to seek again the islands that lay at the edge of the world.

And so it was that I said farewell to my *kunak*, a man of his word, a
man after my heart.

Today, if you sail upon the Volga in a *chayak*, the song of the Cossack
river-men will repeat the name of Stenka Razin, and if you talk to them,
the old Cossacks, many will recall Mark of Astrakhan. He and Razin—
where will you find such men today?

Red Hands

Charny came to himself a little at a time. First he was aware that he sat in a saddle. Then he saw the familiar gray steppe grass and felt the wind in his head.

His head troubled him. It was wet with sweat and it had no lambskin *kalpak* on it. Inasmuch as most of his skull had been shaved a few days ago, it felt cold. A fiery thirst tormented him.

Besides, the level steppe behaved strangely. It rose dizzily and then dropped away from him, although his horse paced along steadily enough. Charny knew what this meant.

"I've been licking the pig," he thought.

He remembered singing a chorus with some fellow Cossacks in a town tavern. After that—night and the saddle and a rushing wind.

"Devil take it all," he muttered. "I've come far."

No town was visible on the swaying steppe. The Cossack bent over and looked down. He had no coat, but his wide leather breeches were there and his prized shagreen boots—he looked on each side to make sure. His shirt appeared torn and stained with tar. What mattered most, he still wore his sword. So, he had not drunk that up.

But the horse! After awhile he drew rein and dismounted, holding firmly to the saddle horn. Streaked with sweat and dust, with burrs clouding its long tail, this black horse was certainly not his. A good horse, however, a wolf-chaser.

"How did I get you, *kunak*?"

Evidently after the drinking bout he had taken a horse from the stable and then raced off into the plane—naturally enough, after so many cups of brandy. It was afternoon now, the sun almost setting, and Charny saw no sign of a trail. Only the waving grass, clusters of dark oaks, the hazy sky—and the brown sail of a boat moving majestically over the grass, far off. The Cossack closed his eyes and looked again. The brown sail was still there.

Well, brandy played tricks like that. Worse than the *myzga*, the mirage. Charny tried to remember whether he had gone north, east, south, or west from the frontier town, but without success.

Leading the horse into the nearest shade he loosened the saddle girth slowly. He searched for a picket rope and found none. Letting out the rein, he slipped it over his shoulder and laid down, his head on his arms. He would sleep for a while and then let the horse find the way to water . . .

Instead, he woke with a start. The red glare of sunset filled the sky, and the wind had ceased. Along the ground he had heard the thudding of hooves on the hard clay. Instantly he leaped to his feet, his hand touching the sword hilt at his belt.

Then he relaxed. Only one rider had come up, a Cossack on a piebald horse—a broad Cossack with long arms, wearing a clean sheepskin coat, a black *kalpak* with a red crown, and polished boots. His was a brown, lined face, like a Tartar's, with tufted mustaches.

"*Tfu!*" grunted the rider. "Draw that curved sword and I'll slap you in the snout."

Charny's head was clearing. The other man had saddlebags, with a rolled-up bearskin and a jug behind the saddle—evidently a registered Cossack, on service. In that Year of the Lord 1684 it was well to look twice at one who rode alone and armed in the eastern steppe. The towns and the Muscovite merchants lay under the sunset to the west, and the steppe here was at the edge of the frontier.

"What man are you?" Charny asked.

"They call me Vash. I patrol from the Zarit *stanitza*. The others turned back, but I kept your trail like a weasel."

Zarit, Charny remembered, was the hamlet where he had been drinking at the tavern. He looked at the man called Vash expectantly as the other dismounted.

"Seventy vests you rode between midnight and now," went on Vash. "Straight over the steppe to the east. Well, I'll take you back."

"Why take me back?"

"Don't you know? Last night you licked the pig—you were dancing the *hopak* in the Cossack's bed* when His Highness, the lieutenant of the *starosta*, rode by. He said something, and you pulled him out of the saddle and used the whip on his hide until he danced. *Tfu!* There was a devil in you—"

"How did I find the horse?"

"It's his Highness's charger—a good one. The *starosta* gave command to all of us on the border patrol to follow and bring you back. They are raging like bulls in a pen, the *starosta* and his men. Come on, it's late."

Charny knew well enough what awaited him at Zarit: the stocks; the scourge; or his ears clipped off. They had his horse and his silver, his *svitza* and his hat, while he had one of their best chargers. So, he had stolen nothing. Moreover, he was tired of the Russian settlements were a man could not even drink without being caged.

"My road is to the east," he decided. "To the devil take your *starosta* and his commands."

Vash considered a moment, his slant eyes measuring the tall fugitive. Then he leaped at Charny, his powerful arms clutching. But Charny was in no mood for a fight. Stepping aside, he drew his curved sword swiftly.

"Steel to you!" shouted Vash, jerking out his own sword.

For a moment the two Cossacks circled wearily, Vash half crouched, his muscles tense, while Charny sidestepped softly, waiting. Then Vash leaped again, his saber swinging over his head. Charny parried the slash at his ribs and drew back while the Zarit Cossack pressed him with cut after cut.

Suddenly the taller man stepped forward, twisting the curved blade of his saber around the other's sword until the hilts locked. Without warning he wrenched the blades toward him, and Vash's sword flashed into the air, falling to the ground behind Charny, who set his foot upon it.

"The devil's in you still!" Vash muttered, rubbing his hand. "Get into the saddle, and may the dogs bite me if I don't carve your ribs there. To fight on a horse—that's the best way. Only sheep-herders fight on their feet."

A smile touched Charny's thin lips. With the red glow of sunset on his half-shaven head, his dark eyes seemed on fire.

"Well, what will you do?" Vash asked irritably. "Don't you see that I'm your prisoner? Do you want me to take grass in my teeth?"

"Do what you like." Charny picked up the other's sword and sheathed his own. "I'm not going back to Zarit to be strung up on a rope."

---

*The trampled earth in front of a tavern door where Cossacks were likely to be found asleep in the morning.

"Well, I can't go off into the steppe without a sword. Now listen, you aren't my captive any longer, that's clear. I won't try to take you back there." Vash's tufted mustache twitched in a grin. "Allah, they say His Highness the lieutenant howled when you kissed his hide with the whip. It's all one to me. Only give me back the sword."

He held out his hand. "Faith of a Cossack. I pledge faith by all the Cossack brotherhood, alive or dead, out yonder." And he motioned to the north and east, to south and west.

He had served, that Vash, in the wars, and his oath was the oath of a Zaporogian—of a free Cossack who had once belonged to the great war encampment of the *siech*. If he gave his word as a Zaporogian, it would be trusted.

Charny handed him back his sword.

"*Aya tak*," he said, "Aye, so. Now give me water from that jug."

Vash sheathed his sword and stared.

"Water! Would I carry water with mother Volga flowing under my snout?"

And, remembering the brown boat's sail on the steppe, Charny laughed. Truly his head had been bitten. Ten minutes later the Cossacks and the horses were drinking at the bank of the wide gray river that flowed soundlessly between borders of high rushes. Charny thrust in his head, snorting, and wringing the water out of his scalp lock. The burning fire left his brain, and all at once he felt ravenously hungry. He found Vash sitting his horse on a sand mound that rose above the rushes. The Cossack of the patrol had barley cakes in his bags, but both of them felt the need of meat or gruel.

With experienced eyes Vash studied the river in the deepening twilight. Swallows flitted overhead; out in midstream a log raft drifted without lights, although the deep notes of a boatman's song came from it over the water. On the far side the gray banks were turning black. Upstream he made out the blur of some large islands. But he shook his head.

"Not a tavern: not a fishing boat. Nothing to eat here."

"Yonder's a fire," observed Charny. He knew nothing of the Volga, but he had been born in the steppe and he had noticed what the other had missed: the thin glow of firelight against trees upstream near the islands.

"Gypsies, it may be." Vash nodded. "Well, God gives."

As they rode north, keeping to the hard ground above the rushes, he explained that this portion of the steppe was deserted except for a few Summer huts of *burlaki* or river-men. Gypsies sometimes followed the river trail. Farther north bands of river pirates haunted the shore, rowing out from inlets to board and capture cargo boats, killing the crews and setting the vessels afire after carrying off what they wanted. To the south near Astrakhan Tartars raided across the Volga in the Winter, to seize cattle and slaves in the villages. Richly laden merchant vessels sailing down river, or carrying salt and fish and sealskins north again, passed this region without stopping.

"We only kill flies," grumbled Vash. There was no support for the Cossacks of the Zarit patrol, except to pick quarrels with the governor's militia. "And kiss the cowgirls when there are any along the river."

It was almost dark by the time they approached the fire, and Vash drew rein with an exclamation. The place seemed to be a large encampment without tents or huts. Along the shore in the firelight some two-score men sat at meat around three smoking pots. Most of them were armed with short sword and pistol, while pikes were stacked in military fashion. A few of them, in fine clothes, looked like Russians. And Vash noticed these had no weapons, although there were two women in their number.

Among the crowd he made out Kalmuks in white felt hats and a scattering of *burlaki*.

"There's no wagon train, no horses," he muttered, spitting out the sunflower seeds he was chewing.

Charny, who was hungry, urged his horse forward. As they came down to the shore some of the men rose to meet them.

"Whose men are you?" demanded Vash.

The strangers made no answer. They stared at the horses, and one went to the top of the rise on which the fire had been built to peer into the darkness behind the Cossacks. Someone else threw a dish of grease on the flames, which soared up, hissing, lighting up the shore.

Vash noticed a figure in a priest's hat and veil seated by the women, who had bold painted faces and the physique of Amazons. At least three of their companions wore the fur-trimmed garments of boyars—noblemen. But these, although they looked curiously at the patrol rider, had nothing to say. Perhaps they spoke only Russian and did not know the Cossack speech.

"Well, people," Vash remarked, "is there no one to bid us to sit down to bread and salt?" The odor of mutton and garlic tickled his nostrils.

A tall man in a red Tartar *khalat* rose from his place and came over to the Cossacks. He had curly hair the color of wheat, and he bore himself as if accustomed to command. With his hands thrust in his girdle he inspected Vash and Charny without haste.

"What seek ye?" he asked curtly. He spoke in the fashion of the Muscovites, like a boyar.

"We are riders of the Zarit patrol—" Vash stretched a pointed to include Charny "and, by Allah, we want to set our fangs in meat."

"Well," said the tall boyar, "I am Kolmar, the lieutenant of Astrakhan, and I have no meat for you thieving dogs." He spoke to one of his followers and turned back to the fire.

Vash glanced anxiously at Charny, who had horsewhipped the lieutenant of a smaller town after drinking brandy. It would not do, he thought, to try that game with this Kolmar. Cossacks would not have turned a hungry man away from such an abundance of food: but these chaps seemed to be Muscovites with a following picked up along the river.

Charny, however, was more interested than angry. Suddenly he reined his horse forward, passing Kolmar and halting to stare at the women and the priest.

"If you have no food for us of the steppe," he said slowly, "give us at least a blessing, little father."

Some of the men laughed, and the bearded priest turned his head as if troubled. Hastily he raised his hand and muttered something.

"Get out!" said the Lord Kolmar softly. "And if you show your head this night you will taste a bullet."

One of the women cried out shrilly but Charny wheeled his horse and trotted off. He headed straight away from the river, as Vash joined him, and kept on until he was beyond the last of the firelight. Then he halted and sat motionless.

"The ox tails—the stall cattle!" muttered Vash. "They had white bread and kegs of mead enough for a barrack. But then they're Muscovites, and God made them so they can't see beyond their whiskers."

"Kegs and chests they had," Charny observed thoughtfully.

His eyes by now were accustomed to the gloom. A half-moon, low over the river, shed an elusive light. To Vash's surprise, he began to quarter the ground at a hand pace, bending down to inspect the light patches of sand between the clumps of dwarf oak and *saxaul*.

"There's no bread here," Vash remarked after he had grown tired of following his champion about.

"Nothing," Charny agreed. "Only the tracks of men who came out of the wood. No carts, no horses, and no tracks of many people."

For a moment a chill of dread touched the Cossack of the patrol, who had all the superstition of those who ride the steppe. Kolmar and his people had food chests and cakes with them, and they could not have carried such things on their shoulders. In fact, they did not seem to have passed over the surface of the steppe. And Vash had seen no sign of a boat. They were there on the shore, waiting by that fire, as if they were dead souls who haunted the river in the hours of darkness. He thought of the florid faces of the women, and the silent priest, and glanced over his shoulder uneasily. True, they were not like honest folk of flesh and blood.

But spirits did not boil mutton over a huge fire, nor did they slake their thirst with honey-mead. Moreover, Kolmar had been a true boyar, ready to blaze away with powder and ball. No, they must have landed from a riverboat, although why they should have done so on this deserted stretch of shore Vash did not know.

"The fire," Charny said softly. "Did you see where it was?"

Hastily Vash glanced over his shoulder, half expecting to find the fire moving away somewhere. But it still flared and smoked on the rise by the shore.

"Devil take it!" he grunted. "Haven't you ever seen a fire before?"

"Not like that."

Vash reflected that he himself would have built a fire in a hollow out of the wind, where it would not catch the eye of roving Tartars. Or, to cook meat, he would have made a small fire between rocks and let it die to embers. But these men made a blaze as if to signal down the river.

"Well, they're Muscovites," he responded. "And they have women to keep warm. Why shouldn't they kindle up?"

Then he started. They had been walking the horses slowly down river, when Charny's mount shied away from a clump of *saxaul*. Something slipped out of the shadowy thicket and sped away soundlessly.

Charny went after it in a minute, lashing his horse through the brush. By the time Vash caught up with him the Cossack had dismounted and was wrestling with a dark figure. A knife flickered in the moonlight as Charny caught the arm of his antagonist and jerked. Charny had muscles of pliant steel in the hundred and eighty pounds of him, and the figure went down on the sand.

Jumping from his saddle, Vash was going to kick the stranger in the head—because a knife in the dark is more to be feared that any sword.

But Charny pulled him back and spoke to the stranger, who made answer in a whisper.

"It's a woman," muttered the Cossack of the patrol, bending down. "A girl. Eh, she's pretty, too. A dove. *Hi—hop!*" He began twirl his long mustache.

"Shut up!" grunted Charny. "She's a Gypsy, and she can take us to some food."

"But—"

Charny took the rein of the black horse in one hand, and he twisted his other fist in the end of the Gypsy girl's long, loose hair. She was barefoot, with a sheepskin *chaban* over her slender shoulders, and she led them swiftly toward the river.

"But," whispered Vash, coming up, "look out for yourself. These Gypsies are witches. They know how to lay spells. They can cut your heart out of your body."

The Gypsy girl laughed softly, hearing this. She did not make any effort to escape from Charny until she scrambled down into the gloom of an oak grove, with a warning cry that sounded like a night bird's.

It was answered from below, and the Cossacks saw that they were at the river's edge, a long musket shot upstream from the fire of the Muscovites. Beneath them, a timber raft was tied to the shore. On the raft whispers sounding faintly and bare feet moved over the logs.

"My people," explained to the girl. "They are honest folk, O my falcons."

Vash doubted this. It would bring bad luck, he thought, to follow this girl of the night. Charny, however, let go the girl and leaped down to the raft.

"I am Yamalian," a gruff voice greeted him. "What would you, Cossack?"

"I," Charny answered, "am a masterless man from Zarit with a stolen horse, and this comrade of mine is a fugitive who has kissed just one girl too many. Give us bread and salt."

A chuckle came out of the darkness.

"Be welcome."

The Tsigans—Gypsies—being horse traders and singers, were on good enough terms with the border Cossacks, who liked to hear the tales they brought up and down the river. They knew more, even, than the Yiddish traders, although how they got their tidings remained a mystery. They drifted over the steppe with their carts and strings of ponies, their hags and children; some of their girls, like Makara who had guided the Cossacks to the raft, were beautiful and fiery in spirit.

Yamalian had two of his sons on the raft. While the Cossacks ate hugely of his kasha and bread washed down with Vash's brandy, the old Gypsy explained they were on their way south to Astrakhan where they would sell their logs and spend the Winter months when the Volga was frozen. They had tied up to the bank for the night.

"Now tell the truth," Charny demanded. "What did you steal from the Muscovites down the shore?"

From the raft the mound with its blazing fire was in plain sight over the fringe of rushes at the shore. Most of Kolmar's man had disappeared, but the women with their boyars and the priest were still to be seen. The Gypsies had not even a lantern on the raft. The only light came from the moon piercing the branches of the oaks.

"Eh, from them—nothing." Yamalian sounded sincere enough and Makara laughed a little.

"How did they come?"

"By boat, in two *saiks*. This morning they passed the raft, O my falcon. Now the *saiks* are hidden in the rushes."

"As you were are hiding in the shadow—why?"

"Because I am afraid."

"When was a Tsigan afraid of darkness? And when did nobles of the north journey with their women in open *saiks*? What kind of priest gives a blessing like a fisherman? Eh, tell."

"I'm afraid. The fate of every man is in God's hands."

"Of what are you afraid?"

The old Gypsy made no answer, but the girl, Makara, said defiantly—

"The red cock."

Charny only shook his head impatiently. Vash, who had been chewing sunflower seeds and spitting them out, leaned forward, startled.

"Eh, the red cock will crow?"

"Before the first light," assented the girl.

"Here?"

"At the fire."

"What is this red cock," demanded Charny, "and his crowing?"

Vash felt for the brandy jug and took a long swallow.

"River pirates," he whispered. "Red hands. After they have attacked and slain, and taken out what they wish, then they kindle up with fire, and the boat goes burning down the river. They say it is the red cock crowing. Allah, we would have had more than bread in our gullets if we had sat down with them."

Many things became clear to Charny—the two score armed men waiting on the shore, their boats concealed in the high rushes. He wondered why they should sit by a fire and why some of them wore the dress of noblemen.

"Red hands down from the north," muttered Vash. "But that Kolmar is a nobleman, devil take me if he isn't. What are the women for?"

Yamalian chuckled.

"Are you a Cossack, to ask?"

"But they're dressed up like peasants, and this Lord Kolmar of Astrakhan has on Tartar rags. Eh, why?"

Makara, who had been watching Charny, leaned forward impatiently.

"When the red hands work, keep your tongue between your teeth."

It did not please the stocky Cossack to be spoken to in this manner by a girl.

"Well," he snorted, "you were spying on them. What did you find out?"

But she shook her head. Charny, the one who had run her down and thrown her to the ground—who had stolen a horse fit for a prince—was the one she wished would look at her.

"What is that?" Charny demanded of Yamalian.

Far up the river a pin-point of light appeared. Presently it vanished, to reappear again.

"It's a boat, the *Kniaz*."

"May the dogs bite me!" Vash clutched at his head. "How do you know?"

Yamalian did not see fit to explain how tidings of the ship's approach had crept down the river ahead of it. He knew the talk of the river-men, the whispers that passed up and down the broad river—and Makara had ears like a cat.

"A rich ship," Vash muttered to Charny. "The last one down before the ice closes up north—for Astrakhan at the Volga mouth, with gold and gear, powder and arms and merchants' goods. *Hi-hop!* The red hands know. They are waiting like wolves." He turned to the Gypsy. "Where's your skiff?"

In spite of the instant protest of the men on the raft, Vash searched until he found a small skiff tied to the logs.

"It's devil's work Kolmar and his lads are about," he explained. "There are honest folk on the *Kniaz*. I'm going to warn them."

"Nay, Falcon," Yamalian objected. "They have cannon, muskets. What harm to them?"

"The devil only knows." Vash considered and shook his head. "It's clear those red hands came to wait for them. Now I must go out on the water and tell them to keep away from the fire. Plague take Makara—if it wasn't for her I would not be able to go."

Charny entered the skiff with him, and a Gypsy took the oars. Yamalian had whispered to him to look out for the skiff. Just as they pushed off the girl jumped in beside Charny.

"See how she loves you," Vash grumbled. "But it's bad luck having her along on the water."

The girl, however, showed no inclination to be put back on the raft.

"*Nà kòn!*" Vash cried. "Make haste."

They met the *Kniaz* about a league upriver. First the patch of square sail, half furled, showed in the moonlight and then the blunt bow of the small bark—that was a large ship on the Volga. A great lantern on the break of the afterdeck gave the light that Charny had seen at first. Little air was stirring, and the ship barely had steerage way in the current. A sailor in the bow took soundings steadily, for the shifting channel and submerged islands made the river treacherous.

"*Hai!*" Vash stood up to hail. "Who commands here?"

"Keep off, you swine!" retorted the leadsman.

Heads began to show along the rail. Light came from the ports of the after castle, and the light wail of a violin ceased. Someone shouted at the skiff in Russian, and a sailor repeated it.

"Have you a message?"

"Aye, so. There is danger down by the islands."

"Come over the side. The serene, mighty lord will speak to you."

At a word from Vash the Gypsy swung the boat in, and the Cossacks hauled themselves up by a rope to the shrouds.

They dropped over the rail and stopped, surprised. A seaman held a blazing pine torch close to their heads, and a half dozen soldiers in helmets and breastplates pointed long pistols at them. Behind these guards stood three officers—one the stout Muscovite ship's captain, another a young ensign in a green uniform, and the third a dry little man who held himself stiff as the gold-headed cane he carried.

"Halt!" he snapped, and put a round piece of glass in his eye to look at them. He said something they did not understand, and the green ensign translated.

"Tell your names, occupations, your master's name and your business upon the river. But first lay down your swords on the deck. It is forbidden to come over the side with small arms."

Instead Charny took a step forward.

"Allah! We have come to warn you."

The officer of the glass gave a second command, and the ensign explained:

"I should count four, and if at the count of four you have not laid down your weapons my men will shoot you. Come now, fear God! One-two-"

The Cossacks exchanged glances. On land they could ever run for it, but here on the cramped deck with the water behind them they were helpless. With a mutter of anger Vash drew his saber and dropped it, while Charny laid his down silently. The ensign picked up the weapons, and the guards lowered their pistols.

It seemed to the Cossacks as if the men on the *Kniaz* were marionettes, bobbing up and down at the pull of invisible strings. First he of the eyeglass snapped out words, then the green ensign sang them out like a parrot, and the seamen ran about or barked orders. Vash peered over the bow and saw that they were approaching the dark blur of the wood where lay the Gypsy raft.

"Look here, Excellencies," he explained, "the devil himself is squatting down behind that bend. Only listen—"

Hastily he told of the meeting with Kolmar and his armed band, of the watch fire and the tidings of the Gypsies.

"May the hangman light my path if they aren't red hands—pirates. If you don't want your hides ripped, keep to the other side of the islands until you are past the fire."

The dry little man glared behind his glass and snapped out questions as a sap log shoots sparks. He ordered Makara and her brother up from the skiff and questioned them without result, because the Gypsies were afraid of the officers.

"What is the name of the leader of this band?" He demanded finally.

"Kolmar, lord lieutenant of Astrakhan." Vash made answer.

The green ensign scowled.

"That is a lie. Here stands his High Well-Born Excellency, Franz, Count of Fugenwald, who has been appointed Lord Lieutenant of Astrakhan by his Imperial Majesty, the tsar of all the Russians."

And he pointed to the erect little German, listening respectfully as Fugenwald rattled forth more long words.

"Moreover, His Excellency says to you that he entertains suspicion aroused by your coming. His Excellency has been warned against the outlaws of the Volga, and he has taken steps to resist them. These four carronades—" the ensign pointed to two pairs of twelve-pounders in position in the waist of the ship—"are charged with chain shot and iron. My twelve men of the Moscow *strelsui* are armed with pikes and pistols, and the twenty members of the crew have swords and axes."

"But for God's sake, go outside the islands. Look!"

Vash pointed at the tree-covered islets dead ahead of the *Kniaz*. But when the ship's captain turned inquiringly to Fugenwald, the German ordered him to keep to the inner channel, to pass close to the fire on the mound. Two seamen swung the long tiller over, and the *Kniaz* turned sluggishly toward the land. Fugenwald and the captain went aft to join a young Russian woman who appeared, wrapped in her cape, at the break of the poop.

"A lady!" muttered Vash. "Give us our swords and let us go."

The ensign shook his head.

"Nay. You two mangy dogs won't sneak off until we find out what your game is. If anything happens here, you'll be hung up on the hooks as a warning to all lawless men." He went to the rail to stare at the fire. "Eh, there are people signaling."

"What will they do?" Charny whispered.

It was the first time he had ventured on the deck of the ship and he did not like it.

"God knows." Vash spat out his sunflower seeds morosely. "These guards are militia—captain's a Russian—commander's a German, and the lady's his wife."

He looked around into the unfriendly faces of the pikemen, several of whom still stood by the Cossacks with drawn pistols. No love was ever lost between the Cossacks and the Muscovite militia. Unseen by the men, Makara slipped away along the rail and vanished into the darkness of the cabin passage.

By now the *Kniaz* was almost abreast of the fire and drawing in toward shore. Fugenwald was holding a spyglass to his eye. Charny climbed up on the spars amidship to see better.

In the firelight on the bank the two women, the priest and the boyars waved and shouted at the ship. One of the men ran down the mound, as if to throw himself into the water. And the cries of the women became distinct.

"Aid! Aid for the lost! Take us in, good people!"

The Countess Fugenwald was urging her husband to send ashore for these castaways who looked like nobles.

"In God's name!" The voice of the priest came over the water. "We were seized and robbed by lawless men. We have nothing left."

Shading his eyes from the lantern light, Charny studied the shore. The chests had vanished, and there was no sign of Kolmar or his men. Nor could he see any trace of the long boats. He glanced around for Makara, but she had disappeared.

Then came a rumble and splash from the bow of the *Kniaz*. The anchor was down, and the bark turned slowly in the channel, until the sail flapped lazily and it brought up, opposite the fire.

"What now?" Charny demanded.

"They've tied the vessel. They're going to send a small boat to the shore to talk to her friends. Hi—wait!"

But the tall Cossack was down from the spars and up the afterdeck ladder with long strides. Grasping the burly ship's master by the arm, he swung him around.

"Eh, haven't you a nose to smell a trap? Loose the boat. Take a whip to her."

Removing his clay pipe from his bearded lips, the Moscow captain pointed with it toward the rail. Seamen stood by the two port carronades with lighted matches in their hands. The pikemen, fully armed, manned the rail, where torches smoked and flared.

"Where's the trap?" The captain growled. "You've been licking the pig this night, my man."

"He wished to turn us aside from rescuing these poor souls," echoed the Russian lady. Pearls glimmered softly on the collar that bound her throat.

Charny went to the rail and stared down. With two sailors, the young ensign was entering Makara's skiff to go to the shore to bring off the priest and the nobles. The ensign stood up, as the skiff pushed into the forest of rushes as high as a man's head along the shore.

And then with a splash a length of the rushes fell down. Orange flashes lighted the faces of the ensign and the two sailors as firearms roared and smoke swirled. A man screamed, and two portions of the rushes began to move toward the side of the *Kniaz*, a stone's throw away. Down in the gloom between the fire on the shore and the torches on the ship the two dark shapes drew nearer with oars swinging at their sides, and men tearing apart the screen of rushes that had hidden the two longboats. But the bodies of the ensign and the two seamen were visible, sprawled in the skiff.

"*Sarin na kitchka!*" voices roared from below. "Death to the white hands!"

Then the pirates were alongside the bark, throwing grapnels over the rail, clutching at the shrouds. Pistols blazed up from the side, and powder wreaths dimmed the torches.

"O Mary, Mother!" cried the Russian woman.

The captain let fall his pipe, shouting hoarsely. No one had fired the cannon, which could not have damaged the boats beneath them. Fugenwald, with an oath, clutched at his sword. But his commands, in German, went unheeded.

Something cold and hard was thrust against Charny's hand, and he gripped the hilt of his saber. Makara had brought it to him, her dark eyes aflame with excitement.

"Strike, Cossack!"

It passed through Charny's brain that even the Gypsies could not fly from the ship. They were all in it together.

"Down with the torches! Shoulder to shoulder. Strike, lads!"

His voice cut through the tumult, as a sailor with a torch staggered and dropped, his face smashed in with an ax. The remaining torches were hurled down into the *saiks*, leaving only the great lantern in the moonlight.

"Back from the rail, you dog-brothers," Vash roared. "Behind the spars with you, bull-tails!"

The Muscovites pikemen, after discharging their pistols into the gloom—their eyes had been dazzled by torchlight—were struggling clumsily at the rail, their long-shafted weapons of little use against the short pikes and knives of the Volga outlaws. Some of the sure-footed sailors were making good play with axes, but the pirates were coming over the rail with a rush.

Kolmar appeared in the shrouds, pistol in one hand, sword in the other.

"Slash the white hands, lads," he laughed. "Ho, women and gold for a frolic!" And, throwing back his head, he howled like a wolf.

Charny had been snorting and stamping with growing eagerness. This fighting at hands' strokes was to his liking.

"Make way for a Cossack!" He called, vaulting the poop rail. "*U-ha!*"

With both knees and the hilt of his sword he struck a Volga man, knocking him to the boards and slashing his body open below the ribs as he rose, dodging the thrust of a pike. The shaggy *burlak* raised the short pike to throw it, but the Cossack's saber whizzed, and the curved blade took off the man's hand.

"*U-ha!*" Charny's war shout. "Come down wolf, and you will howl—"

Kolmar had seen his two men fall, men of the *Kniaz* rallied to Charny's leadership. He hurled the pistol that he had just fired and jumped down into the clear space between the end of the spars and the afterdeck. Snarling, he made at Charny, swinging a heavy cutlass.

Twice he cut at the Cossack's head, and twice he was parried. They were under the lantern, their backs guarded by their men on either side.

When Kolmar felt the weight of the Cossack's blade, he crouched warily.

"Fool," he called softly. "There's gold and gear under your hand. Come over to us. To the fish with the white hands!"

But Charny's saber flashed above his head, dripping blood.

"Your head will go first to the fish," he retorted, laughing.

The voice of Kolmar was the voice of the nobleman, and Charny was not minded to trust a voice any longer. He leaned back as the cutlass swept inside his blade, the point tearing across his chest. Instantly the leader of the outlaws cut down at his knees, and Charny jumped.

"Ho, the Cossack dances!" Kolmar shouted, pressing him.

A pistol roared near Charny, and he had the stench of powder in his throat. He parried a cut, and twisted his blade along about Kolmar's cutlass, locking the hilts and thrusting up. For a moment the two men strained, shoulder to shoulder, steam rising from Kolmar's yellow head. His utmost strength could not force down the Cossack's arm. But his free hand felt at his belt and rose with a knife.

Charny saw the thrust of the knife, felt the steel rip over his shoulder—and wrenched himself free. Kolmar's cutlass slashed down at him, but struck harmlessly against his side, all the force taken from the blow. For the Cossack's blade got home first on the man's bare head, splitting it above the jaw.

Kolmar dropped to his knees, when Charny struck again, severing the spine behind the ears, cutting the head from the body.

"Here's for you, red hands," he called, and caught the smoking head from the boards to hurl it among the Volga man.

A Kalmuk ran at him, but a stocky figure brushed him aside. Vash fought off the Kalmut, shouting:

"*U-ha!*—the Cossacks are dancing. Join in, brothers."

The rush of the outlaws had been stopped at the spars, while the rest of the crew had had time to come up. Some of the armored Muscovites were down, and the rest were fighting with desperation, seeing death at hand. Sight of their leader's head flying through the air brought the Volga men to a stop, and when Charny and Vash pressed around the end of the spars they gave way.

"Come on, dog-brothers," Vash urged.

The curved swords of the Cossacks rose and fell. The outlaws, leaderless, began to drop into the boats. Some leaped the rail, into the water, and climbed into the *saiks*, and in a minute they were clear of the deck, except for the groaning wounded who were soon silenced by the axes of the crew. Mercy was unknown on the Volga.

From the boats the outlaws retreated to the mound, beyond pistol shot. Charny was sitting, panting, on an overturned keg, when he saw Fugenwald striding past and heard a command. With a blinding flash and roar the two carronades were fired, the chain shot and scrap iron sweeping the knoll, scattering the surviving outlaws into the darkness. Only the bodies of three or four men were visible by the fire.

"Eh—" Vash grinned—"His High Mighty Excellency is starting to fight when everything's over. But it was you, dog-brother, who sent the red hands off howling."

"The head," Count Fugenwald explained precisely, "of the man Kolmar has been identified as that of a renegade and a river slayer who has shed blood like water in the northern district. From the scene of his crimes he fled into the steppe. He had the wits of a noble and the cruelty of a Kalmuk. It is apparent now that he laid a trap for this ship, dressing up five of his followers—for two women came with him into the steppe—in the garments of others he had put to death. So, by the discipline of my militia and the destructive fire of my two carronades, we are victorious over the notorious Kolmar and his band."

Approvingly he tapped his eyeglass on the paper in front of him. He was seated on the afterdeck, and the morning mist was clearing away from the *Kniaz*, still at anchor in the river, gray under the first light.

Behind him in the place of the dead lieutenant stood the Russian ship's master who translated his Excellency's words to the two Cossacks who stood before him, silent but with restless eyes.

For an hour the whole ship had been ransacked for the jeweled collar and other valuables of the countess, which had disappeared during the tumult. Nothing had been found.

"However," went on that count, "you two lads bore yourselves well. I commend you and reward you—so!"

He picked up the paper that bore his seal and folded it, handing it to Vash.

"I have written," he explained, "to His Excellency the Governor of Astrakhan to free you, Vash, from patrol duty and bestow upon you the ranking of sergeant in His Excellency's town guard. As for you, Charny, you assured me that you have no duty except that of caring for His Excellency's horses. So I have suggested that you be raised from groom to master of the Zarit stables."

Vash turned the paper in his hands uneasily and passed it to Charny, who looked at it thoughtfully and tucked it into his belt. Both Cossacks were looking over the side, where a log raft was drifting slowly past the *Kniaz*. Behind the raft floated a skiff, and on the raft stood two horses, stamping restlessly. One was a black charger, the other a piebald pony, and their saddles had been removed. Charny nudged Vash, who found his tongue at last.

"We thank your High Well-Born Excellency," he said eagerly, "and we accept the letter joyfully. But we wish to be sent off in a skiff to that raft. Look, our horses are waiting for us there."

Fugenwald glanced through his glass and nodded amiably. After all, he would come to Astrakhan with a reputation.

The Cossacks climbed down into the skiff with alacrity. A few moments later they leaped from it to the raft, shouting farewell to the Russian seamen who headed back into the current.

"Now, you old son of a dog," Vash exclaimed to the anxious Yamalian, "you wanted to get away with our horses."

"As God lives, I heard you were dead."

"In a sow's ear, we were. Makara saw us on our legs."

"But the shore, my Falcon, it was aswarm with outlaws. Truly, I saved the horses for you."

Vash grunted and turned to confront the Gypsy girl, who would come out of the thatch cabin to look at Charny.

"Eh, little hawk, where have you hidden the pearls you snatched from that Russian dove?"

Indifferently Makara glanced at him: but her dark eyes glowed as she stepped before Charny, the wind whipping her dark hair about her throat.

"Will you take—pearls?" she whispered.

Charny smiled down at her.

"Nay, keep the pearls, little Makara. Pearls for a sword. Now I have had enough of the water. My road is on the land. Swing over, Yamalian, swing east."

When they had saddled the horses, and Charny had landed at a point on the east bank of the Volga, Vash followed him, leading the piebald pony.

"How will you get back again?" Charny asked.

The stocky Cossack pulled at his mustache reflectively.

"Then you're not going to Zarit—" he grinned—"to be master of the stables?"

Charny shook his head and drew Fugenwald's letter from his belt, handing it to his companion.

"Not I. You take it."

"I'm not going back. Too many lords and officers. I'll draw my rein with yours, you brother of a dog." Vash stepped to the river's edge and tore the seal from the paper. Then he tore the paper into pieces and scattered them over the water. "Now they can't make me sergeant of the militia."

Charny laughed joyously.

Witch Woman

Beyond doubt, something troubled the girl Ivga. Like a shadow she appeared in the corners of the rooms where Sergei sat; at times, when he looked at her, she smiled suddenly; at times, she wore her sable coat with the white shoulder knot of the unmarried woman.

Sergei did not notice that. He read much by candlelight, pronouncing the words aloud. And once he found Ivga curled up on the Bokhara rug beyond the light. He asked her why she did not go away.

"Because I like to hear the words read," Ivga explained quickly, "and you are the only one who can read them."

"Do you understand them, Ivga, girl?"

"No, but they sound nice—about the heroes and devils and saints."

Pop Opanas, the priest doctor who wore chains under his cassock, understood women much better than the young Sergei Stroganoff. They became hysterical sometimes, the young ones did, he explained, from loneliness. When Ivga's father had died on the frontier, she had come back with a load of furs and two silent Mordva servants, coming down the river to Chusavaya. Instead of going on to Moskva, she had stayed like a shadow in the rooms.

Thinking about that, Sergei shook his head. "If she is lonely, it would be better for her to go to Moskva."

Pop Opanas agreed. He did not want the fur trader's girl at Chusavaya. When she went out at night to the *ploctyad*—the shrine with the great cross of Siberian marble—he followed her. When she came to the lighted candles under the sheltering roof, she did not kneel down to pray. Instead, she looked at the shrine and touched the cat's skull, which was a talisman to aid women in having sons. Standing so near the candles, her face shone white, as if drained of blood. After she had touched the cat's skull, she went away soundlessly.

"My son," Pop Opanas remarked to Sergei after that, "I have had experience at exorcising devils and watching women. And now I have a mind to warn you, to whom I am beholden for my bread and salt. At times forest spirits take human form, and when they take the shape of a young woman, they are apt to be *lieshy*—marsh spirits. The *lieshy* beckon to men, and they are so lovely that ignorant men pant after them to lay hand on them. These marsh girls flit away, shining with white light, and the men who follow, seeing only the light, are drowned in the marshes. So," said Pop Opanas, sniffing among the cups for the strongest brandy, "if the girl Ivga beckons you in the forest, spit three times and cross yourself before you take a step after her."

Ivga heard him say that, as she heard everything. But Sergei Stroganoff only smiled. Of some things he was afraid, yet not of witch women whom he had never seen. He was afraid of the blood that had dried in the ground of Chusavaya estate, because it had been shed by his fathers in making the Stroganoff estate so wide that in his boyhood he had never ridden over land that did not belong to them. Before the Stroganoffs came with a grant of settlement from the Grand Duke of Moskva, who was now called Tsar of All the Russias, this land and these forests had been the hunting ground of the Mordva, the people of the forests.

He thought of this blood, drying under the earth like seed, to fertilize someday and bring forth evil. From the rivers the Stroganoff family had taken gold, from the forests they had drawn animal fur and timber for Chusavaya town. Chusavaya castle was no more than a log fort. They had taken wool from the herds of sheep that grazed where the forest mesh had been cleared; they were mining silver in the hills. Tatar merchants journeyed to Chusavaya gate to trade; *burlaki*, watermen, flocked in from the Volga, to log along the new river. And Sergei Stroganoff, now heir to the lands, was afraid of blood.

Never willingly did he enter the forest to hunt. He had to do it, because his liege men expected it, and they needed meat. By choice, he kept among his books, for he had no company then except the icons blazing on the silk-hung wall. No loud voices disturbed him. When the Tatars drank and bargained, he called for the stewards to settle prices; when the stewards came to him with accounts, he bade them do as they pleased. In this way he bought himself a time of quiet, shrinking from trouble.

He had little weight in his body, and he stooped from sitting long over books. "The life of the old buck is not in him," the Chusavaya stewards said of the young lord. And they whispered that a weakling would not endure long in Chusavaya, where so many vultures came to roost.

Masterless men and others escaping from debt came to the frontier, and stayed on, eating the food of Chusavaya. Sergei had no mind to send them away. He knew it was time to clear the Mordva people from the nearer woodlands, because their trapping thinned out the game, and he imagined himself driving them off, but he could not bring himself to do it.

The night when he found Ivga astray in the forest, he was hunting deer and boar for meat, with the men of Chusavaya driving the animals down to the river where the archers could kill them. The swift water ran with blood in the evening half-light under the tree mesh, and Ivga appeared at his side, riding one of the best Kabardas, sitting astride the birch saddle like a man. He had not noticed her leaving the stables.

"Ride faster!" she cried at him, touching the Kabarda with the whip. The scarf had slipped from her long hair that streamed behind her as she dodged branches, pressing close to him, her thin face shining with joy.

And Sergei rode faster, although there was no road. Nor did he remember to spit three times and cross himself. The mist of the long evening lay around them, and he felt free to leave the hunt to ride with her, wondering, however, why she had come.

Abruptly they came upon a cluster of bark and thatch huts hidden in the bare birch groves—huts where the Mordva people took shelter from the snow. And Sergei caught her rein, pulling in sharply, saying, "It is dangerous here."

Nothing could be seen of the forest folk, who must have hidden themselves at the sound of horses.

"What is dangerous, Sergei?" Ivga cried.

"The arrows from hidden bows."

Ivga shook her head, the dark hair twisting around her throat. "They will not hurt you here. Nay, at Chusavaya is the danger." Her gray eyes seemed to slant as she looked at him. "Will you protect me, Sergei, from everything?"

Sergei felt like saying yes, of course; but he began to think, and he said, "You are alone, girl, and, as you say, Chusavaya is no fit place for you. It seems to me better that you should go to Moskva."

"It seems to you—" Her eyes fastened upon his. "Do you want me to go?"

Then he felt that he did not want her to go. He said, trying to think about it, "But isn't it better?"

Ivga looked down at her hands. "Was that written in the books you read, my lord of Chusavaya? I am only a girl, I do not know."

When he pulled irresolutely at the Kabarda's rein, she struck his hand with her whip. "You wear more chains than Pop Opanas," she whispered. "Ai, I hear them clank and grind."

Twisting the horse's head, she turned and rode away, using the whip, merging into the gray twilight of the forest. Sergei Stroganoff wanted to ride after her, to hear her voice again, and to make certain she was not hurt riding back to the settlement. Instead, because it was near dark, he turned aside to the river to fetch back the huntsmen and the game.

Before the girl Ivga could leave Chusavaya, Irmak came that night. Sergei heard his shout, "Light up, house dogs! Light up, and break open the wine kegs, for Irmak, the son of the Don, is here!"

In truth, Timofeivitch Irmak brought sunlight and sound with him into the log walls of Chusavaya. For he shone like a sun in the honored guest place under the icons.

He shone with white silk *kaftan* and gold-chased breastplate and pigskin boots, when he sprawled at the table, laughing at his own great deeds in the far northeast. "For I am lord of the sun's rising place," he chuckled, "lord of Sibir, where the white lights dance in the Winter's sky."

"Ay, the bears are white there, and the women are black," his *atamans*—officers—echoed, drinking. These *atamans* and a hundred riders had come with Irmak convoying wagon trains of sable and ermine skins, gold and jade and silks from Cathay, as a gift to the tsar in Moskva. They had come back, they said, because they had no more powder. And how could they rule the new empire of Sibir without gunpowder, from the blasting of which the natives ran away like sheep—Tatars and conjurers, reindeer folk and black people of Cathay?

"There is powder in the arsenal here," Sergei put in. "Take what you need, noble sir, for I have need of little, except for hunting."

Big Irmak lifted his eyes and crossed himself. "God gives such an answer to my prayer, Sergei Stroganoff. Give us that powder and ask what you will in payment . . . except the gifts that are for the tsar's majesty," he added quickly.

"We will serve Sergei Stroganoff!" shouted the *atamans*.

Irmak had not taken off his breastplate. It had a double-headed eagle chased upon it in gold. "For the soothsayers of Cathay consulted the stars and swore that I would meet death only from a two-headed eagle. And such a bird is not in the sky."

He did not add that the steel armor kept him safe from an assassin's knife. An outlaw he had been, with his band, before they ventured east of Chusavaya, to conquer Sibir. And Timofeivitch Irmak, who swore that he had never known his own father, had a quick, hard cunning in him. Always he kept near his hand the long steel *kisten*, or war club, with a spiked ball and chain at the end, that he carried instead of a sword.

"With this steel staff I slew Kuchum Khan," he explained. "So I am lord of his lands. I keep it with me for luck, Sergei Stroganoff."

Sergei's curved saber hung on the wall, and he took it down seldom.

"Aye, it is settled here." The bearded Siberian nodded understanding. "You are settled, with sheep and fisheries and mills. But where are the women?" he added, laughing.

His *atamans* said their eyes had beheld no white woman for five years.

"By right, a woman should pour the wine," Irmak pointed out. "You have the name of a good host, Sergei Stroganoff, yet you have had no woman pour the wine."

Sergei explained that he had no women except the housemaids, who were in their barred room.

"You have Ivga," put in Pop Opanas.

When Ivga was called in, she came with a pearl-sewn net of ceremony over her head, and she greeted the noble guests with a clear voice.

Then, in silence, she poured corn brandy into the beakers held out by Sergei and by Irmak, who stared at her hungrily. "Oh, my," he shouted, "a beauty, a dove!"

And the young master of Chusavaya, hearing this said, knew it was true. As soon as Ivga had gone, the Siberian nudged him, smiling. "It feels good in her arms, hey? Have you a son by her yet?"

When Sergei did not answer, Pop Opanas, well sluiced with brandy, leaned over to whisper to the big Irmak, who emptied his beaker in silence.

If he had come like the sun, Timofeivitch Irmak stayed in the house like a storm cloud. Massive and sure of himself, he gave orders and the watermen jumped to obey. Here was a man who could kill with the beat of his arm, and could reward on an impulse. Here was a true leader of men, Sergei thought, when he tried to read in the solitude of his candlelit chamber. To honor his guest, he had given Irmak the great sleeping chamber with the Venetian glass, from which a hidden stairway led down to the stables.

Even when he buried himself in the chronicles of forgotten men, he could hear Irmak's ringing laugh, and the buzz of answering voices. For Irmak stayed, and Ivga stayed, keeping out of the Don Cossack's way like a shadow with veiled face. Often Pop Opanas held the Siberian conquistador in low talk, and Irmak listened, rubbing his beard.

Here, Sergei thought, is a hard man who knows his own mind, and is a fit lord of Chusavaya with its masterless men. Irmak took most of the stored-up gunpowder; he bargained with the Tatar merchants for their brocades and rugs, and got a low price for Sergei from them. "They know I will nail to the door the skin of a man who cheats me," he laughed, white teeth showing in the tangle of his beard. When he rode over the home pastures, his eyes took in everything. When Ivga poured the wine now, he was silent.

Over the wine, Sergei heard a voice down the table, "He's scented his beard with musk; he knows what women are." And another muttered that Timofeivitch would be a true protector for Chusavaya. A hard soul, with no soft spot.

The first clash with Irmak came after the hunting. The Don riders had gone off with plenty of powder, and came back in a snowfall at the end of the day, tired but gleeful.

"Thirty-six they downed," Irmak told Sergei.

"I see no deer."

The son of the Don laughed. "You will not eat this meat, comrade mine. We cleared the skulking Mordvas out of your woods with bullets."

Stung, Sergei flung words at him, "You —— No good will come of that!"

"How, no good?" Irmak watched him, surprised. "Kill a few and the others will bow to you. Otherwise, I have had native arrows in me, boy. Your title to land is better if sealed with blood than with wax." Contemptuously he nodded, when Sergei did not speak. "You are still wet behind the ears."

Sergei shivered, feeling cold, thinking of the blood that had dried long ago in Stroganoff lands. Thinking himself a coward, while this man at his side with the two-headed eagle on his chest had no fear. This man would survive the frontier, while he, Sergei, would not survive.

The hunting of humans in the forest had stirred Irmak's blood, because he pounded with the *kisten* on the table boards that night and called for music with his meat. Some of his men were singing, telling their exploits. Sergei, looking down the row of scarred, openmouthed faces, could not eat. Pop Opanas sighed contentedly over his brandy, as if pleased with what he saw. "So then we'll be joyful," the priest doctor muttered.

As if the hall of Chusavaya belonged to him, Irmak was calling for music and meat, ignoring Sergei. Irmak knew how to provoke a quarrel, and he had already won one dominion by slaying its master. So thought Pop Opanas, rattling the chains under his cassock.

Then he gasped over his brandy. Ivga had come up to the table, clapping her hands. At this late feast they had not expected her, and at first the men from the Don paid little attention to her. But she came close to the long table opposite the icon stand, clapping her hands, and they saw that she had changed her shape. This Ivga was not the veiled girl who had kept beyond the candlelight at night.

Sergei noticed how her face shone white, as if the blood had been drained from it. Her eyes slanting, half closed, avoided his. Pop Opanas saw how she held the cat's skull taken from the *plochtyad*, and how her woolskin jacket gleamed with the wet of snow, because she had come in from the night. When she stamped on the floor boards, the hair on the priest's skull stirred, because, instead of embroidered slippers, she wore moccasins of deerskin that left wet tracks.

When Irmak saw her, his eyes creased as if searching for a trick. Her long hair tangled about her throat, her jacket swung open, showing her bare throat and the shape of her body under the thin long skirt. She smiled at him, and she made music by singing, stamping in time on the floor, drawing near him and retreating. "Tell me, Brother Eagle, is it far to your home—far to the skies of the Donetz shore?"

One by one, the noisy *atamans* fell silent to listen to a song they knew. Pop Opanas thought, She has changed her shape to a witch woman, to a true *lieshy* coming out of the night to lure men after her with voice and eyes. Crossing himself he spat three times.

Irmak stared at her body under the swaying jacket, and thumped the table with his steel staff. "Be quiet, dogs! She sings for me!"

Then the blood rushed to his head, and he shouted, "To the devil with this! Go up to my room, girl!"

Still smiling back at him, Ivga ran to the door that led to the stair. Irmak poured himself a beaker of brandy and got to his feet. The *atamans* stirred, grinning, to look at Sergei.

"She is the guest of Chusavaya," said Sergei.

Irmak Zark laughed. "She seeks the Eagle of the Don. You heard her, cub. Keep away."

Carrying the beaker without spilling the brandy, he strode up the stair. When he did that, Sergei felt cold and weak. His hand reached to the wall behind him for the sword that was hanging there, and his fingers trembled as he buckled it on, following after Irmak, while Pop Opanas pattered at his heels. No one at the table came after them.

Irmak stood within the open door of the great sleeping room, muttering. The room was empty. On the bed, the ermine coverlet lay smooth.

"Oh, my!" breathed the lord of Sibir.

Although the fire made the room hot, a cold current of air swayed the candle flames, billowing out the damask hanging on one wall. Instantly big Irmak went to it, pulling aside the hanging, seeing the blackness of a narrow door in the wall—the escape stair.

Pop Opanas pushed in front of him, babbling, "*Lieshy, lieshy* beckoning you on! Don't follow her into the night!"

"Lies!" cried Sergei.

Irmak scowled at the priest, who was picking up a cat's skull from the floor. "Witch women and vampires don't sing to the Eagle of the Don. She's only a girl."

But he hesitated long enough for Sergei to push by him down the narrow stair. Jumping clear into the stables, Sergei noticed that the wide door was open—a square of half-light showed—while the horses moved restlessly. One was missing.

"She makes herself hard to catch, the darling," observed Irmak's voice behind him.

The man from the Don was moving quickly, jerking a headstall upon a black horse and mounting without a saddle. He rode first, stooping down, through the low doorway, with Sergei close behind on his own horse.

As the two had guessed, dark hoofprints traced a pattern out toward the forest in the fresh snow. An old moon hung low over the pines, and no snow came now from the clear sky. Sergei felt the bite of the night cold, and kneed his racing horse forward.

He was passing the Siberian when they came under the trees. Swinging hard against him, Irmak forced him over, and a dead branch lashed his head. The pain stung him and drove the cold from him. From shadow to moonglow to shadow he followed Irmak, who had to pull in at times to watch the tracks in the snow. He thought only of reaching Ivga then, and taking her away with him. He did not think of Chusavaya.

"Where is the mad girl heading?" muttered the Siberian as they swept under bare birches. Sergei knew she was heading for the river and the huts where she had ventured before. And out of the birches they galloped into the clearing, seeing her still on her shaggy pony in the moonlight by the blackness of the huts. As if held in her place, she waited for them.

Sergei caught sight of the forest men first, where they crouched around the huts and the trees with their bows. Before he could shout or pull aside, he heard the sough of rope in the air. A loop caught his shoulders, jerking him back from his horse.

He felt snow under his hands, and sound roared in his ears, changing swiftly to the familiar rush of the river close by. The rope pressed on his arm, and he threw it clear, seeing bent figures running at him. He smelled the grease on the bodies of the Mordva men who had trapped him, and Ivga, and the Siberian, who lay twisting on the ground beside him. At the same time he thought, They are frightened and dangerous because so many were hunted down. If they manage to kill the two of us they will not spare her.

Because of the urgent need to calm the Mordva men, he rose, stepping toward them and speaking in the same moment, "Stop, animals, or you will be harmed! Stop and listen to me!"

His voice sounded clear, and his mind assured him that these forest folk could not know yet that they had caught Stroganoff and Timofeivitch Irmak and the girl Ivga; they had caught only three Russians riding as if mad into the forest, and if they listened to him, he knew he could calm them. They were hesitating at his voice, drawing closer together, gripping their bows and spears.

"If you harm us," he argued with them, "three hundred riders will come with guns to hunt you like wolves. If you help us, you will be rewarded."

Out of the corner of his eye, he had seen Irmak rising to one knee, feeling at his belt, as if hurt. Suddenly the big man pulled a pistol from his belt, it flashed and roared, and a man in front of them flopped into the snow.

"Cut! Slash!" the Siberian shouted, swinging up his steel club. Frightened by the shot and the swirling smoke, the forest men chattered, huddling together.

The shot rang in Sergei's ears as if it had been directed at him. The powder fumes stung his nostrils, and his mind told him clearly that unless he struck down this man, he would not live again himself. Now he was no longer afraid of himself, and he gripped his sword hilt, slashing at the steel club.

Irmak turned and struck like a wolf. The spiked ball of the club tore across Sergei's chest, driving the breath out of him. "Now you have earned your death," he heard Irmak say.

When he cut swiftly with the sword, the blade clanged off the plate where the two-headed eagle showed in the moonlight. Throwing himself forward, Sergei tried for the Siberian's head, feeling his blade parried, hearing Irmak laugh. But it made no difference now, to be laughed at. Heedless, he jumped forward to grip the other man and drive the steel sword into him.

Without haste, Irmak stepped back to keep clear of Sergei's grasp. Instead of striking again, the Siberian edged back into shadow, keeping Sergei in the light, seeking with a sure instinct for the instant to crush the slight swordsman with a blow.

Feeling behind him for good footing, he bent his body back from a sweep of the sword. Then, with a crash and a tearing of brush, he vanished. The dark patch of ground on which he had stood showed a black hole of crumbling dirt. Checking himself on the edge of the hole, Sergei peered down at black water rushing below him, thinking that the river bank had caved in here.

The white blob of Irmak's face showed down there; his hand clawed out and his hoarse voice screamed. The steel that he wore, the powder horn and the bullet punch were pulling him under. When Sergei stretched a hand down mechanically, Irmak drew away under the water, downstream.

Sergei stared at the black, rushing water, ice-cold to the touch. For a while he waited, hearing the piping voices of the forest folk, "Ai-ai!"

When he was sure that Irmak would not come out of the water, he walked back into the moonlight and tossed away his sword. The forest men crouched at his coming, wondering at the man who had made the armored warrior spitting fire and thunder walk into the river. But Ivga had gone.

The clearing showed no sign of her, and hoof tracks crisscrossed the snow carpet in a tangle, although he sought desperately for her tracks.

"Which way?" he shouted at the tensely watching Mordvas. And they pointed up the knoll behind the huts. Loosening a purse of gold from his belt, he threw it to them, and ran and caught his horse, turning up the knoll.

No path ran here, and the bare birches closed around him. But dark hoofprints led upward along the ground. The prints circled a nest of boulders and ended where Ivga waited in the gray mesh of the birches with the roar of the river rising behind her. Her eyes fastened on the man, and she pulled back on the reins as if mad. The horse, sensing the edge of the ground behind him, reared, circling. Sergei forced his horse forward and swung his arm around the girl, pulling her across to his knees, holding her tight, although she twisted away from him, staring up at him.

"Ivga!" he said sharply. "Be quiet!"

"You are not the same," she whispered "Your eyes and your voice are different."

"I am the same."

"No." She ceased straining away from him, and he felt her quick breath against his throat. Putting his arm under her wolf skin jacket, his fingers closed hard upon the soft flesh, and she became quiet, quivering. "I wanted to jump into the river," she said, "if one of you came after. Because he . . . and you were bewitched. And I—"

"I was not bewitched, Ivga, girl."

"Ai, you were. Your eyes saw only the runes in the books, your ears heard only the nasty whispering of Pop Opanas, your hands gave away what was yours to scheming men. You called for me to pour wine for your guest, Irmak, who had no such spell upon him. You were afraid."

"Pop Opanas was afraid because you took the shape of a *lieshy* tonight."

"I?" Ivga stared, shaking her head. "I could not go away from you to Moskva. I did not know what to do. Nay, I put on the garments of the road, and went out in the snow to pray at the shrine. I couldn't for the anger in me. Then I think I picked up the cat's skull to throw at you, because of that anger, and when I came in I heard your people calling for music for that beast Irmak. Where is he?"

Holding Ivga's body close to his, feeling the tangle of her hair against his throat, Sergei no longer cared what had happened to Irmak. He thought that now there would be no more blood in the ground of Chusavaya, because he would see to that.

"I ran away because I was frightened in the sleeping room." Her head pressed hard against his, and she sighed. "But where is he now?"

"Drowned."

Suddenly Ivga began to cry. "Ai, that will be a calamity for you. His men will storm—Pop Opanas will say I am guilty, and I am. The tsar in Moskva—" She wiped at her eyes. "Now you are well, and I will go on the road to Moskva to explain."

"No," said Sergei. He did not need to think about that, hearing Ivga's voice so close to him. Her hand touched his face, and she tried to wipe the blood away from it with her hair, sobbing. "Listen," he bade her. "That's little to care about. Let Pop Opanas say Irmak was drowned by a marsh witch. His men will say it was the two-headed eagle upon the steel armor that killed him. And when his body is taken to Moskva, the tsar will have Siberia for his own dominion, will he not?"

Ivga lay quiet under his arm, thinking. "Is all that true, Sergei? You are so wise to think of it. I—I can't read or know such things. I am only a girl."

Sergei laughed, looking at the old moon over her bowed head. "That is sufficient," he said.

Sangar

Chilogir, the second, rather more than two hundred years ago, resembled very much his paternal ancestor, the hero, the sword-slayer. On a bluff overlooking a ford in the Yenesei under the snow summits of the Syansk, Chilogir sat his pony, his eyes alert and inquisitive, his leathern face puckered with interest. Yet Chilogir was not known by his skill with the sword; he was *sangar*, a worker of white magic.

He was a gray-haired gnome, an armored dwarf, whose steel-pointed helmet rose scarcely higher than the bare brush of the snow-covered steppe. He was watching the approach of an enemy.

A solitary Cossack was splashing across the ford looking about him like one who had lost his way, as indeed he had. The Cossack regiment that had been sent from Lake Balkash across the Mongolian marches some thousand miles had been freely bled.

It was by then heading back—what remained of it—with a plentitude of wounds to lick and a few captured horses to drive before it.

Borasun had strayed to look for horses. His own mount was badly lamed by an arrow.

Limping across the ford, he scanned the bluff for hostile heads, and searched the snow for hoof marks. Except at the short ravine in front of him the bank rose from the deep water of the Yenesei and Borasun did not see Chilogir until he had mounted the bluff.

"U-ha, Tatar!" he cried. "I want your horse. As for you, old dog face, I'll drop you in the river like a bird with a broken neck."

"*Alash*!" grunted the Tungusi, edging his pony forward for a rush. Borasun also moved forward to put ground between him and the brink of the bank.

Watchfully, they circled. As Borasun had lost his pistols and Chilogir had not his bow with him, both had drawn their swords.

The Tatar saw a slender Cossack with mild brown eyes, hardly more than a boy, but with a long arm and a straight back. Borasun was the most unruly of the *atamans* of the unfortunate regiment—his regiment that had been ordered to harry the Tatars. Half his childhood had been spent in the forests by the rushing Dnieper, or wandering half naked in the Volga steppe.

He had learned early in life the use of a dozen weapons, and seen his masters-at-arms shot down or planted on stakes by Turk and Tatar. Danger was as the breath in his nostrils. Men said an elf of madness danced in his brain.

Once Borasun had dragged the carpets from a mosque near Stamboul, at the threshold of Bagche Serai itself, and had used the carpets for his horse to trample on. He had taken the silk and cloth-of-silver garments of a Polish knight and put them on, only to jump into a tar barrel to show how little he cared for such things.

It was said of him that he had drunk himself snorting with vodka, had leaped in, with boots and coat, to swim the Dnieper—a thing no sober man would care to do. His inn chimney was a steppe fire, and his chair a saddle.

And now Borasun had turned back across the Yenesei among the Tatars for a horse.

Chilogir rushed, slashing at head and stomach. His scimitar gritted on Borasun's saber and he barely avoided the return sweep of the youth's blade.

"To one of us, death; the other, life," shouted the Cossack. "Come back, toad, I can't ride after you—"

The swords clashed, parted and clashed again. Borasun sent the Tatar's helmet spinning over the bluff into the water. Rendered wary by this, Chilogir circled.

Borasun laughed at him and urged his limping horse forward. This time the old man's scimitar brushed his cheek.

"A good one, that!" Borasun pressed forward. "U-ha!"

The quick turns of the Tatar had brought him too near the edge of the bank. The earth gave away under the pony's hind hoofs. Clawing at the bank, warrior and horse disappeared.

Dismounting, the young *ataman* of the Cossacks went to the edge of the bluff some three spear-lengths above the water. He saw the Tatar pony swim against the swift current toward the ford, an arrow-shot away; but the Tatar gnome with Turkish mail under his sheepskin floundered and sank.

"Well, the horse is gone, no doubt of it," thought Borasun, "and his master will soon be spitting water in —— unless—"

On an impulse—he seldom acted otherwise—the youth leaped in the pool without bothering to rid himself of coat or boots. Feeling under water for the scalp lock of his enemy, Borasun gripped Chilogir and swam for shore. No easy matter that. When at last they lay on the rocks Borasun was foredone and Chilogir as limp as a wet sack of meal.

Presently when the young warrior rose to seek his horse the old Tatar rolled over, vomited and stood up.

"*Hai*," grunted Borasun in surprise, "you don't die easily, dog-face."

As they gazed at each other he burst out laughing, the old man looked so like a besotted grandfather. But the Tatar, after steady scrutiny from his green eyes lifted both hands to his forehead and bent his head to Borasun's girdle.

"For saving my life, I will call you nephew and give to you two such horses as you have not seen before this."

Pointing beyond the bluff, he added:

"Come to my yurt in peace. You will eat and drink like a hero, for no man ever goes hungry from the house of Chilogir, the *sangar*."

Borasun considered how much of treachery was behind this offer and judged there was little. Once in the Tatar's hut he knew the inviolate law of hospitality among the high-caste Tatars would protect him. Moreover he lacked both food and a serviceable horse, the last a serious matter. He trusted to his wits to make his escape unmolested.

If he refused Chilogir's offer he departed on a crippled mount with an empty belly and the certainty of swift pursuit at his heels. Borasun could kill the old Tatar easily enough and leave without being followed. But having half frozen himself to save the old chap's life he was in no mood to strike his enemy, now unarmed.

"So be it, uncle," he said. "Let the horses be good ones."

Now Borasun, having left his saber outside the yurt, drank deeply of fermented mare's milk and sour wine. Seated at the guest's side of the fire in the hut, he gorged himself until he sweated with rich mutton, brought by the ancient woman who was Chilogir's wife—and then drank more. But even so he doubted the evidence of his eyes when the Tatar servants of the master of the yurt brought up the two horses for his inspection.

They were little bigger than ponies. They had horns growing in front of their ears, their hoofs were split like an ox's foot.

"I am bewitched," he cried. "These have come from the devil's stable to pay me a visit."

"They are reindeer, good sir," explained the Tatar, not adding that they were his two driving reindeer, not to be sold or killed for food.

"*Ohai!*" The warrior emptied his bowl and rubbed his eyes. "Uncle, 'tis said magicians ride them. I will not."

"No need. They will draw you on a light sledge. See!" Chilogir pointed out the tent's doorway. "Snow falls. It will lie heavy in the mountain passes. My reindeer will take you where no horse can go—aye, and faster. They run with the wind and the wolves cannot catch them. Thus will you go to your own land."

He bent closer to Borasun, his eyes glittering.

"Remember this. He who lays an evil hand upon my reindeer, who does them harm—he will suffer. He may not escape."

In the smoke from the fire the broad-lined face of the gnome who was Chilogir appeared black and his eyes blazed. They were like the eyes of a cat that sees in the dark.

Borasun crossed himself, then laughed.

"I will do them no harm, uncle. *Hai,* if they go fast, 'twill suit my taste. I ride with the whirlwind."

"Upon their ears is the mark of Chilogir, the *sangar*. If the Tatar folk see them in your keeping, Cossack, they will cut you open like a hare. So will I give you a mark by which it will be known that you are the friend of Chilogir."

From the tent wall behind him he drew a broad leather belt, ornamented with iron images of various beasts. At a sign from him the woman strapped it about Borasun, who regarded it with amusement.

"The little daughter of the house should do me this honor," he muttered. "Where is she hiding?"

"Chi-li is my daughter," said Chilogir. "She is riding over the snow on the steppe toward the setting sun. Aye, she was seized by the fellows of your Kazak regiment. They have taken her away."

Borasun felt for his sword, remembered that he had left it outside and shrugged. The Tungusi were wont to guard the virtue of their women closely. It was not well to meddle with the families of the Tungusi.

But Chilogir had given his word that no harm should come to Borasun, and the Cossack felt that his person was reasonably safe from retribution for the carrying-off of Chi-li.

All the same, the brooding quiet of the old man who was called a *sangar* made the youth rather uncomfortable. So he blustered.

"Was she pretty, this Chi-li?"

"Aye, she was a red flower of the steppe. She had not seen fourteen Summers."

"Well, then, she will not be killed."

The green eyes of Chilogir glittered.

"Where will they take her?"

"Over the passes of the Altai to the Kazak steppe, to Tabagatai, our town by the waters of Lake Balkash."

"And will you go there, my nephew?"

"Where else, uncle? Give me some more kumiss. I will take the road tonight, before cock-crow—"

"Chi-li would give the kumiss, if she were here. *Tchai*, there is nothing but smoke in the place where she sat! On the mare's skin, the white mare's skin by the fire. Ha, my woman, give the stranger hero to drink!"

Whether it was the kumiss—the fermented liquids of the Tatars were heady stuff—or his own drowsiness, Borasun did not know. Certainly he heard the old woman lamenting, wailing like a bereaved she wolf.

Deep though he drank, he felt sure that when Chilogir, the old *sangar*, the white conjurer, made the cry of a falcon a hawk answered, though it was night and snowing. When the Tatar uttered the call of a horse, his own beast whinnied; a wolf howled beside the tent.

"Remember," he heard Chilogir saying from very far, "no harm to my reindeer."

The old man stretched his arms out to the west.

"Chi-li, little daughter, I send the reindeer."

When full consciousness returned to him Borasun was leaning back against the wooden support of the sledge, wedged in with furs over which were placed his saddlebags with a fresh supply of frozen meat. The snow was still falling, making the daylight gray about him. His limbs were numb and his eyes ached.

Ahead of him moved the rump of a reindeer; he could see the antlers of the leader farther on. They were moving over the snow carpet with a long swinging gait that caused the isolated firs to flash past quickly.

Borasun could not see the trail they followed. But at the end of that day when the snow ceased, he could make out the white peaks of the Altai against the gray sky. By the contour of the land he knew he was approaching the pass through which he and his comrades had penetrated into Tatary.

The marketplace of Tabagatai was the meeting-place of many races. Wandering Cossack bands rode thither from the Ukraine; the Kirghiz shepherd drove in his flocks to be sold. Solemn lines of camels stalked through the mob, grunting under their burden of trade from the people of the moguls to the people of the tsar.

Thin-faced Moslems squatted in their stalls beside weapons and silverwork for sale, wrinkling their noses at the smells from the fish stall and the cloth booths of bearded and odorous merchants of Moscovy.

Over the snow, trodden into mud here, the smell of camel and horse-flesh vied with sweating humanity. The inns were places of Rabelaisian orgies.

Before the hearth of one hostelry Borasun matched dice with a bearded Cossack colonel, whose skin was marred by wounds and who was blind in one eye. A bottle of *gorilka* stood on the table between them and Borasun had looked long on the bottle. Luck was running against him and the hot blood was rising in his head.

"The devil's in the dice," the young warrior grumbled. "*Hai*, when I crossed the mountain passes from Tartary I heard werewolves howling in the glens and little children vampires flaming in the darkness. Now my luck is bad."

The Cossack, Balabash, crossed himself and murmured a prayer.

"It is true that unburied children make the worst vampires," he admitted sagely. "They cry and cry and climb up behind you. Then when you aren't looking, *psst*—they are sucking the blood out of your neck! How did you escape?"

Borasun jerked his thumb at the inn yard where a curious crowd was staring at the two reindeer. He had driven his unaccustomed beasts hard, but, being dependent on them for his life, had taken as good care of the animals as was within his power.

They had brought him safely over the Sair Pass where the howling of the Winter wind was indeed much like the cry of wolves and where the phosphorescent wood rotting under the snow resembled a green fire in the shadows.

So, going where a horse could not go, he had outdistanced his fellows, without meeting with them. In fact few of that Cossack *kuren* rode back alive from the killing Winter journey over the mountain passes. Those few had promptly sold what booty they had to the shrewd merchants of Tabagatai, in order to join in the general revelry, and drink to the memory of their departed comrades.

Rather proud of his driving reindeer—no such animals had appeared in the town before—Borasun drove them about the place in great style, enlarging on their virtues.

"See, good sirs," he would bellow at the watchers, "here are horses who go before the wind and run away from werewolves. They eat only moss under the snow and bark and such trash. Oh, they are quite a pair, I tell you. I wouldn't sell them; no, I wouldn't think of it."

Now Borasun felt with an unsteady hand in his wallet.

"May I taste a scorpion, Balabash, if you haven't the last of my gold. Well, here's my hat and coat. I'll stake them and win."

But the goddess was perverse. Borasun's gold-inlaid scabbard went the way of his other garments. His sword he would not wager.

"Two hundred thalers," said a voice at his ear, "for your reindeer."

It was Cherkasi, one of the richest of the merchants, a dealer in slaves. He was from Kiev, and it was said no man could outdo him in a bargain. Moreover, having a great store of goods, he was one of the masters of Tabagatai. He was a very tall man, in a soiled mink coat, with a broad face marked with the smallpox.

"Go back to your scavenging, Cherkasi," grunted Borasun; "this is a place for warriors."

The eyes of the merchant puckered. It was said that he got his start as a camp follower who robbed the dead after a battle.

Instead of answering angrily he smiled.

"Two hundred gold thalers," he repeated, "and when you win from the colonel you can buy back your beasts. Here is the gold."

Flushed and unsteady, Borasun stared at the coins. Then he swept them up and cried to Balabash.

"What say you, good sir, at one throw? Your gold against this?"

The Cossack wiped his mustache and nodded.

"So be it."

Borasun lost. He caught up the *gorilka* flask, emptied it, cast it into the fire and straightway went to sleep on the hearth.

> *When the war is over, poor chap, when the war is over,*
> *You will find, poor fellow,*
> *Your wife gone away from home,*
> *And your hide full of wounds.*

Thus sang Colonel Balabash, spreading his feet to the fire and sighing deeply, for he was a melancholy man.

Awake and sober once more, Borasun left the inn and borrowed two hundred thalers from various comrades. Then he swaggered off to the *serai* outside the town wall where Cherkasi kept his pack-animals, his retainers and slaves.

Now reindeer are unusual beasts—peculiar that is, to those who do not understand them. The merchant did not know how to handle the halter-cord that controlled their movements and being unfriendly to animals he did not make any progress with the two deer, who at once became very stupid and obdurate. They would not go where he wanted, nor would they stay when he left them.

Finally, assisted by Kirghiz caravaneers and his henchmen, Cherkasi beat, tugged, and lashed them into the *serai*, where they stood trembling. He wore heavy boots, and the limbs of a reindeer are frail.

Borasun walked through the entrance in the rock wall and growled under his breath when he saw the evidence of mistreatment on the hides of his two pets.

"Here are your two hundred thalers," said the warrior. "I will take back my reindeer."

The merchant sidled forward as Borasun reached for the driving cord.

"Nay, what would you do, Cossack? The reindeer are mine. They are rare beasts, and I will take them to Kiev to sell at a good profit."

"*Hai*, but look here. You said if I had two hundred gold pieces I could buy back the reindeer. Here is your money."

Cherkasi smiled.

"Nay, Sir Cossack. I said if you won from Balabash you could have them back. You did not win. They are mine. Does an *ataman* break his word?"

Scowling, Borasun fingered the wallet.

"Listen to me, you greasy-fingered flesh-seller," he said at last. "These animals saved me my life back yonder in the wilderness. I'll not have them thrashed by a fellow like you. How much do you want for them?"

"From you, nothing. If they are worth so much to you, they are to me. I have some Osmanli lords of Chatagai coming to look at the women your fellow soldiers have transferred to me in trade. They have never seen such deer. They will pay a good price. I will not sell them to you—"

"You rat!"

Borasun's saber was out in a flash. Cherkasi had been waiting for that. He shrank back, calling over his shoulder. Desire for revenge for the hard name Borasun had given him in public outweighed even the chance for gain, at present, in his mind. A half dozen armored soldiers, retainers of the merchant, ran forward at his signal.

"U-ha!" shouted the Cossack. He warded a blow from one of the servants, and cut the man down. A pistol cracked from the group, but Borasun advanced on them, his lean face dark with rage.

"A Cossack fights!" There came a shout from behind him. "Cut, slash!"

And the old Colonel Balabash jumped across the *serai* wall, swinging his saber. Cherkasi raised a cry for help and men were heard running toward the place.

"What is it?" demanded Balabash, ranging himself beside Borasun.

When he heard—for the retainers had drawn back a pace, reluctant to match blows with the two warriors—he became thoughtful.

"This is a knot you can't pick with your sword, *ataman*," he whispered. "Cherkasi is a dog, but he bought the reindeer. If you kill him or his men, he will appeal to the governor of the town. You struck the first blow—"

"One of his men struck first, on my oath!"

"No matter. The governor and the merchants do not love us Cossacks, after they have bought our spoil. They'll hang you off the walls for the kites to dine on. Sheathe your sword and come away."

He was forced to pull the slender Cossack off toward the gate. Borasun called back:

"Harm those beasts and a curse is on you, merchant. That was the word of a magician, Chilogir—"

He shook off the elder's hand and strode past the tents of Cherkasi. The flap of one fell open, and a pretty brown face peered out at the two warriors.

"Chilogir!" Borasun heard a whisper. "*Ai-a*, you wear the belt of Chilogir, my lord. Tell me, what of him? I am Chi-li."

Borasun paused and scratched his head, without heeding the snarls of the merchant at his back. He could not remember where he had heard the name Chi-li. Once, when he had been drinking, it was. She was said to be pretty, he reflected. Well, so she was.

He surveyed the wasted brown cheeks, and the quick eyes under which were deep circles. He could not remember who Chi-li was.

"Whose woman are you, little sparrow?" Balabash asked, twirling his mustache.

"Mine," cried the shrill voice of Cherkasi. "Mine, bought from one of your own comrades, Borasun, for three hundred and twenty thalers. Get along with you! She is my slave and I will sell her to the Turkish lords who pay well for women of other races—"

Perceiving the mute appeal in the eyes of the girl, Borasun could but shake his head. Something that he had meant to do for Chi-li—well, he must have dreamed it.

Seeing that she was staring at his broad leather girdle ornamented with iron images, Borasun unbuckled it and handed the belt to her.

"Keep this thing, then, Chi-li," he grunted.

"So, Cherkasi," murmured Balabash, "you would sell this handsome little mouthful to a Turk, eh? Have you any bowels?"

The merchant refastened the flap of the tent hastily, muttering under his breath. Balabash watched him angrily, and observed,

"How much will you take for her?"

Cherkasi spat and was heard to say to himself that he would have no dealing with such dogs of the steppe.

"Dogs!"

Balabash had his saber halfway out, when Borasun, grinning, caught his arm.

"Have you forgotten the governor and his kites so soon, good sir?"

"True!" The colonel shrugged and linked his arm in that of his comrade. "Cherkasi, you call yourself a Christian, may the devil eat me if you don't. Some day the devil will call you a liar."

So they went off to the inn, being hungry. Already Chi-li, if not the reindeer, had passed from their minds although their hands itched to get at Cherkasi. Behind them a trembling girl stared from the belt to the slit in the felt tent through which she could see the picketed reindeer.

It was toward the end of the second watch of the night and even the bazaar dogs were quiet when Pan Pishnivitz knocked at the inn door. Being a mild man, a Pole, with a secret sense of his own importance as lieutenant of the *voevod*—the governor of Tabagatai, the knock was discreet yet firm. Amid the babble of voices from within it was not heard. Pan Pishnivitz knocked again, more loudly, and felt of the priming of his pistols.

True, he reflected, he had a dozen men at his back, halberdiers and musket men from the governor's castle. And the handful of Cossacks in the tavern were little better than vagabonds—since the country was not at war just then. If Holy Church and the *voevod* and the Empire had been at war and in need of Cossack sabers matters would be different.

So the lieutenant entered with a steady tread and fixed his eye on the hawk-like face of Borasun.

"Cossack," he proclaimed, not without importance, "his Excellency the lord governor of the town and province of Balkash has placed you under arrest to answer for a manifest crime and be punished accordingly." He nodded solemnly, adding: "Be a good fellow, Borasun, and don't stir up a rumpus. If you are to be hanged, you no doubt deserve it; it's your Christian duty to obey the law."

Borasun's black eyes twinkled while he tried to think which of his numerous misdeeds had come to the notice of the governor.

"Is it on account of that dog of Cherkasi's I struck down just before sunset?"

"Not at all, Borasun," replied the lieutenant soothingly. "The dog was a Kirghiz; and he made a pass at you first, I am told. Nay, this is a crime."

Borasun sighed. Luck was a mischievous jade. Already that day Cherkasi had thrown dirt on his beard—or at least on the beard of old Balabash—and he was helpless to take revenge. Moreover Cherkasi was exhibiting his cherished reindeer. Now Borasun was accused of a crime.

He rose.

"What is the charge, Sir Fish—Pish, or whatever your name is?"

"Thieving."

At this the *ataman*'s face flushed dark and the other Cossacks looked up. A group of Muscovite merchants motioned for the innkeeper, to settle their score. Because if there is one thing more than another that a Cossack does not like it is to be called a thief. Blaspheming is the worst crime on his calendar, but stealing is a good second.

A Cossack takes spoil at will; he may fight—preferably with his mates—until the sun is red; he may drink himself staggering, but he will not steal.

So the revelers at the inn stared at the full wallet in Borasun's hand, the gold with which—contrary to Cossack custom—he would not gamble. His mates from the Ukraine knew that it was borrowed, but others did not.

"It is the governor's order," repeated the lieutenant uneasily. "Testimony has been given—"

"What was stolen?"

"The two reindeer bought by Cherkasi, the merchant, and a woman named Chi-li. You and the merchant were at blows about the reindeer, and you were seen by a score of townspeople to talk with the girl and pass something to her, into the tent. Just after nightfall the three vanished as if by witchcraft. You are known to have a quarrel with Cherkasi. Where have you taken his goods?"

"Cherkasi! Does he charge that I am a *thief*?"

The veins stood out on Borasun's forehead and the whites of his eyes turned red.

From the center of the group of men-at-arms Cherkasi, the merchant, lifted his voice defiantly.

"Six hundred—a thousand thalers, I must have out of this Cossack. He swore that I would receive an injury because I kept the reindeer; the girl wore his belt—she has an understanding with him. After nightfall my guard at the *serai* entrance was bowled over by horned beasts and lashed with a whip. Food, furs were taken from the tent of my slaves—most costly furs, gentlemen, I swear. Who ever heard of a slave girl—"

"Oh, we've heard all that before," muttered the lieutenant, who had no liking for the merchant. "And the sledge with the girl went away from all the roads, out on the steppe to the east—"

"This Cossack plotted it, to do me harm. A thousand thalers will not pay for the harm. "

Colonel Balabash rose from his stool by the hearth; his limbs were not as warm as in his youth, and he liked a fire of nights. "Lieutenant Pishnivitz," he said, "the *ataman* Borasun has been by my side since we left the slave sty of Cherkasi. He has had no hand in the escape of the slave. We have been sitting here at the inn since before dusk. Now, sirs," he waved his hand at the Muscovites, "is not this the truth?"

He folded his arms, and his black beard bristled. All those in the room hastened to say that it was the truth. Pishnivitz scratched his head. He had no wish to cross the path of the old colonel, but there was Cherkasi's charge to be disposed of somehow.

Seeing his hesitation, Balabash thrust himself through the soldiers until he faced the merchant, who shrank back as far as he was able. Extending the hilt of his saber under the wrinkled nose of Cherkasi, the colonel roared:

"Smell of that, you jackal—sired spawn of the dung heap. And say whether Balabash lies!"

Cherkasi clawed at his beard and was silent. Satisfied, Balabash returned to his seat by the fire, calling for hot mead to be brought for the soldiers.

After drinking his mead, the lieutenant wiped his mustache and came to a conclusion.

"Good health to you, Colonel. I hope the worthy Cossacks are not angry. I had my duty ——. Now this is what happened. The escape of the woman was the work of magic, of course—"

"And Chersaki would have sold her to a Turk," muttered Balabash.

"White magic, assuredly," nodded Pishnivitz.

"That's it!" roared Borasun, who had been thinking. "I remember now. Chi-li is the child of Chilogir, the Tatar magician. He is calling his reindeer and his daughter to him, a thousand miles away. Cherkasi, the merchant, picketed the reindeer under the nose of the girl who has been their mistress for ten years—"

The Cossacks laughed and piled from the inn to watch Cherkasi, almost beside himself with rage, calling on his servants and armed men to get horses and take up the pursuit of the reindeer somewhere out in the dark steppe.

"They will never overtake reindeer," growled Balabash, whose good humor was restored at sight of Cherkasi's vain search for six hundred thalers.

"I remember, too," assented Borasun, "that Chilogir said misfortune would come upon one who mistreated his reindeer."

"It is true," nodded Pishnivitz sagely. "That was good mead."

"Undoubtedly true," assented Balabash. "Let us have some more of it."

So they departed, singing—

When the war begins, brave chap, when the war begins,
You will find, brave fellow,
That princes give you gold,
And the priest says, "Benedicte."

Beyond the Altai, Chilogir, the Tungusi *sangar*, waited in his tent, until the reindeer he had marked with his mark and sent with the warrior bearing his belt to the place where he knew his daughter would be—waited patiently until his reindeer should return. He knew that they would do so.

Because it is a peculiarity of reindeer that they will not stay with the master who beats them.

The Vampire of Kohr

Snow covered the steppe. Old snow that banked high around the scattered trees and blanketed everything except the dark line of the trail. It formed white caps on the haystacks and on the steep thatched roofs of Gorod town.

Only in the streets of Gorod—a trading town close upon the tsar's eastern frontier—was there smoke and bustle and the chiming of horse bells.

Demid rode into Gorod at noon with a horse between his knees, an empty purse and the ache of hunger beneath his belt. Women who looked twice into his dark face nudged each other and whispered that here was a Cossack coming back from the wars. Tradesmen, glancing at the ragged coat and the shaggy horse, shook their heads, saying that a Cossack was good for nothing except brawling.

But Demid rode on, to the log barracks of the governor's guard, to the smell of hot soup and corn brandy. He dismounted and entered, to stand by the long table where forty men were feeding.

"Eh," he said, "salaam to you. Have you a bowl for a rider from the snow road?"

They grunted and no one made room. They were uncurried devils, those guardsmen of Gorod, who served a hard master, the *starosta*. Aye, they were shifty, masterless men—slant-eyed Kalmuks and bearded Russians who looked out for their own gain—and they had no words for a far-wandering man, a Cossack as wild as a Gypsy or Volga river bandit. Now that snow was deep on the roads, few travelers went from town to town here at the edge of the open steppe. If the Cossack sought food service let him look to himself.

"Go to the tavern," grumbled a pockmarked giant.

Demid had no money. He looked once more at the crowded table, and was turning on his heel when the door opened and a stout sergeant entered.

"Look here, little pigeons," the *essaul* said, "one of you will have to ride to Khor this afternoon. Which is the one?"

For a moment forty heads bent in silence over the kasha bowls. Then the tall, pocked man looked up. "Well, Father Ostap, I'll go."

The sergeant shook his head and spat. "Will you, Gritchka? You'd go as far as the tavern, and come back fit to kiss the pig, and say you'd been to Khor. Come now, it's his Excellency's order. One of you to ride to Khor, patrol the wood for an hour, and come back. I'll stand a glass of corn brandy."

The men at the table said nothing.

"I won't hold back for any man," grumbled Gritchka, "but I won't go after devils."

"Two glasses."

"Make it a jug," suggested Demid, "and I'll go."

The sergeant stared at him. "What manner of man are you?" But he had served his time in the tsar's army, Ostap had. He knew these Don Cossacks who followed the wars, and threw their gold from women to fiddlers, afterward. And then came back licking their wounds to the great steppe that was their home—these steppe-born lads who knew cattle and Tartars and night riding. Good riders and swordsmen—forked lightning on the back of a horse. This Demid was young; he could not know the secret of Khor, and so he might be fool enough to go there, as he offered. Ostap would not have gone for a fistful of ducats, and it was evident that his guardsmen had no mind to go. "Well," he said, rubbing his shaven head, "I'm willing. You'll have to talk to our master. Come along."

His master, the *starosta* of Gorod, was a hard man. So Ostap said as they trudged over the snow, Demid leading his horse. A hard man newly come from Moscow, a man of business, with a hard hand, and new to the steppe. Aye, he clapped a tax on every head and horn and hut, and bade Ostap's lads collect the coins. The *starosta* took in more kopecks than he paid out.

"What is this Khor?" Demid asked. "Where the devils are?"

A farm, said the sergeant, a castle-farm, a few *versts* out of Gorod along the highway. Long ago when Gorod was a small village, the people of Khor were rich and lordly; now there was only one girl on the place and few souls ever saw hair or hide of her. A stone tower in a wood, graves near a deserted chapel, a Tartar village, and a girl mistress of all that. Such was Khor.

"Before last Michaelmas," Ostap added, "we found a trader with his toes turned up in the highroad where it runs through Khor wood. Then we found Togrul, one of my little pigeons. He was a crafty son of a dog, Togrul was; but there he lay by the graves with a hole in his throat and half his blood in the snow. Horse tracks all around, and his sword in its sheath, his pistols primed and charged—untouched." Ostap shook his head moodily. "What manner of thing could come out of the wood and strike down a hard-fighting lad like Togrul as if he were a babe at suck?"

"A lance," said Demid idly, thinking of the horse tracks. He was hungry.

"Would a lance make a hole no larger than a tooth in the vein of his throat?" grumbled the sergeant. "Would Togrul sit there as if saying his prayers while a rider came up and pricked the life out of him? Nay, lad, there are devils in Khor," he admitted honestly. "Think a bit before you ride patrol down there."

"I'll ride through Satan's kitchen," the Cossack answered, "for a dinner of beef and bread."

Ostap spat and crossed himself. "Fear God. Don't jest—it's unlucky."

The *starosta* had more to say. Mikhail, *starosta* of Gorod, was sole lord of the empty land as far as a man could travel in a day, except for the land of Khor. He saw to it that his word was law. Sitting in his high seat by the fire of his hall, his square-cut beard jutting over his collar, he looked from Ostap to the Cossack, noticing Demid's shagreen riding boots and white lambskin *papakh*. Although both the sergeant and the Cossack stood silent, hat in hand, Demid bore himself as if he was at home in a lord's hall, and Mikhail noticed this. But, since the table had been cleared away, he did not bid Demid to sit down to meat and wine.

"You're a likely lad for my service," he said. "Have you any kin in Gorod? No—I see you're a wandering Cossack. Well, times are hard, lad—I can't take another sword into my service. But I'll pay you well to patrol an outlying farm. Eh, what do you say?"

"What is the pay?"

The *starosta* considered. "I confess my own men shirk going to the place. It has a bad name. They say a *vurdalak*, a vampire, roosts there."

Ostap started to spit, and crossed himself covertly instead.

"They have tales to tell," Mikhail resumed, "of this vampire, which seems to change its shape, being sometimes a young woman, sometimes a shining white rider that vanishes into the snow. Old wives' tales—"

"Nay, lord," Ostap broke in stubbornly. "Haven't you ever heard hungry vampires howling in the twilight? They have pallid blue faces and their eyes shine like candles in the dusk when they are hungry. They whine and whine, and if you take them up on the saddle they bite behind the ear or into the throat vein. Once they taste blood—"

"Enough!" Mikhail glanced about slowly, as if ridding himself of some fear. Demid observed that the walls of the hall were hung with a strange variety of weapons, ranging from curious muskets to daggers, not far from the *starosta*'s hand. The muskets looked as if they were charged. "I don't say that vampires and werewolves can't be found. Only, they are human beings that have been turned into beasts. Now the people of Khor are like savages; for generations they have lived with the Tartars and wild herds. No priest is in the chapel there."

"Nay," Ostap assented. "When I rode last to that deserted chapel I was followed by tall shadows that slipped between the trees. As God lives, when I was standing by the graves I heard a woman cry out, like a bird of prey."

"Yes," nodded the *starosta* grimly, "and doings like that frighten my guards away."

"Togrul went into the wood, my lord. Aye, we found his body just where I had been standing."

"I think that more travelers have been slain." The *starosta* turned to Demid. "But their bodies were hidden away—put under the ice somewhere. I think we can uncover a nest of blood-letting thieves in that wood, who have been doing away with solitary travelers. From the top of Khor tower the highway can be seen afar. Those Tartars in the village there must have a hand in it. Togrul saw something evil and so they made crow's meat of him. Now, Cossack, I'll pay you forty silver ducats if you find evidence of thievery and murder—twenty ducats if you find any black magic going on there. Anything, that is, to show there is a witch or human vampire alive there."

"What if I find nothing?"

"Then you will be paid nothing."

"A hard bargain, *starosta*."

Mikhail sat back with a shrug, but he watched the young Cossack. "You are free to do as you like. As for me, too many of my men have sworn they rode through Khor, when they turned back at the windmill. I've seen them do it. If you are man enough to turn the thieves out of their nest, you will have a heavy price paid. What do you say?"

"I will take the patrol. But I must have food."

"When you come back."

Demid smiled, and turned on his heel. When the door had closed behind them Ostap put his wolf skin cap on the back of his shaven head and grunted. "Forty ducats! Why, you can frolic with a princess for that! I've never heard his Excellency say anything more than pennies before. Still, it's a bad place. Are you going, lad?"

Demid swung into the saddle and gathered up the rein. "Which way does Khor lie?"

"Down that street, past the haystacks and the tavern. There's only the one road." Ostap came closer to whisper: "Just the same, if you see a woman or child hungry-looking, jump down quickly and plunge your sword into the ground. The vampire will run up and take hold of the hilt. Then—'In the name of the Father and Son,' you say. She'll slide down the blade and vanish into the ground. Make two cuts, like a cross, over the spot and she can't come up again."

A smile lit up the Cossack's dark face. "Listen, sergeant," he whispered, "I'm brother to the vampires, and I used to train werewolves to bring my supper." He galloped off, turning in the saddle to shout back: "My boots to you, sergeant."

The good people of Gorod hastened to get out of the way of the speeding black horse. Ostap stared after it as if he had seen a ghost rise from the ground.

Khor wood was a dense oak growth surrounding a single hill. On the summit of this hill rose a gray stone tower and the roofs of a manor house. The narrow strip of highroad ran through one edge of the wood, the bare branches almost touching overhead—a good place for an ambush, the Cossack decided.

Along another side of the wood wound a stream, now frozen and hemmed in by alders. Here stood a Tartar village of huts and gray felt tents fenced in with thorn bush. Demid saw several men in wolf skin *shubas* carrying fishing spears. The open steppe around the wood had once been a cattle range, judging by the wrecks of hayricks and barns. A ruined windmill raised skeleton arms against the gray sky. But there were no signs of living cattle—only a few sheep behind fences.

In the wood Demid found a crisscross of trails made by animals and horses. One of these led to a small stone chapel, now boarded up. Beside the chapel the snow rose in short mounds, each one marked by a cross of wood.

The Cossack had dismounted to examine them, when a cold wind swept through the wood, setting the dry snow whirling and dancing around the graves. It struck through his sheepskin *svitza* with an icy touch. At the same time his horse flung up its head, whinnying. Demid looked about him slowly, searching between the trees, until he made out what had caught the attention of his horse.

"Hi, brother—come out!" he called.

A stone's throw from him in a cluster of oak trunks stood a horse and rider, motionless, watching him. The horse was light gray and the rider wore a long, white coat that was almost invisible against the snow. The instant Demid shouted the two wheeled away through the wood.

But the Cossack was not to be left behind. He was in his saddle at once, the big black horse plunging toward the spot where the other had vanished. He saw tracks—caught a glimpse of a gray shape flitting away— and galloped in pursuit.

The gray horse turned and twisted among the thickets. The Cossack, who had chased wolves before now, perceived that it was circling to get past him up the hill. Heading across its track, he leaped a fallen log and came down within lance length of the gray horse's tail. For a moment the white rider tried to shake him off by twisting among the trees at a smashing gallop.

Then the gray horse checked and whirled, rearing. Its hoofs lashed out at the onrushing Cossack. But Demid's horse had played this trick—the dreaded *lava* that the Cossacks taught their chargers—himself. He swerved from the descending hoofs, almost throwing Demid from the saddle.

With an angry cry the rider of the gray horse drew a sword, slashing out at the half-unseated Cossack. Demid had no time to draw his own sword—he threw himself bodily from the saddle, straining every muscle to fall on his feet. As the white rider reined forward to strike again, the Cossack leaped up, catching him about the waist.

So swiftly had he moved, the other was not able to brace himself against the impact and they both came down, rolling in the soft snow. Demid gripped his adversary beneath him, catching the wrist that held the sword and forcing it back into the snow. His right hand grasped the other's throat. And then he loosed his grip with an exclamation.

For the throat beneath his fingers was soft and round, and long dark tresses lay about the small head from which the *papakh* had fallen. A woman's gray eyes looked up into his.

"The devil!" he muttered.

When he drew the sword from her hand she made no resistance. She lay quiet, looking at him steadily. He got to his feet slowly, the blood pounding in his head. Reaching down, he lifted her in his arms. Without doubt she was a woman, light and warm and sweet-smelling. A vampire would have been cold to the touch. Yet her eyes as they searched his face were the eyes of a wild thing.

"Eh, speak!" he whispered.

Well, she was a beauty, with soft, dark lips—her small head as pale as one of the wax figures in church. Demid bent his head, kissed her lips lightly. "Do you greet all strangers with a sword, little lass?" he asked. "Can't you speak? Are you hurt?"

Suddenly the blood flooded her cheeks, and her eyes closed. Demid waited. He did not want to put her down. But she started in his arms, her head turned and her eyes dilated as she stared past him into the wood.

"*Yok! Tzee—tzee, yok!*" she cried shrilly, and the Cossack set her down on her feet.

Behind him in the brush at which she had been looking a brown wrinkled face was drawing back out of sight—a thing malevolent as a demon, wrapped in a wolf skin, with a great bow held fast in its hand.

Demid knew then that he was in peril of his life, and he crouched in the snow, his muscles tense. The thicket ceased quivering, and there was no further sign of the Tartar bowman who had been peering out at him. He heard sounds behind him, and turned his head in time to see the girl going off on the gray horse.

This time Demid made no move to follow. He knew that eyes as keen as wolves' were spying upon him, and he knew that an arrow from a Tartar bow could kill at a hundred paces. "*No—oh, no!*" the girl had cried at the face in the brush.

So she had guardians, in this wood of hers. She, the wild thing, had warned them not to strike down the Cossack, although he had handled her, unwittingly, as roughly as a bear. She had cried out in the Tartar tongue, which Demid understood. Thoughtfully he went to his horse, and when he was in the saddle again he turned back to the highroad that led to Gorod. He was thinking of a splendid dark head lying in the snow beneath him, and nothing else would come into his mind.

That evening be was admitted with Ostap to the hall of the *starosta*, who dismissed the other servants in the room before speaking to him.

"Well, have you news?"

"Yes," said Demid slowly. "This maiden of Khor is no vampire but a woman like any other."

"I did not ask for your thoughts," retorted Mikhail. "Tell me what you saw—what happened?"

The Cossack told about sighting the Lady Ivga—as Ostap called her—and his pursuit of her. Ostap listened to every word, breathing heavily.

"The truth is," commented Mikhail, "that the life was nearly cut out of you, my lad. You should have followed her, tied her up, and brought her in for examination by the boyars and by myself."

Demid shook his head. "If that was the Lady Ivga, we were on her land. Why shouldn't she slash at a man? She's lovely as a deer." He remembered how her eyes had closed when she flushed, and he was silent so long that the two men moved uneasily.

"Look here," Demid went on. "I know how Togrul was slain—with an arrow. It leaves a small cut; still it will drain the blood out of a man."

"We found no arrow," Ostap muttered.

"And I think otherwise," pondered the *starosta*. "What if she had appeared before him in woman's dress—what if she came up to him and put him under the spell of her eyes and then struck him down with a small knife?"

"Ay," put in Ostap heavily, "she's a witch and she has cast a spell on this Cossack."

"If she's a witch, I'm a monk!"

"Now, now, young wildfire. Doesn't she haunt graves, and change her shape? She does, because she rides about in man's dress. Hasn't she long, tangled hair and baneful eyes. You say she has. Did you hear her speak honest Christian words, like 'Get out, you son of a dog?' You did not.

Well, then, she's young and fair, but she's a witch all the same and no good will come of her."

The *starosta* lifted his hand. "I want proof, not words. Go you to the highway of Khor at night, Cossack, and watch what she does in the hours of darkness. There is a moon and you know your way about now. Eh?"

"I'll do that," Demid nodded, "tomorrow night."

"Not for forty good silver ducats of Kiev," said Ostap when they were alone again, "would I do the like of that. Better to follow the hangman's torch than the moon over Khor. Don't you know, *her* brother and grandsire and other men of Khor are in those graves?" He sighed and rubbed his head. "*Akh*, you should have thrust your sword in the ground and said what I told you; then you would be at peace now, instead of rushing about like a wild horse at the end of a rope."

There was no peace in the mind of the Cossack. On the morrow's night when he took the snow road to Khor he galloped as if he were racing the wind. Over his head the cloud wrack passed across the face of the round moon. The bare branches of the wood threshed together as if they were bony fingers of the dead doing a dance in the wind.

A bad night. A bad night to go alone, seeking a witch in that wood. But the Cossack saw gray eyes half closing; he felt the weight of a slender body upon his arm. His blood pounded in his head, and he rode straight as the eagle flies, up the hill to Khor tower. With his stirrup he knocked on the closed wooden gate of the yard.

Round and dark, the tower of Khor rose against the flecked sky. When he beat on the gate an owl swooped away. Steep roof peaks of the log buildings stood against the tower.

"What seek ye?" a man's voice cried.

"The Lady of Khor. Say to her that the Cossack Demid comes as a guest."

"Nay, the *khanim* will see no man from Gorod."

"I am no man of Gorod. No one follows me."

Silence at the gate. Dark figures moving in the shadows of the log wall. A spear point brightening in the moon's light. The black horse snorted, turning restlessly. The gate opened slowly, and Demid rode in, dismounted by the well-sweep, to give his rein to the Tartar who opened the door of the tower. Candlelight flooded the trodden snow, and Demid strode in.

No one was in the round room. A fire blazed in the wide hearth. Bright Turkish rugs covered the floor, and the scent of herbs was in the air. Demid, his *papakh* on his arm, flung himself into a great chair by the hearth.

He did not hear Ivga come in, so quietly did she move over the carpets behind him. She wore no man's garments this time—she was clad in a short shirt and embroidered slippers, in a sleeveless *khalat* that left her arms bare. Her long hair was brushed back and held over her ears by a silver band that was like a diadem. Demid sprang up and bowed to her, and she went close to the fire.

"*Chlieb sol*," she said quietly. "My bread and salt is yours, O guest. It is many a moon since a guest has come to Khor."

Again Demid bowed his head. He could not say anything, because blood was throbbing in his head. The Lady Ivga had changed her shape indeed, and he could not take his eyes from her dark head. When she clapped her hands a Tartar servant entered with a silver goblet. She took this in both hands and held it out to the Cossack. "A greeting to the guest."

"Health to you my lady," he said hoarsely. His hands quivered as he took it from her and drank the corn brandy that was warm and fragrant with spices.

"Are you not afraid, Cossack," she asked, "that the brandy is drugged, and that I am tempting you from your duty?"

"What is that?"

She looked at him, and smiled slowly. "To ride down women in the wood of Khor."

When she smiled the skin of his head tingled, and the breath caught in his throat. "Why did you go in man's dress, with a sword?"

"Because a little while ago when I rode in my own dress, one of the Gorod riders stalked me like a panther. When he tried to put his hands on me, Ghirei, one of my hunters, slew him with an arrow."

"What became of the arrow? It was not found."

"We took it away. After all, that Torgrul was dead. Ghirei caught his horse wandering with a loose rein and rode back to the spot and drew out the arrow without dismounting. If the *starosta*'s men had found the Tartar arrow in that dead rogue, the *starosta* would have taken half the fields of Khor in payment for a life."

Then Demid understood why the only tracks found by the body of Togrul had been those of his own horse. "Why do you tell me this?" he asked.

"I do not know." Ivga did not smile; her gray eyes sought the fire as if to read the answer in the flames. "Perhaps because you come as a guest, after this long time. Perhaps because you are a Cossack, like my grandfather. I don't want you to die," she added impulsively, "as Togrul did."

Forty silver ducats for proof of a slaying, and now he had that proof from her. The price of two years' service in the wars. Yet here, beside Ivga, he thought nothing of that. Togrul, the dog, had been well slain.

"Why did you come to the tower?" she asked suddenly. "You should not have come."

Demid shook his head. How could he have stayed away, after he had held her in his arms? He was frightened, because the wild girl of the snow road had changed into a proud girl of the manor, as remote from his touch as an image in the church. "In Gorod they are saying that you are a witch," he explained, "and your servants rob wayfarers."

"My Tartars!" Her eyes blazed at him. "O fool! My Tartars were born here—aye, their grandsires served Khor, in the day of my grandfather, when the lands of Khor stretched as far as Gorod, which was no more than a village then. We counted our cattle by the hundred on the ranges. Then guests filled the house and there was feasting in this tower. My grandfather was a Cossack, so he had nothing but war in his head. He spent lives and gold and horses with an open hand, and he himself died by the sword. His grave is in the wood." Chin on hand, she gazed into the fire. "Six graves there are that I tend. And the newest is Ivan's. Ivan, my brother, who grew up with me. Ivan was like a Cossack, tall and heedless of everything but his sword and his hunting. He went to serve the tsar in Moscow, taking the strongest of the peasants with him. Whenever he wrote to me he begged for more gold for his debts, his horses—all the things he needed. He used to call me his Devilkin. I sold the cattle and the upper pastureland to send money to him. I was a child, then, and I did not know how to manage such things—"

Ivga looked into the fire. "Then they brought his coffin back to Khor with a letter that said he was a hero. But to me, his Devilkin, he had always been a hero . . . well, that's past. Ivan lived joyfully, but we are poor now. The land that is left is good for wheat, but the rest of the peasants went off to town with their carts. That is because the new *starosta* is building houses there. Now he takes a horn-tax, a head-tax and a fire-tax from us. I went to Gorod to tell him that we had never paid a tax to Gorod, because the land is our freehold. I cannot work the land with Tartars."

Demid nodded assent—he had grown up on the southern cattle range.

"The *starosta* Mikhail said," Ivga went on slowly, "that Khor was an ill place for a woman. He said he would take this land and castle, and give me in exchange a house in town. It had barred windows and the sun did not shine in it. How would I live there, without land and horses? I said I would pay his taxes . . . The Tartars have not left me. They fish the river and they hunt. We sold skins and grapes in the town, to pay the last taxes. Now the *starosta* buys skins only from the traders. The man who was killed on the highroad in our wood was a fur trader on his way from Gorod. My men knew nothing—did not see him. But there were masterless men in the tavern, who knew that the trader had silver on him.

The Cossack also was looking into the fire. He saw how the *starosta* meant to get Khor into his hands. But Demid had no skill to deal with merchants' work—

"This year," added Ivga proudly, "we will be able to sell horses for the money."

"And after that, what?"

After that? There were Turkish yataghans hanging on the walls, gold inlaid; there were holy pictures on the icon stand, with silver frames—Ivga only knew with a deep certainty that this gray tower and its roofs and the graves by the silent chapel were part of her and she could not separate herself from them.

And then the fever that had been rising in the Cossack found a voice. He knelt beside her, pressing his hot head against her knee, and the voice in him begged her to ride with him to the southland where the blue sea water gleamed in the sun. There, he was an *ataman*, a leader of warriors. He would go out on that sea in long boats and take spoil from the Turks. He would bring back silk garments and slaves for her. And his brown hand quivered when it touched the cotton skirt upon her knee.

"Nay," she whispered, stroking his head, "nay, Brother Eagle, where is your home?"

"In the steppe," cried Demid.

"It is far off, where the wind blows and the cries are of war. Do I not know, after Ivan went away?" Her eyes, now that he could not see, had pain and longing in them. "You should not have come to my tower, because, after all, I am a Devilkin."

"I cannot go away."

Then he rose to his feet, his hand on his sword hilt. Silently, moving over the rugs in deerskin boots, a Tartar appeared beside him—holding a bow unstrung, his broad face expressionless.

Demid recognized the face that had looked at him from the thicket.

"*Khanim*," the man said to Ivga, "two riders are upon the road, in the wood."

"What riders?"

"*Khanim*, I do not know. They are calling in a loud voice—*Ai-ai!*"

Demid considered. They might be men who had come after him from Gorod, or belated wayfarers. Here was something that he could see to--there must be no more bloodshed on Ivga's land. "I will go down. Only, do not let these bowmen of yours loose."

"Don't go to the wood," she said quickly. "Stay here. I—I am afraid." She did not know why. A breath of wind from an open door set the candle flames flickering. She touched the Cossack's arm. "Please, do not go away."

But he smiled. "Eh, little Ivga—then I will come back."

He went to his horse and mounted, though she came out into the moonlight and touched his rein, as if to hold him there with her. And she did not go back until he had passed through the palisade gate.

High over the bare trees the moon gleamed on the white snow, outlining the black shadows. As he cantered down a trail toward the chapel and the road, Demid heard a shout. Coming out the highway he saw two riders moving at a foot pace toward Gorod. They were heavy men in sheepskins with saddlebags at their knees. Demid did not know them, but he looked closely at their horses—he had a memory for horses.

"*Hi*, lad," the foremost hailed him, "where lies Gorod tavern? Is that it yonder i' the wood? Faith, we're weary of this accursed road."

"Ride on for half an hour, and you will see the light of the tavern."

"May the dogs bite me!" grumbled the nearer of the two. "A half hour he says. Well, here's something for us all." Lifting the flap of a saddlebag, he drew out a stone jug, and then a glass. Seeing it, the other man came over to them, beating his arms against his shoulders to warm his blood. From the three horses rose thin clouds of steam.

The man with the jug poured out a glassful. He lifted it and grinned at the Cossack. "Here's health to you!"

Behind Demid saddle-leather creaked and steel flicked through the moonlight. But the Cossack had not been watching the jug. He threw his body away from the dagger that whipped past his ear, and as he did so he jerked out his saber with his free hand.

Without turning to look or to set himself, he slashed up and back, wrenching his shoulder around with the force of the blow. His saber's edge caught and cut deep under a man's jaw, and the man fell back without a cry.

The other dropped jug and glass and drew a sword from beneath his coat. He slashed at Demid, who caught the blade with his own, and laughed. This was work for a Cossack. The two weapons parted and clashed. Demid kneed his horse forward until he was shoulder to shoulder with the stranger. Once he slashed the man down the cheek and once over the ribs.

Groaning, the stranger cut wide at the Cossack's head. Demid locked hilts, wrenched the other's saber, sending it flying among the trees.

"Don't strike again!" the man screamed. "For Christ's mercy!"

"Who sent you?" Demid demanded, holding back his arm.

The man was silent. He stared at the wood behind the Cossack. "Hush," he whispered, "or he will hear you."

"He'll hear me," Demid said. Reining back, he glanced at the body of the man who had struck at him first. Beside it lay a strange weapon—a blade as long as a hand, yet no thicker than a straw. An Italian dagger, a stiletto that could slay and leave a mark no larger than a tooth.

Swinging down from the saddle Demid picked it up, thrust it into his belt. "Wait here, dog," he cried at the wounded man. Then he spurred along the road, his eyes questing into the shadows of the forest. When he saw a third horseman motionless there, he plunged in among the trees, the blood-stained saber swinging in his hand.

But this third rider did not run or lift weapon. It was Mikhail the *starosta* with his jutting black beard. Now his hands trembled against his coat and his mouth hung open—for he was shaken by fear, as some men are at the sight of blood.

The Cossack stared into his eyes and then laughed. "*Starosta*," he cried, "forty silver ducats to me! For I have evidence of a murderer in Khor woods."

Still Mikhail said nothing. He was a hard man, who let nothing stand in his way, yet he had no courage to face bare weapons.

"*Starosta*," said the Cossack, "do not mount your slayers on horses that have been tethered at your gate. For a horse is to be known as easily as a man. Now look at this evidence, a dagger from your hall, a man yonder who will talk to the boyars of Gorod. Aye, he will tell those good men how you sent me here by night alone and then tried to have crow's meat made of me so that you, the *starosta*, could find me slain and take Khor as the price of a life."

He stopped, when the *starosta* fumbled in his belt. Mikhail drew out a fistful of coins, and the Cossack struck the fist with the flat of his sword, sending the coins flashing into the snow. Suddenly Demid reached forward his rein hand and caught the *starosta*'s sword from its sheath. Mikhail groaned. He was afraid that his death had come.

"This I will keep, *starosta*," Demid said slowly, "lest you change your mind. If you should—if you should ride back to Gorod without knife or sword, where will you find a friend? Do the boyars love you, after the taxes you plucked from them? Will Ostap and his lads stand at your back after the kopecks you have done them out of? Nay, they would leave you to priest and hangman."

Mikhail moistened his lips and looked from side to side.

"But if you ride on," Demid said, "if you take to the road into the steppe and stay far from Gorod, why then every one will be content. Now it's time for you to take the road. Which way, *starosta*?"

With a cry Mikhail kicked at his horse. He plunged through the drifts to the road. And he turned away from Gorod, past the motionless body in the road, toward the distant, moonlit steppe.

"And now," Demid said to the lady of Khor a half hour later, "you will be well rid of him. Here is his sword to remember him by, and here am I to watch at your gate, for I will never go from Khor again."

He was sure of that, this tall Cossack who sat by the fire, no longer moody but with bright eyes and flushed cheeks, a goblet of brandy in his hand.

But Ivga tossed her head, and her words were like a song. "Did you think, Brother Eagle, I would wed me to a Cossack who cares for naught but his horse and riding to wars—the worthless one!"

Years later a man kept guard at Khor gate. It was Ostap, the sergeant, who had grown fat with good living—for times had changed at Khor. Yes, Ostap, who was too fat for service, sat at the gate and watched the cattle grazing on the uplands, while his Lady Ivga looked to the farm. And when Ivga's children climbed over him they liked best to have him show how Mikhail the *starosta* had vanished long ago, never to appear again.

Then Ostap would pull his sword from its sheath while they watched. "One day, my little pigeons, he was alive and snorting in Gorod town," he would say. "And that night of all nights he vanished. No one ever saw hair or hide of him again. He vanished like this." And Ostap would plunge the point of his sword in the earth. "Zzvt. He went down into the ground like a vampire."

The mistress of Khor must have been happy then, for she was heard singing often in the long months when Demid, her husband, was away at the wars.

He did not write often, that Demid. But he always asked that gold and a horse or two be sent him, and then Ivga saw to it that this was done.

Singing Girl

Ulugh the fisherman nursed a fire of bark and twigs. He rocked on his knees in his smoke-filled hut and sighed. Around him the wind whined like an animal, eddying the smoke and rattling the skins that covered Ulugh's body.

Outside the hut snow blanketed the steppe. Ice bound the river Don from bank to bank. And Ulugh, being a Kalmuk Tatar and weather-wise, knew that snow was coming.

Then he heard, through the voice of wind, the jangle of bit chains and stamp of a horse's hoof.

Thrusting his head out of the horseflap of his hut, he grunted in dismay. Two riders were trotting down the trail to the river bank. The taller of the two carried a jug fondly in the crook of his arm and he sang with a full throat as he dismounted.

"Ai," Ulugh exclaimed *"Kosaki!"*

The tall man staggered as if his legs were unwieldy. "Yes, Dog's-mug," he snorted, "we're Cossacks. And we've come to look for those two sons of dogs, those Muscovites. Where are they?"

"Shut up, Arky," said the other Cossacks "And stop licking the jug." He was younger; his voice quiet. He wore his sword girdle high, like a Tatar, and Ulugh noticed that his broad belt had silver settings for jewels and that the settings were empty. After examining the hut the young Cossack led in the horses and roped them, lifting off the saddles and saddlebags.

These, Ulugh knew, were no wandering settlers. They were *stiepniks,* men born on the steppe. He watched them as a cornered wolf eyes a pair of hunting dogs.

The one called Arky—"Wine"—seated himself on his heels by the fire. Taking a last swallow from the jug, he tipped it up and tossed it aside.

"If it hadn't been for you, Arky," Kalyan grumbled, "we'd be asleep in the barracks at Sarai now. You told the *starosta* you could find those two missing Muscovites."

Arky grinned, and yawned. In another moment he was asleep in his sheepskin.

Kalyan looked at Ulugh across the fire and spoke sharply in the Kalmuk dialect. The great lord of Sarai-town, he explained, the *starosta* himself, was very angry. Many travelers had been lost on the river road that Winter. And now a courier coming down from Moscow had passed two Muscovite merchants with horses and a sledge, near here. The merchants had not appeared in Sarai, twenty versts away. What had happened to them?

Ulugh swore by Allah the All-Wise that he did not know. True, he had seen the sledge standing in the trail. But the men and the horses were gone.

"*Yarou-yarou!*" Ulugh whined, "Take heed. The noble Cossacks must not go near that sledge."

"Why not?" Kalyan demanded.

"Three nights ago a flame moved in the trees as if a demon danced. A wolf howled."

Ulugh would say nothing more, although Arky threatened to put hot coals up his nostrils. And before sunrise the fisherman took himself off to the river.

The Cossacks mounted and went on up the trail. They found the sledge abandoned in the road, its shafts empty.

Kalyan pointed to the ground. A line of tracks left the trail behind the sledge, going toward the fir wood. Dismounting, he led his horse along this fresh trail.

It headed down into the wooded ravine, descending to the river. And the prints in the snow were still clear enough for Kalyan to make out that the two merchants had walked, leading the horses. They had kept to a straight line through the brush, into the first fir growth.

Here the light was dim, and the Cossacks could barely see the tracks. At one place the horses of the Muscovites had circled and plunged, and the men seemed to have followed them about.

Suddenly Kalyan's piebald pony reared. Arky swore fervently. His sorrel had shied, throwing up its head. "Be still, sire of devils!"

Using his whip, he brought the sorrel to a stand, its ears twitching.

He took the rein of Kalyan's piebald, wrapping it around his wrist. "Eh, what's biting them?"

Then he became aware of a third track, a lance length to the side.

"A wolf," he grunted, leaning down to stare at it in the near darkness. "Nay, a grandfather of wolves!"

From pad to claw points the track seemed as large as his clenched fist. Certainly it moved after the boot prints of the men.

As Kalyan followed, in the heart of the wood ahead of them a light flashed up. It burned steadily, as if sheltered from the wind.

"A house," muttered Arky. "Glory to good Saint Nicholas!"

The gate in the dark line of the log palisade stood open. The yard inside was like a hundred other *choutars*—border farms. At one side stood a stable shed. On the other rose the gaunt arms of a windmill. But Kalyan saw no haystack or manure pile, and no dogs rushed out to snarl at the Cossacks. The place might have been deserted, except for the light—the gleam of a candle in the mass of the log house.

When they tethered the horses and strode in, Arky closed the door carefully behind him.

"Bad luck to us," he explained, "if the candle goes out."

And he grunted, pleased. He was standing on a Persian flower-carpet; a tiled stove warmed the long room, silver gleamed on the side table, and somewhere incense burned. The two doors at the ends of the room were closed.

"Hi, inside!" Arky bellowed.

One of the doors opened, and a girl appeared. Such a girl as Arky had not seen before on the border. A pearl-sewn mesh covered the dark hair that fell over her slight shoulders.

"*Chlieb sol!*" Her low voice greeted them, "Be welcome."

She had the large eyes and slim throat of a child. Her cheeks were touched with red, and the heavy silk *sarafan* was much too large for her small figure. Her feet were hidden in red Turkish slippers.

The two Cossacks pulled off their *kalpaks* and bowed low, their long scalp locks slipping down.

"What men are ye?" she asked.

Kalyan flushed, tongue-tied, but Arky answered readily: "Eh, we're Cossacks in from the snow road. Don't be frightened, lass-lady."

"What seek ye?" she asked quietly.

"Only two sons of dogs," Arky explained. "Two Muscovites who lost the way."

"They are not here, Cossack." She stared past him, frowning.

The Cossacks were silent, pondering. Then a clear voice spoke from the shadow of the inner door: "Well, lads, you can't take the road in this storm. So you'll share my bread and salt."

They saw a man with unclipped beard. He was wrapped in a sable coat, with high pigskin boots, and his hands moved restlessly as he came into the light.

"Nay," he said, "I am no merchant of Muscovy such as ye seek. I am Sergey Okol, master of this *choutar*."

"If you know they are merchants," Kalyan answered, "you have seen them, Sergey Okol."

The master of the house shook his head. "Their sledge, yes. I found that. The men, no—I've seen nothing of them." He considered, rubbing his beard. "I know where they are. But you'll not want to follow there, lads."

After Kalyan had stabled the horses, Sergey Okol bade the girl serve them with food while he kept Arky's bowl filled with brandy and afterward honey mead.

Like a shadow the girl came and went, bringing water in a basin to wash their hands and a linen cloth to dry them. "Enough, Sana," said Sergey Okol.

Without a word she took a plate of food to a corner apart from them and began to eat.

"Now," Kalyan asked quietly, "where went the Muscovites?"

"To the devil, truly." Sergey Okol frowned. "The Tatars caught them."

"How caught them?" Arky demanded.

The fools, Sergey Okol explained, went down to the river to try the ice. They were weary of trudging on the trail. And the Tatars watched the river—the Kalmuk horde of Ghirei Khan had made its Winter camp across the river. He had seen the gray devils come down to the bank, to fish through holes in the ice. They watched for human fish, as well.

"Look at that girl, Sana." He lowered his voice, touching his head significantly. "She's out of her mind. She's a *bayadere*, a singing girl of the towns, and she came out with a party of colonists. Poor sheep! They were attacked, on the ice by the devils of the horde. Ay, after nightfall it was. Sana ran toward the wood, with the Kalmuks following. When she reached the trees, they turned back. By the Horned One—'tis a miracle she lived."

"Kalmuks can keep to a snow track in the dark," grunted Arky.

"Not in this wood." Sergey Okol smiled. "They won't come a pace into my trees. They think an evil spirit lives in this place. They say it howls at night when hunger gnaws it."

"Eh—that would be a vampire," announced Arky.

"Not a vampire. I don't know what it is. I found Sana lying in the snow." He hesitated, glancing toward the silent girl. "When I passed that place the next day I found the tracks of a wolf, circled the mark of her body. Now at times she talks about darkness that shuts her in like a prison. But, then," Sergey Okol sighed, "her mind is touched."

Sana had put aside her plate and had taken a doll upon her knee. It was a painted doll, of silk and rags and her fingers worked at it without ceasing.

"You see how it is," Sergey commented. "If she isn't dressing herself, it's the doll."

Stretching his long arms, Kalyan shoved back his bench and went over to the girl.

"What is wrong, lass?" he asked.

Her gray eyes, startled, fastened upon his.

"Go not from the house," she cried. "Go not from the light that burns, into the darkness!"

"Sana!"

With his head Sergey Okol motioned toward the inner room. The girl slipped through the door and Sergey Okol stepped after her, to draw the key from the inside. Closing the door, he locked it, thrusting the key into his sash.

Kalyan picked up his saddlebags and sheepskin and went to the far end of the room. Warily, Arky followed.

"What's biting you, Kalyan?"

"You fool," the young Cossack said softly, "that girl isn't out of her mind."

"Then why—"

"She's playing a part, like a Gypsy. She's afraid."

"Well, why not? Isn't this a haunted place?"

"It may be that," Kalyan admitted. "But don't you see that Sergey Okol's lying?"

Arky rubbed his shaven head dubiously. "Don't think about the girl, just because she has eyes like a dove. Go to sleep, Kalyan."

Whereupon he got his own sheepskin, not too steadily. He put his hand on the stove, found it was comfortably warm, and stretched himself out on top of it. He looked around for the icon, and did not find it. So he made the sign of the cross on his forehead. The wind whirled around the house, and the storm raged. He yawned and rolled over in the sheepskin . . .

By Sana's door lay Sergey Okol, a pistol, primed and cocked, ready to his hand.

Resting against his saddlebags, his eyes half closed, Kalyan was not asleep. He was trying to see with the eyes of his mind what was hidden in the *choutar*. He knew the river, and the evil that was wrought upon it by men. But he felt in this house an evil that was new to him.

The girl's silent appeal to him—as if she had had lifted a mask from her soul for his eyes alone—he did not know what to do about that.

What did she fear? Probably she had seen a wolf, a large wolf, in the ravine. But wolves did not prey upon men; rather, they fled from them. What was there to fear in a solitary wolf? Something that terrified Kalmuks?

Kalyan did not know. He stared at the great candle flickering above the mass of tallow. From the stove Arky's snores resounded. And by the far door Sergey Okol sighed heavily. As Kalyan watched, the candle flame danced and spread skyward, dancing like the souls of the unburied dead that throng the northern sky—howling like wolves—a rush of cold air chilled the Cossack.

Suddenly he woke. The room was dark except for the gray square that he knew was the open door.

Near him a man breathed gustily. "Hey, Kalyan," Arky squatted down beside him, cold sober for once and blurting out words: "Sergey Okol's gone. *Ekh ma*, don't you see how it is, now? Mother of God, why didn't I think? There isn't a holy picture in the place no servants—not a dog. Only listen to the horses! They know—"

"Stop whining."

Running across the room, Kalyan tried the girl's door. It was locked as before, but Sergey Okol had gone from the rug before it.

Outside the house the howl of a wolf quavered.

"It's him," Arky moaned. "It's the werewolf."

Kalyan stopped dead, the hair stirring up the back of his neck.

"In the hours of darkness the animal soul wakes in him, Kalyan. He goes out from the house and his shape changes. Then he cries out and he hunts. Didn't we see his tracks, larger than any wolf's?"

Going to the door, Kalyan looked out. The snow had ceased, and a faint light came through where the clouds had broken overhead. By the feel of the air he judged it was a little before daylight.

"Those merchants ran from the werewolf," Arky muttered. "They never reached the house. Ay, the Kalmuks have heard him howling—they keep away. After sunup, he'll be back in his own shape, when his soul returns to him."

"What's that light?" Kalyan asked.

Above the palisade and beyond the tops of the firs a flame flickered. It seemed to Kalyan that it might be a torch swinging in circles. But it was too far off to be sure.

Running out the palisade gate, he headed toward it, while Arky, unwilling to be left behind, followed panting.

Ahead of them, suddenly, yellow eyes gleamed, close to the ground. A deep snarl sounded, and a clashing of iron. Kalyan knew it was an animal, and probably a wolf. He drew his saber and went forward slowly.

"Don't—" Arky gasped.

Jaws clashed together, and the black shape of the animal sprang toward the Cossacks. Kalyan slashed down swiftly. The steel of his blade clanged strangely, and left his hand. He threw himself on the ground, beneath the wolf. Gripping its head in his arms, he rolled over away from the mad thing that clawed his legs. His sword was gone, but an iron chain struck against his shoulders, pinning him down.

Over the rattling of iron and the wolf's snarling, he heard Arky's fighting yell. Steel whined in the air, and he caught a glimpse of Arky slashing at the writhing animal.

Freeing himself from the chain, Kalyan got to his feet. The blurred shape of the wolf was twitching in the snow.

"*Ekh ma*, you rolled like a stuck pig," Arky commented. He was trembling as he stared at the carcass.

Kalyan grunted, retrieving his saber. Investigating the chain, he found that one end was attached to an iron collar around the wolf's throat, the other to a tree trunk. So, the beast had been tied and, unable to escape, had attacked the men. His sword must have struck the chain, or collar.

"Eh, that ought to do for him," Arky ventured. "Isn't it true if a were-wolf is wounded the same wounds will be on the body of the man the next day?"

"Oxhead! This is no werewolf. How could a werewolf pick up a loaded pistol and walk off with it? Or light a torch in the forest? We'll find your Sergey Okol with a whole hide where that torch is. Come on."

The Cossacks pushed on through the firs, up a rise that overlooked the wooded ravine and the shore. But no light was visible.

"It was near here," Kalyan pondered. "Ay, it—Listen!"

Nothing moved near them. In the stillness of the snow-muffled shore, they heard a faint cry, a woman's voice. It came from the direction of the *choutar*.

Kalyan swore under his breath and plunged back down the slope. Coming into the yard, he headed straight through the door, heedless of what might be awaiting him in the darkness. Once inside he stopped dead, listening.

He heard Arky come in cautiously. The big Cossack went toward his saddlebags and in a moment began to strike sparks against tinder, carrying the flame to a lantern and lighting it.

"There, *kunak*," he grunted, surveying the room, "you see. He isn't here!"

The rug was empty, but the door behind it stood open. Taking the lantern, Kalyan examined the small sleeping room. The only trace of Sana was the impress of her body on the bed, and the painted doll lying askew.

"He's been here," Kalyan said.

The Cossacks tried the other door, which led into a storeroom where dried meat hung with herbs. While Kalyan threw the light behind sacks of grain and casks, Arky examined the liquor kegs with interest, sniffing at them and trying their weight. "It's no use, *kunak*," he grunted, "the man was a wolf, and now the girl's gone. This place is evil. Now after sunup the powers of darkness will cease, and we—" he shook a small keg close to his ear inquisitively, hearing the soft chink of metal that was not iron. "Hi, look at this!"

But Kalyan had gone from the storeroom, leaving the lantern. Outside the house, the sky was turning gray as he hastened to the stable. A horse whinnied behind him, and his piebald pony trotted up, its halter dragging. The two other horses were gone. The saddles, however, were on their pegs. Evidently Sergey Okol had not waited to saddle two mounts.

And he would not go far or fast, riding bareback through fresh snow. Kalyan could see the tracks of the missing horses clearly, in the growing light. To his surprise, they led through a break in the palisade, down toward the river.

"Hi, Kalyan—look!" Arky came shambling up, carrying the small keg. He had pried off the top, and he thrust it under his mate's nose gleefully. It was half full of coins, gleaming softly.

"Gold," Arky whispered. "Ducats, byzants, Arab miskals! Ay, and turquoise and silver bits. *Tfu*—all that didn't come from Moscow. It came over the river, from the east."

Kalyan hefted the keg thoughtfully. If these were Moslem coins, they had come from the Tatars, and surely Serley Okol had not sold furs to the hunters of furs.

"That wolf-soul was rich as a sultan," Arky whispered. "He hid it all in a brandy cask—that's how I found it. Where are the horses, Kalyan?"

Kalyan nodded at the tracks and stepped outside the palisade. In the east an orange streak was spreading, lighting the white channel of the river beneath them.

And out on the river a dozen riders waited, beyond the last firs.

"Tatars!" exclaimed Arky. "Ghirei Khan's men."

Evidently the riders of the horde had not observed the two Cossacks. They seemed to be intent on the wood. After a moment they moved closer together.

Out from the trees two other riders appeared, going toward the Tatars. One a tall man wrapped in black furs, the other a woman.

"Sergey Okol," said Kalyan, "hasn't turned up his toes. There he goes."

"On my horse," groaned Arky, "the son of a dog."

The Muscovite and the girl headed straight across the river. After they had passed, the Tatars fell in behind them—as if expecting them. Another moment, and the riders had climbed the far bank and disappeared.

"*Ta virty, bratik*," Arky exclaimed, "believe me, brother, he's a wolf. Look how the Kalmuks follow him, like a pack." He rattled the keg, lovingly. "Don't they pay him gold? They'd cut us out of our skins. Well, he's left us alive in our hides, Kalyan, and now the sun's up. Saddle your nag, and we'll go back. Eh, Kalyan?"

The young Cossack struck his clenched hands against his head. He had been blind. He, a hunter born on the steppe, had walked unknowing into a baited trap.

"The sledge was the bait upon the road," he muttered. "Ay, the candle was lighted to guide us to the open gate and the open door. And the girl bade us share bread and salt while that wolf-soul watched, to know what manner of men we were. And if we had been merchants of Moscow, new come to the steppe, we would be sold to the Tatars this dawn, with our gear and goods. Like the souls who came hither with Sana. And those others who vanished."

He nodded slowly. "But we were Cossacks, we fools. When Sergey Okol went to signal to the Kalmuks, we didn't sleep like hedgehogs. We slew the wolf and searched for him, and it may be that he felt fear in his heart. Ay, he feared that the girl would betray his secret then. So he bore her off with him—"

Sana had warned him. Her voice had warned him against going out into the darkness.

The hot blood darkened his lean head as he turned on Arky. "Saddle my horse."

This Arky was willing enough to do. He thought Kalyan was coming to his senses, and would go back quietly now to Sarai, with enough gold to let them celebrate all Winter. He was buckling the pony's headstall when Kalyan came striding back from the house. The young Cossack had the doll in one hand and a filled saddlebag in the other.

"Brother," Arky asked, with misgivings, "what have you got there?"

Kalyan swung himself into the saddle and laughed. "Sergey Okol's life."

Catching the bag, Arky loosed the thong and peered into it. His jaw dropped, and he choked. In the bag was the head of the wolf he had slain.

Ghirei Khan, son of Ilbars Khan, Lord of the Little Kalmuk Horde, rocked gently on his heels on the white horse skin at the entrance of his tent. Impassively, he considered how much he would pay for the *ghiaur*—the infidel maid.

For Ghirei Khan had wealth beneath his hand. Uncounted oxen wandered between his gray yurts; his sheep herds stretched as far as his eye could see. Around him stood his chieftains and *mirzas*. They had gold in the hilts of their scimitars. It was profitable to sell as slaves the captives the Wolf sent out on the river ice, with Ulugh as a guide, on the mornings after the Wolf made signal with his torch. They had paid Ulugh the price of the captives.

Now they kept their distance from the Wolf, never having beheld him in human form before. They had heard him howl of nights when hunger gnawed him, over the river. Ulugh the fisher had told them how he went about in the form of a gray wolf dragging a long chain, when he crept out of his human body.

"She has cold blood in her," Ghirei Khan observed to the attentive Ulugh. "A Gypsy would be better."

"It is because her skin is soft," Ulugh urged, "that her blood is cold, as the Lord hath said."

Sergey Okol moved impatiently where he sat on the edge of the horse skin. He wanted to get this business done with. The singing girl, he thought, was not lucky for him. She had managed to stir the suspicions of the Cossacks in spite of all the brandy he had given them.

And for the first time he had had to leave the shelter of his ravine to face these gnome-like Tatars in their encampment. He could not tell what they were thinking, and he had to trust to Ulugh to interpret his words.

"How much will he pay?" Sergey Okol demanded.

"Ai, master," the fisher said, "he has many herds, many handfuls of gold. Do not hurry him. Do not be angry."

Ulugh was afraid of this Muscovite who sold human souls. But more he feared Ghirei Khan, who might order the skin cut from his feet and hands if the fisherman displeased him.

"Let him pay down the gold now," Sergey Okol insisted.

Ulugh said nothing. The Tatars around the yurt turned their heads with guttural exclamations. Some of them caught up the lances they had thrust into the snow. The circle of fur-clad heads broke, and through the opening an enemy of the Kalmuks paced his horse, a *ghiaur* Cossack. He was alone, he held a doll and a saddlebag in his hands, and his sword was sheathed at his hip.

"*W'allah!*" exclaimed Ghirei Khan, surprised, "what is this?"

The Cossack himself answered, swinging down from his saddle: "A gift for the son of Ilbars, khan of the Kalmuks. A mighty gift."

Curiosity kept the Tatars motionless as Kalyan stopped a lance length from Sergey Okol. Loosening the thong of the saddlebag, he flung it down on the snow, and the massive gray head of a wolf rolled out.

Ulugh cried out and drew himself away from it, and even the khan started to his feet.

"Look!" cried Kalyan. "I have slain the spirit of the Wolf. In the hours of darkness I searched for him. For I have the spirit of a great devil in me. I followed the Wolf because he took from me this woman slave. He fled from me, and covered himself with iron—"

The Tatars, drawing back, listened with amazement.

"He sprang at me after he bound himself with iron," Kalyan shouted, "and I strove with him, overpowering him, and cutting off his head. W'allah! Still, he lived. He changed again into human form, and he fled from me, taking the woman with him. Like a serpent he tried to hide himself among the people of the khan. Look at him, how he draws his strength together, to save himself."

Unable to understand, Sergey Okol was glaring about him, his fists clenched at his sides.

"Wah!" cried Ghirei Khan, putting his hand to his mouth.

"But he has lost his power," Kalyan went on. "His spirit is dead. And now he has no place to flee."

Whipping out his saber, he turned on the Muscovite. "The wolf was braver than you. Will you die like a pig?"

The hand that Sergey Okol had thrust inside his coat came out clutching the long pistol. Powder flashed and roared, and the Tatars heard the dull sound of a bullet striking. Kalyan felt a blow against his side. Steadying himself, he leaped forward.

Scrambling to his feet, Sergey Okol snatched at the scimitar hilt in the girdle of the nearest Kalmuk. He flung up the blade, snarling, as Kalyan slashed at his head.

"Hai!" the Cossack shouted, "he feels his death."

Their boots thudded in the hard-packed snow as the two whirled together— Kalyan circling, his blade making rings of steel about the head of the Muscovite.

"True," muttered Ghirei Khan, "now he feels the end of his power."

Lightly the Cossack's blade slid past the other. The curved edge cut deep into the Muscovite's throat, and Sergey Okol moaned, the strength going from his hand. As he staggered, Kalyan slashed down savagely. Sergey Okol's head fell into the snow.

The eyes of the khan gleamed green at this marvelous sight. He bent over the two heads. *"Allah 'im barabat yik caftir,"* he murmured. "God is just and merciful."

Kalyan strode toward the girl, who had hid her face in her arm. Seizing her black hair, he pulled her close to him. "Don't speak," he whispered. Aloud he shouted triumphantly, "The strength of a great devil is in me. Ye have seen! Now am I angered, and my anger will break hard rock asunder and turn aside rushing water—"

Held by his voice, the throng of Tatars moved uneasily, grunting like cattle. For this youth possessed by a spirit spoke words they understood. Moreover, they had heard a bullet strike him, yet he did not bleed like an ordinary soul.

"This maiden is mine," Kalyan roared. "She is no woman of white bones and blood. I made her, for my slave. Aya, I fashioned first a doll of silk—" stooping swiftly, he picked up the doll and tossed it to the feet of Ghirei Khan, "then I breathed upon the doll, and gave life to this elf-maid. The wolf-man carried her off upon his back, leaping over the treetops in the hours of darkness—"

"Kai!" exclaimed Ghirei Khan, stepping back from the doll with the painted cheeks.

"—and if you lay hand on her, a blight will fall on your oxen, and blindness upon your sheep—"

"By Allah," exclaimed the Tatar, "I do not want her. Take her away quickly!"

Kalyan swung her upon the saddle of Arky's sorrel and took the rein of the *choutar* pony, as he mounted his own horse. Lashing the beasts into a gallop he sped away from the staring Tatars toward the river. He did not look back or rein in until he came to the river bank.

Then he relaxed and his words were awkward, shy. "Forgive me, little Sana, that I hauled you about like a slave. I was playing a game with the Kalmuks. I know their minds—like children's. But Sergey Okol didn't, the fool."

Sana's gray eyes were wet with tears. "Nay, he was a hard man, and shrewd. He tried to make you afraid, so that you would steal and fly away; then he could go to Sarai and make complaint to the *starosta*—"

"Ay," said Kalyan gently. His side ached where the Muscovite's bullet had scraped a rib. But his dark eyes glowed as he looked up and down the white frozen river. "He did not know the steppe." Timidly his hand caressed the girl's dark hair—for Kalyan was afraid of her. So white and beautiful she was like an elf-maid, with tears like pearls upon her cheeks.

Suddenly Sana caught his hand, pressing it against her lips. And her lips were warm as those of any flesh-and-blood girl . . .

Ulugh, the fisher, saw them ride away—watching from the dead tree behind his hut. The *choutar* pony was harnessed to the sledge. On the sledge load, upon a Persian carpet, rested a brandy keg. And on this sat the long-legged Arky, swaying, and shouting a song. Behind the sledge rode Kalyan and the girl, their heads close together, their hands clasped.

Ulugh watched them out of sight. Then, with a grunt of relief, he climbed down to his hut, to build up his fire again, and sort out his nets.

The Moon of Shawwul

On the first night of the moon of Shawwul there was calamity, and fire in the city, and a man afflicted of Allah raged near the golden gate with a sword. Many believers died before the first light. But the cause of all this is not known.

From the Annals of the
Othmanli Turks of Constantinople

The *koshevoi*, the chief of all the Cossacks, rose from his seat against the wall of the hut and faced the old men who still sat moodily on the floor, smoking their pipes.

"You have heard the letter—you have listened to the Jew. Now, sir companions, is anything to be done?"

The *koshevoi* was a tall man with a scar that ran from his eye to his jaw. He was a daring leader in battle, but otherwise slow to think and speak. Across his high shoulders was flung a miniver cloak, stained and dusty, and when he faced the elder men his right hand opened and shut as if clasping a sword hilt.

And the veteran Cossacks stroked down their gray mustaches, frowning in silence because it was not customary to speak at once. Few were they—since few Cossacks of the *siech*, the war encampment of the southern steppes, lived to see their hair turn white—in this year of trouble late in the seventeenth century.

"It is true, sir brothers," said one, lifting his head. "And why is it true? Because the Jew who brought the letter is a son of a dog who cannot read Turkish, and his tale is the same as the letter. And he has brought back to us the baton of a Cossack *ataman*."

The *koshevoi* took up from the table a short ivory staff with a cross carved upon one end, the baton of a colonel of a Cossack regiment.

"Aye," said the older men, "that was Kirdyaga's."

By their silence the others assented. Kirdyaga, their companion of the Kuban barracks, had been captured by the Turks when he raided too far beyond the frontier. He was in prison within Constantinople, the city of the sultan, and he had been condemned to die upon the first night of the moon of Shawwul by the Moslem calendar. The worst of it was that the Turks announced that they would torture him by setting him on a stake and letting him wriggle out his life.

Unless—so said the letter—ransom should be paid for the life of Kirdyaga before that night. The ransom must be three thousand gold sequins, or an equivalent in precious stones, and must be paid in Constantinople. As a token the Turks had sent with the letter this baton. And they had sent letter and staff by no worthier hand than that of the ferret-faced Jew in the tall woolen cap and ragged *shuba* who stood shivering by the door, palpably afraid to linger and afraid to beg leave to go.

"Kirdyaga has not asked us to aid him," said the *koshevoi* slowly. "He knows that the Turks are faithless as village dogs."

"Impossible not to aid him," muttered another, taking the pipe from his lips. "To die by steel, that is well enough, but it is another matter to be planted on a stake for slaves and women to pluck at."

"True," assented one whose slant eyes had more than once watched such torture. "By God, that is well said."

"We can gather the gold together."

"Aye, the gold," assented the *koshevoi*, "but how can we send it?"

Again silence followed his words. They could not send the ransom money back by the Jew. Even if Shamoval—he answered to that name— did not make off with it himself, he would be stripped and plundered by Moslem soldiery long before he had covered the two hundred leagues to Constantinople. Nor could the Cossacks entrust the gold to a Turkish officer along the frontier. In that case it would go no farther than the pockets of the officer.

Still, the money must be sent, or the Turks would mock the Cossacks, saying that they cared more for gold than the Cossack colonel who was to be tortured. So in the *koshevoi*'s hut there was silence, until the *koshevoi* himself strode to the open door and looked out.

The only thing that seemed to him possible was to muster the regiments and invade the frontier with fire and sword, to revenge the death of Kirdyaga.

While he pondered he looked up and down the encampment that was called the *siech*, or gathering place. Native-born Cossacks called it their mother, and not untruthfully, because they had given their lives to the *siech*, leaving behind them their villages and families in the steppes.

Long-limbed warriors, sun-darkened, clad each after his own fancy, sat smoking by the barrack walls or gathered in circles about musicians or casks of brandy. The barracks were long huts of wattle and dried clay, and in them were piled blankets and saddles, weapons—lances and Persian scimitars and long, crooked knives called *kindjhals*, the curved yataghans, embossed Turkish pistols, German muskets—for the Cossacks had few arms that they did not take from their enemies. Kegs of powder and cannon were stored in the arsenal by the log church. Only a few horses were to be seen, for the herds of the *siech* were out at pasture under guards.

No wall surrounded the *siech*. It was a point of honor with the Cossacks not to fortify their camp. But except for Gypsy fiddlers and the most daring merchants who came to sell brandy and weapons, no one ventured past that invisible line marking the square of the barracks. No woman was ever seen within the *siech*.

Any man might enter the *siech*, provided he were sound and strong of body. No weaklings could ride with the Cossacks. He was brought to the *koshevoi*, who looked at him and questioned him.

"Do you believe in Christ? And in the holy Church? Well, then, cross yourself and enter whatever barrack you want."

But there were other tests, by the brotherhood. An *oùchar*—a newcomer—might be matched against a full-grown bear, with only a wooden sword given him for weapon. Often he bore the scars of the bear's claws on his hide as long as he lived. Or he would be set in a boat to drift down the cataracts of the river that flowed past the *siech*, or made to ride the unbroken Tartar mustangs. He must fight, at need, but only with his fists, within the limits of the *siech*.

His belongings he could leave by his blankets—his kit and plunder. Gold, if he had any, was given to the keeping of the *kuren ataman*, the captain of the barrack. Theft was almost unheard of and was punished by putting the culprit in the wooden stocks with a club hanging by him, so that the others of the brotherhood could strike him; and when a Cossack of the *siech* did not pay his debts he was chained to the muzzle of a cannon until a companion made good what he owed. A murderer was buried under the coffin of his victim.

When the Cossacks moved out to war the *koshevoi*'s command was the only law. And disobedience meant death by a pistol ball or saber cut.

But while they were in camp they spent their time in revelry, drinking up the spoils of the last campaign. The brotherhood was never the same. Always death thinned its ranks and new faces appeared around the fires. Hither came the riders of the steppes, tired of herding in villages, eager for war that was life itself to them; and hither came fugitives from the law of the cities, from Moscow or Warsaw or Vienna. Some of the dark faces showed the slant eyes and high cheekbones of Tartar blood, others the grace of noble birth; many were scarred and seamed by debauch or suffering or cruelty.

Slender Gypsies sat by massive Russians, a French soldier of hazard matched cups with the son of a Persian emir. No one asked what they had been, and even their names were forgotten, because the Cossacks promptly gave them nicknames and they were known by no other. They became free Cossacks of the *siech*, self-appointed guardians of the steppes that were the frontier of Christendom in this seventeenth century. And they left behind them only the memory of their deeds, sung by the old minstrels.

As the *koshevoi* stood in the door of his hut, by the great drum that was used to gather the brotherhood together, he caught the words of an old Gypsy song, in a full deep voice.

> *My sword is rusty and the blade is dull.*
> *It hangs upon the wall where the spiders make their nest.*

The whine of a fiddle rose above the commotion of shouting where some of the younger men were dancing, their silver heels striking against the hard clay like an axe upon wood, in the *hopák* and *trepák* of the wild Cossack dance. And over the tumult the same strong voice was heard again.

> *And when night falls I hear it whisper-whisper*
> *Take me in your hand and use me—use me!*

The *koshevoi* listened for a moment, then lifted his head as if he had made a decision. He called out in a voice that was pitched to carry over the tumult of hoofs and guns—

"Charnomar!"

The song ceased and the singer strode through the throng toward him.

"Aye, Father."

"Come."

The leader of the Cossacks turned back into the hut, and the man called Charnomar came after him.

He was not so tall as many of the Cossacks, who towered over six feet; nor was he so heavy. Like the others his head was shaved except for the long scalp lock that hung upon one shoulder, but his heavy buckskin breeches and his wide leather belt with its polished silver buckle were like no others in the *siech*. And his sword was a single edged cutlass, almost straight, and heavier than any scimitar or yataghan.

Some Cossacks had found him out at sea, adrift on a splintered boom. They had been fishing off the Dnieper mouth and had heard heavy cannon fire in the offing; they had sailed out to see what was happening in the mist and had come upon this man, who knew nothing of their speech at that time. From Tartars along the shore they learned that an English merchant brig had been attacked by three Turkish galleys and had kept up the fighting until it sank. The Cossacks promptly named him Charnomar—Black Sea. When he was able to talk with them in later years, they had asked him where he came from and he said—

"The sea."

He said also that he was not from the Great Sea—the Mediterranean— but from a wide ocean beyond that and a place called the New World. Of this the Cossacks had never heard. The New World was America.

It was said that Charnomar had been a captive of the Turks on the Barbary Coast. At times he spoke of the Christians he had seen tortured there, and he certainly knew the oaths of the galleys. He made himself at home in the *siech*, or rather in the raids that were launched across the Black Sea to Azov and Sinope, where the Cossacks stormed the citadels and plundered the mosques.

At such times Charnomar's gray eyes glowed and, though he said little, he seemed utterly content. He knew more about navigating than the Cossack *atamans*, and they came to rely upon his strange luck which brought him back alive and laughing out of places where he should have died.

They said of him—

"Upon a horse he is a man, but when he rides the sea he is a devil."

All this passed through the mind of the leader of the Cossacks as he looked at this man who knew more about the sea and the mysteries that lay beyond it than about a horse and the warfare of the steppes. Then he spoke to the old Cossacks.

"This is how it is, sir brothers. The Turks have laid a trap for us; that is what they have done. When did the sultan's dogs ever take ransom for a Cossack of the *siech*? They would like to get their hands on the ransom and the man who brings it. That is all. But if we send nothing, then they will mock at Cossack honor. And it is not to be endured that a brother should die alone and unaided upon the stake."

"Summon the *siech* to march!" growled one of the veterans. "We will answer with swords!"

But the *koshevoi* shook his head. He would have liked nothing better. Yet he knew that the armies of the sultan were too strong to be met in the field by the few thousand Cossacks of the *siech*.

"There is only one road to follow," he said grimly. "To send a Cossack to Constantinople."

"Then the Turks will set up two stakes."

"Perhaps," the *koshevoi* nodded. "Only God knows what will happen. But there is no other way." He looked steadily into Charnomar's gray eyes and explained how Kirdyaga had been taken and what was in the letter. "You know the ways of the Turks," he went on slowly, "and the road over the water. Aye, you stole up on the lighthouse at the straits and blew it up with powder. The Turks put a chain across the Dnieper mouth, and you rode a log down the swift current and broke it. And only God knows why you are still living. But this is another matter. If the Turks seize you, they will put you in the cage, and your sword will not avail you. So, I cannot command you to go to Constantinople, but I ask if you will go with the ransom for Kirdyaga."

The elder Cossacks all looked at Charnomar. It was a mission they could not have undertaken, not the *koshevoi* himself, but in the reckless swing of Charnomar's great shoulders, in the poise of his young head and the gleam of clear gray eyes from his dark face there was no sign of anxiety.

"I'll go," he said. "Only give me jewels, not gold."

Jewels they gave him, the older Cossacks going from one barrack to another and merely saying that the *koshevoi* wanted whatever was finest in the way of precious stones. The softly gleaming heap that lay upon the table within the hour was no larger than a man's fist, doubled up. In it was a string of matched pearls and several large uncut emeralds, greatly desired by Moslems, and rubies that had been pried out of sword hilts. The value of the lot was double the amount of the ransom.

"For," said the chief of the Cossacks, "it is the way of a Turk when he is offered payment, to ask double the price. And besides you will need gold for the road."

He pondered for a moment and called for glasses and a jug of the strong brandy.

"By God," he said, when Charnomar had taken up his glass with the rest, "it's a hard road—a very devil of a road. The Moslem women over yonder, lad, are dark-eyed vixens. Don't talk to them, or they'll destroy you. Keep a sword by you always, and if you're taken by the Moslems, if they beset you, why, strike out and go down with steel in you. That's the best way. And if it happens so, we'll hear of it and remember. Because the Cossacks do not forget."

The old warriors stroked down their mustaches and lifted their glasses. "*Kozatchenky bratiky!*" they said. "To the brotherhood!"

When he reached the corner of his barrack, Charnomar felt a fold of his breeches plucked, and looked down into the thin, eager face of the Jew, Shamoval.

"Ai, noble sir," whispered the man in the *shuba*. "The captain is going to set out on a journey, and in my shop there is everything he will need— soft leather boots and splendid *kaftans*. Such *kaftans* never were seen before! And if the colonel wants saddlebags—"

"To the devil with the saddlebags and you too!"

Charnomar frowned at the trader. He still held in his hand the leather wallet containing the jewels and a sack of gold. Although Shamoval's dark eyes never quite looked at the wallet, they circled around and over it as if it were a magnet from which they could not free themselves. Charnomar reflected that Shamoval had been in the *koshevoi's* hut, unheeded by the Cossacks, and had heard the talk. Jews had a way of wandering all over and there was no telling whether Shamoval would not betake himself to the Turkish posts.

"Where is your shop?" he asked, considering.

Shamoval hastened off across the deserted assembly ground to the traders' streets on the outskirts, where blacksmiths pounded at their anvils and rug merchants and dram sellers sat in their stalls. Only a few Cossacks walked idly through the alleys, because, since it was a time of comparative peace, the brotherhood had spent or drunk up most of its gold. These traders were like the moths that swarm around a light; they gleaned fortunes from the Cossacks, or were plundered and driven out, according to the mood of the warriors.

The Jew's shop was no more than a stall hung with blankets under a thatched roof, with some ordinary saddles and gear stacked in it. But Shamoval lifted the curtain on the inner side, calling out harshly as he did so and whispering to Charnomar to enter.

A clay lamp smoked dimly among shadows that vaguely suggested the presence of a Jewess hidden under quilts in the corner, among rags and sacks of cabbages and piles of broken cord—and two wooden chests, one of which Shamoval dragged out under the lamp.

"Look here," observed Charnomar, "you heard what the *koshevoi* said."

"I?" Shamoval glanced over his shoulder anxiously. "How should I understand what the noble lords were saying? Am I a Cossack, to understand such things? I only heard that the noble captain is going on a journey."

He delved into the chest and began to lay out piles of really costly garments. Charnomar sat down on the other chest and struck a light for his short clay pipe. He noticed that the trader was selecting a strange attire— a fur edged *kaftan*, bright green breeches, a crimson girdle scarf, an embroidered shirt and black velvet vest sewn with seed pearls.

"Here are some of the things the noble captain will need," he explained.

Charnomar pulled at his pipe without answering.

"And riding slippers—" Shamoval hastened off and came back with a pair embroidered with tarnished gold thread. "The man who wore these was a fine, strong hero like you. Only—" he glanced at Charnomar—"that sword won't do at all."

"Why not?"

Shamoval lifted his arms and shoulders. "Doesn't the captain know that such swords were never seen in Constantinople—"

He checked his words suddenly and turned pale, and could not keep from looking fearfully at Charnomar's cutlass.

"So you heard the talk of the Cossacks?" His visitor smiled. "And you've laid out a Circassian swordsman's garments. Why?"

"Emboldened because he was not struck down at once, Shamoval became eloquent.

"Ai, it is certain that the captain must disguise his noble self. And since he can't talk like the Turks and the Greeks—may dogs litter on their graves!—he ought to go as a man from the Circassian mountains. Then every one will take him for a Moslem, but he won't be suspected if he talks in a strange dialect. Many times have I been in the sultan's city, and I've only seen a few Circassians. This one was put to death for something or other and I bought his garments from one of the keepers of the cage before they put an end to him. By everything that's holy, I swear they cost me sixty-two ducats, without the sword and all the daggers the noble lord must wear in his girdle. The keepers took the Circassian's weapons, but I have better ones—if the noble lord will only rise up."

Lifting the cover of the chest upon which Charnomar had been sitting, Shamoval drew out a half dozen swords, and the Cossack picked up one at once. It was a long scimitar with a worn hilt of silver set with smooth turquoises, and the blade was gray, with an inscription near the hilt. Charnomar swung it tentatively and found that it had nearly the weight and feel of his cutlass.

He picked out two long knives and a worn prayer rug and leather saddle bags, and Shamoval announced that the price of everything would be a hundred and twenty and three gold pieces. And he tried not to look at the wallet in the Cossack's hand.

"No one will ever suspect the noble sir if he is dressed like this."

Charnomar selected a saddle with some care, and bade Shamoval send someone for horses, as he intended to set out at once. It was dark before he had completed purchase of a shaggy Kabarda stallion from a Gypsy trader.

"Now, listen, Shamoval," he said reflectively, "you've charged double what these things are worth—"

"Ai—"

"And I'll pay your price, when I come back."

Shamoval raised his hands and clutched at the straggling locks above his ears.

"'Tis impossible!"

"How, impossible?"

"Why—" the trader gulped and seemed to choke over the words. "Why you will never come back. In the first place no one ever bought a prisoner out of the cage. In the second place, you're like all the other Cossacks. You're certain to get into fighting and be killed, or some woman will trick you. You will never come to the *siech* again."

"Then, Shamoval, you will never see your gold."

"Ai—but certainly the noble captain will promise! His promise will be sufficient."

"What promise?"

"Surely the captain has comrades. Just let him promise that if he—that if he doesn't pay, one of his brothers will pay."

"Not a silver *dirhem*!" Charnomar's gray eyes kindled in a smile, and then, before Shamoval could speak again, the eyes changed. "Ay, I'll promise one thing. If you wag your tongue no one will pay."

Shamoval spread out his hands and shook his head so that the tall felt cap flopped from side to side.

"I don't betray secrets," he said seriously, "and as for the Moslems, I spit upon them."

He watched curiously while the Cossack stripped off his old garments and began to clothe himself anew, carefully. Charnomar reflected that the Jew's stall was a good place to change, and since it was dark, no one would notice that a Cossack had gone in, and a Circassian had come out. And it was clear to Shamoval that he knew how the garments should be worn. He wound the shawl girdle above his thighs and let the tasseled ends hang at his hip; he twisted the turban cloth into place and knotted it over one ear. For a moment he held his old cutlass in his hand, then tossed it aside.

Into his girdle under the vest he thrust the sack of jewels and the purse of gold, and then the long scimitar in its leather sheath.

"A pity," muttered Shamoval, "such a splendid weapon to fall to the Moslems."

The Cossack laughed and went out to the shaggy pony that was waiting, hitched to the stall. With a glance at the stars, he mounted and rode off. Once he reined in, to listen to the familiar roar of voices, mellowed by distance, about the fires where mutton and gruel was being issued to the Cossacks at supper. Then he trotted on into the rushes of the river path.

A fortnight later a six-oared felucca with its great sail furled drifted around the lighthouse point and made for the quays of Galats through the evening mist. The felucca had come from Kaffa, along the northern coast of the Black Sea, the Greek captain never daring to lose sight of land, and every Moslem on its deck gave praise to Allah in that sunset prayer because he had been delivered from the sea alive.

Charnomar unrolled his strip of carpet with the others and prostrated himself, because not to do so would have brought instant suspicion upon him. But when his companions filed off into the alleys, he rolled his carpet, put it over his shoulder and wandered along the shore looking for a skiff that would take him across the harbor to Stamboul.*

He walked leisurely, because no one but a madman or a thief or Christian ever hurried within the walls of Islam, with the slow swinging stride of the mountaineer. And a pockmarked waterman about to push off in a skiff already filled with sacks took him for a wanderer out of Asia in search of either wonders or quarrels and good-humoredly indifferent to which it might be. The boatmen of Stamboul have a nose for silver.

"Eh, *chelabim*," he hailed Charnomar, "I go to the marketplace."

Charnomar went down to investigate. He did not answer at once because his Turkish was made up of the speech of the Barbary galleys and the Kuban Cossacks.

"Thy boat," he muttered, "is heavy, and its smell is of fish."

"But the price—the price is small. Six *dirhems*. And in a very little while Allah will cause the dark to come."

Charnomar seated himself clumsily—when did a Circassian know anything about boats?—in the bow of the skiff. But he felt that he should have haggled over the price, because the waterman kept glancing over his shoulder, and when they were within pistol shot of the lights of the Stamboul docks he rested his oars and began to question his passenger.

"Eh, *chelabim*, are you looking for a coffee inn, or perhaps a fine *baya-dere*—a singing girl?"

"Perhaps."

"Then go around the market up the hill. Under the arch is the Kislar Dar,** where the janissaries spend their time. The music there is fine, and the girls come from the Greek islands and Smyrna and all the foreign places. I will show you."

The boatman took up his oars again, palpably eager for a new commission, and Charnomar reflected that it would be well to land with a companion. Already torches were passing along the stone embankment, and the lights gleamed on the shields of armed guards.

---

*The Old City: the Turks never called it Constantinople.
**"The Place of the Girls."

When he climbed up the narrow steps, slippery with damp, into the glare of torchlight and the din of many voices, Charnomar's heartbeat quickened and a slight shiver twitched his shoulders. The shiver was pure excitement, because he stood upon the stones of Stamboul, the citadel of Islam—Stamboul, mistress of the three seas and the mainland of Europe, the gate of Asia, more beautiful than Rome.

More than once he had seen its marble walls, the dark green of its fruit gardens, the domes and slender minarets that had been built upon ancient Christian palaces. That was when he had been chained to the oar of a Barbary galley. For a Christian to enter Stamboul, except on sufferance, afoot and unarmed, was forbidden; for a Christian to wear a weapon, even a knife, was to gamble with death. A Cossack discovered within the city would be hunted down like a wolf found among sheep.

Even the ambassadors of the great kings of France and Holland had their houses across the bay in Pera and came to the city only to petition the sultan or to make gifts, nor could they protect their own followers if the soldiery of Islam desired captives.

So Charnomar breathed deeply, although his dark face was only insolent and expectant when his guide, eager to curry favor with the open-handed swordsman from the hills, cried out loudly:

"'Way for the lord of the hills! Make way, O ye who believe!'"

If the high pitched shout drew the attention of a dozen guards and a hundred loiterers, it also served as introduction, and Charnomar shifted the rug on his shoulder, brushed at his yellow mustache and swaggered onward, taking pains to get out of nobody's way. Instead of striking through the marketplace, where his patron might have been tempted to linger and buy or brawl, the waterman turned aside among uptilted carts and led the Cossack through odorous shadows, past an empty tank, to a flight of wooden steps, narrow and steep and treacherous with mud.

They climbed to where an oil lamp on a courtyard wall revealed the dark mass of an arch overhead. Putting out his hands to steady himself, Charnomar could feel the plaster walls on either side. And as he did so, two tall figures appeared beneath the arch, descending the steps. By their sable-lined *kaftans*, their pearl-sewn turbans and the slender gilded staffs they carried Charnomar recognized the two as janissaries—soldiers of the sultan's guard, slave bred and trained to weapons. More over, they were officers, insolently aware of the fear they inspired.

The waterman shrank back against a wall, trying to salaam and efface himself at the same time. The janissaries brushed past him and looked at Charnomar as hunting dogs eye a wolf. Charnomar guessed that he was expected to retreat before them, but he knew that a Circassian would not give up the path without cause.

"Beggar of the hills!" said one officer pleasantly, when he made no move to yield the steps.

The other had a more pointed tongue.

"O son of nameless fathers," he murmured, "surely thou art coming to visit thy sister within the arch, thy sister, the mother of nameless sons."

They waited to see if this would draw fire from the Circassian.

"Thou wilt know thy sister," the first speaker added, amused. "She wears no veil, yonder."

This was adding injury to insult, and Charnomar answered. He had not spent months on a rower's bench of a Barbary galley without learning the sulphurous language of the slave masters. Moreover, under his calm, he was chilled by a cold hatred of all Turks. So he answered with three words and the waterman yelled in fear and scrambled up the steps.

The janissaries stared until rage overcame their astonishment and the nearest one swung his staff at Charnomar's head. The staff had an iron knob on one end, a steel point on the other.

The blow was hasty, and the Cossack reached up a long arm, grasping the staff under the knob. He pulled down, and toward him, and the janissary was jerked from his footing, scrambled vainly to get his balance on the worn and slippery steps, and ended by plunging past Charnomar fifty feet to the bottom. But the Cossack kept the staff.

With it he parried a savage blow by the janissary's companion. The staffs were rather longer than cudgels, but Charnomar could move his big bulk with surprising swiftness. He had the better position, too, on that treacherous incline, because the man above him could not strike down freely and had to guard his feet.

When the janissary tried to reach for his sword, Charnomar whacked him solidly in the ribs with the iron knob. The soldier kicked out at the Cossack's head, and his ankle was caught by a hand that wrenched him off balance in a second. Clattering and cursing, he went down into darkness.

At once the two lifted the shrill rallying cry of Islam—

"*Ha Muslimin!*"

Charnomar ran up the steps beneath the arch. The waterman had vanished. He found himself in a narrow alley full of subdued sound and movement. He smelled musk and charcoal and cooking, saw the faint gleam of iron lanterns carried by some of the figures in the alley.

Aware of an opening on his right hand, he turned sharply and ducked his head under a low arch. In the gloom beyond he stumbled against animals, laden donkeys by the feel of them. He freed himself and ran on, past the glow of a fire where hooded figures sat about a water pipe. Dimly he saw steps in front of him, and kept on.

The steps led to an open roof where he could make out the line of the parapet against the stars. Voices clamored behind him, and he swung himself over the parapet, hanging by his hands until he felt shrubbery brushing against his feet. Then he released his hold, expecting to drop into soft earth.

But the shrubbery proved to be trees, and Charnomar flung out his arms, falling through the swaying branches of cypresses, a dozen feet or more to the ground. He picked himself up and felt to make certain that his sword was in its sheath. He had thrown away the staff in the beginning.

Above him he heard the *slip-slap* of bare feet, and low voices disputing. In the darkness under the cypresses he could not be seen, and evidently the men above did not think he had gone over a twenty-foot wall. They went elsewhere and Charnomar groped around until he had found his rug.

With this again on his shoulder he moved out from the wall and found himself under clear starlight in a kind of open alley. Dogs snarled at him tentatively, and he investigated farther, bringing up against blank walls until he noticed the arch of a doorway and found it to be open.

He entered at once, because to hesitate would be to show himself a stranger or afraid. A lantern hung from a bracket above the glimmer of water in a stone-bordered tank. Around the tank were masses of tulips and aloes in bloom, and he thought that this must be the garden court of some mosque or tomb—almost certainly a tomb, because it was utterly silent.

He shut the door behind him and went to sit on a bench, not too near the light. Throwing off his rug, he stretched out his legs and sat thinking with one eye on the courtyard door. He was hungry, but the evening was young, and the janissaries had been too angered for him to venture out just yet. Presently they would give up the search and he would go and find a coffee shop.

"O thou man of the hills, what evil hast thou done?"

It was a soft voice, seemingly amused, a woman's voice within a few feet of him. He looked instinctively toward the light, then away. She was sitting a little back from the tank on a strip of carpet under the aloes. After a moment he was certain that no others were with her.

"What is it to thee, O daughter of idleness?" he made response gruffly, for it was audacious in her to speak to him at all.

"Look!"

When he would not do as she said, the woman came and sat on the stone edge of the tank, so near that he could have touched her. Perforce he glanced down. She was a Circassian. He had seen girls like her in the valleys under the Caucasus—girls who wore that same jaunty striped cap with the limp feathers hanging down the mass of her straw-yellow hair. Her fringed shawl, which covered shoulders too slender and vigorous for a Turkish woman, was of soft lamb's wool. And her green leather half-boots were gilded after the manner of the mountain women.

"Peace be upon thee," he said indifferently.

"And upon thee the peace of God, the one God, O my brother!"

There was a hint of meaning in the last word, and Charnomar frowned down upon her, pulling at the end of his mustache. The last thing he wished was to meet with any one from the Circassian hills, and he chose to look annoyed as a warrior should.

"Thy brother was a magpie!" he scoffed, and rose, stretching his long arms, as if too annoyed to sit there longer.

"Wait!"

The Circassian also had gray eyes, though much darker than his by reason of kohl rubbed on the lids. She smelled evasively of aloes and musk, and seemed more than ready to mock him. Because she went unveiled he knew that she must be from the Kislar Dar.

"*Ai-a*, it is two years since I was brought across the sea, and in all that time I have had no speech with one from the hills. What is thy village?"

Charnomar seemed to listen idly.

"Ask the eagles! The eagle is wiser than the magpie."

"Oh, thou art a true *jigit*.* Was it thou who raised the cry and the brawling just now?"

Charnomar smiled. "Ask the Turks!"

---

*A reckless fighter, a daring rider and swordsman, who need not be too clever otherwise.

When he smiled, the harshness left his eyes, and the lines about his wide mouth softened. The girl watched him intently and when he would have moved away, she touched his sleeve.

"Wait! Tell me truly what place thou art from."

Silver bracelets set with amethysts slid upon her arm when she moved. She was a *bayadere*, a girl trained to singing and dancing, brought hither for the amusement of the Turks, and the Cossack reflected that she would doubtless be rewarded if she could point out an armed Christian within the city. That she suspected him was perfectly clear.

"From the sea!" he laughed, meeting her eyes frankly.

"It did not teach thee wisdom. For thou wert sitting with legs stretched out like an unbeliever, and thy talk is like—" She shook her head helplessly. "Thou art no man of the hills."

"What, then?"

For the moment they were alone in the courtyard, and he might have drawn his sword and slain her before she could cry out. The body of a *bayadere* found in a garden tank would have aroused no curiosity in the city. But Charnomar never killed a woman, and he did not think of doing so now.

"It is strange," she whispered. "That *kaftan* and vest—"

She turned her head suddenly. Voices approached the garden, and the door was pushed open. Charnomar saw three Moslems enter, leisurely, as if by right.

The one in advance was an old man in white robes and turban, and the two who attended him were obviously disciples. An imam, an expounder of the law of Islam, and by the same token, an enemy of all infidels.

Before the *bayadere* could speak, Charnomar stepped forward and salaamed.

"O master of wisdom, tell thy servant if this night is the first of the moon of Shawwul?"

The imam answered in measured tones.

"Nay, the second night from this, Shawwul begins."

Something like suspicion touched his thin face, and the two youths stared openly. Charnomar breathed deeply, his ears alert for the first cry of betrayal that might come from the girl. Out of the corner of his eye he saw her rising from the prostration of the dancing girl.

She said nothing at all, and after one glance at her unveiled face, the expounder of the law went on his way toward the tomb. But his disciples

looked back over their shoulders, for the Circassian was well worth looking at twice.

"Come," she whispered the moment they were out of sight. "It is not
safe for thee here. Nay, walk more slowly, a little before me."

"Whither?" the Cossack asked.

"To my place. Oh, thou art a fool! I prayed, here, outside this tomb, for a
man of my people, a man of the hills. When I saw thee wearing the *kaftan*
and vest I thought that God had sent such a man. But thou art a fool!"

The Circassian lived at the top of a ramshackle wooden building, up
flights of dark stairs that were far from quiet. Somewhere a tambourine
jingled monotonously, and a woman sang, and the air was full of the reek
of hubble-bubbles.

"If thou art afraid," he heard the Circassian whisper, "the way is open
to go."

Charnomar did not answer. He had come with her because there were
too many lights and too many janissaries who might be looking for a Circassian swordsman on the prowl for the streets to be safe as yet.

The singing girl drew back a curtain—he could feel the stirring of air
as it fell behind her—and after a moment reappeared with a lamp, holding back the curtain for him to enter.

Her room was carpeted and furnished with no more than a charcoal
brazier, a tabouret or two with a coffee stand, and a chest. But the settee
that ran along the wall was cleanly covered and cushioned, and the air
was fresh because the room opened out into a kind of gallery, screened
by wooden fretwork. Charnomar kicked off his slippers and went and sat
on the divan, and the Circassian laughed softly because this time he sat
upon his heels.

"Tell me truly what thou art!" she demanded.

"First," he responded, "tell me why thou did not betray me to the
imam."

For a moment she looked angry; then it pleased her to mock him again.
"Because thou art a brave—fool."

"Perhaps," he nodded, "because I am a Circassian from the sea—aye,
wearing the garments of the dead."

To his astonishment the singing girl shrank back away from him until her shoulders touched the wall. Her eyes widened and seemed to grow
swiftly darker as her cheeks became bloodless.

"Why?" she whispered. "In the name of the Compassionate—why?"

"To seek vengeance." Charnomar spoke at a venture, unwilling to mention ransom to this girl of the Kislar Dar.

She swayed and brushed back the yellow mass of hair from her forehead. Her eyes were fastened upon him as if she would read the soul within him, the spirit within the lean dark face and the steel-gray eyes. But surely a matter of vengeance could not startle a girl from the hills of the wild clans, who wore thrust in her girdle a curved dagger.

"Indeed, I prayed," she said slowly, "but—how could it happen?"

Charnomar was well content to be silent, until she mastered herself and went into the gallery, presently returning with a small roll of sweetmeat in her hands, fragrant of spice and aloe wood. This was the *ma'jun*, or guest refreshment, and Charnomar took it the more readily because he knew that she meant to offer him food, and the sharing of salt would be a tie between them. Moreover, he was hungry.

"I am Ilga of the Terek people," she said, "and my house is yours."

Deftly she prepared food in a brass pot over the brazier, mutton stew seasoned with garlic and rice with saffron. She moved gracefully, and always swiftly, and in silence. She who had mocked and scolded him was now content to treat him as a guest. More than once he found her looking at him with that strange curiosity. Charnomar was listening to the uproar in the street; for the Turkish soldiers, judging by the sounds, were pillaging the houses, under pretext of searching. More than once he heard a woman wailing, and the clinking of anklets as some girl fled past the curtain.

"What can we do?" the Circassian, Ilga, said calmly. "There are guards in the Kislar Dar—aye, they are the first to enter when the door of looting is open."

She placed food on the tabouret beside him and knelt by the divan to eat.

Charnomar was gathering up the last wad of rice when the curtain was thrust aside and a warrior in mail strode in. He had a shield on one arm and in the fingers of that hand a sack that jingled suggestively when he moved.

"*Ahai*, little pigeon under the roof!"

The Turk, a *sipahi* fully armed, blinked in the dull lamplight and made for the gleam of Ilga's tawny head. He must have emptied more than one cup of wine, because he reached for her shoulder and laughed when he clasped only air. Ilga had drawn away from him and slipped to the divan behind the Cossack.

"Little pigeon flies!"

The *sipahi* peered about him, holding out his bag, which must have contained many rings and anklets taken from more timid girls. Suddenly he cursed harshly, because he had noticed the Cossack in the depths of the divan.

"Out with thee—dog of the hills!"

Evidently he did not think that Charnomar would dare refuse his bidding. Judging by the shield, the *sipahi* was one of the guards of the quarter.

The Cossack got to his feet and confronted the pillager, his hands thrust into his belt.

"Nay," he said, "I will stay and thou wilt go—now."

The *sipahi* fumbled for the hilt of his sword, but his fingers struck the sack and he began to mutter. He was not in any mood to take up weapons and presently when the Cossack did not move or speak, he backed to the door and went out, kicking savagely at Charnomar's slippers.

Ilga ran to the balcony and gazed down at the shifting torches and hurrying figures of the alley until she saw the *sipahi* make his way into the next house. Then she motioned to Charnomar to sit near her.

"Thou art a strange man," she whispered. "*V'allah*, he, that other, was afraid. I think thy heart is against the Turks."

Charnomar said nothing, but the Circassian seemed to read his silence, because she lifted her head as if making swift decision.

"Surely I prayed; many times. Now I will tell thee who thou art and why—why I prayed."

Drawing her feet beneath her, she rested her chin on her hand.

"Thou art the sword that was sent to me."

Charnomar nearly laughed because it seemed to him that she was playing a game. To feed him, praise him and take money from him. That was what such women did.

"By Allah," he said, "I have no money for thee."

Fleetingly she looked up under the mass of her gleaming hair.

"When did I ask? We have shared the salt, thou and I. And now listen. I prayed for blood vengeance upon Kam Mustafa."

The Cossack had heard that name before. Kara Mustafa was *agha* of the *sipahis*, commander of the cavalry of the sultan and more than proud of a reputation for cruelty even among a people that made torture a fine art. He took no prisoners and spared no foeman.

"Two years ago," Ilga said quietly, "the sultan's officers went through our villages, claiming a strong young boy from every family to serve in the army. They took my brother, who was a man grown. Ay, they took me—because Kara Mustafa fancied me. We went down to the sea with them. There was a ship . . . "

She sat, musing upon the happenings of two years ago.

"The ship was crowded with our people of the hills—and Armenians and others. It brought us to Stamboul, and when we were climbing up the steps I ran away. I hid that night in the Jews' quarter under some hides. The Jews were kind and gave me food. Another Circassian woman brought me here, to this place."

Again she fell silent, her eyes fastened on the starlight above the flat roofs of the dwellings.

"Every day I asked for my brother, and after awhile they brought me word of him. The Turks had taken him and stripped off his clothes and thrown him upon the hooks of the wall by the *serai* gate. I put on a veil and went there with the woman who had sheltered me. It was evening, and they were putting lanterns in the galleries of the minarets. All that day he had hung from two hooks; one had caught in his leg, the other in his stomach. After it was dark I called up to him, and he knew me. But he was nearly mad with pain."

Ilga clasped her hands on the Cossack's knee.

"He cried out that Kara Mustafa tortured him because I had fled, and the *agha* had not found me again. *V'allah!* I begged the guards to find Kara Mustafa and make an end of my brother's suffering—the other women going away because of fear. But it was written that my brother should die in that hour. Kara Mustafa is the sword arm of the sultan. And still I, a singing girl, pray that I may see him die, to revenge my brother."

Her eyes blazed suddenly and her hands beat upon Charnomar's knee.

"Now thou hast come in the garments of my people, a swordsman seeking vengeance. If—if I can lead thee to Kara Mustafa wilt thou dare strike him down?"

"The *sipahi agha*?" Charnomar shook his head gravely, "Eh, little maiden, what talk is this? A lord of the Turks is not to be reached so easily."

"But he seeks me—he searches still, they say. And we—"

"Nay, little Ilga. I was sent to do otherwise."

"We have shared the salt."

"And I am bound to aid another."

The light went out of her face, and she went away silently to the divan. She did not make the late-night prayer; and Charnomar thought she
prayed only when the mood was on her. She drew a linen cloak over her
and presently her deep, even breathing told him she was asleep.

Charnomar sat in the darkened gallery, filled with the bittersweet scent
of aloes and rose leaves, watching the street and the lights below until
he dozed, and the distant call of a *muezzin* roused him to see the yellow
eastern sky reflected in the dark waters of the golden horn. Then, without
waking the girl, he went from the room, down to the street.

He went that noon, when the throngs in the streets were greatest and suspicion least, to investigate the lower city where the old *serai** stood. The
sultan now lived in a Summer dwelling upon one of the hills; but the ar-
mory and the prison and the quarters of the chief officers were still in
the old grounds. Two sides of the rambling walls fronted the sea, and one
side toward the city was taken up by the barracks of the *sipahis*. Charnomar went and squatted among some pilgrims who rested in the shade of
poplars by the main gate. Beyond this first wall was a garden—he could
see the lines of elms, and through the foliage the blank white wall and
domes of a church.

This church had been used in other years by the emperors who had
held this last stronghold of Rome. Then the victorious sultans had made
of it a small mosque; and when the *serai* was abandoned as a palace they
had hung its walls with their trophies, the weapons of vanquished kings
and warriors, the rapiers and matchlocks of Christendom ranged among
the jewel-encrusted shields, the inlaid pistols and the gold filled scimitars of Persia. But chiefest of their trophies was the cage, built by captive
metal workers, its bars set into the solid stone flooring of the vault beneath the church.

Here, barred like animals in darkness, were kept the enemies of the sultan, whom he had chief cause to remember. Food was passed in to them
through the grating, and the door of the cage was only opened to conduct
them out to the blinding iron, or the hooks, or stake. When they died be-
times, as often happened, the bodies were thrown over the wall into the
sea. And here, Charnomar knew, was Kirdyaga, the Cossack *ataman*.

*"Palace"; by Italians and others rendered as "seraglio."

By dint of patience and the appearance of good-natured stupidity, he passed the guards of the outer gate. When a Nakshab dervish with a gourd and beggar's staff whined to be allowed to see the courtyard within the gate, Charnomar begged a blessing of the holy man, cursing the guards loudly because they mocked the piety of a man from the East.

The dervish, who had come to beg, fastened himself upon Charnomar until he was pacified with copper and went to squat by the roadway where officials came and went.

"*Ya huk—ya hak!*" the dervish whined, the cry that is as common as the barking of dogs beyond Stamboul.

And Charnomar wandered within the elms of the roadway, chewing mastic and gazing open-eyed upon the gardeners and the strolling men in silk turbans, and the brown-stained wall of a building where great steel hooks projected from the masonry—hooks turned at every angle to catch a falling body.

He was gazing at the hooks, though he was counting the armed Turks in the portico of the prison church near him, when the dervish's wail increased, and hoofs clattered upon the hard clay of the road. He turned in time to see a cavalcade of riders trot past, led by a man in a gold embroidered *khalat* and a small turban the color of steel.

"'Way!" cried one of the attendants. "'Way for the Agha Sipahi!"

Kara Mustafa—Black Mustafa—had the high, square shoulders and dark face of an Egyptian. He rode, as if from habit, with his hand resting on the balled hilt of his scimitar. There was power in the broad figure and both intelligence and cruelty in the blunt head that turned slowly from side to side to scan the crowd. Something in the creases about his throat and the beak of a mouth suggested a lizard.

The beggar rose and advanced into the road, making for Kara Mustafa. With the assurance of a pilgrim and the effrontery of one who has nothing to lose by shame, he grasped at the *agha*'s stirrup.

Whether the horse shied at the staff of the dervish, or whether the leader of the *sipahis* did not choose to be touched by the beggar, the Arab that Kara Mustafa rode flung up its head and swerved. And the instant before it did so, Kara Mustafa drove the point of his iron stirrup into the chest of the dervish.

The *agha* reined in the startled horse without shifting his seat in the saddle. Nor did he look back. The dervish staggered and dropped his staff.

He fell on his knees, his thin arms wrapped around his body. He coughed and spat blood into the dust of the road.

Some of the *sipahis* laughed, but the Turks on guard at the church entrance were silent. They had all seen the dervish fall.

Whereupon Charnomar wandered over to the church portico and seated himself upon the lowest of the marble steps, worn smooth by countless feet of other ages.

"A fine horse," he muttered, after the receding dust of the cavalcade.

It would have seemed strange in a Circassian to take more notice of the dervish than the horse.

"Was the rider the sultan?"

One of the Turks grunted and another yawned and spat.

"Nay, the sword arm of the sultan. Who art thou, to ask?"

The mild-looking Circassian pulled at his mustache, his gray eyes jovial.

"A *jigit*, a rider. Aye, from the sea."

He leaned against a pillar and took from his wallet his short clay pipe and steel and flint.

"It was said to me that an unbeliever would be set upon the stake. Here. I do not see him."

"At sunset, the evening after this one."

"Where is the dog who is to be slain?"

The Turk jerked his head backward.

"Within—aye, within the bars."

"Ah. I have not seen the cage. When I return to my people I would say to them that I have seen the cage."

The Turk shook his head.

"It is not permitted. Go and look at the gaol by the great mosque. Thy people will not know the difference."

Charnomar lighted his pipe and gazed about the garden as if the matter did not concern him overmuch. But he had let the Turk, a hook-nosed swordsman from Albania, see a single gold piece when he replaced the flint and steel. In silence he waited, until the Albanian came and sat beside him.

"The prisoner to go to the stake is a Cossack," the guard whispered. "*Bismillah*—he is the chieftain of a regiment."

Charnomar looked inquisitive.

"Is the prisoner thine?"

"Nay, he belongs to the *rikab aghlalari*, who is the master of the stir-rup, one of the favorites of the sultan."

Charnomar fixed the name in his mind, while the Albanian pon-dered.

"Eh," he said, "for a price—for a very little price thou canst see the Cossack. Come to this place at the hour of evening prayer on the morrow. Then will the dog of an infidel be led out."

"*V'allah*! For nothing at all, an hour later, I could see him at the stake."

"But here we will bind him, and set him face to tail upon a mule, to lead through the streets. That will be a tale to tell in thy village."

"Perhaps." Charnomar looked disappointed. "And yet it is in my mind to see the cage. I am no beggar. I have gold."

Again the soldier hesitated. Punishment in the *serai* was swift and sure for one who disobeyed an order. But the Circassian seemed guileless and stubborn—and much might be done with gold.

"An order has been given, to find a man with a mule," the guard whis-pered. "At sunset, tomorrow, come thou to the gate—that one where the dervish squirms. Come thou at the hour I said—and wait. I will do what may be done. But bring a purse with thee."

Charnomar clapped his hand upon his girdle, nodded, and with a whis-pered "*Insh'allah!*" stowed away his pipe and, after gazing openly at the weapons of the guard, turned his back upon the portico.

By the time he had left the gate he had wandered over most of the gardens and knew its plan; he had studied the prison church and had noticed one other entrance—a narrow door iron studded and almost certainly kept barred. And he had aroused the greed of one of the guards without draw-ing suspicion upon himself. He was reasonably sure the Albanian would pass him in to see Kirdyaga, and he meant to bring two horses with him, instead of the mule.

Not until he had decided this did he go in search of the house of the master of the stirrup, to make the attempt to ransom Kirdyaga.

Twenty-four hours later Charnomar made his way through the ever-in-creasing throngs of the horse market that had once been the forum of The-odosius. There was little buying and selling. The midafternoon sun had baked the mud of the streets and the stench vied with the heat, and the flies were a torment. The Cossack wandered among the traders until he found a wizened Tartar sitting on a sheepskin with his back against the soiled marble block of a pedestal that lacked a column. From the Tartar Charnomar bought two shaggy ponies that looked both evil and ill-used but had a turn of speed and endurance. He knew the breed.

For both ponies he bought bridles and saddles, and he mounted one, leading the other through the alleys to the khan of the Bokharians, a great hostelry for wayfarers that was half a sleeping court and half a stable. Here he fed and watered his beasts, loosened the girths and left them tied. Three hours of sunlight remained, before the time when he was to go to see the cage.

The khan was near the Place of the Girls and Charnomar made his way back to the scene of his meeting with the janissaries. He did not hurry; he even stopped at a weapon seller's stall, and selected a heavy scimitar with a fine edge. He placed this, in its leather sheath, in his girdle.

The weapon seller, who had got his price without much haggling, waxed curious.

"Is not one sword enough?"

"Perhaps. But this night will be the first of the moon of Shawwul, and—who knows—I may have need of the two."

"Verily, the moon of Shawwul begins—aye, and the first of the three holy days."

With the first darkness, when a black thread could no longer be distinguished from a white one, would begin the festival of the Bairam of Ramadan. Already, as Charnomar wandered forth again, merchants were leaving their stalls. Many had put on gleaming robes of crimson and gold; the horses that pressed past him in the dust had caparisonings of white and cloth of silver; through the throngs bobbed the white caps of the dervishes and over the tumult of feet and voices resounded the cry of beggars. The month of fasting was at an end and with the first of the holy days came feasting.

The wisest of the Greeks and Jews were leaving the city, because in the first evening of the great Bairam armed Islam exulted, and a drunken soldier might see fit to try his sword on an unbeliever, and pave his way to Paradise thereby.

But Charnomar, wearing openly his two swords, seemed perfectly happy as he sought out the coffee house where Ilga the Circassian had told him she sang in the afternoon. He went down the steps into the cool gloom where the figures sitting against the wall sipped noisily at their bowls and argued in whispers. A boy dressed as a Mamluk stood at the entrance and sprinkled him with rose water, and Charnomar tossed the boy, who expected copper, a silver coin.

"*Giaba*," he cried at the proprietor, snapping his fingers.

Should not a warrior from the hills, on the eve of a festival, buy coffee for all his companions in merriment? And for himself he had brandy in the coffee.

"Eh," he said to the gloom at large, "where is the music—where is the singer?"

"By and by," explained the Turk who was master of the place, "the fiddles will play, and there will be the shadow puppet show."

"Nay, bring out a singing girl."

"The *bayadere*? She sings only for the *chelabilar*, the lords!"

"Allah! Am I not a personage?" Charnomar smiled, laying his hands on his two sword hilts, and the Turk waddled off into the curtains. When he returned, Ilga appeared behind him, and the sipping and whispering ceased, because her face, unveiled beneath the tawny hair, drew their eyes instantly. And even in the haze of smoke they recognized beauty.

"The Yataghan!" Charnomar cried. "The song of the sword that whispered!"

"He is a little drunk," the Turk admonished her, "but he is a man of thy hills—"

"O son of a bath tender," laughed Charnomar, "I am very drunk, and I will give gold to this singer. Go back to thy sitting place!"

Ilga saluted him, sinking gracefully upon her knee, but her eyes under the long lashes were both eager and disturbed.

"Nay," Charnomar insisted, "sit by me, here! Am I not the one to pay? Knowest thou the song? Thus it begins."

Reaching out his long arm he took from her the three-stringed lute, and swept his powerful fingers across it. She lifted her head and nodded.

My sword is rusty and the blade is dull—

Her full, soft voice swelled and sank in the wild and yet sad measure of the Circassian song. And when she had made an end, he called for coffee to be served her, his fingers still wandering over the lute. Fifty pairs of eyes were upon them.

"Are not the gates open?" she said under her breath. *"Ai,* in a little while it will be sundown, and the beginning of the festival. Before then, thou must go!"

"Why?" Charnomar wondered aloud. "Verily, by Allah, this is a splendid city, and soon the cannon will fire, and the minarets be lighted!"

To mark the hour of sunset, he had heard that guns would thunder from the forts. To mark the eve of the holy day, lanterns would be hung in the galleries of the towers.

To the watchers it appeared beyond doubt that the wide-shouldered Circassian had had too much of *raki* and coffee.

"And why hast thou come to this place?" she demanded softly.

"To say farewell to thee," he whispered, and then raised his voice again. "For the sight of thee is pleasing to me. O little pigeon of the loft, I will sing of thy charms. Aye, one by one. First of thy sun gold hair—"

Some of the watchers smiled and resumed their talk. With an exclamation Ilga snatched the lute from him, and picked up the bowl of steaming black juice that had been set before her on a wooden platter.

"O fool!" she cried aloud, and then almost inaudibly, "I know now who thou art. Aye, a Cossack—an unbeliever and friend of the unbelievers. At the time of the late afternoon prayer, yesterday, thou wert at the house of the master of the stirrup, talking with his treasurer. To him thou gavest a great sum in jewels, for the ransom of a Cossack prisoner, saying that thou wert sent by the brotherhood of the Cossacks. Is not the tale true?"

"It is thy tale, Charnomar smiled. "Say on!"

"The servant of the treasurer told it in the Kislar Dar, and it was related to me—that a heedless Circassian hath acted as the emissary of the Cossacks."

"Then," Charnomar mused, "the servants of the master of the stirrup do not know who I am?"

"Ai-a, their talk was of the jewels. They think thee a besotted hillman, who served the foes of Islam."

"And thou?"

"Ohai, Charnomar, I know well thou art not of my people. Thy speech, thy way of sitting, the mission that brought thee. I think the janissaries were hunting thee that first night with cause. Thou art an enemy of Islam and thy life is forfeit, if I choose."

The Cossack took up his bowl of coffee and drank it slowly, with loud sips. His fingers on the hot bowl were steady, and when he set it down, he had made a decision.

"True, little Ilga—thou hast spoken the truth."

He heard the catch of her breath, and was aware that her head turned toward him swiftly, and he was grateful for the obscurity in which they sat.

"Did the master of the stirrup free thy—thy brother in arms?" she asked after a little silence.

"I gave them," he explained, "the missive that was sent to the Cossacks. And the sum of the ransom in jewels. Many men came in to question me, and to ask each for more payment. I gave them the last of the jewels, but did not show any gold. I promised that more gold would be given after the Cossack colonel was freed. So, in the end, the master of the stirrup made out a paper to release the captive."

"And thou, O fool?"

"They told me to go to the courtyard of the cage tomorrow morning and the Cossack would be given to me. That was the order in the paper. I have it here."

"Hast thou read the writing?"

"Nay, how could I? But it has a seal."

"And wilt thou go to the cage with it?"

For a moment the Cossack was silent. Ilga knew his secret, but she had shared bread and salt with him and, beyond that, instinct whispered that she would not betray him. And Charnomar had found that the boldest action was often the safest.

"Aye," he said, "but not tomorrow. I shall go this evening. The men of the master of the stirrup are too fond of gold to keep faith altogether."

"And yet thou knowest not what is written in the paper!"

"No help for it, little Ilga. At least it bears a seal. I have two horses and I shall say that the Cossack colonel is sold to me. A little more gold—" he grinned—"they may hand him over. If not, we may cut a way out with swords."

She shook her head quietly.

"Can the trapped panther free himself from the cage with his teeth? Do not go."

"Didst thou not go to sit by thy brother who was hanging on the hooks?"

"Aye—"

"I came to Stamboul to free the Cossack colonel from torture. Shall I turn back now, saying to the Cossacks that I became afraid of a paper and a woman's word?"

"Nothing will change thy mind?"

Charnomar made no response, but the singing girl understood his silence. She rose, gathering her dolman about her slender shoulders, shaking back the mass of tawny hair.

"Then come with me. I know an Armenian who can read the paper. Nay—wilt thou go blindly into the trap?"

Again she called to him to follow her, and the men in the place looked up curiously. Charnomar strode after her to the curtains in the rear, and through a passage that opened into an alley deep in shadow where the dogs snarled among piles of refuse. Ilga hastened on, past courtyard walls to a narrow stair that led to a balcony.

The Cossack lengthened his stride to keep up with her, but the swift-footed girl disappeared within the arch of the balcony a moment before him, and he took his time in making certain that no men loitered in the alley before he followed her, bending his head to pass under the smoke-blackened beams.

On a worn carpet an old man in a skullcap sat, with a book resting upon a frame before him. The level sunlight gleamed on his white beard and thin, pallid hands. Ilga's eyes blazed as she held out her hand for the missive, and Charnomar drew the rolled paper from his girdle.

The Armenian glanced at the seal and fingered his beard.

"*Eh, chelabim*," he muttered, reading over a second time the few lines of writing. "It is like the Turks, this."

"What says it?" demanded Ilga.

"It is an order from Hassan Bey, the master of the stirrup, to the officer of the cage. It says that the officer should seize the bearer and put him to death at once."

"O blind fool!" Ilga whispered.

Charnomar stretched out his hand for the order, and replaced it in his sash.

"I had thought the Turks meant to trick me, by sending the prisoner to the stake this evening," he said grimly, "and giving me no more than his body tomorrow. Now that Hassan Bey has been paid, he wishes to do away also with the man who paid him. I had not thought of that."

"What wilt thou do?" demanded the singing girl anxiously.

"I must take two horses to the gate of the *serai*."

"And then? *V'allah!*" She shivered a little, as if the cold wind from the strait had come into the balcony. "Nay, I know. Thou wilt try to aid thy brother with the sword. I am afraid!"

"Why?" Charnomar smiled, because he could not understand her moods. "What harm to thee?"

"At first," she said swiftly, "I would have let thee die, to harm Kara Mustafa. I planned that when I first saw thee. I led thee to my place to persuade thee. But the next day, when I woke and found thee gone, my mind was otherwise."

Suddenly she came close to him, resting her cheek against his shoulder.

"May Allah shield thee—I am afraid. The *serai* is an evil place, and I— I would like to go with thee from this city. I love thee. May God have pity upon me! Let us take the horses and go back to my people of the hills."

Slowly the Cossack shook his head.

"Nay," he responded, placing his hand on the tawny head. "Do thou stay with this man of learning."

But Ilga sprang away from him, her eyes gleaming with tears.

"Shall I not go to the cage with the man I love—I, who have seen my brother die? I will wait at the gate."

"May Allah shield thee, then," cried Charnomar impatiently. "Come, if thou wilt."

He strode away and Ilga followed. The man in the skullcap watched them pass from the alley and push into the throngs outside. Down by the sea a cannon boomed.

The Armenian sighed, shook his head, and turned a page of the book on the stand beside him.

The sun had gone down in the mist, and one by one the minarets of the *serai* were outlined in light against the gray twilight, as lanterns were hung in the galleries. The throng that had gathered in front of the main gate of the palace pressed closer, to watch the lights and await the coming of the prisoner who was to be led through the streets to the stake.

By the courtyard wall a mountebank was setting up a puppet show, and cloaked figures had already seated themselves expectantly before the curtain. The jingling of a tambourine chimed in the hum of voices that swelled and sank as Turkish officers appeared and passed through the gate.

Some of the officers stopped at a table under an awning hung with colored lanterns. The table was set with rolls of tobacco, boxes of mastic and ambergris. Behind the table appeared a thin head under a long cloth cap that flapped from side to side. The head hovered anxiously as a bird over its nest, sometimes smiling, sometimes exclaiming, and always bowing profoundly before the Turks. Shamoval, the Jew of Stamboul, had returned to set up shop at the beginning of the festival.

"Great, mighty lords," he cried, "here are ribbons and sweets, and bracelets for the pretty girls—and at such prices!"

While he cried out his small eyes pierced the throng like lances. Shamoval, as well as the others, had come to see the torture of the Cossack colonel. But unlike the others, he had money at stake on the issue. He hoped earnestly that Charnomar had left Stamboul before now.

And so, when he saw two Circassians ride up to the gate on their shaggy horses, he uttered an exclamation of fear and anguish. In spite of the beauty of the girl who rode unveiled among these Moslems, he had eyes only for Charnomar, who dismounted some distance from the gate and led his two horses forward.

Shamoval saw the Circassian girl slip from the saddle and go out of the crowd to the entrance of an alley. Here she stood where she could look through the open gate, and Shamoval muttered to himself, shaking his head, because he distrusted all singing girls.

"*Ai!*" he cried, clutching at the sleeve of an officer who was sniffing at a box of mastic to learn whether there was opium in it. "Look, noble lord!" He lowered his voice. "This mountain *jigit* with the horses—he is—"

Something caught in Shamoval's throat and he could not go on. He would be rewarded if he pointed out a Cossack. But he could not bring himself to say the words. And then perhaps Charnomar had only come here by chance, and would not run any mad risk.

"He is bringing the horse to mount the dog of a Cossack, who will be taken to the stake," grunted the Turk, evidently in good humor.

"Holy Saints!"

Shamoval's mouth dropped open and he trembled. Again he started to speak, and only groaned.

Taking the two horses by the reins, Charnomar advanced to the soldiers at the open gate, spoke to them briefly and passed on, into the palace grounds, where Shamoval could no longer see him.

The Cossack knotted the reins of the two ponies and made fast a loop to the low-hanging branch of an elm some distance to the side of the road and a stone's throw from the prison church. He took his time about this, because he wanted to make certain where the Turkish soldiers were. Seven at the outer gate, ten or twelve at the portico of the church: an occasional officer with servants riding out of the grounds. Over there, in the gloom under the high walls of the cavalry barrack, perhaps a score of *sipahis* sitting and lying about a fountain.

He was glad that no mounted *sipahis* were about. If he could get Kirdyaga into the saddle of a horse . . .

"That's the only way out," he thought.

The master of the stirrup had tricked him, and it was useless now to show the order that had been given him. Only one thing was possible— to try to cut a way out of the city. A guard would be sent to escort Kirdyaga to the stake. It would be dark by then. And if the guard were janissaries on foot, Charnomar could bring his horse close to Kirdyaga, in the streets, let the captive know what he meant to do, and whip up the horses suddenly. After that, he did not know. The gates were locked. But Kirdyaga would be in the saddle of a horse, with a sword in his hand, and he would not go to the stake.

"What is this?" growled a voice. "Thou hast brought horses instead of the mule that was ordered."

The Albanian had left his comrades of the watch and come to meet the Cossack in no gentle mood.

"Nay," Charnomar made answer, "they are my horses. I do not ride mules through the streets."

"May Allah not prosper thee! O dog without wit, didst thou think to ride like a lord among the *sipahis* who are to take the Cossack to the stake?"

"What *sipahis?*"

"*Mas'allah!* The twenty and the officer who will have charge of the captive. It is past the time of their coming." The broad face of the swordsman glowered under the massive white turban.

Charnomar knew that there would be no chance to cut Kirdyaga free from a score of lancers. That way, also, was closed.

"Where are the sequins that were promised?" demanded the soldier.

Feeling in his wallet the Cossack drew out a single gold piece and gave it to the Albanian who peered at it and spat.

"One! May jackals tear thee—"

"No more, until I have seen the cage."

Charnomar's voice was low and unhurried, but the Albanian saw fit not to argue. He stowed away the coin and led the way to the portico.

On the steps the Cossack glanced over his shoulder. The road through the garden was deserted; he heard no hoofs. Twilight had closed in upon the white walls of the *serai*. The hooks overhead were no longer visible. In the minarets the lanterns glowed, tracing spears of light against the purple sky. One of the soldiers was tuning a flute, and Charnomar hummed under his breath as he waited for the Albanian, who had disappeared into the church.

At any time the *sipahis* might come up and after that Kirdyaga was doomed. The only remaining chance was that the Turks might let Charnomar go down to the prisoners with only a single guard, or two. A slight chance. But the thought of it was like wine to the big Cossack and he waited cheerfully for the least bit of luck.

A lantern came swinging between the pillars and was lifted high. A gaunt man, beardless, in a black robe, peered out and asked sullenly—

"Where is the one who would smell of death?"

Charnomar ascended the steps and almost laughed as he did so.

"Here, O thou father of vultures."

The lantern was thrust close to his eyes, then the keeper of the church grunted and turned, signing for him to follow. They passed under a doorless arch, into the cold gloom of the stone nave.

Nothing within looked like a church. The swinging lantern flickered over rows of swords on the walls, the steel blades tarnished and dull. Charnomar saw costly shields heaped in the corners and long Indian matchlocks stacked here and there. The statues and mosaic work had been knocked out by the Turks and the altar, dimly seen under the dome, dismantled.

The air was heavy with tobacco smoke and an odor less pleasing. The flapping of their slippers on the slabs echoed overhead, swiftly, because the keeper hurried, looking over his shoulder to see that Charnomar did not try to snatch up any of the weapons.

Four men seated around a brazier on the raised chancel looked up at Charnomar, stared at his sword hilts and the wallet in his girdle. One had a beard stained red in the Persian fashion.

"What is this?" he asked.

"The mule driver who comes to take the Cossack," responded the keeper. "It is time."

He of the red beard yawned and spat and stretched out a muscular hand for the lantern. The others rolled off their haunches and stood up. One, who looked like an Italian renegade, had a long pistol in his belt, but all carried swords. The keeper saw fit to say nothing more, and Charnomar hoped that the four would not go down together to the vaults.

But the four filed off, opening a door at the side of the chancel. Charnomar heard them descending steps.

"Go, if thou wilt," the keeper muttered. "It is down there—the cage."

Charnomar gained the head of the stairs and kicked off his slippers. There was light enough to see the last of the four passing around a turn in the stairs. The air in the passage was close and foul with stale filth. What good to go down there, with four armed men? Two he could cut down, but not four.

He slipped down the steps and around the turning. One more flight of steps. The Turks tramped off into the shadows of the vault. Charnomar moved after them, his big body swinging soundlessly over the stone flagging. He stopped in the shadow of a heavy pillar.

Holding the lantern high, the man with the red beard was peering through a line of rusty iron bars. In the center of the vault these bars had been set in the flooring and the ceiling, making an enclosure some ten paces long and three broad. And in this space without so much as a quilt or a mattress a score of men were crowded. Outstretched on remnants of sheepskins, or on the stones greasy from the contact of their bodies and darkened with stains, some lay blinking at the lantern. Others squatted against the bars, shielding their eyes from the light. Charnomar noticed one who wore a silk *khalat* and embroidered sash.

By their heavy breathing and restless movements, some must have been ill. The coughing as the guards approached the gate in the bars sounded like the subdued barking of dogs. They were housed worse than dogs—these doomed men of the cage.

Evidently they had shown their teeth in the past, because two of the Turks drew their swords, while a third fumbled with a heavy key in the lock. The gate, a square of smaller bars, rasped open, and the red beard spat through it.

"May God be with ye!" he mocked them. "Send forth the Cossack unbeliever."

The coughing ceased while the listeners hung upon the words.

"He will go to the spit," remarked the man with the pistol, "now that he has been roasted enough."

Charnomar understood the words when the Cossack emerged from the gate. The hair had grown upon his shaven scalp, so the long lock looked like a plume hanging from a tuft. But around the brow the hair had been burned and the skin seared with hot irons.

This torture had taken the sight from one eye, because he turned his gray head from side to side to see his way. He was bare to the belt and through the hair of his chest a great cross had been burned, so that the cracked red flesh showed clear. Only a spark of vitality remained in Kirdyaga's shattered body, but he held his head up and he stood before the Turks not as a slave but as a foeman unarmed.

At sight of him Charnomar strode toward the five men.

"O brothers," he inquired, "is this the unbeliever?"

"And thou, son of a mule—who summoned thee?" demanded the leader of the guards, he of the red beard.

Charnomar's gray eyes surveyed him grimly. "It was written I should come—to bid thee hasten. Verily there is little life in the accursed unbeliever."

Yellow teeth shone through the red beard.

"Verily and indeed, as thou sayest. Look!" The Turk thrust his foot against Kirdyaga's hip and pointed at deep swollen gashes under the captive's shoulder blades.

"Thus he hung from the hooks."

"Aye, he tasted of hell!" Charnomar nodded understanding and pressed closer to stare at Kirdyaga's wounds. "Ho, he will whine, at the stake, like a ripped cat."

"Nay, he does not cry out."

Kirdyaga, standing passive as a wearied horse, waited for the talk to cease. And Charnomar knew that the old Cossack was so maimed that he wished for death more than anything else.

"Look how he eyes the swords," he grinned. "Allah, he would like to have one in his hand again! *Hai*—" he drew a scimitar and balanced it in both hands out of Kirdyaga's reach—"the old eagle lifts his head." He spat into Kirdyaga's face and the two Turks who had stepped past him to close the gate turned to watch the mocking of the captive. "There is life in him yet. Eh, Kirdyaga!"

"What didst thou call him?" demanded the red beard, who thought he had missed a jest.

"*Kirdyaga, ataman!*"

The good eye of the tormented man turned full upon Charnomar, gleaming strangely.

Charnomar tossed the scimitar in the air toward him, and took a single step past him. For that instant the eyes of all the Turks were upon the steel blade, and in the next second Charnomar had set his hands against the shoulders of the two guards standing at the open gate and thrust. He put all the power of his shoulders into the thrust, and the two were taken off balance. They plunged through the gate and fell headlong. Whereupon Charnomar slammed shut the gate and turned the key.

There had not been a sound other than that. The scimitar had not fallen to the stones, and the onlookers had not yet bethought them of shouting. A single glance showed Charnomar that the old Cossack had caught the scimitar by the hilt as it fell, as a swordsman could be trusted to do by instinct.

The red beard had put down the lantern and drawn his own weapon, his eyes bewildered. He cut hastily at Kirdyaga, but Charnomar parried the cut and knocked up the Turk's blade. The long scimitar of the young Cossack slashed the burly leader under the ribs, and blood darkened the man's girdle and breeches.

"Ha, *Muslimin!*" the red beard groaned and fell forward.

Charnomar turned to look for the other Turk and found him cocking his pistol, feeling with hasty fingers at the priming. He fired as the young Cossack leaped toward him, but the ball went wide, tearing through the sleeve of Charnomar's coat.

Then the Turk lifted the pistol to throw it, reaching at the same instant for a curved knife behind his hip. Suddenly he screamed, standing rigid, still clutching the smoking pistol. Charnomar had thrust the point of the scimitar under the man's heart and twisted it upward. The soldier's knees bent and his head and arms fell forward.

"A good blow!" Kirdyaga spoke for the first time—a quivering growl, as if the sound of his own voice was strange to him.

"Health to you, Sir Colonel!" Charnomar grinned at him. "The brothers of the *siech* sent me to greet you."

"Alone?"

"Aye."

Charnomar had stepped to the cage to see what had happened to the other two guards. And for a moment the Cossacks stared silently.

Where the Turks had fallen were two piles of writhing, gasping figures. The Turks were not visible. They had fallen among the captives, and all the inmates of the cage, even one too ill to do more than crawl, had scrambled upon them, gripping and tearing and clutching at their weapons.

A man's leg rose out of the tangle, kicking. A deep groan resounded to the vaulted roof. Some of the captives began to get to their feet. One held a sword, its channels dark with blood. He was the wearer of the silk *khalat*. For the other weapon they were still struggling, until a bearded negro came erect with it and lashed about him, half maddened with the lust of fighting, trampling on the torn body of the soldier who had been alive and careless of harm five minutes before.

"In the name of Allah the Compassionate," cried the first noble, "open the cage!"

They pressed against the bars, peering through the smoke at Charnomar.

"O thou brother of misfortune, open swiftly!"

In the confusion of the struggle it did not occur to them that Charnomar might be anything but a Moslem like themselves. If they thought at all, or cared, they must have reasoned that he quarreled with the guards. Life is strong even in condemned men, and only one thing was in their minds, to escape from the cage. They were all doomed to torment in various ways.

"O ye dead men!" Charnomar cried back at them. "Will ye come forth to your graves?"

They shouted in unison, half crazed with dread that the Turks would come and bind them. And Charnomar turned the key in the gate. Kirdyaga picked up the lantern and stepped aside.

But the men of the cage did not wait for light. All of them knew that weapons were to be had in the church above them, and they rushed up the stairs, the giant negro in the lead, the sick man staggering behind. In a moment the Cossacks heard a frightened yell, and Charnomar wondered what had happened to the keeper who had lingered by the brazier. Shouts echoed down the stairway faintly, and in the distance sounded the clashing of steel.

"Come," Charnomar said.

But Kirdyaga shook his gray, scarred head. He drew closer to Charnomar and bent to look in his face.

"Nay, for me the road is closed. Eh, you are brave. You may get out. Give me your pipe and some tobacco. I have a sword and Satan will have new servants before they make an end of me."

Charnomar shook his head.

"It is night. I have horses waiting. Once in the saddle, who knows? Come!"

The gaunt colonel's mustache twitched in a grim smile.

"How far could I ride with this?" He pointed to the sear of the cross on his chest. "You are young. Maybe girls are waiting for you somewhere or other."

"If you stay, I stay."

"A thousand devils take you!" Kirdyaga turned toward the stair unsteadily. "Where are the horses?"

He mustered his strength as he climbed the steps, breathing heavily. At the top Charnomar ran out into the chancel to see what was happening at the main entrance.

"Hide of the devil," he whispered, "the *sipahis* have come up."

Horses were plunging outside the portico. He heard rather than saw them. Smoking torches swung wildly through the outer garden. The tall negro, the tunic torn from his shoulders, stood in the portico, a sword in one hand, an ax in the other. Many of the captives had been soldiers, and they had had their pick of many weapons. With nothing to hope for except a swift death, they had cut their way through the guards who had come into the church to investigate the pistol shot, and had fallen upon the surprised *sipahis* like maddened wolves. Their outcry—*Allah-ilal-lahu*—mingled with the rallying shout of the soldiers. Charnomar was well content.

He ran back, took the lantern from Kirdyaga and searched along the corridor for the small door he had noticed when he had examined the garden. It was closed and barred, but in another moment he had blown out the lantern and opened the door.

Taking Kirdyaga by the arm, he walked to the elms where the horses were tethered. The janissaries at the outer gate of the garden were hurrying toward the church, and *sipahis* were running up from their barrack. Turbaned heads appeared under the lights of distant balconies, but no one saw the two Cossacks moving under the trees. The garden was a bedlam of struggling figures and galloping horses.

Charnomar found the two ponies where he had left them, and he helped the old Cossack to mount.

"Keep behind me and keep your mouth shut."

Grunting with satisfaction, Kirdyaga thrust his feet into the stirrups and trotted after Charnomar, who kneed his horse to a gallop as soon as they reached the road.

"*Ahai!*" he shouted, and the throng of merrymakers who had pushed into the open gate gave way hastily.

In Stamboul only Turks might ride and a rider with a drawn sword would not be tolerant of delay. No guards were there, but no guards were needed to open a way.

As Kirdyaga passed through, the crowd yelled with fear and astonishment.

Even Shamoval looked up, who was scurrying about like a long-eared rabbit, trying to get his belongings packed and away.

Charnomar looked over the tossing heads, to where Ilga had taken her stand to watch. And he reined in so suddenly that his pony reared.

The puppet showman had kindled oil lamps behind his curtain and the light from these lamps fell upon the Circassian girl. She was straining desperately to free herself from a Moslem who had gripped the tangle of her long hair.

And this man, who sat easily in the saddle of a restless black stallion, whose cloth of gold cloak gleamed in the strong light, over silvered mail, was Kara Mustafa. He had found Ilga and caught her. Another Turkish nobleman was maneuvering his horse behind the girl, trying to grip her arms and lift her to Mustafa's saddle.

Perhaps the leader of the *sipahis* had come to take charge of Kirdyaga's execution; perhaps he had come when he heard the fighting. But once he had seen the girl he paid no heed to events within the *serai*. His broad chin was outthrust, his thick lips grimaced, and his eyes were no more than slits.

Before Charnomar could move he heard a hoarse shout behind him—"*Khosh aha-ar!*"

Kirdyaga, striking his pony with the flat of his blade, had wheeled into the throng and headed for Kara Mustafa, ten paces distant.

Excitement had gripped the old Cossack when he mounted to the saddle. Sight of the Turkish commander in his shining dress had stirred the embers of old hatreds. His one eye was fastened upon the grinning face of Kara Mustafa.

Quickly Charnomar wheeled his pony. But Kirdyaga was ahead of him, almost upon the lord of the *sipahis*.

Mustafa had seen him at once, had released Ilga and gripped the hilt of his scimitar. Clad in mail from throat to knee, a skilled swordsman, he seemed as eager for the meeting as the gaunt Cossack.

"'Tis a sick dog," he cried to the other Turk. "Nay, I will give him his death."

He started to draw his sword and shouted in sudden fury. Ilga wrapped her arms about his forearm. She was on his sword side and she flung all her weight upon him so that he could not shake her off at once.

He lifted his left hand to strike her, but changed his mind, to jerk at the reins, to wheel his horse away from the Cossack. But Kirdyaga crashed into him, and the long scimitar slashed under his chin.

"*Hai!*" the old Cossack shouted.

All his strength had gone into the blow, enough to drive the curving steel through to the Turk's spine. Kara Mustafa gripped convulsively with his knees and Kirdyaga could not free the blade. At the same instant Mustafa's companion struck Kirdyaga's unguarded head. The steel split the skull and when the Turk wrenched it free, Kirdyaga fell voiceless to the ground.

Charnomar came in with a rush, and the Moslem nobleman turned to meet him agilely. The curved blades clashed and parted and clashed again. The Turk's horse reared. Charnomar closed in—he had need to make an end at once—and caught the Moslem's downward cut on the back of his own scimitar.

Leaning forward before the other could pull away, he drove his hilt into his adversary's throat and when the Turk swayed back in the saddle he pushed the point of his blade deep into the rider's side.

The Turk's horse became frantic and reared, throwing the dying man to the ground. But Charnomar caught the rein and swung the horse to his other side.

"Mount," he called to Ilga.

While the girl was climbing into the saddle, he looked down at Kirdy-aga. The old Cossack was dead, a grim smile on his gaunt, scarred face. Beside him the glittering body of Kara Mustafa still moved convulsively, the dark face knotted in agony, the sword still locked deep under the chin.

Charnomar felt in his own girdle for the written order that had been given him by the Turks. He tossed it down beside Kara Mustafa, for the men of the *serai* to find and wonder at. Ilga uttered an exclamation. He looked up quickly.

The throng by the puppet show had fled at the first flash of the swords; but now the men had stopped to look. The showman, a miniature wooden warrior on each fist, was cursing and praying at the same time; the Jew Shamoval was tearing at his earlocks in an agony of suspense. A janissary thrust his way forward, raising his rallying cry.

"Hai Muslimin!"

As soon as the Cossack and the Circassian girl turned and whipped their rearing horses into the darkness of the alley, din broke out behind them. Presently Charnomar heard the familiar thudding of racing horses.

"The *sipahis*," he said, listening to the shouts of the riders.

"Aye," she nodded, "and the gates are closed."

She rode as if at home in the saddle—what Circassian was not?—her tawny hair streaming behind her, the dolman flapping on her slender shoulders and her arms straining at the reins; for the black horse was not used to women. But there was no fear in her voice and she seemed more than happy.

"Go toward the Kislar Dar," the Cossack urged her. "Knowest thou the way?"

"Aye," she cried, wrestling with the charger until she had turned him aside into what seemed a pit of obscurity.

The alley was too narrow for them to keep together and Charnomar took the rear. Again Ilga turned off, this time into a nearly deserted street, where shadows flitted away from the galloping horses.

Listening, Charnomar thought that the *sipahis* had divided at the turnings, not knowing which way the fugitives had gone. Obscurity deepened to darkness, and the walls brushed his knees. Ilga reined in her charger and seemed to be searching for something.

Presently she stopped and he heard her spring down.

"Here are stairs," she whispered. "Be quick. Let the horses go."

Charnomar dismounted and struck his pony with the flat of his blade. The two beasts made off into the darkness. Ilga's choice was wise, because they climbed the steps and passed unheeded through narrow alleys to the end of the Kislar Dar and the arch that led down to the harbor. Here Charnomar stopped again to listen, and was aware of bands of horsemen moving through the streets about him. In the direction of the *serai* smoke rose against the stars. But down by the docks all was quiet under a haze of mist.

"The way is clear to thy house," he said at length.

She laughed under her breath. "I held Kara Mustafa's swordarm as he was cut down. And he was a favorite of the sultan. I dare go to no house."

The Cossack bent his head and took her chin in his hand, to look full into her eyes.

"Eh, little Ilga, this afternoon there was fear in thee, without cause. Now they hunt thee, and thou art minded to laugh."

At this she clasped warm fingers about his hard wrist.

"Before sunset I was not afraid. I was angry, because thy thoughts were all of the other Cossack. So I told the Armenian to say to thee, in reading the letter that thy brother in arms was dead. But he would not. He read truly from the letter. Verily, the old warrior was brave, and thou art a swordsman . . . " Her eyes closed and she sighed a little, being weary. "It was written, and who may alter what is written? We have come to this place, but the gates are closed."

Charnomar laughed. "One road is always open."

The moon of Shawwul had grown full and passed. The Koshevoi Ataman, the chief of all the Cossacks, was walking outside the lines of the camp, through the shops. There were many shops, and all were thronged with warriors buying vodka or brandy or rare Turkish pistols or costly green and red silk shirts. For the Cossacks had returned from a raid on Azov, and they were drinking up the plunder that had weighted their saddle bags.

The *koshevoi* himself wore over his wide shoulders a *kaftan* of ermine and red velvet, and he carried his pipe and tobacco in a girdle bag of cloth of gold. He did not walk too steadily, perhaps because he had been so long in the saddle. As he passed an open stall he heard his name called in a strange fashion.

"Lord Colonel! Lord Colonel!"

Checking his stride, he stopped, then took another step to regain his balance, and poised himself with his booted feet wide apart. Before him a thin head in a gray felt cap bobbed up and down. It was Shamoval in his ragged *shuba*, his dark eyes bright with excitement.

"Doesn't the noble colonel remember me?"

"What's that?" growled the *koshevoi*. "Stand still—don't jerk."

Shamoval ceased bowing and shouted. Fiddles were whining near them, and muskets were barking where the Cossacks were burning powder, and he thought the colonel had grown a little deaf.

"I've been to Constantinople again."

"*Tá nitchògo*," grumbled the leader, "what is it to me if you've been to Satan and pared his hoofs?"

"Will the Colonel only listen? I saw the Cossack captain, Charnomar."

"He isn't a *sotnik*, he's the luckiest son of a dog alive."

Shamoval wagged his head so vigorously that the felt cap flopped around again.

"Only, he's not alive any more."

"How, not alive?" The tall Cossack remembered Charnomar, and that the young warrior had been sent on an almost hopeless mission. "Did he fall into the hands of the Turks? Was he tortured?"

"Tortured?" Shamoval flung up his hands. "May I never live another moment if he didn't torture the Moslems. This is how it was. When I set up my stand at the *serai* gate, I saw him ride up, with two swords in his girdle, and two horses—and a girl on the other horse—"

"A woman? You lie, you—"

"May God smite me, if I lie! Why should I lie to the lord Colonel? The young Cossack went into the palace grounds, and after a little while the great lord, the commander of the Turks' cavalry came up—"

"Kara Mustafa?"

"That's how it was. He came with twenty *sipahis* but when he saw the girl waiting—what a beauty she was, with hair like gold!—he started to take her on his saddle because she was beautiful."

"To the devil with Kara Mustafa and the girl! What happened?"

"Calamity happened. *Ai*, a battle began in the palace grounds. Such a battle, as if regiments were charging! All over the place the Turks were running. Then Charnomar came out of the gate with an old Cossack."

The *koshevoi* bent his head to listen intently while Shamoval told how Kara Mustafa had been cut down, and Kirdyaga had died, and how Charnomar had killed the Turk who was an officer, and had gone off with his horse.

"Holy saints, what a heedless youth the Cossack was!" The trader lifted his eyes and shoulders at the same time. "The horse was worth fifty sequins of Venetian weight, but the *sipahis* found it abandoned in the alleys. Then there was more calamity because the great sultan—may dogs litter on his grave—was very angry, and the master of the stirrup was hung out of a window by the neck, because of a paper he had written, and because the Cossack had been seen talking to his treasurer. The sultan was very angry because of the death of Kara Mustafa. Then the Cossack took a ship."

"How, a ship?" demanded the *koshevoi*, pulling at his mustache with satisfaction.

"A felucca with one sail had just come over from Galats or Scudari to bring some Turks to the festival. The Cossack and the girl hailed the felucca and promised the master gold if he would take them over across the port. They paid the gold, but as soon as the sail was up the Cossack threw the master of the ship into the water. The Turk swam ashore, and said that the soldier was afflicted of God or bewitched by the girl. He heard the girl singing in the mist. Then the Turks sent the oared galleys from Sarai Point to bring him back. And that is why the noble Cossack is no longer living. Because the Turks did not find him in the port or the strait, or anywhere. They did not find the ship or the girl." Shamoval wagged his head sadly. "And the lord Cossack was in debt to me, a hundred and twenty-three gold sequins."

For a long time the *koshevoi* reflected. Then his mustache twitched in a smile.

"If Charnomar got to sea, he's safe. The devil himself could not pull that brother of a dog down, at sea. But the girl must have bewitched him, because he has not come back."

He drew the wallet from his pipe case and tossed it to Shamoval, who caught it deftly and immediately weighed it in his hand. "He was a good Cossack. I'll pay his debt."

By Midwinter there was a new *koshevoi* in command of the camp. The leader with the scar did not return from an Autumn campaign across the border, and with him died the older Cossacks who had been in his hut the day that Charnomar was sent away. And Shamoval no longer had his stall near the *siech*, because the Cossacks had been cut up in the campaign, and there were few men in the barracks. Along the trampled snow only an occasional blacksmith's shop or tavern was open.

Still Cossacks drifted in to the *siech*—youths from the steppe camps, veteran warriors tired of village life, adventurers who had turned their backs on the cities. More and more gathered at the cooks' fires in the barracks at evening, greeting old companions, or asking for friends who were no longer in the ranks. Some brought their sons, who listened in awe to the tales that were repeated while the kasha bowls were emptied and the brandy cask opened.

So the faces of the men in the Kuban barrack were almost all strange when Charnomar came in alone at the supper hour and flung his saddle bags in a corner near the fire.

The *kuren ataman* stared at him over his pipe, because Charnomar was bareheaded, and his skull, where he had worn the turban, was lighter than his weather-darkened face. And his green breeches were stained and faded by salt water and the mud. The barrack leader looked at his much-worn riding slippers.

"*Cherkess?*" he asked. "Circassian?"

Charnomar shook his head. This *ataman* was a new man who did not know him. He went over to the rack and took up a bowl, filling it with barley gruel from the pot. Then he borrowed a cup and dipped it into the brandy cask.

"Health to you, sir brothers," he said.

A short and powerful man who had been lying in his blankets, sat up and looked over toward the fire.

"By God, that's Charnomar back again," he shouted, and came over to the group. "That brother of a dog always turns up."

Others who had known Charnomar pushed the strangers aside from the fire and struck his shoulders with their fists. "Eh, we heard you'd left your bones in the sultan's horse yard."

"Nay, we heard you had found an island out in the sea—an island ruled by a witch who took you down under the water with her."

"Give us the tale," urged the first speaker.

Charnomar looked at them, smiling. He was glad to be back. From Sarai Point at Stamboul he had made the slaves of the felucca head down the length of the Black Sea, and he had wandered with Ilga to her village on the Terek in the Caucasus. But he was a man of few words and he did not know how to tell the story.

"I've been down the sea a bit," he said, and lifted his cup. "To the brotherhood!"

"To luck!" one repeated.

Again Charnomar smiled. "Nay—to the singing girl."

Cossack Wolf

The airplane came over after moonset, waking Yarak. He sat up with a snort. By the drone of the motor, he knew it to be a machine, and in consequence something with which he had no concern.

But in thinking about a machine, he remembered Kirdy, his grandson and the only human being for whom Yarak cared. Kirdy rode, instead of a horse, the biggest of the machines that roared up and down the valley road, going from Novocherkessk to the Kavkas—the Caucasus Mountains. It was, in fact, a military road.

And Kirdy had told his grandfather Yarak that he had a girl now. This girl, Ileana by name, he had added, was a black-browed Cossack beauty, a perfect delight. And while Kirdy was absent, driving his convoy car, he had wanted Grandfather Yarak to look out for Ileana who would soon be in town. She was, Yarak calculated, down there in the town now. But Yarak had reasons, both personal and potent, for not showing his gray mustache and his six-feet-three of ambling height down in the town.

"Devil take the girls," he muttered, "the darlings!"

He pulled his sheepskin jacket around him; he felt for and jerked down a slab of salt fish hanging over his head and munched it.

All at once he felt thirsty. He had passed a hard Autumn hunting down meat and skins, without tasting anything stronger than red Georgian wine, out of bottles. Somewhere in the town of Kizlyar there would be a jug of brandy, and Yarak meant to find it.

"Promised that dog of a Kirdy to watch out for Ileana," he told himself. "Can't go back on a given word. Impossible."

Gathering up his musket and powder horn and belt bullet mold, the Cossack tightened his belt, pulled the lambskin *kalpak* on his shaven head, scooped up a handful of old snow outside the door of his hut to ease his throat, wiped his hands on his greasy breeches and was ready for the raid into town.

Almost at once Yarak scented something unusual about the town of Kizlyar. On the uplands, where the snow ended, the black goats and cattle were wandering unattended even by dogs.

When he skirted the outlying farms he saw carts standing, their poles in the air. When he entered the town, he saw crowds in the streets. And an explanation occurred to him. A *tamasha*—a festival. That was the reason why the people were in the streets, instead of on the farms. And if it was a festival, he might find a jug to lick.

Then his nose caught the unmistakable odor of alcohol. Across the square Cossacks clustered like flies around some tables, and there Yarak found the source of the odor. The merry boys were drinking vodka out of small glasses.

"Here's a *dyadya*," shouted one, "a grandfather come along."

"A steppe wolf," said another.

Thus encouraged, Yarak shoved into the group and emptied the first glass he saw without a hand on it. Colorless and tasteless, made out of potatoes, the alcohol still moistened his throat. "Health to you, brothers," he grunted.

Some of them carried old rifles. A big man in a business suit brought a bottle out of the store and filled glasses all around. He did this several times before Yarak realized the extraordinary truth. No one was paying. Instantly he held out his glass, and the big man filled it up.

"Glory to God," said Yarak, who was beginning to think kindly of Kizlyar and its festival, "this is a day of days."

"A hard day," said the big man, "a day of misfortune. Why should any comrade pay today?"

Fluent Ukrainian he spoke—not through his nose like the Russians. And yet, Yarak thought, not like a Cossack born.

"Well, brother, it's all the same," he remarked politely. "Good or bad. Sometimes you ride, sometimes you carry your saddle. *Nichevo!*"

"Old wolf," laughed the big man. "Steppe wolf. Have you heard?" He leaned closer. "The wires to Moscow are down."

"What of it?" demanded Yarak.

"Can't get any news from the north." The big man shook his head. "They say rifles are being sent from Novocherkassk. But—who knows?"

One of the drinkers shoved in his face. "Well, how can we know, Menelitza? It's true, all the same, that the Division had to get out."

"True enough." Menelitza nodded. "And even if we get the rifles, what good will they do as long as the soldiers have cleared out?"

All this sounded vaguely familiar to Yarak. He began to warm up, in the midst of all this festival. Then he bethought him of that girl.

"*Het!*" he said, loud. "Which of you brothers of dogs knows a girl named Ileana?"

The big man Menelitza was the only one to pay attention to him. "Ileana what and who?" he asked.

"Black brows. A perfect beauty."

"*Tfu!* That's Ileana. Certainly, she's curator of the Ithnolo-logikul Museum."

Yarak blinked. "The Ith—"

"The museum of old days and people." Menelitza pointed impatiently. "Over there. She's making a speech."

Confused by these strange directions, Yarak gathered up his musket and wandered along the square to a doorway where bunting was fastened. Sure enough, here he heard a young woman's voice. Going in he saw little at first except a crowd of bareheaded men and silent women with kerchiefs. Then he sighted something really extraordinary. Along the wall stood glass cases.

And in those cases, stuck up somehow, the red and green and gold-embroidered *svitzas* of Cossack leaders of long-forgotten times, ranged beside gold-chased yataghans, jeweled belts and ivory batons. The costumes and weapons of Cossack Koshevoi Atamans. Yes, in the corner stood the staff and crosspiece hung with gray buffalo tails, and surmounted by a shining cross. The *buntchauk*—the standard itself of a day long before Yarak's birth. He recognized these trappings with surprise.

Then he was aware of the girl Ileana. Before a small metal box on a stick she stood, tossing her head and crying out " . . . brother comrades of the Ukraine, this is the day when the workers will be shoulder to shoulder with the soldiers. Remember Cossack glory of old days when the Koshevoi Ataman ordered all the projects of the steppes and gave commands in every district. . . ."

Ileana's face glowed as she tore off words. She was a short girl, but with a wide forehead and dark eyes. Strong, supple shoulders she had, and Yarak thought she would breed strong sons. Only she wore boots, and she had cut her hair off at the ears.

"She has a devil in her, that one," he thought.

Then he stared. Behind her, in a long blue silk coat stood Ghirei Khan, the Tatar horse breeder. His mahogany face was pinched with age, his shoulders bent. Uneasily Ghirei Khan took snuff from his belt and shoved it up his squat nose. He sneezed loud, in a fashion Yarak well remembered. Long and bitter had been the feud between the Tatar khan and Yarak, forty years ago, and since then they had not poured water on their swords. They had never made peace.

And here, taking snuff, dressed up in his glory, Ghirei Khan had been brought out by this Ileana for the crowd to see. Nay more, she was even praising Ghirei Khan, "He was a Tatar, but he took the prize of the Kavkaz region for raising the black Kabardian horses two years ago. Now Ghirei Khan stands like a rock with us. So do the Circassians and the Lezghians—shoulder to shoulder with the Cossack comrades!"

What was she saying? Ghirei Khan a stock breeder, a comrade of the Cossacks. That could never be. Ghirei Khan, Yarak knew, was just as much a Tatar as he ever was. Restlessly, he listened to the flow of Ileana's speech.

"It will be like the day of Mazeppa," cried Ileana, tossing her black hair, "when Mazeppa the greatest of the Cossacks rode the steppes like a storm, striking down the foes of our Russian land!"

That was too much for Yarak, who was well warmed up inside. Here was Kirdy's girl making a speech like a book, putting that son of a dog Ghirei Khan on parade, and now lying about Mazeppa. Festival or no festival, Yarak began to grow angry. He pushed through the crowd and spat. "Het!" he yelled. "Shut your mouth, girl. Mazeppa! Mazeppa, the son of a Turkish bath tender, dressed himself up like a she-actor in silk. He sold himself for a woman, and rode with the Swedes, the spawn out of a dunghill—"

And that was as far as he got. Some of the Cossacks began to hit him on the head, and Yarak, aroused, swung his gun. He kicked out at their belts, and swept the musket around like a flail. He howled like a wolf. Ileana stopped talking at the box and ran at him.

She pushed between the Cossacks and hung on Yarak's musket, her eyes blazing. "You drinker of vodka!" she cried. Very angry was Ileana. "I was addressing the Terek district."

"I don't care what you were doing," said Yarak, "but you don't know anything about Mazeppa. A girl like you!"

"A drinker like you!"

To call three glasses of vodka drinking! "Listen, sparrow!" Yarak growled. "Why didn't you ask me about Cossack glory first? Now Khmielnitski was a *koshevoi* for you! What a fire he lighted on the steppes! And Sayaidnitski now, even the Turks trembled his name was spoken. *They* rode the steppes, they did."

Some of the older Cossacks, listening, nodded agreement.

"You've been reading books in university, girl," Yarak went on sternly "You don't know true from false. Just as Kirdy said."

Ileana looked at him. "What did Kirdy say?"

"For me to look out for you."

"Are you the *dyadya*—Yarak?"

"Of course I'm the grandsire!"

"And he sent you. To—to look after me?"

Yarak nodded triumphantly. That was the truth. Ileana hesitated. She seemed, all at once, to be tired. After speaking to the men around the metal box, she took Yarak out of the museum, paying no more attention to Ghirei Khan. "Come!" she said.

"Where?" he demanded.

"You spoiled my speech," she said "I'm taking you back to Kirdy."

At once every other thought went out of Yarak's mind. Kirdy, son of his son, was here in town. This festival day seemed to have brought everyone to Kizlyar. But what was Kirdy doing here when he should have been riding his machine?

He was lying asleep, wrapped in his coat, on the seat of his truck. Vigorously Ileana shook him. "Your grandfather ruined an air talk. He's been drinking. Take him away somewhere."

Yawning, Kirdy grinned at her. His broad brown face was unshaved.

"Eh, Kirdy," said Yarak, pulling at his mustache.

"Health to you, old one. Don't bother the girls. They're busy."

Again Ileana's eyes blazed. She had a temper, that one. "Can't you do anything but sleep?"

"What's to do? Can't get anywhere without juice."

Striking her fists against the seat door, Ileara stormed at him. "Can't—
can't! That's all you say. Nothing will be accomplished unless it is *planned*.
First, think of something and then do the best you can."

"You got that out of the book, dearest," grinned Kirdy.

"Dumbhead!"

Fully expecting his grandson to swipe the girl, Yarak stepped back. But
Kirdy only laughed. "She bites hard, doesn't she, Grandfather?"

Wiping the mud from her hands, Ileana turned away. "Two men—and
all you're good for is to soak up vodka and sleep. You are both as brave
as pigs."

Red surged up into Kirdy's face and his grin vanished.

"Pigs are brave enough," objected Yarak, who had had experience with
wild boar. "Only they have more sense than men. They smell an enemy's
track and they go away, because they want to keep on eating and living.
There's a mound of sense in pigs."

But Ileana went on walking away, not looking back.

"Why don't you take a whip to her, and then kiss her afterward?" demanded Yarak. "That's the thing to do!"

"They've taught her too much at school." Kirdy thought for a moment.
"Look here, Yarak, you'd better make yourself scarce. There's a lot going
on that you haven't caught up with. Ileana thinks we ought to dash up
to Novocherkassk without any benzine, and fetch a convoy load of rifles.
You'd better head up to the hut."

"Then you come!"

"Can't leave the machine."

Without a word the old Cossack started back to the hills. He had a feeling
that, somehow, he had offended Ileana, and made trouble for Kirdy, and
he went away quickly in spite of it being a festival day.

When, about noon, he heard a shot echo, he went to a knoll to look
down into the valley.

What he saw interested him immediately. Far down, the ribbon of the
road wound through some bare hillocks. On the height nearest him, dozens of Cossacks were coming from town, to throw themselves down and
crawl to the edge, by the road. Yarak's keen eyes observed that they all
had guns.

Evidently they were setting an ambush over the deserted road. But he
couldn't think whom they'd be after. He was inclined to run down and

join them, but reflected it would be better to see what might be at the other end of the ambush.

It was not long before he saw it. A gray truck, crawling along the road.

Others appeared after it. Presently he saw that they were filled with men, and he sat down expectantly to watch. Those men also had guns.

The ambush had been set barely in time. Squirts of smoke ran along the hillocks where the Cossacks lay, and Yarak heard the familiar faint thud thud of the heavy Trokhlini rifles. The first truck on the road stopped abruptly and then began to back slowly. The sharper explosion of rifles came from it. The men in it were kneeling.

Down the road to the west, men jumped from the oncoming trucks and deployed to either side. A large plane appeared from the west following the road, and circled over the hillocks above the Cossacks. After a while Yarak saw the sharp bursts of howitzer shells exploding along the hillocks. But he could not make out where the howitzers were hidden.

The Cossacks changed their position, to escape the bursts, although they kept on firing.

Then Yarak saw the bicycles. They came up, two abreast along a cattle lane extending behind the hillocks. Very fast the bicycles came on, scattering mud. The explosion of their motors mingled with the firing.

Excited, Yarak jumped up. "Look behind your tails, dog-brothers!" he shouted. His voice did not carry to the Cossacks, unaware of their danger. Gray-green figures slipped off the bicycles and ran among the hillocks behind the Cossacks, carrying heavy weapons. And Yarak heard the clatter of machine guns and automatic rifles.

"*Tfu!*" he grunted. Those Cossacks down there didn't have the sense of pigs. In a few moments they were shot or herded together, to surrender to the bearers of the machine guns. From his vantage point Yarak saw that not one Cossack escaped from the ambush which had turned into a death trap. Yarak was glad he had not hurried down to join them.

He watched, with appreciation, the businesslike behavior of the soldiers from the road. Patrols were sent out from the hillocks. Officers scanned the road ahead with glasses. Slowly the truck convoy moved up and swung out into the grazing land on either side.

The gray-green men placed their prisoners in the center of the truck encampment they were making. They even took time and pains to drive in the herds of half-wild cattle from the neighboring pastures.

When one of the patrols began working toward his observation post, Yarak headed back toward Kizlyar, five miles away. It was sunset by then and he did not think they would make any farther advance.

This was no steppe feud, he decided. It was a raid in strength, with machines. It was war. But who were the raiders?

Hot with his news, he entered Kizlyar by moonrise. And he found that his news had got there before him. No electric lights showed in the streets of Kizlyar. The lines of stalled trucks waited there, stark in the moonlight. Machines, it seemed, no longer stirred there. But Yarak could not find his grandson at the trucks. He traipsed into the square where men were gathered, arguing, and looked around for Kirdy. The big Menelitza was talking loud in front of his cafe. He looked taller and more like a soldier in the moonlight.

"Nothing to do now," he was saying, "but get away. They didn't send the rifles. You can't hold the road with pitchforks—"

Ileana's small figure appeared before Menelitza. "Only wait!" she cried at the listening men. "The rifles and cartridges will come."

The crowd fidgeted. Yarak shoved forward, catching the girl's arm.

"Where's that cub of a Kirdy?"

When she didn't answer he pulled her along with him. "Look, sparrow, that vodka chap isn't talking through his shirttail. It's true."

"He's sabotaging our morale. And Novocherkassk assigned me to keep up the morale here."

Yarak spat. What words from a girl!

This, however, was a danger he could deal with. "We'll find Kirdy," he whispered, "and look around for some salt and bread, and track out to my hut."

"Never!" said Ileana, gulping, She swallowed hard. "Kirdy isn't here."

"Where is he?"

"He took a rifle and went down the road with the others."

"Then he's captured!" Yarak wouldn't think that Kirdy, the little devil, could be killed. A Cossack wasn't dead until his head was cut off. Certainly, he would be a prisoner.

"It's all the same." Ileana tossed her head. "Maybe they will keep the Cossack boys for hostages for a while. Only they'll stand them up and shoot them afterward, for being guerrillas—no uniforms."

And quite suddenly Ileana began to sob, digging her fists into her cheeks. Leaning against Yarak's greasy sheepskin, she cried away like an ordinary uneducated girl. For a moment Yarak considered. It would be necessary, he saw at once, to get Kirdy out of the lines of the gray-green men. Immediately. Pulling at his mustache, he pondered ways and means. A horse was the first thing. No plan could be made without a horse—

"He didn't speak to me," Ileana wept "when he went away. Aia-a!"

Women, Yarak understood, had to cry at a time like this. Gently he shook her. "Listen dearest girl. Pay attention now. Tell me—are those raiders Turks?"

"No—o," she gulped.

"Austrians?"

Ileana shook her head, miserably. "Worse than that. They are Germans."

Rapidly Yarak reviewed what he knew about Germans in that late war. They couldn't be bought. They wouldn't be caught napping. They were *educated* soldiers. With Germans there was only one thing to do.

"Wait here," he told the girl.

Germans, he reflected, knew so much that if they saw something that puzzled them they would forget everything else until they found out what it was. They were just like sheep—mountain sheep—in that respect. What he could do after he had caught their attention Yarak didn't know. He muttered, "God gives." But he would need a horse to get near Kirdy. A Cossack needed a horse above everything.

Heading for the nearest carts, he searched in vain for any sign of a horse.

Then, half wrapped in a blanket in one of the carts, Yarak sighted a jug. It had a cork in it. Instinctively he glanced around, and pulled the cork. And, as if a miracle had come to pass, he smelled the rich fragrance of corn brandy. "*Tfu!*" he said, and in a second was back in the shadow of a house with the jug. Here in his hand was comfort in the cold of the night, and inspiration. Yarak tilted the jug and drank deep and long.

Immediately inspiration came to him. If there was a horse in town, it would be Ghirei Khan's. That Tatar would not come in, unless in the saddle. Moreover, no one but Ghirei Khan would be likely to know where that horse was put up.

Quickly he searched the square for the Tatar and found him sitting at an empty table watching events.

At sight of the old Cossack, Ghirei Khan reached at his belt for the knife that was not there. Old and enduring as their two lives was the feud between them. Honored now by memory—it had been the high endeavor of their youth and their prime. Yarak chose his words carefully, in the Tatar's speech. *"Yok,"* he said. "No. I come not with steel and fire this time."

The Tatar turned his head a little, waiting suspiciously.

"A son of my son," Yarak urged, "and a grandson of a Tatar woman, is captive down the road."

Ghirei Khan snarled, listening.

"I have never asked a gift from Ghirei Khan," Yarak went on. "Give me only a horse tonight, now." He laid his musket down on the table, and thought of the right words: "Don't you remember? You would have cut out my heart on account of that woman. *Aya tak*—ay, so it was. You came across the Terek like a black storm—you set fire to the steppe grass—you drove off our cattle, and left our outriders lying in their blood."

A grunt came from the Tatar's thin lips. Yarak set the jug down by him, and uncorked it. "Here—drink while you remember. You are full of years and honor now. And why have you such honor with the Urusse? Because of our hatred. By it, you became the Lion of the Terek, the avenger. I have on me the mark of your bullet, and the scar of your knife."

Gratified, Ghirei Khan lifted the jug, pouring the mellow brandy down his throat. "God gives." He reflected pleasantly thinking of their magnificent hatred. He and the Cossack were indeed made great by that. And to the great in soul, a gift is a small thing. He drank again. "The horse," he said, "is in the little house behind the big talking house."

One minute after that, Yarak was kicking open the doors of the outhouse behind the museum. Inside, he found a horse tethered—a long-tailed black Kabardian, plump and sleek, with its Arab strain showing in the small, lifted head. In two minutes he had tightened the girth and led the animal outside. This was a horse fit for a Cossack *hetman*.

As he was thinking that, he passed the rear door of the museum. It stood open, and there was no evidence of anyone inside. Then the corn brandy glowed and warmed his throat, and the fullness of his inspiration came upon him. Dragging the horse with him, he made his way into the museum, straight to the glass cases, half visible in the moonlight. With his heel he shattered the nearest glass.

Ten minutes later, the crowd in the square outside was shocked into silence. From the entrance of the museum plunged a rider on an almost unmanageable horse.

In that moonlight he looked startling enough, on the plunging Tatar stallion and gleaming saddle. He wore the red embroidered *svitza* of a Cossack Koshevoi Ataman; his belt shone with jewels, his hand raised the staff of the ancient *buntchauk* with its flying tails and cross.

"*Het!*" the apparition shouted, and careened across the square through the staring Cossacks.

They ran out to look after him, for the black horse went through the streets like a gust of wind. Menelitza, of the free vodka, stopped his talk to stare. Ileana gasped. For here was the very spirit of the free Ukraine. And yet she knew that no spirits could ride this earth.

"Khmielnitski!" a man shouted.

And a whisper ran through those people, the incurably superstitious folk of the Ukraine. A sign had appeared in their streets. Out of the Ethnological Museum. It pointed down the road toward the enemy.

Yarak, as soon as he had got the horse in hand, put him into a steady gallop westward. He grudged every minute necessary to get him to the German lines. When he sighted the dark hillocks he lifted the standard pole with an effort. A rifle spat fire in front of him, and he reined in.

"Hi, fools," he shouted, "come out."

No one came, but no more rifles barked. Waving his *buntchauk*, Yarak walked the horse forward, for the time he thought it would take an outpost to summon an officer. Clearly, on that road, they could see he was alone.

Presently two figures appeared out of the shadow beside him. One, who held an automatic revolver, peered up at him and felt over him for weapons, while the other watched the road. After a moment, they led the horse on to where a car waited without lights.

An officer got out of the car—an Amrikan, Yarak thought. He was lean and hard and quick. Pulling Yarak's arm, he brought the old Cossack down out of the saddle, and stared at his regalia, which might or might not be a uniform. He stared at the clumsy standard, and grunted when he noticed what a fine horse the Kabardian was.

He said something to the two soldiers and one fell in behind when the underofficer led Yarak, gripping his arm tight, back along a path through the machines that were parked around the encampment. Yarak held tight to the *buntchauk*.

In that clear moonlight the Cossack's eyes missed little. First he spotted the prisoners sitting huddled on the ground. They seemed to be all alive, although hurt. The guards pacing around them carried small automatic rifles, without bayonets. Bad, that. On some of the cars, other soldiers sat at ease behind machine guns. Yarak also recognized an armored car, and small cannon of a type unfamiliar to him (for this was a German Bahnbrecher brigade, with antitank guns). Not a horse in the encampment. Only, up the slope from the machines, he spotted the dark masses of restless cattle.

A second officer strode out to them, with his tunic unbuttoned, walking like one who gave orders. For a moment in the haze of moonlight he considered Yarak, who looked, with his beard and the flowing animal tails of the standard, like some figure out of the archaic past. The newcomer held out a tobacco pouch. "Tobacco for you," he said in good Ukrainian.

"No," said Yarak, loud. "Not for me—Colonel Commander."

This officer sniffed the Cossack's breath. "Drunk!"

Yarak thought about that, and decided to risk a shout. He did not think he could get closer to the prisoners. "That's a lie!" he yelped. "That dog won't bite—"

"Shut your noise. Tell me—what's this thing you have brought?"

He poked his finger at the standard, which puzzled him. The other officer was running his hand over the black horse, admiringly, holding fast to the rein. Off in the haze some of the prisoners turned their heads.

"It's a *buntchauk*, Sir Colonel. It's a *sign*," Yarak said in a loud voice.

"A flag of truce? From Kizlyar? You bring a message?"

"Of course I do," Yarak yelled. "Certainly it's a sign, Kirdy. No truce. Not a bit of that. This *buntchauk* is a sign for the animals. They'll all follow it, even cattle. Eh, they'll jump when it comes. Don't you believe me? I'll show you, Sir Colonel. In just two little minutes Look—"

"*Dyadya!*" Kirdy's voice echoed from the men on the ground.

The officer wasn't napping. His hard fist jolted Yarak's mouth, and he barked a command to the armed soldier. In the same second the Amrikan started to lead the Kabardian horse away. Yarak thought that these were hard souls, quick as devils.

As the soldier reached for his collar, Yarak yelped. Reeling away, he pushed the standard pole into the ground as if to steady himself.

"Drunk as a pig," grunted the officer.

Two steps away Yarak took, and vaulted, holding to the pole. He smacked hard into the saddle of the black horse, which circled, startled. Somehow, Yarak held on to the pole, and the end of it caught the under-officer in the face. With one foot in a stirrup, Yarak kicked the Kabardian, which jumped between the men. It plunged between two cars, and leaped an antitank gun as Yarak gripped the reins and held himself firm. A shot behind him and the crack of a bullet past his head sounded together, as Yarak turned the frantic horse toward the edge of the dark herd of cattle.

More shots ripped out. The Cossack, however, was a shadow speeding through the haze, around the herd. Lifting himself in the saddle, he waved the standard with its flying tails, and he howled like a wolf.

"Het-het!" he wailed, circling behind the plunging steers. Frightened by the shooting and the apparition of the rider, the cattle started stampeding downhill.

The longhorns jostled together, moving faster. A machine gun flickered at them, and they struck the line of cars like a black flood, pouring through them. They plunged through the encampment, and the German guards and prisoners jumped for their lives. For a moment the Bahnbrecher brigade, the sleepers rousing, thought of nothing except climbing into the cars, and when fire was opened on the prisoners, they were off in the shadows of the hillocks.

At the edge of the stampede, Yarak flourished his standard. The black Kabardian kept its feet, drawing away from the cattle.

Yarak headed in the direction the Germans were firing, where the Cossacks had vanished. As he passed through a patch of moonlight, one of the fugitives turned in front of him, and caught his stirrup. "Hang on, cub," he grunted.

He felt a jerk as the boy swung himself up behind. "Eh, Kirdy'" he growled. "To be caught by bicycles!"

After full daylight, when the Bahnbrecher brigade moved cautiously up the road to occupy Kizlyar, they found the town buried under smoke, its streets burning, along with the convoy of stranded trucks.

Groups of Cossacks were moving, far away, driving their cattle up into the forest at the snow line.

In one of those groups Menelitza, the vodka distiller, labored under sacks of bread and potatoes. And Ghirei Khan, reeling slightly, clung silently to the rein of his prize black Kabardian, uninjured after the ride of the night.

The girl Ileana, a bag of salt on her shoulder, helped Kirdy to start the gray buffalo in the hollows and the wandering black goats up toward the highlands. She did not cry now. The rifles had not come from Novocherkassk, and Kizlyar was lost. But she could feel Kirdy's hard arm around her waist and hear his living voice.

"We've got the cattle," Kirdy was saying, "so we'll live through the Winter well enough."

He was laughing as he pointed out Yarak, ahead of them. Somehow, Ileana realized, Kirdy didn't seem to be beaten by misfortune. "Look at the father now," Kirdy chuckled. "He has it all planned out. We're going to put up in his hut. Next Summer, when the grass is dry, we're going to burn the steppes and scorch out all those machines."

Like a patriarch of old time, Yarak stalked ahead of them, his standard on his shoulders. He carried also a jug.

In one day he had dealt with machines and education. Now he was leading his flock home to his house, as a Cossack should.

The Stone Woman

Late that afternoon, Uncle Yarak found the flag. Actually, the wind whirled it along the ground in front of him, and he picked it up, not understanding that it was a flag but thinking that he might make use of that small piece of cloth. He was picking his way along the road to the Dnieper River, heading toward the setting sun. Instead of following the road itself, Yarak kept to the tall grass and the gullies at the side, his blue eyes under shaggy brows questing through the underbrush, his lean, sun-blackened head bent. One hand held a loaded musket, low. A full powder ham weighed down the pocket of his stained breeches, and the rest of his equipment consisted of a steel knife blade, bits of flint, and a bullet punch.

The steppe grass, that mesh of wild wheat, thornbush and stalks of the Ukraine, rose as high as his chest. Down in the gullies where pine growth screened the sandbanks, Yarak could stand up to his six-feet-three of height. "The sky," he repeated to himself, "is a Cossack's rooftop, the saddle's his home."

Yarak, however, had neither horse nor saddle. No horses were to be found here, far from home and behind the German lines. Moreover, a man with a musket on a horse would have been visible a half mile away, over the steppes. And Yarak had discovered by experience that to be sighted from the road was to earn a greeting in the form of a burst of bullets.

On his part he had a shooting feud with the mechanical monsters that passed along the road; with the tanks and armored cars and supply trucks of every nature that chugged back and forth through the billowing dust, usually in herds. He was trying to hunt down such German machines—so far without any luck. The herds of machines passed by for the most part, he noticed, at night and at speed. If they would venture off the road, he might set fire to the steppe grass to windward of them and damage the machines by the resulting furnace-like flame . . .

Toward sunset, he saw the grass stirring on a knoll in front of him. It was not a wind gust striking the grass, because the tops did not bend. Cautiously he investigated, to see if it was a pig moving away. On the summit of the knoll he found a small space beaten down.

"*Lopazik,*" he grunted. Beyond doubt, it was a lair where something quite different from a wild pig had been hiding out. A small sheepskin lay on the ground with a bottle, which Yarak found to contain nothing but water: At the end of that hot day he was thirsty enough, but he wanted more than water.

There was also a small tin box which had in it a flower-embroidered cap, some printed pages much soiled and illustrated with women's dresses. In the papers, three matches had been tucked away carefully. Yarak decided that the occupant of the *lopazik* had been a woman, and a small woman. "*Hai, dushenka,*" he called, low. "Hi, darling!" And got no answer.

He did see, however, that from this lair by the road, a ruined village was visible, and, nearer than the village, a mound upon which stood the gray figure of a woman looking his way. To this, Yarak paid no attention. Such mounds and such gray motionless women were found often enough in the steppes, watching the east. The figures were stone, and Yarak knew them as the stone *babas.* Usually, he was careful to keep his distance from them.

This time, because he was thirsty, he decided to investigate the village which appeared to be empty. He ambled into the cottages, and stopped, puzzled.

These houses sprawled an either side of the road, and those nearest the road had one side crushed in. Between their thatched roofs, over the road itself, wires and poles were stretched with a network of pine branches woven through them. But no living person remained in the village, to sit in the shade of the makeshift canopy. Yet the ground around Yarak reeked with fresh oil. He felt that this place had been occupied very recently and then abandoned.

Before he could investigate, the Cossack sighted a plume of dust down the road, and he headed toward the nearest high grass, which happened to be around the mound where the stone statue stood.

Three mechanical monsters approached the village and slowed down, turning in under the camouflage. The first, an armored car, was followed by two tank trucks. The Magyar beside the driver of the armored car put away his field glasses.

"Thought I saw two of them stirring around," he said. "One certainly had a rifle."

The captain commanding the detachment, a heavy man who had been a factory manager two years before, said nothing. He was standing on the step, to watch the area of the sky for any sign of hostile planes. The two tank trucks behind him contained gasoline.

"You thought," he muttered presently. The Magyar, commanding the armored car section, seemed to him to be careless. The captain's copy of the *Militar-Wochenblatt* stated that "The members of the Supply Organization work with unflinching force and unswerving care of detail along the roads which are the arteries of the army structure."

While the captain was maneuvering, without the loss of a minute, the two gasoline trucks into two ruined houses where they would be screened from the air, the Magyar merely told his section sergeant to search the high grass around the mound. The sergeant and his men came back with Yarak, whom they had found lying in the grass.

A search of the old Cossack, however, yielded no trace of weapons. He had got rid of his musket, powder horn and bullet punch. For a moment the officer studied his prisoner. "You," he snapped in good Ukrainian, "where is your chum hiding?"

"*Chelom, dobrodiou,*" Yarak responded instantly. "The forehead to you, master. There's no chum."

"That's a lie. Where did you hide your rifle?"

"A rifle? Haven't any such. Not a smell of one."

"Lie number two." The Magyar spoke to a soldier who snapped the bolt of his carbine. "I saw the rifle with my glasses. Now spit out one more lie and you'll have a bullet through your guts. Understand, Uncle?"

"Yes," said Yarak moodily, cursing himself silently for not getting into cover quicker.

"Turn around," ordered the Magyar.

Yarak did so, flinching inwardly.

"Where did you get that flag?"

Starting to ask what the German was talking about, Yarak checked himself, remembering the bullet which would, from that position, go through his kidneys. And he recollected the small streamer of white, red and green silk that he had found and tied to the back of his belt, for convenience. Evidently that was what German officers meant by a flag. Carefully and truthfully, he answered.

"Captain," the Magyar interpreted, "he swears he found it near the road, and he uses it like any other piece of clean cloth. Clean! Come to think of it, it's a Turkish idea of sanitation. Also, he says he does not know that it is an Italian flag—doesn't know what Italian is. Now—what will the captain do with it?"

Exasperated, the commander eyed the soiled emblem of Italy. Lacking imagination, he could not think what to do with the flag—especially with his section sergeant and four men looking on. So he snapped at his lieutenant: "Over there—look over there, Sartlov, and you will perceive the second Russian whom you have failed to find." And he pointed with satisfaction at the woman's figure on top of the overgrown mound.

Now the Magyar's eyes were better than those of his captain, who wore glasses. Moreover, he had been through the campaign in the Ukraine, while the captain was newly arrived in that area. He said briskly: "Right— maybe. Let's have a look at her."

Escorting Yarak, the two officers walked across a plowed field to the mound, which was smooth and regular in shape. They left the sergeant and the men to other duties. As soon as they were out in the field, the Magyar jerked loose the knot that tied the flag to Yarak's rear, and dropped it between two furrows.

Meanwhile, as he had hoped, his captain had identified the woman on the mound.

"So—it is a statue, Sartlov. And still distinctly I remember you said you saw a woman moving."

"I did . . . something moving. Maybe a boy."

"Or a woman, let us say." Irritatingly, the captain pricked at him. "But why is this statue sited in a field? Observe, the regular mound makes for it a base."

"Oh, they're scattered through the steppes hereabouts. Ancient steles—you always find them on a mound." A flicker of interest warmed the young officer's voice: "And always facing due east. Always solitary, like this woman—as far as Manchukuo. Curious things."

"Russian?"

"Older—"

Abruptly Yarak came to a halt at the edge of the high grass. He had been pondering anxiously the hiding place of his musket and powder, there in the mound. *"Kurgan plocho—strashno!"* he muttered. "Mound haunted—by spirits."

The Magyar's narrow eyes shifted moodily to his prisoner. "Another lie!"

"Het!" Yarak spat. "True enough. Doesn't the noble officer know about the stone *babas?* They watch, here in the steppes. Bad luck to monkey with them. Don't step on the mound. Look—the people here wouldn't plow close to the mound. That's why grass grows over it."

Out to the east, the shadow of the stone woman stretched. A kind of skullcap covered her rudely shaped head, and her hands were clasped on her girdle. Dust swirled up from the grass around her.

"I suppose this *baba's* spirit haunts the mound, of nights?"

"Certainly. The hours of darkness are not good here at the mound. We Cossacks know that."

Something vaguely remembered tugged at Sartlov—back in his homeland, a white *Schloss* standing deserted on a dark mountain ridge: A medieval castle, avoided by the modern villagers simply because it was old and deserted. No, more than that. The girl. That one with the stiff embroidery on her jacket, who used to walk up with him to the *Schloss* of evenings. She used a kind of balsam oil in her hair and she had strength in her young arms. Perhaps she had really loved him. She had never said much . . . that was it. The hour of darkness, the ruin on the height, and that girl who had been amusing, until she took to crying . . .

Seeing that he was making an impression, Yarak gave tongue fiercely: *"Ekhma!* Keep away from these women, noble commander. With human beings you can deal, somehow. But the spirits aren't the same at all. The stone *babas* don't keep their watch for nothing. Try to move one from her place and see what happens."

"Well, what happens?" Sartlov's mind was off still in the shadow of that other ruin.

"Why, with a horse and a rope you can pull a *baba* to the east, that way. But you couldn't pull her away, to the west, with one of your machines over there. Impossible!"

"What's he saying?" demanded the captain.

"He's afraid of this mound. Although, come to think of it, we found him under cover in the grass. The Cossack's right one way—these kurgans are really burial mounds. Archaeologists have been at work on them

and have uncovered ninth-century burials. Local people are always superstitious about burials before their time."

"You are unusually partial to Slav superstitions, Sartlov."

The Magyar smiled. "I am partial to women."

The captain grunted and led the way back to the cottages, as if washing his hands of a bad business.

"Don't try to escape," Sartlov warned the Cossack.

Yarak hung back, in the plowed field. Paying no more attention to
him, the officers headed for a table under the camouflage. On that table,
gray soldiers were breaking out tins and curiously shaped bottles. They
poured white liquid from these bottles into glasses, and the two gray officers drank quickly from the glasses. Beyond a doubt, Yarak thought, men
did not drink water like that. He licked his lips and reflected.

Somewhere in the red haze the sun was setting. But a sentry at the
edge of the field was watching him, and the sentry had a carbine. No two
ways about it. Yarak, who had done no harm to these soldiers and who
had told only the simple truth, was still a prisoner. Shambling back to
the edge of the mound, being careful to keep in sight, he squatted down
to think things over.

From this vantage point, he could dive down into the mound and recover his musket and ammunition. Only, then he would have to emerge
again under fire from the carbines of the gray soldiers. That dog wouldn't
bite. On the other hand, he could keep quiet where he was, hoping that
they might forget about him, until after dark—

"Ayaa—hi—lahaa!"

The skin along the back of Yarak's neck moved of its own accord, and
his nerves tingled. This soft, whispering herder's cry seemed to come from
the ground behind him, and a woman's cry at that. Hastily, he glanced
up at the stone *baba*.

"Don't move, blind ox!" said the voice.

Already dusk was obscuring the gray walls of the cottages, and no living
being was nearer than the motionless sentry who could not be expected
to know a Tatar herder's cry.

"In here," the voice whispered. "In the grave place."

If she was down in the mound, Yarak reflected, she must be where his
musket was. "Where are you from, girl? How did you get here?"

"Shut your mouth!" The voice quivered excitedly. "I crawled. If you are faithful to the Russian land, don't come in here!"

Yarak did not care at the moment about the Russian land. But he was mortally concerned about his musket. If these gray soldiers were going to shoot him through the guts, he intended to plug them instead. If a strange woman, who might or might not have anything to do with the stone *baba*, was down there with his musket, ordering him to keep out, the matter required careful thinking. "Listen, *dushenka*, did you see a musket there, by the bones?"

"No," The voice quickened hopefully: "Is there one, Uncle?"

Inwardly Yarak swore. It had been a mistake to mention the gun. But how was he to know? Luck certainly had been against him since he sighted the motor trucks.

"Who are you?" he demanded. "And what the devil are you doing in the grave?"

"I'm just somebody, old comrade," explained the girl. "And I'm on a mission. Don't gab so loud!"

"Devil fly away with you!"

"Wait just for a couple of hours. Then it will be over—"

The sentry, either because he heard Yarak or because it was getting dark, was moving over to the Cossack. Yarak hesitated and decided that fate was against him. "Shut your noise," he whispered to the ground behind him.

Stopping by Yarak, the sentry jerked his head toward the cottages. "March!" Slowly Yarak arose and marched.

No gleam of light showed at the table where the officers sat. The sergeant made Yarak sit against the house wall, and in that position he could smell the fragrance of the bottles. More than vodka—probably rum or kummel. The Germans seemed to be waiting there, with their tank cars put inside the houses, and only once did the younger one speak to Yarak.

"Is your woman up to anything, Russky?"

Yarak started, and then realized that the officers apparently had seen only the stone *baba*. "No, nothing," he muttered. "Only, keep away from the kurgan, or it will be bad for you."

"Superstition has been the curse of the Slavs. You accept fate, good or bad. It's your kismet—it's been like that ever since the first of your race emerged from the swamps that bred you. Indeed yes, Cossack, the Slavs, your remote forefathers used to run off into their swamps to escape an enemy—"

"That's a lie!" Yarak yelped.

His rage seemed to please the young officer. "It's an ethnological truth. How else did the English word slave come to be, unless from Slav? That's why you'll accept the rule of a master. You'll be better off so old wolf."

Yarak did not agree with the young officer on this point. But he said nothing because, at that moment he heard a confused rumbling down the road. The ground shook under him. Black shapes larger than buffalo appeared, hissing and grinding—a whole line of them. Under the camouflage they stopped close together, and men climbed out of their tops. Yarak, interested, recognized these black monsters as the tanks, which until then he had seen only from afar along the roads.

Immediately the tanks began to refill with fuel from the waiting gasoline trucks. The Germans who had captured Yarak began to talk with the others who had come from the machines. Although it was full dark by then, with all the stars out, no one lighted even a cigarette.

Apparently the Cossack did not stir. Actually, he was edging himself closer to the table. Stretching out a long arm, he grasped a bottle, which turned out to be shaped like a dog. From this he drank quickly and silently, and set the bottle back in its place.

The liquor, more fiery than vodka, warmed Yarak's gullet.

His thoughts now began to grow urgent. His anger against the young officer who had said that he, Yarak, had been born in a swamp, increased. Into this anger intruded the German tanks, which—as he now understood—had been the cause of his present plight. Obviously the German officers had come to this village to refuel the black monsters.

"Eh, you are big enough," Yarak muttered, "but you are like the blind steers that have to be led along the roads. A horse is better, because if the road is lost the rider can let go the reins and the horse will find his way, even in a snowstorm. That's the truth—"

Off in the field the sentry called out something, and the Cossack, glancing that way, became filled with misgiving. A faint light showed along the mound. A glow within the ground fell upon the figure of the stone woman. From beneath her, a spiral of smoke rose.

This phenomenon, Yarak knew, would lead to fresh trouble. And so it proved. The Germans on the road stopped talking. The sergeant grabbed Yarak's shoulder and hauled him up, striding toward the mound.

At first they could not find the source of the light. The Magyar officer came up and led them around the base of the kurgan.

Here, almost covered by the rank waist-high grass, a trench showed, extending into the kurgan. A little way along the trench, a fire of dry grass and sticks burned. The wind whipped the flames up and down.

Immediately the big sergeant ran into the trench, stamping out the fire. Then the Magyar lieutenant pushed Yarak into the trench. When they reached the smoking embers, the officer switched on an electric torch.

The Germans saw what Yarak feared they would see, the black opening of a tunnel where the trench ran underground into the kurgan.

"Old work," said Sartlov to the sergeant. "Looks more like an excavation than a bombproof."

He had seen such excavations of tumuli before, and he reasoned that if Russian archaeologists had supervised the digging, they would have tunneled in at the grave level rather than open up the whole of the mound. Pushing Yarak ahead of himself and the sergeant, he called down into the tunnel. No one answered.

"That fire," the sergeant said, "was lighted just about three minutes ago."

The Magyar considered, his bony face tense. And he smiled. "Old wolf," he said gently, "we'll have a look at your chum who lights a signal flare so promptly when the Panzers arrive."

Yarak did not understand the officer well. But he caught the word *kunak*—chum—and he guessed a good bit. His thoughts were shifting very quickly around the musket he had hidden in the grave and the girl somebody who was probably hiding there, as stupid as a fox.

"Look," he argued, "it's nobody but a woman in the kurgan—"

"I've heard lies aplenty in my time," said the officer, "but nothing to match yours."

Shoving the Cossack ahead of them, the Germans entered the tunnel and felt their way down the steps cut in the earth. Ahead of them, the officer flashed his beam. The sergeant drew out his pistol.

They found themselves in a cavern so low that Yarak had to stoop. Around them the earth walls showed no other entrance. A heap of bones lay on one side, and these Sartlov identified with a glance as human. Since they were blackened with fire, he guessed that the bodies laid in this tomb had been burned centuries before. Probably the excavators had removed any objects spared by the funeral pyre. Then he whistled softly, steadying the beam from the torch.

The light shone full upon Somebody, pressed against the earth wall. She was panting with fright, her slant Tatar eyes gleaming. She wore men's trousers, and her hair had been clipped short. One hand, tight-clenched, held something.

"What in the name of a thousand devils," demanded the officer, "is this?"

"The girl in the kurgan," growled Yarak.

He noticed that she was stiff with fright. When the officer questioned her, the only thing she would say was that her name was Atzai, a Tatar name. They made her open her hand and saw that she held only two matches.

"Why did you start that fire?" the officer asked for the dozenth time.

Atzai would not explain.

"Very well. You do not know, I suppose. Then, why are you sticking here in this grave, which is not exactly a recreation spot?"

The sergeant, satisfied that only the girl was present in the cavern, put away his pistol and waited indifferently.

Atzai's eyes half closed and speech bubbled out of her: "Because I was afraid."

"Of what, pray?"

"Of you. Of all of them. The Fascists rape and kill."

The German considered her small face curiously. It was coated with dust and sweat, and yet if washed off, it would be handsome enough. Atzai's slim body did not seem to be more than fifteen years old. "We are not Fascisti," he said thoughtfully.

Yarak thought that the girl was lying. Yes, she was screening her eyes and playing a part. Scared of something no doubt of that—but not of the officer.

"*Chelorn, dobrodiou,*" he said to the officer. "The forehead to you, lord. Let her go. She has seen too much killing. Her mind isn't what it ought to be. Yes, that's how it is." He gained inspiration as he harangued. "The little child is afraid of the dark—she lights fires—"

"Shut up!" The officer was frowning, piecing things together in his mind. "When I believe you, Cossack, my platoon will walk on water." He thrust the torch closer to Atzai's eyes. "So. You knew she was here. And you gave us that tale about the haunted kurgan. The spirits that come out after dark—"

For a second, a memory touched the Magyar . . . of the twilight hour and the castle of his homeland. Then he heard the planes.

It was the faintest droning sound, far off. But Atzai heard it and she gasped. She jumped from the wall, between the men, out of the beam of light, before the officer could get in her way. Toward the entrance she scurried.

The sergeant shouted after her, reaching for her. The sudden rush touched off Yarak's nerves. Things were warming up. He hooked out his foot, tripping the sergeant.

When he moved, the lank Cossack moved quickly. He dived down behind the bones and came up with his musket. Lurching up, the sergeant found the barrel of the long weapon pointed at his stomach.

Hearing the hammer of the strange weapon click back, he peered at it in the half-glow. The beam of the officer's torch had followed the flying girl.

"*Het!*" yelped Yarak, his gray mustache bristling.

The Magyar took several seconds to study what was happening. He decided quickly enough not to move from where he was. Holding the torch motionless, he spoke sharply:

"Cossack, put that antique down. If it goes off, it will fire one bullet and it might hurt one of us. I grant you that. Whereupon our pistols would fill your carcass with holes. Can you understand that?"

His words came curt and crisp. As he talked, behind the light, his left hand was freeing the flap of his automatic pistol.

"*Tfu!*" Yarak spat and shouted, "you talk too much!"

The officer's hand closed on the butt of his pistol. "Besides," his voice went on, "there are two hundred men outside, who would cut the hide off you—"

Hot rage gripped Yarak and he swung the muzzle of the musket, jerking the trigger. The cap flashed, the gun thundered into Sartlov's face.

Heavy smoke rolled around the sergeant. The torch dropped, rolling along the dirt, and the sergeant could see nothing. Nor could he hear the Cossack.

He heard, however, strange sounds. A snapping and crackling outside the grave chamber, and men shouting, far off. Also, through the drifting smoke, a red glow lighted the entrance of the chamber. Freeing his pistol, he moved his head, to catch the Cossack's outline against the glow. The dense powder smoke stung his eyes.

Then something smashed against his jaw. Loose powder filled his nostrils and eyes. He swore, crouching, to wipe at his face.

Yarak, having thrown his loaded powder horn, felt that the grave chamber was becoming unsafe for him. Too much was happening for him to understand clearly. The grass was burning outside, and he ran back to the trench with his musket. Sheets of flame and smoke, twisted by the wind gusts, whipped over the trench, and he scrambled through on all fours.

He plunged out into the smoke and found men running up to the fire which crackled over the mound, from the trench. Waving his musket, his scalp smarting from sparks, he leaped away, running.

The Germans seemed to be too busy to pay any attention to him. With blankets and rifle butts they were beating at the fire. As Yarak ran, the glare of the fire grew brighter. In that wind, the dry grass went up with a roar. Yarak ran on to the first cover he could find, a pile of rocks. Here he flung himself down.

"Come on, Uncle," Atzai's voice called in his ear. "Come away, you blind ox."

"Not yet," panted Yarak, who wanted to see what was happening among the houses.

The Tatar girl pulled at his arm. She was lying there behind the rocks, biting her lips, pressing one fist against her chest. In that hand she still held one match.

"Don't you see? They aren't following," he explained to her.

The girl moaned with excitement. "Look up, Uncle," she gasped.

Up there, black shapes were passing across the stars. A whining came out of the air over the roaring of the planes. And then it happened.

Explosions ripped the village, flashing like lightning, sending dirt flying skyward. Yarak flattened down, stunned. Another line of bursts struck full over the blazing mound.

The Germans vanished from around the mound in a mighty dust cloud. "Eh!" Yarak yelped. "The sky is shooting down."

The sky was exploding down on the village, where the stone walls melted, and dead branches and human bodies shot away like wisps of straw. The sky was tearing at the earth, around the lighted mound. And the girl, shivering beside him, was crying out. "It's our planes . . . they kept coming over the road at night . . . now they have a light to see the tanks. I thought they would come down if only they could see. I waited . . . "

Yarak remembered the lair where this schoolgirl had watched, hiding herself. From the black monsters crowded close together along the road, guns belched up at the shapes circling across the stars. Some of the tanks were moving away.

A bomb struck into a housetop, and flaming gasoline shot up. Bombs struck among the tanks, jerking them across the road so that they ground together. Then lines of tracer bullets flowed down from above, on the tangled clusters of mechanical monsters. The dust cloud, rising from the road, was lighted by the fiercely burning gasoline.

The Cossack was awed by this insensate fury of the sky. "The whole herd is trapped," he grunted.

Atzai was looking up at him, crying with excitement. He patted her shoulder. Had she not set the trap for the herd? "And they said we ran away to hide in swamps."

In the first lull in the bombing he made the girl run off toward her lair. He headed through the dust clouds into the village.

The captain, hugging the ground beside a rubble of stones, lifted his head in the interval of quiet. It was unbelievably bad luck, this attack, which had been provided against with such care. Where had his lieutenant disappeared? How had the ancient grave mound become a lighted beacon at the time of the passing of the planes?

Over at that mound, smoke rose around the stone woman, like incense at the end of a ritual of burial. It was fantastic.

By the glare of the burning gasoline, the captain saw a wild figure flourishing a musket rush at the table. This figure grasped two bottles and vanished with a yell into the curtain of dust.

The captain did not know how he was going to put all this into his report.

City Under the Sea

Uncle Yarak sat on a sandbank overlooking a river that flowed into the Black Sea. Trouble lay heavily upon his Cossack spirit and he did not know what to do about it.

He had to think of something to do. A plan—that was it. But how could he think of a plan without lighting his pipe? To strike a match in that clear, starlit night, might be to draw a shot from a German patrol along the opposite bank. A drink of brandy would be helpful in making a plan, but brandy had not refreshed his throat in the ten days he had spent wandering to this jumping-off place.

"*Ekh ma*," he sighed. "There's nothing to help."

A shadow appeared on the surface of the water, and he heard a humming sound above the rush of the current over the shoals. Abruptly he sat up, the wiry steppe grass cutting through his shirt sleeves. Something was coming up from the depths of the narrow river.

"The city—" he muttered.

Never before now had the old Cossack laid eyes on the long line of the sea, or the ships that plied the waters thereof. Yet he knew the legend of the city. In bygone days, on an island in this same Black Sea, good people had lived in a city that was attacked by pagan Turks. The people of the city prayed to the Lord for deliverance from their peril. And when the Turks swarmed over the island, it settled and vanished beneath the sea with all its people. Even now, on holy days, the bells of that city could be heard ringing beneath the waters.

Yarak watched the shadow in mid-channel hopefully for a moment, and then spat. "*Tfu!* There are no bells."

Luck, undoubtedly, had deserted him for these last ten days. All because he had spoken to a strange woman. The next time he would cross himself and spit three times before speaking to a strange woman. And he peered morosely at the woman curled up asleep in the sand beside him.

Her tawny hair stretched over her arm, her smart chamois jacket was wrapped tight about her small body. She breathed evenly, as if unconscious of hunger and danger.

"*Shepheardsismailiahaleptaganrog*," Yarak repeated softly to himself. That was where she said she had come from. It didn't make sense. She couldn't speak intelligently—not a bit of Ukrainian, the Cossack speech, and only enough Russian to ask for things like water and watermelons and the sea. She had been able to make Uncle Yarak understand that she wanted to go down to the sea.

Be-ty she called herself, when the sergeant of the guerrilla patrol had turned her over to Yarak, explaining that she was dumb, being a foreign woman. She had lost her way, getting around the Kharkov lines, and she said her car had broken down. The sergeant, who had other matters to attend to, had made Yarak promise to take her where she wanted to go.

Well, he had done that. He had brought her to the sea, because she wanted to go to the sea. It had not been easy, because German forces happened to occupy that section of the coast through which the Cossack had had to make his way at night, scavenging food where he could, with the foreign woman following obediently behind.

And when, at last, he had shown her the dark line of the sea above the sand hillocks, she had sat down suddenly, not smiling any more. She had wiped at her eyes. Something had gone wrong. Be-ty would not follow him any more. Probably she was sick, and possibly she might be dying. Yarak did not want that to happen. The dumb woman was young, and lovely when she smiled.

But what was he going to do with her here in this sandy waste, without food, with only German patrols watching the empty river?

Yarak chewed his cold pipe, peering into the haze of starlight. He heard a splash upstream that might have been a fish. Up there something moved, looking like a pair of tree trunks, drifting. It did not, however, swing out with the current when it approached the sand bar. Yarak's eyes, accustomed to darkness, were keen.

"Ghar," he whispered at the blond woman. Then, remembering that ordinary speech meant nothing to her, he laid his fingers against her throat, waking her quietly.

"*Whatstheshow?*" she whispered, her eyes opening. With his hand on her mouth, he pressed her head back into the sand. Then he started down to the water's edge.

Bending his six-foot-three of height to keep himself below the skyline, he made his way out to some rocks in a clump of rushes, without a sound. For a moment he studied the drifting logs which had navigated the point upstream. Two and perhaps three men lay stretched on the raft, and the starlight above picked out a rifle barrel.

"U-u-haa!" he called softly, close to the water, watching the rifle. The logs hesitated and turned in, with a faint splashing. "Eh, rivermen." Yarak grinned at the clumsy way they handled their raft. "Eh, say."

"You say," a voice grumbled.

The men on the logs were investigating the river. They wanted to know where the German posts were. Yarak explained that a field hospital had been set up three versts away at Chovno village, and that the Germans patrolled the vicinity on foot. "Where are you heading?" he asked, hopefully.

"None of your business, Cossack."

The men on the raft would only say that they had holed up along the river. They were trying to observe what the Germans were doing. Earlier that night they had found a foreigner.

Yarak pricked up his ears. "What kind of a foreigner?"

"How do we know what kind? A foreigner."

"I thought you were *burlaki*—rivermen."

"Sure we're from the river. The Amur, brother."

"Where's that?"

"District of Siberia."

Yarak swore. He did find out where the stray Siberians had their quarters—in a ravine behind the third point, upstream. There they had left the foreigner.

When they had floated on, Yarak started upstream along the bank. He thought: If these Siberian soldiers had a foreign man, and he, Yarak, had a foreign woman on his hands, he could lead the man to the woman. The man would know what to do for her. Then the blonde woman would get over her sickness, and what was more to the point, Yarak would be relieved of his responsibility . . . At the edge of the upstream ravine, he went slowly, calling "U-u-haal!" No answer came.

At once Yarak stopped, pulling out the Turkish knife that he had acquired in his wandering. Carefully he listened to the faint humming that was made up of the murmur of the river, the buzz and chirping of insects. He caught a swish of the air, and ducked. Something rattled against the slope above him, and he heard the sharp thud of feet.

The Cossack rolled over on his back, kicking up and slashing with the knife. His booted foot jammed against the hurtling body, but his knife blade cut only air.

Rolling to his feet, Yarak prepared to strike again. Something harder than a fist smashed against his cheekbone.

Flashes of light spurted before his eyes, which watered, blinding him. "Dog's tail!" he yelped, startled.

Nothing more hit him. Instead, after a moment's silence a voice spoke curtly:

"You're Russian?"

"No—Cossack!"

By now Yarak could make out his assailant—a shorter, slender man holding a cudgel. This foreigner spoke Russian quick enough, but with an accent. He kept his distance from Yarak's long arm.

"Who are you and where are you from, brother?" Yarak asked, quieting down.

"Did you see the sun set, Cossack?"

"Yes."

"Well, that's where I'm from. Part of my name is Jan."

Evidently this foreigner did not want to say much about himself. So Yarak explained how he was in trouble with a woman. "She's a foreigner like you. Maybe she's dying. How can I tell?" And he added craftily, "She's pretty as a sunflower—a regular girl!"

The stranger listened without any emotion. "Sounds fishy. What's she carrying?"

"Carrying? A handbag. And a handkerchief."

"What color's her hair?"

"Like ripe wheat."

"All right. Hand over that butcher's knife."

And the foreigner would not move until Yarak laid down the curved knife. Picking it up, he reached under a bush and pulled something out. Yarak caught the clink of glass. "Vodka?" he cried.

"Cognac." Jan put a bottle in each pocket of his tunic without offering the Cossack a swallow. "Good French cognac, fresh from Chovno. Take off!" He picked up something else, resembling a sledge hammer. "And if you're taking me anywhere except to that *dushenka* you describe, Cossack, you'll feed the birds."

Yarak felt both thirsty and angry. "*Het!* I'm not lying, Jan. I'm Yarak— in the last war essaul of the Terek Division. The Savage Division."

For the first time the stranger laughed. "The Savage Division of the last war would be the school children of this one."

Morosely, Yarak stepped out. He recognized what Jan was carrying in hand. A German stick grenade, undoubtedly looted with the good liquor from the stores at Chovno. Jan had a hard soul—he had a devil in him.

To his great relief he found Be-ty sitting alone in the waste of sand, waiting patiently.

At sight of her Jan stopped instantly. "Marya!" he breathed. He said something Yarak did not understand while the girl only stared up, puzzled.

Certainly these foreigners had a strange way of greeting each other, Jan trembling as if he were stepping a grave, and the girl as silent as a stone. Presently they began to talk, but not Russian.

"What is she?" Yarak asked curiously.

Jan kept staring at her hair, until she brushed it back with her hands unthinkingly. "A nurse," he said. "An English nurse, named Betty. But she can speak some German." He had ceased to the think about Yarak. "She came from Shepheard's in Cairo, through Ismialia Halep to Taganrog, last Winter—or so she says."

"What kind of sickness has she?"

"No kind. You've walked her for a week, with only black bread and barley to chew, down to this wilderness."

"It's the sea, where she wanted to go."

"Not much it isn't. There's more than one sea, Cossack. She wanted to go around the Kavkaz, to the Caspian."

The muscles twitched in Jan's face, as if he were frightened. The girl watched him quietly. When she spoke and touched his arm, he pulled away.

Be-ty smiled and drew a cup from her handbag. And Jan uncorked one of the bottles to pour into the cup. The sharp odor of strong cognac struck

Yarak's nostrils, and he moved over. Jan pushed him away. "Not for you, *stiepnik*. The lady needs it."

He called her lady, now, and not *dushenka*. "But there are two bottles." Yarak's throat felt dry.

And plainly Jan thirsted for the good drink as much as Yarak.

The girl seemed to know that, because after she sipped at the cognac she held out the white cup to Jan. He took it, hesitating. "Captain Jan Slowycky," he muttered, "escaped from Czersk prison. The forehead to you, lady."

Giving up hope of the bottles, Yarak wandered off toward the river. This Jan, he reflected, who was no older than Be-ty, had a black devil in him. It happened that way with men who had been in prison. Jan's mind was sick, and Yarak did not know what he could do about that.

Suddenly, he stopped and spat. The river beyond the sand bar had changed. The shadow along the surface was rising, coming up.

Something like a house took shape, with a cannon on top of it. Then out of this house the figures of men climbed.

"Ekh!" Yarak muttered, the back of his neck feeling cold. Mirrored above the gleam of the water, the monster of the unknown, vasty deep drifted closer to the steep bank opposite, and stopped. The men on it lowered what seemed to be a mattress to the water, and four of them climbed into it, rowing into the loom of the land across from him.

Fascinated, the Cossack watched, at the end of his sand bar. If these specters rang bells, they must be denizens of the city under the sea. Instead of bells, Yarak heard Jan's voice. Singing.

As he scrambled back, he heard the words: "When the bread is hot from the oven, dear girl you will burn your fingers. Wait!"

Within the screen of grass, Jan was emptying the cup. "When the kiss is hot, on your, lips, dear girl . . . you must never wait. Hurry!"

Beside him Be-ty sat silent.

"Shut up, and listen, Jan," the Cossack exclaimed. "In the river a city is coming up, with men climbing out."

"In a pig's eye!"

Jan laughed and poured himself more cognac from a bottle that Yarak judged to be more than half empty already.

"Ghosts on the water," Jan said. "Cossack, I used to sit like this on the stone steps, while Marya made tea. At her house you know—or you don't know. To the devil with tea! She had hair like gold, and she looked into my eye's—not afraid. I'd kiss her hand. Like two kids."

"Stop licking the drink. It's the girl's."

"Not this girl's. She's alive, isn't she?" Jan filled his cup carefully. "When I was out of Czersk, I got down to the Tatras to look for her at the old place. The farm people told me about Marya. She'd had typhus, and before she was well, she had been sent with the family out of their house, north to the swamps. For the water sports, the Nazis said. You know, cutting timber in the bogs, poling rafts. I didn't find her. It was like chasing a ghost over the swamps—"

The girl Be-ty had been watching his face in the starlight, and she took the cup away from him. Jan stopped talking.

"There's a gun on the river now, Jan," Yarak insisted.

He took Jan's arm, leading him down to the sand bar. For a long time Jan stared at the shape on the water. "Undersea boat," he said. Leaning close to the water, he listened. "It's not Russian they're speaking over there."

"Four men rowed ashore. Without a boat." Yarak pointed to the far bank, hidden in the murk.

"They're Germans, all right. Probably going to communicate with Chovno."

The thing out of the sea was an enemy warship, Jan insisted.

"Impossible," Yarak grunted. He knew that ships sailed on top of the water; they did not emerge from the depths like a sturgeon coming up to feed.

Jan peered at him curiously. "You believe in a city of dead people coming up out of the water, but you balk at a submarine."

"Oh, crickey!"

Quietly the girl Be-ty had come up behind them. And she knew more than Jan about the black shape moored in the river. She said it would have a searchlight and machine gun on the little house that she called a conning tower, and a small boat made of rubber, blown up so it would float. In this berth at the river mouth it could lie hidden for the night, and it would be off by daybreak. It showed no lights, to prevent observation from the air.

"*Tfu!*" Yarak shook his head. A machine such as that to swim around in the water like a fish. It could not be.

Jan, squatting down close to the water, did not move. He was like a man bound tight with wire cords. "There are only four of the water sporters on deck," he whispered, "and, I think, two on shore over there."

Then Yarak heard a sound that sent him crawling back hastily through the grass. Heavy feet were moving in the dry growth about the camp site, and his sharp ears caught the clink of a glass bottle. As he suspected, he found the Siberian guerrillas there, nosing about. They had found the cognac and the girl's bag.

"Hi, *kunaks*," Yarak hailed softly, "those are the foreign lady's bottles. Look here—there's a German machine lying like a fish in the shallows of the river."

Invitingly he pointed down at the bank. A short, stocky figure stepped up to him. "We aren't blind, Uncle. Sure it's there. Only we haven't any *kriga*—net traps big enough to catch that fish."

Those Siberians had the bottles, and Yarak counted eight men with four long, old-fashioned rifles among them. He did not argue with the stocky man, the section leader called Kem by the others. Then Jan appeared with the girl, and Jan picked up the stick bomb from the ground. He spoke with the ring of command in his voice:

"Army men, can you find your way through to your lines?"

"Yes," said Kem, "when we're ready to go."

"Well, it's time you took off, with this lady. She's a nurse and she'll end up by getting killed here. See that she's put on a train to the Kavkaz, to Tiflis. There'll be other English people in Tiflis. You won't want to stick around here."

"Why not?" demanded Kem. "And what makes you think you can give the orders?"

"It will be too hot around here for you, after an hour. I'm through giving orders. I'm going over to the other bank to give them this cocktail."

Jan's voice was flat, as he showed Kem the stick bomb. The Siberians crowded around, muttering. No use throwing one bomb, the Germans had sentries on shore, and a party coming back from Chovno. And their searchlight could show up all the bank there.

Kem hesitated, and put down the cognac. "We have some dynamite, from Chovno, but we couldn't find any detonators. We're keeping it for the roads."

"Well, you can't worry a submarine by exploding dynamite in the open air—if you could explode it."

"I know that." The Siberian seemed angered. "Didn't I graduate at the Ural Kuznetsk chemico-metallurgical combination?" He laughed. "For cultural upliftment."

"May the dogs bite your cultural upliftment!" Yarak pushed up to them, snorting. It had taken a long time to convince him; but if the soldiers also believed the leviathan from the deep to be a warship, it must be so. Although it seemed to him something of a miracle that such a ship could be. "You didn't learn much on the Amur. You've got a raft, haven't you, Kem? Then hand over the dynamite and I'll take it down alongside that machine."

"The forehead to you, Yarak! So you'll cripple the submarine by yourself."

"*Tfu!* I was doing things like that when you were still wet behind the ears." Yarak felt provoked. First the officer Jan had slighted the Savage Division of the real war, and now this man from the Amur made a jest of him. Yarak felt hot under his skull. "I've taken a log down a river at night with Tatars watching. And they don't need searchlights to see at night."

He explained how it was done. Not by splashing around like the men from the Amur, but by drifting with the current. Not by lying on the logs but by swimming behind them.

"Only one thing is needed," he added. "A diversion. If you Siberian fly killers can get up on the bank over there, throw in a stone for the boat boys to look at."

"What did you say?" Kem asked.

"A diversion. To make them look the other way."

For a moment the officer and Kem stared at the gaunt Cossack. They seemed to find much to think about in what he said. Jan shifted the bomb in his hand, and Kem breathed hard through his teeth. "Uncle," he said, "will you try your luck like that?"

"Stop talking, and fetch the dynamite."

They were starting up the river, when Jan put out his hand. The girl was waiting there, not knowing what they meant to do. Yarak saw the officer go up to her and talk, strained. It was as if Jan had been pulled toward her.

"She wants to come with us," he explained quickly. "She says she wants to share our luck."

His voice was glad, and he took the girl's hand, bending over to kiss it. Be-ty moved unexpectedly. She brushed back the tangle of her hair and she smiled at Jan, putting her arms around him. Tight she held to him, whispering.

When he lifted his head, Jan's face was not hard as before. He looked like a boy, troubled and determined. His fingers held to the girl's hand.

Yarak thought that Jan was no longer afraid of a ghost. This girl had somehow driven the black devil out of him. Well, that was how it happened, with a girl.

The Pole held his body straight in the torn tunic. Taking the lead, he walked fast, motioning Kem to keep up with him. Yarak could hear them talking, low-voiced, up at the guerrillas' hideout.

And there they lost no time rooting heavy boxes out of the brush. Lugging the boxes down to the shore, they worked over them, while Yarak inspected the log raft. Not satisfied, he searched out a dead branch and puffed up rushes by the roots. Kem came over to watch him curiously, while the others laid a half dozen dynamite boxes close together on the two logs of the raft.

Over these boxes, Yarak wedged the branch, and stuck rushes in between the logs. He noticed that the wooden boxes bore numbers and marking.

The others were wading across the river from shoal to shoal, Jan carrying the girl. Some of the Siberians seemed to be carrying packs.

"Wait for as long as it takes to milk a cow," Kem explained. "Then shove off." He calculated a moment. "That gives us time to get around to the bank."

"Don't forget to make the diversion," Yarak warned. Then he thought of something. "How will the dynamite go off?"

He did not know much about the explosive qualities of dynamite, but Kem, understood such chemicals, "Don't worry, Uncle. It will go off, at the submarine." He hesitated, watching Yarak. "Only you'd better get away from the raft before then. Understand? Well, that's all you need to know."

And he ran after the file, now lost in the gloom of the opposite bank.

Stripped from his shaven forehead to his toes, Yarak shoved his driftwood raft out into mid-current. When he felt the tug of the current, he spat three times and crossed himself, to ward off bad luck. After a while he let himself into the water, holding on to the end of a log, guiding it. With his head screened by the branch he watched the outline of the high bank, and peered ahead for the little house on top of the boat. He only moved his legs to guide his floating bomb.

When he lifted his head he sighted the leviathan of the deep closer than he had expected. From the water it loomed up, high. He caught a faint humming and a clank of metal as men moved about the house.

The current, he calculated, was taking his float near the outer side of the monster, and he did not dare, now, to change its course. Lowering himself down, he waited for the splash of a stone, or some diversion from the bank. Surely, he thought, the *kunaks* up on the bank, twenty paces away, could spot him by now.

But no diversion came. Yarak could make out the rubber boat tied to the shore ahead of him, and hear men moving there. No other sound broke the quiet of the river. And he was bearing down steadily upon the giant from under the sea.

"The brothers of a dog!" he thought bitterly, trying to swing the logs closer to the submarine.

Suddenly a flashlight blinked at the water. Then a glow of light dazzled Yarak. The Germans had turned their searchlight on the driftwood, now only a stone's throw away.

Yarak kept his head still, swearing silently. He heard the crack of a single shot. Water sprayed beside him. A second shot from the conning tower ripped through one of the boxes. Yarak wondered again what made dynamite explode. And, hastily, he released the logs, letting himself sink into the water. Then he turned to swim against the current.

The glow faded from the water around him, and he came up to breathe.

Twenty feet away, the searchlight held on the logs, now almost at the submarine's bow. Its glow showed a man in a jersey out on the runway aiming a rifle at the suspicious floating mass. An officer climbed out of the tower, and shouted as if angry. The rifleman held his fire, while the others clustered around him, peering at the boxes which they could see plainly now.

Then the quiet of the river was shattered. Four shots flashed from the bank above the submarine, and Yarak recognized the roar of the heavy Russian Trokhlini rifles. Another volley cracked down, bullets whining off the steel decks, and some of the crew tumbling down where they stood.

The survivors jumped away from the light, and again the officer shouted. The searchlight swung around and up, across the face of the bank. Nothing showed there except brush.

From aft the conning tower, a machine gun rattled and spat at the bank, following the finger of light. The Germans, Yarak thought, were quick as devils to shoot. And by now his dynamite would be drifting harmlessly out to sea—

He caught the splash of paddles coming out from the bank before he saw, in the glow under the lightbeam, the rubber boat drawing near the submarine. Four men were hunched over in the strange craft, racing toward the iron ladder under the conning tower. Yarak wondered if the officers had returned from shore. Then he stared, fascinated.

The men in the boat were not Germans. When they grasped the ladder two of them went up with knives in their hands. The machine gun stopped, and the sailor with the rifle jumped for the ladder. At the same instant Kem jumped for the rifleman, and the two of them splashed into the water.

The two guerrillas following swung heavy packs over their heads. The packs dropped down the hatch. Another sailed in after them.

At the rail of the conning tower, the German officer stepped into the light, firing a revolver. Beneath him Jan held to the ladder with one hand. The other hand swung the stick bomb up. It dropped after the bundles into the steel hatch. And Jan let go his hold, to drop back into the water.

"*Ekh ma!*" Yarak breathed. The machine gun cut loose again. And with it the water shook around Yarak, and a blast shot up from the conning tower

The submarine swayed; and vapor boiled around it coming out of the hatch and the seams of the deck. The searchlight dimmed out and smoke spread over the water.

Yarak found himself clawing toward the shore across from him, shaking his head, to clear it. Looking back, he caught the splash of paddles, where the rubber boat was again in motion toward the high bank. Some of the boarding party, then, had got away.

The smoke closed down on him, and the reek of oil made him cough. Shivering with the chill of the river, the Cossack climbed out on the shoal. At once, his bare legs laboring through the grass, he made for his camp site.

There lay the two cognac bottles where they had been left. Yarak shook the one that felt half empty. He took a long swallow, to drive the chill out of his body. "Eh," he muttered "I was the diversion."

Immediately he felt warmed inside, but not outside so he took another long swallow. "Eh, the firing from the boat was the diversion for the boat."

He felt comfortable, now that he understood everything. The dog brothers, he thought—they bit hard. They left him the boxes and took the dynamite with them.

Upstream, when he sat down to put on his clothes, he saw the guerrillas making back across the ford. He counted nine, with the Polish officer and the wondering girl among them. He heard Kem telling the survivors to get their rolls together and start east to the next post. "Brothers, soldiers," Yarak called after them, "that was done like Cossacks."

Overhead the finger of a searchlight probed the sky to the west; a patrol hurried down the far bank. Yarak felt a glow of contentment, and, crawling back into the rocks, he wrapped himself in his coat. Putting the remaining bottle in a convenient pocket of the coat, he dozed happily.

The Two Swords of Genghis Khan

There are several motor routes from the U.S.S.R. into China, none of them good. They cross the mountain ranges of mid-Asia and what is known as the Gobi Desert. The Kurdai–Luntai route, hitherto unmapped, was discovered by the army of the United States. It was discovered accidentally. It might never have been found and mapped if the tribe of Dungans had not cherished a superstitious fear of the ghost of Genghis Khan, or if Uncle Yarak had been able to find any war in the settlement of Kurdai.

On that particular day, the soul of Yarak the Cossack was sick. Sitting moodily on a gasoline tin, he polished his sword with the tail of his shirt, wholly heedless of the scenic beauty of the bare heights around him. There was nothing else for him to do in this place.

"*Tfu*," muttered Yarak. "The devil has flown away with this war."

It had been in the west, where the sun set—no doubt of that. But he had heard there was also war in the place of the sun's rising. Whereupon he had contrived to get himself as far to the east as possible, to Kurdai, and had found himself in the shacks of a construction camp where a battalion of soldiers labored at laying the roadbed of a railroad.

Yarak had no desire to work upon a railroad. In other and better days now long vanished, he had played his part in these barrens of central Asia as a Cossack should, with a *kuniaki*—a little horse—between his knees and a real saber at his side. Then he had stalked and killed his enemies and possessed himself of their weapons. He had kissed the Dungan girls, at night, after washing down his meat with corn brandy as clear as crystal.

When Yarak thought of that brandy, he got to his feet. If he could not fight, he would drink. Only he had no coin to buy brandy, nor did he own anything fit to sell for money—except this sword.

It wasn't much of a sword, being an ancient yataghan with some writing on its steel that he had picked up unseen at a market. Moodily, he considered it, and brightened. It wasn't worth ten kopecks but he could think up a legend about it. Yarak knew plenty of legends—more than these ignorant Russians.

To think, with Yarak, was to act. In a minute he had drawn the officer of the battalion aside and exhibited the yataghan. He had found it in a kurgan, a tomb mound, very ancient. This was a lie.

"Look at the writing on it," he urged. "It's old, that's what." He lowered his voice: "It's the sword of Genghis Khan."

Without haste the captain inspected the yataghan. He knew Yarak. "The sword of Genghis Khan?" He laughed. "With Arabic writing on it? Pin your shirt tail with it. It's not worth ten kopecks."

"May the dogs bite you, Brother Captain Ilytch," growled Yarak.

The engineer captain considered. "Tell you a what, Uncle. Sell it to the Amrikans."

"The which?"

"The Amrikans. They don't know anything, Yarak. Look at them over there—reading a book to find out where they are. They're dumb but they have coin."

So it happened that Yarak sallied forth across the roadbed to try his luck with the Amrikans.

Five of them were clustered about a sixth, reading a book, on the running board of a motor truck. The seventh was a woman, also reading from a book leaning against a new command car. Yarak noticed that their uniforms differed from the Russian gray and their cars shone like new.

The woman wore boots of a kind and trim khaki. She had a clean, lovely face and her gray eyes looked full at Yarak with surprise as he strode toward her.

What a woman like this was doing with the strange Amrikans Yarak did not know. But young as she was and dumb, he liked her looks. He put one arm around her and, with the other, displayed the ancient curved yataghan.

"*Hai, dushenka,*" he growled invitingly. "Hi, darling, do you want to buy a sword cheap, for brandy money? And such a sword!"

The darling said something Yarak could not understand, although he knew most of the dialects of central Asia. Then a man's arm with stripes on it was shoved against Yarak's chest. A stocky soldier appeared in front of him, shoving hard.

"*Het!*" Yarak yelled.

He kicked out at the offending soldier's thigh, and the soldier dodged, swinging a heavy fist below Yarak's belt. This heavy Amrikan had gray hair and he breathed like a bull. Pained, Yarak jabbed him in the throat and swung up the yataghan. The soldier reached for an ax. Before either one could land a blow, in between them jumped the girl.

She seemed to Yarak to be an angry girl.

"Fold up, you zombie!" said Nurse Branson crisply, keeping her slender person between Yarak and the sergeant.

In a previous war, Sergeant Lanihan had served in a regiment known, for good cause, as the "Infighting Irish." Now he was ready to go and he protested: "The guy made a pass at you with a knife."

"Oh—rats!" said she, and she looked at the officer wearily. "Can't you do anything?"

"I—I'm sorry, Kitty." The officer flushed.

Now Kitty Branson had been through a good deal, and all of it unexpected. The transport plane bearing her and this Captain Whittaker with other officers had made an emergency landing through the overcast on unknown terrain, shaking up its passengers. True, they had been picked up after due time by cars summoned from the nearest emergency field by radio. Thereupon, this same Sergeant Lanihan had lost his way driving back to the field, in the enveloping mist that Captain Whittaker called clouds.

There being no roads, apparently, and the leading cars being lost to sight, Sergeant Lanihan had relied mistakenly upon his compass, forgetting that the metal and electric system of a motorcar had more attraction for a magnetized needle than the true north. The truck, containing a 60 mm mortar detail and several rifles, had followed Lanihan's car obediently.

Now, after a foodless day and a sleepless night, they were lost. All that Captain Whittaker could say for certain was that they were nine thousand one hundred and eighty feet over sea level.

Feeling their way through the clouds, they had stumbled upon this battalion of Russian engineers. But they could not communicate with the Russians, owing to the barrier of language.

Surveying Yarak's six foot three of height, his gaunt, pockmarked face and flowing mustache, Kitty Branson longed for the gift of free speech.

She had a manual of Russian phrases with her and she had been able to ask these Russian engineers for bread. But when she tried to ask for the landing field, they brought her out a cot.

"Are we going to stay here," Kitty inquired in clear Boston accents, "making signs for the Red army to feed us, until they get that railroad built, and a Trans-Siberian express comes along to take us somewhere?"

Far overhead, a plane droned past, invisible above the drifting clouds. Bitterly, Kitty reflected that the crew in that plane was probably American, perhaps searching for them at that moment.

"How about it, Captain?" she asked, with malice.

The bars upon Noble Whittaker's shoulders were shining and unscarred. He had worn his uniform for no more than three months. Never had he been placed in command of men or set his foot upon the soil of Asia before now. Shy and spectacled, he had one enthusiasm—map making. Upon a drafting board, with the skill of an artist, he had brought to life the delicate contours of elevations, the dark shadings of depressions, the tracery of rivers. He had dreamed of so delineating this misty mid-region of Asia, which of all the areas upon the globe, not excepting the North Polar region, was the least known topographically. And to carry out this dream, the Army had clothed him and sent him forth—but not to give orders to fighting men.

Technically, Whittaker was not in command of this mixed detail, but he was the only officer present and he felt the weight of full responsibility resting on his slender shoulders. It was up to him to get them all out—somewhere, somehow.

Then came the flash of inspiration. He remembered that the pilots in the transport plane had talked about another emergency field set up near a place called Luntai.

"Wait a minute," he said eagerly, and he had Lanihan unlock the rear compartment of the car, so he could get at his map case. When Lanihan obeyed reluctantly a half dozen bottles were revealed among the assorted baggage.

Yarak, watching the strange actions of the Amrikans, moved up instantly. Some of the bottles held a brownish liquor that might well be brandy; some, square in shape, contained liquor clear as crystal—unmistakably vodka. His thirst increased.

Meanwhile the officer was regarding a map very thoughtfully. He had found Luntai. "Ask that Cossack," he demanded, "if he knows the bearing of Luntai. That is—where it is."

In grim silence, Kitty extracted her Russian phrase book. *"Piu na Luntai?"* she gave forth presently.

Yarak pricked up his ears. Two generations of wandering had tuned his ears to the dialects of Asia, and he decided the Amrikan girl was trying to speak Russian, which he knew almost as well as his native Ukrainian. Whereupon the following dialogue ensued:

Yarak: "That way, darling." He pointed, and Whittaker by use of the compass took a bearing of almost due southeast. It looked about right to him.

Whittaker: "Does he know the road, there?"

Kitty: "Road to Luntai?"

Yarak: "There isn't a road. But I know the way through the mountains like my doorstep. Look, Commander, that way." His eyes quested along the mountain barrier and spotted a ravine through which large birds were flying. Yarak had no notion of the way to Luntai, but he knew that such birds did not enter a ravine unless it led somewhere.

Whittaker (studying the ravine entrance through his field glasses and observing a track of some sort): "Will he guide us there—for pay, of course?"

Kitty (having difficulty with this): "Will you go there—leading us—for money?"

Yarak: "Certainly."

It was just as Brother Ilytch had said. These Amrikans could not do anything without reading books and looking at maps. Moreover they had money. But Yarak was chiefly interested in the bottles.

He spat three times and crossed himself. His problem was solved. With these Amrikans, he would go out of railroad building Kurdai, and when they drank the good brandy and vodka, Yarak also would drink.

If not, he need only wait until there was an accident and then he'd abstract a couple of bottles from the rump of the small car. Knowing these mountains, he did not think these Amrikans would go far on their way.

As for Luntai, Yarak had no wish to go there, beyond the mountains. In the memory of man, no Christian souls and no wheeled vehicles had gone there. On the contrary, Yarak would wait for the accident to happen.

Meanwhile the Kurdai–Luntai expedition was being launched in a fashion unforeseen by anyone but Whittaker, who was making something like a speech to the four enlisted men.

"It's really up to you guys to decide. We can stock up with chow and gas by purchase from the Russians, I hope. Enough to last for five days or a week. Then we can proceed in one of two directions. Lanihan can try to guide us back to his field."

There was silence at this. "We just as well try to fly," said one of the mortar detail at length, "than follow him around any more."

"What's the other direction?" demanded Lanihan, and added, "Sir?"

"China."

No one said anything. Kitty looked at the captain curiously.

Whittaker explained about the AAF's emergency field. It meant a hundred miles through the mountains, and then thirty miles or so across the barren Gobi Desert. Perhaps they could get the cars through the mountains, if the gas held out. They'd have to take their luck with water.

"The printed maps are lousy about detail," he assured his audience. "But I think I can pick up Luntai."

Whittaker tried to keep enthusiasm out of his voice. He wanted earnestly to explore these unmapped mountains.

The enlisted personnel looked at him, looked at the sergeant and voted to try for Luntai. They were tired of chasing mist in this no man's land, and China sounded good to them.

"If you find it," said Lanihan sourly.

"What about you, Miss Branson?" Whittaker asked.

"I seem to remember that Marco Polo was the only European who found a road ready for him in this part of the world."

Whittaker nodded. His shyness had vanished. "Yes. I figured we'd have to make our own."

Kitty looked at him with respect. Right or wrong, he had guts.

During the next five days, Sergeant Lanihan decided that the track they followed—Marco Polo or no Marco Polo—had been made by animals, and that those animals had been goats.

For five days, Yarak found his hopes unfulfilled. These Amrikans did not open up a bottle even when they cooked supper. Moreover, he could not manage to break into the rump of the car with any tool he found handy. The girl, for some reason best known to her, kept the key of the compartment.

They escaped an accident by a succession of miracles. They climbed steadily into the silence of the heights, where they could look down on the eagles when the cloud rift cleared. Where the slope was too steep, they made the smaller car haul itself up by a wire cable, and then the small machine towed up the big one.

Where a sandstone outcropping blocked the way, the noncom cleared it by accurate blasts from the small trench mortar. Where a gray glacier-fed torrent had torn out the track, they rushed the cars through. Finally the track failed altogether, but the Amrikans slid the machines down a rubble slope on the cable and followed the dry bed of a stream out upon a plain bare of everything except gray tamarisk and dead reeds. Here the ground unexpectedly gave off heat like a covered oven.

Yarak decided that, although the devils of the mountain pass had been strong, the devils in the Amrikans were stronger. At every point, the Amrikan officer had sketched in his compass bearings on a new map, taking observations of the drift of the mountain range and the summits when he could. Under his pencil, the road through the pass took shape.

Then on the sixth day, the accident happened that Yarak had expected hitherto in vain.

It began with a stoppage in the thermostat on the truck, due probably to bad water. While Lanihan and his gang were investigating the thermostat—and digging for water—Whittaker searched the plain with his glasses and observed no sign of Luntai. He was in the Gobi Desert, but where in the Gobi Desert he did not know.

To his questioning, via Kitty, Yarak returned only evasive answers. Luntai was a town, he admitted, yet it wasn't. In what direction it lay, he would not say.

So Whittaker took Kitty and the Cossack in the command car and went forth to investigate the gray plain upon which appeared no sizable tree, or any building built by the hands of men.

"It looks empty," Kitty observed, "and dead." After those five days she was the worse for wear and she was hot. "Are you sure Luntai is a town?"

"No," said Whittaker.

Through his field glasses, he saw what looked like a division of infantry, standing in open order on an endless parade ground. But when he headed the command car toward them, the formation turned out to be a few square miles of desiccated and iron-hard poplar forest. Only the lower trunks of the trees survived, poking upright in billows of sand.

Steering between sand dunes, drawing away from Lanihan and the truck, Whittaker came upon some strange sights. All around him the roof beams and gates of wooden houses, gnawed by sun and sand, projected from the ground.

"Luntai!" said Yarak, peering at them.

A few holes had been dug down into the sand-buried houses. Horse tracks crisscrossed the loose sand but not even a lizard seemed to be alive and crawling in the ruins.

"This," said Kitty emphatically, "is the grandfather of all the ghost towns. I don't like it."

Whittaker assured her they must have come upon one of the sand-buried cities of the Gobi. A couple of millenniums ago, the remnant of a salt inland sea had moistened this vast depression. The bed of the sea had dried up into salt crust, and the encroaching sands had buried the houses of Luntai, preserving them in that bone-dry atmosphere. Triumphantly, he pointed out how this was proof that the Kurdai–Luntai road had once been a caravan route across Asia.

"You're a good guesser," Kitty admitted wearily, wiping the sweat out of her eyes. After the icy-cold of the heights the heat from the ground made her dizzy and she felt like crying. Noble Whittaker didn't seem to think of anything but a line on the map.

That moment Yarak sighted the Dungans. They came galloping over the mounds of sand, sun-blackened riders in flapping sheepskins, on shaggy ponies, with a tall swordsman leading them.

"*Kubardar bratsui!*" Yarak yelled, and slid out of the car.

Neither Whittaker nor Kitty understood his warning. The tribesmen flowed in like a human tide on their horses, making for the motorcar.

Whittaker reached for a pistol, then took count of the numbers of the Dungans. He did not know what they were. He looked for the damaged truck, but it was out of sight.

Yarak perceived that at last an accident was happening to the Amrikans. Taking up a large rock hastily, he smashed it down on the handle of the luggage compartment. The lid opened to his pull, and he extracted deftly two of the bottles, one brown, one white.

He had had experience with the tribes of the Gobi region; he proceeded to get himself out of visual range. Jumping into a hollow, he crawled off between the sand dunes. He did not think the Amrikans would get any farther, and he had saved at least two of the bottles.

Lying prone in the sand, he looked back and saw the wave of horse-men swirl around the car. In their black sheepskins, the Dungans looked like animals.

Dismounting, they pulled the Amrikans out of the car. They knocked Whittaker down and trampled on him. Then they began snatching at the crates of stores.

"*Tzee-tzee!*" their voices chanted around the leader on the white horse.

Unobserved, Yarak caught the rein of a wandering horse. It was a good, swift-paced Kabarda pony, and before the tribesmen sighted him he was a half mile off, heading back toward the hills.

Beyond the first rise, Yarak dismounted to watch his back track. All this rapid exertion made him sweat. The ground was hot under his knees. Gratefully, he ripped the fastening off a bottle and drank.

It was the white liquor and it tasted much like vodka. Smiling, Yarak opened the brown bottle and tried it also. It had the pungent flavor of brandy and Yarok sighed with satisfaction. At leisure, he quaffed from the square white bottle, and then from the brown.

A sense of increasing comfort pervaded him. The ill luck of the Am-rikans had been his good fortune. Now he had a horse and most of two bottles.

With this assurance of well-being, however, a vague discomfort as-sailed his Cossack spirit. The liquor of the Amrikans was good liquor. They had come over the mountain pass in their machines like devils. They had been like *kunaks*, brothers of the road. And now, by force of an accident, he had to leave them.

The dumb lady had smiled at him, like a merry girl. When the Dun-gans discovered she was young, they wouldn't leave much of her.

"*Tfu,*" he muttered. "Impossible to ride off and leave a girl like that." But he couldn't think of anything else to do.

Then he heard the chugging of a motor, and the truck came surging up to the rise, its injury repaired. "Het!" yelled Yarak, pulling his horse over to it. The truck stopped suddenly.

Sergeant Lanihan and the half squad surveyed the scene below them in the sand-buried city of Luntai. "Hell's bells!" said the sergeant and let the truck slide back out of view.

He reflected that he had in the truck only the 60-mm mortar and several rifles. Also, he knew that the Asiatics swarming around the captain and the lady were at present beyond the mortar's effective range. He wanted time to size up the picture.

"Are they Japs, Sarge?" someone asked.

Lanihan did not answer because he did not know.

Then Yarak came up, jabbering and gesticulating. The eyes of the Cossack gleamed under shaggy brows, and his breath gave out with gin and whisky, although Lanihan could see no bottle on him.

The sergeant knew no Russian and less Ukrainian, but in days gone by, he had argued with Frogs in similar situations. Bending his ear attentively, he tried to make out what this Cossack was saying but it made no sense.

When Yarak mounted the Kabarda and went swinging off to the side, back toward Luntai, Lanihan nodded to his henchmen. He had a reputation to maintain, and that reputation had suffered recently.

He thought he could guess what Yarak was doing.

"Co-ordinate on this, you guys," he told his excited detail. "Maybe them's Japs, an' maybe they ain't. The Cossack's gone to find out. But never mind him. We got to move quick. We couldn't find our way out of here without that captain."

With the Kabarda between his knees, Yarak trotted up to the Dungans in the ruined city. His mind was alert with drink, and he was shaping a stratagem. Tribesmen like these could be frightened by something they did not understand—by the supernatural.

The Dungans, beholding him returning of his own accord and alone on one of their horses, watched him with great and growing curiosity.

"*Chorziaka*," he growled at them, "insects out of a dunghill, make way for me."

He saw the two Amrikans and was relieved that neither the girl nor the officer called out to him. They were not afraid of the Dungans.

Kicking his way through the armed crowd, he dismounted and strode up to the leader of the riders, who now sat upon a horsehide in the shadow of a gate. A heavy man, with a scar closing one eye, he looked like a hard soul. Silent, he sat on his ankles instead of his heels in a curious fashion.

"Yah Beg," said Yarak. "Chieftain, I have come where the spoil is gathered. I have come for my share."

The strange Beg rolled his good eye up at the empty hillside and back at Yarak. "A dog barks at the wind," he rasped. "And who art thou?" He hissed the words as if they were strange to his tongue.

"One man," replied Yarak modestly, pleased with his stratagem. "Yet a mighty manslayer. The sword I carry is a sword of power."

Behind him, the tribesmen breathed audibly and strained closer to hear. Yarak turned on them, touched the ivory hilt of his yataghan and shouted, "Tell me, jackals, what spirit rides in the night over these mountains when the sand dunes sound with the beat of drums?"

"The spirit of Genghis Khan!" voices clamored.

"True. And this is the sword of Genghis Khan, taken from the tomb of Genghis Khan!"

His words brought instant silence. The tribesmen gaped at him, their hands on their mouths. Yarak put his hands on his hips proudly.

"Thou?" yelled one. "That is a lie and a poor one."

Gripping their rifles, they surged around him, staring at the ancient yataghan. "Our leader has the sword of Genghis Khan!" they chanted, and they pointed at the chieftain, who did not sit like a tribesman of the Gobi. "The power is in him. In the night, his eyes see. No bullet can harm him. Ai-a, all who follow him shall slay and be victorious over the Christians."

The leader of the Dungans had indeed a sword different from any Yarak had seen—long, in a black lacquer sheath, with a shining hilt.

"From the place of the sun's rising, from *Jih pen kuo*, he has come," the Dungans cried. "These rifles he gave us, to slay the western Christians."

Laughter shook the crowd. Yarak noticed that the rifles were serviceable, with a bolt action. He spat vigorously.

"Bow down, Cossack," rasped the chieftain. "For I set my foot where the spirit horde stands guard. When the white spirit horse came, in the seventh moon, I took this sword from the grave of Genghis Khan. No enemy can stand before me. Bow down."

Silently the seated man drew a blade of polished steel. Yarak felt a chill of fear. But he had no mind to bend his head, to have it cut off by that sword. He slid a glance toward the two Amrikans. They were empty-handed, their arms tied, and on the height behind them, there was no sign of soldiers or truck.

"Then prove it!" he shouted. "A dog can bark, a lama can lie. I have the true sword. It is your head that will fall."

He began to feel uneasy. The Dungans patted their hands on their hips, overjoyed by the challenge to their swordsman. The chieftain lifted the long shining blade of the sword gently and stepped forward arrogantly. The Dungans surged back. So did Yarak.

Rather he jumped back, and swung himself into the saddle of the Kabarda pony. "*Het*," he shouted, "to the saddle, thou. Are we to fight like women, in the dirt?"

So quickly had he moved that the Dungans had not been able to stop him mounting. Moreover, they appeared supremely confident in the prowess of their swordsman. That person hesitated, then swung himself not too easily into the saddle of his fine white horse.

Instantly, Yarak rode at him, swinging the yataghan. As he suspected, the strange Japanese was a poorer rider than swordsman. Circling him, Yarak cut savagely, whirled the Kabarda and slashed again.

Each blow fell against the rigid blade of the long, tapering sword. A chill of misgiving went through the Cossack. The stranger used the sword as if it were part of him. The razor point flashed at Yarak's belt, and the Cossack almost lost his seat. That sword had a power in it.

Yarak felt afraid. He was tired and panting. The stranger pressed him inexorably. Yarak whirled the Kabarda, kicking the little horse. He would have to use his pony more than his sword.

As he streaked away toward the hills, with the swordsman two lengths behind him, the greater part of the Dungans scrambled into their saddles and whipped after the fighters, yelping with excitement.

Watching back as he rode, Yarak gripped the Kabarda with his knees. The little horse was strange to him, but nimble on its feet—racing with its head tossing up, alert. Yarak crossed himself with his sword hand and decided to risk a trick.

Savagely he jerked the rein around and up. The startled horse missed stride and spun on its heels. With all the strength of his arm, Yarak pulled up its head.

He pulled the rearing Kabarda around and full into the racing white horse that had no time to swerve. The Kabarda's hoofs struck into the head of the white horse. Yarak slashed down with the yataghan.

This was the *lava*, an old saber trick of the Cossacks. The white horse fell heavily. The Japanese shot out of the saddle with his head half off. The blade of the yataghan had caught his neck. Hurriedly Yarak dismounted and caught up the strange sword.

Waving the two weapons, he yelled at the oncoming Dungans, "Which sword has power? Which, now, is the sword of Genghis Khan?"

Bending down from the saddle, the tribesmen glared at the body of their leader, with the blood running out of it. The power of magic had not protected him, who had given them rifles to slay these Westerners.

Cra-ash! Something exploded sharply at the edge of the surging crowd. It was followed by the crack of high-powered rifles.

Yarak jumped, then looked over his shoulder. Momentarily he had forgotten the other Amrikans. He saw them now.

Over the ridge, two hundred yards away, one driver steered the truck. Beside him two riflemen advanced on foot. Two others were reloading the trench mortar hastily. Sergeant Lanihan's detail had all the appearance of the advance point of a strong force.

"*Het!*" Yarak yelped.

The second burst came full among the Dungans. This firepower stunned and awed them. As one man, they headed off into the sand dunes, lashing their horses. After that, it seemed only natural to Kitty that Captain Whittaker should sight a plane when it was no more than a speck on the vaulting skyline. It seemed only natural that he should plot its course, and that finally they should arrive at an American emergency landing field—a cluster of brown tents ranged along a clear stretch of clay, all ferried in by transport.

Not until they had eaten canned soup and prunes and slept the clock around on real cots, not until Whittaker completed his sketch survey of the way they had come and showed it to the major commanding the field, not till then did Kitty realize that the captain had accomplished a small miracle.

The major stared. "You came through the mountains?" he exclaimed incredulously. "From Kurdai to Luntai? By my map, it's impossible."

"We had an excellent guide," Whittaker said. "He knew an old caravan route."

"Great Scott!" The major beamed. "This means we can supply the field overland—by truck."

Kitty heard the wind beating at the sand dunes with a roar like that of drums and she went out into the night to wait for Noble Whittaker. When he had finished with the major, he found her and she pointed out how bright the stars were.

He peered up at them intently. "That's Orion," he said, "just south of here."

Kitty stared at him for a moment and then smiled. For all he was a man of courage, he was also a man of maps. One day perhaps she might draw him a map, a different sort of map than any he was accustomed to reading, but he would follow it.

She took his arm and said, "Let's find Yarak. We haven't thanked him."

"Nor paid him," said Whittaker.

It was not hard to find Yarak. Something like a free-for-all was taking place at the campfire, where most of the enlisted personnel of the field gathered around the gaunt Cossack who had taken his stand on a gasoline drum. Voices cracked out and fists were thrust up at him.

On the drum beside him rested a bottle of Kentucky bourbon and another of gin, now empty, Whittaker observed. Above the tumult, Yarak waved the long curiously shaped sword of ancient workmanship. In the upraised fists of the American soldiers, Kitty sighted bank notes and Chinese silver.

"He's auctioning off the sword," she laughed, "of that Japanese officer."

The Phantom Caravan

No war had come to the land where Usbekistan borders Afghanistan. No plane traversed the hard blue sky over the ruins of Samarkand and no machines raised the red dust along roads where pack horses plodded. Fighting machines and petrol had been sucked away beyond the Volga and men of fighting age had followed them, leaving only obsolete machines in the vicinity. A rusted Italian machine gun or a Lebel single-shot rifle with cartridges fetched their weight in silver here, for they gave their owners power.

While Soviet troops policed the railroad, the borderland of the hills served at night as a pathway for horse thieves and armed men of ill will. The Black Sheep Turkomans took to raiding again. And the name of Zarafak, the Gold Finder, became a powerful one.

Yarak the Cossack, journeying homeward to the west by horseback, had encountered the strength of Zarafak and was now considering its consequences ruefully. He sat on a park bench under silvery poplars over which shown the splendor of the blue-tiled dome and chewed meditatively on the stem of his cherry wood pipe. "When the Devil is afraid," he muttered disconsolately, "he sends a woman."

It was unquestionably true. Regardless of the first mother, Eva, had not Kleopatra beguiled the good soldier Marka Antonius to his ruin so that he killed himself with his own saber? No doubt. And he, Yarak, formerly of the Savage Division in the old war and participant in his good *sablianka* upon the battle fronts of this new war had been beguiled likewise by the words of a yellow-haired girl who chewed sunflower seeds. Such woman as she and Kleopatra seduced men to sit on doorsteps of a home and think of cattle and mattress beds and children. That was how they tempted an otherwise right-thinking man.

Yarak spat three times carefully, and went over in his mind the steps leading to his downfall.

First his coming into Samarkand at moonrise, leading his horse, looking for vodka and companionship. He found no lighted shops or barracks or soldiers. Only, in this silent city, the shining blue dome arising from the poplar grove and having all the appearance of a palace. It struck Yarak as strange.

Then he sighted this girl sitting on the doorstep of the small house, with her yellow hair unbound, weeping quietly.

"*Eh*, say, girl," he demanded, "what has happened here? Is this a place of the dead?"

It was the old city, she explained, wiping her face with her sleeve. The ruined city of Tamerlane, the Lame. Tamerlane, a limping Turkish conqueror, had built himself a palace with the loot of the world five centuries and a half ago. When he tired of war, he passed his time among the pleasure gardens.

Yarak pondered the words of the girl, Praska, who sat here alone because her man was serving in the west. So the thought came to him. Why should he, Yarak, endure another Winter of war? He had wealth in his saddle roll. Like Tamerlane, he could settle down in an *izba* of his own, with smoked fish hanging to the rafters, a keg of vodka by the head of his bed, and a hawk on its perch by the door. He could pass his days so in luxury, perhaps hiring a *bandura* player to sing the old songs of the Cossack brotherhood.

After all, he was old. Certain parts of his six-foot body ached when the Winter frost set in. Was it not better to sit like a nabob smoking his pipe on the sunny side of his house, than to live in the saddle like this, following after battles like a dog after a caravan? Certainly it was better.

That was how the girl Praska put a thought into his head as if she had been a *koldun*, a magician.

To think with Yarak was to act. At once he wanted to turn his property into money.

"Eh, say," he asked, "where is a trader, a money changer?"

"Over in this new city, by the station."

Yarak peered at her curiously. "What makes you cry, girl?"

Praska looked up at him with wet eyes. "Nothing," she said. "I'm not crying. Don't hang around here, grandfather."

Full of his new thought, Yarak climbed into the saddle and put his horse to a trot. Passing the twin towers of a giant ruined mosque, he looked for the road out. And off in the moonlight he saw lanterns move.

Heading toward it, he found, instead of a road, the wide crumbling gateway of a *serai*. Beyond the gateway moved man and animals. There were plenty of such deserted caravansary along the old roads here, but seldom with people in them. Entering, Yarak found a score of horses being loaded by men in black sheepskin hats—Turkomans, who were evidently preparing to take the road.

He stopped because he had no desire to interfere with tribesmen who chose to be on the move at night. But the lantern moved over to him, and the man who held at it—whose massive fat was bound up in a shining blue *khalat*—demanded, "Well, what, Cossack?"

"Nothing, brother," Yarak explained. "I am looking for a trader."

"Dismount, then. For here is a buyer of goods."

He pointed and Yarak saw, up on the balcony of the *serai*, a well-dressed European sorting papers into a box.

Yarak presented himself before the master of the caravan with his pack. Out of the saddle roll he shook his wealth—bits of jade and carved ivory, American paper money, a blue enamel triptych from some forgotten church, a fine Afghan yataghan and other stuff he had acquired during his wandering in ways that he chose not to explain. In the wake of the war's devastation it was not hard to pick up wealth like this.

"How much for the lot, in gold?" he asked.

The trader looked at the jade and the triptych carefully, close to the light. He had a pale face like a moon.

"Pay him twenty pounds, Yussuf" he said, his long fingers putting in the jade away in a box.

"Gold," insisted Yarak, who knew how worthless most paper currencies were.

The big man in the *khalat* showed his broken teeth in a grin. "Ai, Cossack—gold, for stolen articles?"

The trader closed the box carefully, and spoke without expression. "Possession of gold is illegal, Cossack. It would mean the taste of a Soviet prison. You will be paid in good foreign currency. Look."

The man called Yussuf counted out a sheaf of soiled bank notes, pinkish blue in color and ornamented with a woman's head. Yarak spat.

"That dog won't bite," he snarled.

Moon-face closed his box and locked it. "A bargain is a bargain," he said.

Yussuf, grinning, picked up the lantern. Behind him, Yarak heard a familiar *clack*. Turning his head, he observed a Turkoman closing the breach of a sawed-off rifle. Quickly he went down to his horse. He did not want to lose the animal, which was a good one.

The next morning he showed his beautiful engraved bank notes to an officer at the railroad station and discover that he had been paid in Syrian paper pounds which could not be used in Soviet territory and were worth little in any case. The officer wanted to know where Yarak got such money, and Yarak explained that he had found it in a deserted caravansary. The caravansary was, in truth, deserted that sunrise.

So, thinking it over, Yarak blamed the girl Praska for his loss. Morosely he rode back to the little house by the tiled dome. He strode in through the door and stopped, surprised at what he saw. The main room, instead of a bed and furnishing, had only a row of empty glass cases and a chest with traces of gilt upon it, likewise empty. Wondering what sort of house this might be, he passed into the rear room, where he discovered Praska heating water for tea in a samovar. Beside the stove stood her cot, neatly made up. Evidently she lived in this kitchen.

"What kind of nest is this?" he demanded.

Not a nest, Praska informed him—a museum, closed since the war. She was, she explained, in charge of the valuable exhibits in the showcases, the bits of gold work and turquoise jewelry and several fine Korans, all belonging to the time of Tamerlane. But these exhibits had been stolen while she had been away yesterday evening at the railway station watching the train coming in.

Yarak pondered this. "Eh," he ventured, "did you see the Turkoman horse caravan yesterday?"

Praska shook her head. She had seen only Yarak. As for tribesmen, they would not have known about the exhibits. Whoever would have broken into the house for the old Korans and jewels from the tomb?

"What tomb?" demanded Yarak.

"This one." Praska nodded toward that tiled edifice under the towered dome. "The Gur Amur where Tamerlane is buried in his tomb."

"But you said it was a palace."

It was true, she explained, that Tamerlane started to build the mosques and palaces of Samarkand, now in ruins; but he died of a sickness before the city was finished, and he'd been buried there in the place now known as his tomb.

"Eh, that's the truth of it," Yarak muttered. "When he turned his horse from the path of war and settled down he became sick and died."

The kettle dropped from Praska's hand as she looked past Yarak, and the blood drained from her face as if the hand of a ghost had touched her.

Yarak peered over his shoulder and beheld a stocky man coming up the path to the kitchen door. Coming slowly, dragging one leg, with a blanket roll on his shoulder. He wore infantry boots.

"Michael!" gasped the girl.

Past Yarak she flew, to be grasped in Michael's arms, her golden hair pressing against his shoulder. "Michael—you did not come on the train. I thought for months you did not come, and I thought—"

"I came by road, riding trucks."

Praska's eyes gleamed under the tangle of her hair and she flew around the kitchen, getting a bench for the limping man, pouring out hot tea for him fresh from the samovar. And when he explained that he had come on indefinite leave with the injury to his leg, it was as if new life coursed through her.

"Glory to God," she cried. "Listen to the man! And I was thinking that he was off dancing with the Polish girls."

The lines of the soldier's face shifted as he smiled. "Devilkin," he said. He rubbed his red thatch as he told how he had been injured while investigating the working of a new Niemtsev mine. In his pack he had some detonating mechanisms from captured mines brought back to show Praska, with some fringed Italian silk for a shawl for her. He had been two years at the war, seeing much of the world, Praska knew. And she knew that he would never walk far again with that leg.

Michael limped with him along the path when Yarak went to mount his horse, and Praska brought along bread for the Cossack to take with him. When he undid his saddle pack to put in the two small Korans and a silver-guilt bracelet fell out. Yarak stared at them, puzzled, but the girl examined them and cried out. "*Akh*—from the museum!"

"That's a lie, girl," Yarak growled. Certainly these things could not have come from her museum, because they could only have been put into his roll in one way—by the broken-toothed Yussuf, when he, Yarak had traded last night with a master of the caravan.

Defiantly, Praska tossed her head. Who, she asked, had seen anything of the night-prowling caravan, except Yarak? And where had the bracelet and the Korans been, but in the Cossack's pack?

Yarak nodded. That was true enough. The night-riding devils had branded him a thief. Then he remembered the bank notes and produced them.

"They were here, all right, girl. Look what they gave me."

Michael examined one of the notes curiously. "For what," he wondered, "did they give it to you?"

Yarak considered, not wishing to explain all that he had been looting. "*Het*," he growled. "For an old yataghan, soldier—and the paper money isn't good, even for a glass of *vodka*."

"It was more than a yataghan you sold." Michael nodded reflectively. "And these traders, they are invisible."

"How invisible?"

"Gold finders. They keep behind the front lines. They show up when we're someplace else."

"Looters?" demanded Yarak.

"Buyers. The war bred 'em, uncle."

This Michael had been through two Summer campaigns and a Winter in the Caucasus, where he had smelled out the black markets. But the Zafaraks, the gold finders, were no ordinary black market dealers. They stacked up cheap paper money, bought for a few kopeks on the ruble, and they searched for valuables like silverware, weapons, good boots, quinine, and especially the old gold coins that still trickled through the bazaars, along with the new American bills. They bought up good land, where the owners had been killed, and even valuable manuscripts, postage stamps, fine paintings.

Such things they carted from one place to another, to sell later in good markets, where rising prices rose still higher in inflated paper. They thrived on the destruction of the wars because the authorities could spare neither time nor men to investigate their network.

"Like wolves," Yarak nodded, "they feed well on the battlefield. And who will ride off to hunt wolves?"

"That's how it is, brother. These wolves who lifted Praska's collection, they may travel as merchants or tribesmen or whatever, to Baghdad or Kandahar to sell the things—"

"But it's that Tartaristan Historical Museum collection of the Tamerlane relics," cried Praska.

"And who knows that in Baghdad or Kandahar?" asked the red-haired soldier. His arm squeezed her waist. "Don't run after the water in the river, my sweet."

Shoving him away, Praska wiped her eyes. Michael, she said indignantly, clearly did not understand how her pride was broken because she had lost the priceless things entrusted to her. They meant little to him.

Yarak looked at her and saw that she had a conviction. A *dushenka* like Praska, with a young warm body, ought to be thinking about kisses and children. Instead, she grieved for a vanished collection.

"Listen," Michael argued reasonably, "it isn't as if you'd had guards for this dumb museum. You aren't to blame. How can you keep out a dozen men with rifles—unless you'd had a booby trap over the door, and a mine—"

"You think you know everything. I'm not dumb. I'm only—" she flung up her head, in a temper. "I'm going after the sons of dogs and bring back the collection."

Michael shook his red head. "You are dumb. Supposing you could ever find them, will you charm their rifles by smiling at them? Look here, Praska, you just report it at the station."

Of all things, the one thing Praska would not do was report her loss. The Cossack, she said, could find her a horse. As for Michael, he could not ride on account of his leg.

"I suppose," Michael growled, "you'd like me to sit here alone with the door locked, to keep people away until you get back with the curios?"

"Certainly," she cried.

"Find your own gatekeeper, Curator Praska." The soldier's lips grinned at her. "There are plenty of other girls over in the city."

Yarak pondered. He had his own ax to grind with the gold finders, and something Michael had said made him thoughtful. "*Eh*, brother, easy enough to follow wolves. If you could make me a trap to take along."

Going into the ravaged display room, he contemplated the empty carved and gilded chest, the only thing left there. He, like Michael, had had experience with booby traps, and he began to vision the discomfiture of the broken-toothed Yussuf and Moon-face. Moreover, in this way he could escape beyond reach of Praska's tongue.

Behind him he heard the girl's voice, low and coaxing. "Can you really trail those horses, Uncle Yarak?"

The Cossack snorted. Could he follow more than a score of unshod Turkoman ponies, weighted down with packs, along dust-padded roads? "Go back to your kitchen, girl," he muttered. "I am not yet blind. I will find them."

Praska's eyes blinked. "That I must go with you, to identify the stolen articles," she announced calmly. "Otherwise you would not know them."

So two days later Yarak found himself questing along the Samarkand desert road, leading another horse with the chest lashed to it. The silent Michael had worked for a day and a half over the chest. From time to time Yarak glanced back uneasily at it as it jolted. He distrusted machines.

Heartily he regretted his rash promise to Praska. She had begged a good horse from the soldiers at the railroad, and now she rode as if possessed, without stopping to rest the horses or let them roll.

At first the tracks of the trader's caravan had been clear enough. Then the trail turned away from the railroad onto an old caravan track that skirted the edge of the desert where a haze lay over the baked ground. "The Red Sands," Yarak muttered, shaking his head. "Not good, Praska. At the first wind the tracks will be blotted out."

As Yarak had prophesied, all tracks were swept off the dry ground by the wind. At the next village nothing had been seen of the trader or his men.

"But we are close to Bokhara now," the girl insisted. "And if they have come to Bokhara, they will be seen."

Yarak was not so sure of that. The Turkomans and Moon-face, their master, managed to keep out of sight . . . And when the road led to the flat roofs of the desert city of Bokhara, the military guard at the old towered gate informed Praska that no such caravan had entered. "For a couple of years, sweet," the section leader assured Praska tranquilly.

"Ei, girl," barked Yarak cheerfully. "Now they're gone, like water down the river—as Michael said."

Praska looked at him and her lips moved soundlessly. Then, when they had ridden out of hearing of the soldiers, she turned in the saddle, her little chin thrust out. "Cossack," she demanded, "who has seen this caravan of yours—except you?"

"No one," Yarak admitted.

"Then if you do not find it, everyone will say that you lied about it, and if you lied, it will appear as if you were the thief. Think, old wolf. If the caravan didn't sit down by the road, and it did not go into the city, where is it now? Think quickly."

Yarak understood clearly. There would be no silencing this girl's tongue until the traders were found. And no one could find them except himself.

Savagely he smacked the flank of his horse and the beast stumbled as it broke into a trot. A bad omen, that. Jerking up its head, he reined up a rise by the road. Here he could see the outskirts of Bokhara, the olive groves and the wandering goatherds, the black tents of some Turkomans. Horses grazed near the tents, but no European like Moon-face would take up his quarters here.

"What is that stink?" asked Praska, who have followed him close.

"Bones," Yarak muttered instantly. "Bones of the dead."

"What?"

Yarak pointed over to the left, where the high clay walls of an abandoned mosque crowned a rise. Around it the barren rocky clay was strewn with stone slabs. Once, as the Cossack knew, Bokhara had been esteemed a holy city of the Usbek Muslims and its suburbs were filled with shallow graves, so thickly that old graves had been dug up to make room for the new. Close against the mosque clustered the beehive tombs of the richer or more celebrated dead, their names now forgotten.

Certainly the mosque was abandoned now. But the Cossack observed horse tracks crossing the road to it and leaving it. In the soft dust the tracks were clear and must be recent.

"Look," said Praska suddenly, "at Samarkand your gold finders kept out of sight in a ruin."

Yarak grunted. The caravan must have disappeared by breaking up around here. The horses might be over in the Turkoman *kibitka*, and the men—

"Stay where you are, child," he urged. "Talk to yourself."

He turned down to the road, and picked up the tracks crossing it, unshod pony tracks. Near the courtyard gate he lifted his glance and saw fresh dung inside. In the courtyard there was no trace of anything living. There was water, however, in the well. The Turkoman horses might have come here to drink.

His beast thrust forward to drink thirstily. Then it flung up its head, ears pointing toward the doorway of the mosque building where no curtain hung. The burning afternoon sunlight laid a square of light within it and in the obscurity beyond Yarak could see no movement, nor did he hear a sound. But something in there had disturbed his horse.

Dismounting, Yarak strode toward the door. Simultaneously a man appeared, coming out. A short man in a long padded *khalat*, his face shadowed by a voluminous turban wound in the Bokhara fashion.

"Wayfarer," he asked, "what you seek in the house of Allah?"

The familiar phrase, *"bait-ullah,"* was muttered crisply, not in the rapid mummering of an Usbek *mullah* such as Yarak had known in years gone by. Under the turban was a young face with broad cheek bones and thin lips. It might be Malay, it might be Japanese, but it could hardly be the face of an aged, bent caretaker in an abandoned house of Allah. Yarak stopped with a snort.

He carried no war weapon of any kind, owing to the law in Usbekistan. But he noticed the ivory hilt of a knife in the *mullah's* girdle.

Then he heard the trend of horses behind him, and Praska's musical voice.

She had come after Yarak, and now she was driving the pack horse away from the well while the man in the mosque stared up from slant eyes at the tawny mane of her hair.

The skin at the back of Yarak's neck grew cold. He remembered how his horse had stumbled a while back. "Go on, girl," he said sharply. "Don't dismount here."

While Praska looked at him, surprised, the *mullah* took the rein of her horse. "Nay, rest here, woman," he said. "Stop and rest, out of the sun."

Pulling at her rein and drawing the pack horse after him, the *mullah* started into the mosque. Yarak followed swiftly.

For a moment, coming out of the glare, he could see nothing in the half-darkness. The *mullah* was drawing the horses toward the dais where the *kiblah* should be, and where a pair of indistinct figures showed.

Yarak, peering through the dimness, recognized the two figures, Moon-face, in his dark European clothes, and pock-marked Yussuf, of the broken-toothed grin. So also did Praska recognize them from Yarak's description and before he could stop her, she gave tongue.

"Hey! Aren't those the ones who looted the museum?"

"What museum, girl?" Moon-face asked. His name, he explained, was Nabi, and anyone could tell her that he was the head of the importing firm of Nabi and Mitsui, now closed by the war. There was no museum in Bokhara, and for months he had not left the city. That afternoon he had taken a walk out to the old mosque with his servant—he nodded to Yussuf.

Praska's small face was puzzled but determined. "You have my collection! You gave the paper money to the Cossack."

Smiling, the gentleman-importer Nabi shook his head. He had nothing of hers.

"*Kahnim*," observed Yussuf respectfully, his hands crossed over his big stomach, "Lady, someone has been lying to you." He nodded at Yarak. "Do you trust that Cossack?"

Praska hesitated. These men seemed to be what they said, yet their words sounded false. Their eyes were too watchful. "Yes," she cried, "and I'm going to search until I've found what I lost."

"Dismount, and we will help the young lady," Nabi replied respectfully, and ordered Yussuf to unload their visitor's chest.

"Take your hands off that," Yarak growled at Yussuf. "There's a mine packed in that chest: we're taking it to the military. Don't interfere with us."

Yussuf lifted down the chest. "A dog bays at the moon," he said.

Yarak kept his eyes on the chest. He and Praska had meant to set a trap for the traders, and now they were caught themselves because of Praska's stubbornness. No help for it now. He had to get Praska away from that chest and the men. Suddenly he reached for the *mullah*, who held her rein.

Even as the *mullah* turned, Yarak's hand came away with the ivory-hilted knife. Stepping back, the Cossack howled like a wolf and jabbed the point of the knife deep into the flank of Praska's horse. The pony jumped, whirled, and plunged toward the sunlit doorway with the startled Praska clinging to the saddle. The rein ripped from the hand of the *mullah*, who was thrown off balance.

Nobi pulled a revolver from under his coat. Watching Praska's pony bolt across the courtyard, he laughed. "Now, Cossack, the lady will not find you when she comes back. And no one will find you." He lifted the revolver. Then, "What's in that thing?" he barked at Yussuf.

Yarak swallowed hard and hung onto the knife, watching the lid of the chest as Yussuf lifted it. Within the chest women's clothes were packed neatly around a large metal box that looked like a jewel box.

"Here's what the old dog had hidden," Yussuf muttered, pulling at it. Instantly Yarak flung himself down. And Yussuf felt the box catch on something. He heard a *click* in the depths of the chest—

Yarak felt the blast of the explosion. Metal fragments crackled around him on the tiles of the floor. The frightened packhorse, over by the wall, plunged toward the door. Yarak's head sang, but he could move his limbs. Raising his head, he made out the three men who had been standing over the chest lying sprawled among its fragments, badly injured.

"*Het*," he coughed, and got up. Michael's booby trap had worked.

He had started to investigate, when he heard rapid footsteps, echoing under the dome of the mosque, but he could see no other person moving, until the figure of a man hurried out of a narrow door in the darkness back of the dais. This man, like Moon-face, wore European clothes, and carried a rifle. He stopped dead when he beheld the floor behind the dais. Then, swearing, he shot at Yarak.

Yarak dove down beside the prostate Nobi, and caught up the revolver. He rolled over, using Nabi for a shield, and fired up through the murk, emptying the cylinder. The man on the dais, reloading as he ran, stumbled and fell.

For a moment Yarak watched him but he did not move. Thoughtfully the old Cossack felt in Nabi's pockets. He found, as he expected, some loose cartridges. With these he reloaded the revolver, cautiously watching the shadows of the mosque around him.

A half hour later Praska returned with her pony and three soldiers and the section leader of the gate guard. They found four wounded men lying among fragments of splintered wood and clothing, with a loaded revolver and rifle on the floor by them, and the Cossack sitting on the dais, smoking as he contemplated the scene.

Yarak's gaunt face was tranquil and around him hung an elusive odor of spirits. The section leader later identified the silent Nabi as a well-known Laventine importer who had quartered two foreigners in his home in Bokhara. The three had been known to take sightseeing trips on horseback out into the country.

"It looks like a battle," the section leader observed, puzzled, "but these firearms are loaded." He looked at Yarak. "What is the truth of it, uncle?"

Out of the corner of his eye, Yarak watched Praska. For once, seeing the four men laid out, the girl held her tongue. Yarak grinned cheerfully. Vodka warmed his veins and his mind was clear and easy at last. "Not a battle, brother," he said shaking his head and pulled at his white mustache.

"Nothing like that. We were passing by because as you know, Praska, this little love, was looking for a collection she lost. Isn't it so, Praska?"

The girl nodded.

"Well, these good people invited us in, out of the sun," Yarak explained. "Eh, they were examining a German booby trap of a mine and it went off. You can see for yourself. As God lives, that's the truth."

"Where did they get the mine?"

"Where?" Yarak's gaze wandered around the empty mosque, to the *kiblah* platform and to the narrow door, almost invisible behind it. "Out of that," he pointed.

Beyond the door lay a passage, lighted only by openings in the brick roof, and a row of heavy wooden doors set in the outer wall at intervals of a dozen feet. All the doors were dust coated, banked up with the accumulated rubble of years—except one, that looked as if it had been opened recently.

"Tombs," grunted the section leader who had been there before. "Nothing inside but stiffs."

Then he sniffed curiously. Through the dry, moldy odor of the place cut the fragrance of vodka. The section leader bent closer to the door and thrust it open.

Within that tomb lay no shrouded bodies. The soldiers gazed incredulous, at paintings stacked against the side of the tomb, and piles of rugs, boxes that held jewelry, shining ivory and jade, and sacks of gold.

"Like a bank vault," muttered the section leader, peering into the boxes. By the door stood several bottles of brandy and vodka, one of the latter half empty.

"The Tamerlane collection!" shrilled Praska, and, diving into the piles, she began to pull out gold-inlaid scimitars, old Korans, silver and turquoise jewelry. It did not seem to Yarak that this collection of the girl's was so valuable after all.

"Now you've found your collection—" the Cossack spoke up.

"Not mine," said Praska, "Michael's." She nodded brightly. "His leg is so hurt, Cossack, that he will want something to do with his hands. Isn't the war nearly over? He can't go on finding mines now, or putting them together. He must have work to do, in our *izba*, or he will wander off."

Now Yarak understood. All the time this girl had been thinking of her nest, her *izba*. She was making it ready for the man, so he would not sit with empty hands on the doorstep, watching people walking by along the road, eyeing other girls.

Praska laughed happily. "Look for your wealth, uncle. Didn't you say you had wealth? Now you can settle down at a cottage of your own."

The soldiers looked at him curiously. Yarak considered with bent head. When he had had wealth, matters had not gone well with him.

"No, girl," he said, "that's well enough for a woman. But what did you tell me in the moonlight? This Tamerlane settled down with his wealth, and straight away he died, so they put him in a tomb. And these gold finders outside, they retired during the war, and what happened to them? It's a dangerous thing to do, and that's God's truth."

With a nod, he left the searchers, taking with him only one bottle of brandy and one of vodka. And even for these, he gave the soldiers payment in foreign bank notes.

He went out to his saddle horse, to the road that led toward the west, where battles were still being fought.

Wolf-Hounds of the Steppe

Chapter I
Pulling Up His Stakes

'Twas early evening on the steppe, and the level rays of the setting sun gilded the cartwheel which hung on a pole in front of the abode of Paul Ostalim, blacksmith. The cartwheel indicated to passers-by on the highway the presence of a smithy in the gully shaded by willows. Like all the other hamlets of the steppe in southern Russia, Ostalim's cottage was in a ravine. This was for two reasons: first, the brooklet in the gully; second, protection from the bands of marauders who made the steppe a battleground in the last quarter of the sixteenth century.

The sun also revealed the tall figure of Ostalim leaning against the pole where he could command a view of the highway. Bareheaded the smith was, with brown curls falling to his powerful shoulders, his arms crossed over the sheepskin *svitza* which covered his broad chest. Unlike most of his brother Cossacks, he was plainly dressed in baggy trousers supported by a broad leather belt, and heavy brown boots blackened by his trade. With one foot he was caressing the back of a borzoi, one of his splendid pair of wolfhounds which served as companions in the lonely hamlet, and a smile twitched at his black mustache, and shone in his brown eyes as the dog gave a sigh of contentment.

The next instant master and dog were keenly alert, for sounds heralding the approach of travelers echoed along the road. Without moving from his place by the pole, Ostalim's gaze searched the approaching dust cloud and identified it as harmless. For he saw a *tarataika*, or carriage, of a wealthy man drawn by two shaggy ponies, accompanied by two Cossacks on horseback, and in it was seated a woman.

In a moment the carriage had come to a halt before the smithy, and one of the mounted Cossacks was whirling his horse in a dashing fashion before the eyes of the woman. This rider attracted Ostalim's gaze by the splendor of his attire, which consisted of red leather boots, a red cloak held by a flowered belt, a black sheepskin hat, and a saber of Turkish design in a gold-chased scabbard. Jewels glittered at the Cossack's throat and on his fingers, which the smith observed to be overslender for much use of the sword.

"Hey, smith!" called he of the finery. "My horse has cast a shoe. Busy yourself with getting ready another, and you would have a gold piece instead of a lash across that broad back of yours."

Ostalim liked neither the other's words nor the covert look that the rider shot at the occupant of the carriage, as if to call attention to his elegant manners. Little was visible of the girl except a bright, smiling face, and a pair of dark eyes shaded on either side by two long ringlets, for she was wrapped in a long cloak and hood. But her dress and the carriage proclaimed that she was the daughter of some patrician, and Ostalim thought to himself that she was not one to endure lightly the overbearing manner of her escort.

"In truth," he said mildly, "I am no shoer of horses, honorable sir, but a maker of swords and spears and such-like. Wherefore, you will see that it is not possible for me to minister to your need. It is not far, however, to the *sloboda* Ruvno, where you may find a proper blacksmith."

The brows of the Cossack addressed knitted together, and he drew his horse nearer to Ostalim.

"I see that you are a surly rascal," he growled, "and will have the scourge instead of the gold piece. Shoe my horse for me or you sleep tonight on broken bones."

"Hold that lively tongue of yours, Stepan Vertivitch!" broke in his companion, a powerful Cossack with a good-humored, red face, who measured many feet about the belt. "Do you not see that the smith speaks truth? There are several goodly swords within his shop, not to mention a pistol or two."

"Then why does the lying dog hang a cart wheel before his door?" snarled Vertivitch. "Are we to sit here and quarrel while the light fails and Mirovna Cherevaty longs to join her father before the feast at Ruvno tonight?"

"Mirovna Cherevaty may go to her father," replied the stout Cossack, who seemed to enjoy his companion's bad temper, "while you sit here and quarrel, Stepan Vertivitch, for I am a good enough man to take her to the feast."

Vertivitch's reply was to free the stout whip that he carried at his side and raise it over the smith's shoulder. Ostalim made no movement beyond a narrowing of the eyes, but the two borzoi rose to their feet with a menacing growl.

At once the voice of the girl broke the tense silence. "Put up your whip, Stepan Vertivitch," she called in a clear voice. "You will not shoe your horse any quicker with a scourge. As for you, smith, what is your name?"

"Paul Ostalim, Lady," replied that individual calmly.

"Ostalim?" Her brow wrinkled in perplexity. "I have heard the name before surely. Indeed I am in great distress, honorable sir, because we are already late upon our journey. I have come from friends in Kiev with Stepan Vertivitch to a feast tonight at the house of my father, *ataman* of Ruvno, and the horse of the Cossack delays us, having fallen lame with no shoe. Cannot you shoe the horse, so that we may proceed?"

She leaned forward from the carriage as she spoke, and Ostalim met the eager appeal of her eyes with his steadfast scrutiny.

"Be quiet, fools!" he muttered to the dogs, and added: "It is not well that the daughter of Ataman Cherevaty be kept from her home at nightfall because of an ill-shod horse. I have some skill at shoeing my own horse, and I might make shift to remedy the trouble for the lady, as she asks it. But let there be no more talk of whips."

It was the work of only a few minutes for the smith to shoe Vertivitch's steed, which he did calmly without heeding the gibes that the dandy cast upon his own plain attire. When the work was done he arose with his tools, and would have withdrawn into the cottage when the other stopped him.

"Here's for your trouble, smith," he cried, throwing a gold coin on the ground, "and thank the lady for saving you from the hiding you deserve." With which he spurred off down the road, his red coat fluttering gayly, his seat in the saddle as sure as that of a Tartar. Ostalim dropped his tools, and his hand flew to his side, where no sword hung.

As the carriage followed the rider, Ostalim caught sight of a pretty face turned toward him, the hood thrown back, revealing a mass of black curls. "Come to the feast tonight, Paul Ostalim," he heard, "and say that Mirovna Cherevaty bids you, if any ask."

"Aye, come, smith," echoed the fat Cossack good-naturedly; "there will be rare corn brandy flowing."

Carriage and riders alike were hidden in the dust cloud along the road, but Paul Ostalim remained standing, looking after them for a long time. His mind was filled with wonder, the sight of a laughing, dark-eyed face turned back to him, of dainty white teeth, and a little hand that waved him at the same time a farewell and an invitation. Rare was the sight to the smith, and he found that his heart was pounding against his coat.

A sigh escaped him; then he straightened with sudden determination, picked up his tools, and entered the shop. He went to the pallet that served as his bed, and drew from under the clothes a long, curved sword with a jeweled hilt. Paul Ostalim had not been to the university at Kiev and he could not read, yet he knew by heart the words chased on the scabbard in silver. "The sword of Koshevoi Ataman Dmitri Ostalim," he said to himself as his finger traced out the words and he patted the curving scabbard with reverence.

Then fastening the sword to his belt, he filled his tobacco pouch, selected two of the best Turkish pistols from the group in the shop, and took up his sheepskin hat. At the door of the cottage, he paused long enough to draw the heavy post from the ground with a single heave of his powerful shoulders and hurl it into the bushes. This done, he entered the stable, untethered his horse, and with a last look at the hamlet where he had lived for the twenty-two years of his lonely life, set out on the road to Ruvno. At his heels trotted the two borzoi.

As the rider vanished around a bend in the road, the sun dipped out of sight, and the silence of night, broken only by a light wind that stirred the grass, fell upon the steppe.

Chapter II
At the Feast of Cherevaty

There was a reason for the feast that night at the house of Ataman Cherevaty. As *ataman*, or captain of a Cossack regiment, he was going to lead the young Cossacks of the Ruvno district to the *siech* the next morning. Hence the feast was a farewell to the village on the part of Cherevaty and the striplings, among the latter Stepan Vertivitch and his stout companion in arms, Rashov.

For the *siech* was none other than the Zaporogian Siech, or war encampment of the Cossacks on the Dnieper islands, where they faced the hostile
Tartars across the water. To go to the *siech* was the dream of every young
man who could swing a sword or ride a horse, for there manly honor was
to be won and the fighting for which the Cossacks longed.

Not that the Ukraine was actually at war. Constant fighting ruled
along the borders; battles with Turk, Pole, and Tartar who threatened
the three sides of southern Russia with fire and pillage and cared little
whether their governments were at peace or not. In truth, the Ukraine
was the war border of Russia, the white kingdom, and the *sieches* were
the outposts of the Ukraine.

Little wonder, then, that the business of the Cossacks of Ruvno, who
were within a day's march of the Dnieper, was fighting. Were they not
the darlings of Tsar Ivan Grozny, the august ruler who bore the surname
"the terrible" on the lips of his enemies?

To Cherevaty the evening was doubly festive for the reason that it welcomed home Mirovna from Kiev, with the Cossack Vertivitch, who was
to be Cherevaty's right-hand man in the Ruvno *kuren*, or encampment.
Cherevaty was kindly disposed toward the young student from Kiev, because the elder Vertivitch had been his comrade in arms, and he was more
than anxious for Stepan to win the renown at the *siech* without which it
is not considered fitting for any Cossack to marry.

Hence it was that late in the evening he nudged Rashov with his elbow
and pointed to the corner where the young Cossack and his daughter were
seated. To make his meaning quite clear, the big warrior took pains to lay
his finger alongside his nose and to wink several times.

"Ho!" exclaimed Rashov in reply, filling the cup of corn brandy which
had been upset by the *ataman*'s nudge. "So that's the chimney the devil is
flying down! Nevertheless, I have seen not one but many courtings, and
to my mind they were two-handed affairs, while Stepan seems to be carrying on his battle single-handed."

"That is nothing, Rashov," returned the warrior, stroking his long black
mustache. "Devil take it, would you have the girl lead in the attack? No,
Mirovna has learned true maiden manners at Kiev, and she is but feigning
coldness to bring the Cossack more fully to her feet. The match pleases
me, for no man who is not warrior born and proved shall wed Mirovna."

"That is true, honorable sir," admitted Rashov, draining his cup, "for
I have heard you swear it upon a holy cross before witnesses. Still, to my

thinking Mirovna is a girl who will do the deciding for herself. In truth, there is no woman within a hundred versts of Ruvno to compare with her."

A second time Cherevaty nudged his companion and pointed across the room. On the long bench that ran around the room he had spied a stranger. "Who is that Cossack, Rashov?" he asked in surprise. "The one in the brown coat with the dusty boots; he came in only a moment ago."

Rashov glanced in the direction that the other indicated and laughed. "A smith he is, come on the bidding of Mirovna, to whom he rendered a service on the road."

"Ha!" exclaimed Cherevaty, and strode over to Ostalim, for the hospitality of a Cossack is as open-handed as his enmity. "How like you the brandy, honorable sir?" he asked. "And it warms you not enough, sit on the stove for a while."

This invitation was a mark of consideration, for the great stove that occupied a recess in the back of the cottage was covered with planks which often offered a resting place to the large limbs of the Ruvno Ataman. Ostalim flushed as he felt the gaze of those in the room bent upon him. He had slipped in only a brief while ago after a long hard ride, and the splendor of the large room, with its painted walls, the whips and rare weapons on the window ledges, and the many goblets of elegant workmanship, booty from the Anatolian coast, awed him not a little.

He had early spied out Mirovna and Stepan, and his brow darkened momentarily, clearing when his gaze wandered over the throng of warlike Cossacks, already booted and garbed for the departure of the morrow and in high glee. This was the fellowship he longed to join.

To the *ataman*'s greeting he replied respectfully, for Cherevaty's face was familiar to him. "The brandy warms my heart, honorable sir," he said lightly. "Tomorrow there will be no drinking for this distinguished company, for I hear that you will set out for the *siech* to reinforce the Ruvno kuren. Are many going?"

"A fair lot," replied the *ataman*; "about threescore young men—sixty-two in all."

"Sixty-three, rather," declared Ostalim boldly, although his heart was beating painfully. "I would like to join the Ruvno *kuren*, and go with you to the *siech* on the morrow. It was for that I came here at your daughter's bidding. With the Tartars pressing against us on the Dnieper another sword will be welcome, without doubt."

Cherevaty frowned. It was one thing to welcome this stranger to his house, but to take him to the *siech* with his chosen band was a horse of another color. He knew nothing of the Cossack, whose attire was certainly not that of a warrior.

While he was debating the matter, Stepan, who had been watching him from the others side of the room, stepped to his side and said loudly: "It is fitting that you should be warned against this fellow who tries to enter the society of proven Cossacks. He is no other than a smith, who shoes horses by the highway, and the sword that he carries is probably one of his stock. As to his clothes, you can see for yourself that they indicate no rank. Why should such a stranger come with the men from Ruvno?"

Ostalim placed his two hands on the table and smiled across it at Vertivitch. "The Cossack has made a mistake if he thinks that I am begging to accompany him to the *siech*. I claim a place in the *kuren* of Ataman Cherevaty by right of rank, for my father was a famous leader. As for a red coat and tasseled boots, the first Tartar I meet will supply me with those."

"Then prove your father's rank, smith," returned the other, "and we will know how much truth there is in your words."

"Aye, smith," agreed Cherevaty thoughtfully, "that is the way to decide the matter. What claim have you to high Cossack rank?"

Ostalim's hand went to his sword; then he hesitated. "To tell my father's name and rank would avail nothing," he said shortly, looking at Stepan; "and you like not my company. My father was known by his deeds. I claim no rank other than that I shall win for myself. On these terms do I ride with you to the *siech* or not?"

"If you go," retorted Vertivitch, "I shall not be in the company."

Several of the others in the crowd who had come from Kiev at the same time as Stepan murmured agreement to what the student said. Hearing this, the *ataman* raised his hand as if to render his decision, when Ostalim forestalled him.

"I shall not force my company upon the Cossacks of Ruvno," he said in a clear voice. "Rather than make it needful for Ataman Cherevaty to decide one way or the other, I withdraw my offer."

"Doubtless," sneered Vertivitch, who was pleased with his victory, "you wish to return to your anvil and cottage, where there is less danger of meeting with the Tartars. There you will be able to get gold coins for mending the swords of braver men who know how to use them."

"That I stand ready to use my saber," cried Ostalim, "I shall prove to you without further delay, to the satisfaction of every one here. Come, man, let's see the light of your blade!" With which he drew his own curved saber and laid it on the table, the jeweled hilt tightly gripped in his scarred hand.

As Vertivitch hesitated, the *ataman* stepped between them. "Are you children," he growled, "to quarrel over going to the *siech* when our enemies, the Tartars, are at the banks of the river? Your squabbles must be settled another time. As for you, smith, unless you can show us good reason for joining our company on the morrow, go back to your shop."

"My goal," said Ostalim, replacing his weapon, "is the camp, and since I am forbidden your company, I shall go alone and join another *kuren* that is readier to greet a brother in arms."

"By the devil's carcass," cried a hearty voice, "I like the way this rooster crows! Perchance there will be more fighting with a bird of this sort than with Stepan Vertivitch. You shall not go alone, Paul Ostalim, for I will come with you."

The giant Cossack clapped the other cordially on the back. Ostalim was grateful for the offer of company on his trip, but he was not allowed time to express it, for the big Rashov hurried him from the room to the stable, in order, as he said, to get a nap in the hay before starting.

The good intention of the two friends, however, was not to be carried out at once; instead, there was a further scene of leave-taking. Rashov was arranging some straw into a suitable bed by the side of his horse, admiring Ostalim's dogs the while, when he held up his hand for silence and chuckled. "By the sound of it" he whispered, "our friend Stepan is not content with his farewell at the hands of the beauty, Mirovna."

Ostalim waited for no more, but strode to the door of the stable which opened into the courtyard. The glazed windows of the cottage lighted up the space, aided by the torches of several maidservants who had come out with Mirovna to draw more wine for the men. Apparently, Vertivitch had seized the opportunity to have a moment alone with the girl, and the two stood within a few paces of the stable door. Owing to the flickering light of the torches, they did not see the smith, who stood in the shadows.

The Cossack was bending over the girl, his face close to hers, and his words came to the ears of Ostalim. "Your father has said that we are to be married," the dandy was urging, "and it is but right for me to claim a kiss as farewell. Your father——"

"Has told me that the man who marries me must be of good Cossack blood, and proved at the *siech*," retorted Mirovna with spirit. "When you come back from war, and the village can hear of how you have borne yourself, then it will be time to talk of marriage."

Rashov had joined the smith at the door, and now he whispered approvingly: "That's talk for you; she can handle Stepan without——What are you doing?"

Vertivitch had decided to get by force what he could not by argument— a farewell kiss from Mirovna, who was not as docile as the beauties of Kiev. His reward was a stinging blow in the face that made him give back a pace. Then he caught the girl roughly by the shoulders, angered at her display of temper. This earned him another and more formidable adversary, for Ostalim sprang from the stable door and tore his hands from the girl's shoulders.

Before the dandy was quite aware what was happening, the smith gripped him by arm and leg, lifted him clear of the ground, and threw him, with stunning force, into the center of a patch of mud. So severe was the fall that Vertivitch lay prostrate for some time.

Meanwhile, Mirovna thought it best to return to the house, to which the maids had fled at the start of the struggle. Seeing that she hesitated in the semidarkness at the mud bed, Ostalim picked her up bodily with a sweep of his heavy arms and bore her across to the threshold of the cottage.

"Sometimes, lady," he said, setting her down, "dusty boots are useful."

"But ill-mannered, sir," she returned, freeing herself from his grasp. "You have the insolence of a peasant."

"If you want manners, lady," said Ostalim, pointing to where Stepan was extricating himself from the mud, "you will find them there."

When he returned to the stable, Rashov surveyed him with amusement. "Have you done enough mischief for one day, Paul?" he inquired. "First you bandy words with the *ataman*; then, after throwing the *ataman*'s favorite into the mud, you quarrel with the *ataman*'s daughter. If you are content, we will crawl into our straw blankets."

Chapter III
Across the Steppe

Rashov proved to be a most useful companion on the journey to the *siech* the next day. He knew the direction to take across the level sward of the steppe, for there was no road running from the village to the camp, and he told Ostalim tales of the great camp of ten thousand Cossacks, the Koshevoi Ataman, or war chief, and the war treasure of gold hidden in the swamps of the Dnieper bank by the Koshevoi Ataman and a few of his trusted captains, which was to be used only in time of war.

Ostalim listened greedily, and remembered what he was told. He was eager to take the shortest way to the camp, but Rashov cautioned him against it, choosing the lower land by the river instead, remarking that, unlike the sea, the bottom of the land was a safer place to travel than the top.

So the two friends picked a course bordering on the fields of high rushes that lined the Dnieper bank, keeping on their right the grass of the steppe with its myriad cornflowers winking up at them. Rashov was in high good humor, for he had secured a goodly ration from Mirovna before setting out, and, as he explained, while no Cossack would drink on the march, still there was no ban against eating.

They made no halt for the midday meal, but took cheese and barley cakes from their capacious pockets and proceeded to make a meal on horseback. It was in the act of biting into a cake that Rashov paused and jerked his head toward the rushes. A peculiar cry, high and quavering, came to Ostalim's ears.

"A gull," explained the stout Cossack indifferently; "probably its nest is in the reeds."

"Its nest must be a boat, then," said Ostalim, who was listening intently. "I have heard gulls before, but never of that kind. I'll wager that bird has two arms and legs, as well as a mustache and saber."

"If the wind lies that way," returned his companion, "we'll have a look at our gull. If he proves to be a Tartar you can trim his wings for him."

Cautiously the two pushed into the forest of reeds which closed around them to the height of their heads. The horses were soon trampling in water, as the cry of the gull came nearer to them. When the water was over the horses' fetlocks they emerged into a narrow channel in the rushes. A few yards away a boat was moored, well concealed, and in it a man was bent over the oars.

Ostalim had never seen a figure like it before, and even Rashov gave a whistle of surprise as he caught sight of the man at the oars in the heavy skiff. The stranger's start of alarm at seeing them changed in an instant to joy, and he stretched out his arms, bound by chains to the seat.

"Cossacks, brothers!" he cried in a weak voice. "Blessed the day on which I see the faces of men from the *siech*. Tell me, honorable sirs, did you see a band of Tartars prowling through the rushes? They are my masters, who forced me to row to the Ukraine shore and stay here in the skiff while they explored the higher ground. Undo these chains——"

"By the devil's scalp lock!" echoed Rashov, pushing forward. "A galley slave and a Cossack once by the look of him. Speak, man, are these precious masters of yours in the vicinity? How came they to the shore of Ukraine?"

"They are a short way out on the steppe," explained the rower, who Ostalim saw to be a powerful man, his back, burned brown by the sun, bent double, his scarred hands and arms calloused by chains and oars. The only clothing he wore was a loin cloth. "They wished to see whether reinforcements came to the *siech* from the villages, for the Tartars are moving against the Cossacks by trickery. It is planned to lure the band from the *siech* across the Dnieper, and when they are——"

"It would be better, Rashov," suggested Ostalim, "to free this man first and find out what he has to tell us afterward. At any moment the others may return, and he possesses a secret worth more to Cossackdom than the lives of either of us."

"True, by my faith!" snorted Rashov, leaping from his horse. "I would have gossiped like an old shrew. Paul, you have skill with chains, see what you can do with these trinkets while I lend an ear to the approach of our friends from the steppe."

Already Ostalim was bending over the rower, examining the irons. Seizing one of the oars, he twisted it through a chain, and, resting the end of the oar on the side of the skiff, heaved sharply on the other. The rower bent his head to still a cry of pain, as the iron bit deep into his flesh, but the staples came out with a rasp, and one chain was dangling free. Another moment and the man was freed from the boat, although the chains still clung to his limbs.

With a cry of triumph, the crippled Cossack picked up one of the heavy oars and crashed its butt through the bottom of the skiff.

As he did so, Rashov made a gesture of warning. "The rushes are moving half a verst away," he whispered, "and we had best leave the boat to the Tartars. I'll wager the sight will not be to their liking."

Finding that the chained Cossack could barely walk, Ostalim swung him into his own saddle and ran beside the horse through the rushes after Rashov, until they had put a safe distance between them and the disabled skiff. The ground was firmer here, and the trio could sit down without fear of discovery on the part of the Tartars. Ostalim insisted on the rower eating some barley cake before hearing his story, and Rashov proffered his pipe.

"Such food, honorable sirs!" cried the Cossack gratefully. "Indeed it seems from heaven, so good it tastes." Then his brow darkened, and he flung a look over his shoulder in the way they had come. "But it is sinful to waste time in eating when the golden treasure of the *siech* is in danger."

"Say you so, honorable sir?" asked Ostalim. "Whence comes danger to the war treasure, hidden where none can find it in the swamps of the Dnieper?"

"The Tartars have keen eyes," returned the other gloomily, "and they must have seen men go to the spot where the treasure is buried with chests and return empty-handed. So long as the Cossacks are encamped in the *siech*, it would be folly for them to attempt to steal it. But their cursed devil brains have hatched a scheme which bids fair to deceive the wisest of the *atamans*, even the Koshevoi Ataman himself. Nine years have I been a slave to the vermin, and I know the spider's web that they spin for their victims. Not only is the treasure to be seized, but Ruvno and the nearby villages will be laid waste."

Rashov would have broken into a string of oaths, but Ostalim checked him and urged the stranger to tell what he knew.

"It is this way," began the Cossack. "So long as the ten thousand fighting men remain in the *siech* the treasure is safe. The Tartars plan to divide into two parties. One is to approach the shore of the Dnieper opposite the camp, burning the villages there, until the Cossacks rise in anger and sally across the river after them. Then by a crafty retreat the devils will entice our men several days' march from the river. Meanwhile the other part of their forces will emerge from hiding and gain the swamp where the treasure is hid. Once the gold hoard of the *siech*, which is our sinews of war, is in their hands, they will turn north and ravage the villages as long as the absence of the men from the *siech* will permit them. When forced to do so, they will flee back across the Dnieper with their booty."

"A plot of the devil!" snarled Rashov, fingering his sword. "How came it to your ears?"

"Once I was sleeping," explained the other, "and they thought that I had died of the blows they had given me, so they talked freely. Their spies are everywhere on this shore, and there is talk of traitors in the *siech* who have been won over with gold."

"That is not to be believed!" exclaimed Ostalim. "How comes it that you know the Tartars have really discovered the hiding place of the gold hoard?"

The Cossack's eyes flashed, and he raised his hand proudly. "Nine years ago," he said, "I was an *ataman* in the ranks of the *siech*, and the secret of the place was told me. The Tartars could not make me reveal it by tortures when they tore loose the flesh of my arms and cracked the bones of my back. Yet they know the secret now, for I have heard them describe the place in my hearing."

"Then there is no time to be lost," said Ostalim. "And this is what we will do. You, Rashov, go with the *ataman* to the place where the gold is hidden—not to the spot, but near it—and hide in the rushes to keep watch. Meanwhile I will ride to the *siech* and put the tale of what we have heard in the ears of the Koshevoi Ataman, together with the account of the spies we met on this shore."

"The plan is good, Cossack," approved the old *ataman*, a gleam in his faded eyes. "Would I could ride with you and swing a sword with the strength of your lusty arm."

"Yours is the gray head that plans, honorable sir," replied Ostalim respectfully. "And that is worth a hundred blades of the keenest steel. My father was such a man, and something of his cunning I have learned while a boy."

"You will be a man in short order, Paul," observed Rashov jestingly, "when you enter the Zaporogian Siech with such tidings. By my faith you told us what to do as coolly as if you were an *ataman* and we the striplings. I spoke truth when I said there would be fighting if I came with you——"

He broke off, for Ostalim had wheeled his horse, settled himself firmly in the seat, and whirled off through the reeds in the direction where Rashov had told him the *siech* lay. Although there was care on his brow, his heart was alight, for was he not bringing to the waiting ten thousand such tidings as had not come in a generation, which would bring him the honor that was due him by birth?

Chapter IV
Lack of Foresight

The *siech* was awake and stirring. After months of idleness the Cossack warriors heard the whisper of war in the wind that came to them across the Dnieper. Some who had been guzzling beer for weeks took their swords to the armorer to be sharpened; others examined their horses and trappings to see if all were in order for a march. Throughout the entire encampment there was a buzz of preparation as the various *kurens* assembled their quota of men under the *atamans*.

In the center square of the *siech*, loaded wagons rumbled down to the river bank, bearing all the supplies, powder, and weapons of the Cossacks; in the square also stood the tall figure of the Koshevoi Ataman, or war chief, in whose hands rested the authority of life and death over the Cossacks—a gray-mustached veteran of a hundred battles.

Above the turmoil of blacksmiths' hammers, the creaking of wagons, and the commands of the *atamans* rang the excited shouts of the young Cossacks who were going into war for the first time, and who could hardly keep themselves from springing into the river on their horses at the first sight of the Tartar bands. It needed all the wisdom of the older men to restrain the striplings until night, when the last of the reinforcements from villages like Ruvno would be in and darkness would cover the crossing of the river.

But the Cossacks under Ataman Cherevaty were late in coming, and the Koshevoi Ataman was still at his post in the square late in the afternoon when a dusty rider trotted in through the kurens and dismounted before him. Ostalim had lost no time in arriving at the encampment, as his tired horse and the dust on his garments showed.

The glance of the war chief swept quickly over the plain attire of the new arrival, and he frowned slightly. This was no ordinary Cossack. "Speak," he said sharply, "and tell your business; minutes are not to be wasted when the Zaporogian Siech prepares for war."

"That is the truth, honorable sir," returned Ostalim. "Wherefore, will you give order to beat the drum that shall summon the *rada* council of the *siech*? I have news of the movements of the Tartar folk that will open wide the eyes of the Cossacks. A trap has been set for you, honorable sir."

"You have important news?" The war chief measured glances with Ostalim. "Then the *rada* drums shall beat that the *siech* may hear your tidings."

He spoke a word to a Cossack who stood behind him, and the roll of the kettledrums began to echo through the encampment. At once the Koshevoi Ataman picked up the mace that was his symbol of office; the judge of the army emerged from a *kuren* carrying his heavy seal and accompanied by the scribe. From all quarters the Cossacks flocked round the square, wondering at the summoning of the council on the eve of departure.

Every head was bared as the war chief stepped forward with Ostalim at his side and lifted his hand for silence.

In accordance with custom, the war chief addressed the assembly slowly, with his eyes on the ground to show that he weighed his words carefully. "A messenger has come to us, honorable sirs," he said, "who has tidings of such importance that he asked for the calling of the council. Let us hear what he has to say, for it concerns the Tartar folk."

A murmur went through the gathering at this, and there was much craning of necks to see the unknown messenger, and a greater murmur when it was seen that the newcomer was clad in none of the Cossack trappings except a sword.

"These are my tidings, honorable sirs," began Ostalim steadily, although his heart was fluttering under the gaze of the ten thousand. "On the bank of the Dnieper, coming from Ruvno with the Cossack Rashov, I learned from an escaped galley slave that the Tartars were in truth assembled on the other bank of the river. They are divided into two parts, and their purpose is for one part to draw you across and far into their territory, when the second half of them will steal our war treasure."

"That is impossible, Cossack," cried the Koshevoi Ataman sternly, "for none save my lieutenants know where it is hidden."

"The Cossack who escaped from them knows the hiding place, and he learned that they found it out. That is not all our enemies plan, for they will sweep up the river bank and lay waste the village of Ruvno with others as long as they may do so with safety."

The Koshevoi Ataman shook his head. It was true that he had heard reports of Tartar detachments seen on this side of the Dnieper, but the main body of the enemy were in full view on the other side of the river, where the smoke of burning hamlets was rising to the sky and there were appeals for assistance. How was he to test the truth of the words of the unknown Cossack?

"Have you proof?" he demanded.

"None other than that you may find the galley slave with the Cossack Rashov by the war treasure when you send Cossacks to protect it."

"Are you known to any here?"

Ostalim scanned the faces before him, and found that all were strangers. In his haste to bring the tidings to the *siech* he had not thought of how they would be received, and he had no proof to offer.

"I am known to the Ataman Cherevaty, honorable sir," he said after a moment's thought. "He will be here with the men from Ruvno presently."

At this point there was a commotion in the gathering. A group of elegantly clothed Cossacks who came from the Polish frontier and wore gold braid in their coats were murmuring against the interruption by the strange rider in the dusty clothes. Those around them took up the whisper, and it became a loud muttering. The Cossacks of the *siech* were not men to dally with. Few would pause to heed the words of Ostalim; they were eager to be off after the foe across the river.

Only the Koshevoi Ataman seemed willing to consider the message Ostalim brought. "What is your name?" he asked.

"My father——" Ostalim's eyes flashed proudly as he began his reply, when a shout went up from the throng. The assembled Cossacks parted on both sides of a lane, down which spurred at full speed a rider on a foam-flecked horse.

Without a pause the daring Cossack swept up to the group around the Koshevoi Ataman and flung himself from his horse. Ostalim saw that his sword was naked in his hand and that he wore no hat.

"Honorable sir," cried the newcomer, "how is it that the *siech* stands idle when Cossack blood flows on this side of the Dnieper? Have the Zaporoghi taken to beer brewing that such things should be allowed to go unpunished?"

"Cossack blood never goes unavenged," said the war chief proudly. "What has happened?"

"Ataman Cherevaty has been waylaid along the trail from Ruvno by the Tartars. I was in his band, and the foe dashed out on us from a thicket. Many good Cossacks lie dead on the steppe, while the Tartars bear away spoils of swords and rich cloaks. Cherevaty and his lieutenant Stepan Vertivitch and a dozen others survive, but they are prisoners, carried to the river, while the *siech* gossips in council like the fat Poles."

A shout of anger went up at the man's words that echoed through the kurens. Ostalim tried to make himself heard in the uproar, but was silenced by the Koshevoi Ataman, who grasped his arm sternly.

"Before we take up the pursuit of the dogs who have captured the worthy Ataman Cherevaty," he cried, "what punishment shall be the reward of the false Cossack who tried to lead us astray? He has told us that the Tartars plan to seize the war treasure when they have attacked our brave Cossacks and carried them across the river. He has come from the river bank where the Tartars must have landed. He is known to none of the Cossacks of the *siech*. What is the will of the *rada*?"

"Death!" cried the same group of dandies who had started the first commotion. "He is no Cossack, but an enemy who seeks to betray us. To the river with him!"

Some voices from groups of the older men opposed this, and Ostalim was grateful to them as he heard the veterans say he should be brought with the army until the truth of his words could be proved. The Koshevoi Ataman listened to both factions; then he raised his hand for silence. Instantly quiet prevailed in the square.

"One law of Cossackdom compels us to go after our brothers who have been made captive," he said, "and another gives death as the reward for false news in time of war. Whether this man is a spy or not, I shall leave his punishment to the army. He shall be placed in the stocks and a club laid by him. Any man believing him guilty may strike him with the club, according to the measure of his strength. Those who believe him innocent of wrong will not touch the club. Meanwhile, forward to the river."

At the sentence, Ostalim started forward to make an appeal, but two giant Cossacks grasped him and tore his sword from his belt. Vainly he tried to speak to the war chief. He was dragged away to one side, where the stocks stood.

Before he realized what was happening, his captors had thrust his legs into stout wooden blocks set in the ground, which were clamped tight and locked. His sword was flung down on the ground at his feet. It was growing dark, and the Cossacks brought two large torches which they stuck upright in the ground on either side of him. By their light he could see the ranks of Cossacks hastening by him to the river.

Worse than his own plight was his failure to make plain the treachery of the Tartars. He cursed his haste which had brought him alone. Rashov was known in the *siech*, and they might have listened to him. But the mischief was done, and his own life was forfeited in disgrace for his momentary lack of foresight. He had heard from Rashov how men in the stocks were clubbed to death without mercy.

This was his entry into the *siech* that he had planned for so long! He was thankful that his father was dead and could not learn of it; even his father's sword was in the dust and would be unnoticed, for which he was thankful now. There was no one else to care whether he lived or died, except perhaps Rashov and Mirovna Cherevaty, who had thought enough of him to quarrel with him.

So far he had been left in peace, the Cossacks being busied with their departure for the river, but now he found himself in the center of a group that he recognized as the Cossacks from the west with their gold braid. He read no mercy in their eyes by the flickering torchlight. It was curious that this group, among the thousands, should be so interested in his death, and the words of the escaped rower returned to his mind—that there were spies in the camp itself.

He shut his eyes and clenched his teeth as the first of the group stepped up to him with raised club. He made no plea for mercy, resolving to submit to punishment in silence.

But the blow did not fall, and he opened his eyes in surprise. There was a commotion in the circle, and a big figure pushed through the others to a place in front of him. "Pardon me, honorable sirs," he heard a familiar voice; "but I insist on seeing the fun in spite of your objection."

Rashov broke off to stare blankly at Ostalim. "May the devil roast me if it isn't my friend Paul," he cried, "strung up and trussed like a ripe pullet. What is the meaning of this?"

"The man is a traitor," growled one of the Cossacks, "and the Koshevoi Ataman has decreed his death, as is fitting."

"Not so," broke in Ostalim. "The Koshevoi Ataman said only that those who believed me guilty of false tidings should beat me with the club."

"Ha! So that's the beer you beauties have been brewing here?" Rashov planted himself by the side of his friend and whipped out his sword. "The Koshevoi Ataman is a wise man," he said, laughing, "and if you choose to do so, lay on with the club. Only when you have done so I shall roll your head in the dust like an overripe plum. Who is the first to lay on?"

The man who had the club stepped back hastily, and the others showed no signs of being willing to take Rashov at his word. After whispering together and scowling at the pair of friends, they drew off, leaving Ostalim unharmed. No others came to molest them, although they waited until the last of the army had disappeared in the darkness by the river bank.

When the camp was deserted, Rashov lost no time in freeing his friend, declaring, as he pried the stocks apart with his saber, that the mandate of the Koshevoi Ataman had been fulfilled and that they were free to look after their own skins. They had the camp to themselves, for every one of the Cossacks had gone with the army that was already crossing the Dnieper under the protecting shadow of darkness.

"How comes it, Rashov," inquired Ostalim, rubbing his ankles to restore the circulation, "that you are here and not at the war chest with our friend the rower?"

The big Cossack rubbed his chin thoughtfully, as though the matter was new to him. "A man must eat," he said finally, "and two men must eat more. Wherefore I came but to procure necessary bread and brandy."

"That is a lie," interrupted Ostalim calmly.

Rashov's red face flamed purple; and he clutched his sword. "By my faith," he snarled, "and I had not shared bread and salt and brandy with you, and were we not brothers in arms, I'd split your skull for you, handsome as it may be, for those words."

"Talk not of splitting skulls between two brothers," replied Ostalim, "when I owe my life to you. I have not marched and slept with you without knowing that you would not leave a post of duty without greater excuse than hunger. There was another reason."

"Well, your brain is keen as your sword, Paul," admitted Rashov ruefully, "and I did but try to frighten you with my talk. As for the reason, the truth is that our rower, in spite of dire need of food, thought naught of it, but sent me to confirm your words to the *siech* when I told him that you were unknown to the Cossacks. A wise move, but I came too late."

"Not so; you came in good time, Rashov. What think you of the warriors who would have beaten me?"

"Their hands looked whiter than their conscience. I liked not the breed. What *kuren* do they claim?"

"I know not, except that they were pleased to wish my death. Come, my blood is back into its channels again." Ostalim buckled on his sword and summoned to him the two borzoi who had kept at his feet through all the turmoil of the camp. "It is the law of Cossackdom that we may not leave a comrade in danger to seek safety, and so we must return to the swamp—on foot—for our horses were carried off."

As the two friends left the camp behind them, Rashov caught Ostalim's arm and pointed back. In the circle of torchlight stood a full-armed Tartar, mounted on a beautiful Arab steed, his swarthy face peering suspiciously into the shadows. The enemy had come to the Zaporogian Siech.

Chapter V
To Save the Treasure

In the reeds which concealed him from view the old rower raised his head and listened. For several hours he had waited in the darkness for the coming of the Cossacks from the *siech*, and now he was beginning to suspect that something had happened to delay them. There had not been a sound in the swamp after the departure of Rashov, save the crying of the gulls overhead and the slinking sounds of small animals moving about near him. Now he heard a new sound, as of a heavy body splashing in toward him from the river.

The war treasure was hidden, he knew, in a hillock under the trunks of two great, fallen willows, a few paces from where he sat, and he wondered if the Tartars were coming already for their booty. If so, he reflected, they would find only a naked man without weapons to combat them, and he resolved that they would not take him back to the galley. He would lose his life in defending the treasure that he had helped to mass together ten years before, and that would be more fitting than to perish of abuse at the hands of the Tartars.

The footsteps neared him quickly, and his keen ear made out one person approaching alone. He crouched down in the reeds and waited until the newcomer was abreast of him; then he crept forward like a stalking tiger, and, when he made out a shadow loom beside him, sprang on the other's shoulders.

With surprising ease he bore his enemy to the ground, and gripped the two arms that might reach for a sword in a steel-like clutch; the years of rowing had given him the arms and shoulders of a giant. Then he relaxed his grasp as quickly.

The figure under him gave forth a cry—a woman's cry of surprise and hurt, followed by a muffled sob.

"A woman!" he muttered. He drew back and felt her short skirt and slender boots to make sure his ears had told him the truth. "What do you here?"

"You are a Cossack," she echoed gladly as she sat up. "I feared I had fallen in with a Tartar. Indeed," her voice saddened, "none have better right here than I, for I have heard that my father and his men have been attacked and killed near this spot. I came to search for his body, if I could find it, and bear it to Ruvno from further injury."

"Ha, you are a good girl!" returned the Cossack, patting her shoulder, "and it grieves me that I hurt you. Who was your father?"

"Demid Cherevaty," she said sadly, "*ataman* of the Ruvno kuren. They set upon him foully from the thicket where he rode to the *siech* with Stepan Vertivitch and his men. Few escaped the slaughter. No one suspected that the Tartars dared come to this side of the river so near the *siech*."

An exclamation escaped the rower, and he bent closer in the darkness. He could see little of the girl, save her eyes gleaming from the mass of dark hair which lay disheveled over her slender shoulders.

"Did you say Stepan Vertivitch, of Ruvno?" he demanded sharply.

"No other. He was a close intimate of my father, who wished him to marry me, but I would not, owing to things that I had heard about the youth in Kiev. Still, now he has lost his life, for there is no hope for a Cossack who falls into Tartar hands, I should not speak ill of him, should I? His fate has been that of his father, the warrior Vertivitch, who was *ataman* of Ruvno, and who was taken by the Tartars and lost to Cossackdom."

"Aye," remarked the rower bitterly, "like his father, doomed to torment. Tell me more of the lad. Was he a promising fighter? Does he deal a hefty blow with his fist, and ride his horse fearlessly? Was he honored by the Cossacks of Ruvno?"

The girl seemed to hesitate. "It is not fitting that ill should be said of one who fought bravely and was overcome by numbers," she said thoughtfully. "Those who escaped the fight and came to Ruvno with the news said that Stepan defended himself against all the Tartar horde, and that he was the last to give in, still unwounded. And I know that he is my father's favorite, for he shared with me the secret of the hiding place of the war chest, which my father told him as a token of his trust. Also his love for me was great."

"Whence did the Tartars go with their prisoners?" the rower asked, after weighing her words in silence. "Did they return across the river?"

"So it is reported. They were seen to enter the swamps along the river bank, where they disappeared. Already the men from the *siech* have taken up the pursuit across the river. But I felt in my heart that the Tartars might have killed my father before they crossed, wherefore I came here tonight in a sailing skiff from the village, because I could not rest until I knew the truth."

The rower patted her head roughly in sympathy. The cry of a gull over-head broke into his meditation, and he climbed clumsily to his feet, draw-ing up the girl.

"Listen, little one," he whispered. "Your father's capture was a part of the Tartar plan, as cunning as a devil's snare. Those who waylaid him and his men have not returned across the river; they are concealed near us in the swamps, waiting until the last of the men from the *siech* are over the Dnieper. At dawn they will come here to seize the war treasure, and there will be none to defend it. For Ostalim and Rashov would have returned with at least a *kuren* if they had been able to do so. Something has hindered them."

"Ostalim, the smith?" cried the girl. "He is a stranger to the *siech*, and no warrior proved."

"Strange," remarked the rower, "for he bore himself like a man who knew his strength, and I would swear that he would not leave me in peril, contrary to the Cossack law. Yet he has not come back, and it is within an hour or two of dawn. Soon the Tartars will be here for the war treasure, and they will find only an old man and a girl, of all the ten thousand."

"The war treasure! This is the spot!" The girl drew a quick breath. "Why, it is all the wealth of the *siech*, gotten together for twenty years——"

"It lies there, beneath the trunks of the willows that you see as shad-ows among the rushes." The old man pointed out the place. "If we could manage to save a part of it——"

"We can," cried Mirovna quickly. "Don't you see how it can be done? My boat lies only a few paces away in the rushes, where there is a chan-nel. We still have a little time before it is light. I am strong, and I can help you carry the chests to the boat. Once clear of the reeds we shall be safe from the Tartars."

"Well planned, little one!" cried the rower in high glee. "The thought is worthy of your father, who was once my brother-in-arms. Come, let us see what an old man and a girl can do, eh?"

The thought of saving the war treasure put new life into the rower's shattered limbs, and he lost no time in tearing aside the covering of earth and branches that concealed the treasure under the willow trunks. Down on her knees, the girl worked beside him, giving a soft cry as the tops of the chests were disclosed.

The gold they contained made the chests weighty beyond the strength of the two to carry, despite the iron muscles of the rower. But the old man hastily contrived a pronged branch by which they could drag the precious objects to the boat through the mud and water of the marsh. By placing the branch slanting against the side of the boat, they were able to push their burden over the rail without actually lifting it. As soon as they had disposed of one chest they hurried back for another, panting from their labors.

As they labored, they watched the red glow that meant the coming of dawn. The red glint changed to orange and pale yellow, while a gray light began to steal among the reeds that lay to the east. Before long they were able to make out each other's faces, streaked with sweat and mud, but the last of the chests was on the heavy skiff, which the rower pushed farther into the channel against the danger of grounding under the weightier cargo, and they clambered aboard.

As they did so the swamp to the south, in the direction of the camp, echoed with the tramp of running men, while several shots rang out. Hastily the rower seized one of the large oars and began to push into the mud bed with it to set the vessel in motion. The skiff, with its mast and sail and fifty feet of clumsy construction, was no light craft, and for several seconds it hesitated, as if unwilling to move forward at all.

Meanwhile the splashing in the reeds came nearer, and two large wolfhounds sprang out into the channel, swimming as they reached the deeper water and barking with excitement. At their heels plunged a big figure of a Cossack, without hat or pistols, his boots coated with mud, and the finery of his attire smirched with many a fall into the swamp.

Sighting the boat and Mirovna, he gave a shout of surprise. "Forward, Ostalim!" Rashov bellowed, waving his sword. "By the beer mug of my grandfather, if angels haven't sent us a boat and manned it themselves. Leave the Tartars and come and see it with your own eyes."

Saying which, the fat Cossack lost no time in scrambling over the rail of the skiff, no easy task for a man of his weight, after thoughtfully helping the dogs to do the same first.

"Ostalim!" cried Mirovna, listening to the noises of the pursuit in the swamp. "He came with you? Are there others?"

"I would there were, lady," said Rashov ruefully; "but the two of us came alone on foot from the *siech*, being chased into the bargain by a horde of rascally heathen from across the river, who were concealed in the swamp. By my faith, the ground is foul with them! It was only by luck and the dexterous use of our pistols that we are here at all. Ha! Here comes my brother-in-arms."

The boat was already under way when Ostalim emerged from the rushes into the channel and Rashov helped him to climb over the rail. His first act was to seize the hand of the rower, who was shoving into deep water with all his strength.

"Hold!" cried Ostalim, panting. "There is another Cossack escaped. I saw Stepan Vertivitch running through the reeds, a naked saber in his hand, with a pack of Tartars at his heels. He will be here directly."

A spasm crossed the face of the old man as he heard this, and his hands knotted on the oar. He peered through the rushes in the gray light, as if his heart were fixed on what might come from them. Angrily he shook off Ostalim's restraining hand, and gave a mighty thrust to the oar, sending the craft a dozen paces out into the channel.

"Are we women," he cried roughly, "to wait with the treasure of twenty years to save the life of one Cossack, and a stripling at that? Little thanks would we get from the Koshevoi Ataman for lightly risking our precious cargo. On to the river!"

In spite of what he said, his eyes roved eagerly around the swamp, until well clear of the rushes, without catching sight of what he sought. Ostalim and Rashov, realizing the truth of the old man's words, had flung themselves, exhausted, on the bottom of the boat.

Mirovna was the first to speak. "Look!" she cried. "On the shore. Several regiments of Tartars are moving toward Ruvno on the higher land. And—see! On the river by the *siech* two of the enemy sailing ships are headed this way."

Chapter VI
The Peril on the River

Mirovna's cry brought the two Cossacks to their feet in short order, and they saw that she spoke the truth. The sun was now well up, and the river banks were in plain sight. Against the sky line on the side nearest them they could see rank after rank of Tartar helmets moving in the direction of Ruvno, which lay some ten miles off. Ostalim guessed that these were the ones who had been hidden in the swamp, where they had come during the night, and that they had emerged as soon as scouts reported the *siech* deserted.

Moreover, the two sailing craft were in motion in their direction, although still three or four miles off. The light breeze which had sprung up from the south favored the Tartar craft which were making two paces to their one, even under the skillful handling of the old rower, who had arranged the sail cunningly to get the full strength of the light air.

There was no sign of the regiments of the *siech*, who had made the crossing with true Cossack swiftness and vanished into the wooded hills on the farther side of the river in pursuit of those who—as they imagined—had carried off their comrades. Ruvno itself lay around a bend in the river, and was hidden from them.

Mirovna and the three men in the sailing skiff were being rapidly overhauled by the two faster craft of the enemy, and were without a friend in sight. At their feet, in the stout wooden chests, was the treasure of the *siech*, worth the ransom of five rich towns, or the plunder of a dozen heavy-laden merchant fleets.

Ostalim drew the members of his little party together in a council to discuss their position, and to see if any hope of escape offered. All but one were silent.

"As Cossacks," said the old man thoughtfully, brushing back the matted hair which hung over his faded eyes, "we have but one duty, and that is to save the war treasure if it can be done. Already we have sacrificed one life of a brother to do it—and that was no easy matter for me"—his heavy voice faltered as he said it—"and we hold our lives lightly, if we may succeed in any way. Have I spoken truly?"

"That is the truth, honorable sir," replied Ostalim respectfully; "but how are we to save the treasure, even at the cost of our lives? And we must remember that there is a woman on the ship, to whom we owe protection not less than——"

"Not so," cried Mirovna with a toss of her black head. "Think you that a Cossack daughter will ask to survive her father, at such a price! What is your plan, honorable sir?"

"Well spoken, little one," approved the old man gravely. "Such words become the child of an *ataman*. My plan offers small chance of escape; but it may help to save the treasure for the *siech*. By continuing on our present course we may win to Ruvno before the pursuing craft, yet we cannot hope to outspeed the mounted Tartar regiments ashore, who will be there before we can. By steering for the other shore, however, we could land one of our number before we were overhauled. This man could make his way through the thick woods that lie along this way without being seen, and perchance he could regain the ten thousand on their march by midday, when they could return to the river. It might be that the treasure could be recovered by such means. What think you?"

"Let us try it, honorable sir," cried the girl eagerly, "and by landing both the young Cossacks, the chance of success would be doubled."

"That would leave no one on the skiff to protect you, Mirovna Chere-vaty," objected Ostalim, who was loath to leave the girl to the mercy of the Tartar folk to whom compassion is an unknown word.

"It would be better for you to remain, Ostalim," rejoined the old man, with a glance at the pursuing craft astern, "for you are looked upon with suspicion at the *siech*, and a message by you would be worth less than naught. No, Rashov must go, and God speed him on his journey."

"I would be a fat swine," cried Rashov indignantly, "to leave you to fall into the hands of the villainy over yonder. In faith, you had all bet-ter come——"

"And abandon the treasure, Rashov?" put in Mirovna. "No, the advice of the gray-haired sir is always better than the words of youth. After the fate of my father, and the destruction of Ruvno which must come soon at the hands of the Tartars, my danger is a very little thing. We shall all pray that you may win through to the ten thousand and tell them what ills are endured by the Cossack folk."

"It grieves me," mourned the honest Cossack, "to do this, and should I succeed, I swear by the holy church bells that your graves shall be as thickly adorned with Tartar heads as a pudding with raisins. The Koshe-voi Ataman is as wily in war as a wolf, and he will see that vengeance is not denied any Cossacks who die today. Only I would not see the beau-tiful head of Mirovna swing at a Tartar's belt by those raven locks, and friend Ostalim here, who is the son of a Koshevoi Ataman——"

"Ha, is that truth?" The old rower peered at Ostalim, as he guided the skiff nearer the shore. "I thought that his face recalled another to my mind-one of a brave warrior."

"Koshevoi Ataman Dmitri Ostalim was my father," said Ostalim proudly. "You can see his name on this sword, which was once a terror to Tartar and Pole in his hand."

The old rower glanced at the inlaid scabbard and a smile of recollection warmed his lined face. "It is in truth the sword of the Bogatyr* Ostalim," he cried. "Why does not the son acknowledge the father? If the war chief of the *siech* had seen this sword he might have believed your tale."

"There was no time to show the sword," explained Ostalim regretfully. "And as for not speaking of it in Ruvno, certain Cossacks with jewels and tassels on their trappings mocked at my plain coat and dusty boots, and I

---

*"Hero."

would not tell them my father's name until I had shown them that I was in truth fitted to take the place of the son of Koshevoi Ataman Dmitri Ostalim."

"That was wrong, Ostalim," said Mirovna sadly. "If you had told my father he would have trusted you instead of the gallant from Kiev and perhaps they might not have fallen into the ambush, for you are a brave warrior."

"In spite of my dusty boots?"

"In spite of them, and your rough manners."

For a second the brown eyes of Ostalim looked into the black eyes of the girl, and though the sadness still lay on her heart, it beat to a faster tune. For Ostalim thought of the little hand that waved him a greeting from the carriage as he stood in the door of the shop, and Mirovna thought of the strong arms that had picked her up lightly and set her down at her door two nights ago.

Then their thoughts were broken into by a cry from the rower, who had steered the ship to within arm's length of the rushes along the shore. "Jump!" he cried to Rashov, who stood poised on the rail. The big Cossack gave a farewell wave of his hand to Ostalim and the girl, and sprang in the water with a splash like a small whale. Finding firm footing, he waded ashore through the reeds, and turned to wave to the boat again before he plunged into the woods.

As he did so, the brush parted behind him, and four horsemen spurred forward. Mirovna gave a shrill cry of warning and Rashov wheeled, drawing his sword, just as the horsemen closed in upon him. For a moment those in the boat saw the giant Cossack defend himself ably, warding off the blows of his enemies, and even throwing one from his horse. Rashov tried to spring on the loose mount, but as he swung his big bulk upward, one of the hostile sabers glanced off his head, sending hat and rider headlong to earth, where both lay passive.

After watching the boat for a moment, the horsemen wheeled and rode back into the wood. As they did so Ostalim gave an exclamation. He had recognized, by their gold-broidered cloaks and tasseled hats, the same men who had been so anxious for his death in the *siech*.

How came they back to the Dnieper? Where had they left the others of their company? With a heart heavy for the fate of his friend, Ostalim turned to the river. Once more they were headed out to midstream, but their pursuers in the meanwhile had cut down the distance between them to a scant mile.

"That was our last hope," said Mirovna sadly. "Poor Rashov—he fought nobly against a treacherous attack. Our enemies seem to be everywhere, and no Cossacks will come to our aid."

"Can we win to Ruvno now, think you?" Ostalim inquired of the rower, but received a shake of the head for reply. It was easy to see that the other craft were gaining rapidly on them. The light wind had given place to little better than a calm, and the Tartars were urging their craft forward with oars which gave them a decided advantage. The light of hope which had gleamed for a while in Mirovna's eyes faded, and she bowed her dark head on her knees.

"Death is a sore thing for a beautiful lady like that," said the rower, sighing, as he watched her; "while it comes to me as a rest from pain, it despoils her of a fair, full life. Would I could save her, for her father's sake."

"Would I could save her for her own," Ostalim put in, his gaze fixed hungrily on the dark head, the slender shoulders in the silk smock, and the white hands clasped over the girl's knees.

"There is no hope now," whispered the rower, bending closer, "and, as for those dogs of Tartars, I have been their prisoner for long years, and I know the river is better for the daughter of Ataman Cherevaty than their hands, so while you keep the devils away with your good sword, I shall cast her over the side and see that she does not rise again and——"

"That will be a kindness, honorable sir," said the girl, smiling, to the men who had not thought that she heard what they said; "and it is what I wish," she added.

Ostalim's heart rebelled as he heard the girl's words. Much as he valued the treasure of the *siech*, he found it in his heart to wish it at the bottom of the river, if the girl were safe. Fain would he have sheltered her from harm with his own body, if it were possible. It was a bitter thing to have found love, as Paul Ostalim had done, at the gates of death, and to see the fate of his beloved. But he could not wish it otherwise.

In his anger he drew the blade that hung by his side and waved it at the approaching vessels that were now rapidly overhauling them.

But the sword of Dmitri Ostalim availed little when the Tartars swept alongside. No sooner had the other ship come within two paces of the skiff than a dozen swarthy warriors sprang over the side to the deck of the smaller craft. So quick were they that Ostalim scarce had time to cut one man down before he was gripped on every side and flung to the deck under a struggling mass.

The rower was seized in the act of throwing the girl from the side, and a heavy blow quieted his struggles. A sword flashed twice and the dogs were silent.

Chapter VII
The Real Reason

For the second time in two days Paul Ostalim was bound hand and foot and at the mercy of his enemies. Only this time there was no stout Rashov to come to his assistance, and his plight was doubly hard to bear because of the nearness of Mirovna. The girl was not laid helpless in the bottom of the boat, like Ostalim; a stout rope around her waist bound her to the mast of the skiff, and her little fingers were powerless to untie the knot.

The boat, looted of the gold chests, was ashore in a cove near the village of Ruvno, where it had been steered by the Tartars, who, to Ostalim's surprise, inflicted no further injury on them, but hurried off with the treasure across the river. The sail of the skiff, torn down by the invaders, covered the fore part of the vessel, and the oars had been recovered. Of the veteran *ataman* there was no sign.

Ostalim had found, after a few brief struggles, that it was hopeless to try to lose his bonds. The sailors had tied him with cruel ingenuity so that each movement caused him pain. He stifled his involuntary groan, and managed to smile at Mirovna. The body of the girl drooped forward from the waist from weariness, so that the little gold cross around her white throat hung loosely against the coin necklace. Her dark hair flooded down to her waist, and she was forced to push it aside to look at Ostalim.

Suddenly her eyes widened and she gave a quick gasp. The sound of a horse's gallop reached Ostalim's ears, coming rapidly nearer, and in another moment the rider dismounted by the boat. Mirovna shrank back against the mast and hid her face in her hands.

"Why play at coquetry here?" said a mocking voice that rang familiarly in Ostalim's ears, although the speaker was hidden from him. "You had your fill of that at Kiev at my expense——"

"Stepan Vertivitch!" cried Ostalim, in astonishment; "did you, too, escape from the Tartars in the swamp? We gave you up for lost."

"So the good Paul Ostalim is still alive," purred the smooth voice. "Good—excellent! We can now repay him for that blow in the stable yard—in full. In this way two debts can be settled at once."

Something in the words struck a chill to the helpless Cossack. That Vertivitch bore him ill will, he knew, but surely the man would help

Mirovna, for, after all, he was a Cossack of Ruvno, and an intimate of old Cherevaty.

"Your score with me, Stepan," he said quickly, "can be settled any time—here if you wish. Only help the lady Mirovna to get free of the Tartar ranks, and safely away from here where the danger is pressing. Perhaps there is security in Ruvno."

"For me, yes," admitted Vertivitch, coming to the side of the boat where he could see Ostalim. As they exchanged glances the captive's brow darkened. A change had taken place in the dandy's attire. Instead of sheepskin hat and *svitza*, he now wore a bronze helmet surmounted by a white plume, a gold-broidered *kaftan* falling over his graceful shoulders, and a silk belt holding his sword.

"Since when," demanded Ostalim wrathfully, "have you been a Pole, Stepan Vertivitch? Have the Tartars turned your heart to milk and forced you to renounce your church and people to save your life——"

"Nay, Cossack," returned the other, smiling as he stroked his mustache; "you wrong both my intelligence and foresight. I have become a Pole of my own accord, months ago, when I lived with a gay group of comrades in Kiev who were planning to deal a heavy blow at Cossackdom. They needed a secret—a certain secret—to make their plan sure of success, and this I furnished them, at a price."

"The hiding place of the war treasure!" cried Mirovna in horror; "you learned it from my father who trusted you. You betrayed it to the Tartars!"

The dandy bowed gracefully, and stepped into the boat within arm's reach of the girl, regarding her admiringly, while she shook the heavy masses of hair about her face to escape his look.

"You are more intelligent than our trusted friend here, Mirovna," admitted Vertivitch; "yet you have only yourself to thank for your present plight. You encouraged my suit in Kiev; then turned cold all of a sudden and scorned me——"

"That is false, Stepan Vertivitch," cried the girl. "I did but smile on you once when we first met, before I knew of your wasteful, villainous life. Later, I told you that I had no love for you, yet you persisted, until I asked my father to bring me home to Ruvno."

"You smiled on me, Mirovna," Vertivitch returned, pushing aside the dark hair to stare into her face which was turned toward him defiantly; "and that made you my one desire. I vowed to have you at all costs. When

you came home, I completed my arrangements with the Poles, knowing that they might be useful to me, and came with you. But that pig of
a Rashov joined us. Then at Ruvno I gained your father's support to my
suit, and you spurned me in the stable yard before the maids. You set your
gallant on me, the worthy smith——"

"A lie," broke in Ostalim sternly. "If there were any name worse than
traitor and dishonored warrior, you deserve it. If only these bonds were
loosened I would oppose the naked hands of a true Cossack against a traitor's sword!"

"So this rooster, as Rashov might say, can crow," sneered Stepan, fingering the hilt of his saber. "After all, good smith, what is a true Cossack?
A dog that is taught to fight by his master the tsar; a robber, trained to
plunder and lay waste the border marches from childhood, until he roasts
alive in the brazen belly of a Polish ox, or has his veins ripped out by a
Tartar dagger. A dog's life!"

"The life of a borzoi, Stepan," retorted Ostalim proudly. "The watchdog that guards the gates of our Russian land, and protects the Orthodox
Church. The Cossacks live with sword in hand, and surely that is better
than idling in silks and jewels in towns and hiring men to do your fighting. Your father, who was a great warrior, found no fault with such a life,
and the tsar himself called him *bogatyr*."

"Speak not of my father, and you value the few minutes that remain
to you of life," snarled the other; "he is dead, taken captive by the Tartar
folk a dozen years ago. I am free to avenge my slight at the white hands
of Mirovna. Would you know how it happened?"

"Tell me," said Mirovna suddenly, drawing deep breath. It seemed that
out of the corner of her eye she had seen the heavy cloth of the sail move.
"I would know it all."

"Willingly," returned Vertivitch with a smile, sitting where he could
watch Ostalim and the girl, with his back to the bow of the ship. "I would
please you, Mirovna, for you are a beautiful slave, and you will adorn my
home across the Dnieper as a flower blooms in a desert. Before I left Kiev
I cast my fortunes, like dice, with those of the brave Poles who were my
companions. But the dice were loaded, Mirovna; I saw to that. They left
for the *siech*, disguised as Cossacks from the Polish border, and I swore
to bring them the hiding place of the war treasure. This secret I got from
your father the night in Ruvno, for he trusted me——"

Mirovna drew back from the traitor with a cry of dismay. Again she
saw the pile of sailcloth move.

"According to our agreement," went on Vertivitch, "the Poles, who were in league with the common enemies of Cossackdom, the Tartars, arranged to have our wily allies from across the river waylay Cherevaty and the party from Ruvno. In this way I entered the ranks of the Tartars, only to find that the gold treasure was gone from its hiding place. Our scheme was working well, the ten thousand dogs from the *siech* were across the river, and my friends, the Poles, were with them, watching everything that occurred. Four of them returned to tell of your unlucky visit to the camp, and how the wise Koshevoi Ataman had put you in the stocks.

"The tale delighted me," he continued, "and my happiness was full when, with the war treasure on the river, we captured the proud beauty Mirovna"—he broke off to run his hand over the girl's slender shoulders in spite of her shrinking—"and my good smith whom I had sworn to chastise. I persuaded the Tartars to let me have the two of you for slaves, and they agreed willingly, being full of the gold hoard. So instead of having the task of breaking into Ruvno, which is resisting our attack with surprising strength, I came to claim my two slaves. Does not my story interest you, Mirovna?"

"It is a recital of villainy," retorted the girl, her heart beating as she followed the stirring of the sail behind Ostalim. To keep his attention fixed upon her, she hurried on:

"You would have me for a slave, Stepan Vertivitch? Truly, an unwilling slave is a bad bargain, for rather than have you for master I would follow the most barbarous of the Tartar horde. You would get little good of your prize—for I would have my Tartar stick a knife into your back, knowing that you betrayed my father. Still, for a price, I would be a willing slave."

"And the price?" demanded Stepan, his face flushing.

"The release of Ostalim. Not later, but now—at once. When he is freed of his bonds and set loose in the brush, I shall go with you, and not make resistance. You have broken my heart already with the loss of my father; loss of the daughter is not so great, after that. But Ostalim is the son of a true Cossack, and he will be the leader the Ruvno people in the future. His freedom is the price of my consent."

"No, Mirovna," cried Ostalim angrily; "that cannot be. My life is not to be bought at such a price——"

A glance from the girl, a quick, warning signal, silenced him.

"You pledge your word that this will be so?" asked Stepan thoughtfully.

"My word, and it will not be broken," replied Mirovna, smiling.

"Why are you so eager to win the freedom of this fellow?"

"He has risked his life to defend me."

"That is not the only reason?"

"He is the son of a Koshevoi Ataman, a wolf leader of the wolf-hounds."

"Bah! The real reason?"

Mirovna's dark head lifted proudly, and her eyes sought Ostalim's. One hand stretched out to him anxiously. "Because I love him," she said, in a low voice, "and the Cossack race is true to its love. The love of the wolf is not to be set aside."

"Ha, there we have the truth!" snarled Stepan, drawing his sword; "there the woman spoke truly. Think you I would tear the wolf breed apart, and have my life forfeited by the vengeance of a Cossack? Rather, he shall die at once!"

Heedless of the girl's wild cry, Vertivitch stepped past her and bent over Ostalim, his bare sword lying loosely against the captive's chest, a deadly anger blazing in his eyes. Ostalim's gaze did not meet his, but sought Mirovna eagerly. It was useless for him to resist, for he was helpless to move. He strained to meet the girl's eyes, when he gave a quick cry of astonishment. At the same instant, Vertivitch wheeled, sword in hand.

Chapter VIII
Face to Face

Beside Mirovna stood the figure of the old rower. With his hair matted with blood about his face, and his scarred, half-naked body, he presented a fierce aspect. One hand supported him on his weak legs by clutching the mast; the other was stretched out toward Vertivitch. His teeth were bared in a snarl that rumbled in his throat like a growl.

"Spawn of the devil!" he hissed at Vertivitch; "hyena of the wolf breed! Traitor to breed and faith, bought over by gold to betray your comrades and the *siech*! I had thought you dead at the hands of the Tartars in brave fight. If any man had said to me that this was true, he would have paid for it with his life. Yet I have heard it from your lips."

Anger strangled the old man as he lurched forward and gripped the dumfounded Stepan by the shoulders.

The Cossack gave a broken cry as he caught sight of the other's face. "My father!" he whispered, staring into the face that was so near his own.

"Nay, traitor!" roared the enraged *ataman*; "no father of yours. Have I not heard from your lips how you plotted with our enemies to betray the Cossacks, while I lay under the sail where I fell when the Tartars boarded us. Such a tale of villainy has not come to my ears in ten years of slavery at Tartar hands. Worse than the scum of Turks is a traitor to the *siech*."

A Cossack father is judge and priest to his son. He may punish as he sees fit for any wrongdoing, and the son is powerless in his hands. The old *ataman* was crippled, while Stepan was strong and with a sword in his hand. Yet the memory of his childhood flooded back on him, and he trembled before the rage of the father whom he had thought dead.

"For ten years," went on old Vertivitch, "I toiled at the galley oars and thought of the time when my son would have strength in his arm to avenge me. When I heard from Mirovna that you had defended yourself well against the Tartars, my heart leaped, even though you had been taken captive. Bah! Doubtless the Tartars whirled their creeses about your head and smiled, knowing you were bought over to their side."

"If you had not been taken from me——" began Stepan faintly.

"Aye, say you so? Look at Ostalim whose father died at my side. Is he a renegade? Is Mirovna less courageous because her father is lost? No more words after what you have said when you thought yourself master here——"

"We *are* masters," snarled Stepan, shaking off the spell of fear of his father; "the Cossacks are miles away, except those shut up in Ruvno, and the war treasure is ours. The Tartars and Poles are victors, and my sword is with the victors."

"Be not so sure, traitor. The Koshevoi Ataman is not to be caught asleep. Matters here have gone too smoothly, methinks, for the heathen. They have not felt the full measure of Cossack strength. It is no easy matter to catch the wolf unawares."

"The wolf is trapped, old man," retorted Vertivitch, with a laugh, "and I have seen the trap close on him. When your famous ten thousand return from their chase, they will be ambushed like Cherevaty and his men, and their fate will be the same!"

This was more than the *ataman* could endure. He seized Stepan's sword arm with one knotted hand. With the other he felt for his son's throat, snarling like an angry dog. In an effort to free his arm Stepan brought the sword down heavily on the ship's rail and the blade was snapped in two.

Old Vertivitch had the strength of two men in his arms and shoulders and he crushed down the other's resistance in a hug that lifted him clear of his feet. With a crash the pair came down on the thwarts of the boat struggling in desperate silence.

With a wrench Stepan tore his father's hand from his throat and gasped: "On the shore—the Tartars——"

"He lies!" cried Mirovna, who was following the struggle with burning eyes.

Too late old Vertivitch saw that she spoke the truth. In the instant that he relaxed his taut muscles to look toward the shore, Stepan tore himself free. Before the iron clutch of the Cossack could descend upon him, he was over the side of the ship, to the shore.

"Treacherous spawn!" growled the *ataman*, crossing his arms over his panting chest. "You are free now; go for your friends, the Tartars; tell them where true Cossacks can be found."

Stepan ran to his horse, staggering from exhaustion; but as he leaped to his seat, the gay smile returned to his lips, and he adjusted his *kaftan* which had been disarranged in the fight. Wheeling his impatient horse, he darted up the slope to a ridge where he could command a view of the steppe.

The *ataman* lost no time in hastening to Ostalim and undoing the bonds which kept the young Cossack helpless. Then Mirovna was released, and Ostalim turned, his arm about the girl, to face the shore and what might come therefrom.

Stepan had wheeled about and was galloping down to the river again, the feathers in his helmet dancing in the wind, straight for the boat. Shouts echoed after him from the plain. Ostalim's arm tightened about Mirovna as he made out a number of horsemen speeding after the flying renegade. To his surprise, instead of drawing up at the boat, Stepan dashed into the water, and headed his horse across the river, where the two were soon swimming. The *kaftan* was flung from his shoulders and floated on the water near them.

"What means this?" cried the girl, wondering.

Ostalim had been watching the approaching riders, and now he gave a shout of joy. "It means," he said, laughing, "that we are safe from Stepan Vertivitch, for a time, at least. Look, Mirovna, is not that stout figure known to you?"

"Cossacks!" she cried; "and there is Rashov, and the one in the lead ——"

One of the riders spurred up to them and whirled his horse on the shore by the boat. "The Koshevoi Ataman comes," he cried; "whither went the Tartar we saw on the ridge?"

As Ostalim pointed out the swimming Stepan, already safe from pursuit, the erect figure of the gray-mustached war chief of the *siech* appeared beside the boat, scanning the occupants swiftly. His gaze lingered on the old Vertivitch who stood silently by the mast, his arms crossed, his head hanging in shame.

"Who is this man?" he demanded. "I know his face."

"It is Ataman Vertivitch, honorable sir," said Rashov; "he has escaped from the Tartars."

"Vertivitch!" exclaimed the war chief, pressing to the side of the boat. "The *bogatyr* of Ruvno. Happy is this day for Cossackdom, by the light of my faith!" he swore.

"Ha!" growled the old *ataman*, his face lighting up; "it is good that the Koshevoi Ataman is not tricked by the Tartars and scheming Poles. I have said that he would fall in no trap, and my words are proved true. But how comes it that you are here, honorable sir, without the ten thousand?"

"The ten thousand are here with me, honorable sir," answered the war chief respectfully, pulling at his gray mustache. "At dawn this morning we fell upon half the Tartar strength across the river and drove them in flight. Then, for we knew of the trap, we hastened back to the river and caught the boats with the treasure. Already Ruvno is freed from the invaders who are defeated on every hand."

"By my faith, but this is welcome news," swore Vertivitch. "Glad am I that I have lived to see this day. But how——"

"Your pardon, sir," broke in the war chief, wheeling his horse. Summoning his followers together he rode back to the plain where the battle was still raging. Only Rashov remained, grinning with pleasure to see his friends again.

"That is a Koshevoi Ataman for you," said Vertivitch admiringly. Then his head drooped and he folded his arms in sorrow, remembering his son.

Ostalim motioned to Rashov. "Unravel this mystery for us, good Rashov," he cried. "Are my eyes turned liars, or did I see you struck down by the treacherous Poles?"

"Comfort yourself, Paul," returned Rashov; "your good sense remains to you as I can see by what you are doing with your arm——" Mirovna freed herself, blushing. "In truth I did but sham dead, as the foe were too many for me. Some good brandy has quite restored me. And as to our being here—did you think that the old wolf of the *siech* was to be trapped like a jackal? The secret is bare in two words. The Koshevoi Ataman had an eye in Kiev that was wide open, and watched the movements of the Poles, with our friend Vertivitch. This eye came to Ruvno with Vertivitch," he went on, "and brought the news to the Koshevoi Ataman, who, like the wise wolf he is, planned to enter the trap set for him, and turn upon his enemies. Hence he had you tied to the stocks in the camp, although he saw to it that no man laid a club upon you. He had to do so, to quiet the suspicions of our friends, the Poles, until he got across the river. He also saw to it that Ruvno was well defended, to engage the interest of the Tartars here until the ten thousand could get back from their feast across the river and settle the reckoning as it should be settled. At midday I saw the ten thousand swim their horses across the river, and I came to look for you. The rest you know."

"And my father," cried Mirovna appealingly.

Rashov stretched his arm toward Ruvno. "It will go hard, lady," he said cheerily, "if we find him not before nightfall."

"But this eye of the war chief at Kiev?" inquired Ostalim.

"Rashov; none other," said Rashov, twirling his mustache, well satisfied. "He sent you to the *siech* with the tidings already known to the war chief, because, by the devil, he wanted you to show your mettle. And you have done so. The Koshevoi Ataman thinks well of you. Why not smile, old man," he turned to the *ataman*, "when everything goes so well?"

"Not when I have lost my son, a traitor," replied Vertivitch. "I am alone in the world."

"Not so," said Ostalim gently, "for I have no father except you, and you will accept me as your son."

"Aye," said the old man slowly; "you are truly the son I should have chosen. I shall find comfort in you, the son of my friend."

"Not only comfort, by the looks of it," added Rashov, with a twinkle in his eye, "but a daughter as well. And grandchildren, many of them. Devil take me, if I don't go for the *batko** this minute to make the wedlock fast. A few minutes and I shall be back."

---

*"Priest."

Ostalim half put out his hand to check his hasty friend. Then, with a glance at Mirovna, he drew it back again. The girl had made no objection In fact, sitting demurely by his side, like all the maidens who approached the threshold of marriage since the world began, she was anxiously arranging the disordered mass of her hair with the water for a mirror, the ten fingers of her white hands for a comb.

Appendix

Adventure magazine, where many of the tales in this volume first appeared, maintained a letter column titled "The Camp-fire." As a descrip-tor, "letter column" does not quite do this regular feature justice. *Ad-venture* was published two and sometimes three times a month, and as a result of this frequency and the interchange of ideas it fostered "The Camp-Fire" was really more like an Internet bulletin board of today than a letter column found in today's quarterly or even monthly magazines. It featured letters from readers, editorial notes, and essays from writers. If a reader had a question or even a quibble with a story he could write in and the odds were that the letter would not only be printed but that the story's author would draft a response.

Harold Lamb and other contributors frequently wrote lengthy letters that further explained some of the historical details that appeared in their stories. The letters about the stories included in this volume, with introductory comments by *Adventure* editor Arthur Sullivant Hoffman, follow, and appear in order of publication. The date of the issue of *Adventure* is indicated, along with the title of the Lamb story that appeared in the issue. Lamb did not write a letter about every story.

August 20, 1922: "Sangar"

Something from Harold Lamb concerning the Tungusi who figure in his story in this issue:

Any one who meddles with them is likely to be out of luck. More than three hundred years ago the Imperial Russian Government made this discovery when it tried to subject the Tungusi.

The Tungusi were nomad Tartar tribes who wandered over the most fertile part of the Mongolian steppe, where the river Yenesai drains from the Syansk mountains. Russian explorers reported that there were Steppe, Forest and Fisher Tungusi, and all were *sangars*—men who worked white magic.

This was probably because the Tungusi lived to themselves and kept the customs of the time of Genghis Khan, which rather mystified the first white men who visited them. Then provincial officials looked them over from afar, saw that they kept animals, and named them Horse, Reindeer and Dog Tungusi, admitting that the Tungusi could not be made to pay taxes.

This was because the Tungusi riders liked fighting with the bow, so that no one cared to face them with a musket until the musket became a rifle that could be loaded as fast as the Tungusi could deliver themselves of arrows. Also, the man who closed with the Tungusi, thinking that the tribesmen disliked cold steel, was out of luck.

Lastly, the Imperial Russian Government classified the Tungusi as Wandering, Nomadic and Sedentary—the last one alone paying taxes. It is a matter of record that the Sedentary Tungusi number less than one percent of the whole. Also that the most incorrigible are the Wandering (alias Steppe and Reindeer) Tungusi.

The Chinese called them the Chih-mao-tze, the Red Haired People, and let it go at that, being careful not to meddle with the clansmen or their animals.

On the other hand the Cossacks, the ancient and honorable foe of the Tatars, were ordered to meddle with the Tungusi. It was the Cossacks who called them *sangars*, white magicians, nearly three hundred years ago.

Such things as talking to horses and summoning reindeer from a thousand miles away are not so easily explained by any administrative bureau. But strangers riding through the Tungusi steppe are careful not to do any injury to the private reindeer of the natives. It is one game preserve where no liberties are taken.

No laws have ever been written about the reindeer of the Tungusi. It is a case, one might say, of unwritten law.

November 20, 1925: "Mark of Astrakhan"

Something from Harold Lamb in connection with his novelette in this issue. And, following his talk to Camp-fire, part of a personal letter he wrote me that covers a bit of the same ground but is interesting nevertheless:

Stenka Razin was the Robin Hood of the Cossacks. In the course of the last three centuries many legends have gathered around his name; popular superstition, mellowed with time, has credited him with supernatural powers.

If you were to travel by any chance on the great Volga through the southern steppe, the river-men would entertain you endlessly—if they happened to be Cossacks—with stories about Stenka Razin's exploits.

But his revolt, his expeditions, and the brief and colorful kingdom he established are recorded in history. For a while he was a thorn in the frontiers of two kingdoms—Muscovy and Persia.

As for Mark—he existed. I have his own account of the taking of Astrakhan, corroborated by the adventurer Jean Sturys, the Hollander. From Astrakhan to the Volga mouths, and the execution at the Kremyl, the main incidents of the story actually happened.

The battle between Stenka Razin's men and the Persian fleet probably took place before the capture of Astrakhan. It is given clearly enough by Petis de la Croix, in his annals of the seventeenth century—the trick played by Stenka Razin, the death of the ten thousand. The incidents of the story, of course, appear to take place within a few months, instead of two or three years, as was actually the case.

Some readers may be curious about the word "alkali" in Central Asia at this early date. I was curious when I found "al-kali grass" mentioned by a European voyager there, long before the desert regions of America were explored. On investigation "al-kali" proved to be correct, *al-qali*, "roasted"—pure Arabic. In the deserts of Central Asia soap was made out of the ashes of the burned alkali grass.

This story is probably the first narrative to be written in English about the exploits of Stenka Razin. By great good luck in gathering material it was possible to *uncover* this story. Down to almost the smallest details it is a narrative of things that happened and men that existed.

The songs of the Volga pirates, the Round-head colonel, Mark himself, the capture of Astrakhan and the battle of the Volga pirates and the Moslems in the inland sea—all these are reality. The "man who was called a Walloon" played his part on the stage of life nearly three hundred years ago, just as he is shown in the story. The fat Polish colonel *did* accuse Mark as to his cannon, as told in the story.

Stenka Razin's actions, his character, and his end are all drawn from life.

Mark is not his real name—he was known as a Captain Butler. And the character of Uncle Kosta, who tells the story, and the niece of the Round-head colonel are imaginary. Also, the actual date of the battle on the Caspian is uncertain—it may well have taken place before the events of the story.

As to Mark's real identity—his youth and reasons for coming to Astrakhan—I have had to improvise. But I had his letters written from Astrakhan, splendid stuff, and the journal of the adventurer Jean Struys to compare them with, and the book of the priest-wanderer, Father Avril (who passed through Astrakhan a few years later) for further corroboration. Also the legends told me by the Cossacks as to Stenka Razin, and, to check these, the Moslem annals translated by Petis de la Croix some two hundred years ago.

So, from different men, in different languages and from various ages of the past, come these details of what happened on the inland sea in the year 1670.

As I said before, this story has been *uncovered* from the past, rather than *made up*. And I have tried to tell it as Uncle Kosta would actually have told it. Hence the brief prelude.

December 8, 1926: "The Wolf Master"

The *koshevoi* of the wolves is an old Cossack legend and is undoubtedly based on some actual happening. Just what it was no one knows. The Cossacks, by the way, used to call the wolves "gray friends" and the picture of St. Ulass and the wolf may still be seen in their churches.

As for the False Dmitri—he is one of the weirdest figures of history. His character is summed up very well by one historian, Ustrialof, in these words: "Since he was the head of many tsardoms that had submitted to the Russian scepter, not being satisfied with the title of tsar he took the name of emperor . . . but while he understood the necessities of the empire, he did not understand his own situation. He aroused against himself universal hatred, and the annals hint at unheard-of crimes and call him by the name of God-detested man."

An adventurer, who made himself a great emperor, aided by no more than his own wit; a man of unknown origin, who revealed real ability to rule when he had stolen the throne, and might have made the best of monarchs, except for one thing. Himself.

As to what befell him in the Terem that night, it is one of the secrets of medieval Russia. And about the most reliable account of the events of that night is the journal of Captain Margaret, French soldier of fortune.

The events are related in the story as Margaret and Bertrand told them— the mystery of the three missing horses, the beard on the dead man that did not look as if it had been shaved before then, the letter to the boyars and all the rest. Bamanof and Tevakel Khan and Ilbars Sultan were living men, and the raid of the Turkomans on the Golden Horde took place about this time—though the name of the Turkoman chieftain is not known to me.

As to the legend of the Earth Girdle—it bobs up in Europe, Persia and Arabia. In Europe, at least as late as 1630, it is the *Cingulus Mundi*, and in the tale of Abou Ishak it is the mountain Câf. I have in my library a map published by Petit de la Croix about 1710 that shows a single mountain barrier stretching down mid-Asia and this barrier is named Câf.

Modern exploration has cleared up the geography of high Asia sufficiently to show that this "rampart" is in reality a system of many mountain ranges extending northeast from Afghanistan to Lake Baikal, rather than north and south.

But there are regions behind the Gobi still unexplored, and one chap, Thomas Atkinson, observed some curious ruins above Lake Zaizan Nor—the ruins that appear in the story as the city of the Golden Horde (which once ruled the country).

Atkinson saw a granite plateau standing out of a mountain range, and observed on nearer approach that the mass was in reality a number of isolated rock bulks that had the appearance of the ruined edifices of a vast city.

At least one ruin in this place was man-made—and during an earlier age—an enclosure nearly half a mile in length, surrounded by a wall of large stone blocks with smaller fitted between. Some portions were six feet high and seven thick. Where the wall was no more than two feet, Atkinson jumped his horse over it, and his two Cossacks followed him, but nothing could induce the native Kirghiz to enter the ruin. They rode around and waited for him on the other side.

They explained the ruins—which had the appearance of fortifications, towers, and pyramids—were the abode of "Shaitain" and it was not healthy to graze herds nearby after dusk.

The Kirghiz are descendants of the Golden Horde. There are many such basalt and limestone formations in the loess regions of Central Asia, and plenty of abandoned cities, the prey of encroaching sands, plague or invasion. And the ruins of nature are often similar to the ruins left by men.

About the Author

Harold Lamb (1892-1962) was born in Alpine NJ, the son of Eliza Rollinson and Frederick Lamb, a renowned stain glass designer, painter, and writer. Lamb later described himself as having been born with damaged eyes, ears, and speech, adding that by adulthood these problems had mostly righted themselves. He was never very comfortable in crowds or cities and found school "a torment." He had two main refuges when growing up— his grandfather's library and the outdoors. Lamb loved tennis and played the game well into his later years.

Lamb attended Columbia, where he first dug into the histories of Eastern civilizations, ever after his lifelong fascination. He served briefly in World War I as an infantryman but saw no action. In 1917 he married Ruth Barbour, and by all accounts their marriage was a long and happy one. They had two children, Frederick and Cary. Arthur Sullivant Hoffman, the chief editor of *Adventure* magazine, recognized Lamb's storytelling skills and encouraged him to write about the subjects he most loved. For the next twenty years or so, historical fiction set in the remote East flowed from Lamb's pen, and he quickly became one of *Adventure's* most popular writers. Lamb did not stop with fiction, however, and soon began to draft biographies and screenplays. By the time the pulp magazine market dried up, Lamb was an established and recognized historian, and for the rest of his life he produced respected biographies and histories, earning numerous awards, including one from the Persian government for his two-volume history of the Crusades.

Lamb knew many languages: by his own account, French, Latin, ancient Persian, some Arabic, a smattering of Turkish, a bit of Manchu-Tartar, and medieval Ukrainian. He traveled throughout Asia, visiting most of the places he wrote about, and during World War II he was on covert assignment overseas for the U.S. government. He is remembered today both for his scholarly histories and for his swashbuckling tales of daring Cossacks and Crusaders. "Life is good, after all," Lamb once wrote, "when a man can go where he wants to, and write about what he likes best."

Source Acknowledgments

These stories were originally published in *Adventure* magazine: "Sangar," August 20, 1922; "Mark of Astrakhan," November 20, 1925; "The Wolf Master," December 8, 1926; "The Moon of Shawwul," August 15, 1928; "The Outrider," September 15, 1929; "Koum," July 15, 1931; "Over the River," August 15, 1931; "The Post in the Steppe," January 15, 1932.

These stories were originally published in *Collier's* magazine: "The Vampire of Khor," January 6, 1934; "The Devil's Song," April 10, 1937; "Singing Girl," June 24, 1939; "Cossack Wolf," February 28, 1942; "The Stone Woman," September 26, 1942; "City under the Sea," January 2, 1943; "The Two Swords of Genghis Khan," February 5, 1944.

"Red Hands" was originally published in *The Big Magazine*, March 1935.

"The Phantom Caravan" was originally published in *Argosy*, January 1944.

"Witch Woman" was originally published in the *Saturday Evening Post*, October 5, 1946.

"Wolf-Hounds of the Steppe" was originally published in *Top Notch*, July 15, 1917.

www.ingramcontent.com/pod-product-compliance
Ingram Content Group UK Ltd.
Pitfield, Milton Keynes, MK11 3LW, UK
UKHW022046060225
454777UK00012B/992